In the Eye of the Sun

IN THE EYE OF THE SUN

AHDAF SOUEIF

PANTHEON BOOKS
NEW YORK

For Robbie

Library of Congress Cataloging-in-
Publication Data
Soueif, Ahdaf.
In the eye of the sun/Ahdaf Soueif.
p. cm.
ISBN0-679-40948-3
1. Egyptians—England—Fiction. I.
Title.
PR6069.078I5 1993
823'.914—dc20   92–41012
                                    CIP

Manufactured in the United States of
America
First American Edition

9 8 7 6 5 4 3 2 1

contents

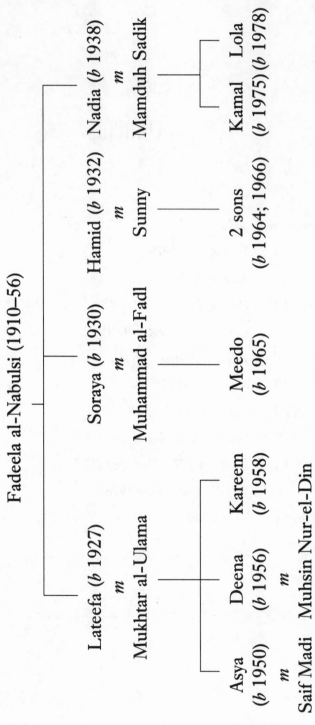

Ismail Mursi (1900–1973)
m
Fadeela al-Nabulsi (1910–56)

Lateefa (*b* 1927)
m
Mukhtar al-Ulama

Soraya (*b* 1930)
m
Muhammad al-Fadl

Hamid (*b* 1932)
m
Sunny

Nadia (*b* 1938)
m
Mamduh Sadik

Asya
(*b* 1950)
m
Saif Madi

Deena
(*b* 1956)
m
Muhsin Nur-el-Din

Kareem
(*b* 1958)

Meedo
(*b* 1965)

2 sons
(*b* 1964; 1966)

Kamal   Lola
(*b* 1975) (*b* 1978)

...and we do not expect people to be moved by what is not unusual. That element of tragedy which lies in the very fact of frequency, has not yet wrought itself into the coarse emotion of mankind; and perhaps our frames could hardly bear much of it. If we had a keen vision and feeling for all ordinary human life, it would be like hearing the grass grow and the squirrel's heart beat, and we should die of that roar which lies on the other side of silence.

—GEORGE ELIOT
Middlemarch

i

July - August 1979

Scene 1

Saturday, 28 July 1979
London

– used to it – although sometimes the very fact of my having grown used to it strikes me as the oddest thing of all! But then as Dada Zeina (and the vast majority of grown-ups) would say: one gets used to anything. So Chrissie, dear, I've been notching them up again (although not at the moment, of course, with Khalu and Nadia both here) – nothing serious – just broadening my base, so to speak, and am looking forward to telling – and hearing – many stories in two months' time (your children permitting of course), although I guess there may not be Arabiscos still for tea. Is it all really as different as I hear it is? Not *everything* can change though, can it? I mean, there must be *some* things that stay as they are; after all, it's only been five years, and while that's very long for you and me it isn't long at all in the history of a country –

Asya looks up from her letter-pad: her uncle sits in her new armchair with the vaguely Andalusian design in red and gold velvet and gazes out through the french windows and across the small south-facing balcony. What is he looking at? What can he see from where he sits? Only an elaborate arrangement of fragile lines and angles black against the clear blue sky: the aerials and the antennae on top of the Czechoslovak embassy building. Were he to stand up he would see the grey bulk of the Cromwell Hospital – still under construction but functioning nevertheless. And in the foreground, between her house and the hospital, a long, white wall well on its way to being completely covered with green creepers.

He sits and stares without moving for a while, then raises his right hand and slips it under the back of his chequered beige wool shooting cap so that the brim falls at a rakish angle over his eyes – and rubs the back of his head. He adjusts the cap and reaches towards the black ash table and picks up his diary once again. He smooths it out on his knee and holds it open with the heel of his right hand. Then he turns backwards one page, then two, then forward to where he had first opened it. He rests his palm on the diary and sits back frowning.

Asya moves from where she has been sitting at the old gate-leg table. She walks over to him and bends and puts her arm around his shoulders.

'I'll make you some coffee, Khalu.'

He does not look up but says, 'I seem to have lost a day somewhere –'

3

'Well, don't try to find it this minute. You're still tired.' She pats his shoulder. 'Come on, put the diary away. Do you want a biscuit with the coffee? Or some cake?'

He looks up at her with her brother's eyes – and her mother's. Where did they get these eyes? They aren't her grandmother's; *her* eyes had been green. And they aren't her grandfather's either. Ismail Mursi's eyes had been black black: deep and shining and looking as though they were lined with kohl – like Nasser's. Typical Upper Egyptian eyes. His son's are a gentle hazel and she notes – suddenly and with a slight surprise as she does each time – slightly mismatched: the right eye now looks puzzled, anxious; the left eye is – as usual – blank.

Then he looks down at the diary. He closes it.

'Let's go out. Let's go for a walk.'

'Do you think –' she hesitates. 'I mean, can you – manage?'

'Of course I can.'

An impatient, arrogant note has come into his voice. Her grandfather's. But her grandfather would have stood up and walked out. His son, Hamid Mursi, continues, 'There's a place in Kensington High Street that makes good espresso. And you can have some ice-cream.'

Asya smiles. I am twenty-nine, she thinks. But you are still my uncle; my only uncle. And I still like ice-cream.

She stands back and watches him lever himself up with his right hand, wait a few seconds till he steadies, then walk to the bedroom to find his shoes. He comes back with them on and carrying his jacket in his right hand. She takes it from him and stands behind him, holding it for him to get into. Then she comes round to his front and reaches up and straightens his tie – a deep red silk with a scattering of tiny dark green circles – and he says, 'I shan't bother with the arm this time.' So she does up the two buttons of his jacket and he pushes the end of his left sleeve into its breast with his right hand and she slides her own hand into the crook of his right elbow and they set off.

Outside, the sunshine makes them blink and she digs into her handbag and finds his sunglasses and hers before they start walking down the dappled Kensington streets. In Addison Gardens they stand aside for two young nannies in striped uniforms pushing their prams home from Holland Park. The nannies look up from their conversation and smile their thanks. What they see is a tall man in his middle age standing erect and looking a bit military with his left hand tucked into the breast of his jacket. His jacket is a beige tweed and he wears a white shirt and a tie and a woollen shooting cap on this warm July afternoon. He has on a pair of gold-rimmed sunglasses and he is foreign of course. Darkish. Could be Spanish – or Greek – or Arab. So could the woman who holds on to his arm – his daughter maybe? Or could be a young wife. She is somewhere in her middle twenties, goodlooking, with black eyes and lots of long black

hair. She wears a loose blue cotton skirt and a sleeveless fuchsia top from
French Connection and she has earrings, bangles, open-toed shoes and
toenails to match. She carries a big bright mirror-work bag that Oxfam
just up the road had in their window for three pounds last month and
round her neck she has a single strand of pearls. Real ones. When the
nannies look back a couple of minutes later they see the couple turning
into Allen Street. They are walking slowly – somehow more stately than
strolling – arm in arm, and do not alter their step even as they cross the
road.

'This is it,' says Hamid Mursi.

They find a table in a patch of shade and Asya asks for a chocolate ice-
cream with caramel sauce while her uncle orders a 'doppio 'spresso, per
favore' and for a moment enjoys the sounds of Italian on his own tongue.
She watches as he glances with automatic interest at a tableful of tanned
blondes. But in seconds his face takes on its abstracted look again. The
end of the left arm still sits – Napoleonic fashion – in the breast of the
jacket. But the right hand has slipped back into the pocket that holds the
diary. Oh brother of my mother. First dashing young man of my girlhood
– he looks up and finds her staring at him and raises his eyebrows
questioningly.

'I was just thinking' – she smiles – 'that you look a bit like Napoleon.'

'He was a dwarf.' He gives her a wide smile. 'I'd make two of him.'

'Even Napoleon you'll take on, Khalu?'

'Asya, dear, I must be keeping you from all sorts of things.'

She smiles and shakes her head.

'You're keeping me from nothing. It's a weekend anyway.'

'I don't mean just now.'

'I'm doing everything I want to do.'

'All right. But you know you don't have to spend every minute with
me? It's enough that we have your lovely flat as a home in this country.'

'It's OK. Really. It's just so nice having you here – even under the
circumstances.'

And what about all the time you've given *me*. The bits of your life – no,
of *my* life that you've given me? The 'quick spins' to Port Said and
Ismailia when I was small and your black Austin was the first and only car
in the family? The wild games on the stairs of Grandfather's house so I
wouldn't hear my mother's screams when Kareem was being born? The
summer days in Alexandria when you taught me to swim? The summer
nights when you let me come with you and your amazingly beautiful new
bride to the open-air cinema? Asya smiles. One night they had wandered
into the cinema, bought their drinks and sat down. The film was called *A
Rage to Live* and starred Susanne Pleshette, whose pictures Asya had
seen in magazines and who she thought was terrific. She had played a
small-town girl and Asya (although she was eleven and did not really

understand what was happening and only learned the word 'nympho-
maniac' a few years later when she saw the woman in Fellini's *Satyricon*
who lies tied down to her bed in a tent in the fairground while her
husband desperately rounds up one man after another to dive into the
tent and into her. As long as some man is inside her she lies still. She
cannot fold her arms round him but her face looks tender and serene –
even beatific. The moment she is left empty, however, she snarls and
writhes and gnashes her teeth and strains to break free from her bonds
and gouge out the eyes of her keeper: her husband) – Asya was spell-
bound. She had noticed her uncle conferring with Tante Sunny and,
halfway through, he had said lightly, 'This is a bit of a silly film, isn't it?
Shall we go?' But Asya had merely shaken her head and they had had to
sit at her side through many torrid scenes and seductions before
Pleshette arrived at her awesomely moral end. Afterwards, over pancakes
stuffed with mincemeat in the marketplace at Sidi Bishr, with the big
gas-lamps glaring in the night and the sounds of the nearby funfair
drifting on the wind and the sea a mass of dark movement on the other
side of the road, he had obviously felt he ought to say, 'She was ill, you
know, she wasn't normal. It was a silly film.' Neither Asya nor he has
mentioned that night since. Now she looks at him and smiles. She taps
pink fingernails on the table to catch his attention.

'Khalu, aren't you a bit too hot in this jacket?'

A look of uncertainty crosses his face, then he says, 'No. No, it's just
right. I'm a little cold.'

He orders a second espresso and she has one too. Then he takes his
diary out of his pocket and opens it on the table in front of him.

Alexandria. The beach at Sidi Bishr. The sun has set and all the
parasols have been gathered. A few people still loiter on the beach.
Mama Deela, Asya's grandmother, and Tante Soraya, Mama Deela's
second daughter, are standing at the edge of the water looking out to sea
while what must have been a four-year-old Asya, wrapped in a blue and
white striped towelling robe, snatches a few last moments of play at their
feet. Eventually, a swimmer can be seen rounding the back of the rock
island which sits about two hundred metres out to sea and represents –
after the bobbing red buoys – the final boundary known to bathers in the
sheltered bay. He approaches with leisurely freestyle strokes, his feet
making hardly a ripple in the water behind him. Mama Deela starts
unfolding a large bath-towel.

Tante Soraya says, 'I told you not to worry.'

'It's just that he might catch cold.'

'Hamid never catches cold. He never even feels the cold.'

'Stop it, Soraya: you'll evil-eye your brother.'

Uncle Hamid wades out of the sea, hitches up his navy blue swimsuit
and shakes himself over Asya, who squeals and looks up for more. His

mother wraps the towel around his shoulders and he says, 'You're still here? I thought you'd have gone home.'

'Mama has been worrying about you,' Tante Soraya says reproachfully.

'Mama always worries about me,' he says as he uses a corner of the towel to dry his face. He puts a damp hand on the shoulder of his mother's pale green dress. 'You shouldn't worry about me.'

'Come on, come on.' Mama Deela pats his hand and starts to walk heavily homeward. 'Come. Otherwise it will be time for evening prayers before I've done the sunset ones. And you're going to catch cold.'

For how could Fadeela al-Nabulsi stop worrying about her only son? She had started twenty-two years ago before he was even born, as she lay on her bed with her hand on her belly, attending to the kicks of the new child while she watched its older brother die. She had two daughters, Lateefa and Soraya, and she knew that her third child, her first-born son, was going to die. She had known it for more than a year. He was two now and he could speak and sing and laugh but he could not stand or walk. Lateefa had to carry him everywhere for she herself had been unwell since his birth. And he was heavy and swollen. Swollen and swelling more and more every day and nobody knew what to do for him. He was a placid, happy child and sometimes she could hardly bear to look at him. But he was Lateefa's responsibility now, and even though she was not yet six she looked after him and took him everywhere on her bony little hip, and she, Fadeela, was now five months pregnant and still ill and in bed concentrating on the new baby growing inside her and praying for a boy – a healthy boy to bear his father's name and partner him in his business. What would Mama Deela have felt if she had been there when he finally did? When he sat in his father's shop that first day – under his own portrait taken thirteen years earlier when he was just twenty-one – and said hesitantly, 'Maybe you could let me do the books?' And the old man had grunted and shambled off to the back of the big dark shop and made some show of looking for things in various desk drawers, then vanished upstairs into the workrooms where he stayed with his carpenters and polishers and upholsterers till night-time, and his son sat under his triumphant portrait and considered what he should now do with what was left to him of his life.

She had been spared all that, for she had died in 1956, when Hamid was just twenty-three. There is a photo – it must have been taken a few weeks after that summer evening on the beach – showing Mama Deela standing in the desert. Her dress is blown by the wind and she holds on to it with her right hand while she raises her left to her head to secure her *tarha*. She squints a little into the sunlight and looks, as she does in all of the few photos of her that exist, part proud, part embarrassed. At her right her son stands tall and handsome. His feet are wide apart and both his hands

7

are on his hips. He wears baggy white shorts, a sleeveless vest and a thin, Spanish-style moustache. Tante Soraya, not quite twenty-four, stands on the other side of her mother looking very pretty and windswept in a long, light cloche skirt and a shirt with sleeves rolled up to the elbow, her bare feet dug into the sand. Near her feet sits Asya in dark trousers and a white shirt with a white ribbon in her hair. And next to Asya and looking up at her brother sits Nadia, his youngest sister: sixteen, with curly hair and round glasses. Hamid has got his first job – with an oil company drilling in the Sinai – and his mother and the two of his sisters who were in Egypt had brought Asya with them and come up for a few days to inspect his new whitewashed bungalow and help him set up home. In her room in the north of England many years later (nineteen years later to be exact), Asya had spent what must have been hours staring at this photograph. It had amazed her then that Mama Deela was only forty-four when it was taken. How proud she must have been on that day – and how relieved. She had borne him without mishap. When he was only one year old she had pulled him back – with the help of God – from the brink of the grave. She had seen him through school. She had seen him arrested and imprisoned for two whole years during which her heart and blood had turned sluggish with grief. She had rejoiced in his release and in his graduation, and even though he had not joined his father – Ismail was, after all, a hard man to work with, he was a hard man to live with – the business would always be there and Hamid was in a pioneering, responsible job, a job fitting for a man: for a fine strong decent clever man, as her son had turned out to be. And his future lay before him. Maybe one day, when he'd first stood on his own feet, he would join his father –

'This won't do.'

'What won't do, Khalu?'

'It's Saturday today? Right?'

'Right.'

'I came out of hospital yesterday, Friday, and I went in the day before, Thursday. But I can't remember anything from Wednesday.'

'No. You went into hospital Wednesday.'

'But I went in one day and came out the next.'

'No, Khalu. You went in on Wednesday. You stayed in Thursday – you were having the treatment – and you came out Friday – yesterday – evening.'

'Then it's Thursday that I don't remember?'

'Don't you remember any of it?'

He shakes his head.

'Don't you remember suddenly waking and looking to see if you were still hooked up, and then the pretty Australian nurse came in to check the drip – you don't remember anything?'

Again he shakes his head.

'She said, "OK Mr Mursi?" and you said, "Nurse, where's my ice-pack?" She just looked at you. You looked completely wide awake. Then you said, "I understand the ice-pack stops the hair falling out. I haven't got many hairs left and each one of them is precious to me. Each one of them is *known* to me. If I lose any of them I shall be very unhappy. I shall sue the hospital." '

Hamid Mursi is grinning; his right eye is alive, interested. He throws back his head and laughs.

'I said that?'

'Yes you did, and then you closed your eyes and fell asleep. Nadia had to follow her into the corridor and convince her you were joking – or delirious.'

He pushes his cap over the bridge of his nose and rubs the back of his head, still smiling. Then he nods admiringly.

'That's not bad. That's good.'

'She was going to stop the treatment.'

He shrugs and signals the waitress.

'Nadia must be home by now,' he says. As he adjusts the cap he says, 'A lot of the hair – not that there was a lot to begin with – but a lot of what there was – has fallen out.'

'It will grow again,' Asya says.

'Yes,' he says. 'Yes, I know it will.'

Scene 2

Later that evening

They sit on the balcony looking silently at the sky. A warm, moonlit, July night. Rod Stewart is on the record-player and a supper of cheeses, cold roast beef, salads and yoghurt is spread out on the low bamboo table in front of them. Mint tea is brewing in the teapot and three small glasses stand ready for it. Asya al-Ulama and Nadia Mursi share the cane two-seater while Hamid Mursi, wrapped in his woollen cloak with his beige shooting cap still on his head, sits in the woven armchair and longs for a brandy.

Nadia takes up more than her fair share of the small sofa, but Asya is glad of the comforting solidity of her presence. Asya glances at her aunt. She is looking into her tea as though she could read the leaves – but there are no leaves, for this has been made with teabags. What is she thinking of? Of her brother sitting to her left? Or of the two small children she has left in Lateefa's care in Alexandria so that she could be here with him? How awful to think that even as they sit here the cells are growing. Asya kicks gently at the brick wall. She misses her cottage up in the north. Khalu would have enjoyed it: he would have liked her tiny stream and the horses grazing in the field and the smell of the wood fire in the evening. She kicks again at the brick wall. She had wanted to plant ivy and roses on this balcony, but if she was going to Cairo soon – and for long stretches – who would water them and look after them?

Nadia says, 'I don't know, Hamid. I don't know if it's wise –'
'It's finished, Nadia. It's finished,' Hamid says, but gently.
'I see Khalu's point,' Asya says.
'Of course,' says Nadia. 'His point is very clear. But still –'
'It's not possible, Nadia,' says Hamid. 'It's not reasonable. If the cells were responding to the treatment even – that would be something. But they're not and all the rest of me is suffering. I'm becoming confused. I'm losing days. And the cells are simply unaffected.'
'I spoke to Tony and to June Hampshire today and they both confirmed that it can take three to four treatments before the response begins, and they strongly recommended that you continue for a bit.'
He shakes his head. 'I can't do it. What did Shnayerson say in New York? He said if it were his case he would operate.'
Nadia nods. 'It's a different approach; they're much more aggressive in America.'
'Fine. That's what I want. We get in there and we carve the bastards out. No more treatments.'
Nadia looks at him silently for a while. Then she says, 'I'll call Tony. I'll ask him to recommend a surgeon.'

Scene 3

Monday, 30 July 1979

Nadia sits in front of Mr Haygold's desk as he goes through her brother's file. 'He's South African,' Tony had said, 'but he's good.' Which meant he was terrific. A National Health practice in the Marsden and a private practice in the Cromwell. Two thousand pounds to pick up his scalpel. And he is young – mid-thirties – and looks like Robert Redford. She sighs quietly and slips her right foot out of her too-tight shoe.

'So' – he turns back to the beginning – 'an extremely fit forty-nine-year-old man – weight in indoor clothes seventy-one kilos – automobile accident twelve years ago – several fractures including ribs, scapula and base of skull – damaged left hand – neurologic damage to the olfactory and left optic nerves – blindness in left eye – disuse atrophy of left upper extremity – necessary for him to wear a cast on and off for two years and left with atrophy of some of the muscles of the hand –'

He looks up at her. Her face is neutral but intent. Her green eyes seem slightly unfocused.

'Pretty bad eh?'

She nods. 'He was lucky to come out of it alive.'

'Career?'

'He was an engineer. He lost his job and became unemployable.'

'Ah! Insurance?'

'No.'

'Damages?'

'He got what they called "compensation": seven thousand Egyptian pounds after nine years.'

'Well!' He makes a face. 'What does he live on? Private means?'

'Our father died in seventy-three. He took over his business.'

'Family?'

'Yes. He has a wife and two sons. The boys are both at university now.'

He looks back at the report. ' "June 1974 the patient noted the appearance of a mass in thenar side of left hand. Biopsy revealed a low-grade fibro-sarcoma – led to below the elbow amputation August seventy-four. Clinical examination reveals normal heart-rate 102 a minute – blood pressure 126 over 70 – right pupil reacts to light – lens clear – conjunctivae of good colour – tendon reflexes normal in legs – foot pulses palpable." Right.' He opens a large brown envelope with a stiff cardboard back. 'And now it's hitting the lungs –'

He clips eight cat-scan sheets on to his lantern and narrows his eyes at them. Nadia waits.

'The left lung.'

'Yes,' she says.

Now she pushes her foot back into her shoe and gets up and leans over to peer at the scan sheets with him.

'You see there,' she says, 'they all seem to be clustered in the lower node.'

'Yes. The lower quarter, say, or maybe third.'

'So, it would be possible to go in and clear –'

'He's not responding to treatment?'

Nadia sits down in her chair. 'No.'

'He's had' – he looks down at the reports – 'cytoxan 600, vincristine 2, actinomycin 2·5 and DTIC 500. And how many times?'

'Twice. And the carcinoma is proliferating. He is also reacting badly to the treatment.'

'Well –' He sits back. 'It's your field too.' He offers her the field with outstretched hands. 'Tony says you've worked with him. What would you recommend?'

Nadia looks at him. She takes off her glasses and closes her eyes and rubs the bridge of her nose with her thumb and forefinger. Then she puts her glasses back on again and opens her eyes.

'If I didn't know him I would recommend he continue with the treatment – at least once more – and if there is still no response then we should consider a switch to either adriamycin or high-dose methotrexate as single agents. But he is completely against this; his whole – leaning is towards surgery.'

'June Hampshire is giving the treatment; I'm sure she would think he ought to continue.'

'What did Tony say to you, Mr Haygold?'

The surgeon shrugs. 'Noncommittal. You know Tony. He's seen it all.'

'Yes,' says Nadia. 'But he's been very good.'

'I'm sure he has.' Haygold sits forward suddenly, both tanned forearms on the desk. His shirt is a brilliant white and his tie a brilliant turquoise. 'You see, there's another reason why I wouldn't want to do it.' He turns back to the lantern and points. 'On the right lung, look, there's a shadow. Only one, I know, but definitely there. You can see it.' He jabs his finger at three scan sheets one after the other. 'Here and here and here.'

'I know,' Nadia says, 'I saw it too. But it's ill-defined. It needn't even be a carcinoma.'

'Does it show on any previous scan?'

'No.'

'Does your brother know about it?'

'Yes.' Nadia takes an envelope from her handbag. 'We went to the

States between the two treatments.'

Haygold sits back in his chair and looks at her with new interest. 'Yeah? Who d'you see?'

'We saw Shnayerson at Sloane-Kettering. This is his report.' Nadia places the envelope on the desk and the surgeon picks it up.

' "Forty-nine-year-old white male –" da dada – "showed the presence of three pulmonary metastases. The largest measures about three centimetres and the smallest approximately one by two centimetres. All three nodules are confined to the left lung. A recent CTT scan and full chest tomography shows that there is no other metastasis – find this to be a malignant schwannoma. It is my opinion that we should not wait too long to perform radical surgery." Radical eh? "My decision to do surgery at this time is based on several factors. First, the above lesion in the left lower lobe involves the chest wall as well as the pleura. It may begin to involve more chest wall and become less operable if the lesions do not respond to chemotherapy. All three lesions look as if they are surgically resectable now, however this latter lesion will be a problem. Secondly, malignant schwannomas notoriously are resistant to chemotherapy, however we have recently had some success with cis-platinum in combination with adriamycin. It would be my plan to treat him with this combination chemotherapy following successful surgery. Also I think he is definitely a surgical candidate since he has three large solitary metastases and no evidence of any smaller metastasis in the remainder of the left lung field and the right lung field is completely clear." ' Haygold looks up. 'But of course the right lung is no longer clear.'

Nadia nods.

He picks up the report again. ' "The surgery will be difficult and should be done by a very experienced thoracic surgeon in the field of surgical oncology. To this end I have suggested Dr Geoffrey Winfrey at the Jackson Memorial Hospital in Miami, Florida, or Dr Frank Junior at the Memorial Sloane-Kettering Cancer Centre in New York. The above two surgeons have had extensive experience in this type of surgery and in particular in resecting lesions that might involve the chest wall. The patient may need chest wall resection and reconstruction of that area during the surgery. The success of his treatment will depend on the adequacy of the surgery, even with postoperative chemotherapy, this will not prevent the local recurrence if radical surgery is not performed." ' Haygold nods. 'They are certainly aggressive over there.'

'Yes – and my brother responds to that: he wants to get in there and fight it. But of course the costs in the States are prohibitive.'

There was silence. And then, 'You're really asking me to do this, aren't you?'

'Yes.'

'Even though he might come back in six months' time with a definite carcinoma on the right lung?'

Nadia smiles. 'But then again, he might not.'

'I'll have to see him,' the surgeon says. He leans back in his chair and looks at Nadia. She nods.

Scene 4

Tuesday, 31 July 1979

Hamid Mursi sits in front of Mr Haygold's desk. His file is in front of the surgeon and his lungs are displayed in eight scan sheets on the lantern.

On the desk beside his file is a small silver statue: a slender figure – you cannot tell if it is male or female – stands on the tips of the toes of its right foot. Its arms are stretched upwards and its hands have just caught a small silver disc. Its left leg is extended behind it, toes pointing. It has been caught in mid-pirouette.

'So Mr Mursi, you really want to go ahead with this?'

'Yes,' Hamid smiles.

'You will undergo major surgery. This is major surgery, right?' Haygold looks round at Nadia who nods. 'About as major as you can get,' he continues. 'We'll open up the left side of your chest and take out from one quarter to one third of the lung. It looks as if we should be able to clear it completely –'

'Good.'

'For the moment. However, there is this mysterious shadow on the right lung.'

'I know about that, Dr Haygold.'

'And we can't open up both sides at once. So – depending on the behaviour of this shadow – we'll probably have to open up the right side later, after you've recovered completely. That's another major surgery.'

Hamid nods.

'And I have to make *sure*, Mr Mursi, that you understand that I believe that there is a very real chance that the carcinoma will regroup and grow again in the left lung so that in five, six months you will be back to where you are now – having gone through the trauma of one, maybe two big operations.'

'Dr Haygold, those five or six months would be free of medication?'

'After your convalescence in hospital, yes.'

14

'So I would function normally?'

'After recovery and until a relapse occurs – yes.'

'Do I understand that there is not a very big chance that I do not survive the operation itself?'

'Only the normal odds in major surgery.'

'And when you go in there you will eliminate every single cell of cancer you can find?'

'I will do my very best for you, of course.'

'When can we do it?'

'Well' – the surgeon pauses for a moment – 'I have a space in the Cromwell the day after tomorrow – in the evening.'

'Good. We will be there. It will be convenient for my sister and my niece: it is right next door to where we are living.'

Hamid Mursi stands up and, smiling, holds out his hand to the doctor.

Out in the street he steers the two women towards a taxi.

'Come on, come on. We're going to go home and change, then we're going out to celebrate. Nadia will find us a concert, she's good at that. And Asya will book us a restaurant for after, she's good at *that*. Six months without medication! With a clear head! Come on, girls: we're going to celebrate!'

In one of the tapestried armchairs of L'Epicure, Hamid Mursi raises his glass of champagne –

'I think we should drink to Mr Haygold,' Nadia says, 'since he's the cause of this celebration. To Chris Haygold!' She raises her glass.

'Dr Haygold!' Hamid raises his glass and drinks.

'May his hand be steady and his eye be straight!' Asya raises her glass. How odd that he should be South African. Might he have known Mario? Or known of him? It would depend where he was brought up of course – but he is English – and in two days Khalu will be on the operating table and this man will swiftly and precisely run a knife down his chest –

'Will you both stop looking so worried? I thought the music would brighten you up,' Hamid says.

'You're taking a big risk, Khalu,' Asya says.

'Listen, Asya,' her uncle says. 'Those drugs are terrible. And my heart feels that they won't do me any good.' He turns to Nadia. 'I know that you believe they are best –'

'No,' Nadia says, 'I don't. I just believe they keep your options open for longer. And I'm afraid for you. Surgery is traumatic, but if it works it's best of all.'

'Good. Then we agree. And there isn't a risk of not surviving the surgery –'

'Not if Haygold is as good as they say he is.'

15

'So the danger is in a relapse – after, say, six months?'

'Yes.'

He sits back comfortably. 'I need those six months. I have our father's business, don't forget. And that belongs to all of us, you and Lateefa and Soraya and all our children –'

'Hamid, none of us –'

'There are some things that we have to be serious about,' her brother interrupts. 'We all have children. This is the eldest' – he rests his right hand on Asya's shoulder – 'and the smallest is only one year old: your own daughter. I have to sort everything out. Six months with a clear head are very important to me. And if there is a relapse at the end I won't be worse off than I am now – and my mind at least will be easy. I will be very grateful for six months. Now, can we all forget about this until Thursday? Come on. Let's look at the menu. What shall we eat?'

'They ought to bring Haygold to Alexandria University for a day,' Nadia says to her brother when they've ordered. '*That* could do with radical surgery –'

'I bet I know who you would want to be the first to be carved out,' Hamid says.

'Absolutely,' Nadia says. 'You're right. My so-called husband. But there are a few others whose departure would improve matters. And while we're about it we can prescribe radical surgery for the country – and the whole Arab world.'

'Surgery for the Arab world? That's impossible.' Hamid smiles. 'Who would you take out of Lebanon? And what about Israel? And lots of people would now say eliminate Egypt altogether –'

'You'd have to make sure Haygold's on your side,' says Asya. 'like he knows you're the one who's paying him.'

'Well, the "Collider" of Iraq probably sees himself as a Haygold figure,' Hamid says. 'A couple of hours in his National Assembly resecting a few cells – and his republic is as good as new.'

'That seems to have been pretty bad though,' says Asya. 'Really spooky.'

'The story will come out some time,' says Nadia, 'and it will turn out to have been terrible.'

'They're particularly brutal, the coups they have there,' says Hamid.

'I remember when 'Abd el-Kareem Qassem was overthrown,' Asya says, 'and Mummy hid the newspapers and I found them, and they had these awful pictures of him and his men being dragged about after they were killed.'

' "My son, what aileth the sheep that she is skinned after she hath been slain?" ' Nadia quotes.

'Ah, but still,' says Asya, 'even in coups it takes a certain type to hire a photographer to record the corpses being kicked around.'

16

'It doesn't matter to the sheep,' says Hamid, 'but it tells you something about the chap who's skinning it. This man isn't the one who overthrew Qassem though.'

'Isn't it odd about his name,' says Asya. 'I mean, imagine if he'd been named "Collider" and been a meek little knock-kneed chap –'

'There was practically a call to arms in the *Telegraph* yesterday,' says Hamid. 'Did you see it?'

'No.' Asya and Nadia shake their heads.

'They're worried about Russian influence: "Soviet control over Iraq's oil and" – some word like "unrestricted" – "use of naval bases in the Gulf." And they urge that this "should evoke some reaction in London and Washington".'

'London and Washington have got Kuwaiti and Saudi and Gulf Oil. Plus their own. Do they have to have Iraq's as well?'

'America is worried now it has lost Iran – for a while anyway.'

'The *flambé* for madame?'

'Yes, please,' says Asya, sitting back to make room for the waiter.

'That's really "the wheel of fortune", isn't it – the Persian thing?' says Asya, leaning over to cut up her uncle's escalope milanese. 'One minute he's Eternal Shah of the Peacock Throne, the next he's running away and he's got – ill, and has nowhere to go.'

'Well, Sadat has kindly offered him asylum,' says Nadia.

'Sadat loves it all.' Hamid smiles. 'He's really enjoying it, "my friend Jimmy" and "my brother Henry" and Marcos and the Shah –'

'Do you think it might happen to *him*?' asks Asya. 'Three years ago Deena told me he was encouraging the Islamic groups, now he seems to be threatening them.'

'They're growing very strong,' Nadia says, extricating a curled-up prawn from her sea-food salad and putting it in her mouth. 'You wouldn't recognise the University now, Asya: half the girls are wearing the *hijab*; a particular angular version of the *hijab* that makes them look like the Sphinx –'

'But I don't understand how they can – I mean religion for me and Chrissie and everyone was Ramadan and our grandparents praying and things like that –'

'It *is* understandable though,' Hamid says. 'People have to have something to hope for.'

'But there's lots,' Asya says. 'There are the things we've always hoped for –'

'Yes, but it's all changed –'

'Your generation was brought up on 'Abd el-Nasser's speeches; on "Non-Alignment" and "Socialism" –'

'Yes,' Asya agrees. 'And "Arab Unity" and "The Palestinian Cause" –'

'So they find it difficult to accept the open-door economic policy and begging for US AID and bilateral peace with Israel –'

'The worst thing,' says Asya, 'is this terrible rift between us and the rest of the Arab world.'

'There you are, you see. Because you were brought up believing in Egypt's position – its role in the Arab world –'

'And meanwhile there's real economic hardship at home,' Nadia says. 'You can't imagine. I mean if you were to look for a flat in Cairo these days – forget it.'

'So really,' says Hamid, 'it's neither one thing nor the other. The kids see their ideals being dismantled, and they see no gain to themselves – in fact the opposite. They have to look for *something* –'

'Something that's theirs,' says Nadia. 'You'll see the change when you come back.'

'I've been so looking forward to coming back,' says Asya, 'and so dreading it.'

'Dreading it?' Nadia says. 'Why dreading it?'

'Well, because – I suppose primarily because of – of the Saif thing, you know. And because everything must have changed so – and I've been holding on to things as they were –'

Her uncle reaches across and pats her hand. 'Not *everything* has changed. And what *has* – well, you're young and strong; you'll find your way. Here: I want to drink to the health of Asya who for the last month has provided us with a home and wonderful hospitality in this country of brilliant surgeons and great concert-halls and excellent food! To Asya!'

'Absolutely! To Asya!' Nadia raises her glass and drinks.

Scene 5

Thursday, 2 August 1979

They drift around the reception areas of the hospital surveying the different nationalities – mostly robed Arabs, Asya has never seen so many robed Arabs – the glass display cases, the florists and newsagents, the deep armchairs and deep-pile carpets – 'more like an airport than a hospital,' says Asya, 'but nice.' They loiter in the luxurious powder-rooms and brush their hair and redo their make-up and spray themselves with eau de toilette. They go down to the staff canteen where Nadia has pulled strings to get them admitted and sit in front of coffee and cakes.

They sit on sofas in the lobby and read the day's papers. Asya thinks how 'gauche' it feels, somehow, to be sitting here so anxiously when it is just another evening's work for all the staff. 'These Arabs,' they must be thinking. 'You get one bloke ill – and his extended family has to all come along with him.' Well, it's sort of true. And now Lateefa, Asya's mother, is on her way too. She had managed to make herself stay in Egypt as long as it was chemotherapy. But for surgery she has handed over Nadia's children to Tante Soraya and is flying over tomorrow. Khalu Hamid has been four hours in theatre. Asya tries not to think of Chrissie's father. This is different: Uncle Sidki hadn't had an operation, Uncle Sidki hadn't had Nadia to make them do the things he might have wanted done – and yet – anything can happen. Nobody is protected, not really.

'Nadia,' she says, 'you know, Saif once sent you some car brochures.'

'Did he?' says Nadia. 'I don't remember.'

'But do you remember if you'd ever asked him for any car brochures? Two summers ago, if you'd been thinking of changing your car?'

Nadia looks at her niece a little oddly, then shakes her head. 'I don't remember,' she says.

At last, when they have exhausted all the public facilities of the hospital, when Nadia has said for the sixth time, 'He insisted on doing it,' and Asya has thought for the hundredth time, 'But of course he's going to be all right' – as they sit silently doing nothing on a sofa in the lobby, they see the lift doors open and Chris Haygold walk out. His step is jaunty, his jacket is slung over his shoulder, his shirtsleeves are rolled up and he is whistling. They both watch him approach and as he draws near they stand up. The surgeon winks at them and pauses – ready for flight.

'Wonderful. Wonderful. Cleaned it out completely. Lucky formation. He's comfortable. Good night.'

At Information they are told that Mr Mursi is in intensive care and that they can't even peep at him through the panel till next day.

Scene 6

Friday, 3 August 1979

(1) Large picture of abdominal area of pink dress: a slim waist flaring out into hips. Text: 'Here is a woman.'

(2) Superimpose line-drawing of female reproductive organs. Text: 'These are the reproductive organs of a grown woman. This is the uterus – also known as the womb and the home of the child "*beit el-weld*". This is the vagina – and up here are the ovaries.'

(3) Superimpose drawing of released ovum in fallopian tube. Text: 'The ovaries' job is to release the eggs out of which every new baby is created. God in His wisdom has given each woman two ovaries. Each ovary, with the grace of God, produces an egg every eight weeks. The ovaries alternate in the production of eggs.' Here invite audience participation by asking: 'So how often is a new egg released into the womb?' Correct answer: every four weeks.

It is possible here (depending on time available, sex and qualification of extension personnel and other situational factors) to invite more audience participation by asking the women whether they do, in fact, get their menstrual periods every twenty-eight days. Or more? Or less? After discussion, assure them that variations from twenty-eight days are normal.

(4) Superimpose line-drawing of spermatozoa swimming up the vagina. Text: 'When copulation takes place between a man and his wife, the sperm of the man, by the will of God, are released into the woman. They swim up through the vagina and through the womb and eventually – if such be the will of God – one of them will meet the ripe egg up here in the tube. The sperm is a human cell. And the egg is a human cell. The sperm and the egg desire union even as the man and the woman desire union – and out of this union a new human being is, by the will of God, created. Now, if for any reason a man and his wife have decided –'

Oh dear – how is this going to go down now?

If for any reason a couple have decided to thwart the will of God already mentioned – how many? one, two, five times above, if, for any reason, a couple have decided to render this twin miracle of ovum and sperm as nought, we will show you how to implement that blasphemous decision.

Shit. This won't do. OK. Go back and cross out all those references to the will and grace of God. Now what? Now it doesn't sound like the way anyone would talk in Arabic, let alone in a village. Far too definite and cocksure – so to speak. Positively asking for misfortune. Asya sits back in her chair and throws her pencil on the desk. Behind her, the window looks out on the bustle and the one-way traffic of Long Acre. At her left hand is a pile of rough sketches of figures using a variety of contraceptive devices. Next to them is a pile of detailed medical notes on the use, reliability and side-effects of each device. And next to that is another pile containing the directives of the Egyptian Higher Council for Family Planning concerning the formulation of the messages it would use in its forthcoming campaign. A fourth pile contains a number of pertinent quotes from the Qur'an and the Traditions compiled by Citadel Publishing Inc.'s religious advisor for the Visual Aids Project from the School of Oriental and African Studies. On the desk also are an A3 sketch-pad, five sharpened pencils and the blunted one Asya has just thrown down and a large Staedtler eraser. She has finally learned why she should call them 'erasers' and not 'rubbers' as she used to. At her right hand there is a telephone and she is waiting for it to ring. She and Nadia had left the house together that morning and her aunt had turned into the hospital while Asya had crossed the Cromwell Road and gone on to catch the underground from Earls Court station. That had been – Asya checks her watch – almost three hours ago and Nadia still hadn't phoned to tell her how her uncle was doing. Does that mean something has gone wrong? She reaches for the handbag hanging from the back of her chair and rummages in it for her address book. She picks up the receiver and dials the hospital.

'Good morning. You have a patient by the name of Hamid Mursi who was admitted for surgery yesterday. Last night he was in intensive care. I want to find out how he is, please.'

'. . .'

'Mr Haygold's.'

'. . .'

'Yes, I'm his niece.'

'. . .'

'No, that would be my aunt: his sister.'

The door opens and Gus comes in, bleary-eyed and grinning. He waves a blue envelope at her. She smiles and pats the desk and he puts the envelope down and leaves, giving her a wobbly 'thumbs-up' on his way out.

'Yes? He's still in there?'

'. . .'

'Thank you. Bye.'

No change. Still in intensive care. So why had Nadia not phoned her? The blue airmail envelope lying in front of Asya is addressed in her sister's large scrawl. But the stamp is a British one and the postmark W2. So Deena must have given it to someone to mail. Asya slips it into her bag to read over lunch. The phone rings.

'Asya?'

'Nadia!'

'I'm sorry I didn't call you before, dear. I went over to Mr Haygold's and had a long talk with him and I've just got back to the hospital and checked on your uncle and he's fine.'

'I just called the hospital. They said he was still in intensive care.'

'He'll probably stay there two or three days. I haven't been inside. But I've talked to the sister and he's fine.'

'Good. Nadia, Mummy's plane gets in at five.'

'I know. Are you going to be able to make it?'

'I don't think so. I'd have to leave the office at four to get home and collect the car and drive out to Heathrow. And it'll be the rush hour. And we have a meeting which won't end till five anyway.'

'OK, then. I'll go.'

'But you're not driving.'

'No. But at least I'll be there. We'll take a taxi back.'

'Are you sure?'

'Yes, of course. Absolutely.'

'Then I'll come straight to the hospital. About six.'

'Fine. We'll meet there.'

Asya pulls her hair to one side and twists it into a rope. She tugs at it with her left hand while she retrieves her pencil with her right. She puts the pencil in her mouth and bites it, then puts it down and lets go of her hair and leafs through the images. Her task right now is to co-ordinate the images and the notes in a practical sequence; to formulate a 'message', and to fashion out of the notes two sets of text to accompany each image: one set detailed and technical for the extension personnel; the health workers, teachers, outreach workers, and village leaders all over the Third World whom Citadel Publishing Inc. were hoping would use their new educational device – and the other text, simple and punchy for those same health workers, teachers, outreach workers and village leaders to deliver to their target audience: the men, women and children of the villages of the Third World – starting with the Arab Middle East – starting with Egypt.

In the plan-chest in the left-hand corner are the prototypes of the two modules Asya has already finished: 'Environmental Hygiene' and 'Infant Diarrhoea and Dehydration'. Each series of four images is stapled to a blank A3 sheet – and under them the two accompanying texts are neatly written out in Arabic. Under the Arabic you can read the English translation: 'The river is the lifeline of your village. Discourage your children from urinating in it.' 'Cleanliness is a component of faith. Always wash your hands after performing natural functions.' Others are yet to come. 'Basic Arabic for Nigerians', 'Immunisation' etc. But the one to hand is easily the most difficult. 'Discuss the matter with your husband' should come under the image of the two smiling faces that had been delivered with such labour from the design department: one moustached and male, the other long-haired and female, both a warm, toasted colour meant to appeal to third-worldeans from Chile to Afghanistan. But Asya truly cannot imagine any Egyptian *fallaha* – take Dada Sayyida for example – discussing any such thing with her husband. What would she do? He comes back from the fields at sunset and washes, ablutes and prays the sunset prayers. She puts his supper on the *tabliyya* and after he's eaten she makes him a glass of tea. Their three children are out playing in the moonlight – but what if they are asleep in the corner of the room? She says, 'Let's go for a walk I want to talk to you'? Of course not. OK. So he's finished supper and he starts looking around for his slippers so he can go out and meet his mates, and she takes the plunge and says, 'Abu Muhammad. I was kind of thinking maybe that maybe we might sort of – I mean three kids – in the face of the enemy – are enough for now wouldn't you say? And if we want more later we're still young and God is generous'? It just doesn't feel right. Asya can see the man pausing in his search for the slippers and gaping at the wife who has never before in his presence strung together a sentence one third the length of this one. And yet the Higher Council for Family Planning's policy is clear: the government is not and cannot be seen to be coercing the populace into family-planning practices. The government is not aiming its message solely at women. The family-planning message should not be divisive for the family; the whole family must see that it is in their interest to practise family planning: 'A Small Family is a Happy Family'. Well, Asya tells herself, just write 'Talk about Family Planning with your husband'. But she can't. She puts the pencil down. You'll just lose them if you kick off with something that they think you ought to know is absurd. And she will be the one right there on the spot; testing the stuff out – seeing if it was going to work. It will be bad enough when they ask her how many children she's got and she has to say 'none'. At twenty-nine – thirty by then. Those women would be twenty-four with five kids. Well, but they won't know she is thirty. She can easily pass for – what – twenty-six? And she had been studying. 'Completing her education' as they would say. Even so. Asya is, as she had told her uncle and Nadia, partly dreading it. She has not been to Egypt for five years. And she has not been to a village in, what? Seven years maybe. And soon, in October – in two months – it will all begin.

23

Where will Khalu be then? Will he still be here? Or will he be home and well? She is lucky, really; she knows that. Fresh from the viva for her Ph.D she had fallen into this job, and now that she is preparing to go back to Cairo and teach in her old department Citadel are saying that it suits them just fine that she should be in the Middle East and would she go on working for them there? Yes she will, and gladly too, as long as it is on projects like this, for she welcomes the chance to be involved, to have something to contribute, to be part of real life and not just teaching English Literature in Cairo University – but now these prototypes have to be finished and dummied up ready for testing and there is no one whose advice she can seek. She is meant to be the expert at 'communicating with Arabs' – who could she have asked? She can hear Saif saying, 'What, family planning and empty talk? These are poor people; they can't see tomorrow and you want them to see nine months from now?'

'That isn't true. Of course they know about planning. They know when to plant which crop; they know when to get their children into the fields to clean up the cotton –'

'Yes, but these are natural processes. Try getting them to plant some new strain of something, to try a new method of irrigation –'

'But they must see that it's better for them if they only have two or three kids –'

'Nonsense. Their children are their work-force, their ornament, their providers in old age – you know all that, Princess; why are you coming on like some European?'

Asya shakes her head. Well, Mummy will be here tonight. Maybe she can come up with something. She looks at her watch. One o'clock.

Asya stands in the take-out queue. She does not want to sit at a table and chat. She wants to get back to her office. She wants to stay near the phone – and to read her sister's letter. And she has just started reading *Chéri*. She waves at her boss's secretary who is making her way out of the coffee-shop with his carton of tomato soup and his two roast-beef sandwiches and her own carton of Cottage Cheese with Pineapple and a packet of two brown Ryvitas. Asya gets her purse out of her handbag. Deena's letter peeps out from where it nestles in between the pages of *Chéri*. She can see bits of her own address: the characters big and untidy; ill-formed like a child's. Deena is twenty-three now – teaching physics at Cairo University and thought to be brilliant. She already has her MA and a couple of her papers have been published in Hungarian journals – in English, Asya imagines, although they don't seem to use much language in that kind of paper. Asya hasn't seen her since July 1976 when Deena had come and stayed for three weeks in the cottage up north at the end of the summer. She had written to Muhsin Nur-el-Din practically every day and when she went back to Cairo she married him. Unlike Asya, she could not be persuaded by her parents to wait till she had finished college before she married. Well, it was a different time, and besides, Deena had always been more forceful. So she had married Muhsin Nur-el-Din despite her parents' mild attempts at discouragement; attempts which she had dismissed as being 'based upon entirely bourgeois reasons', as indeed they were, for he was a nice enough chap and kind and thoughtful and intelligent and he obviously cared for her. It was just that they couldn't quite see where he was going. True enough, he was in the prestigious Faculty of Economics and Political Science – but he *was* still a student, although five years older than Deena. 'But,' Deena had countered, 'this is not his real career, his real life's work. He is only at college as long as the "movement" wants him to be there.' She told them, somewhat proudly, that he belonged to a left-wing organisation – a liberal intellectual left-wing organisation – which by right, of course, and under any decent system of government, would be a legitimate political party, but in Egypt's repressive climate had to work underground. She would tell them no more about it for their sakes as well as his – but she assured them that she was not a member nor about to become one – just a sort of auxiliary – a sympathiser. Lateefa had twisted her lips and her eyes had looked sad and bewildered behind her spectacles. This is how she always looks when she comes up against some intransigent, wrong-headed decision taken by one of her children. She would go round looking surprised and hurt for a day or so, and then she would collect herself and gather her resources and set about discovering how she could help them implement their decision with minimum damage to everything that she wanted them to hold on to. But Deena's father, Mukhtar al-Ulama, and her uncle Hamid Mursi, who in their idealistic youth had had dealings with the 'National Democratic League' and 'Bread and Freedom' respectively, found no ground on which to object to Deena's choice. Except that each separately pointed out to her that his affiliation with left-wing underground organisations inspired by liberal intellectual ideals had ended in pointless disaster: for Mukhtar al-Ulama had been jailed for one year, and Hamid Mursi for two, and everything else had continued exactly as it would have done had they spared themselves and their families that particular unpleasantness.

But Deena now combined her own natural idealistic fervour with passion and compassion for the pleasant, undogmatic young revolutionary who might possibly not change the course of history but was, nevertheless, prepared to make the sacrifice of deliberately flunking his college exams year after year upon the orders of his organisation for the furtherance of some future, general good. So she married Muhsin Nur-el-Din and her parents bought them a little flat in the ugly new residential area that was springing up in place of the fields and meadows that used to border the Pyramid Road, even though everyone concerned

25

disapproved strongly of the trend to build on priceless agricultural land and – what's worse – to use the black silt which had taken thousands of years to get to its present state of richness and fertility to do it; to take the provident earth and bake it hard in ovens and throw up leaning, ill-finished buildings that would never even be painted – but what could you do? For you could not find a hole to pass a needle through in Cairo today unless you were a thief or a foreigner – or both.

Over the last year Asya has been regaled by members of her family who have passed through London – and even by Deena's letters – with tales of the new in-laws – and she has created an image of a farming family straight out of World Literature. The mother is a silent, still-faced, black-clad figure out of Lorca: small, but the centre of power. Her domain is the large, crumbling farmhouse and her vocation is to keep the family going. The two sisters, married into neighbouring farming famil-ies, are sometimes from Grimm and sometimes from Louisa May Alcott. The brothers are a couple of well-meaning buffoons out of Dickens or Fielding: they are dogged by disaster. If they decide to boycott the whole-saler who cheats them and market their vegetables themselves, their tomatoes rot in their slatted wooden boxes because they have not con-sidered how they will transport the boxes from their land to the nearest town or, better still, to Damanhur, the big, hungry city that stands only twenty kilometres away. If they buy a donkey as an initial step to provid-ing their own transport it reveals itself to be rabid by spending its first night biting all the cattle in whose barn it is supposed to be making its new home. So the tomatoes once again rot in their boxes and the cow, the buffalo, the two sheep and three goats are all dead into the bargain.

The mother, by sheer will-power, keeps the family going. This she did mainly by raising poultry and rabbits for the dinner table, by milking the cow, the buffalo and the goats and by churning butter, fermenting cheese and soothing yoghurt out of cow, buffalo and goats' milk, before the cow, the buffalo and the goats were all killed by the donkey. And by the occasional discreet sale. Her gold had gone first: her bridal necklace and – one by one – her dozen heavy bangles. She keeps her flat wedding band and her round earrings – for how can she be seen without them? But the handful of gold sovereigns her grandmother had given her for a wedding present saw her two daughters married and then – bit by bit – the furniture had had to go: carved beds, framed mirrors, walnut commodes had all gone, until most of the rooms of the large, sad house now sat empty. But the rooms were locked and abandoned anyway, for who was going to clean them? And who was there to use them?

The father, a dreamy, expansive sort of man from Tolstoy, a failed and impoverished Levin, owns the only pair of long rubber boots in Beheira Province – if not in the whole of agricultural Egypt. And in them he tramps through his fields, inspecting the crops, dreaming up new systems of irrigation, encouraging the odd day-labourer who still works for him, maybe even lending him a hand. If, however, he comes upon a scrap of print – any scrap of print – a child's precious schoolbook lost in a field on the way home, a sheet from a newspaper dancing across the hedgerows – there are no hedgerows in Egypt, Asya reminds herself. No matter then: dancing across the fields, a double-page spread from a glossy magazine fashioned into a cone in which somebody has carried home five piastres' worth of sugar, he will pick it up and, looking around for the nearest tree, will seat himself comfortably in its shade, carefully smooth out his find, and proceed to read. And there he will be found when the time comes to go home for dinner. He will greet the person who had found him with pleased looks and – even if it is some small child sent out to fetch him – he will immediately engage in a lively critical discussion of what he has just read and all the things it makes him think of. He has many half-formulated ideas and theories about many subjects: Methods of Agriculture, Bringing Up Boys, the Capitalist System, the Inevitability of History, Sufism; they are all subjects that he has read about and that had exercised his thoughts and his imagination before his grandfather's library had had to be sold.

He knows – he fully accepts – that it had to be sold. Boys had to be educated and girls had to be married and life in this world needs money and the land yields food and shelter but no cash. Still. Sometimes his fingers long for the feel of a once-familiar volume. And sometimes he longs to read again a particular formation of words of which he remembers only the rhythm. But his library is gone. His subjects continue, though, to occupy his thoughts – particularly the Inevitability of History – and he turns them in his head this way and that – but for any new ideas or any voice other than his own he is dependent on bits of paper fluttering in the wind. He chases after these bits of paper, but always goes home eventually. And he always eats the food his wife silently places before him on their old, chipped, marble-topped table, and he always extols the dexterity of her hands which have prepared it. And he sleeps at her side in the big, brass, four-poster bed with the billowing, white, much-mended mosquito-netting that had belonged to his father and his father's father before him. And every morning he rises at daybreak, washes and prays the morning prayers, and asks for the blessing and mercy of God to envelop his wife, his two daughters, his three sons and the souls of his father and mother, drags on his khaki trousers and his two or three heavy sweaters and his groin-length boots, picks up the large hunk of home-made bread with honey and clotted cream that his wife has prepared for him and strides purposefully out into the fields.

His youngest son – her brother-in-law – is an object of much specu-lation to Asya. He is only one year younger than herself and she has him figured out as more of a Romantic Revolutionary than a Molotov-Cocktail-Throwing Revolutionary. The kind of young man who would have slotted perfectly into the London School of Economics in the late sixties – and gone on to join the Labour Party. His 'organisation', as far as she can make out, consists of himself, one wild-eyed friend named (or maybe code-named) 'Zuku', who keeps everyone up late into the night talking about the ultimate necessity of armed confrontation with the government, and one other very serious young man known as el-Prof who teaches in the Department of Arabic at Ein Shams University and lives in Nawwaz Pasha's mausoleum in the City of the Dead and writes publishable, alienated short stories in a Pinteresque style. Their activities are described by Tante Soraya as 'sitting around every evening in Deena's flat talking and drinking tea and staying up till dawn and being in no fit state to do any work next day'. The Palestinian flag and a poster of Che Guevara and the banned songs of the blind Sheikh Imam seem to figure prominently in these scenes, and so do a wide variety of books ranging from *One Hundred Years of Solitude* to *Das Kapital* to Son'alla Ibrahim's *The Smell of It* to all the Amnesty International reports on human rights abuses in Egypt and Israel and the rest of the Arab countries and South America. And that is it. Or maybe that only seems to be it. Maybe they do other things that nobody knows about. But when? As far as anyone could see Muhsin's whereabouts are always known. He is always around. Well, perhaps that is just this 'cell'. Perhaps all over the country there are other, more active, 'cells'. And perhaps there *is* a 'popular base' that they are in touch with. A popular base that will leap into organised, effective action when the moment comes and the word is given. But the family doubt it. And Asya doubts it. And Deena will not say. Deena is totally loyal to Muhsin and appears to be still in love with him after three years of marriage and a baby boy. Muhsin himself seems somewhat quixotic to Asya. A Don Quixote, however, with no Sancho and in place of Rosinante he now has a Lada. He had at last been allowed (or allowed himself) to graduate from his faculty but he would not take any teaching or civil service job because he would not collaborate with the government at any level, and he would not take any job in the private sector because he disapproved totally of the private sector and the fat cats who ran it. So Asya and Deena's brother, Kareem, who had just graduated from engineering and taken a job with a multinational out on an oil rig in the Gulf, sent his younger sister his first salary – which he said he wouldn't need because he was staying on the rig for another six weeks and by then he would have cashed his next salary – and with it Deena and Muhsin had bought the Lada. The Lada was painted, metered and licensed as a taxi and Muhsin was in business. He would drive the Lada, and a third of its income would be his, a third would be Kareem's, and a third would be ploughed back into the business. The

28

job would give him even more opportunities for contact with 'the people' and hence of pursuing his real mission, and as long as he did not overcharge – which of course he wouldn't – he need not accuse himself of being a 'petty capitalist' or 'on the make' or any such thing. The current talk was, Nadia had said, that far from overcharging his fares he undercharged them, and sometimes even refused the money if his client looked like someone who could do with the thirty piastres Muhsin was about to take off him or her. And, Nadia had said, the Lada was mainly being used as free transport with driver for any member of anybody's family and friends who needed a lift to hospital, or to school, or to the cemeteries, or to the doctor, or to their home village. 'Well,' Uncle Hamid had said, 'he is a gallant, helpful young man, just not altogether practical.'

'But he needs to be practical,' Nadia had argued. 'His wife, all right, has a job. But he has a child now.'

'That's true,' said Hamid, 'I agree with you. But also think how many times you had to send your children to Cairo and he drove up to Alexandria to collect them. Or when Soraya had to go to the doctor with her leg and her husband was away and I was in hospital – who would have taken her? These things count too, you know.'

'Yes, they count. Of course they count,' said Nadia. 'But still: God preserve both their families, for without their presents of cash and food I don't know how Muhsin and Deena would live.'

Asya has never met Muhsin but hopes to do so next month when she goes to Cairo. If all this latest business is over by then, that is – Nadia seems to think it will be: 'The government can't take much notice of a bunch of dreamy kids,' she says. But Khalu Hamid had said, 'They're not kids any more – and anyway, since when did a government let even a bunch of dreamy kids get away with anything if it could stop them?'

Asya had tried to get the details of the story but nobody seemed to know a great deal. A midnight raid by the Mabahith on the unused servants' quarters attached to Asya's parents' house had yielded some rusty bits of metal which upon examination had turned out to be parts of an old Katyusha rocket. The police had been apologetic and deferential to Professor Mukhtar al-Ulama. After all, he was Dean of the Faculty of Arts, an ex-Minister of Culture and a respected public figure. They were sure he knew nothing about all this – if he could just inform them of the whereabouts of his son-in-law, Mr Muhsin Nur-el-Din? Mukhtar al-Ulama, looking at the metal fragments displayed for his benefit in a box carried by a dull-featured young peasant dressed up as a policeman, had said courteously that he did not doubt that the police could – without his assistance – find the address of anyone whom they wished to question, bade them goodnight and opened the door to usher them out. He sat up in his maroon silk dressing-gown till two o'clock in the morning however, for the visit had brought back memories and had shaken him more than he would admit – and he was angry. Deena had no telephone so he could not call her. Lateefa was in Alexandria taking over from Nadia the running of her household so that Nadia could travel to England with her brother. Hamid was ill and he could not call him at this hour. He could not call anybody at this hour. And in late June the heat did not go away at night-time; it settled heavy and clammy on top of everything. Professor al-Ulama, who had a deep-rooted dislike of sitting, let alone sleeping, in the breeze from a fan, knew it was going to be a difficult night – and it was. In the morning he sent an office-boy round to his daughter's flat with a curt summons. Contrite, Deena admitted to having allowed the mutilated Katyusha part to be hidden in the servants' quarters of her parents' home: 'Nobody ever used those two rooms, Daddy, and we meant to get rid of the bits very soon.'

He berated her for irresponsibility, foolishness etc. and confiscated her keys to his house. When his anger had abated and she had made him a cup of turkish coffee medium sugar he had remembered what the 'find' had actually looked like and asked, 'But what were you – they – planning to use it for?'

She had looked slightly baffled. She had shrugged. 'I don't know. Maybe they thought they could make something with it.'

'Are there other bits hidden in other places?'

'No. I mean as far as we know, there aren't. Actually, I really believe there aren't.'

'In that case this is completely absurd.'

She had hung her head. 'I know.'

'Then why did you have anything to do with it? Anything at all?'

'Zuku seemed to really care. I don't know where he got the bits but he was so pleased with them. Then his wife wouldn't let him keep them so he brought them round to us and Muhsin put them under our bed, but I knew we'd forget them and in a while Ahmad would probably find them and try to eat them, and they are so rusty –'

'So you brought them here.'

'Yes.'

'How long have they been here?'

'About three months.'

'You would probably have forgotten them for years.'

She had said nothing.

'They wanted to know where Muhsin was.'

'They came round to our flat last night. But he's at the village. His sister has just had a baby.'

'What will he do?'

'I sent word straight away. I expect he'll stay there for a few days.'

'But that's where they'll go next. They might be there already.'

'Daddy. Even *they* know it's absurd. What have they got? Five pieces of rusty metal? What could we do with them? *Throw* them at somebody?'

Her father had looked at her: her bravado was coming back. 'Deena,' he had said, 'one: the government is not rational. Two: the government is scared. Three: they are looking for scapegoats, to make examples of them.'

And there the story stayed. Muhsin had remained hidden in the village. The police had not found him. In a few days they would get bored with looking and Muhsin would go back to Cairo. In fact he might be there already.

And when she gets to Cairo Asya is really looking forward to meeting him. She has seen photographs of him – mostly, of course, with the child. A tall, slightly scruffy, slim, dark-skinned, brown-eyed, specifically Egyptian-looking young man with crinkly hair and a pleasant smile.

Asya settles into her chair. She swivels it so that she is sitting sideways to the desk. From the window to her left the sunshine falls across the corner of the leather top of the desk. She unwraps her cream cheese and anchovy in French bread and opens her seasoned tomato juice and spreads a paper napkin over her knees and puts *Chéri* and Deena's letter on top of an image of a woman with a pleased smile holding up a pessary between two fingers. She puts her feet up in the patch of sunlight on her desk and crosses them. For a moment she admires the slender brown feet with the now orange nails looking so good in strappy yellow summer shoes – then she reaches for the letter.

Cairo, 28 July 1979

Dearest Asya,

You will have heard that Muhsin has been 'on the run' since 25 June. Officially, of course, he was not 'on the run' since, officially, there was no warrant out for his arrest. It was just that if they found him they would take him. So he has been hiding and we have been waiting for it all to blow over. At first he was at his home village but he was told they were coming for him there so he got away. They stationed four Central Security guys in his parents' yard and they harassed the village dreadfully, so he could not go back there. On 16 July we heard that they had got Zuku. I didn't know about el-Prof but I thought – because of where he lives – he would be harder to find. Two days after hearing about Zuku I lost touch with Muhsin. All our contacts went dead. I checked the police stations; he had not been through any and the Public Prosecutor had no record of an arrest. But they had pulled their men out of the village and so I knew they had him. In the end – on the 24th – we learnt that he was in the Citadel jail. It is a sort of almost military jail which does not come

31

under the official Prison Organisation. I went there and of course they said he was not there and they did not know anything about him and all that. However, Daddy spoke to some people and two of our friends who are lawyers helped and I was able to see him yesterday. I am telling you all this because you are in England and in publishing and have friends in newspapers and all that. It may be a naïve thought but perhaps you could do something? I saw him yesterday and he said el-Prof was there too. He almost could not speak. He could not look at me. They have all been tortured: they have been beaten everywhere, *everywhere* on their bodies and their heads, they have been held down and raped, they have been hung upside-down –

The hand holding the letter falls into Asya's lap. Asya lifts her feet off the desk and sits up straight. Her heart is beating so hard she almost cannot breathe. She stands up and walks to the window. In the street people come and go. A delivery van is parked on the yellow line and the driver is arguing with the traffic warden. The sun shines. She walks back to the desk and sits down. She smooths the letter out and reads.

– they have been hung upside down for hours and had live wires put inside them. He said Zuku was paralysed from the waist down and that he himself was so afraid, he would do anything to get out. But there is nothing he can do. He was crying and he could not look at me at all.

If you can do something and need detailed information or anything at all, write to the address on the back of this envelope before 7 August. If you cannot do anything don't worry, I will get him out somehow.

I cannot believe how your newspapers there keep making like Sadat is this wonderful humanitarian hero. The only people he is 'humanitarian' to are the Israelis.

I am sure you will not tell Khalu any of this now. Ahmad is fine and looking forward to seeing 'Tante Asya'.

Much love,
Deena

Scene 7

Later that evening

He is sitting in a metallic chair. From the armpits down he is swaddled in white wraps. One arm is on an armrest and his head is leaning against the back of the chair. He appears to be part of a big, complex piece of machinery; hundreds of different-coloured wires and tubes loop themselves around him, attach themselves to him, enter him and exit to loop around again and plug themselves into a number of large instruments of varying heights that surround him. Behind his back red pulses appear and disappear and green dotted lines hesitate their way across a bank of screens. His mouth hangs slightly open and he appears to be asleep. He is almost bald. Asya peers further into the room. She can make out two figures lying in their beds with sheets and blankets over them. A green curtain is drawn across the far right-hand corner. At a desk, with her back to the glass panel through which Asya is looking, a uniformed nurse sits working by the light of a desk-lamp. Asya looks at her uncle. His face is bruised and swollen. He looks strange. Remote, yet terribly familiar. She has seen this face before, this bruised and swollen face. Only last time it was more vivid: there were more purple patches and weals and clots of red. And the swelling on the left side had been so exaggerated that Asya had not believed that Khalu would ever look like himself again. But this time he looks so weak. His one wrist is frail and thin. He had not seemed so weak, so tired then. But that was many years ago and he is older now.

Scene 8

May 1967
Cairo

In May of every year, Egypt is gripped by exam fever. The exam that matters more than all the others put together is the General Certificate of Secondary Education: the Thanawiyya 'Ama. Your performance in this exam, taken at the age of seventeen, determines which college and which university you get into. And therefore it is very likely to determine the whole course of your future life and status in this world. In May of 1967 two hundred and seventy-three thousand, five hundred and sixty-six Egyptian teenagers are preparing to sit the Thanawiyya 'Ama. Among them is Asya al-Ulama. Because of the importance of this exam her mother, Lateefa Mursi, has since March abdicated her study to her daughter. It is a tiny room which just about takes a desk and a chair and a narrow couch. But it has a window which looks out on to Hasan Pasha Sabri Street (Brazil Street now, but everybody still calls it by its old name), the main shopping street of Zamalek – and over the al-Ahram petrol station on the corner, to the health club and then the Officers' Club on 26th July Street. And it has a wallful of Lateefa's books and a door that Asya can close. Behind this closed door Asya now spends most of her time with her books and with glass after glass of iced mango sherbet with the frosted outside of which she can cool her upper arms and her face between sips. School is over – and the two hundred and seventy-three thousand, five hundred and sixty-six seventeen-year-olds have been given four weeks for concentrated studying. The exams are scheduled to begin on Saturday, the tenth of June.

On the fifteenth of May Hamid Mursi drops by his eldest sister's flat at lunch-time. He has just the week before come back from London, from a six-month course in systems engineering. The first person in his company to get ready to 'interface' with computers. He has already been up to the company oil-fields in Abu-Rdeis for three days and is back in Cairo settling into a new work routine. His second son is now almost nine months old and both he and his older brother, who is two and a half, are at Hamid's mother-in-law's for an extended visit while his wife prepares for the discussion of her Ph.D thesis on 'Images of Women in the Egyptian Press since the Revolution'. He has, at the family's insistence, got rid of his old black Austin. He had had her for fourteen years and was sorry to see her go, but his wife Sunny, and Soraya, his sister, had gone on so about how old and unsafe it felt that he had sold it to a car mechanic friend and bought himself a brand new silver Citroën Deux Chevaux which is the very most he can afford – and even so he has had to borrow from his father which he hates doing. He is thirty-six – clean-shaven now, tall and broad-shouldered with thinning hair – but with the same gentle eyes and quick temper he has always had.

They sit down to table in the inner living-room, as far from the sun-baked outer walls of the flat as possible, and Asya pulls a white T-shirt over her cotton camisole and joins them, for Khalu Hamid talks to her in just the same way that he talks to her mother and father and does not think that she is weird just because she is seventeen. Besides, everything is pretty exciting right now with all this talk of war. Of course everybody says there isn't going to be a war – that it's all politics and bluff and newspaper-talk.

But if there *is* going to be a war – after the exams – then Asya wants to volunteer to do nursing. She had been in England in 1956 – and, of course, too small. But this time she is seventeen and right here and can certainly do something useful like caring for the wounded.

'Well, Khalu, what's your opinion? Is there going to be war?'

She is permitted the initiative in lunch-table conversations much more now that she is studying for the Thanawiyya 'Ama. As a rule she does not care, but with Khalu Hamid there it's a privilege worth having. Deena and Kareem are inside, getting ready to go to the club with Dada Zeina for an afternoon in the pool.

'I don't really know,' says Hamid, carefully dissecting a chicken thigh. 'A lot of their actions seem to point to war. And a lot of others to point away from it.'

'The Americans won't permit them to fight,' says Asya's father.

The Americans, the Americans, what have the Americans got to do with it? thinks Asya.

'Not unless they can be beaten once and for all,' says Lateefa.

'Well,' says Asya, 'the army is on full alert and the papers say all the reservists are being mobilised.'

'Yes, but that just happened yesterday,' Hamid says, 'and at the same time everyone knows that they've hardly got a budget. Since the beginning of the year the reserves on duty have been down thirty per cent – to save money. You can't fight a war on impulse.'

'What about the Yugoslavs – the UN forces? They've all gone. Would he have asked them to leave if he wasn't going to fight?'

'Maybe he thought they wouldn't go so quickly –' says Lateefa.

'But he must be willing to chance a war?' Asya insists.

'Maybe he shouldn't have ordered them out – yet,' her mother says.

'But he *had* to,' says Asya. 'Have you forgotten what the Arabs were saying? And we can't just sit here and let the Israelis invade Syria – after all, we have a mutual defence pact –'

'You know,' says Hamid Mursi slowly, pouring himself some iced water, 'in Abu-Rdeis some people are saying that there *are* no new Israeli troops on the Syrian border –'

They are quiet for a while and Lateefa helps them all to salad; then Mukhtar al-Ulama says, 'And what's all this business of Montgomery lecturing at the Military Academy the day before yesterday, a coincidence?'

'That must have been arranged months ago,' says Lateefa. 'For his twenty-fifth anniversary.'

'They just didn't cancel it,' adds Hamid, 'and suddenly the old man is here with his lecture all prepared –'

'Well, let's hope it had some useful message for them,' says Asya's father sitting back and starting to load his pipe.

35

'I can't believe they really mean to go to war,' reflects Hamid Mursi. 'Half the army is still in the Yemen, and yet –'

'The other half is very visible,' says Lateefa grimly. 'The Officers' Club is full day and night and those huge trucks of theirs are screeching about on the roads all the time.'

After lunch Hamid Mursi had gone into Deena and Kareem's room and chatted with them for a bit and at four he had left the Ulamas' apartment. In the street he exchanged greetings with 'Abd el-Hadi, the old porter, who was drowsing on his bench in a spot of shade, and climbed into his Deux Chevaux. It was like climbing into an oven. He opened all the windows and drove up to Hasan Pasha Sabri Street where Asya, watching from her window, saw him turn left, get into the right-hand lane, nip through the petrol station and come out on 26th July Street where she could no longer see him. She pulled her shutters closed and settled into her siesta. He felt the car bump over the pot-holes at the petrol station exit. It had no suspension to speak of and no upholstery at all but he was getting rather fond of it. Anyway, leather seats would have made it even hotter right now. As he drove up 26th July Street he was thinking of his mother. He often thought of her these days; of how delighted she had been with the Austin and how terrified of it. What would she have thought of this one? He remembered the day he had brought the Austin home and Fadeela al-Nabulsi – who hardly ever went out any more – had come limping and leaning on his arm down the stairs to look at her, all shiny black curves and gleaming chrome, and then, with less difficulty than he had expected, she had been persuaded to climb in and he had taken her for a gentle drive. After a while, when he turned to look at her, he saw a face that took him back to his earliest childhood: a laughing, girlish face, flushed with colour, green eyes shining and chestnut hair off which the black *tarha* had slipped – untidy in the breeze. That night she had called him into her room and given him a string of lapis prayer-beads which had come with her father from Nablus and made him promise to always keep them in the car. If he did not want to hang them from the rear-view mirror, that was fine – but keep them somewhere in the car. He glanced at his rear-view mirror. Nothing. He should remember to put the beads in *this* car now: for his mother's sake. He was coming to the lights at the intersection of 26th July with Shagaret al-Durr Street. They were yellow. In front of him was a covered army truck. For a moment he debated whether to swerve past it and cut through the yellow light. Up ahead he could see Zamalek Bridge and, just to the left of that, his home. He pressed his brakes. He regretted that his two small sons would not be there when he got home but of course Sunny had to work. His rear-view mirror was still empty. People were still having their siesta. It would be five o'clock before the streets began to get crowded. How hot it was, and it was only May. He took out a folded white linen handkerchief and mopped at his forehead and his neck. He pressed the clutch with his left foot, shifted into first and rested his right foot lightly on the gas. He smiled a little at himself: taxi-driver habits, bad for the clutch, but he wanted to get home. He was directly in front of the Officers' Club and through the open gates he could see a lot of men in khaki moving about and, beyond them, the stage where many of the official celebrations of the Revolution took place. What things would be like on the next 23rd July was anybody's guess, but the chances were that the crisis would have blown over and there would be an extravagance of Fifteenth Anniversary parties. The lights changed to green. He glanced in his mirror and saw another covered army truck coming up fast behind him. He eased his left foot slightly off the clutch and put a little pressure on the gas but the truck in front of him did not move. He looked again in his mirror, the sons of bitches, he thought, the sons of bitches – and then he heard the crash.

Witnesses said that the army truck had come roaring up behind the Citroën, thrown it forward, then smashed it into the back of the army truck waiting in front. They said the Deux Chevaux had crumpled like a piece of chocolate paper – but the truck had not quite stopped yet and had gone on to mount her like a bull elephant. They said nobody believed the man inside would be alive and many people had uttered the Shahada on his behalf. They said the two soldiers driving the two trucks had jumped out and cursed each other and started to fight. Nobody had come near them – for they were army. But when twenty men had put their shoulders to the mounted truck and pushed it off, and when the ambulance and the military police and the ordinary police had arrived, and as they started to cut through the metal and the clothes and the blood and to ease out the body of the driver, the torn lips had moved in the bruised and swollen face, and when several people had yelled at the crowd to shut up and several others had bent their heads to the whispering mouth they made out a six-digit figure that the man was repeating over and over and over again: nine oh three one one one. The man was unconscious but his lips kept whispering nine oh three one one one. Then someone went and used the phone in the gas station on the corner and dialled the number, which was on a downtown exchange, and when he described the car and what he could of the man who had been in it, he found he was talking to the man's father – God grant him patience – so he told him what had happened to the car and to his son.

That evening, while the weather was turning pleasantly cool and Khalu Hamid was in intensive care in the Qasr and Tante Sunny sat on a wooden stool outside his door, and Ismail Mursi and Lateefa and her husband Mukhtar al-Ulama, and Soraya and her husband Muhammad al-Fadl (for Nadia, who could have handled all this, had left a year ago to study in the United States), and, of course, Sheikh Zayid – while they were all making phone-calls and running errands and rounding up doctors, and Deena and Kareem and Dada Zeina were still unknowingly out at the club – Asya went to look at the car. It stood, as reported, just outside the gate to the Officers' Club. Apart from the wheels, it did not look like a car any more but like an empty cigarette packet that had been crushed in a fist then thrown on the road. Around it was a sagging police cordon – and nothing else. No other car, no lamp-post; no indication of how this had come about. Just one crumpled little car in a sober position, waiting at a traffic light.

Two days later Asya went with her mother to the Qasr el-'Eini. The Qasr is like a bazaar: people on the floor, people on benches, a man sitting dead still against the wall with a bloodied bandage round his head, a young girl bent over her stomach, weeping, babies screaming on their mothers' knees and on their mothers' shoulders and at their mothers' feet, student nurses in grubby uniforms, sisters in clean uniforms, fat orderlies shuffling along in slippers with buckets of water and disinfectant and striding young medics with stethoscopes dangling casually from their necks. The doctor friend who accompanies Asya and Lateefa bends over a nurse and she replies, 'Ah. The army accident. Please come with me.'

They follow her down the long corridors. For Asya, all this is almost entertainment. It is certainly a break from studying. She looks around to see if any of the young doctors are romantic-looking. She is not enormously, heart-stoppingly concerned about Khalu for everything always turns out all right in the end and grown-ups always look after themselves and after everybody else as well. It's true that Mama Deela died and so did Daddy's father, Geddu Ulama, but they were old and Khalu isn't.

The sister stops in front of a door with a glass panel.

'You can look at him through here – but you can't go in.' Then, as they move forward, she adds 'It has been written that he should have a new life. His mother must have prayed for him night and day.'

Asya looks at Khalu. At least, her mother says it's Khalu. It could have been anybody for all it is is a human form covered in wraps and bandages and connected with different-coloured wires and tubes to what must be ten different bits of machinery. The left side of the face is a swollen, purple mass.

II

May - June 1967

*...car je ne veux pas dire qu'un éternel été
fasse une vie toujours joyeuse. Le soleil
noir de la mélancolie, qui verse des rayons
obscures sur le front de l'ange rêveur
d'Albert Dürer, se lève aussi parfois aux
planes lumineuses du Nil, comme sur les
bords du Rhin, dans un froid paysage
d'Allemagne.*

— *Les Femmes du Caire,*
GÉRARD DE NERVAL

Scene 1

Thursday, 18 May 1967: morning
New York
Secretary-General U Thant receives the Israeli representative who presents his government's view 'that the United Nations Emergency Forces withdrawal (from the Egyptian/Israeli boundaries) should not be achieved by a unilateral (Egyptian) request alone' and asserts 'Israel's right to a voice in the matter'. When, however, the Secretary-General raises the possibility of stationing UNEF on the Israeli side of the line, the representative replies that this would be 'entirely unacceptable to his government'.

Afternoon
Secretary-General U Thant meets with the UNEF Advisory Committee and decides to 'comply with (Egypt's) demand' and remove UNEF from Egyptian territory.

Evening
U Thant sends instructions to the UNEF Commander in the Sinai.

Scene 2

Monday, 22 May 1967
Aqaba
President Gamal 'Abd el-Nasser closes the Straits of Tiran to Israeli shipping:

– This is an affirmation of our rights and our sovereignty over the Aqaba Gulf. The Aqaba Gulf constitutes our Egyptian territorial waters. Under no circumstances will we allow the Israeli flag to pass through the Aqaba Gulf.
The Jews threaten war. We tell them: You are welcome, we are ready for war. Our armed forces and all our people are ready for war, but under no circumstances will we abandon any of our rights. This water is ours.

41

Scene 3

Tuesday, 23 May 1967
Tel Aviv
Prime Minister Eshkol declares in Parliament: 'The Knesset knows that any interference with freedom of shipping in the Gulf and in the Straits constitutes a flagrant violation of international law . . . It constitutes an act of aggression against Israel.'

Scene 4

Tuesday, 30 May 1967
Jerusalem
Foreign Minister Abba Eban: 'Less than two weeks ago a change took place in the security balance in this region. The two most spectacular signs of this change were the illegal attempt to blockade the international passageway at the Straits of Tiran and the Gulf of Aqaba and the abnormal build-up of Egyptian troops on the Israeli frontier. The government and people of Israel intend to ensure that these two changes are rescinded, and in the shortest possible time.'

Scene 5

Friday, 2 June 1967: morning
Cairo
British MP Christopher Mayhew interviewing Nasser: 'And if they do not attack, will you let them alone?'

Nasser: 'Yes, we will leave them alone. We have no intention of attacking Israel.'

Evening
Field Marshal 'Abdul-Hakim 'Amer's office on the
sixth floor of the General Headquarters Building in
Heliopolis
Nasser heads a Military Conference attended by Muhammad Hassanein Heikal and Field Marshal 'Abdul-Hakim 'Amer, Defence Minister Shams Badran and other top military personnel. He tells them he expects Israel to strike within seventy-two hours, i.e. on 5 June, and informs them of his decision to wait for Israel to strike the first blow. Egypt will only retaliate. This is so as not to lose the good will of the Superpowers – in particular the United States who would definitely support Israel in the event of an Egyptian attack.

Sidki Mahmoud, Commander of the air force, estimates that allowing Israel the first blow will result in a loss of 15 to 20 per cent of Egypt's air power and have a bad effect on the morale of the air force.

Nasser reminds him that military strategy is merely an implementation of a nation's foreign policy.

Field Marshal 'Amer assures the President of the readiness of his troops and their ability to fight a retaliatory war – 'Be it on my head, Chief' – and brings the meeting to a quick conclusion.

Scene 6

Sunday, 4 June 1967
Zamalek, Cairo
A tall glass and a jug of sherbet. Some days it is mango and others it is strawberry. But they both taste the same: sugared water with a whiff of boiled sweets. Ice-cubes – lots of them – float in the coloured water: suspended, pushing away from the bottom of the jug, jostling for space, bobbing around, breaking the surface. When you pour, you let one, maybe two, cubes come clinking out into the glass, then you use the tips of your fingers to imprison the rest in the jug while you finish pouring. Otherwise they will all come tumbling out and you will end up with great

big splashes all over the desk and the books. You have to lick your fingers carefully right away or they'll get sticky. As you lick one, the other dries. The glass is beaded all over with frosted droplets. It has to stand on a saucer – or a piece of folded tissue paper. Asya holds the glass and presses it to her cheeks – each in turn – and then to her temples and the middle of her forehead. The most delicious of all is pressing it to her upper arms; up, near the shoulder, pressing it to the soft, springy flesh at the front and the back of the arms. Sometimes, with her finger, she traces patterns in the frosted beading, but it isn't like a window-pane where you have lots of room; it is only a glass.

She presses the soles of her bare feet on to the cool tiles of the floor and tries to concentrate. If she can be certain of having memorised the 'Socialist Laws of July' she can treat herself to fifteen minutes of reading. Soon it will be six-fifteen and time to open the blinds.

The afternoon is the time for memorising and the morning the time for brainwork. Not that there is much brainwork to any of this. Arabic grammar is about the only thing that can count as brainwork, parsing sentences: the Deed, the Doer and the Done-To; the Added and the Added-To; the Attribute and the State; the Circumstances of Time and Place and, most problematic of all: the Built upon the Unknown, in which the logical Done-To assumes the form and function of the Doer. These have to be worked out. Everything else, when you come down to it, is memorising.

Her study schedule is taped to the wall in front of the desk, slightly to the left. Saturday ten to twelve: Geography; twelve to two: Arabic Grammar; five to six: Sociology; nine to eleven: National Education. Two to five is taken up by lunch and the siesta, and in the siesta, just before she falls asleep, she can read a chapter or so of a novel – legitimately. Seven to nine is supper and a standing dispensation to watch the newly acquired television. At seven all of Cairo is immobilised as people watch the nightly twenty minutes of *Peyton Place*. All her friends are crazy about Alison, but Asya likes Betty who is dark and sad and is carrying Ryan O'Neill's illegitimate baby. Kareem and Deena watch it too and then they all sit out on the balcony eating cheese and olives and yoghurt and grapes. When Deena and Kareem go off to bed, Asya goes back to her mother's study and closes the door.

On the wall to the left of the desk there are her mother's bookshelves, and when Pakistan's annual tonnage of jute (when she had asked M. Maurice, her geography teacher, what jute was, he had said it was mainly used for making sacks – and yet it seemed to be an essential crop – surely the essential crop ought to be what went *into* the sacks?) threatens to overwhelm her, Asya reaches out for one of her mother's books. This is not the best selection; the really good stuff, the novels, short-story collections and plays are all in the bookcases in the living-room. Here it is mainly eighteenth-century and some letters. But it almost doesn't matter what she reaches out for: it is bound to be better than what she is studying.

Secreted inside the top drawer of the desk, the page gleams out at her. She keeps the drawer pushed to. She can see maybe five lines of print at a time and by simply leaning forward slightly she can push the drawer to with her midriff if anyone comes into the room. Occasionally, as she reaches for a book or even as she reads, she argues with herself that she should not be doing this; that it is ridiculous; that in a few short weeks she will be free to read whatever she likes – and openly; that, come October, reading these books will itself (incredible thought) be her work. In vain. It is always 'just one more page: just till the end of this chapter and then I'll stop I promise I'll stop'. And still she reads. Even *Robinson Crusoe* is preferable, it seems, to the details of the Sykes/Picot agreement:

> The British and French Governments, as the protectors of the Arab State, shall agree that they will not themselves acquire and will not consent to a third Power acquiring territorial possessions in the Arabian peninsula, nor consent to a third Power installing a naval base either on the east coast, or on the islands, of the Red Sea. This, however, shall not prevent such adjustment of the Aden frontier as may be necessary in consequence of recent Turkish aggression.
>
> The negotiations with the Arabs as to the boundaries of the Arab State or Confederation of Arab States shall be continued through the same channel as heretofore on behalf of the two Powers.
>
> It is agreed that measures to control the importation of arms into the Arab territories will be considered by the two Governments.

Today is Sunday. Ten to twelve: Arabic. Twelve to two: Philosophy. Five to seven: History. Six o'clock: one hour to go for History to be over – and then release into the living-room and the company of her brother and sister and the black and white television. Since it is Sunday her father is out at his clinic. And her mother is probably locked away in her bedroom surrounded by hundreds of university students' exam papers. Asya knows these papers so well. They have been arriving at the house regularly every June since she can remember. Her parents would come back from work with a car-bootful of them. 'Am Abd el-Hadi was too grand to pick them up himself but his small Nubian assistant would – under strict surveillance – pile them into the lift and then out again into the flat. Her mother's lot have rough grey-green covers. Her father's are always a polished white. They come in bundles of one hundred, arranged back to front in alternating tens and bound and knotted in several tight loops of skin-scraping string. At the top of each bundle, a tatty piece of lined paper proclaims from behind the string: English, Two,

45

Shakespeare – or English, Three, Civilisation, or etc. etc. The top corner of each one of those papers – the corner which has the student's name and serial number written on it – is neatly folded back in a triangle. It is glued and sealed in red wax with the seal of the university. Her mother always has many more papers than her father. Her father's papers would be placed neatly on a table in his study and he would go in there and close the door. Her mother's would go into her bedroom: on her desk, under her desk, in her wardrobe beneath her dresses, in the shoe cupboard attached to the dressing table. Sometimes even under the bed. There is an atmosphere of drama and danger as long as these papers are in the house. For these are Exams; People's Futures; the culmination of a Whole Academic Year's Worth of Work and, as Asya understands it, mislaying just one of these close-scribbled, grey-covered books, or – possibly worse – causing the red seal to look as though it had been interfered with – would result in what amounted to a speedy court-martial for the parent whose paper it was and everlasting shame for the other.

In other years, when Asya had not been studying for her Thanawiyya, when school exams had ended well before university exams, Asya had helped her mother with the papers. Not with actually correcting them, of course, but with everything else. If Lateefa was correcting only one question, Asya would find it and lay the papers on top of one another open at the right page. If her mother was correcting the whole paper, or if she was the last to correct a section. Asya would copy out the marks from inside the paper into the spaces on the cover, add them up and write them out in letters as well as numbers. Then she would have the thrill of drawing a red circle round the grade that didn't make the passing 60 per cent. It was a piercing and complex thrill: part embarrassment, part sympathy and part exultation. It was not as perfect as it could have been, however, for this was still Egypt in the sixties and the only red pens available were biros that were scratchy and dry and impeded the free movement of the hand on the rough, grey paper. Asya did not know about felt-tips or markers but she imagined a pen that would allow her effortlessly to circle all those failing grades with one fluid movement of her hand.

Six-fifteen. Asya puts down her pencil and stands up. She opens the window and secures it. Then she opens the blinds and flings them wide and leans out. Directly opposite, the sun is preparing to set behind the high wall of the Officers' Club. Khalu Hamid has been moved out of intensive care today but is still in the Qasr. His sisters and his wife are taking it in turns to look after him, and this evening Tante Soraya is the one staying with him. Asya focuses her gaze closer. On the eighth floor of the grey building just across Hasan Pasha Sabri Street the Lebanese family are seated with their tray of tea as usual. The father, a small man with an unconvincing pot-belly and upright grey hair, looks normal from a distance, but when Asya had seen him close to in the Nouvelle Pharmacie Victoria downstairs she had seen that he was stubbly around the chin and too bright in the eyes and looked like someone with whom something was going wrong. The mother seems normal and sedate, but maybe that is because she is always sitting down with her broad back turned to the street and Asya can never make out much about her. In the five weeks or so since Asya has started observing her neighbours so closely, she has never once managed to catch the Lebanese mother in motion: either she is sitting, with her back to the railings, or she is not there. There is a daughter: a little girl of maybe eleven or twelve; blonde and very clean-looking, with hair pulled back into ribbons and the pink and grey check uniform of the Manor House School around the corner. Mainly, though, there is a son. Tall, he stands, and always a little separate, in a grey shirt and white trousers, maybe with his foot resting on the low stone wall beneath the railings. Lately, he has begun to incline his head just slightly when Asya appears at her window and she permits herself a curt nod back and then turns away. After all, he too is studying for the Thanawiyya. She knows, because late at night, after midnight, when everybody has gone to bed and everything is dark, the kids who are studying for the Thanawiyya all have their lights burning and each occasionally wanders out on to a balcony, holding a book, and trying to catch a breath of unheated air.

There is another boy in the Victorian mansion-type redbrick building to the left. On the fifth floor. From this distance he promises to be very good-looking: fair-skinned with a lot of smooth, dark hair. He walks out on to the small corner balcony – which must be the balcony of his room – in blue jeans and a string vest and unseeingly stretches and flexes his muscles and swings his arms about. This unseeingness of his, the way he never looks around, makes Asya suspect he is with the Frères Jesuits. His father – tall, grey-haired, distinguished even in a similar string vest and pyjama trousers – sits on the long balcony at the other end of their flat drinking tea with his wife. Above them, the famous painter Asya had been introduced to and admired by last summer paces among the shrubs on his splendid roof terrace and shows off his marble one-armed bending Greek to a grey-haired woman: obviously foreign.

The ones who stay up latest, though, whose light is always on after Asya has switched off hers, are the twins. In the white building to the right, on the fourth floor, the twins were, Asya had thought, the eldest of five sisters, all – from this distance – looking very similar in waisted dresses with lace collars and straight black hair in bangs and pigtails. There is an older woman, fair and plump and red-haired, and Asya had assumed she was their mother until Dada Zeina informed her shortly that she was their elder sister and was bringing them up. Something about Dada Zeina's tone had reminded Asya of a feeling she had had once that her mother disliked that building. She had watched the flat. The five girls were always properly dressed, combed, clean, with books in their hands. The older woman, the redhead, was always laughing. She seemed to have a huge collection of nighties and matching peignoirs and would stand on the balcony in them, unembarrassed. Sometimes Asya could actually see the shadows of the dark bra and panties circling the white body under the semi-transparent blue or pink material. Sometimes she had a young man in her bedroom and would stand in full view of the nieghbours laughing and kissing him until he stepped over and pulled the blinds. Once, with his mouth on her shoulder, she had turned and looked full at Asya, then waved her hand. The man had raised his head and looked, then smiled and waved. Asya had retreated primly and crossly and closed the blinds. Then, almost immediately, she had hated herself and wished she had smiled and waved right back. She dreamed up scenes in which she was with them; sometimes being introduced to strange and wonderful feelings; other times being subjected to painful yet exhilarating ones. But never again did she stare straight at them. She conceals herself behind the right-hand blind and peeps out and is sometimes, late at night, rewarded by seeing, in one window, the two neat twins reading in their books, and, in the next window, their elder sister sharing a watermelon with her lover.

It is almost seven o'clock and both Sykes/Picot and the Socialist Laws of July are still insecure. Still, there are two History sessions left to go before the exam. If there really is no war. Asya stretches against the window-frame. Monday, Tuesday, Wednesday, Thursday, Friday. Five days to go. And then the exams. One week. Then a week which hardly counts because once you start the actual exams time goes very, very fast. And then – oh and then the club, the pool, a couple of parties perhaps, and then join the Civil Defence which had been opened to volunteers last Monday. Learn how to dress wounds and comfort victims of shock. Maybe even learn to shoot and never ever again Geography or History or Sociology but only fiction and drama, fiction and drama and poetry for ever and ever and ever.

Scene 7

Monday, 5 June 1967: 6 a.m.

Sinai

The leadership at the front, having been informed the previous day that Field Marshal 'Abdul-Hakim 'Amer will visit them today, begin to move, mostly by helicopter, from their various bases, to be at Bir Timada Airport when his plane arrives.

7.30 a.m.

Israeli troops attack and occupy Um Bassis in the Sinai. No news of this first blow reaches headquarters.

8 a.m.

The leadership of the front congregates at Bir Timada Airport in the Sinai.

8 a.m.

Israeli planes start to leave their bases heading for targets in Egypt. These massive movements are seen by Commander 'Abd el-Mon'im Riyadh on the Jordanian front and reported immediately to Cairo: 'Grapes. Grapes. Grapes.' In Cairo, the wireless operator is unaware that the code has been changed in the early hours of the morning. He tries to decode the message and fails. 'Grapes. Grapes. Grapes.' The message fails to reach headquarters.

8.30 a.m.

The assembled leaders at Bir Timada Airport see an approaching aeroplane and stand in line to receive the Field Marshal while a military band prepares to play. The one plane is followed by several others which proceed to bomb the airport: the runways, the operations room, communications and fuel depots. The leaders dive to the ground. Pilots run to their planes. A few manage to take off, the rest are killed on the runways.

8.35 a.m.

The pilot of 'Amer's plane approaching the Suez Canal area sees Israeli planes bombing one of the Canal airports. He takes evasive action and heads back to Cairo International Airport. From the air 'Amer and air-force Chief Sidki send commands to the leaderless air force to attack.

8.40 a.m.

Cairo, Heliopolis

'Amer's plane arrives at Cairo Airport and he and his chiefs can find no transport to headquarters except one very old taxi with a very old driver wearing thick spectacles. He drives them very slowly to the operations room in nearby Heliopolis.

8.45 a.m.

Sinai

Israeli planes finish attacking and destroying most of the Egyptian air force as it sits on 'secret' military runways. The runways too are rendered useless.

9 a.m.

Cairo, Giza

The morning session of exams begins at Cairo University.

9 a.m.

Cairo, Zamalek

Soraya Mursi phones her sister Lateefa to say that they can hear what sounds like bombs from the direction of Abbassiya.

Asya al-Ulama stretches, listens to the phone ring in the living-room, and decides to stay in bed for ten more minutes.

9 a.m.

Cairo

The radio and television services begin to broadcast one announcement after another counting the number of enemy planes shot down from the Egyptian skies.

9.30 a.m.

Sinai

The order goes to General Sidki al-Ghoul, Commander of the Fourth Armoured Division stationed in Timada, to move to defend the southern section of the front line.

The Second Battalion of the Fourth, under General Kamal Hassan Ali, moves eastward and takes up its position from the Contilla to the Mazallat on the front line.

9.30 a.m.

Giza

The exam season. One of the best times for trade as far as 'Am Salih is concerned. 'Am Salih has a kiosk on the broad pavement just outside the tall black iron railings that surround the main campus of Cairo University. It is on the corner, the north-eastern corner, although he would probably not think to describe it like that. He thinks that it is, praise God, in a not-bad position because although it misses the stream of students heading from the main campus gates between the two gardens and down to the river, and although it is too far from the Faculty of Engineering to benefit from the affluence which undoubtedly lies therein, it is in a good position to catch all those students who turn left towards the 'University City' or the sports fields. It is also bang opposite the entrance to Applied Arts where the students don't seem to have much to do and like to hang around outside holding their giant rulers and triangles and hoping the girls from the snob departments of English and French will mistake them for genuine engineers from across the way. Also it catches the fringes of the trade that is to be had from the poor but populous district of Bein es-Sarayat, which begins immediately after the 'City' and stretches all the way to the railway tracks of the Upper Egypt Line by the side of which he lives with his wife Sayyida and their remaining seven children. Eleven she had borne him in all and seven of them still live although two are blind but God has mercy on His worshippers and the eldest girl has a good voice and is already making a living reciting the Qur'an for the women at funerals and such and as for the little one God grant him, her father, strength and ability until they find something for her too.

'Am Salih sells cold drinks and cigarettes. On a couple of shelves in his kiosk he also has some dusty packets of Arabisco biscuits and thin bars of Corona chocolate in faded red and yellow wrappers. During term-time, when the students are around and trade is brisk, Sayyida stands with him all day. She sets up a primus behind the kiosk, balances a big, black frying-pan on it and spends the day frying *ta'miyya* and stuffing it into sandwiches with salad for anyone who has three piastres to spend on lunch or breakfast. Together they manage to make a living. Without her he would probably have gone bust long ago. Life isn't easy for a man like him; even though he now sits elevated on a little cart with a decent covering over his stumps. He has put on weight with the years and it is an effort turning the wheels to propel himself around. Nowadays his son, Muhammad, who is twenty, pushes him down here every morning and opens up the kiosk for him. He can manage after that. Especially in the dead time in the summer when it is only every so often that some clerical worker or some student from the 'City' with no home to go to or not enough money to take him there would stop for a tepid cola or two cigarettes from the open pack of Cleopatras. Now, at exam time, Muhammad helps him with the early trade. He leaves at a quarter to nine when the students are all sitting in rows in the giant exam tents – may

God grant them all success and calm their parents' hearts – and there they will stay till midday, when they will come spilling out into the blistering heat of the sun and stand around drinking cola or Spathis and waving their question sheets and comparing their answers. By then Sayyida will be there. She will come with his lunch in the middle of the day. He had tried to tell her not to: the walk is too hot for her, she can get sunstroke. He could eat anything – he doesn't know what that anything would be but still that was what he had said to her. And she had said that the children would be all right and why should he not have a few bits and pieces from his own home to keep him going until supper-time? So she would put out the food for the children and let their sister, not the eldest for she was blind, but Haniyya, the second one, the pretty one, the one who looked like her mother – she would let Haniyya look after them and she would place his lunch on a tray and balance it on her head all the way from the railway track to his kiosk, and there she would help him until the last student had melted away in the heat; then she would place his food in front of him and sit herself down on a sheet of newspaper on the ground by the front wheel of his cart and eat with him. And when, having eaten, he dozed off in the heat, she would push him into the shade and make sure his head was resting against the railings of the university, then sit down and swish away the flies and tend the kiosk until he woke up. She is a good wife to him. Has always been a good wife to him and looked after him and taken account of him, and she had borne him eleven children seven of whom survived and the youngest was only two and was the apple of his eye.

After his son has left and the morning has quietened and heated up round him, 'Am Salih takes down his small Czechoslovak transistor radio from the shelf and switches it on. The voice of Fayda Kamel rings out in mid-song:

'. . . my wea-pon
I have yearned for you in my stru-ggle.
Speak up and say "I'm awa-a-ake" –
Oh war! It's been a long ti-i-i-ime –'

He places the radio on his stump and lights a Cleopatra and the voice of Ahmad Sa'eed, Chief Broadcaster on Voice of the Arabs, interrupts the song: 'The number of enemy aircraft shot down by our glorious air force is now twelve. The Zionist enemy, after his treacherous attack on our sacred land this morning, is learning to his cost that Egypt is not a power to be trifled with . . .'

'It's been a long time for the ma-a-sses
As they come thundering along . . .'

The song fades back in and 'Am Salih slams his fist down on his right

52

stump. 'You sons of bitches,' he cries out loud in admiration, 'you're really going to fight! You're going to fight and be men and get Palestine back after all these years!'

12.30 p.m.
The Command Room in Heliopolis
Field Marshal 'Amer tells guests (old comrades who have come to offer their services) that the enemy has now lost seventy-three planes.

The guests notice that air-force Commander Sidki Mahmoud is constantly on the phone and that he appears to be weeping. His Field Marshal tries to buck him up.

'Amer: 'Come, come man. Pull yourself together. How many planes have we brought down till now? Seventy-three, right? That's right. What more do you want? What have you got to be unhappy about now?'

12.30 p.m.
Outside Cairo University, Giza
The students have come streaming out of the exam tents to the news of war. They stand around in buzzing groups under the scorching sun. Under the scorching sun 'Am Salih is propelling himself furiously up and down his pavement. Up and around and down and around and up and around – the radio clutched upon his stumps is going full blast, there are specks of foam at the corners of his mouth and his voice is hoarse. 'Seventy-three – seventy-three and pray for the Prophet. We'll show 'em. Them and the other pimps. So no one can say one word about us after this. No one would dare open his eye in our faces –'

Sayyida, in her hot black overdress and *tarha*, trots plumply to and fro trying to catch and keep him every time he comes wheeling back to her. 'What are you doing to yourself, Abu Muhammad? What are you going to gain from all of this, man? May seventy-three afreets ride on their backs all of them. Come here. Just come here a minute. You're going to harm yourself, by the Prophet, you're going to harm yourself.'

12.30 p.m.
Zamalek, Cairo
Asya goes down to the Sunni's for sticky tape, blue paper and drawing pins. Her mother, of course, had not wanted her to, but Dada Zeina had had to go and join the queues that were forming to stock up with sugar and tea and oil and flour and Lateefa had had no choice. The Sunni's is where you get useful things like exercise books, sewing needles, balloons for birthdays, squared paper and rice paper and fireworks and passe-partout and elastic bands. Across the narrow road is the Sudanese where you get things that are – on the whole – bad for you, like cola and Spathis

and Rocketa chewy chocolate that sticks to your teeth and – in moments of extreme daring and abandonment – two cigarettes from the pack of Belmonts that he keeps open on his counter.

The atmosphere in the street is festive. Wherever there is a radio, people gather in small excited groups.

The little crowd in Ghattas's ironing shop are smoking their *shishas* while from the radio placed in front of a calendar depicting a shining blond Christ the Shepherd with arms extended in invitation Fayda Kamel sings:

'I am the Nile: the grave of invaders
I am the people: waiting for the tyrants
I am death in every inch of land
If your enemy, Egypt, appears from afar.'

By the time Asya gets to the next radio at the greengrocer's, Ahmad Sa'eed is jubilantly announcing the shooting down of seventy-three enemy aircraft. The large and terrifying wife of the greengrocer is bargaining viciously with her clients and using the cane, with which she normally beats her two daughters, to slash at the huge oak around which her fruit is displayed. 'If I were a man. If only I were a man. You wouldn't see me here today. By the grave of my mother I'd be at the Canal if I had to get there on foot.' Her husband, the greengrocer, sits in his usual dim corner by the okra, spaced out, his hashish-filled cigarette in his hand.

Asya takes her time for she knows she probably will not be allowed out again soon. She passes by the post office where she waves at 'Am Ibrahim who sells the stamps, then she doubles back and crosses 26th July Street to Simonds where she sits on a bar-stool and treats herself to a large *chocolat glacé* and a strawberry tart with lots of cream. Then she goes to 'Am el-Sunni whose shop is practically just a counter wedged into a wall. He stands behind his counter, tall and dark and courteous in a white turban, and he can instantly produce whatever items you ask for and in any quantity you desire and is never known to have run out of anything.

Afternoon
Timada, the Sinai
The Israeli offensive has come from the north. The order goes to General al-Ghoul to retrieve the Second Battalion of the Fourth Armoured Division from its position at the Contilla in the east.

The battalion spends the rest of the day and part of the night moving back west to Timada. They lose three tanks.

Evening

Zamalek, Cairo

'*J'avouerai même qu'à défault de bruillard, la poussière est un triste voile aux clartés d'un jour d'Orient –*'

Nine to eleven is still French. Exams in the universities have been discontinued as of midday – but there has been no news yet that the Thanawiyya 'Ama will be postponed. Asya sits in front of her books. There is nothing else to do. Her mother has categorically refused to allow her to join the Civil Defence. 'Let's just wait and see what's going to happen –'

'We're always waiting, waiting, *waiting* to see what's going to happen –'

'It's the reasonable thing to do. This isn't a game, this isn't theatre. This is a *war.*'

'*Exactly,*' Asya had shouted. 'What more can happen? What is it we have to wait for? We have gone to *war!*'

'You are not going out. You are going to carry on with your work until we find out whether exams are postponed or what.'

'If everyone were like us nothing would *ever* happen. Everyone would just sit around with their books and wait to see "what will happen", wait for things to blow over – wait for *life* to blow over –'

But it was no use. And her father would only be worse. The only reason he isn't here right now, putting his foot down, is that he is out helping to move Uncle Hamid from the Qasr to Grandfather's house. Uncle Hamid is still in bad shape but they've all decided he will be safer and they'll be able to look after him better in his father's house. So today they are moving him back into his old, sunny room in 'Ataba; the room Mama Deela had died in. And Tante Sunny is going to go over and stay with him there. And now here Asya sits – with the iced sherbet and the *Oeuvres choisis.* There has been no *Peyton Place,* of course. Television is showing patriotic songs and footage of past military parades. And every once in a while announcing the growing number of enemy planes brought down. It seems to be going pretty well, although it isn't very clever not to say anything about our own losses since everybody knows there are bound to be some. Asya presses the cold glass to her right temple. It is so hot and now she cannot even open the window or peep through it to see how the other students are doing. All morning she and Kareem and Deena had been busy and by lunch-time the fanlights on the doors were already crisscrossed with sticky brown tape and covered with the opaque purply-blue paper that Asya for years has used to cover her English exercise books. Brown for Arabic, green for Science, yellow for Maths and French, red for History and Geography and blue for English. Asya has always preferred the brighter, more transparent, more crackly blue paper – but there is no doubt that the thicker, opaque type is more durable, does not tear at the edges, lasts for the whole eight months of the school year and is definitely more suited for the blacking-out job it is now doing on all the fanlights and all the windows of the flat.

Evening
Operations Room, Heliopolis

Field Marshal 'Amer is busy answering the phone and making calls to various small outposts of the army. He has severed all communications with his Chiefs of Staff.

Enter Nasser looking pale and concerned.

Nasser: 'I know for sure that there are no American or British planes fighting in this war. They are all Israeli.'

Shams Badran, Minister of Defence and one of 'Amer's closest friends, hands Nasser a report. Nasser sits on the edge of 'Amer's desk and starts to read the report. He looks at 'Amer.

Nasser: 'Rafah is lost, al-'Arish is under attack, Gaza is under siege and Khan Younis will be next . . .'

Field Marshal 'Amer does not reply.

Nasser: 'I have to know the truth of the situation because I have to make a decision on the proposals put to the Security Council . . .'

'Amer continues to be busy with his phones and does not reply.

11.15 p.m.
Zamalek

Suddenly Asya can no longer bear it. She switches off her desk lamp, makes sure her door is firmly closed, and in total darkness she turns the handle of the window and pulls it open. She twists the knob on the blinds and pushes them open just a little bit and puts her face between them. The night air is cool and pleasant. There is no moon and the stars shimmer brightly in the black sky. She looks round at the buildings, massive bulks of a different shade of blackness from the air around them: not one gleam betrays a Thanawiyya 'Ama student doggedly memorising his lessons or a plump courtesan entertaining a lover. Down below, the street is an abyss of darkness. Her eyes go automatically to the two spots where the gas-lamps have always burned all night: the greengrocer's to the left and the bakery to the right. Nothing. Blackness. She can make out nothing at all.

Evening
Operations Room

A retired general arrives and finds Field Marshal 'Amer busy trying to get in touch with an officer in 'Arish Airport: General el-Deeb.

'Amer: 'Deeb, Deeb, I've called you before. I said send a fifty-seven millimetre anti-tank gun to el-'Arish. Deeb, there are enemy tanks in el-'Arish.'

Retired General: 'But how could the enemy tanks have got to 'Arish? Our forces are covering the front.'

'Amer: 'I've lost the son-of-a-bitch.'

Retired General (agitated): 'How could the tanks have got to el-'Arish, Mr Field-Marshal?'

'Amer (looks at him): 'What? Oh well, they just kind of sneaked in.' He gets through. 'Hey, Deeb. Have you sent that gun yet?'

'. . .'

'Amer: 'Send them the gun, Deeb, they need it.'

'. . .'

'Amer: 'The Israelis may not get as far as you if you send the gun into town.'

'. . .'

'Amer: 'You son of a bitch! I'm going to kill you when I set eyes on you. Send them the gun, you son of a whore!'

Scene 8

Tuesday, 6 June 1967: morning
Cairo
Al Akhbar newspaper proclaims eighty-six Israeli planes down.
The BBC and all foreign stations are jammed.
Cairo Radio continues to broadcast news of Israeli planes shot down and nationalist songs:

'Leave my skies for my skies will burn you,
Leave my Canal for my waters will drown you,
And beware the land for my land is explosive.
This land is mine
And here my father sacrificed . . .'

Gaza, Palestine
United Nations Emergency Forces post at Gaza hit by the Israelis.
Fifteen Indian soldiers killed.

Timada, Sinai
General al-Ghoul receives an order to retreat with the Fourth Armoured
Division to the Second Line and defend the Sinai Passes.

12.45 p.m.
Gaza, Palestine
General 'Abd el-Mon'im al Huseini surrenders Gaza.

Afternoon
Operations Room, Heliopolis
Field Marshal 'Amer summons Chief of Staff Muhammad Fawzi.
    'Amer: 'I want you to draw up a plan for the immediate withdrawal of
our forces to the west of the Canal.'
    Fawzi: 'Sir, our armed forces are doing well. Apart from the Seventh
in the North they're holding fast –'
    'Amer: 'You've got twenty minutes.'
    Twenty minutes pass and Fawzi returns with three senior officers and
a broad plan to withdraw the army over four days.
    'Amer: 'You want four days and three nights, Fawzi?' Laughs bitterly.
'I've already given the order to withdraw within twenty-four hours.'

Midnight
Sinai, the Passes
The Fourth Armoured Division has taken up its position in the Passes
and is poised to defend them.

Scene 9

Wednesday, 7 June 1967: dawn
Palestine
Khan Younis falls.

The Passes
The order comes by phone from General Salah Muhsin, Commander of
the army. The Fourth Armoured Division is to withdraw west of the
Canal. The withdrawal will start at noon.

General al-Ghoul: 'Sir, my division is practically untouched. Why would I withdraw? And to withdraw at noon, in the eye of the sun, I'd be asking the Israelis to bomb it. My tanks will be trapped –'

General Muhsin: 'These are the Field Marshal's orders. Maybe he's prepared some air cover for you.'

General al-Ghoul: 'Sir. I beg of you. Check with the Field Marshal again. The enemy has control of the air. If we have to withdraw, let's at least do it at night –'

General Muhsin: 'You have your orders, General. Carry them out.'

10 a.m.
Cairo

The Thanawiyya 'Ama has been indefinitely postponed. The sirens sound continually over Cairo. The BBC has been jammed for two days and Cairo Radio continues to play martial music and nationalist songs – but without announcements.

12 p.m.

The radio announces: 'Our troops are valiantly holding the Second Line of Defence.'

How, wonders Asya, do we go from shooting down a hundred and fifty planes and incurring minimum casualties to holding the second line of defence?

Straggling, dazed-looking soldiers begin to appear on the streets of Cairo.

Afternoon
The Crossing south of the Bitter Lakes

The Fourth Armoured Division has completed its retreat from the Passes and is crossing the Suez Canal at the southern point. The division has been distributed by the communications officers at the crossing: some units are sent to Ismailia, some towards Cairo. The Second Brigade has been told to camp in the Gardens of al-Tahira Palace in Cairo.

General al-Ghoul heads for the Command in Ismailia. There he finds General Salah Muhsin on the phone. As he waits he hears General Muhsin say, 'No, no, sir. The Fourth Division has not returned. These are just some light elements. No, sir. The division is in the Passes. Yes, sir, all of the Fourth Division is in the Passes.'

General Muhsin puts the phone down and turns to General al-Ghoul.

General Muhsin: 'What brings you here?'

General al-Ghoul: 'You, sir. You recalled me. You said withdraw at noon. You said they were the Field Marshal's orders –'

General Muhsin: 'The orders have been changed.'

General al-Ghoul: 'Changed? When were they changed? Why was I not told?'

General Muhsin: 'Listen, General. Go back. Go back at once.'

General al-Ghoul: 'Go back where?'

General Muhsin: 'Back to the Passes.'

General al-Ghoul: 'The Passes? Go back to the Passes.' Shouting. 'What the hell do you think I'm running here? A bicycle? This, sir, is an armoured division. Your officers have sent parts of it to Cairo. You think we can just turn around and head back? Where are our supply lines? Where was our air cover? We have no fuel –'

General Muhsin: 'General, these are your orders. I've told you: get back to the Passes. Now go.

Evening

Cairo

The sirens sound almost continuously along with the thud of anti-aircraft guns. Cairo is completely dark and a curfew has been imposed. Brick walls and sandbags have appeared at the entrances to all buildings. The few cars which are allowed in the streets at night have their headlights painted blue. Army units are to be found on bridges and near electricity and water stations – on guard.

An entire armoured battalion is observed marching mysteriously through Cairo from the north. It sets up camp in the gardens of al-Tahira presidential palace. Panic spreads among the units guarding the palace. Is this a coup? Should they attack?

The battalion is revealed to be the Second Battalion of the Fourth Armoured Division, the flower of the army. The command comes through to send it immediately back to Ismailia.

'I saw the battalion and I was appalled,' Salah al-Hadidi, Commander of the Army in Cairo, is to say many years later. 'Appalled at the condition of these men and the obvious physical and psychological exhaustion they were suffering from. They appeared to have spent the previous two days in constant movement, in combat and under threat from enemy aeroplanes, and were in total confusion as to their next set of orders.'

Zamalek

Pointless now to study or revise. Impossible to work. Impossible to do anything except chafe and fret and fight with Lateefa who now wants her children to remain in the inner living-room of their flat and not even sit – with the windows closed – in the outer rooms where the walls could fall in on top of them at any moment. Dada Zeina cannot come any more. She has to stay in her own home and look after her own children. No shops are open to be sent to buy anything from. To go to the club would

60

be unthinkable. Apart from the odd phone conversation with a friend, the world has been narrowed down to the inner living-room. Even novels are no good any more: Asya opens *Madame Bovary*, *Middlemarch*, *Anna Karenina*, and closes them again. Out there, there is the world and action and history taking shape. And in here: waiting, helplessness – paralysis.

Scene 10

Thursday, 8 June 1967: 2 a.m.
The Bitter Lakes
The fuel arrives at last and the reassembled Fourth Armoured Division refills itself.

4 a.m.
The Division heads back for the Passes.

As it crosses the Western Sinai it comes across large numbers of soldiers dragging themselves in the opposite direction: westwards towards the Canal, suffering badly from burns, wounds and thirst.

7 a.m.
The Division enters into combat. In the absence of any air cover, all the tanks are bombed, enemy aircraft flying so close that the soldiers swear they could see the pilots clearly. A rocket for each tank followed by a burst of napalm.

No communication is possible with any of the commands in Ismailia or Suez. Headquarters in Cairo appear to have closed down.

The Fourth Armoured Division is wiped out.

Scene 11

Friday, 9 June 1967: evening

President Nasser addresses the nation. From somewhere private. No audience. No applause. There he is: the big square head, the magnetic eyes, the massive shoulders, the pause before he speaks. What have you done to us, Chief? Oh, what have you done to us?

'I tell you truthfully and putting aside any factors on which I might have based my attitude during the crisis, that I am ready to bear the whole responsibility for what has happened. I have taken a decision in which I am asking you all to help me. I have decided to give up completely and finally every official post and every political role and to return to the ranks of the masses and do my duty with them like every other citizen.

'In accordance with Article 110 of the Provisional Constitution pro-mulgated in March 1964 I have entrusted my colleague, friend and brother Zakariyya Muhyi-d-Din with taking over the post of President and carrying out the constitutional provisions on this point. After this decision, I place everything I have at his disposal in dealing with the grave situation through which our people are passing.'

They've got you now, they've got you. They've wanted to for fifteen years and now they have. A terrible sadness. A desolation. Asya sobs in front of the television. Kareem and Deena sit mutely miserable. Their father and mother go into their bedroom, saying nothing and closing the door. And is this a time to go away? OK, maybe you are responsible. In fact, of course you are responsible. But how can we let you go? What shall we do without you?

Last winter Asya had seen him; not just passing by in a motorcade as she – as everyone – had often seen him, but much closer, in a concert to celebrate the new session of the National Assembly.

It had been a top-notch affair. In the huge, domed Festival Hall of Cairo University, Ummu Kulthoum would sing for the President and his guests. The stalls, the boxes, the circle and the galleries were full to capacity when 'Abd el-Nasser had walked in at half past eight. In the whirlpool of bodyguards, photographers and ushers surrounding him, he was the still centre; he stood out. Taller than any man there – except possibly his friend Field Marshal 'Amer who kept abreast with him but was colourless and bland. The eye immediately went to the magnificent head and shoulders rising above the crowd. The heart leapt in his presence. His raised hand waved in greeting, the black eyebrows and the eyes crinkled up with a smile. The audience rose to its feet in an ecstasy of applause. ('But what about the purges? Here: in this very university?' whispered a quiet voice in her head. 'What about the concentration camps? The torture of both the leftists and the Muslim Brotherhood?' I don't know. I don't know. Maybe he never knew of it. How can one man know everything? 'What about Salah Nasr and the Mukhabarat, the huge intelligence organisation that has been turned against the people?' What do I know of government? How do I know what he knows? He nationalised the Canal, he got rid of the British Occupation, he gave us back our dignity – and at home, what about the clinics he's building everywhere? What about the High Dam? What about electricity for the peasants and land reform and education? He has to be a good man.) When he reached the middle of the front row he turned and faced the audience. His smile was wide and shining. He raised both arms above his head. 'Amer sat down abruptly. Nasser clasped both hands together and beamed around the auditorium. He gave one last wave, then turned and sat down next to the Field Marshal.

Ummu Kulthoum stands in a long grey gown of French dentelle, with the famous dark glasses on her thyroid-bulged eyes and the famous long silk handkerchief clasped in her right hand. The legendary voice soars and drops in the concert-hall. Up and down and around and up and down and around:

> 'O my heart do not ask where is love,
> It was a fort of my imagination – and it fell.
> Let's drink together over its ruins
> Let's drink and let my tears slake my thirst –'

A thirty-two-line lyric is made to last for two hours.

> 'My yearning for you burns into my side
> And the seconds are live coals in my blood.

> Give me my freedom! Let loose my hands!
> I have given you my all and held back nothing.
> I ache with your bonds drawing blood from my wrists
> Why do I hold on to them when they have availed me nothing?
> Why do I hold on to vows you have broken
> And this pain of imprisonment when the world is mine?'

For a moment the audience is apprehensive. Would he perhaps think that this was a veiled reference to his Mukhabarat? How very audacious she is. Who else would have dared to sing this stanza – even though it is in a love-song? Then the Chief is seen to laugh and clap his hands and the audience goes wild: 'Tani,' 'Encore,' 'Bis,' they cry. And it is only when she has repeated the stanza four times that they allow her to go on:

> 'Where from my eye is a magical lover?

In him is dignity and majesty and bashfulness.
Confident of step he walks a monarch,
Unjustly beautiful, melodiously proud,
His enchantment is perfumed like the breath of gods,
His absent gaze is the dream of nightfall.'

Don't go. Oh, please don't go. Stay and we'll all sort it out together. I can't bear how sad you look. I can't bear what they've done to you. It can't be that bad. Nothing can be that bad. We'll all sort it out – together.

11 p.m.
The people of Cairo are pouring into the streets. They are heading for 'Abd el-Nasser's house in Heliopolis. They are begging him to stay.

Scene 12

Saturday, 10 June 1967
'Abd el-Nasser announces his decision to submit to the will of the people. He will remain as President.

Field Marshal 'Abdul-Hakim 'Amer is given the choice of departing immediately for any country in the world. He refuses and barricades himself in his villa with his family, his bodyguards and his close friends.

Scene 13

Monday, 10 July 1967: midday
Cairo, Midan el-'Ataba-l-Khadra
The Place of the Green Threshold: the absolute centre of the city. Some ten acres of land encircled by massive, Italianate, colonnaded buildings. In the middle is a lush garden – for this is where the Eastern Desert ends

and the rich earth of the Nile valley begins. The hills of the Eastern Desert come rolling down Shari' al-Azhar and Shari' Muhammad 'Ali but they stop here: at the Green Threshold. On the circumference of the garden yellow trams crawl lazily like fat caterpillars. Seven roads converge on 'Ataba and branch away from it: one to each district of the city. Shari' al-Azhar leads east: to the mosques and bazaars of the Fatimids and from there to the cemeteries and the Eastern Desert. Shari' Farouk leads north: to Abbassiya and Heliopolis. Shari' Klut Bey goes northwest, through the whores' district in Azbakiyya to the railway station at Rameses. Shari' 'Adli and Shari' Sarwat go west, through Midan el-Opera towards the Nile and Zamalek and then Giza and the Western Desert. Shari' 'Abd el-'Aziz runs south to 'Abdin palace and the slaughterhouse and Coptic Cairo, and Shari' Muhammad 'Ali, with its musicians and dancers and printing presses and revolutionary coffee-houses, leads south-east to the Gate of the People and up to the Citadel of Salah-u-din and the cemeteries and the desert once again.

Arranged around Midan el-'Ataba-l-Khadra are the National Theatre, the Central Post Office, the Fire Brigade and the Central Market. And on Morgan Street, facing the big covered market, is the furniture shop of Ismail Mursi. Today Ismail Mursi sits in his shop – under the photograph of his son, twenty-three years old and so serious with his steel-rimmed glasses – and cannot find it in his heart to put on his jacket and go chasing debts or orders in government offices or making courtesy calls on business rivals. 'Waste' is the word that keeps coming to his mind. 'All gone to waste.' These past few weeks have knocked the strength out of everyone, and as if that were not enough today he has learnt the extent of the damage his son had suffered. His only son.

'Praise God and thank Him, 'Am Mursi.'

Sheikh Zayid, his friend and companion of forty years, sits telling his beads beside him. Mursi shrugs and whisks at a fly with his horse-tail whisk with the leather handle.

'Praise God and thank Him,' Sheikh Zayid says again. 'There isn't a family in this country that hasn't lost a son or a brother this summer. You still have your son. A bit of time and care and he'll be like iron again.'

Waste, Ismail Mursi thinks. Everything. Waste. He reaches into his trouser pocket and takes out his silver snuff-box. He puts his fly-whisk down across his knees and sits holding the snuff-box in his left hand and tapping its lid with the forefinger of his right. Zayid cares for the boy, of course; many a time when Hamid was small and got too tired to walk Zayid had hoisted him on to his shoulders and walked along. He had taught him to swim when he was four and had smuggled him money when he was in jail and had stood by him at his wedding like a second father. And just the other day, when they brought him home from hospital – on the first day of the war with the sirens wailing and the thud of the guns rolling down Farouk Street – who had practically carried the boy from the hospital to his bedroom? Sheikh Zayid. But still, he was not his son. Flesh of his flesh and blood of his blood. Zayid's own son had, it was true, been shunted into Sinai with the Reserves, but he was back now and at work as though nothing had happened.

'How's Yosri doing?' Mursi asks, opening the box and taking out a careful pinch of snuff.

'We thank God.' Sheikh Zayid raises his hands for a moment helplessly. 'He's always frowning and looks – what's that word they keep using – depressed. But we thank God and praise Him all the same.'

Ismail Mursi pushes the pinch of snuff into his nose. He closes his eyes and pulls in his breath loudly, then wipes a crumpled white handkerchief across his face. He makes sure the snuff-box is shut tight, then pushes it back into his pocket without offering it to his friend.

'And who's not depressed?' he asks.

Sheikh Zayid raises his eyebrows so that even the prayer-spot in the middle of his forehead looks wrinkled. He tells his beads. He does not take snuff. He does not drink beer. He does not even smoke cigarettes – only a *shisha* from time to time. His piety, his helpfulness and the dark *zebibah* engraved in the centre of his forehead through repeated pressings to the floor in prayer had all earned him the title 'Sheikh' instead of the secular "Am' that Ismail Mursi goes by. He glances at his friend from under heavy lids then turns to see if the *shisha* boy from the coffee-shop is anywhere in sight.

He knows what 'Am Mursi is feeling. The labour of years, everything he'd done, the money he'd made, the business he'd built up, were – in the end – all for Hamid. The boy hadn't turned out exactly as his father had wished – hard-nosed and practical – but that was the way of the world, and he was a good boy; warm-hearted and straight and he was doing well and what had happened to him had been on nobody's mind –

'Let's get up and stretch our legs,' Ismail Mursi says standing up suddenly. 'We'll go to Mahmoud's and order some grilled fish for the house for lunch – and for us too.' He shrugs into his jacket.

Outside, Farrag, the foreman, gets to his feet. His master makes a vague motion towards him with his hand but Sheikh Zayid salaams him politely and the man stands and watches the two friends walk down Morgan Street towards Shari' Muhammad 'Ali. They walk slowly in the centre of the road where there is no shade – 'Am Mursi's shoulders hunched up in his jacket, making the same vague gesture with his hand at the men who greet him from their shops on either side of the road, Sheikh Zayid straight-backed and big-boned looking twice as tall as the older man and courteously raising his hand to his head when somebody calls out to him by name.

Ismail Mursi is walking down the street he has known for fifty-eight years and feeling dislocated. He has not been feeling himself since the accident – but the boy had been alive and he had told himself he would pull through. When the phone-call came God had been good to him and numbed his senses so that he was able to phone Hamid's sisters and send for Sheikh Zayid – but when he had arrived at the Qasr and followed the nurse down those long, soul-darkening corridors he had felt his heart becoming more and more constrained so that by the time they had arrived at intensive care he could hardly draw his breath, and when he had looked through the panel – he shakes his head as he walks down Morgan Street, trying to shake away that other head on the other side of the panel: the face bloodied and broken and purple, the eyes sealed, the swollen tongue pushing through the bruised lips; trying to shake away the memory of the moment when he, Ismail Mursi, the Sa'idi from Bani Murr, who was respected and feared in all corners of the furniture trade, and whose word was law in the 'Ataba Market, had sat on a bench in a hospital corridor, hidden his face in his hands and wept out loud like a woman.

9 p.m.

Still with hunched shoulders Ismail Mursi negotiates the wheelbarrows, pot-holes and parked trucks of Morgan Street to its northern end. He crosses Shari' al-Azhar and starts up Shari' Farouk (now Shari' el-Geish of course, he thinks bitterly) where he has to cross again. He could do this route with closed eyes. In fact he almost *is* doing it with closed eyes for he never once looks around him. Forty-two years he has walked from his home to his shop and from his shop to his home. He had taken the flat in Shari' Farouk in 1925 when he had decided to get married, and he had brought his bride to it that same year. All his children had been born there, and one – God have mercy on his soul – had died there. And their mother had died there too. Fadeela. As he walks into the marble entrance hall he remembers her. The face she lifted towards him was anxious, the eyes, still green and soft and perfectly aligned, were troubled. 'It's Hamid, Si Ismail, Hamid. I don't know what's the matter with him. All day he's had a raging fever. Suppositories I've tried. Cold compresses with vinegar all day. I don't know what to do.' The year was 1933. As he steps into the old, creaking lift he remembers turning left off the hall of his flat, and there in the large bed with the carved headboard that came from his own workshop his son lay quiet and still. He had never seen him so quiet and still. He had walked up to the bed and put his hand on the damp forehead and the boy had looked up at him silently. 'He isn't even crying,' Fadeela's voice said behind him. The lift shudders to a stop and he walks out. On the terrace that leads to his flat he pauses and looks down. Cairo is still dark. The windows are still papered over and the street-lamps are unlit. The globe on top of the old

67

Averino building has been broken and there is a gaping, jagged-edged hole where half the world used to be. He puts his key in the lock and goes in. To the left, the door of Hamid's room is closed. The glass panels are papered over but under the door there is a faint gleam of light. Only the night-light burns in the hall but the old clock chimes nine times and Soraya walks in from the corridor and says, 'Good evening, Father.'

Ismail Mursi grunts and shoves past his daughter and into the second room on the left and closes his door. He turns on the light and sits down heavily on his bed. She had sat next door, Fadeela, with the boy on her knee. For days on end she had sat there. After the doctor – el-Manzalawi Pasha himself he had brought in – had said there was nothing more he could do. She had sat and held the boy on her knee. She had lost one already and was not going to let go of the second. So she had sat and held him on her knee. Soraya was four and Lateefa was seven and they had brought her compresses for Hamid and tea for herself for she would eat nothing. And her women friends had come and gone. Illnesses, marriages, deaths, these things are all for women. He bends down and takes off his shoes and socks. His bare feet find his slippers exactly where they are supposed to be, then he pushes them off again as he loosens his belt and undoes the buttons of his flies. He stands up and steps out of his trousers and leaves them on the floor where they have fallen. He pushes his feet back into the slippers and shuffles over to the hanger where he hooks his jacket. He fumbles a bit with the buttons at his wrists, then he gets his shirt off and lets that too drop to the floor. From his wardrobe he takes a fresh *galabiyya* and puts it on. He throws a fresh towel over his shoulder then walks down the long, long corridor to the bathroom. As he passes the living-room he sees Soraya, sitting in the corner of the sofa, sewing, while Ne'ma, the servant girl, sits on the floor close up to the television which is switched on very low. Muhammad al-Fadl is probably already asleep with the baby, as usual.

When Ismail Mursi comes back to the living-room and sits himself down in his armchair facing the television, Soraya speaks sharply to Ne'ma.

'Come on, Ne'ma. You'd better get to bed. Meedo will be waking you up early in the morning.'

The girl pouts at Soraya and smiles at Ismail Mursi.

'But I'm not sleepy yet, Sett Soraya.'

'Come on, come on.' Soraya is impatient. 'We have lots to do tomorrow. Get up.'

Ismail Mursi thinks that Soraya's face is hardening. She is the most beautiful of his daughters. Truly beautiful. Not her mother's looks. Only Hamid had those. But beautiful. There was a time when she was in her early twenties when she looked like a film star. American or Italian. Something like that. But now she is thirty-seven and her face is hardening. The girl Ne'ma stands up in stages like a camel: first she shows one plump white leg to just above the knee. Then she bends right over so he can see the outline of her rump just two arm's-lengths away from him. Then she straightens and faces him and smooths her smock down over her thighs.

'Shall I prepare you some supper, Sidi, before I go to bed?'

Soraya stands up.

'*I'm* going to prepare supper. You go get to sleep. Now.'

Ismail Mursi feels the familiar reassuring tingle around his groin but right now he is not disposed to think about it – or even to resent Soraya for continually thwarting him. His thoughts are on his son. The sight of one eye gone for ever. No possibility of reconnecting the nerve. The eye itself is still there. Yes. But useless. One hand too. Crushed. Useless. The most they could do was make him a special glove which would be strapped to the wrist and into which the fingers could be stuffed. Just to make him more comfortable. A couple of teeth knocked out. A broken jaw. And the brain? The brain, doctor? he had asked. Yes, it will be affected. But not much, and only in the areas of memory and concentration. Memory and concentration? The boy's work is all with figures, with machines, with computers. What is he going to do?

'How's he been today?'

Soraya sets his tray down in front of him and hands him a plate and a napkin. On the tray there is some yoghurt, honey, dried bread, a glass of tea and a small saucer with his tablets. She goes back to her sofa.

'We praise God.'

'Isn't he any better?'

'Yes.' She bends over her sewing. 'He's better.'

'Did anyone come to see him?'

'His friends are on the phone all day.'

He breaks the bread. 'If Nadia were here –'

'What can she do that we haven't done? The best doctors have seen him.'

He spoons the yoghurt into his mouth. On television a group of carefully poised men in dark suits are singing:

'Retur-ning
Retur-ning
We are returning –'

He sits back with his glass of tea.

'Is his wife with him?'

'No, she's with the children tonight. She'll be back tomorrow.'

When he has finished his tea, Ismail Mursi puts down the glass. He crumples his napkin into the tray and stands up.

69

'Goodnight, Father,' Soraya says without looking up.

As he turns slowly he sees himself in the mirror at the back of his wife's glass display cabinet. In the front, just over his chest, is the small blue opaline vase he had bought Fadeela for the first birthday she had spent with him: her fifteenth birthday.

Ismail Mursi stops at the basin in the corridor and rinses out his mouth and hawks and blows his nose. In the big, dark hall he hesitates, then bears left. Quietly, he opens the door of Hamid's room, and there in the large bed with the carved headboard that had come from his own workshop so many years ago his son lies. Quiet and still. Only once before in his life does he remember him so quiet and still. His mother had sat there, just *there*, cross-legged on the corner of the carpet, bending over the limp baby while the sunlight touched her chestnut hair and the two little girls brought her cold water and Zayid sat discreetly on the terrace to be on hand when the inevitable finally happened – and the women came and went and scolded her and remonstrated with her:

'Let him go. He's practically gone already.'

'Sett Fadeela, this is sinful. Let him go in peace. It's God's will.'

'You're torturing him like this. Torturing him. Can't you see he *wants* to go?'

But she shook her head and would not speak and would not let Hamid go, and when she lifted her face to her husband there were dark bruises under her green eyes and she would not speak but she would not for one moment separate the boy from her own body: she held on to him, and after three nights he swallowed down a spoonful of cool water and then he licked a drop of honey off her finger and he came back to her. And some people shook their heads and said that she had cheated death and death was not to be cheated. But Hamid had come back to her and filled the house with his life and his noise –

Hamid's eyes are open in his bruised face. He is looking at his father. Ismail Mursi keeps his hand on the doorknob.

'How are you now, son?'

'I'm fine, Father. Thank you.'

'You're better, aren't you?'

'Yes, Father. Much better.'

'Do you want anything?'

'No thank you, Father. Everything's just fine.'

'Good. Well. Goodnight, then.'

'Goodnight, Father.'

Ismail Mursi holds on to the doorknob for another moment, then lets it go and shuffles down the hall to his room. He sits down heavily on his bed and switches on his reading-lamp. The girl Ne'ma is in her bed in the little room off the kitchen. He switches on the radio and starts fiddling with the knobs trying to tune in to the BBC Arabic service. The sons of bitches are still jamming it. Through the interference he can hear Soraya steal into the room next door to bathe her brother's face in cold water, to prop him up and coax him into eating a few mouthfuls of food and drinking half a glass – just half for my sake, for our mother's sake, Hamid – of hot tea with honey and lemon to build him up.

III

October 1967 - May 1968

Scene 1

October 1967
Cairo

A girl comes out from between the benches and steps on to the wooden platform. She grins over her shoulder – presumably at her friends – looks for a piece of chalk, finds it and begins to write on the freshly polished blackboard. Asya will not remember what she wrote. In fact, she will not remember if she read what the girl wrote. What she will always remember is that she wore a straight brown skirt which just covered her knees and, over it, a large white shirt with a brown diamond print. She also wore brown court shoes with a low, square heel and on the third finger of her right hand she wore a plain gold ring. In this, Asya's first memory of her, she is vivid, confident, almost exuberant. Asya will also believe that she had thought immediately, We will be friends. How much of this is accurate? How much is a mounting and framing that took place later? She cannot honestly tell. But friends they did become despite the efforts of the Greek.

The Greek had been to school with Chrissie (that's the girl's name) – in fact there was a whole bunch of girls that had come from the Manor House School, and Chrissie had never been best friends with Mariana (that's the Greek) but Mariana made it her business to be affronted at Chrissie's taking up with Asya. As it happened, Asya too knew Mariana. They had already once been rivals. That other time, ten years before, it had been over a blonde, green-eyed girl who lived in the apartment block off Midan el-'Ataba where both Asya's and Mariana's grandparents lived. The little blonde had the glamour of a father whose name – even though it was engraved in brass on the door of their third-floor apartment – could not be mentioned. He had, Lateefa Mursi had told her daughter briefly when her questions became too insistent, been an officer high up in King Farouk's army and was therefore now in prison. Asya could not see the inevitability of that 'therefore'.

'What had he done?'
'He was in the King's army.'
'But what had he actually done?'
'Nothing.'
'But the Free Officers were officers in the King's army?'
'But he didn't belong to the Free Officers.'
'So are all the officers who didn't belong to them in prison now?'
'No.'
'Only some?'

75

'Yes.'

'Why?'

And so it went on; Asya's questions, Lateefa's attempts to neutralise if not actually to answer them. Eventually, several years later, when his children were almost grown, the man with the engraved name slipped quietly back into their apartment. A tall, fair, Circassian-looking man in civilian clothes with hair already white, he proceeded to spend what remained of his life being unobtrusive. Asya used to see him sometimes as she sat in the sunshine or watered the plants outside her grandfather's front door; she would see him going out at sunset, not raising his eyes from the worn black and white tiles of the floor. And she would imagine that he was on his way to secret meetings in dark rooms thick with conspiracy and cigarette smoke, with maps on the walls pierced with flagged pins at strategic points. She was never quite clear what she thought they needed the maps for, but there they were up on the wall, with pins from whose heads flew tiny triangular standards in red, green and blue for all the world like an operations room in a Second World War movie. The maps gave added boldness to this vision for they were maps of Cairo and no maps of Cairo were available in those years, and why they weren't was another question you weren't supposed to ask. It was as though it was totally plain that anyone who needed a map of the city had no business being there anyway and could be up to no good. In any case, this particular Colonel never did carry out a coup, so evidently – with or without a map – his meetings came to nothing. Which, Asya would come to believe, is what most meetings of this nature (and, indeed, of most other natures too, probably) come to in the end. For even this, her less-than-microscopic patch of history, is more or less a record of meetings which, in the end, came to nothing; the meetings of Mukhtar al-Ulama and his 'National Democratic League', of Hamid Mursi and 'Bread and Freedom' and – a generation later and partaking of the general decline – the meetings, under the black and white Che poster of Muhsin Nur-el-Din and his friends: events resulting in nothing except a few years in jail, a few buckets of cold water in your face if you were lucky, bare wires between your toes if you weren't. Well, the Colonel had already had his few years in jail and now was probably on his way to Groppi's to have a coffee or a beer with one of the few remaining friends who acknowledged him. Or maybe he was on his way to visit a second wife or a burdensome sister of whom Asya had never heard. But back in those late fifties years when he was absent, it became an act of daring to read Hamdi al-Dafrawi's name on the brass plaque: to mouth it silently while waiting for the door to open. An act of dissidence against Asya knew not what, possibly against the power of her mother's arbitrary 'therefore'; an act of illicit pleasure.

There were other unusual pleasures to be had inside the flat, for the absent Colonel had a pretty wife who sat around all day in frilly house-dresses painting her nails and a son who disdained to speak to his younger sister or her friends so that (at least for Asya, whose only brother was still in his first year of life) it became a treat merely to catch a glimpse of him in the depths of one of their dark corridors. As for Asya's little blonde friend, she (unlike the other girls in the building who were timid and well-bred) had a free and uninhibited nature. This was proved conclusively when she got married. She was seventeen and just out of school and – in the manner of young brides – made a habit of taking her washing home to her mother. Her mother – in the manner of mothers – made a habit of tut-tutting over the state of her laundry:

'Look at these sheets! All these stains! How can you do that? I've used up my eyesight embroidering these sheets for you and they'll soon be threadbare with so much washing. I thought you would, one day, pass them on to your daughters. I just don't understand –'

It was a warm autumn day when her mother said this for maybe the twentieth time and anyone who had their kitchen window open suddenly heard the young bride's voice ringing through the stairwell:

'All *right*. Since you don't understand I'll *make* you understand. You know what these stains are, Mama? They're my husband's semen. *Semen*. SEMEN. MY HUSBAND'S SEMEN.'

Over the years Asya carries with her an image of the young bride continuing to shout and sing those words as she dances down the long dark corridors after her mother, who has dropped the sheets and fled, her frilly house-dress flapping behind her, her hands over her ears. But it probably isn't true. At the time of their friendship, when they were both eight, Asya's friend had a talent for inventing naughty games, and that year the two girls wriggled away many a summer afternoon on over-stuffed and brocaded sofas in hushed and shaded drawing-rooms, taking turns at pretending to be moustached and unprincipled seducers of young girls. What the little blonde did on other afternoons with Mariana Asya did not know, but what she did know, as she skipped up the one flight of stairs back to her grandfather's flat at the end of an afternoon at the Dafrawis', was that if she looked at Nina's window next door she would see the sulky face of Mariana palely watching her.

And there was her sad face again, ten years later, on that early October day; Asya's first day at university. When after class Asya looked around for the girl with the big shirt and the big smile, she saw her in a group, being talked to by her old rival. At first Asya thought Mariana was pleased to be central: the one who knew them both. But one morning, two weeks into the first term, Chrissie whispered, 'I've something to show you.' Chrissie and Asya ran upstairs to the Department of History and climbed out of the french windows of the end classroom and on to the out-of-bounds terrace. They sat on the tiled floor, undetectable from the ground below, and Chrissie dug into her book-bag.

My Beloved Friend . . . I believed university would afford us the opportunity to continue walking together on the beautiful path of friendship we started at school . . . The clever fox, Asya, took you from me . . . I cannot share . . . You must choose . . . etc.

It was while they giggled and exclaimed over the letter that they truly became friends: inseparable.

Scene 2

Chrissie and Asya. Chrissie and Asya sit side by side. Chrissie is fairer than Asya. Asya's hair is thicker than Chrissie's. Chrissie is a little taller than Asya. Asya is a little rounder than Chrissie. Chrissie is in a constant nurturing of her flaking nails. Asya, whose nails are a perfect, pearly oval, envies Chrissie her naturally smooth legs and wages unceasing war on the little hairs that keep reappearing on her own. Chrissie and Asya skip Latin, go to the zoo, read in the library. Asya is clever in class. Chrissie is smart outside it. Asya interprets Auden to Chrissie. Chrissie explains the world to Asya.

'Chrissie' is not Chrissie's real name of course. Her real name is 'Carima' – but she was born in England and lived there for the first five years of her life and that is how she came to be called 'Chrissie'. She does not recognise 'Carima', will never answer to it, and even talks – occasionally – of having it officially changed.

Chrissie's home is in Dokki – between the university in Giza and Asya's home in Zamalek. Chrissie's home is what Asya thinks of as a 'proper' home – meaning that it is unlike Asya's own home which is determinedly untraditional. Asya's home has modern paintings by friends of her parents. It has geometric rugs and elongated African statuettes. It has studies and sitting-rooms and no dining-room or drawing-room. Chrissie's home has an entrance hall with red plush armchairs and a piano and on the wall a huge painting of Roman gladiators preparing themselves in the arena of a packed amphitheatre. It has a drawing-room with gilt French furniture upholstered in grey brocade, marble-topped tables, a good Persian carpet, a glass display cabinet

78

with some Dresden shepherdesses, Sèvres demi-tasses, crystal glasses, a few rolled-up bits of string and a framed photograph of a young Uncle Sidki, Chrissie's father, shaking hands with a smiling and uniformed Colonel Nasser. The walls are panelled in pale grey, brocade-like wallpaper, and on them are displayed some choice family photos. The most striking, to Asya's eye, is one which shows Tante Muneera, Chrissie's mother, at the age of eighteen. She is Asya and Chrissie's own age, but the difference, the style, the *glamour* – Muneera al-Tarabulsi is in a dark, close-fitting sheath, with a transparent outer dress of sequined tulle. She leans against a round table over which the tulle is spread out so that it forms a circle behind her. A nonsensical little confection of tulle gleams in her hair. Her head is bent modestly, but she glances up and into the camera with shining eyes and a demure smile. A few days after this photo was taken she was married to her cousin, Chrissie's father. This was 1945. The war was over. Muhammad Pasha al-Tarabulsi and his brother Sidki Pasha al-Tarabulsi threw a big party in the grounds of the old family palace in Hilmiyya to celebrate the marriage of their two children. Coloured lights were strung up between the trees. *Sofragis* in white circled among the guests with trays of sherbet and sugar-coated almonds. The couple spent three days in Alexandria, and then came home – to this flat. A wedding photo hangs on the wall. A traditional pose: the groom's right arm encircles the shoulders of his bride. He is at least nine inches taller than she. She holds a bouquet, her train swirls around her feet and ripples into the foreground of the photo till it is cut short by the frame. Five years after meeting Chrissie, blown up on a big screen in a dark cinema, Asya sees the face in this photo. Chrissie's young father is Michael Corleone; his black hair is combed back and he stares fixedly at the camera. He is madly in love with his bride. After they marry, his love blossoms into an obsession: he buys her jewellery, he chooses her clothes, he kisses her fingers one by one. Soon she conceives his first child and he carries her up and down the three flights of stairs to their apartment – to *this* apartment. This son will eventually divide them but Sidki al-Tarabulsi does not know that. This is his seed taking root: his cousin, his childhood sweetheart, his bride, is growing big with his child. Her arms, her wrists, her ankles are still frail and delicate but her small breasts grow round and hot and she puts aside her virginal timidity and comes to him with desire. She is in her seventh month when she is summoned to her father's death-bed. She sits on a low chair next to the bed for twenty-seven hours. Her husband comes and goes and comes and goes. Finally he can stand it no longer. She is pale and exhausted with weeping and waiting. She is harming herself and their child. He insists that she leave with him and return later. And when she will neither move nor answer, but just sits there, palely, with great, green, red-rimmed eyes, he loses his temper and, grabbing her arm, he drags her out of her chair and away from his dying uncle. He has to half pull half carry her out of the house and into his car while she struggles and kicks and bites his hand and screams that he is mad. At home he puts her to bed and she immediately falls asleep. When she wakes five hours later, her father is dead. Her husband kisses the purple bruises on her arms and weeps over them. On his knees, he begs her to forgive him and swears he will shoot himself if she does not – and that night their first son, Taha Sidki al-Tarabulsi, is born and placed in an incubator where he will stay for five weeks and emerge to grow into his father's scourge and his mother's greatest sorrow. She bore her husband three more sons and a daughter. And there are photos of them all on the wall. Taha, aged two, leaning between his parents over a ship's rail. Taha, aged five, in a duffle coat and sailor's cap walking beside a slim, trousered, fur-jacketed Tante Muneera on a windswept Brighton beach while she pushes a buggy containing a plump, smiling one-year-old Chrissie. One large photograph shows Uncle Sidki with his arms around Tante Muneera and their five children: Taha is frowning, Chrissie grins, the rest look non-committal. The youngest of the boys is ten now and Chrissie tells Asya that since the day he was born he sleeps between his father and mother in their big double bed. Asya says, 'So that means . . .?' and Chrissie nods: 'Never.'

Over the years Sidki al-Tarabulsi has acquired a good professional reputation; the post of Minister of Health, a few women 'friends', a considerable girth and an eclectic collection of pornography. Asya and Chrissie raid this when they can. Italian girls sucking on huge penises, two French girls engaged in a frilly *soixante-neuf,* Danish women being mounted by large hounds. Asya has read the *Kama Sutra* and the *Perfumed Garden* of the Sheikh Nefzawi and she has seen some Japanese and Indian classical drawings, but all of this has never seemed to have anything to do with real people. The Indians were engaged in stylised, improbable, mystical acrobatics – while the Japanese paintings presented themselves as an ornamental design: a woman's vagina echoed by the flowers in her kimono and her hair; a slender, plume-like object emerging from a profusion of patterned textiles suddenly becoming recognisable as a penis. And the features are always abstracted, decorous, like the faces of Pharaonic statues. This is her first exposure to modern pornography and the first few times she could only glance at a page then slam the magazine shut, her heart pounding. Chrissie, who had found this cache five years before, laughs at her. She laughs even more when Asya begs to be left alone with the magazines.

'I can't look at them if you're looking at me,' Asya explains. Left alone, Asya studies the photos. She studies the expressions on the faces of the women; the men mostly have no faces: they are cut off somewhere in the middle of the trunk; and the dogs too have not much expression; apart from the odd tongue hanging out they could have been up to anything. Asya tries to imagine Uncle Sidki leafing through these magazines. She can only see him either laughing or looking cross – and neither expression fits. She tries to imagine some relationship, some common ground, between Tante Muneera and the tousled, splayed, pouting girls in the photos. But Tante Muneera, lifting her eyes from her sewing to glance at the television, or urging one of her children to eat, or placing a glass of tea silently in front of her husband, does not seem to inhabit the same world as these girls. Yet 'things' used to happen. Must have used to happen. At least up until ten years ago and in that very bedroom the door of which is almost always pushed to. Until Uncle Sidki dies, and then it will always stand wide open. But that has not happened yet. Uncle Sidki is still, in a sense, obsessed by his wife; she cannot do the smallest thing in his presence without eliciting a comment from him. His first words to whichever of his children he happens to see when he comes home from work at three o'clock are invariably, 'Where's your mother?' In the family living-room he will often raise his eyes from his newspaper to check if she is around. 'Why have you made more tea?' he grumbles before he drinks the glass she places in front of him. 'You're going to blind yourself with all this sewing!' – 'I said I don't want another piece of chicken.' His wife mostly meets all this with silence – sometimes friendly and sometimes pained – and carries on sewing or putting food on his plate. In company, exchanging wisecracks with a friend or a relative, if he likes something he's said he will turn and seek her out, and if she does not meet his eye he will call out in his heavy voice, 'Hear that, Muneera? Did you hear that?' and then he will repeat it for her benefit.

Scene 3

Thursday, 16 November 1967
Cairo

The grounds of Cairo University on the very edge of the city. A long wooden shed on the boundary of a playing-field. The shed has two doors. A line of girls stretches across the field in the winter sunshine. It winds lazily into one door and emerges from the other animated, dispersed, rushing off in different directions. Chrissie, Asya, Mimi and Noora form a unit in the line. Together they enter the shed. A counter runs the length of the darkness inside, and behind the counter stands a woman who has the appearance and deportment of a weary gym mistress. As each girl approaches, the gym mistress reaches for a wrapped-up bundle from the shelves behind her and lobs it over the counter saying, 'Wash, iron and gym shoes.' Out in the sunshine again the four of them examine their bundles. Each one consists of a khaki skirt, shirt and cap and a white canvas belt.

'Comme ça!' exclaims Mimi, holding the unravelled clothing in delicate fingertips and raising her fine eyebrows. 'Without any measurement or anything?'

'You think this is Saint-Laurent, do you?' asks Chrissie. 'Saint-Laurent, Giza.' Asya giggles.

Noora is looking at the belt.

'This is a good belt,' she says seriously. 'I'd quite like to keep it.'

The four friends take a bus back to the university. At their college coffee-shop they sort through the clothes and try to distribute them rationally. Noora is the tallest and the thinnest. Mimi is the broadest across the hips but the smallest in the waist. Asya and Chrissie are much alike, but Tante Muneera can adjust Chrissie's uniform so Asya takes the uniform that fits her the best.

Saturday, 18 November

Skirts tightened and shortened and washed and ironed, shirts with sharp creases down the sleeves, belts nipping into waists and caps set jauntily on to freshly shampooed heads, the girl cadets of the Cairo University Military Training Course, 1967, converge upon the playing-fields at Giza at half past eight on Saturday morning. It is right and it is fitting that military training should thus take precedence over academic subjects in a country that is – after all – at war. Every student entering university in this autumn of 1967 is right now somewhere on a field or a patch of desert beginning a two-week course of training. The boys will have two weeks of combat training, while the girls will have one week of combat and one of nursing. Here on this field the girls divide into 'battalions' of forty each. Chrissie, Asya, Mimi and Noora manage to stay in the same battalion. Each battalion is made to form a square, each of its four sides consisting of ten girls standing at arm's-length to each other. In the middle of each square stands a weary-looking gym teacher. And now, standing 'at ease', the girls listen to a long discourse on the importance of military training. Asya looks around her. Noora is standing tall and straight. Her fringe covers her eyebrows and her black braid, falling over her shoulder, reaches almost to her waist. She looks attentive but abstracted. She could stand there all day, at ease, staring ahead and oblivious of all around her. Mimi, next to her, looks bored already; she shifts her weight from foot to foot, adjusts her cap, examines her fingernails and wishes she were sitting in a comfortable chair with a nice, hot, glass of tea. Asya catches Chrissie's eye and Chrissie gives her a wide grin, then looks seriously back towards the gym teacher.

At eleven, the first shift of primary schoolchildren are released from the classrooms of the neighbouring Abu-l-rish. They spot the activity in the university playing-fields and swarm on to the wire fences to get a good look. For the rest of the day, they hang there, a hundred kids or so, in grubby beige uniforms, their satchels thrown to the ground: yelling, waving, laughing and singing mock-patriotic songs. Soldiers come on to the field pushing wheelbarrows. The wheelbarrows are piled high with machine-guns. The soldiers move round the squares: for each girl, one machine-gun. Now things are looking up. The rest of the morning is spent sitting on the grass learning how to dismantle, clean and assemble the Repeating Gun Port-Said.

The rest of the week is spent practising dismantling, cleaning and assembling the Port-Said; running with the Port-Said, climbing rope-ladders with the Port-Said, wriggling over sand with the Port-Said, squirming through barbed wire with the Port-Said. Actions all accompanied by the comments, the encouragement, the cheers, of an ever-increasing number of ill-fed, ill-washed but happy children, hanging on to a wire fence.

Thursday, 23 November

The girls present themselves at the Sa'idiyya Secondary School for Boys for their Military Training Test. The boys have been confined to their classrooms for the day but they hang out of the windows, laughing, whistling and shouting. Paper boats and aeroplanes with names and phone numbers written on them come floating down on to the heads and shoulders of the group of girls standing at one end of the football ground. Along the sideline there is a row of five targets.

A young officer steps up to Mimi who has strayed slightly from the group.

'Please come forward, miss. We'll take you first.'

He hands her a Port-Said and some bullets.

'See that target there straight ahead of you? Load your gun and aim for the centre: the red dot. One bullet at a time.'

Mimi looks at the bullets then at him.

'But I've never fired a shot before,' she says.

'You've been in military training for a week.'

'But I haven't fired; we had no – no ammunition.'

'Load your gun, miss.'

'I don't know how to load it –' Her voice is getting louder and she looks around at her friends.

'You've held a Port-Said before?'

'Yes.'

'Open it.'

Mimi opens the gun and the officer loads it.

'There. See. Like this. OK. It's loaded and ready.'

Mimi holds the gun and looks at him. He looks at her.

'Why are you looking at me? Your target is over *there*. Fire.'

She lifts the gun into position against her shoulder, then lowers it. A soldier is strolling behind the targets.

'Go ahead. Fire. What are you waiting for?'

'That man. Isn't he afraid something will happen to him?'

'What man?'

'That man there. Behind the targets.'

'That's a soldier.'

'I know he's a soldier. But I might shoot him.'

'You're supposed to aim at the target: the red dot.'

'And if I hit him?'

The officer turns towards the targets.

'Hey, *you* – you donkey walking over there,' he yells, 'get out of the way.'

From across the football pitch the soldier gazes back at him, shading his eyes with his hand.

'I said get out of the way. The lady won't fire as long as you're there. Are we going to stay here all day? *Move.*'

The soldier strolls off and Mimi once more raises the gun to her shoulder and peers over the top of the barrel. The officer hurries to her side.

'Not like this. Not like this. What have they been teaching you there? Here. Like *this* –'

He is now standing behind her; his arms under her arms, holding the gun in place.

'Now. Just look through there. Aim. And fire. Go on. I'm holding it for you. Just aim and fire. I said F I R E.'

Mimi averts her face, closes her eyes and presses the trigger. A long burst of machine-gun fire follows and then she bends double over her gun. Chrissie, Noora and Asya rush over and try to straighten her up but she is hysterical with laughter. Her target is unmarked. The young officer looks at her blankly, then puts the minimum passing grade of 60 per cent on her card and walks off to the next group. Two soldiers are now strolling among the targets.

Saturday, 25 November

Chrissie and Asya are detailed to the Mabarret Muhammad 'Ali Hospital off Qasr el-'Eini Street. Freshly washed, pressed and shampooed they arrive on Saturday morning at eight-thirty and sit in Casualty for an hour until a sister is free to take them around.

'And in here is the burns unit. This is the one that will be of most use to you I should think in military training, although the causes of the burns we get here are of course quite different: domestic accidents mostly, and mostly, of course, women and children. This woman, here: this is a boiling-water injury' – pulling back the sheet – 'worse, you see, around the face and neck than on the legs. Her husband threw the pan at her and he aimed high. This one' – pulling back the sheet – 'kerosene. Very severe.' In a lower voice, 'Set fire to herself. Very common. A couple of cases every week. Young girls, mostly. A fight with her family. Wants to marry her cousin or whatever and they won't let her so she rushes into the kitchen, pours kerosene over herself and throws a lit match on to her dress. She's not likely to marry anyone now. Now, this one was just unfortunate. Caught her hair in the primus as she was bending over the washing. Whole head on fire. Panicked. By the time a neighbour came – well, you can see –'

Asya and Chrissie sit silently wherever they are put. They decline offers of tea. Their fresh clothes and wholesome bodies seem to Asya offensive in this place so rich in burns, growths, sores and fractures. This place where children too sick to cry and for whom there are no beds lie on corridor floors in nests made up of bits of spare clothing while their mothers sit silently on the tiles beside them.

'Chrissie. This is dreadful,' whispers Asya. 'Dreadful.'

'Yes,' whispers Chrissie.

'It's not right,' whispers Asya.

'No,' whispers Chrissie.

'What can we do?'

'How do you mean?'

'Well, what can we *do*?'

'About *them* you mean?'

'Yes.'

'Nothing,' says Chrissie.

In one ward a nurse is standing over an old man. She is young and cheerful and is preparing an injection. She holds the hypodermic up to the light and squints at it, pushing the plunger till the liquid spurts slightly out of the needle. Then she catches sight of Chrissie and Asya and motions them over, smiling.

'You're the military training students, aren't you? Here, d'you want to practise giving injections? You can give him this.'

She holds the syringe out towards them. Chrissie, whose father is a doctor, already knows how to give injections and says so. The nurse offers the syringe to Asya. Asya has always felt nauseous at the very thought of injections but she steps forward.

'How do I do it?'

The nurse pulls the sheet off the old man.

'On your side, 'Am Muhammad. Go on.'

He turns over, unobjecting, and she pulls down his striped green and white pyjama trousers and rubs at a spot above his exposed left buttock with a piece of cotton wool dipped in alcohol and holds out the syringe to Asya.

'There. See where I disinfected it? Just aim there.'

But Asya can't look at the old man's bare buttock, his tired, neutral face; can't imagine sticking a needle into him just like that, can't bear that he should let her, that he just lies there with his pyjama trousers pulled down; he doesn't sit up and shout, 'What the hell is this? Am I a pillow that you train her on me?' She cannot so much as touch the syringe. She backs off. The nurse shrugs, bends, aims and pushes the needle home.

Sunday, 26 November

Chrissie and Asya walk into the Mabarret Muhammad 'Ali at eight-thirty. They sign on and walk out again. They walk briskly in the cool morning air through the downtown streets to Midan Soliman Pasha. They go into Groppi's and order tea and English cake. When it is ten o'clock they walk up the road to Cinema Qasr el-Nil where they watch Jane Fonda reject her husband in *The Chapman Report*. At one o'clock they are back at the hospital, signing off.

Cinema Cairo is showing *Un Homme et une Femme*, Cinema Metro *Come September*, Cinema Odeon the Russian *Hamlet* and Cinema Miami, Abd el-Halim Hafez and Shadya in *Idol of the People*. On Thursday at one o'clock as they sign off they present their cards and each gets an 80 per cent grade.

Scene 4

Thursday, 7 December 1967: 3.30 p.m.
At the Tarabulsis'

The family have sat down to eat and Asya is with them. Tante Muneera is ladling out *mulukhiyya* for everyone. Chrissie holds out the dishes for her. As Chrissie puts the full dish down in front of Taha, her elder brother, he gives a low moan and pushes his chair back. His father, Dr Sidki al-Tarabulsi, looks up with a face of stone and his mother pauses with her ladle in the air. Taha stands up and lurches to his room. He shuts the door. Even as it closes, his mother's hand is on the knob. She slips in and reshuts the door behind her. Sounds of whisperings, remonstrations, low moans and one loud bang as of a fist on wood come from within. Asya doesn't know what to make of all this. She glances round: Chrissie has finished serving the soup. She and her three brothers are eating with carefully blank faces. Uncle Sidki has bent that same stony face to his dish and is eating too. When he finishes, Chrissie starts serving rice and vegetables but he pushes his plate aside, wipes his mouth with his napkin, throws it down, and gets up. He walks heavily to the closed door and pushes it open suddenly so that it bangs loudly against the wall. His wife is sitting on the side of the bed leaning over the prostrate figure of her son, whose face, marked with deep lines, is drenched in tears. Sidki al-Tarabulsi walks in, grabs his wife's arm, pulls her up and out of the room and back to the dining-table where he pushes her into her chair. He motions to his second son to close the door of Taha's room. Tante Muneera looks up at her husband, weeping, and whispers, 'Sidki, it's Taha. Taha, my son.' But he stands over her and shouts at her to eat. Once she makes as if to get up but he raises his hand and she sits still. She keeps her handkerchief over her mouth and will not eat.

'If he wants to starve himself to death, let him,' rages her husband. 'Why should you stop him? What has he brought us but long faces and misery? And you're responsible. Yes, you. You encourage him. These are not the actions of men. He's twenty-two years old. He's an adult. And don't tell me – Copt or no Copt, if he were a man he'd go and marry her – not sit here and lament like a woman. And if it hadn't been this it would have been something else. He is mad. He *looks* for misery. Upon my honour, you're not going back into his room or paying any attention to him until he straightens himself out.'

Chrissie and Asya have been given the formal dining-room for their semi-exclusive use. It opens – as does the drawing-room – off the entrance hall to the left of the front door and is separated from the main body of the flat by a long corridor. It is a large room with magnolia walls, a 'massif' dining-table to seat twelve, two ornate sideboards full of Sèvres and Alpaca, and a Queen Anne gilt couch with a large gilt-framed mirror above it. French windows open on to the balcony which encircles two sides of the flat. When Asya and Chrissie are not sitting on the couch, they sit in two bamboo armchairs on the balcony and stare out across the rooftops of Giza to the faint silhouette of the pyramids fifteen kilometres away. Or they stand at the rails where, if you lean over and look to the left, you can see a bit of the Nile and the trees of Gezira Island across it. Beyond those trees is Asya's home. Chrissie and Asya have a stash of Arabisco biscuits in one of the sideboards which they dunk into their tea. Arabiscos are square with delicately festooned edges. They are wrapped in silver paper with blue and red lettering. They come seven to a pack, which always strikes Asya as odd since there is no way you can share them out fairly. But Asya and Chrissie prefer 'Arabiscos' to 'Maries' – the other tea biscuit available in their socialist self-sufficient state – because they are always slightly on the burnt side while Maries are doughy and unbaked. So they sit on the gilt Queen Anne couch, their shoes off and a tray of tea and fourteen Arabisco biscuits between them. Chrissie tells Asya about Taha's hopeless love for a Coptic girl – 'and not only does he choose a Copt, but her father is actually a priest – so there's no hope of his ever agreeing to let her marry Taha; Taha just sits there all woebegone as you see, waiting for her to phone him – and when she phones him he becomes even more miserable –'

Also on the gilded couch, Chrissie hands Asya a black and white passport-size photo of a young man. He seems very serious. He has dark hair cut short, a square chin with a dimple in it, and he is looking intensely into the camera. On the back is written, 'For Chrissie. May 1st, 1967.' Chrissie says, 'That's Issam.' Issam is Chrissie's cousin, the son of her mother's sister, Tante Rita. 'They live in Alexandria and we spent all our summers there. We would stay at the big house in Shatby, but every day the whole family – at least the children – all got together on the beach. We had two cabins at Stanley and we played there all day. He was six years older than me and I thought he always saw me as a child. But he was my favourite cousin and really I admired him very much. He never talked a lot. He was more manly than any of my other cousins – or my brother – but also kinder. Then, in January last year – sixty-six – he came to Cairo in the mid-term vacation and of course he stayed with us. On the nineteenth of January, it was a Wednesday, we were standing on the balcony here, waiting for his mother to come back from her shopping. She was at Buccilati – you know Tante Rita used to paint? It was six o'clock and almost dark. I was leaning on the railings and suddenly he put his hand over mine. "Chrissie," he said, "I love you." I turned and looked at him for a moment, then I looked back at the road with my heart absolutely shaking. Taha could have come into the room behind us or even on to the balcony itself at any moment. But I didn't move my hand. Issam said, "And you love me. In June, when I graduate, I shall speak to my uncle." He took his hand away and just then the light went on behind us and I heard Taha say, "Has my aunt not come back yet?" I, of course, could not speak at all and left them and went inside to my room and my mother saw me and followed me and closed the door and said, "What's the matter, Chrissie? What's wrong?"

'I said, "Nothing's wrong, Mama."

'She said, "Well, what is it? Why is your face so changed? What's happened?" and I said, "Issam."

'She said, "Has he spoken to you?"

'I nodded. She said, "Chrissie, do you want him?"

'I nodded. She hugged me and kissed me and wept a little and said, "He asked my permission to speak to you. He is a good boy and when he graduates your father will find no fault with him. He's my sister's son and he will look after you and treat you as you should be treated." She thought for a moment and said, "He should speak to your brother now and to your father as soon as his college results come out."

'I said, "Mamma, please don't make him speak to Taha."

'And of course at once her face turned all bleak and sad. "Why, Chrissie? This is the right procedure: he speaks to your brother first."

'I begged, "Not Taha, Mama, please. He'll knot it all up, you know he will!"

'Tears came to her eyes again. "Your brother will be hurt. He will be slighted to be passed over in this manner."

'"You always take Taha's side, Mama. Always. This is something that's mine. Think of me. Taha will surely come up with problems."

'So, Issam didn't talk to Taha, but he made a point of being particularly friendly and attentive to him over the next six months – and in June, as soon as his exam results were out, he came and spoke to my father. My father said he'd "think about it" and of course he made all the usual objections. "He's a kid" – "What are they going to live on?" and so on and so on. And I heard my mother say to him, "Sidki. The moment you graduated you asked for me. And my father said the things that you are saying now. Yet, here we are. Issam is a good, straight, responsible boy and he's her cousin and already a son to both of us." And eventually he agreed. But he said no marriage or even an official engagement before Issam had finished his one year of military service. Issam insisted that some formal promise be made and his parents and my mother backed him up and in September they read the Fatiha and we put the gold bands on each other's fingers. He was allowed to come and see me whenever he wanted and we could sit alone – but always here – in the house.'

'Did you ever – do – anything?' asks Asya.

'Kissing only,' says Chrissie. 'And once he put his hand on my knee and slid it under the hem of my dress. I felt my whole body melting – but then we heard Taha in the next room and I jumped up. Taha, of course, since the Fatiha, was going round with a face as long as a hand-span. But we wouldn't let him make us miserable.'

Issam, as a favour to his father who was a general in the army, served his army conscription as a Reserve Engineer Officer to the Second Battalion of the Fourth Armoured Division. In May 1967 he was ordered with the Battalion into the Sinai. He came to see Chrissie before he left and he gave her the small photo, the most recent one he had. On 7 June he phoned Chrissie on a distant, crackling line. She thought he sounded terrible. She asked where he was phoning from and he said, 'We're in

Cairo but our location is secret and we have to stay with the unit.' He said, 'I'll come to you as soon as I can.' He never came back. His father, the General, and his father's brother – a general in the police – pulled every string they possessed but they found nothing. He was never reported killed. He was never reported captured. He just did not come back. In the weeks to follow, when the full extent of the catastrophe that had befallen the country started to be guessed at, when solitary soldiers came limping back barefoot from the Sinai to tell of heroism and chaos and betrayal, and the sight of beribboned and starred khaki sent crowds into a frenzy of anger so that ranking officers had to wear civvies or not show themselves on the street – that was when stories started to appear. One soldier phoned to say that a friend had seen Issam: dead amid the debris of men and trucks and equipment in the Mitla Pass. Another said that he was among the soldiers captured by the enemy and would no doubt be released. And a phone-call came from an officer who had been asked by a dying soldier to inform Lt Issam al-Uthmanli's family that he had seen him – and that he was alive but would never come home because he had lost a leg. Tante Rita had not mourned him. She still believed he would return. The war was now six months begun and finished. The dead had been counted and some captives released. The last stragglers had dragged themselves home, their feet and brains burnt by the sands and the sun of the now-occupied Sinai. The country mourned the loss of the 'desert of the turquoise' and, although not everyone yet knew it, it also mourned the loss of the Great Arab Dream. Nasser nursed his diabetes and his broken heart. 'Amer, his best friend and Chief of Staff, his son's namesake and his other son's father-in-law, his old comrade-in-arms, died poisoned under arrest at the presidential rest-house at the pyramids. Among the men from the armed forces unaccounted for was Lt Issam al-Uthmanli.

Chrissie wept when she spoke of him, and yet it could not be said that she was surrounded by a permanent tragic aura. Hearing her story, Asya thinks back to that first morning. She tries to recall the girl in the big shirt, laughing in the sunshine and holding a piece of chalk in her hand. No hint of tragedy. And yet it was undoubtedly there. Does time really heal? Asya has not yet suffered a great sorrow – a loss, a tragedy. What does it feel like? What does it *really* feel like to miss someone and know you would probably miss them for ever?

Asya admires Chrissie. Chrissie is always – or almost always – practical and down-to-earth. She sees what people are up to. She laughs at Asya and scratches gently at the balloons of her foolishness and fantasy. She stays out of family quarrels and finds ways of comforting her mother. But no one can comfort Tante Muneera for Taha. Her eldest, her first-born, her darling. He of the sad face and the deep lines etched around his mouth and on his brow from before he was even twenty. As he passes

90

with bowed head where she sits sewing in the hall she feels a darkness, a foreboding. Let him marry a Christian if that will bring him comfort. They too are people of the Book. And the Prophet, the blessings of God be upon him, loved Mariam the Copt who was sent to him as a gift from Egypt. He loved her for her softness and her curly hair. He loved her so that when she conceived she conceived of a boy, Ibrahim, his only son, whose death he so sadly mourned two years later. Muneera shakes her head over the buttons of her son's shirt. Taha's blood has risen for the girl and what is he to do? This is not something you decide with your mind. But the girl's family – for them it is serious; and her father is a priest. She sighs. Marriage would be good for him. Get him out of himself and out of his father's way. He's a good boy. A bit closed-in but tender-hearted. And he's in the university and will get a Ph.D and any girl would wish for him. And he goes and falls in love with a Copt. And his sister – biting off the thread of the last button and screwing up her eyes against the light to rethread her needle, Muneera thinks of Chrissie. She'd thought she had her settled and taken care of and then, just like that, the boy is gone. She will not lack for suitors but she doesn't care for any of her other cousins and a relative is better than a stranger. And three more boys – squinting at the needle – may God preserve them all. And the youngest only ten. The last of the cluster, precious as her eyes. She blinks and tucks her slim legs under her and rubs her eyes. It's been getting harder to thread her needle lately. Is she wrong to have the little one still sleep next to her? But he is so accustomed to it now – how can she suddenly send him away? And Sidki is so violent. Violent in every-thing he does. And she can no longer bear it. He had been furious when she had started taking the baby to bed, but that was ten years ago and he has not said anything for a long time now. It isn't as if nothing ever happens. He still catches her alone sometimes or in Alexandria when the boys sleep with their cousins. But of course she's not as interested as she used to be and he is too rough. She knows it is her duty. It's her duty to ask him every night. Every night a woman should ask her husband three times if he wants anything. And only then can she fall asleep with an easy conscience. But really, she cannot suddenly turn the boy out of her bed. And besides she has to think of Taha. It would kill him if he thought his father so much as touched her. She would be too ashamed to walk out of her bedroom and face him if she slept alone with Sidki.

Scene 5

December 1967
Cairo

Asya has a crush on the Professor of Poetry. Asya's crushes are usually from a safe distance and for a short duration. Chrissie tries to talk her out of this one, but it is no use. Asya sits in the front row and gazes at the Professor and cannot respond to a whisper or pass back a note.

A poet and a playwright; first Egyptian head of an Egyptian Department of English. In Asya's mind there is a pantomime of the previous British head – fifteen years or so back – handing her Professor the department in the small, formal office, under the faded, somewhat sly gaze of the portrait of Shakespeare. The Englishman (whose name she does not know but whom she imagines as white-haired and stooping with a droopy moustache) bows stiffly and hands over the department. The Professor puts out his hand and takes it. He cups it in both hands and with a movement at once disdainful and courteous he stands aside to let the older man pass. Asya looks closely at the department and sees that it is one of those flat-bottomed crystal balls she had loved playing with when she was a child. Inside it a few red-roofed houses, a weather-cock on a steeple, the sign of a pub. As the Professor moves his hand, snowflakes drift dreamily about and settle on the sloping roofs and on the shining surface of the street.

The Professor is probably nearing sixty now – though no one knows for sure. He has a deep voice, bloodshot eyes – which when they rest on you transform you either into a worm or – no, not a princess, but a small, beloved child. He has a handkerchief in his sleeve and what everybody agrees is a terrifically ugly face, except Asya, who describes it as his '*beauté mal*'. He is a 'controversial figure' and is constantly under attack in the newspapers for the symbolism of his plays, the harshness of his criticism, the number of his divorces, the rumours of his affairs, the handkerchief in his sleeve, the dandiness of his clothes and the Britishness of his English. It is he who introduces the freshmen to literature. 'Ladies and Gentlemen –'

The veined, protruding eyes survey the one hundred and three students filling the amphitheatre as though they were not worth even crushing beneath the heel of his expensive moccasin boot – gone are the small, brilliant groups of twelve and fifteen, of which every member was to become a writer or a critic or a big name of some kind. And yet to come are the mobs of three and four hundred squeezing into the cracks of the wall, oozing out of windows, listening in loudspeakers in other rooms, hiding inside 'Islamic' clothing and destined to use up their lives trying to make sure they stay alive. This is late 1967: the turning-point. Standards are falling, but they still exist. Excellence is possible although no longer likely. And if the Professor looks scornful now what will he look like if God grants him life and he surveys that same amphitheatre on a November morning some twelve years later?

'Ladies and Gentlemen, you are here to study poetry.'

The way he says 'poetry' makes it sound important, resonant, colossal, terrifying.

'Ladies and Gentlemen, what is poetry?'

'. . .'

'What – is – a poem?'

'. . .'

'Is it a donkey pulling a cart?'

'. . .'

'Is it a piece of cake?' A few nervous giggles. 'Perhaps you think it is.' Giggles subside. 'I will repeat my question. What, Ladies and Gentlemen, is a poem?'

Most of the one hundred and three, of course, neither know nor care. The bulk of the class is made up of presentable upwardly mobile girls who want to 'improve their English' so that they can get jobs in translation, newspapers, banks, indiscriminately. Then there is the closed-rank contingent from the few foreign schools that remain in Cairo who are here to get a classy degree from a chic department while they wait to get married. Chrissie belongs to these. Then there are the hugely outnumbered boys: two handsome dilettantes with perfect English and a pair of Harley-Davidsons parked by the university railings, and a handful of earnest, hardworking young men with heartbreaking English. These last are probably the only ones who really would like to know the answer to the question. And Asya, whose desire to join the department was so unswerving (apart from one brief disloyal hesitation as she considered the trendy Faculty of Economics and Political Science) that she wrote 'Dept of English, Faculty of Arts, Cairo U.' sixteen times in the sixteen slots labelled 'Choice 1', 'Choice 2' etc. on her university application form and thus invalidated it.

She had come home carrying a new application form; defeated. She had sat down at the kitchen table and filled out fifteen slots with the legitimate choices 'they' had asked for:

(2) Dept of Sociology, Faculty of Arts, Cairo University.
(3) Dept of Auditing, Faculty of Commerce, Cairo University.
(4) Dept of Trees, Faculty of Agriculture, Cairo University.

'They', of course, would not see the joke. They could not know how inevitable it was that she should read Literature. And now here she is, in

93

the front row of Room Thirteen, gazing up at the Professor who gazes back with 'frog's eyes' says Chrissie.

'Mysterious, hooded eyes,' says Asya, 'eyes that have seen everything.'

'Ladies and Gentlemen, what is a poem?'

Asya puts up her hand.

'Is it an expression of emotion?'

The eyes focus on her. He knows her. He has known her since she was born. He has taught her mother before her. But nothing in his look betrays this and Asya is grateful. Above all she wants to belong. To belong to the body of students. If she is to be singled out let it be for merit. Merit that no one can mistake or deny. Not for her parents.

'If I scream, young lady, is that a poem?'

'N-no . . .'

'And yet it is an expression of emotion?'

'Yes.'

'So, what is a poem?'

A formalised expression of emotion? A lyrical expression of ideas? A this, a that and nothing would do, and at the end, 'A poem, Ladies and Gentlemen, is – simply – what it *is*. We can ask no more of poetry than that it should *be.*'

He pushes his chair back. Stands. Surveys the room. Steps down from the podium and out of the door.

'Isn't he brilliant?' breathes Asya, her eyes shining.

'That's what we put down in the exam?' asks Chrissie. 'A poem is what it is?'

'Why are you thinking about the exam now? Just *listen* to him.'

So Chrissie and Asya listen. Arnold, Pater, Poe and Eliot. The Objective Correlative. The Creative Mind as Catalyst. The Image. What is the effect of 'O my love is like a red, red rose'? What is the value of 'The barge she sat in like a burnished throne'? The Designed Effect and the End in the Beginning. The world, for Asya, takes on a new pattern. Into the dustbin go the subjective scanned verses of her middle teens. A poem is of the self but beyond the self. The supreme achievement of life is to create an object of beauty; to create the designed effect, to see the end in the beginning.

'Decadence' scream the literary pages of the national newspapers. 'It is a well-known fact that the doctrine of "Art for Art's Sake" found acceptance – even in the land of its origin – among a few misguided and uncommitted so-called artist members of the upper class who lived in ivory towers. To adopt that doctrine in this country is an outrage. Now, more than ever, at this crucial point of our history, of our national struggle, intellectuals and artists alike should be committed to the single cause of our nation. Art is – and *should* be – at the service of Society. Art is at the service of the Revolution. Will there be no end to British imperialism?'

But the Professor is a man who thrives on the rage and hatred of his rivals – and the devotion of his disciples. Asya watches him cross the garden between the department and the main building of the faculty. He walks with the practised, unseeing face of a man used to being recognised, pointed at, pointed out. A cigar smoulders in the corner of his mouth. The creases on his beige trousers are razor sharp. His jacket is cut long and loose. Everybody knows his clothes are made by Abbas the Mute – the most skilled and expensive tailor in Cairo – who charges an exorbitant fifty Egyptian pounds to cut one suit. For these are still the years of austerity – of import restrictions and hardly any foreign travel. And Cairo still abounds in nimble-fingered tailors and Armenian shirt-makers. The Professor's cravat is of patterned silk and must have come from Paris, and he is not merely an academic – but an artist. His plays are performed, his stories are read by thousands, his criticism angers and inspires. Oh heady days. Heady, heady days. Beauty is the ultimate Good. To be legitimately out of the house from eight in the morning to seven-thirty in the evening six days a week. To be able to wander into the Zoo and the Botanical Gardens without having to ask your parents' permission. The Literary Society is in full swing. Poetry and prose pace forth: austere and crafted. Pity the poor fools who believe in outpourings of raw emotion.

The students and the industrial workers are demanding the right to free speech; the right to participate in politics. The cafeteria of the Faculty of Arts serves the most delicious spiced sausage sandwiches and mint tea at three piastres a throw and over the sausages or the *basbousa* and tea you can shape the world.

'OK, OK. So who was responsible, then?'

'For what, specifically? You've got to be specific –'

'For everything. For all the decisions taken. For example, who was responsible for pushing Reserve forces into the Sinai without any arms – and for the arms never arriving?'

'We never heard the end of the "Scandal of the Dud Arms of Forty-eight". The reason our armies were beaten in the first war. They were ready enough then to blame the Palace –'

'And this is a scandal on an even larger scale. These people didn't even *have* weapons.'

'And what about the decision to retreat? A massacre.'

'You take twenty-six days to push your forces into the battlefield and then you give them one day to withdraw –'

'That's if you can call them forces. Eighty-five thousand Reserves, suddenly called up, milling around in the desert –'

'You order them to withdraw in one day, with no air cover, then you go

95

ahead and start blowing up the bridges across the Canal so most of them can't even get back over.'

Asya glances at Chrissie who is concentrating on stirring three spoonfuls of sugar into her tea.

'The Israelis were shooting them like you shoot rabbits.'

'A fighting force made up of eighty-five per cent Reservists!'

How can she bear it? wonders Asya. She must be listening to this sort of thing all the time. She looks over at her other two girlfriends: Mimi also is watching Chrissie, but Noora is in a dream, slowly and absently brushing her cheek with the end of her braid –

'Did you see that bastard, Shedeed, saying, "What have the Israelis gained anyway? A few sandhills?" '

'It's his father's Sinai. This country belongs to the bastards; they can throw away a few sandhills whenever they like.'

'Whole families have been packing and leaving since June – and not Jewish ones this time –'

'It's like forty-eight and fifty-six all over again.'

'Things won't go on like this.'

'But he's more powerful than ever. Didn't we all rush out into the streets on the ninth and the tenth and beg him to stay?'

'Don't leave us, Chief! Oh Boss, Boss don't leave us.'

'That was a crisis. It's understandable. It's not a mandate for him to do whatever he likes.'

'So who's going to stop him?'

'Everybody. People are fed up. They want things put right and they want things out in the open. You can't blame June on a few air-force officers then hope to bury it.'

'The Palestinians aren't going to keep quiet any more; that's for sure.'

Bassam, the Palestinian in the group, has been gazing at Noora. Now he rouses himself and nods.

'Absolutely. It's been a lousy deal all along and now we'll be worse off than ever: Gaza, the West Bank, Jerusalem, all gone.'

'You guys are right to think you've been used, you know –'

'It's a game of governments –'

'It's a question of participation –'

'If this were a true socialist state –'

'A true democracy –'

'June would not have been possible.'

'A true democracy? Man, we don't even have a constitution.'

'A "provisional" constitution we've had for almost four years now.'

'The newspapers simply publish government lies –'

'Remember Ahmad Sa'eed in June?'

'They've disappeared him behind the sun.'

'Are you going to blame him personally?'

'But look even here: inside the university. Before you can put up a poster you have to clear it with the Guard.'

'We had more freedom at school.'

Participation. Life. Students from Egypt, Libya, Sudan, Algeria, Morocco, Iraq, Jordan, Palestine, Syria and Yemen all sit round the same table. News of unrest comes from the universities of Europe and the United States. Poetry and Politics. Never mind the defeat. Never mind the 'Setback' and Sinai and what remained of Palestine gone. The young have a voice and the voice shall be heard. Bassam, the Palestinian, and Hani, one of the Harley-Davidson boys, both play the guitar and the campus rings to songs of exile and yearning:

'Where is Ramallah?
Where is Ramallah?
Tell me, O traveller,
Where is Ramallah?'

Asya is organising an evening of poems and music. She walks around with a navy-blue clipboard.

Scene 6

Sunday, 6 January 1968
Cairo

She was coming out of the library carrying a dark blue vinyl clipboard. She had a large plaster on her knee. She was wearing a short, straight, blue and grey check skirt, a nondescript pullover and the most atrocious blue corduroy blazer I had ever seen. She had fantastic hair and eyes, good legs (apart from the plaster) and far too much make-up on. She had even drawn those spider-like lower lashes they paint on so carefully under their eyes. I'd been told she spoke English as though she'd 'just come over from Oxford'.

'What have you done to your leg?'

'I fell.'

A touching mixture of defiance and uncertainty – probably good boobs under there too – but you couldn't really tell with all that woollen stuff she was wearing.

'My name is Saif Madi. And you are Asya.'

I held out my hand and she stepped forward a little awkwardly – and took it. In days and drawing-rooms and restaurants to come, as she entered with a smooth and practised stride, I would remember the haltingness of that first step with which she entered my heart.

Sunday, 6 January 1968

I've met him today, I'm sure. His name is Saif Madi – a name with rhythm and resonance. He is 26 – eight years older than me. He speaks terrific English and I absolutely know he's read just about everything. Chrissie thinks this is just another of my 'naughtinesses'. But I know it's not. He wears a tweed jacket and Hush Puppies and glasses and smokes a pipe. I know the obvious analysis is the 'father-figure/father-fixation' one, but really he's utterly unlike my father. For one thing he has a moustache. I never thought I could fall in love with a man with a moustache.

I noticed him as I came out of the library. He was standing at the bottom of the steps looking out over the garden towards the department and he looked completely different from everybody else. I walked down slowly, looking at him, and he turned and said, 'What have you done to your knee?' It was the first thing he said to me. His handshake is strong and firm. I hate people who just pass you their hand to do with as you please. Ugh. They make me think of Uriah Heep. He's nothing, NOTHING like that. His hand was warm and dry. We walked over to Chrissie, Mimi, Bassam, Noora and the others in the cafeteria and later he interrupted something I was saying to ask, 'How old are you anyway?'

'Eighteen.'

'I bet you're not eighteen yet.'

'Well, I will be. In two months.'

And his grin of triumph.

I've come home all shivery and I sort of feel my heart filling my whole body –

Skip the tremulous bit. The purple passage. Everyone's been through it. There it is, though, that seminal image: the shining marble of the library steps, the garden with the flower-beds, and beyond the garden, the long low building, housing – oh happy coincidence, blessed omen – the Department of English on the ground floor; and above it – '*May no other man be above you. May he be your partner in this world and the next*' – the Department of History where Saif Madi is registered as an external, 'mature' student. The mellow stone of the buildings, the dome of the University Festival Hall, the cafeteria, bright with parasols, populous with friends, and the warm, gentle winter sunshine all taken utterly for granted – all hers by right. The armful of books: Pater, Heraclitus and that stream that you could never step into twice. Later, whichever way you turn, it's the same old puddle. But at not-quite-eighteen, what fantastic notions: not a world there for the taking – but worlds. Anyway – he had a great handshake. And his hands were warm in winter and cool in summer. He was proud of that inbuilt thermostat. Just as he was proud of his perfect feet and his smooth, muscled, brown back. '*So what the hell did you feel when you touched the bastard? Did you run your hands over his pimply white back while he screwed you?*' His clothes were always terrific and he was thinning a bit on top but wasn't bothered. What she will remember most vividly later is the schoolboy grin breaking through all that grown-upness.

Scene 7

February 1968
Cairo

The very first memory of Soraya's life is of her mother sitting cross-legged on a red carpet; only her lips move as she whispers passages from the Qur'an over the small still baby who lies in her lap. Hamid. How would Fadeela have felt now? Grateful, thinks her daughter. Grateful, as she had been every time her son had walked out of the sea undrowned, every evening he had arrived home at the end of another day: safe. As she had been when, after twenty-four months of absence, he had arrived on the doorstep: Sheikh Zayid's arm round his shoulders, pale but healthy and looking slightly embarrassed. Every day for two years Fadeela had wept and prayed and washed and cooked, and every day either Soraya or Lateefa had carried food and fresh linen to the prison at the Citadel. For a moment Soraya has a vivid image of her brother as he stood in the dock among his comrades. How many had they been? Almost twenty years on, now, she cannot remember. But they had all stood silent and unmoving after one of them had declared their refusal to recognise the court. He had been eighteen. In a white buttoned-up shirt with no tie and the steel-rimmed spectacles that misleadingly made him look so serious and which he had just started to wear. And how angry their father had been. Soraya glances at Ismail Mursi, who is concentrating on his food. For his son to first get mixed up in a lot of communist rubbish. *Then* to get caught visiting a flat where they stored subversive leaflets. *Then* to reject the court and turn down the defence lawyer his father had commissioned;

99

Saba Pasha himself, the best, the most prestigious lawyer in the whole country. 'I wash my hands of him,' he had raged. 'I swear I'll marry again and beget me another son. Sons even. Why not? Sons who would stand by me and who would know the worth of what I do!' He hadn't, of course – as far as they know anyway. And Hamid had eventually come out of jail. He had finished college and grown a moustache, but instead of joining his father's business as Ismail Mursi had always, though with less and less conviction, hoped, he had found a job with an Italian company in the oil-fields of Sinai. Two years later he had buried his mother and then after four years he had fallen in love and got married, and there she sits now, his wife of seven years, beautiful and groomed and cool as ever, never looking at him and daintily picking her way though her salad. Soraya allows herself to look at Hamid where he sits at the far end of the table. He is watching the football match on the television behind her head and trying to eat. Occasionally he bends down and says something to one of the three small children playing around under the table. From this angle his face is almost normal: the face she has watched – watched over – through so many years. So many versions of Hamid she remembers as she watches that gloved left hand stiffly supporting the knife in the roast lamb where the right hand has placed it: the little boy she walked to school every morning so spruce and shiny, and picked up every afternoon scruffy and grazed, his *tarboosh* white with dust from having been used as a football; the twelve-year-old who refused to leave the hospital and sat up with his mother all night when she had the accident; the sixteen-year-old in a fury numbering his clothes-hangers and writing his name on each one to prevent his sisters pinching them –

Her father holds out his plate and motions towards the platter of stuffed vine-leaves. Hamid puts down the knife he holds in his right hand and passes his father's plate to Asya who passes it to Lateefa who heaps several vine-leaves on to it.

'Do you want some yoghurt salad next to it, Father?'

Ismail Mursi shakes his head, and his plate travels back to its place in front of him. This is where he eats – where he has always eaten – every Friday afternoon: at the head of his table, surrounded by his family. In the far corner the football flickers on the large black and white television. Behind him the great glass-panelled doors that lead into the drawing-room shine with a thousand tiny pin-pricks of light. 'English' glass they call it. Sixty panels of English glass refracting the February sunshine that comes in through the open windows of the dining-room. Sixty panels and not one of them broken or changed in the thirty-seven years Soraya has lived in this house, eaten in this room. Thirty-seven years. She had been born in this house and lived in it all her life except for the three years she had lived alone with her husband in a small flat the other side of Falaki. Muhammad al-Fadl sits on her right, next to Hamid's wife. He has stopped eating long ago and is gazing at the football. He is not a good eater; doesn't really care for food. Doesn't really care for football either; he is just watching it because it's on and he's sitting in front of it. What *does* he care for? He cares for Meedo, she has to give him that. What else? Her glance slides over him. An undistinguished man. She can never remember his face when he is not right there in front of her. And sometimes she is surprised to come across him – to come across him in her life so to speak: walking down the long corridor of her father's house or sleeping in the large canopied bed she shares with him in what used to be her mother's room. Her mother's room where they had all been born and where her mother had had her accident and where she had died. The room from the balcony of which she had watched her mother's coffin as it left the house on the shoulders of the men: Ismail Mursi, Hamid, Sheikh Zayid and Fadeela's three brothers. 'Speeding along,' Soraya's uncles had said, looking accusingly at their sister's husband. 'Light and happy to be going even though she was only forty-six.' But before she had died Fadeela had fixed Soraya, Hamid and Nadia with her straight green eye while the eye that had wandered had looked vaguely out of the window, and she had said, 'Look after your father.'

Soraya looks at her father. Ever since she can remember he has sat down to eat against this backdrop of shimmering glass. She watches him. He eats singlemindedly; not looking at the football or attending to anything going on around him. He finishes what is on his plate, then indicates with a curt nod of the head the dish he wants to be served from next. He only ever tries one dish at a time. When he has finished he will drink a glassful of iced water, wipe his mouth, throw his napkin down on the table and rise. Everybody else will stop eating for a moment as he makes his way round the table and out of the room. From the basin in the corridor will come the sounds of his washing and spitting and brushing of teeth. Then he will come back into the room and sit down in his armchair with its back to his wife's display cabinet. He will look around and growl, 'Where's the tea?' and when it has arrived and stands steaming by his side on the small table which all his children and grandchildren had at one time or another turned upside-down and used as a train, he will rest his head against the velvet-upholstered back of the chair and fall asleep. He would sleep for about an hour – unless his grandchildren took their noisy play out of the room or somebody switched off the television, when he would start awake in the silence – first confused, and then angry. He is more or less angry all the time now: angry that he didn't remarry, angry that business is bad after the war, angry that Hamid has had an accident. He is even angry that Hamid is offering to join him in the shop, although everyone agrees that this is the best thing that Hamid can do now and his father had always wanted him there, hadn't he? And when Dr Mukhtar, in his role of eldest son, had spoken to Ismail Mursi about it he had agreed. Not very willingly, but he had agreed. And yet Farrag said that yesterday, when Hamid, having sat uselessly behind the desk in the shop all morning, had finally said, 'Maybe you could let me do the books?' his father had made some incomprehensible sounds and wandered off to the back of the shop then up the stairs to the workrooms where he had remained for the rest of the day. What could Hamid have done? Chased after him? No one can blame him if he stays away after that. But of course he won't. It is his business after all – in the end. *Their* business – all of them. And it's his right to be involved in it.

Soraya looks at Hamid still manoeuvring that clumsy left hand around the fork. Asya keeps glancing at him out of the corner of her eye. Soraya knows she wants to offer her help, to cut up the food for her uncle, but she does not want to risk offending him or drawing attention to Sunny's neglect. Soraya smiles at her niece and nods invitingly towards the serving-dish still heaped with grilled chicken quarters. Asya smiles back and pats her tummy and mimes full-up-ness, then goes on picking separate grains of rice off her plate and pretending she is still eating. Her 'first-born', her 'eldest child', Soraya always says of her niece. For she had been 19 when Asya was born, and since Lateefa was working and studying and married and busy, Soraya and Fadeela had together looked after the little girl all day long, sending her home only for bed-time. She had been such a pretty child and Soraya had always dressed her and had sewn and embroidered for her the most exquisite little bibs, dresses, nighties and party-frocks that a little girl had ever had. Even her vests and knickers had been scalloped and edged in toning colours. It seemed like only yesterday she was wedging her tiny feet into her aunt's high heels, stealing the nail varnish and the kohl and dabbing herself with perfume to go playing on the marble stairs in the sunshine catching baby cockroaches; capturing them alive for Nadia's anatomy classes. And now there she is: eighteen and at university and almost a bride. 'May God send her happiness,' prays her aunt who in her heart of hearts no longer believes in happiness.

She looks briefly at Asya's father, sitting up very straight across the table from his daughter, between Hamid's wife and Sheikh Zayid, who has finished eating and is quietly fingering his prayer-beads. Mukhtar al-Ulama has just accepted the post of Minister of Culture, with misgivings. His place is in the university, he says. If he had wanted to be a politician he would have been one long ago. He had neither served the government nor fought it. But now, in the wake of the defeat, intellectuals are being urged to forgo their isolation, to put their ideas at the service of their country, to assume practical responsibilities. He eats meticulously. Only allowing on his plate what he knows he can finish. He avoids ill-defined foods like *bamia* and *mulukhiyya*, eats his rice with a fork instead of with a spoon like everyone else and never touches anything – not even the chicken – with his fingers.

Hamid has put down his knife and fork and picked up the drumstick with his right hand, the left resting at last on the table in front of him. What is he going to do? His two sons are playing with Meedo under the table. Their father is unemployable, and anyway there is no more Sinai and there are no more oil-fields. There is no more Canal, the country is in ruins and Sunny is cold-hearted and will be no comfort to him. He has started court proceedings against the army but a court case will take years and in the end bring him – what? Compensation comes only from God. What has happened has happened and what has been lost has been lost for ever.

Scene 8

February 1968
Cairo
The military court delivers its verdicts on charges of negligence brought against the leaders of the Egyptian air force. The feeling in the country is that the sentences are too lenient. The storm that has been brewing since June erupts. The workers in the munitions factories in Helwan decide to commemorate the 21st of February of twenty-two years ago: 'Bloody Thursday'. They organise a demonstration and plan to march on Parliament and on the presidential palace in Abdin. But their (Arab Socialist Union Party) leaders persuade them to confine it to the ASU Headquarters of Helwan Zone – which happens to be near Helwan Police Station.

21 February
The steel and munitions workers march through the streets of Helwan. They clash with the police outside Helwan Police Station and scores are injured.

At the universities in Cairo and Alexandria the events planned in memory of Bloody Thursday are turning into a series of confrontations in which officials find themselves fielding the students' questions on the political situation and the military trials. News of the events in Helwan reaches the students and they take their protest on to the city streets in the first demonstrations since 1954.

103

24 February

A delegation is formed from among the thousands of students demonstrating outside Parliament. The delegation is to present the demands of the student body to the Speaker of Parliament: Anwar el-Sadat. The students register their names as required, then express their fears that they might be arrested. Mr Sadat gives them his word of honour that that will not happen and hands over his personal phone number in case they are molested in any way. He then reprimands them because, 'With your demonstrations you gave courage to elements which had been eradicated or had retreated [from our society]. A car was spotted today touring the schools in the Heliopolis area and inciting students to strike. The passengers in the car were sons of the old feudalists.'

Later that night, the members of the delegation are arrested in their homes.

25 February

Al-Ahram publishes an order by the Minister of the Interior banning demonstrations on the ground that 'other elements' had infiltrated student ranks. Any breach of the ban would be 'an insult to the national struggle at a time when the Arab nation is having to face a wide-ranging conspiracy by imperialist forces and Israel'.

The government has decided to close down the universities but the students, angered at the arrests of the previous night, call for a sit-in at the Faculty of Engineering:

> Let every free man among you know that freedom is to be taken not to be given, to be extorted not to be donated. Since we do not have enough power to impose our demands we have found that the only way to let the people hear our voice . . . and to force the ruling power to respect our freedoms . . . is to resort to passive resistance in the form of a full-scale sit-in.

Riot police besiege the college but the students bombard them with stones and small rocks and the police withdraw to the adjacent Zoo and Botanical Gardens while parents and faculty members are brought in to put pressure on the students to end the sit-in. The students, meanwhile, formulate their demands:

(1) the release of all arrested colleagues;
(2) the formulation of an effective policy for the liberation of Palestine;
(3) the creation of a truly representative parliament in a real and sound representative system;
(4) the reconstitution of the youth organisations;
(5) freedom of expression and of the press;

(6) the withdrawal of Intelligence personnel from the universities and the removal of the apparatus of the Mukhabarat from domestic matters;

(7) a declaration of the extent of the air-force officers' responsibility in the Setback;

(8) a serious investigation of the workers' incident in Helwan;

(9) the dismissal of al-Lethi 'Abd el-Nasser: Nasser's brother in charge of the ASU in Alexandria.

28 February

As the uprising dies down in the rest of the country the students agree to end their sit-in and to present – once again – their demands to the Speaker of Parliament. They are moved from the Faculty of Engineering to Parliament in a fleet of government cars and there enter into fierce debate with ministers and representatives. When they ask that their declaration and demands be published in the press, Mr Sadat says, 'I reject this declaration in form and content . . . I read it last night . . . Isn't it that of "freedom to be taken not to be given"? . . . I say no to this . . . This declaration has been based on bad temper and not on our democratic discussion of today.'

The uprising ends, having resulted in the deaths of two workers, the injury of seventy-seven civilians and one hundred and forty-six police and the arrest of six hundred and thirty-five civilians – among them Hani, who was revving up his Harley-Davidson and chanting 'Spiro Spathis – Betrayed the People'.

Ten days later, the arrested students are released, but the Minister of the Interior keeps some of them in custody without the knowledge of the Public Prosecutor. Among them is Hani, who is unable to explain the hidden meaning behind 'Spiro Spathis – Betrayed the People'.

Two weeks later President Nasser interprets the students' battle-cry of 'Freedom': 'It means we should educate them, offer them jobs after graduation, get them married and provide them with houses!'

Scene 9

'Una niña bonita
Sentada al balcón
Ella queria mi alma
Yo le di mi corazón
Ella queria mi alma
Yo le dije – Adios.'

I tried to tell her. I gave her Lorca, L'Etranger, The Blood of Others,
Saint-Exupéry. The lot. At the Hotel Omar Khayyam I bought her her first
Tom Collins and watched as she sipped at it carefully.
'Are you always so silent or only when you're with me?'
Confused, she raises her eyes to mine for a moment and then lowers them.
'I don't know.'
'Talk to me.'
'What about?'
There is true helplessness in her voice.
'Anything. Anything you like.'
'Well, ask me something then.'
'Do you think we are in dead man's alley where the blind men lost their
bones?'
She picks it up, of course, and smiles and shakes her head, but that is all. In
the months to come this exchange will be repeated like a refrain, with her 'I don't
knows' and her 'About whats?' becoming tinged with desperation. Later, I
forbade her to say, 'I don't know' – but that afternoon, the afternoon of her first
Tom Collins, I took her to the rock garden and into the maze Lutfallah had had
built when this was still his palace. We walked round the maze in silence as
darkness fell and then I took her in my arms and kissed her. Apart from a
momentary drawing back and an intake of breath, she did not resist, and within
moments her arms were around my waist and she was kissing me back. It was
seven months to the day since Didi had left Egypt. I whispered, 'Marry me,' into
her neck and kissed her again and again. When I felt her legs giving way, I
propped her against the rock wall and pressed my mouth hard to her lips, her
face, her neck, her shoulders. Eventually, fifteen minutes late for her seven
o'clock curfew, I walked her home.

Sunday, 17 March 1968

Yesterday I had my first alcoholic drink ever. In the Omar Khayyam. We sat on the terrace overlooking the gardens. The pathways are lined with statues of half-naked ladies with Grecian chignons and chopped-off arms. It, the drink, was a 'John Collins' and it's made with gin and lemonade. I didn't feel any different, though: drunk or anything I mean. I mean, I'm so constantly breathless when I'm with him anyway. But I don't know why I can't seem to talk to him at all. I talk plenty to everyone else, but he seems so clever, I just don't want to look stupid in front of him by saying something not particularly profound. When we'd finished our drinks he said, 'Let's go for a walk.' We walked round the gardens and looked at the pool and he pointed out his bungalow (he's giving a course and the company has put them all in this hotel), then he took me into the rock maze. He was walking ahead of me because he knows the way through the maze and also he was holding aside branches and twigs and things so I could pass. We came to a clear bit and I was just walking along behind him when he suddenly stopped and turned around. I just sort of walked into him and he put his hands on my shoulders and kissed me. His hands were on my shoulders and his lips were on mine and it was like – like electricity jolting me and a great heat-lamp being suddenly turned on and all my blood turned into hot quicksilver and went racing madly through my body. And of course I was terrified that someone might come along and find us but also I could not make myself pull away. His lips are terrific: warm and not hard but kind of firm with a promise of softness underneath. The moustache doesn't really get in the way as I had thought it might. My heart was absolutely pounding in my throat and in my fingertips and the backs of my knees and later I found that I was leaning against the rock wall and my arms were round his waist. I felt there was such – almost desperation in the way he kissed me, like this was something he so badly needed to do. His mouth was on my neck and I opened my eyes and leaned my head back against the rock and looked at the stars and could not believe that all this was happening to me. Then he said, 'Marry me,' and it seemed terribly quick but also completely inevitable and I said, 'Yes.' Then he held me and kissed me very very hard so my head was actually banged into the wall once. I loved it; I loved being in his arms and holding him and kissing him instead of sitting on the other side of the table trying to think of something to say. Then he walked me home. He has the most wonderful way possible of leaving my hand when he's been holding it: his hand kind of lingers – like he really regrets letting go – but without being yucky or anything. Upstairs, I was ten minutes late and I had to rush and get dressed because we were going to the opera. In the bathroom mirror I saw a drop of blood on my lower lip. I licked it away but it came back. When I went into my mother's room to get my pearl bracelet from the secret drawer in her wardrobe I couldn't hold it back so I said, 'He's asked me to marry him.'

And she actually said, 'Who?'

'Why, Saif of course, Mummy!'

She kind of looked at me, then sat down on the edge of her bed (they're in a twin-bed phase right now) and said, 'You haven't given him an answer yet have you?'

'I said "yes".'

'Oh. Oh.'

It was like something had hurt her. She said, 'You're not even eighteen yet –' looking all bewildered.

'I will be next week,' I said, and licked a fresh drop of blood off my lip.

Then I saw tears in my mother's eyes. I'd only ever seen tears in my mother's eyes twice: once when we were in England in 1956 and all the Suez stuff was happening and her mother died in Cairo. And once – a year later – after the only row I've ever seen my parents having. And now her eyes had gone all wet and red and small and she sat on the edge of the bed – even though she knew we were getting late and my father was ready and waiting for us outside – and said, 'But you can't make such an important decision just like that. You can't determine the rest of your life suddenly one night when you're not yet eighteen.'

And I felt suddenly and for the first time in my life that I was wiser and stronger than she was, and I kissed her and said, 'Don't worry, Mummy. I know what I'm doing.'

Then Daddy knocked loudly and opened the door and looked at us with astonished displeasure:

'Are you ready? Shall I call the lift?'

I sat in the dark box. Red plush and gilt everywhere. I love the opera house – and how wonderfully fitting that we should be coming here tonight. I listened to *Don Giovanni* and gazed up as I always do at the oval portraits of Scarlatti, Donizetti, Puccini and Verdi along the rim of the pale blue cupola with their names picked out in gold. I looked at the gigantic chandelier and the draped 'loges' and I dreamed of how – after our engagement – he will join us in our box – probably for the very next season. What will he think when he sees me for the first time in evening dress? If he sits across from me our eyes will meet – keep meeting. If he sits near I can stroke the fine black hair on the back of his hand. I love his hands: brown and square with strong, blunt fingers. I sucked at my bruised lower lip and dreamed of making love with him here: surrounded by the music of Mozart and the red velvet of the loge, starting with kisses as he leans from his chair to mine, then standing, leaning against the moiré silk wall, my silver dress against the red silk covered by the black of his evening suit, his hand lifting the silver up, and up, sliding under it, then, as he lifts his mouth from mine and looks at me, I would hold his eyes and slowly lie down for him on the red velvet chaise-longue –

Scene 10

Saturday, 30 March 1968
Cairo

 ' "My bounty is as boundless as the sea,
My love as deep: the more I give to thee,
The more I have, for both are infinite." '

He ducks his head and glowers over his horn-rimmed glasses. They are down almost to the tip of his nose; another two millimetres and they will slip over it and fall crashing to the floor. The class holds its breath. Dr Minyawi seems to have forgotten that he is standing on top of a rickety wooden chair placed dangerously near the edge of the dusty podium. A hundred or so faces, carefully expressionless, gaze at him from the tiers of Room Thirteen. Asya and Chrissie kick each other under their bench.

'Well?' he snaps, staring round the class. 'Well? Well? What does this mean? What is odd about this construction?'

'That it is a paradox,' he answers himself. ' "The more I give to thee, the more I have." A paradox. Yes? And the paradox is sometimes the only way to express the truth.'

He had shambled in at precisely eleven o'clock, climbed the podium and slammed three dull-coloured files on to the massive desk, causing a small cloud of dust to rise into the air and hover for a moment before it dispersed and settled once again. 'Am 'Ali (or Dr 'Ali as the students call him), the cleaner, coffee-maker, telephone-answerer and student-frightener of the department, is having the off period that coincides with the blowing of the winds of the Khamaseen: each year he fights, and loses, a battle against the dust that they carry into every corner of every room in the department. Each year, as the first fine particles catch in the hair of his nostrils, 'Am 'Ali mobilises his underlings, collects his buckets and his rags and his brushes, and prepares for war. But when for the fifth day running he has vigorously polished the first of a row of benches and turned around to find it already covered with a fine layer of red dust; when he opens a brand-new, sealed packet of coffee to find the red film lying on top of the soft black powder – then he gives up. He wraps his distinguished, silvered head in a grey shawl and does not bother to clean any room except the one in which the Professor himself is just about to give a lecture. And if any of the faculty order tea or coffee, they just have to drink it as it comes: tasting of the winds of the Khamaseen.

Dr Minyawi had stood behind the desk. He had gripped the back of the wooden chair and leaned forward.

' "He jests at *sca-a-ars* who never felt a wound!" '

The last students had settled down and they were sitting there with biros in their hands and sheets of fresh, blank paper on their desks. He had surveyed them bitterly.

' "He jests at scars who never felt a wound!" '

He had looked around, then suddenly staggered backwards, throwing his right hand up as though against a powerful glare.

' "But, soft! What light through yonder window breaks?
It is the east, and Juliet is the sun –" '

He had grabbed the chair in both hands, pulled it out from behind the desk and banged it down at the front of the podium. One of the legs buckled slightly. He stared angrily round the class then clambered on to the chair, straightened up, composed his features and gazed into the distance.

' "Ay me!" ' he sighed on a high-pitched drawn-out quaver, and his round face shone and his green jacket flapped as he jumped down, turned and fell to his knees on the floorboards, stretching his right arm up into the air.

' "She speaks.
O, speak again, bright angel, for thou art
As glorious to this night, being o'er my head,
As is a winged messenger of heaven –" '

Asya had gazed at him. You could see the grey stubble on his chin. You could see the tiny motes of spit flying out with every plosive, every sibilant and every fricative; the residue settling into white flecks in the corners of his mouth. His jacket is shiny with age and his socks are a pukey yellow and there they are again as once more he mounts the chair – which amazingly does not collapse – and then rears back violently.

' "What man art thou, that, thus [spit] bes[spit]creen'd in night,
so stumblest[spit] on my couns[spit]el?" '

And yet he's married. *Marri-éd*. And fairly recently too. He has a small baby. It's unimaginable. Not to think of him actually doing it even – even just the preliminaries. How can his wife bear it? A nudge from Chrissie, and a note is passed across. Asya unfolds it: 'You are staring horribly.'

'Well. Just look at him!' Asya writes back.

Chrissie scribbles: 'Still. Don't stare like that.'

'Why does he have to do this?' Asya whispers, crumpling up the note. 'Why can't he do *Macbeth*?'

'Shhhh.'

' "Fain would I dwell on form, fain, fain deny
What I have spoke; but farewell compliment!
Dost thou love me?" '

The falsetto melts with tenderness. No, it is too much. Asya draws her hands over her face as she tries to hold back the fit of giggles that threatens her. Think of something terrible. Something unfunny. But she can only think of Dr Minyawi approaching Mrs Minyawi, his soul bursting with paradoxical truths, his arms stretched out, his eyes glazed, his voice a-quaver. He couldn't. He couldn't possibly. And yet he must have. At least once. Asya tries to imagine Dr Minyawi in the Omar Khayyam maze; tries to imagine what it would feel like to be the object of those arms reaching out, the hands ready to clasp, the face drawing near, the lips – no. No, no, *no* –

' "– the more I give to thee,
The more I have, for both are infinite." '

He ducks his head and glowers over his horn-rimmed glasses. In one of the glass panels of the door, to his left and invisible to him, the gaunt, shawl-encircled features of 'Am 'Ali suddenly materialise. He peers suspiciously through the glass, and as the students catch sight of him a ripple of suppressed laughter passes through the room.

'Well?' snaps Dr Minyawi, staring around the class. 'As I have said before, Shakespeare's dramatic tools are irony and paradox –'

But 'Am 'Ali, disturbed by the thudding noises he keeps hearing as Dr Minyawi leaps from the chair to the podium and from the podium to the chair, has come to investigate. Asya thinks that, framed like this, rising out of the darkness, he looks more than ever like a character from an Eisenstein movie: Ivan the Terrible, say. She puts her face in her hands and prays that this class should end before she bursts into laughter. 'Am 'Ali frowns at the students shifting slightly on their benches. Then he hears another thud. He opens the door and puts his head around the corner.

' "O blessed, blessed night! I am afeard,
Being in night, all this is but a dream –" '

111

Dr Minyawi stares angrily at 'Am 'Ali. Sweat shines on his face. 'Am 'Ali scrutinizes the teacher, then nods slowly to himself. He leaves the room and closes the door behind him with a slight slam. Asya slips a folded note to Chrissie: 'Let's go see the film.'

'What film?' Chrissie writes back.

'Zeffirelli. *Romeo and Juliet.*'

'You mean you want to wipe out this version?'

'He's HORRIBLE. And he SPITS.'

'You prefer il Dottore Piemontese?'

'But of course. Gli Italiani sono sempre cute. Let's go see the film.'

'OK. Thursday?'

'Not Thursday. Seeing Saif.'

'Your mother knows?'

'No. Wednesday?'

'You have Italian.'

'D. Piemontese is not coming this week.'

'OK.'

'So! So!' Dr Minyawi is shouting at his students. 'What are you sniggering at? Love?' he shouts. 'You think that love is to be sniggered at? You think you know all about love? You think you know what love is? I tell you. You know nothing. *I* know about love.' The class holds its breath. 'I love my child.' The class breathes again. 'I love my cat.' He looks around. 'And I love my wife.' Silence. 'It is all the same. It is love. Yes. It is *love*. To love your child. To love your cat. To love your wife. Love,' he shouts, 'is – infinite.'

Scene 11

April 1968

Cairo

'He came home yesterday looking as though he'd had a terrible shock. And he locked himself up in his room and wouldn't speak to anyone. I coax him: "Taha, shall I get you some supper?", "Taha, shall I make you a glass of tea?" All he would say was, "I don't want anything." I beg him. It's still no use. At last this morning I conjured him by my life and if he held me dear. I vowed I would wish myself dead, and he opened the door.'

Muneera al-Tarabulsi pauses. She turns her reddened, swollen eyes on her daughter's friend who has been summoned over by an urgent – whispered – phone-call from Chrissie.

'I can't tell you, Asya. He was sitting on his bed in pyjama-trousers and a vest and I can't *tell* you what he looked like: a human being who had not closed his eyes all night.

' "What is it, Taha? What is it, my son?"

' "I saw her, Mama. I saw her."

' "Saw who, my darling?" I thought he meant he'd seen that girl he's in love with. The Coptic girl. And maybe she'd told him something that upset him. What else could she tell him? It would have to be something to upset him.

' "Chrissie. My sister. I saw her with my own two eyes."

' "Saw her? How do you mean "saw her"? What are you talking about?" My child, I was confused. I started thinking maybe he'd seen his sister in a dream and it had been a bad dream and had worried him. Then he said, "Yesterday. I saw her in the street." I said, "What of it, Taha? She has to walk in the street. How else will she come and go?" He *hit* his desk with his fist closed like this – I swear by God I jumped – and said, "Don't you understand, Mother? I saw her with a man. *My sister.* Walking in the street with a man." '

Asya glances at Chrissie sitting in a grey armchair, her elbows on her knees and her head in her hands. The chandelier is not lit and the shutters are closed. They have not spoken since the phone-call. 'Look, can you come over?'

Chrissie's voice had been low. Asya had realised she must be whispering into the mouthpiece and found herself whispering back.

'What's up? What's the matter?'

'It's Taha. But listen: I can't really talk. He saw me yesterday. With Bassam. In the street. He's locked himself up in his room and Mama – I can't talk. Come if you can but if you can't it's OK.'

The receiver had fallen silent. Asya had tried one tentative 'Chrissie?' then put the phone down. Now that was really bad, bad luck, she had thought. Bassam was nothing at all to do with Chrissie; he was miserably in love with Noora and had probably been going on to Chrissie about it. And where had Asya herself been? Why hadn't she been with Chrissie as she normally would have been? Because Saif had had a free afternoon and she had been with him in the maze of the Omar Khayyam –

'I couldn't speak,' says Chrissie's mother. 'I couldn't speak; my breath just went. But after a bit I collected myself and said, "For sure it's a colleague, Taha; one of her colleagues. Chrissie's my daughter and I know her –" His blood seemed to boil right over. "You always defend her. You always keep her secrets. That was fine as long as she was at school. But now look what's happening. *Now*," he said, "it's a matter of

113

reputation; the *whole* family's reputation. And that's why my father has to know about it." So he's sitting there waiting till his father gets back from Alexandria and then he's going to tell him. I pleaded with him and begged him but it was no use.' The tears start running down Muneera's face again. ' "She's his daughter," he says, "and he can deal with her as he sees fit." And there he is, sitting inside on his bed. And Sidki, may he come home safely, please God – is due back any minute. Oh Chrissie, Chrissie. Did you have to walk with that boy in the street? Don't you know what your brother is like? Don't you know what your father is like?'

'Mama! Did I know that Taha would be on that bus? Isn't he always at his own university in Heliopolis? The other side of the world?'

Chrissie is impatient but she has been crying too.

'Yes, but why would you walk with a young man in the street anyway? Didn't you know what could happen?'

'I've already told you. Mama: he was talking about things and he was very unhappy and you know I had to get home by six so I said why didn't he walk with me to the bus stop just outside the campus gates? We walked to the bus stop and when the bus came it was very crowded so I thought I'd better walk a bit further and catch the trolley-bus. We walked along by the Zoo towards the trolley-bus stop and that's where Taha saw us. And now he's making out like he saw us hiding in the bushes. All I did was walk in the street –'

'All you *did*? *All* you did? Good. Fine. Say that to your father. Tell him all you did was walk in the street with a young man. See what he's going to do –'

'Tante Muneera! Bassam is just a colleague. What's really happening is that he admires a friend of ours only he's afraid to tell her –'

'So he's telling my daughter instead? What has Chrissie got to do with these things? I don't understand. And you, Asya! Where were you? Why did you leave your friend on her own to get into trouble like this? Where were you? Aren't you two together all the time?'

Chrissie looks at Asya quickly.

'Mama, I've told you twice: there was a film on at the Italian Cultural Institute in Zamalek and Asya went to it because it was useful to her. You know she's doing an extra course in Italian. I've told you –'

'Then if you didn't have lectures why didn't you come home earlier, Chrissie? Why did –'

'We had lectures but Asya thought that – just this once – she would skip the lecture and catch up on it later. The film was only showing once.'

Muneera turns to Asya again. 'And does your mother know you were at the Italian what's-it-called and not at college?'

Asya looks at Chrissie.

'Yes!' Chrissie has both hands on her knees and is leaning forward

114

now, shouting. '*Yes*, she knows. Because her family is *civilised*. They let her *do* things. *Reasonable* things. They *talk* to each other there; it's not all screaming and shouting –'

'Chrissie, Chrissie,' cries Asya. 'Stop it.' She runs over and hugs her friend, then sits on the arm of her chair keeping her hand on Chrissie's shoulder.

'Tante, Chrissie just didn't think. Because she really, really wasn't doing anything wrong. We're all just a group of friends and this guy, Bassam, he's very serious but he just can't bring himself to tell the girl herself –'

'So he tells Chrissie.' Muneera is a bit quieter now after her daughter's outburst. 'This boy, he's in the same class as you?'

'Yes.'

'So he's – what? Nineteen?'

'He's twenty,' mutters Asya.

'You are all children. *Children*. And you don't know what you're doing. And in any case, he admires a girl, one of his colleagues. Why doesn't he go and tell her? Or, better still, tell her brother. Doesn't she have brothers this friend of yours? If his intentions are honourable that's what he should do. And he knows that very well. Who is the girl he admires?'

Asya glances down at Chrissie. Chrissie shrugs.

'It's Noora,' says Asya.

'Noora al-Manesterli?'

'Yes, Tante. And you know how vague she is. He can't tell if she feels anything for him. And he's Palestinian –'

'Palestinian?' Muneera claps her hand to her mouth. '*Palestinian*? And he's going and falling in love with Noora al-Manesterli? I swear her father will have him jailed. What has he got –'

'Yes, well, he realises all that. That's why he's so hesitant about speaking to her. But in fact he's from a very good family. He's a Huseini. His uncle is the governor of Gaza and they have houses and lands in Nablus –'

'Governor of Gaza? Houses and lands in Nablus? Houses and lands in the palm of the Devil. Are you all mad? Don't you live in this world? Tomorrow his mother could go out shopping and come back to find she hasn't got a house to put her shopping in. And he's falling in love with Noora al-Manesterli? Her father –'

'So what does that mean, Tante?' Asya knows this is not the moment for arguing but she cannot help it. 'That Palestinians shouldn't fall in love? Shouldn't –'

'They should fall in love, yes, fall in love as much as they want to: with their own people. Among themselves. They shouldn't spread their disasters over other people's daughters. Oh God, God –' Muneera strikes her thighs with her open palms. 'I had thought we might get the boy himself

115

to phone Taha and explain. But a *Palestinian*. It'll be a black day if Chrissie's father hears all this. And he'll be coming home any minute –'

'What are we going to do, Tante? What can we do?'

'I don't know, child. I don't know.' Muneera looks at her daughter. 'Maybe if Asya spoke to Taha?'

'Asya speak to Taha? No, Mama, no. He won't listen. All he'll do is be nasty to her –'

'He might. He might listen to her. He thinks well of her, and if she told it to him calmly and reasonably – will you talk to him, Asya?'

'Yes, Tante. If that's what you see.'

'Mama, don't make her do this –'

'Come with me – come with me –'

Muneera is already up and nudging Asya down the long corridor towards the private rooms of the house.

'You talk to him, Asya, yes? He's very kind really; it's just that he's the quick-tempered, nervous type –'

'You'll be there, Tante, won't you?' Asya asks quickly.

'No, no, dear, I think it's better if you talk to him alone. I know he thinks highly of you and if you talk to him –'

'But Tante, I can't just go into his bedroom on my own –'

'Darling, these are exceptional circumstances, and after all, Taha is like your brother –'

Asya's hands are cold and clammy. She puts them in the pockets of her loose cotton jacket and runs her tongue over her dry lips. She knows Taha doesn't like her – and she doesn't like him. Whenever she saw him he'd be frowning at the floor. They only ever mumbled 'Good afternoon' at each other when they couldn't avoid it. He'd probably get even angrier at her coming in like this –

'Taha. Asya's here. She'd like a couple of words with you.'

Tante Muneera has knocked on the door, pushed Asya gently into the room and closed the door behind her.

Taha is sitting on his bed facing her. His back is against the dark headboard and his legs are stretched out in front of him. Asya retreats two steps so that her shoulderblades are touching the door. He wears beige and white striped pyjama-trousers and a white cotton vest. His shoulders and chest are more muscular than she would have expected and his feet are white and long and delicate. He is staring at them and his face is set and hard. Her hands are still in her pockets and her back against the door. He raises his face and looks straight at her.

'So? What is it you're going to say? You're going to tell me some fairy-tale in defence of your friend? Yes?'

Asya looks at him. This is the first time he's addressed a sentence to her. And she was right. He doesn't like her. She isn't going to be able to persuade him –

116

'Well? You're supposed to be tactful. Diplomatic. "Eloquent" your friend says. Are you going to get her out of this?'

His arms are folded across his chest. His chest is muscular but his chin is weak –

'Taha,' Asya begins. 'Look. Chrissie has not done anything wrong. Don't you know your sister?'

'So I was imagining things? You're telling me I'm mad?'

'No of course you weren't imagining things. She was in the street with our colleague –'

'Ah!'

'But the street is a public place. She wasn't hiding. She wasn't doing anything wrong.'

'She was walking in the street with a man –' His voice has risen.

'Not a man.'

'Not a man?' He stares at her.

'I mean he's just a *young* man. One of our colleagues. A boy almost. They were having a totally normal conversation on the way out of class and he walked with her to the bus stop –'

'A totally normal conversation? And why should he have this totally normal conversation with my sister in particular? There's no one else for him to have a totally normal conversation with?'

'Taha. You know what it's like at college –'

'You, for example. Why wasn't he having a totally normal conversation with you? Where were you? Why weren't you with your friend?'

Asya remembers Chrissie's lie.

'I had to go to the Italian Institute because of something to do with a course I'm taking. So I left early. Chrissie –'

'You're doing Italian as well? Praise be to God who has created all this!' He looks her up and down, presenting her to herself with a wave of his arm before folding it back across his chest. It feels so odd, being alone in the bedroom with him: a man, undressed and sitting on his bed. This is the first time Asya has been alone in a room with a man – and a closed door behind her. If this were a story she would now offer herself to him – as ransom for Chrissie. She would sit on the side of the bed and he would reach up and pull her down.

'I've always wanted to do this,' he would say against her mouth as he picked at the buttons of her shirt.

'You can do what you like to me,' she would whisper, 'but I have to stay a virgin. Please remember that.' And even though they didn't like each other – maybe *because* they didn't like each other – it would be –

'Well,' he says, 'since you've got nothing more to say –'

'Taha, please. You've got it all wrong. Really you have –'

'She was walking in the street with a man. And they were on their own. Isn't that so?'

117

'Yes, but –'

'There are no buts. That's what happened and that's what I shall tell her father. If you have anything else to say, you can say it to him. And tell my mother it was not a good idea to send you in like this.'

Muneera and Chrissie look up at her. Asya shakes her head.

Chrissie says, 'Didn't I tell you?' to her mother.

Muneera cries, 'So nothing is any use at all?' and jumps up and runs inside.

The two girls go into the dining-room and sit on the Queen Anne sofa under the gilt-framed mirror.

'How was it with Saif yesterday?' Chrissie whispers, grinning.

'Oh Chrissie, be quiet,' Asya whispers back. 'I wish I hadn't gone. I wish I hadn't gone and I'd stayed at college with you. What's going to happen now?'

'I don't know.'

'Well, what are we going to do?'

Chrissie shrugs. 'Nothing. What *can* we do?'

There is silence. Then Chrissie asks, 'Was it difficult for you to come here? What did you say?'

'My father wasn't there, luckily. I told Mama you had a problem –'

'*That's* for sure –'

'– with the Pater and Poe essay due tomorrow.' Asya looks at Chrissie. 'Have you done it?'

'You must be joking. Have *you*?'

'Not yet. I wanted to ask you for some things from your notes.'

Chrissie points to the blue folder lying on the sideboard. 'They're over there. When do you have to be home?'

'Six.' Asya looks at her watch. It is five o'clock.

'You'd really better *be* back at six,' says Chrissie. 'If Tante Lateefa phones here –'

'I know. I know. Chrissie, all that stuff about the Italian Cultural Institute –'

'I had to think of *some*thing, didn't I?'

'Yes, but –'

'Look, if they suspect you for a moment they'll say I can't see you; can't even *speak* to you.'

'I know. But supposing they check?'

'There *was* a film on yesterday. From five. What time did you go home?'

'Seven.'

'So you *could* have been there. They can't check that. You wouldn't even think of keeping the ticket. And it's right next to the Omar Khayyam if anyone saw you on the street or anything –'

'And if Tante Muneera phones my mother?'

'She won't. And even if she did, you just tell your ma it's true: you'd just suddenly found out about it and wanted to go. And you didn't tell her later because you knew she wouldn't like you having gone without telling her in the first place. She'll forgive you. It's only a cultural misdemeanor.' Chrissie smiles.

'What was the film?' asks Asya.

'*Rome: Open City* –' Chrissie says.

'He won't. He just won't.' Tante Muneera is standing in the doorway. 'I told him, "This is it. I'm not going to plead with you any more. I'll ask you for just one thing: your father will be very tired when he comes home. He'll have been driving for at least three hours and he's been sitting on committees for five days. He'll have just climbed the stairs with a heavy briefcase. Have mercy on *him* if you won't have mercy on your sister, let him catch his breath. Let him have something to eat and have a nap and a shower. After that, do what you want and may God forgive you." He stared at me and said, "You're so worried about him? You're worried about *him* and not worried about our family's reputation –"

They hear the light on the landing clicking on. Then a thump and the jangle of keys. Chrissie and Asya back off to the far corner of the dining-room, while Muneera glides into a chair in the entrance hall and turns her head towards the sounds of arrival. The key turns in the lock, and as he comes through the door Dr Sidki al-Tarabulsi, opening his mouth to call out for his wife, sees her sitting in the half-light on the red velvet armchair under the great tableau of the Roman gladiators and the cheering crowds.

'Salamu Aleikum,' he greets her, panting with the effort of climbing the stairs.

'Praise God for your safe return,' she replies as she rises and comes towards him.

'Why are you sitting in the dark like this?' he asks.

She takes his bag and his briefcase. 'Oh, I just sat down for two minutes,' she says lightly.

As she turns towards the interior of the flat, he sees her face clearly in the light from the corridor.

'What's the matter with your eyes? Have you been crying or what?'

'No, no, Sidki. What have I got to cry about? My eyes are just hurting me a bit. That's why I was sitting in the dark: to rest them. I'll get you something to eat. You haven't had lunch, have you?'

Her mother's voice and her father's heavy tread fade down the corridor. Chrissie looks at Asya.

'Perhaps it's better if you go.'

'I'm going to stay with you.'

'There isn't anything you can do any more.'

119

'Do you *want* me to go?'

'No, of course I don't want you to go –'

'Then I'm staying with you.'

They sit side by side on the sofa listening to the silence coming from inside the flat. Time passes. Then they hear the crash of a door and Muneera's voice crying out, 'Sidki!'

They hear Chrissie's father roar, 'WHERE IS SHE?' and Muneera cry out, 'Sidki! Wait! Listen to me! Just listen to me!'

Chrissie has gone white and is now standing behind the dining-room table holding on to its edge with two hands. The noises approaching rapidly along the corridor sound like those of a multitude; a stampede. Then Sidki al-Tarabulsi appears at the door of the dining-room. He is so big that he seems to block the doorway. He is still in his jacket and tie. His shoes are dusty and his face shines with sweat. His eyes are bloodshot and he is breathing heavily. His wife is hanging on to both his arms and looking up at him. She is like a sash draped across his massive body. He loosens her hands and places her carefully to one side then steps into the room. He stands at the opposite end of the table from Chrissie, staring at her. Muneera is poised in the doorway breathing fast and whispering Chrissie's name. Sidki looks down at the table for a few moments. Asya, standing behind Chrissie, looks at the table too. There are reflections in the sheet of glass that covers and protects the mahogany surface. There is a bowl of fruit, two silver candlesticks and three heavy crystal ashtrays. Sidki's hands are clenched tight on the back of a dining chair, his knuckles white. He speaks steadily, keeping his voice even and low.

'From today, you are not going to university any more. It's over. You will stay at home and help your mother until you get married.' He lifts his eyes to see Muneera, Chrissie and Asya all staring at him. His voice rises. 'Is this understood? This is my word and I've said it.'

'The girl's future, Sidki –'

'But Uncle Sidki –'

'Father, I haven't –'

When he hears his daughter address him, Sidki al-Tarabulsi reaches for the largest, heaviest ashtray and hurls it at her. It crashes into the wall behind her head. Asya has jumped sideways and now feels her heart throbbing in her throat. Chrissie has not moved.

Muneera screams, 'Sidki!' and leaps forward to fling her arms around him.

'You're answering me, you criminal? You're opening your mouth and answering me? You say "Father" to me?'

He is trying to move towards Chrissie but Muneera is holding him back. He grabs his wife's shoulders and pushes her away from him, and as she comes forward again he swings out at her. The blow from the back of his right hand catches her on the chest and she falls against the doorpost and sinks, silent and open-mouthed, to the floor, her hand to her chest. Taha appears in the doorway and falls to his knees next to her. Chrissie says, 'Go!' and Asya makes for the sideboard and picks up the blue file. Sidki has got round the dining-table and caught his daughter's arm in his left hand.

'You've forgotten whose daughter you are? Forgotten who your grandfathers were? You would shame me in front of people? You would drag the Tarabulsi name in the mud?'

His open right palm smashes into her face. Chrissie says nothing but raises her free arm to protect her eyes.

'You're walking in the street? With a man?' Asya winces as she hears the second blow. In the doorway Taha is weeping and stroking his mother's face and kissing her hands. Behind him Chrissie breaks free from her father. She races past Asya through the entrance hall, hissing 'Go!' as she makes for the bathroom and the only lockable door in the house. Uncle Sidki kicks his son out of the way and comes crashing after Chrissie. Asya lets herself out of the flat and closes the door. Pausing on the landing, feeling sick, she checks her watch: it is twenty to six. She starts to run down the stairs. He can't mean it. He can't possibly mean it. He won't keep Chrissie from college. She holds on to the blue file as she races into the street looking round for a taxi. She'll have to write two essays for tomorrow, and make them different.

Scene 12

May 1968
Alexandria

There is no new country, no new sea.
Only the same old city
Shadows you night and day.

I walked from the train station to Cecil's Hotel where she was staying with her parents. The wind was blowing in from the sea and I felt its salt taste in my mouth as I walked down Shari' Sa'd. It's almost eleven months since I was here last. Mid-July. When I walked this street at night with Didi and she wept and begged me to tell her she had to stay. To make her stay. And I wouldn't. I wouldn't.

All our furniture was ready. Delivered even. The Queen Anne bedroom, the Sheraton dining-room, the Aubusson, the works. Piled up in one of the spare rooms in her parents' summer apartment. She held on to my arm and wept and stumbled so that we had to leave Shari' Sa'd and thread our way through the narrower, darker streets behind the Nabi Danial. I said, 'It's your decision. You have to choose.' And as she wept and clung to my arm I knew that she would choose to go with her parents. We walked around for a couple of hours and then I took her home and her mother stared at me with hostility, but I had not done what she feared. I had done something worse. Back in the spring. But she didn't know about that.

Down the screened corridor, behind the third door on the left, our furniture was stacked and covered in dust-sheets. Hashim Bey was in Cairo attending to some last-minute business. I said goodbye to Didi and smiled at her. She stood at the door of the apartment and cried. I walked by the Graeco-Roman museum, dark and barricaded with sandbags, along the street and up to the station. I stood on the platform and watched my train leave for Cairo. Then I sat on a bench and lit a cigarette. I took the next train. Didi never came to Cairo of course. Shahir called me three days later and said they'd gone. He's my best friend but even so he couldn't understand why I wasn't on that ship to Canada.

You will spend your life
In the same dim suburb.
In the same house grow grey.

In the months that followed, I knew what I wanted. I wanted no more changes. My room to be always my room. My wife to be always my wife.

May 1968

He looked so French, so Aristide Bruant-ish with his padded navy-blue cotton army jacket and his huge red scarf thrown around his neck and over one shoulder. I saw the glow of his cigarette as he waited for me in the shadows round the corner from the main entrance of the hotel. What I wanted to do was walk into his arms. What I wanted to do was lean my back against the hard wall of the Cecil Hotel and feel the softness of his jacket, his darkness, his warmth and weight press in upon me. I wanted to kiss his mouth and smell the Rothmans on his breath. But of course I stood in front of him with my hands in the pockets of the pink wool coat that I knew he liked and he smiled and said, 'You look like a kitten.'

I said, 'I think I'm OK for two hours,' and we started to walk.

122

After a few steps he took my hand.

We crossed the Corniche road and turned left and walked for a bit to get out of sight of the hotel. Then we stopped and stood leaning on the low stone wall and looked at the sea, black and restless against the rocks, and I thought of my great-grandmother who had lived to a very old age and whom they say I had seen once when I was very small lying on what was shortly to become her death-bed and who had until the end of her life insisted on coming once a year to Alexandria. And when the family arrived at the summer house, and before the old lady would suffer her bags to be unpacked, before she would even drink a cup of coffee or a glass of tea, she would demand to be taken to the beach. And she would walk barefoot and unassisted till she stood on the curved line of foam that the waves left on the wet sand and there she would raise her hands to her head and cry, 'As-salamu alaikum, ya Malik!'

Then she would sit down on the chair that had been carried by one of her sons or grandsons and silently contemplate the power and the might of that undulating blue expanse before returning home. I could not cry out, like her, 'As-salamu alaikum, O King!' But I always felt that tug at my heart when I came upon the sea after an absence. I felt the tug at my heart – and said nothing.

We looked at the lights of the fort of Quait-bay gleaming across the water, then we walked on until we came to the great square of the Mosque of Sidi el-Mursi Abu-l-Abbas and we crossed and started cutting through the narrow streets behind it aiming for the Nabi Danial and Shari' Sa'd. Holding on to his hand, feeling the edge of his sleeve brush my wrist, smelling the Monsieur de Givenchy and the Rothmans and the scent of the sea, all the feelings I have for the city at last reach a focus. Every year in the summer for as long as I can remember – and beyond: to what I know only from photographs – we have come here. My grandmother had inherited a plot of land in Miami. Miami, Alexandria, that is. It was about an acre, I suppose, and it was planted with date-palms and in the middle of the date-palms stood a two-storey wooden chalet painted white and green. In June, when school broke up, this was where we would come. Dada Zeina and one or two other servants would come first, on the train, to open the house and air the rooms and stock up with food. And then we would drive up. We children and nannies would stay for the whole summer, while the grown-ups would come and go. A wooden deck ran around both floors of the house, and on the second, just outside my window, there was a long wooden table. There the grown-ups would sit and eat in the evening while I drifted off to sleep behind the thin wall, watching the light of their big gas-lamp flickering through the slats of my shutters and listening to the rise and fall of their conversation against the whisper of the palm-fronds in the evening breeze. Alexandria meant waiting to grow up.

How long does one have to wait to grow up?

Juliet was only fourteen.

'What satisfaction can'st thou have tonight?'

Olivia Hussey had been so beautiful: the long hair, the white nightie, the big eyes – she had hesitated just a fraction after 'What': 'What – satisfaction can'st thou have tonight?'

'Do you want to sit down somewhere? An ice-cream? We could go to the Elite.'

'Oh yes, please.' I squeezed his arm.

'Shore of Alexan-dria
Oh shore of lo-ove.
We came to Alexan-dria
And we fell in lo-ove.
Oh blissful breeze
Oh contented evenings
I carry you in my eyes –'

Alexandria is summers and beaches and wet hair and the songs of Fairuz and 'Abd el-Halim and a feeling as present and powerful as being in love. Or maybe it *was* being in love: in love with the heat of the day and the wind that blew at night and the spray of waves against rock at Bir Mas'oud and the soft, untanned skin behind my knee and the hair bleached golden on my arms and the smell of grilled sweetcorn waved towards me by a huge ostrich-feather fan and all the young men bronzed on the seashore and all the older men in restaurants and coffee-shops and the sight of ships, small and mysterious and faraway, vanishing into the horizon. And now you. Here. For real. Mine. So I hold on to your arm and walk through the streets, and I touch your knee with mine and eat my ice-cream soda and watch two Greek sailors dancing together on the dance floor.

We don't talk much, but what I want to say to you is that learning to play backgammon with my grandfather under our parasol by the sea and eating my first lobster and all the books I've read and the songs I've heard and stories Dada Zeina's told me and the days of my childhood and the nights I've tasted the sea and waited for life to begin are now part of loving you; that I love both your smiles: the lop-sided ironical one and the wide, mischievous grin; and I love your eyes that go soft and vulnerable when you take off your

124

glasses; and I love the spring in your step and your moustache and the way you call me 'Princess', and how we touch each other all the time and we don't really seem to need to talk – except that you do say, 'I want to grow old with you.'

IV

August 1968 - September 1969

The glare of that much-mentioned
brilliance, love,
    Broke out, to show
Its bright incipience sailing above,
Still promising to solve, and satisfy,
And set unchangeably in order. So
    To pile them back, to cry,
Was hard, without lamely admitting
how
It had not done so then, and could not
now.

—PHILIP LARKIN,
'*Love Songs in Age*'

Scene 1

August 1968
Beirut

She holds his hand and gazes out of the window at everything he points out to her. But later she will remember only an impression of sun-lit trees and busy streets, the feel of his hand holding hers, the smell of Rothmans and Monsieur de Givenchy, and in her head over and over again I am in love with you yes I am in love with you yes – Easy to shrug off the mild dalliance with the young priest on the plane. It was her first plane ride after all and she hadn't actually fancied him or anything: he was too slim and pale and his lips were too thin and his light blue eyes were rimmed with pink. His dog-collar had intrigued her and when her fingers had tightened on the armrest as the plane roared at the edge of the runway and she had felt a hand covering hers she had kept her face turned towards the small window. And when they had levelled out and the desert down below looked like a school project in papier mâché and you could see tracks and patterns that you'd never have dreamed were there, she had turned and looked at him and smiled. He had smiled too as he let her take away her hand and she had wondered if he was simply being pastor-like and had chatted to him happily but had not mentioned the fact that on this, her first solo trip away from home, she was on a clandestine and definitely sinful assignation that was due to begin in about one hour: as soon as the plane touched down in Beirut Airport.

Saif opens the door with a key and they enter a dim and cluttered living-room. He walks ahead. Even carrying her suitcase there is that slight spring to his every step. She carries her beige handbag and – main symbol of adulthood – her vanity case. At the far end of the living-room he unlocks a door into a big, light bedroom and steps aside to let her pass. He follows her in and closes the door behind them. He puts her suitcase down on the bed, turns and gathers her into his arms. He slips his hand under her hair and rubs the back of her neck and smiles at her. 'I'd better go tell the Contessa you're here.'

Across the room french windows open on to a small balcony with two chairs and wrought-iron railings and outside the roofs slope down to Ras Beirut: the wide bay and the San George nestle in a cosy fold in the Mediterranean. She leans her forehead against the window-pane. Four days. Four days to walk and talk and swim and ski and shop – and make love. Would they? Would Beirut be the place where it actually happened?

129

Does she want it to happen? Beyond the door the man she loves is making arrangements with the owner of the Pensione Margareta: a countess, an émigrée, a White Russian. He will come back to her and they will go out to dinner. They will sit at sidewalk cafés and they will stroll back at any hour which suits them and then – and then? And then they will at the very least do what they have been doing since March but in a big, double bed, and, content, she will fall asleep and lie close to him till morning. And when they wake up they will choose what to do with the day. Together. This, then, is *it*. Must be it; the very stuff, the very essence of grown-upness. To prove it her handbag sits on the table. Her passport and foreign currency are in it. Her suitcase is on the bed.

She opens the suitcase and flings back its lid. Then she stops: no. First the vanity case. Her vanity case is his gift and makes her think of the opera-house every time she opens it: it is made of white leather and lined with red satin. On the inside of its lid a large mirror shines in a frame of pleated red silk. The case is full of creams, body lotions, mascara, eau de toilette, clear lip gloss and tinted lip gloss, enamelled butterflies for her hair, pearly nail varnish, silver bracelets, a gold ring with a turquoise stone and – her current favourite – a pair of clip-on earrings made of tiny pieces of pink quartz: large and round they look like two discs of crystallised candyfloss. The room is big and the bed – she lingers over it: it is going to be the first time they lie together in a bed actually made for two. High and soft-looking with a white cotton coverlet and lots of cushions. *Un letto matrimoniale. Matrimoniale.* What had Saif told the Contessa? That they were married? Engaged? In love? Does it matter? This is not the Omar Khayyam where you dread the appearance of the hotel detective at the door of the bungalow. This is Beirut: Beirut where you can do anything and it's OK. Beirut, the capital of a country with a history of hospitality to fugitives, to the oppressed. Besides, she is grown-up. Grown-up, she shrugs and goes to unpack her summer dresses and hang them in the huge old-fashioned wardrobe that reminds her of the furniture in her grandfather's house. Each dress unfolds with a thought of someone back home: the web of pink silk crocheted by Tante Muneera – what would she think if she knew? The turquoise shift with white daisies embroidered by Tante Soraya, what would *she* think if she knew? And as for Grandmama Malak, Daddy's mother, who would uncover her hair only for the few minutes it took to brush it every morning and every evening – amazing how none of them seems to have anything to do with her any more. Amazing how totally she does not feel any – embarrassment, even. Flowered pants, a long, loose white shirt and a necklace of seashells. She isn't even supposed to be in Beirut. Isn't even supposed to be in *Lebanon*. She should be in London, waiting for Nadia to arrive from New York and registering in and preparing for the summer course she is going to take at University College. Nadia is going to sit for her fellowship at the end of the year and she had written to Lateefa offering to put Asya up in London for the summer and pay her fees for a month at the university. And Asya had immediately seen this as a way to meet Saif – to meet him away from home.

It had needed a lot of fixing and lying and rushing around to arrange to fly to London via Beirut where Saif could legitimately be on company business. If they knew – but they did not know and could never guess or even believe that she could be so – so – so what? What was it that she would call –

Saif comes back and the Contessa comes with him. She is tall and straight and has bouffant chestnut hair and wonderfully manicured nails, but her eyes are old and dull and her ringed hands are veined.

'Bonjour!'

'Bonjour, Comtesse!'

'I hope you will be comfortable. Mr Madi's father is an old friend of mine, yes?'

'I am sure I will, thank you. It is very beautiful.'

The old lady waves a hand that offers the antique furniture, the luxurious linen, the photographs on the walls and the city beyond them. She turns.

'Allons, ma'm'selle! I show you the bathroom.'

Asya glances at Saif. So it is 'Ma'm'selle'. Well, that suits her better. It is great to be sinful. Sinful in Beirut! She follows the Contessa through the dark living-room and down a long corridor. Why does she have to see the bathroom? Bathrooms are boring; somewhere to be out of as quickly as possible. Their bathroom at home had white chinaware and black marble on the walls and the floor. There was one bar of soap on the basin and one on the side of the bath and one on the bidet. The bar of soap on the side of the bath was accompanied by a loofah and a pumice stone. Above the basin there was one glass shelf with one yellow tube of neatly squeezed Kolynos toothpaste and five toothbrushes in carefully distinct colours. Asya's is always blue. There was also her father's shaving brush, his tube of Palmolive shaving cream and his razor. And there were two towels and a roll of toilet paper. Nothing else was allowed to stay in the bathroom. If she took a book in there and forgot it, it was, 'What's this book doing in the bathroom? It was lying on its face. Books can get ruined like this.' And once when she had left a tube of Clearasil on the shelf her father had brushed his teeth with it.

'Your father is very cross with you,' her mother had said.

'Why?'

'What was this doing in the bathroom?'

'I was using it.'

'Why did you leave it in the bathroom?'

'I forgot it. What's the big problem?'

131

'Your father brushed his teeth with it.'

'It says on it it's for the skin. It's not a toothpaste –'

'Well, he didn't read it.'

Asya could just see her father's face as, mouth full of paste, he brushes away in his vest and pyjama-trousers – and then the look of surprise; displeased surprise, as the familiar Kolynos taste fails to hit his palate. He would have picked up the tube he had just used and scrutinised it. He would need his glasses of course to do that, so he would have had to reach for them and put them on – with his mouth still full of Clearasil – then he would have examined the tube and when he read 'for the treatment of spots and acne' his face would have creased with disgust and he would quickly have spat out the cream and rinsed out his mouth. Asya could see him dangling the Clearasil tube between the thumb and index finger of his left hand and depositing it on her mother's desk.

'There you are, madam. See what they are leaving in the bathroom these days.'

Lateefa would have studied the tube over the rim of her spectacles:

'This is Asya's.'

'Asya's or the afreet's I've just brushed my teeth with it and it was something disgusting.'

'But it says here that it's for the skin: "external" –'

'And is one supposed to wake up each day and study what's written on the tubes in one's bathroom? If I find anything like this in the bathroom again I swear I'll throw it straight into the dustbin –'

'All right, all right,' Lateefa would have said, hurriedly covering the tube with her hand. 'I'll speak to the children.' A tube of Clearasil was hard to come by. This one had been sent by Nadia from New York via a chain of five people when Asya had discovered a small pink spot near her ear one day and proceeded to make everybody miserable about it.

Now Lateefa handed it back.

'So would you please keep it in your room and don't create problems for us with your father?'

'How come we don't brush our teeth with his shaving-cream then go rushing off to complain?'

'Asya! You keep your stuff in your room or it'll get thrown in the dustbin. Understand?'

A door opens at the end of the long corridor. The Contessa's bathroom is like an extension of her living-room: magazines, plants, postcards, framed photographs, jars of soap-balls and bowls of pot-pourri crowd together on various lace-covered surfaces. The shower-curtains too are of lined lace, and next to the handbasin are shelves and shelves stacked with perfumes, powders, creams, varnishes, sprays and paints. Asya stares around her in delight.

132

'This,' says the Contessa, pointing at the shelves and looking slightly suspicious, 'is for me, eh?'

'Oh yes, of course,' says Asya quickly. Over the basin is the clearest, most brightly lit mirror she has ever seen; in it, a pretty girl with long black hair, laughing eyes and a face shining with happiness smiles at the world. This is Life. More than just Life: this is Colette come true. She turns to the Contessa.

'I think it is all just too, too beautiful.'

The Contessa regards her for a moment, then shrugs:

'Eh bon! For me, I will use the bathroom between the ten and the eleven in the morning and between the six and the seven in the evening.'

They walk through Hamra and miraculously find a free table at the Horseshoe. They sit under the striped green and white awning and Asya is not afraid that someone will see her. He has a scotch on ice and she orders a Campari because of the sound of the word and because its red is so pretty. When it comes she finds it bitter but she won't say and so she sits sucking on bitter ice-cubes and listening to the languages of the world flowing around her.

In a store in Ashrafiyya she sees a plate: matt white with a cluster of small, stylised birds in smudged blue. Saif's arm squeezes her shoulders.

'It's always blue, isn't it, Princess? What is it with you and blue? OK. Come on: we'll buy some. How many do you want?'

'Well,' Asya hesitates, 'what – I mean what – what will they –'

'They'll be the first thing we buy for our house, silly. How many shall we get?'

'Two.'

'Two?'

'No?'

'People usually get twelve – or at least six.'

'All I want is two.'

'We might have visitors – sometimes.' He smiles.

'But these are just so pretty. Can't they be just for us? Our very, very own?'

Saif shrugs. 'Sure they can. We'll buy a set for two.'

In the Hôtel Martinez they order *soupe à l'oignon gratinée* and when her eyes meet his as the strands of melted cheese stretch between the toasted bread and her spoon, Asya feels that she is at the very centre, the very hub of Life.

He wears desert boots, blue jeans and light blue linen shirts with the sleeves rolled up. He wears thick white cotton socks with the jeans and fine black cotton socks with everything else. He says he will never wear any other colour socks. He uses an old-fashioned silver razor and his fresh ultra-white underwear is tumbled into an untidy heap on a shelf in the wardrobe. Because he does not yet own a Patek Philippe, a Rolex is tied to his left wrist with a black strap.

'No,' Dada Zeina had declared. She had frowned down at the chicken she was plucking. 'No. This is not normal.'

Asya sat on a wooden chair by the side of the kitchen sink. Her bare legs were stretched out in front of her and her feet rested on another wooden chair. She wore a dark blue T-shirt and white cotton panties and her hair was braided and pinned out of the way in a tight knot. In her hand was the ball of caramel-coloured *halawa* which she was now pasting on to the outside of her right leg.

'What do you mean "not normal"? He *is* normal –'

'It's not normal that he shouldn't want to do anything –'

'Did I say that he doesn't want to do anything? Of course he wants to.'

'How do you know?'

Asya had glanced up, but from that side she could see only Dada Zeina's bad eye: the skin scarred and shrunk and tightened around an eyeball that had gone yellow; the colour of a bad egg. A useless eyeball which nevertheless continues to swivel and roll in unison with its black, sparkling twin. When Dada Zeina had been new and Asya had been eight years old and frank she had asked her about it and Dada Zeina had said that when she was six an abscess had grown on her eyelid which her grandmother had bandaged over too tight so that when it had – unnoticed – burst, it had run into the eye and ruined it. But three years ago when Deena at the age of eleven had asked her the same thing Dada Zeina had said that when she was five and helping her grandmother clean out the chicken run, the cockerel had flown at her and pecked out her eye. 'When my uncle came back at the end of the day he said, "Who shall we find to marry her now?" and grabbed hold of the cockerel and slaughtered it, and my Grandmother said, "What's the use of slaughtering the cock? We'll just have to get another one, or are all these hens going to sit here barren?" And when God allowed, my cousin asked for me anyway and married me and I wasn't even fifteen.' Asya had almost said but what about the abscess? But then she hadn't. She told herself it didn't matter but, since then, every time she looked at Dada Zeina, the eye – and its two attendant histories – troubled her.

'I feel him,' she had said, 'when we're together.'

Dada Zeina threw her a look out of her good eye. She had to turn right round to do it.

'I mean – I don't mean I feel his feelings. I mean I feel *him*. His body. I feel things happening to it.'

'Well then?'

Asya tore off the *halawa* and examined the smooth patch on her leg. Then she looked at the dark hairs uprooted and embedded in the sweet paste with their follicles sticking upwards. She kneaded the *halawa* and

134

started spreading it over the same leg but lower down, nearer the ankle.

'Well then what?'

'Well then, why doesn't he try to do something? Mind you, I'm never saying you should let him, but why doesn't he try?'

'But he does things. He does plenty. I've told you.'

'You told me he feels your breasts and kisses you.'

Asya winced, then tore off the *halawa*.

'Isn't that right?'

'Yes. But you mustn't say it like that. You mustn't say the words.'

'And then what?' Dada Zeina had her whole hand up to her wrist inside the chicken. She tugged out its entrails and bent over, tilting her head to examine them closely.

'What?' Asya had asked.

'Is that all?'

'It's enough.'

'What do you mean it's enough?'

Asya had smiled up at her. 'It's very nice. Mmmmmmmm.'

Dada Zeina shook her head as she separated the innards.

'He never touches you underneath?'

'No.'

'And you're happy like this?'

'Yes.'

'And what about him?'

'I guess he must be happy too.'

'Are you silly? A man has to arrive at his end. Does he?'

'I don't know. I don't think so.'

'Well that's what isn't normal. And isn't good either.'

Asya tore off the *halawa* once more.

'First it was, "Be careful, Asya. Look after yourself. Don't go to his room at the hotel. Men turn into wild beasts. In a second he changes so that you don't know him. Take care, Asya. You're well brought up. You know right from wrong. And that's the biggest wrong –" '

'Of course it's the biggest wrong!'

'Now you're telling me he isn't normal –'

'Yes, child. It isn't normal for a man to be with the girl he loves, and on their own, and not do something.'

Dada Zeina bundled up the chicken's feathers, its entrails, its clawed feet, its beak and the bony tips of its wings into an old newspaper and pushed them into the dustbin. She scooped up some flour from the dish she had already prepared next to her and started to rub the bird with it – hard. She up-ended the chicken, sprinkled flour inside it, pushed her hand in after the flour, and rubbed. Asya was concentrating on the tiny hairs that grew on her knee.

'Well there you are. He doesn't want to do the "biggest wrong".'

'What are you telling me?'

'It's *true*.' Asya looked up. 'Aren't you going to finish with that chicken and come and help me? It's true. He doesn't want to do anything until we're married. For *my* sake. Because he really loves me.'

'Is this what he said to you?' Dada Zeina had rinsed the chicken and was now rubbing it with salt. The bird was pink and glowing.

'Yes. He said so the very first time we went to his room. So that I wouldn't worry about being with him.'

Dada Zeina shook her head. 'No man behaves like this. You've been together more than five months –'

'Look.' Asya leaned back for a moment. 'The truth is it's also for his own sake. So he doesn't one day think that maybe I married him just because we'd already done it.'

Dada Zeina plunged the chicken into the pot of boiling water on the cooker and counted out four cardamom seeds. She put each one between her teeth and carefully split it, then she dropped them in with the chicken.

'Who thinks?'

'Him.' Asya lowered her right foot to the floor and, bending over, started to spread the *halawa* on to the outside of her left leg.

'Thinks what?'

'Not now. Later. I mean maybe he thinks – now – that if we do it – now – and then we get married later then maybe after that he might think that maybe I only married him because I couldn't marry anyone else because I'd already done it with him. And of course he wouldn't want to think that. So – oh please won't you come? I'll never get finished like this.'

'I'm coming, I'm coming. Be patient.' Dada Zeina sizzled some butter in the small frying-pan and quickly fried the cluster of soft embryo eggs she had found inside the chicken. She added the chicken's liver and heart, threw some salt over the whole lot then spooned them out on to a green plastic plate. She handed Asya a damp towel.

'Clean your fingers.'

She put a fork and a hunk of bread next to the food and handed the plate to Asya.

'Here. Eat.' She wiped her hands on her *galabiyya*. 'Lift your foot.'

She sat down on the chair opposite and took the *halawa* from Asya's fingers. 'In the name of God the Compassionate, the Merciful –' Then she started to work quickly and ruthlessly on the left leg. Asya caught her breath.

'Goodness. It hurts so much when you do it.'

'So we're going to sit here all day while you pat gingerly at your legs? Come on, let's get it done.'

After a moment Dada Zeina had glanced at Asya.

'I don't know about all this thinking this and thinking that but there are

136

other things you can do that can make it all right for him. It doesn't have to be inside inside. Because being suffocated isn't good for him. And you want to marry him, don't you? But you still have to be careful.'

Dada Zeina hadn't a clue how much it hurt. Her own legs, which Asya thought were like tree-trunks but of which she herself was very proud – and certainly she did not lack admirers down in the street – were completely free of hair – naturally. She boasted she had never put the *halawa* to them. But of course she did her underneath. Asya shuddered. When Asya had asked her if it hurt she had said, 'Like fire. But you get used to it.'

'Well anyway,' said Asya, 'I know he's normal because . . .' You had to eat the eggs in the whole cluster because if you tried to break one of them off they would run. They were delicious, not really like proper eggs, finished eggs as it were. Except they *were* a bit of course. They were the Ideal Egg. The potential egg; the egg that had not yet realised its imperfections – Asya put a piece of bread in her mouth. 'Because he has known other women.'

'He told you that?'

'No. One of his friends did. You know, the one I didn't like. He said there'd been a Greek one for a year: Adriana. Then that he'd lived with a Frenchwoman in Paris for three months, and then he was engaged to a girl at AUC called Didi Hashim who was terribly in love with him but who had to leave Egypt with her family after the war.'

'Have you finished eating?'

'Yes, praise God. Thank you, Dada.'

'Stand on the chair now and turn around so I can do the backs of your legs.'

Asya put her plate and fork in the sink and jumped on to the chair. She winced as the *halawa* pulled at the skin of the back of her right thigh.

'I was really miserable when he told me that, really *really* miserable and jealous. But then – I guess it must be better if he has experience. Or what?'

'Spread your legs a little so I can get at this bit. A woman can't be happy with a man who's raw.'

'Well he's not "raw".'

'And a man who's been around can't ever limit himself to his own house.'

'Dada Zeina: you don't want him raw, and you don't want him experienced. And the solution?'

'They're a bad species and not to be trusted. We can't do without them, but we have to be careful. That's it. Do you want under your arms done?'

'Yes but do it gently.'

'All right. Come on then. Take that vest off and sit down and hold your arm up. High. There.' Asya gasped. 'Come on, just once more. Now the other. Have you no endurance at all? What are you going to do when you get married? Eh? It's over, it's over. You're the one who wanted it done, aren't you? Now run to the bathroom before your father gets home. It'll all cool down under the shower.'

They walk from the Hôtel Martinez to the Pensione Margareta. A cool breeze blows from the green mountains above the city and down below the sea lies quiet and dark. There are people still in the cafés and on the streets. Men's heads turn to follow her as she goes by and three silver-haired ladies sipping their coffees and chatting in French smile kindly at them both. Saif carries the box of plates with the smudged blue bird in his left hand. He puts his right hand on her shoulder. 'Tomorrow,' he says, 'I'm hiring a car. We'll drive to Ba'albek and come back by way of Jounieh. You'll like that.'

She has a shower and washes herself carefully. She rubs body lotion on her legs and arms and everywhere she can reach and Ma Griffe into her neck, under her arms, between her legs, on her wrists and behind her knees. She cleans her teeth, inspects her eyebrows and brushes some mascara on to her lashes. Then she puts on fresh white panties and a bra and puts her dress and shoes back on. She brushes her hair and goes back to their room. He is standing in the window in jeans and bare feet, looking out. His shoulders and back are bare and he has a white towel around his neck. She touches his back and he turns and buries his face in her neck.

'Mmmm. You smell nice.'

Holding each other close they step out on to their balcony and stand for a few moments looking down at the silent city. Suddenly, to the south, a volley of shots rings out. Asya looks at Saif. He shrugs. 'A wedding somewhere. That's how they celebrate, the Lebanese.'

When he's left the room she takes off her dress and hangs it in the wardrobe. All her nighties are little-girl nighties with smocking and rosebuds but she had brought one with her anyway to avoid rousing suspicion as she packed. A pink one. She can't possibly wear it. She finds the white lace slip she has stolen from her mother and taken in at the sides. She considers the bra and panties: normally of course she would not sleep in her underwear, but it seems dreadfully forward to volunteer to take them off. She puts the slip on on top of them, closes the wardrobe door, brushes her hair once again and jumps into bed quickly when she hears a sound outside the door. She lies waiting for him.

He pads quietly in on bare feet and closes and locks the door behind him. He throws the towel on to the window-seat and lights a cigarette, then comes and sits on the edge of the bed. He balances the cigarette on the edge of the ashtray and pushes off his jeans and pants and swings his legs under the covers. He puts an arm across her as he lies back and finishes his cigarette. Then he turns and starts to kiss her. In the Omar Khayyam he had always kepts his jeans on and through the denim she had felt him harden. Here in Beirut she feels him warm and growing: moving against her body. But she is too shy to look. She wants to put her hand down there and feel him but what would he think of her?

When he has kissed her for a bit and stroked her back and rubbed her neck and undone her bra and is nibbling at her breasts, Asya puts her hand on Saif's hair and makes her offer. 'Darling,' she whispers, 'darling, you know – if you want – it's really all right. I'm not afraid or anything.'

He lifts his head. 'What are you talking about, Princess?'

'If you want to, you know, make love properly' – she moves still closer to him – 'then that's all right. I love you.'

'I love you too, Princess.'

'Well?'

'No – no.' He looks into her eyes. 'It wouldn't be a good idea.'

'Oh! Well, OK.'

'See, now you're relieved.'

'No . . . I'm not – at least I don't think I am. Oh Saif, I don't know. No, I know I'm not –'

'Hush.' He bends his head and kisses her.

'Saif.' She strokes the back of his head. 'Saif – maybe there's something – if there's anything – you know –'

'It's OK, sweetie. It's OK. Just relax. Come on, turn around. Let me feel you. Yes, like that –'

Before she falls asleep Asya murmurs, 'It's so wonderful being in a big bed.'

'Yes.'

'And it's so wonderful not being afraid someone will knock at the door.'

'Yes.'

'And we don't even have to sing an *aubade* and part at dawn.'

'No.'

' "It is. It is. It is the lark that sings so out of tune –" '

'Go to sleep now, Princess.'

'I am going to love you for ever and ever.'

'Good,' he says. 'I'm counting on you. Now go to sleep.'

At sunrise Asya wakes. She creeps out of the room. In the bathroom she pees then washes herself on the bidet with warm water. She brushes her teeth and washes her face and puts on moisturiser and mascara. She brushes her hair and sprays on some more Ma Griffe. Then she creeps back into the bedroom and into bed. This is the first time she has seen him asleep. He sleeps quietly, on his side, turned away from her. His face is blank. She arranges herself in bed and lies still. She tries to fall asleep tidily so that when he wakes up and sees her he will think her pretty.

She frightened me. She frightened me with her candour, her optimism, her faith. She did not even know she possessed these things. She took it all as given. She truly thought that you could shape life as you pleased; that if you wanted something you would get it, that if you did certain things, others would necessarily follow. She was so open, so vulnerable. She knew nothing. Nothing at all. I thought of Adriana with her accident and her reconstructed face. I thought of Danielle waiting for Shazli in her miserable room above the rue de la Huchette and meanwhile making do with me. I thought of Didi, secure and freezing in Vancouver. I thought of my mother – and Asya. I said to her once – lightly, 'Les choses sont contre nous,' and she stared at me with those fantastic black eyes and asked, 'Quelles "choses"?'

A red BMW. Hairpin bends and mountain slopes covered in cypress trees. The great ruins of Ba'albek surrounded by fields of marijuana all the way north into Turkey.

'Have you ever tried it?' Asya asks.

'What? Hashish? No.'

'I'd like to try it one day.'

'It's nothing. It's just stupid.'

'How do you know if you've never tried it?'

'I've seen other people try it. Lots. It doesn't do anything.'

'It must do *something* otherwise people wouldn't be on it, would they?'

'And anyway it's harmful.'

'I know that. Everybody knows that. But it isn't harmful to try it just *once*? I'd like to try *everything*. Even if it's just once.'

But Saif has walked away, kicking at a stone as he walks.

The drive back is silent, but in Jounieh his mood clears. They eat grilled fish and he has a beer and she has iced Coke and as night falls the little town sparkles by the sea.

'If you just carried on walking along this coast,' says Asya, 'you'd walk into Israel. Isn't that amazing? I've never been so close to it before.'

'You'd walk into a few Palestinian camps first.'

'Oh!' says Asya and they are both silent for a moment.

'Saif?' asks Asya. 'What did you do in June?'

'I joined the Civil Defence. I haven't done army service; when my turn came they wouldn't take me because I wore glasses. They weren't so desperate then. But in June I joined the Civil Defence and I went to Ismailia. By the time they got us there, there wasn't a lot we could do.'

'I tried to join the Civil Defence.'

'You?'

'Yes. But my mother wouldn't let me. First she said let's wait and see what happens, then she said it's all over anyway.'

'She was right; it would have been a waste of time.'

Beirut is hot. At eleven the sun is beating down on the city and Asya and Saif are reclining on sun-loungers on the terrace of the San George with a large pitcher of lemonade sweating on the table beside them. Saif is in white swimming trunks and Asya is in an orange bikini which she had saved up her pocket-money for and which her parents do not know she possesses. Already when she lifts the elastic edge on the pants and peeps inside she can see lighter skin. It seems to her that the tan she is getting here in Beirut is better, more golden, than the one she gets in Alexandria or by the pool at the Gezira Club.

Saif is a serious swimmer. He dives sharp and clean and stays under water for what seems a long time. He surfaces in one smooth movement blowing a tall jet of the Mediterranean into the air. His eyes are brown and deep and he smiles at her but she knows he can't see without his glasses. He is happy in the water: changing strokes, lying on his back, executing somersaults, playing on his own like some creature of the sea. Asya uses the steps to go down into the water. She prefers the sensation you get from diving: going from very hot to cold to just right all within two seconds, but now she does not want to get her hair wet; it takes three hours and a performance to dry, and their time together is short. They swim out to a small wooden platform: Saif streamlined, cutting through the water, Asya leisurely, head up with hair piled on top, sunglasses and earrings firmly in place. On the platform Asya lies down in the full glare of the sun while Saif sits on the edge keeping his feet in the water.

'You are a brilliant swimmer. You look so at home in the water.'

'I used to swim for the club,' he says.

'Why did you stop?'

He shrugs. 'I just stopped.'

Into the bright silence comes a distant buzz; a whirr. Asya lifts herself up on one elbow and shades her eyes with her hand: in the distance a small powercraft is speeding over the still water. Behind it, ploughing up two straight seams of foam, two water-skiers hang taut against an invisible line; they draw apart and then move closer – 'as stiffe twin compasses are two' thinks Asya – and then one of them sinks slowly into the sea and the boat starts arcing back in a wide circle.

'Saif? The – your – the girl you were engaged to. Could she not have stayed?'

He looks up briefly and frowns, trying to see her face through the glare of the sun and without his glasses.

'She believed she couldn't,' he says.

'Why?'

'I don't know.'

'Did you not ask her to stay?'

'No.'

'Why not?'

'She had to make up her own mind. Why are you asking all these questions now?'

'Did you make love to her? Properly?'

'Yes.'

'Completely?'

'Asya –'

'Please. I just want to know. Did you?'

'Yes.'

'In the Omar Khayyam?'

'No. How could it have been in the Omar Khayyam? There wasn't a course or anything on then. I hadn't even joined the company yet.'

'Where then?'

'Why?'

'Please. Please tell me.'

'In their flat in Alexandria. It was empty. In her father's study. On a chair. It was she who did it really. I need a fag. Come on, let's go back.'

The water scarcely parts as he dives. Asya stays on her elbow for a moment longer. She sees Saif sitting on an upright chair at the side of a big dark desk. She sees, sitting astride him, Didi Hashim. Her hair is in a sleek black bob. Her thighs are slender and polished. She holds his face and her nail varnish glints orange against his cheek as she bends to kiss him. Asya gasps and sits up straight. She lowers herself carefully into the water. Of course he should have told her. What else could he have done? She had asked him. Anyway, she'd been thinking up so many different scenes; it was better to have just one. She could forget it more easily. When she gets to the terrace Saif has almost finished his cigarette. He pours her a glass of lemonade. She says, 'Gosh it's so hot,' and he says, 'Would you like to go skiing?'

'Water-skiing? I'd get my hair wet –'

'No, no. Real skiing. Up in the mountains. Shall we go?'

They leave Beirut and start driving up the mountain road. The road winds and stretches and curves. On one side the tree-covered slopes strain upwards; on the other they drop sharply away. And once in a while, growing out of the mountain and clinging to it: a village. A village with fountains and courtyards and houses of honey-coloured stone that glow with the sunlight that has soaked into them over hundreds of years. They stop in Zahlé and at a table under a spreading cypress they eat *mezzeh* and drink red wine. A group of young locals converge on the fountain in the middle of the square. They wear cut-off jeans and cool, loose, pastel-coloured T-shirts. They sit around the fountain in the sunshine which here, halfway up the mountain, has become benignly mellow. They hold slim green bottles of Seven-Up and laugh and talk and occasionally throw a bright yellow ball to or at one another. They are all good-looking: long-haired and bronzed and at ease. From somewhere across the square the voice of Fairuz floats by in an unfamiliar song and for a moment Asya envies the young Lebanese their localness, their belonging. For a moment – before she remembers that that is what she does *not* want – the square flickers with the possibility of a life lived entirely in one place: marrying the boy next door and settling across the road from his parents and yours. Wheeling beautiful babies round to be admired by aunts and grandparents. Holidays up in the snow or down by the sea and life lived daily on the mountainside among people you'd always known in a village dappled with sunlight –

'That's going to be the next big thing,' says Saif.

'What is?'

'Seven-Up. There's going to be a big drive to get it into the Middle East.'

Closer to the top the villages are scarce and so are the trees. The sunshine is white and flat and the air is cold. As they spiral upwards the snow begins. In Feraya muffled-up people are skiing.

Scene 2

November 1968

Cairo

'Your kind of scene is better. Honestly. No, I'm serious: your dad shouts and does his thing and then it's all over. It's not silences and atmospheres and avoided subjects –'

'How can you talk like that?' Chrissie is incredulous. She stops on the pathway and stares at her friend. 'Don't you remember that scene in April? You were actually there –'

Asya pulls at her friend's arm and they walk on.

'Of course I remember. But it wasn't *that* bad.'

Chrissie and Asya are walking along the pebbled mosaics laid over a hundred years ago for the pleasure of the Khedive Ismail. The pebbles are black and white and varying shades of grey. Their patterns are intricate and Asya is secretly trying to follow one particular pattern with the toe of her right shoe as she walks. Beside them the trees bank up to the suspended bridge she used to love so much when she was small, and to their left the giraffes stand elegantly patient with their heads craning dangerously over the spiked points of their iron railings.

'It wasn't that bad? Asya, for my whole life I will never forget what your face looked like that day.'

'*My* face? But of course my face would look dreadful. Because I'd never seen anything like that before. But if you're used to it –'

'Nobody's used to it. You never get used to it. You're always afraid. You're afraid all the time. Ask my mother.'

'Is that true? Really true?'

'Yes. You're always afraid. Of course time passes and he's nice and laughs with you and of course you feel that you love him, but all the time you know that at any moment he can erupt. That ashtray could have killed me.'

Asya shudders. 'Don't say that.'

To their left a gate leads into an enclosure.

'Do you want to see the hippos?' Asya asks. Chrissie shrugs and they walk on until they come to the monkey clearing. But Asya doesn't much care for monkeys.

'OK, Chrissie. That was a horrible scene. But then it's over. And when it's over it's *really* over. Finished. And three weeks later Tante Muneera says, "For my sake let Chrissie attend the exams," and there you are in the exam tent with the rest of us.'

'Yes, but my mother has to beg him and weep and go through a whole routine and for my sake this and for my sake that – *you* can *talk* to your father. You can actually *discuss* things.'

They stand looking at the polar bear's cage.

'You can discuss things, sure, but you can't *change* anything. Honestly, Chrissie. He knows where he stands from the beginning and he doesn't move. Honestly. Not one little centimetre. It's bad enough when you're discussing abstract things, theoretical stuff or politics or something, but when it comes to something real it's dreadful. He listens and talks but his position is fixed from the start and that's that.'

The polar bear, when you examine him, doesn't look too good: his thick, shaggy coat has gone yellow and its underside is wispy and almost grey. He has a shallow, dirty-looking pool in the interior of his cage, and a few rocks. But he ignores them and stays close to the bars. Up and down he pads, up . . . and down. Each time he comes to the wall he looks as if he is about to walk into it. Then he swings his head up and out of the way just in time. He turns and – without missing a beat – pads back. Nine to the left and swing and round and nine to the right and swing and –

'Once when I was small,' says Asya, 'I got really upset over this bear. I couldn't stand it that he kept coming up against the wall. It seemed so horrible. And then my father, to comfort me, said they had hardly any memory, polar bears. "See how small his head is," he said. I said, "So he doesn't know he's already come up against this wall a few thousand times?" and he said, "No," and I started to cry. It seemed even worse that every single time he thought he was going to get away, to simply walk away, just like that – and every time he found a wall.' Asya looks at Chrissie. 'What do you think, Chrissie? Which is worse?'

'Well. I don't know. Maybe it's better to have hope.'

'Even if that hope is always going to be destroyed? Always always always?'

'But he doesn't know it's always going to be destroyed.'

'But maybe if he did know then he could resign himself. He might even start enjoying his filthy pool and his slimy rocks –'

'I went up thumping
Came down thumping
Saw the bear
Cracking pumpkin
Seeds –'

Two boys – youths – had come up close to the cage and were staring at them and singing the old rhyme. Apprentices of some sort, out for the day, Asya thinks. Flared trousers, platform shoes, quiffed hair stiff with soap, big smiles, bad teeth. She stares at them and their faces turn hostile. Chrissie plucks at her arm and says loudly, 'Come on: let's get back to my mother and the children or they'll all start worrying.'

Safely round the corner, Asya grins at her.

' "My mother and the children"! How can you dream up things so quickly?'

'Phew. If they knew we were on our own we'd never get rid of them.'

'And then Taha would catch us both coming out of the Zoo arm in arm with those two –'

'Be quiet, Asya, be quiet. Don't even joke about it. It would be enough for him to see us coming out on our own. I don't even know why we are here. Why couldn't we have stayed at college?'

'There's nothing wrong in coming to the Zoo, just the two of us. All we're doing is having a walk and looking at the animals.'

'Yes, but you do know what will happen if your parents or my parents find out. We're supposed to be at college. It won't be too bad for you; you can talk to them –'

'Again, Chrissie, again?'

'Well, anyway, tell me about your pa. What did he say in the end?'

'He said no.'

'Just like that? That's it?'

'You see, you keep saying I can talk to him. But he has this whole technique that he uses against you. Like if you don't keep it all measured and low-key it's, "No no. This is mere emotionality. We don't want to get emotional." And then you just have to shut up. Because you can't say, "*Why* don't we want to get emotional? It's an emotional subject." You can't question his basic premises like "Reason Is More Valid Than Emotion" and so you look like you accept them and then you're sunk. Because you haven't got an argument. There is no *reasonable* reason why we should get married now. The only argument I have now is emotional: that we are in love and want to be together and why spend another three years being apart and skipping around avoiding detection and being home by seven-thirty and all that nerve-racking stuff when we could be together now?'

'But what did you exactly say to him?'

'That Saif and I wanted to get married and that we were going to get married one day and so why should that day not be now?'

'And?'

'He said, "For these grave things it is best to wait."'

' "But why, Daddy? Do you think he's unsuitable in some way?"

' "No, my dear, as far as I know there is no objection to him."

' "Then why? Why? Are you hoping it will pass? Because it won't, you know."

' "Believe me. It is best to wait. And also it will interfere with your studies."

' "But even when I finish I'll still be doing an MA. Then a Ph.D. In fact I'll be busier than now because I'll be working *and* studying. Why won't it interfere then?"

' "Believe me, Asya. It is best to wait. Do you think I have anything other than your good in mind?" '

'It would be impossible to have a discussion like this with *my* father.'

'Yes, but Chrissie, where does it get me?'

'Can't your mother help?'

'No. The most she could do was get his permission for me to talk to him about it. And she did that. You see, *your* mother can actually make your father change his mind –'

'Well, you'll just have to wait a bit and try again.'

'I can't try again. I can't have another conversation like this with him. And besides, if I go on about how much I want to be with Saif they'll get frightened and start to watch me more carefully. Oh, it's such a dreadful waste of time. We could do all sorts of wonderful things together. Do you know he went all the way around the Sinai once? He has maps and photos and everything.'

They have come to an empty stretch of pathway with a recessed bench and a drinking fountain. The November sun shines down on the two girls

146

and on the puddle under the fountain and the three scraggy pigeons drinking out of it. Chrissie sits on the bench and Asya walks round and round the maze of coloured but dull and dusty pebbles. 'If these were mine,' says Asya, 'I'd polish every stone. They're so beautiful. My mother says when they first brought me here I spent the day looking for bottle-tops and wouldn't look at the animals. I'm sure I was looking at these pebbles. Come on, Chrissie: let's climb the hill and walk across the suspended bridge. I used to love that. Dada Zeina couldn't get me off it.

'And,' she says as they labour up the steep steps, 'it's so horrible. It's so horrible having to rush off at seven every time we meet. Especially after Beirut —'

'Don't mention Beirut. I just don't know how you dared to do that or how you got away with it. I would have died. I was actually dying here every day until I heard you'd got to England and were safely with your aunt and it was over. So just forget Beirut —'

'But Chrissie, we don't even have anywhere to be alone together any more. The courses are over so he doesn't have the room at the Omar Khayyam. We meet at the club and walk around and hold hands and have these long, long silences, and then I phone him late at night after my parents are asleep and we have some more long, long silences — and I can't bear it.'

'But that's how it is for everybody.'

'I know, I know, but I can't *bear* it. Oh! Look!'

A rope is stretched across the foot of the suspended bridge. A handwritten notice is nailed up to a tree. It says: 'Bridge Closed For Perils.'

'Come on,' says Chrissie, 'it's almost five. We'd better go.'

They start walking down the steps.

'Can't Saif borrow someone's flat?' asks Chrissie. 'All that AUC crowd; someone must have a flat you can use.'

'No, I don't know. I guess he wouldn't do that.' They walk in silence for a bit and then Asya says, 'I go to him in his office, but we can only kiss, and it's just so terrifying —'

Scene 3

Saturday, 4 January 1969

Cairo

On the phone he sounds curt. 'I can't make it tomorrow.'

Asya's heart suddenly doubles its weight. Her right arm holding the phone starts to ache. Has he stopped loving her? Stopped, just like that? What should she say? Just 'fine'? 'OK'? But what about Beirut? What about – what about everything?

'Why?' she asks.

'I'm not feeling too well.'

'What's the matter, Saif? What's wrong?'

'Maybe a flu. I don't know.' Should she? Should she? Should she? What if he doesn't want her to? She would never have let a flu keep her away from him. What if he just wants to be on his own? But how can she bear it? How can she bear not to see him?

'Would you like – I mean, I could come to you –'

'Would you do that?' He sounds surprised.

'Well, if you can't come into town. And if you'd like me to –'

'Yes. Yes, of *course* I'd like you to. What time can you leave college?'

'Twelve.'

'It'll take you an hour. You don't know Heliopolis, do you?'

'Not really, no.'

'I'll wait for you. Take the Nozha metro to the end. I'll wait for you there.'

'But should you be out? If you're ill?'

'I'll be fine.'

Sunday, 5 January

Deena turns the corner into her father's study. The hall light, dim behind her, makes her brushed cotton nightdress faintly transparent. She is almost thirteen, thin and barefoot, and is walking cautiously slow and close to the wall. She whispers, 'Asya?' In this dark she cannot see, but she is guided by the quiet sobs that come from the far corner, from behind her father's desk. She negotiates the two armchairs, the coffee-table with the black glass top and the standard lamp with the huge shade. 'Asya?' Her sister is a lump of denser darkness on the floor in the cramped space between their father's desk and the bookcase-lined wall. Her back is against the desk and she is weeping. 'Asya!' Deena bends down and puts her arm around her sister's shoulders. 'Ya-ya, darling.' She uses Asya's baby-name, the name Kareem used to call her when he could manage nothing else. 'Come out of here.'

Asya carries on crying. Now Deena can see that she is cradling something on her lap: the heavy black telephone. Deena picks it up and puts it back on the telephone table next to their father's swivelling desk-chair, then puts her arm around her sister's shoulders again, pulling at her gently.

'Asya, come on. Let's get out of here.'

Asya draws a long shuddering breath and stays on the floor.

'Asya, it's after midnight, if Daddy wakes and finds us here – please, Asya, you're frightening me, come on, please *please* let's go inside –'

Asya stands up and allows her sister to lead her around the standard lamp, the coffee-table and the two armchairs, round the corner of the desk, and out into the hall. In the inner hall they tiptoe past their parents' bedroom. Kareem's door is open; he is asleep and his quilt is in a heap at the foot of his bed. Asya goes in and pulls it over him. Deena relaxes: now they are legitimate; now it doesn't matter if their parents wake up. Except that Asya is still crying. She watches her sister draw the sleeve of her nightie across her face.

Asya goes into their room and closes the door. Deena is sitting on her sister's bed. 'What is it? What's the matter? Why are you crying?' Asya sits down next to her and starts to cry again. 'Hush! You're going to wake them up. What *is* it? Have you quarrelled with him?'

'No.' Asya shakes her head. Then she lifts her face and looks at Deena.

The sisters' room is divided by a screen. Each half has a single bed, a wardrobe, a desk, a rug and bookcases full of books. Asya's side has a long mirror. Deena's side is in chaos: books and papers spill out of open desk drawers, various odd socks peep out from under the bed, a heap of polished pebbles sits in the middle of the floor and two of her own drawings on pages torn untidily out of a sketchbook are pinned on the wall. Asya's side is neat: the quilt on her bed is smooth, her books stand in straight rows, her papers lie in coloured folders aligned on top of each other. On the wall she has a Toulouse-Lautrec lithograph, 'Aristide Bruant dans son cabaret', a poster showing a young man holding a gun and wearing the Palestinian *kaffeya* with the legend: 'Children of '48: Commandos of '68', a larger banner in black lettering which reads 'facciamo l'amore non la guerra' and some necklaces made of shells and wooden beads. She had also had photographs of napalmed Vietnamese children but her father had made her take them down.

'Well, why are you crying then? Please, Asya, what is it?'

Deena has always shared in the ups and downs of Asya's romantic life; when she was eight she had given up a week's pocket-money so that Asya, fourteen, could buy a birthday present (a silver wrist-chain) for her school boyfriend, the handsome, goal-scoring Hilal al-Yafi, who had already bought Asya a silver butterfly brooch for *her* birthday.

'Was it something that happened when you went there today? You've been looking odd ever since you got back. What *is* it?'

'I'm going to tell you. But, Deena, you must promise me never *ever* to tell anyone. Promise?'

Deena stares at Asya. 'Yes, of course. Promise.'

'Well' – Asya takes a deep breath – 'when I got there, he was waiting for me at the end of the metro and it was all very nice and he seemed really touched that I'd gone. Really. He even told me that it hadn't been true that he was ill and the truth was that he was broke and couldn't take me anywhere and of course I said what on earth did being broke matter but obviously it meant a lot to him and it meant a lot that he had kind of confessed it, and he was all unshaven and miserable but it was OK between us. More than OK: it felt real and close and we walked to their house and his mother was really nice and welcoming only I wasn't sure she was his mother because of how he had described her.' Asya is crying again. 'Anyway, she gave us lunch and she was really nice and of course she *was* his mother, and after lunch he vanished and I was chatting to her while we were clearing up and I said something about his dog – you know I'd told you he'd told me he had a German Shepherd – and then I understood' – Asya can now hardly speak for weeping and Deena leans forward and puts her hand on her arm – 'I understood that the dog is dead.'

Asya stops to get her breath back. She finds a tissue and blows her nose.

'The dog has been dead for seven years. She said it had jumped off the roof and died in the courtyard and Saif had been heartbroken.'

'I don't understand.'

'He made me think the dog was alive; was *around*.'

'Maybe you got it wrong.'

'Deena, you know when he was in the Omar Khayyam? The first time I went there with him, while we were having a drink, he said that if I'd gone there the day before I would have seen his dog. He said he'd brought his dog – his German Shepherd – brought it there the day before and it had nipped an old lady's ankle. A *Swiss* old lady's ankle.' Asya starts to laugh.

'Please don't,' says Deena. 'Don't start to laugh and cry together, Ya-ya. It makes you ill.'

' "Only playfully," he said. "He'd only nipped her playfully. But the manager banned him and I had to take him home." He'd had to take him home and the dog had been dead for seven years; jumped off the lousy roof.'

She laughs and sobs and crumples the tissue she is holding, tosses it into her waste-paper basket and reaches for another. She looks at her sister.

'You're not to tell *anyone* any of this. *Ever.*'

'I know.'

'Except, of course, Kareem.'

'I know.'

'He said his mother was tall and had long brown hair. Well, she's short and has short black hair. That's why I was confused when I first saw her. I thought she must be an aunt or something, but then she was behaving like it was completely her own house so I thought maybe she was his mother, but she didn't look anything like what he'd described. Not worse or better or anything: just different. It was really only when he actually called her "Mama" while we sat at the table that I was completely sure. And then I thought, well, I must have got it wrong. But I couldn't see *how* I could have got it wrong. And then when the dog thing came up – Oh, Deena, what am I going to do?'

'He's telling you . . . fibs.'

'That's what anybody would say. But it isn't true. Fibs have a point to them. I don't see any point to these – stories. They don't make him look better or anything. I don't think you can call them fibs. Do you think maybe he doesn't know?'

'Doesn't know that his dog is dead? And that his mother has short black hair?'

'Well, if he'd thought he'd told me something that wasn't true, surely he'd have tried to stop me finding out it wasn't true? So he'd have not wanted me to meet his mother or go to his home. Or if he'd wanted me to go but realised – I mean, he could have said something on the way from the metro. Even made up another story to cover up the first one, like, "Imagine, my mother has just had her hair dyed and cut," or something. But he didn't say *anything*. It was like there was nothing wrong at all.'

'Maybe he thinks you won't remember.'

'Won't remember what?'

'Won't remember these things he's told you.'

'But then he'd have to think I don't remember anything he tells me; *anything at all.*'

'Asya, why were you crying next to the phone just now?'

'All day I thought maybe by the evening – maybe when he's had time to think. Maybe he'll find it easier to explain on the phone than face to face. But he was just – just normal. Like nothing at all had happened. He even asked me why I was sounding odd.'

'Didn't *you* ask *him* anything?'

'No.'

'Aren't you going to?'

'No, of *course* not. How *can* I? "Why did you tell me your dog was alive when he was dead?" "Why did you tell me your room was upstairs when it's downstairs?" '

'Did he really? About his room?'

'Yes.'

'Maybe he's moved rooms since he told you?'

'He said there were some stairs off the hall and you went up the stairs and there was a little lobby and his room was just off it. So after we'd cleared lunch and I was hanging about the kitchen with his mother she said, "You go and see Saif now, dear," and I thought how sweet and understanding of her, and I saw a flight of stairs outside the kitchen door and headed for it, and she looked at me all surprised and said, "There's nothing up there. Just the roof. Saif's room is over that way: across the hall." And it *is* off a little lobby, only it's not upstairs. What am I going to do? Oh, Deena, what am I going to do?'

Deena puts her arms round her sister. 'Hush, Ya-ya, hush. What's it like? His room?'

'It's lovely. It's really really nice.'

'It is perfect. It is big and his bed is kind of between single and double with a soft, dark red eiderdown. And he has loads of books and records and magazines. And he has a veranda with a climbing ivy and a small love-seat covered in striped white on white satin and shaded by a pear tree growing just next to the balustrade. I stood outside until I'd stopped being surprised at being downstairs instead of upstairs – it was like finding you were looking at a map the wrong way up – and then I knocked and went in. He was lying on the bed and the room was full of Joan Baez and the smell of his cigarettes.

'Plaisir d'amour
Ne dure qu'un moment,
Chagrin d'amour
dure toute la vie-ie-ie . . .'

'I stood in the doorway expecting him to say something about the room or about his mother but he patted the space next to him and I kicked off my shoes and lay down, and oh the absolute relief of being in his arms again after all this time. Four months. Four months without this – and now relief. Relief so intense that it hurt. And hurt and hurt again, and afterwards he brought me a tray with tea and biscuits out on the veranda and watched me while I ate, and smiled at me and stroked my hair and we listened to Joan Baez and waited for six o'clock when I had to go home.'

She liked men who smoked a pipe and wore well-used tweed jackets and desert boots.

She liked Joan Baez and Bob Dylan and Sayyid Darwish and Simon and Garfunkel and the old songs of Abd el-Wahab.

She had strong views on almost everything.

She had great faith in our country.

She was very pretty, delicate and warm. She was also kind and considerate.

She had a wonderful fairytale-ish atmosphere about her. It frightened me. I thought it unsuitable for the times.

She was well read.

She was committed.

She had a good sense of humour.

She was adventurous and had courage. But at the same time she was very careful with people's feelings and beliefs, and was forgiving, especially to me.

Scene 4

Winter and spring 1969

The Stage of Resilience and Defiance is over and the Stage of Active Defence is well under way. In March, the War of Attrition will start throughout the Suez Canal Zone.

Sinai has been severed and the Canal Zone – a powerhouse of the economy – is paralysed. The great oil refineries stand idle and are subject to periodic disciplinary bombing by the enemy. The Canal itself, that unnaturally straight path of shining blue water which has become so much a part of the country's myth – just say its name and you will see the labourers in their peasant underwear bent double under their burdens of stones and earth, sweating under the whip, dying – twenty thousand of them – to fulfil the dream of the Turkish Khedive and his French friend Ferdinand de Lesseps. You will see the Grand Inauguration; the cloth of gold marquees standing erect, the crowned heads feasting and the Treasury of Egypt bankrupt. You will see the Zoo and the Opera House and Pyramid Boulevard: all built for the same celebrations and inspired by the same ambition: to bring Egypt that little bit closer to the West, to Europe. And you will see the country staggering under the weight of its debt and then the debtors closing in: the Bombardment of Alexandria and the landing of an Army of Occupation, 'Orabi Pasha in exile and all the riches of Egypt controlled by foreign hands, and nowhere is this more obvious than in the Suez Canal Company: a state within a state. You will see ninety years of the great ships of the world steam through, the small

153

native boats pulling nimbly alongside with supplies and cries of 'baksheesh' – and then you will see Gamal 'Abd el-Nasser crackling in black and white, his arms raised in greeting to the thundering crowds: one million citizens gather in the great square of Manshiyya behind the Mosque of Sidi el-Mursi Abu-l-Abbas: 'We will reclaim our rights in the Suez Canal. We will reclaim our rights and we will build the High Dam. Egypt was for the Canal. Now let the Canal be for Egypt. In the name of the Nation, I declare the Suez Canal Company an Egyptian –'

You will see the crowd surge and roar and break.

How good you look, boy,
With your hand on the rudder,
And victory has lit on the Canal
A wedding procession.
Our Chief declared
There's no impossible –

You will see Port Said bombed and defiant and the great statue of de Lesseps at the mouth of the Canal overturned into its depths and the High Dam gushing with water and electricity. You will see for eleven years every schoolchild in the land come to stare at the Canal and listen to the recitative of its status: a symbol of freedom, of strength, of victory –

– And this Canal now lies defeated and stagnant; the great ships lie rusting under its still surface and the enemy builds the Barlev line along its Eastern bank and trains his guns on the red-roofed villas of Ismailia and Suez. The fields of strawberries and sugarbeet lie uncultivated, the stores unmanned. Six hundred thousand embittered citizens have been evacuated. They take refuge in the capital and the City Victorious groans under the new burden placed upon it.

In the newspapers, the drawing-rooms, the secret cells beginning to form, in the coffee-shops and in the university the debate continues.

'They are changing things. Of course they are.'

'Name one. Name one thing that's really changed.'

'We don't have to get the Guards' authorisation before we pin things up on the wall.'

Chrissie and Asya and Mimi and Noora and Bassam are sitting in the cafeteria. They have some others with them: two young men who are admirers of Asya and one who is trying for Chrissie. But Chrissie is not interested in him. Mimi has no admirers in college but she has at least one official suitor a month introduced by Father Boulos from the Church.

'But the Guard are still here; they still have an office at the main entrance to every college.'

'But we don't have to ask them.'

'Why are they here?'

154

'You have to have some way of guaranteeing law and order –'

'They don't have a Guard in every bank, in every company. They don't even have one at AUC. Why do they only put them in the national universities?'

Asya has, all in all, six declared admirers: four at university and two at the club. They have declared themselves only to Chrissie, not to her, and Chrissie has fielded their declarations. So now Asya can enjoy their company, or, rather, enjoy herself in their company, while pretending ignorance of their hopes. Asya finds that when she is with them she feels good: she feels pretty and clever and – wanted.

'How about the Youth Organisation? They've disbanded it as we requested.'

'What do you call the Socialist Vanguard then? It's still a way of containing youth and the energies of youth. It's just using a different name –'

'It has a different constitution.'

'Oh *honestly*! How can you –'

Rivalry lends virulence to conflicting views. Chrissie avoids looking at her admirer. Asya gazes fondly at both of hers. Chrissie kicks her under the table and frowns.

'What about what he just said about detentions?'

'That they won't detain people without due process of law? Big deal. That's their game, you see. You remove all basic rights from people. Then you dribble a couple of them back and everybody falls to the ground and kisses your feet –'

'Well of course they want to stay in control. They *are* the government. They can't just let the lid blow off the whole thing. They're under pressure from every side: a no war no peace situation, the Canal closed and the economy going to pieces and Israel spreading like a cancer. They're raiding us way into the Delta, man, *and* in the Sa'id. The people see that the government can't even protect schoolchildren –'

'They say the Chief is ill –'

'And who wouldn't be ill in his situation?'

'No, but seriously ill.'

'He's brought it all upon himself –'

'And upon us.'

'How is it all going, then? Huh? Huh?'

Napoleon is there. He stands towering over the small group, a pile of paperbacks clasped under one arm, the other arm stowed away behind his back, his head thrown proudly back, his thick frizzy hair cut at an angle, his upper teeth – as always – chewing furiously at his lower lip.

'How are you doing then? Huh? Asya? Noora? How is it all going? Bassam? Any news from home?'

'They are well, praise be to God,' Bassam says quietly.

'Praise be to God. Praise be to God. It will all be mended. It will all return. That is History. Asya!' He stares at Chrissie; each time he sees her it is as if for the first time. 'Asya!'

Asya cannot use his name because she can never remember it. So she smiles at him politely. 'Hi!' Among themselves, all the students call him Napoleon.

'And your friend –' He points. Chrissie stares intently at her empty glass.

'Chrissie,' says Asya.

'Chrissie. Chrissie. That is not an Arabic name. Is she not Arab? Hm?'

Chrissie will not speak so Asya says, 'It's Carima, really.'

'Call her Carima, then. Far better. Far better. We must all do our bit. Good. Good. Right. Keep it up, then. Keep it up.' He nods curtly at each one of them, then moves slowly away, surveying the cafeteria and the grounds as he goes.

'How long has he been here?'

'They say ten years.'

'This place is full of crazies.'

'And not just the students.'

'Thank goodness it's only the Faculty of Arts,' says Mimi, who rarely speaks.

'What do you mean?'

'Well, imagine if it had been Medicine or Engineering or something serious.'

'How can you say that?' Asya is aghast. 'What can possibly be more serious than Art?'

Mimi looks blank and Noora intervenes.

'I suppose it has been said that Art sometimes benefits from a touch of madness.'

Bassam is quietly, over the weeks and months, drawing closer to Noora. He writes her beautiful, oblique poems and silently accompanies her on her long trance-like expeditions around the Islamic ruins in the old quarter. Noora is as vague as ever but nowadays she seems to drift gently into the seat next to him – if it's free.

'A touch –' begins Asya.

'Hey, Asya! Tell them about today in class: Mahrous and Dr Mostanser. That was dreadful,' says Chrissie.

'Oh, heavens!' remembers Asya. 'That was just too funny. You know Mahrous?' turning to her audience.

'No.'

'Yes you do. He *always* comes to the Literary Society meetings. He's the very serious boy with the very short hair and the peasant accent? Yes, you *do* know him: he wrote the story about the little boy and the pyramid. Right? Right. And you know Dr Mostanser? He's the very intense-looking guy. The big guy with very black hair and a very fine pale skin pulled tight across his face, and he walks around glaring, right? Well, we're doing the *Poetics* with him and he'd been going on and on about the Unities like they were the Ten Commandments and then Mahrous puts up his hand and says in his best peasant accent, "But, Doctor, zis unity now not necessary." So Dr Mostanser goes all snooty and aloof' – Asya draws herself up and looks down her nose at her friends – ' "I beg your pardon?"

' "Zis unity in modern is not necessary. Yoonescu –"

' "We are not here to discuss Ionesco. This is not a class in modern literature. You may, in the fullness of time, arrive at modern literature in your final year. Meanwhile, you are in your second year and we are discussing Aristotle; the father, the progenitor, of all literary theory –"

' "But Aristotel say we must have ze unity and now it is proof is not necessary."

'Dr Mostanser becomes very, very tall and his eyes get brighter and brighter. He comes up very close to Mahrous and drops his voice right down.

' "Are you trying to say that Aristotle was – *wrong*?"

' "Mahrous doesn't answer and Dr Mostanser starts to turn away. "Aristotle, therefore, declares that three unities are always necessary: the unity of place –" and then Mahrous bursts out behind him, "Is not always enough always just Aristotel say, Aristotel say. Maybe I, Mahrous, say –" and Dr Mostanser turned around and punched him.'

'He hit him?'

'He *punched* him.'

'Straight in the face,' adds Chrissie.

'Knocked him down on top of the boys sitting next to him,' says Asya.

'Was he hurt?'

'There was blood all over his face but he was squaring up and yelling, "You want fight? You want fight?" And Dr Mostanser went for him again but Hani and another boy got between them and Chrissie ran and got Dr 'Ali.'

'He put a stop to it, of course?'

'Of course. He led Dr Mostanser away. Probably reminded him he could be court-martialled or whatever it is for hitting a student.'

'He's gone for one before, I've heard.'

'Yes. He wears gym shoes when he's invigilating exams so he can sneak up on you –'

Asya is happy: her story is a success. Everybody is laughing and commenting. She feels pretty oh so pretty and witty and bright and she could never have told this story if Saif had been there. Of course she feels pretty with Saif and she loves and adores him but she doesn't feel clever or quick when he's around. It's because he's so much cleverer himself. He's really the real thing. These guys only admire her because they don't know any better. But she likes being with them – and then she sees Saif on Sundays. Alone. At his house. She knows all the ways there now: routes and alternative routes. The metro costs five piastres – but it takes an hour. A taxi takes half an hour and costs fifty-two piastres and three for the driver is fifty-five. Best of all is when Asya borrows her mother's Fiat. Then she can make it from Zamalek to Heliopolis in twelve minutes. And on Sundays there isn't much traffic about. Their Golden Sunday Afternoons she calls them to herself. She loves the time she spends in his room, browsing through his bookshelves: Camus and Saint-Exupéry, Sartre and Pinter and Harold Robbins and de Beauvoir. Asimov and Hemingway and Le Carré and *Playboy*. Stacks of *Playboy* lying around openly. And he refers to articles and jokes in them – but not to the pictures. She doesn't even know if he looks at the pictures – well, of course he looks, don't be ridiculous – but she doesn't know for sure. She never looks at them either – when he's around. But she sneaks glances at the centrefolds whenever he's out of the room and then is smitten with misery because they are so beautiful. Tante Adeela is not beautiful. She has a very strong face, hard even, except for the eyes. She now loves Tante Adeela, his mother, and spends all of Sunday morning with her in the Madis' large bright kitchen. Tante Adeela teaches her to make *pasta al forno* and rice and *mulukhiyya* and tries to teach her to make stuffed vineleaves and tells her stories about Saif when he was a child. Saif never sits with them, of course. He might wander through to see what lunch was going to be, peering into the casseroles and asking, 'What is this shit?' Dada Wageeda, his old nanny, grey and dried-up like a stick, would say, 'You don't like it, don't eat,' and wave a wooden spoon at him. 'Go eat somewhere else.' He might steal a biscuit still warm from the oven. He might drop a kiss upon his mother's head or pat Dada Wageeda's shoulder absently as he passes by, and if he makes himself a glass of tea he would always offer to make tea for everyone else, but if his mother or Dada Wageeda started to speak to him he seemed to attend only to the first three words or so and then he went blank. Asya could see that he was only waiting for the sounds to cease so he could go away, but the women would continue chattering happily as they rubbed raw egg into the pasta or crumbled butter into the flour. They did not even seem to mind when he did not wait for the end of the sentence but wandered off, lighting a cigarette as he went. And always Tante Adeela would offer, 'Go with him, Asya, go. Why are you sitting here?' But Asya always stayed. It appeared unseemly to her to lock herself in with Saif so early in the day. And he did not look as though he expected her to anyway; whenever she went in he would be reading, or drawing what she had now learned were flowcharts, or he would be out on the veranda, silent and smoking. And besides it was fun watching Tante Adeela cook. In Asya's home food preparations were minimal. The Ulamas always ate their meat grilled or boiled and their vegetables sautéed or in a salad. And it was all done by Dada Zeina; Lateefa never sat in the kitchen and cooked – unless they were having guests, and then she cooked standing up and in a hurry. So Asya stayed in the kitchen with Tante Adeela, and Tante Adeela always said, after Saif had been and gone, 'He's a good boy, Saif; kind and tender-hearted,' but she always seemed to say it with a touch of sadness. And Dada Wageeda at the sink with her arms in lather up to the elbow would add, 'His heart is green! If only he would learn to pick his clothes up off the floor!'

'You're the one who spoilt him, Wageeda, and it's no use complaining now.' Tante Adeela turned to Asya. 'It's exactly the same as when he was at school: he comes home from work at the end of the day and he's carrying his tie in his hand, he's already ripped it off in the car, and he drops it on the floor just inside the front door. He makes straight for the shower taking his clothes off along the way and letting them fall on the floor wherever he happens to be.'

'His wardrobe would be a dustbin if I didn't tidy it up myself.'

'It's true, Wageeda, may God give you health –'

'Every week. Every week I go in there and get everything out and sort it and fold it and put it back in neat piles: the vests with the vests and the pants with –'

'Wageeda! I swear if you went in one day and found it all tidy you would be miserable and come running to complain. Anyway, it's all in Asya's hands now. You'll have to teach him, Asya.'

Asya shrugs happily. What does it matter if he throws his clothes on the floor? She can just see him in the shower all brown and gleaming, his face raised and his eyes closed, enjoying the water pouring down over him; first steaming hot and then a burst of cold –

'He'll always be loyal to you, Asya. He'll carry you in his eyes and will always be faithful –'

At the word 'faithful' Asya feels a pain. A pain in her heart: she immediately has an image of him being unfaithful. She sees Saif, still in the shower, but now next to the gleaming body there appears another – paler and shorter and wonderfully curved: a Botticelli Grace with her arms raised. Saif puts his hands around the girl's waist and pulls her in with him under the water. He folds his arms around her and bends his head to hers.

'Tante,' says Asya in a low voice. 'Tante? Do you have a photograph of Didi Hashim?'

Tante Adeela looks up at her, surprised, then she glances behind her back at the open kitchen door. 'A photo of Didi? Why, Asya? What would you want with that?'

Asya is tracing patterns with her finger on the white formica table-top.

'I just want to see what she looked like.'

Tante Adeela shrugs slightly. 'I must have one. I'll look for it for you after lunch.'

But now the subject has been broached Asya can't let it go:

'I don't understand how she could have left him.'

'Didi?' Tante Adeela glances over her shoulder again at the kitchen door. She drops her voice. 'Poor girl. I swear I was so unhappy for her. And for him of course. She really loved him. She loved him with all her heart. But her parents kept buzzing into her ears. Her mother specially. From the beginning they weren't truly happy about the engagement; they thought he wouldn't be able to support her in the proper manner. Well, of course he's just starting out. And they could have helped them. But when they decided to leave after the war they kept on and on at her. Her mother even came to visit me. "Saif is like my son, Adeela Hanim, but put yourself in my place: Didi is our only child; what would we do without her? And we shall be in Canada; at the other end of the earth. We won't be able to look after her."

'I said to her – I'm telling you this freely, Asya; it's a story that is past and ended but you ought to know it – I said to her, "My son will look after your daughter. He will be her husband and her father and her brother. I know him. And as far as we are concerned they can marry tomorrow and Didi can move in with us and share his room until God widens the path for them and they get their own place. Didi knows that she would be our daughter and the decision should be hers. She must do as she thinks fit." '

'And she saw fit to leave the boy and break his heart,' Dada Wageeda says from the sink.

'Enough, Wageeda, enough. And lower your voice. God has His own wisdom in His every act – "And ye might hate a thing and yet it prove a benefit to ye".'

' "And God the Magnificent has spoken truth",' completes Dada Wageeda.

'Anyway, this has all passed and now we have Asya.' Tante Adeela reaches out and pats Asya's hand.

Asya tortures herself with the thought of Didi Hashim. But it is a kinder, more homely pain than the German Shepherd Torture or the Room Upstairs Torture. She waits in dread for others to unfold. She tries not to build on information he gives her and she is cautious in front of others in case she unknowingly contradicts him. She watches him and wonders what he thinks. Has he forgotten that he'd told her his room was upstairs? Or does he think she's forgotten that he'd told her his room was upstairs? Or does he believe his room *is* upstairs? And his dog is asleep on the landing outside it right now?

But she still loves sitting at their lunch table with him and Tante

Adeela, and sometimes his father and sometimes his two brothers, and listening to his jokes and the banter and the football talk so different from the serious conversations that go on around their own lunch table at home. And even though Saif is always first to leave – blessing his mother's hands, carrying his plate into the kitchen and then disappearing into his room – she does not mind because now, at siesta time, she can follow him. And this is what she loves most of all: she loves lying next to him on his soft red eiderdown, kissing him and feeling him stroke her while Bob Dylan plays in the background and the shadow of each leaf of his pear tree grows sharp on the sunlit patch of wooden floor just inside the window.

And the sunlit patch moves as the weeks go by until one Sunday Asya suddenly sees that where before it had touched the edge of the bookcase now it has moved away and is starting to climb the wall next to the bed. Asya watches it and listens:

'Whatever patterns you have in your mind
I'll show them to you and you'll see them shine –'

She wonders if the shadows she sees now are different from the ones she – well, of course they are different, but are they the shadows of different leaves than the ones she was watching twenty-seven weeks ago? And then she wonders why she feels so sad. It is Sunday afternoon, and she is sad. She is lying in his arms, and she is sad. They have just made – after their fashion – love, and she is sad. Saif is stroking her arm. Should she tell him about the sunlight, 'the sunlight in the garden hardens and grows cold / you cannot cage –' oh, stop it. It is just – it's always on Sunday. Always on Sunday. And always after lunch. And always the same.

'Lay lady lay,
Lay across my big brass bed –'

'What is it, sweetie?'
'What? Nothing. Nothing at all.'
'Are you all right?'
'Yes, of course I am.'
'Was it nice?'
'Yes. Yes, oh *yes*.'
'What was it like?'
'It was like – like starbursts; one after the other. Oh, I do *love* you.'

He lights a cigarette. What can they do after all? She has college and he has work and this is Egypt and she has to be home by seven-thirty and that is it. If only they could get married: then they could do everything; go out to dinner, trek across the – no, they couldn't trek across the Sinai any more; that was gone. But they could maybe travel to the Oases? They

161

could go dancing. They could visit friends. They could make love –
properly. And in different ways and different times and different places.

'Saif?'

'Yes, Princess?'

'What about you?'

'What about me?'

'You know what I mean.'

'I'm OK. I'm fine. Really.'

'You can't be. You can't always be OK like this.'

'But I am, so stop going on about it.'

'Listen. Surely there must be some way to – there must be more – I
mean, can't I –'

'No. No. I don't want any of that. We'll wait and do it properly – when
we're married.'

'Well, then, let's not do this any more either.'

'Look, come on, Princess, what's the matter? Don't you like what we
do?'

'I do, you *know* I do. But I don't like – I don't like nothing happening
for you.'

'Everything happens for me. It doesn't have to be so localised, does it?
I love being with you.'

Lying in his arms, smelling his Rothmans and his Monsieur de
Givenchy, she remembers a story he had told her last year when he was
staying at the Omar Khayyam. A group of them had got pissed, he'd said,
and very late at night they had pushed over one of the marble statues in
the garden. Asya had seen those statues, she had watched them when she
used to sit with him in the gardens of the hotel: the ladies in the Greek
mode, armless and bare-breasted with some drapery falling modestly
around their thighs. Saif and his friends had pulled and dragged at the
statue until they got her to the bungalow of one of the instructors: Peter,
who was drunk and asleep. They had lifted her into his bed and under
the covers next to him. He had laughed as he described Peter rolling over
in his sleep and cuddling up to her. And he had laughed as he described
Peter, hung-over, next morning, refusing to let her go: 'He just kept hold
of her, stroking her face and saying sadly over and over, "She's so
perfect." ' Asya can see the marble lady lying in the disordered bed. Her
eyes are open but sightless. Her sharp stone nipples point up at the
ceiling. Her arms are cut off above the elbow. Over her, the man
laments.

She does not know why she has remembered this story. She does not
even know if it is true.

Scene 5

Italy

And now it is Sunday and Asya is not with Saif. In a decorous one-piece black swimsuit, she is lying face-down on an emerald-green lilo on the polished deck of a white yacht. Her right cheek is resting on the page she's been trying to prepare for tomorrow's class.

S'i' credesse che mia risposta fosse
A persona che mai tornasse al mondo,
Questa fiamma staria senza più scosse;
Ma però che gia mai di questo fondo
Non torno vivo alcun, s'i' odo il vero,
Senza tema d'infamia ti rispondo.

Il uso del Soggiuntivo. This was how you would be able to tell if the person you were talking to was una persona colta or not. It is odd, she thinks drowsily, to be dealing in this way with a passage she had always thought of more as a prelude to something else. There is no yellow fog here. Not even in London – any more. London where she will meet Saif in exactly twenty-two days. For a moment Asya thinks of Saif. She thinks of him all the time of course, but at a tangent; she tries not to let herself think of him head on for fear that her missing of him would overwhelm her and she would be helpless with misery. She half opens her eyes and sees, through the white railings, the vivid blue of Trasimeno as pretty as a painted ship, upon a painted ocean. She closes her eyes again. She has had a glass of cold white wine and she is sleepy and content. Somewhere behind her she can hear Eva and Carlo splashing in the water. Bobba has retired with the old man into his cabin and Umberto – where is Umberto? She opens her eyes and raises herself slightly on one elbow: a young man is lying on a sun-lounger. His feet are crossed and his hands are folded lightly over his belly. He is slight but beautiful and his pale body is gleaming with sun-tan oil. Buried in the black hair of his chest she catches the glint of his crucifix. A soft white fisherman's hat is tilted over his eyes and he is fast asleep. Asya settles down again. He had rubbed her back and shoulders with Ambre Solaire. His touch had been straightforward and firm – and different. His scent too had been different: slightly more lemony, more obvious. Saif would have liked it here on the yacht in the middle of the lake with the mountains showing blue-grey in the distance. And it wasn't hypocritical to think that. She was doing nothing she couldn't have done if he'd been there. But then she wouldn't have been asked here in the first place, would she? Well, no. No, she wouldn't. She knew that now, but she hadn't known it when Eva had come up to her on Friday, her fourth lonely day at the Università degli Stranieri, and held out her hand and said, 'My name is Eva. I am from Innsbruck. Sunday we are going on excursion to Lago Trasimeno for swimming and water-ski with some friends. We like to invite you.' Asya had said, 'Yes, thank you.'

And part of why she had said yes was just because she could not believe it could be that simple. Not, 'I'll have to ask my mother and let you know,' and then activating the whole ponderous machinery: 'But who are these girls? Whose yacht is it? How will you get there? What time will you be back? Is there a phone? Well, you'll have to ask your father –' and on it would go into the next round. Not, 'I'll ask Saif if he'd like to come,' but I know he won't want to. And then again: 'Who are these people? Oh, Asya, they're probably a bunch of jerks, it'll be deadly. I've been water-skiing a hundred times and in Beirut you didn't even *want* to water-ski. Is there something particularly special about this lake? Well, sure we'll go if you want to.'

Just, 'Yes.'

She could wake up, have a shower, get dressed and go out. She could come back, let herself in, have another shower, and go to bed. She didn't have to speak to anyone. She didn't even have to *see* anyone.

And he wouldn't really have liked it anyway. He wouldn't have liked the people; he *would* have thought they were jerks. He would have been contemptuous, for example, of the gold chain round Umberto's neck. And yet why not, she thought rebelliously, why should a man not wear a gold chain if he wished? Or a ring? Or, indeed, an earring? Well, perhaps not an earring. Not unless it was the right earring and he looked perfectly magnificent in it. Like Franco Nero maybe in *The Virgin and the Gipsy*. An Italian again. They really are terrific though. Partly it's the language of course. 'Tanto gentile e tanto onesta pare –' in what other language would such an – an unromantic sentence sound like that? Even a phrase like 'Vesti la giubba' could contain such amazing pathos. 'Umberto'. How wonderful to be named in so kingly a fashion. Of course people are called 'Farouk' and 'Fuad' and 'Charles' and 'Louis' but those names can hardly be said to have the same ring to them. 'Ferdinand' almost made it. She had used to think that 'Rudolph' was romantic because of Rudolph Rassendyl until she'd learned about Rudolph the Red-Nosed Reindeer. But 'Umber-to'. 'Umberto' was a good name. 'È un bello nome,' she had said to him as they drove west from Perugia towards Trasimeno.

'Pensi?' He had laughed.

They had picked her up in Carlo's car and she was sitting in the back between Umberto and Bobba, a Yugoslav blonde who was also on Asya's Corso Medio at the Università.

'Pensi?'

His arm had lain casually across the back of the seat and she had only met him ten minutes ago and he was friendly and easy to be with. And she had not yet started feeling awkward. It was only when they were on the yacht and obviously not expecting anyone else that she had seen it was a pairing situation – but by then they were casting off and what could she do? She'd have had to make some sort of a scene and she'd have looked quite mad. And she wasn't mad. Only embarrassed. Embarrassed because he, and the other two men, would think that she was knowingly here to partner some man she'd never seen before in her life. He seemed OK though. The nicest of the three men by a long way. The owner of the yacht had been on board to greet them. He was already in his swimsuit and he was old and leathery under his tan. Carlo was very loud and hearty and soon he and the athletic, bronzed Eva were pushing each other into the water, spluttering and laughing and turning somersaults. Umberto was OK. He was courteous and friendly but not over-friendly and she found herself wondering why he was there. Yes, it seemed he was a good friend of Carlo's, but he didn't look as though he needed someone to fix him up with a date. Her Italian, however, would not have stretched to the delicacy of tone her question would have required; it would have come out as a bald, 'Why are you here?' And so she'd left it, and here they were: sleeping innocently in the sunshine.

It had been so wonderful of the Italian Institute to give her this scholarship. True she had worked for it for two years, but you could hardly call it work: reading their terrific poetry and listening to their terrific operas and discussing their terrific painting/sculpture/ architecture. It was a shame that she had been so miserable on her one night in Rome and had passed through it so blindly. Maybe she could go back. She and her mother had had to plan so carefully to get her father to agree to let her come to Europe on her own. Her mother had had to point out to him privately that it would look very bad if he, the Egyptian Minister of Culture, were to turn down a scholarship offered to his daughter by his Italian counterpart. And Asya had had to go round for days looking quiet and responsible and sometimes appearing at home around sixish as though she wanted to be home and staying out late did not matter to her at all. And she hadn't, in fact, stayed out late since she'd been here. Sunday evening in Rome she had been all shivery and almost ill with loneliness and with missing Saif. She had even missed her parents. And she had missed Deena. And Kareem. And she had stayed in her room at Papa Germano's listening to the American kids shouting and laughing in the hall until it was Monday morning and time to catch her train to Perugia. Her spirits had lifted a little when she saw the narrow, cobbled, Etruscan streets and when she saw her own large-windowed room and her carved oak bed in the Signora Alunni's establishment, but when she had gone out for a walk on Monday evening and seen the promenade from the old Clock Tower to the Hotel Brufani buzzing with students in groups and couples all her loneliness had returned and she had sadly walked back down the stairway cut into the mountainside and along the road at the bottom until she reached the Signora's flat and her room.

The old man comes out of the cabin followed by Bobba. She has her sunglasses on and she is adjusting the pants of her red bikini. She walks over to a lilo with a white towel spread on it and lies down on her back. The old man looks down over the side of the yacht and shouts something to Carlo, then he wanders into the cabin and comes back with a tall, clinking, sweating glass. He stretches himself out on a recliner with a blue mattress. Asya hears Eva and Carlo climb on to the deck. She sees Eva, dripping with water, bend over the old man and kiss him, then she sees Carlo and Eva walk into the cabin with their arms round each other. They close the door. On the wooden deck a trail of wet footprints remain. Asya closes her eyes. Soon she is asleep.

When she wakes up it is late afternoon and the men are talking of turning towards land. Carlo seems to be suggesting that they all go on somewhere else, but the old man who owns the yacht shakes his head and puts up his hand as though he's had enough. Bobba clamours and pouts at him from her lilo then stands up and walks over and sits herself down on his knee. She strokes his face and tweaks playfully at his ears while Carlo and Eva laugh. He sits silent and still, watching her and smiling. Then he parts his knees and lets her drop on to the deck. Carlo and Eva laugh even louder and Bobba, after she has collected her scattered white limbs and put her sunglasses back on, laughs too. Asya glances at Umberto: he is smiling. Only the old man is not laughing, not even smiling any more. Asya feels her head burn and her hands go cold. She stares intently at the rivets in the wooden planks of the deck, and after a moment she reaches for her long white shirt and slips it on over her swimsuit. Later, she silently follows the others as they leave the yacht.

Wedged again between Bobba and Umberto in the back of the car, she shrinks away when Umberto stretches his arm across the back of the seat. He does not try to speak to her but says something to Carlo which she does not understand. Carlo pulls up in a street which is not the street where she lives and Umberto gets out and holds open the door. From inside the car she looks up at him.

'Vieni, vieni,' he says. 'I take you home. They go somewheres.'

Asya gets out and climbs into the dark blue car which he unlocks. The seats are white leather and probably what they call 'bucket seats' only she doesn't care. Later she will wonder why she wasn't frightened, terrified

166

even. He could have taken her anywhere; he could have killed her. She didn't know a thing about him. They could have all killed her and cut her up into little tiny pieces and emptied her out into Lago Trasimeno, and no one would have ever found out. No one had known where she was. She had just said yes and gone and no one – *no one* had known where she was.

'Che cosa c'è?' asks Umberto after driving for a bit in silence.

'Nothing,' mutters Asya, staring out of her window.

He drives silently some more, then he asks, 'È la Bobba?'

Asya cannot speak. But she nods.

He turns and looks at her. 'Ma, fa niente. It is nothing.'

'It is *not* nothing. It is *terrible*. It is terrible and humiliating and exploitative' – Asya is actually emphasising each adjective with a bang of her fist on her knee – 'and she lent herself to it and –' She is silent.

He shrugs elegant shoulders in a dazzling white shirt. 'Non ti spiace; lo conosce lei. She know everything.'

Asya sits in silence until he parks outside the Signora's. Of course he wouldn't understand; he'd been smiling too. Not laughing it's true but –

'Thank you very much for bringing me home.'

'Aspetti, 'spetti, Asya' – he puts his hand on hers and the way he draws out the first letter of her name is so musical – 'la cena. Dinner. Have dinner with me, yes?'

'No,' says Asya. 'No. Grazie.' And she opens the door and hurries into the house.

Had she forgotten him? In just seven days had she forgotten him? No no, of course she hadn't. But how could she have done what she did? Oh how could she have done it? And it was no use looking surprised and asking, but what had she done? It was no use claiming not to have done anything. She had and she knew it. She had lent herself to a cheap, a vulgar situation. And she had enjoyed it: enjoyed being there in the boat in the sunshine. Enjoyed it more because she had a good-looking man in attendance. She had enjoyed the – the feeling of anything being possible which had filled the place. She had – although it made her ill to admit it – been excited by the thought that behind the closed door of the cabin Bobba was doing it with the old man – and doing it without love or talk of love. *That* was the terrible thing. She had been fascinated by the casual way Carlo and Eva took their turn in the cabin. It was like queueing for the ping-pong table – or for school dinner. And she had liked the feel of Umberto's hands massaging oil into her shoulders. She had breathed in his scent and permitted herself to speculate on what his narrow, clean-shaven lips might feel like on hers. And how can she even *dare* to think in terms of 'doing' or 'not doing'? Had she not always believed that it was in '*wanting* to do' that the real issue lay?

167

'I wouldn't wish some man to deny himself something he wanted and then make a terrific virtue of it,' she had said fiercely to her mother during one of their heated theoretical discussions.

'But what matters is whether he actually sleeps with her or doesn't sleep with her –'

'No. What matters is whether he *wants* to sleep with her. If somebody is in love with you, they don't *want* to sleep with anyone else. And if they *want* to sleep with someone else then they're not in love with you. Sure, if a man is free then he can want to sleep with everybody – but not if he's in love.'

'I don't know,' Lateefa had said doubtfully.

'What don't you know, Mummy?'

'Well, I don't know if you can have a rule about "wanting". I think the most you can hope for –'

'But it's not a rule,' Asya had insisted. 'It's not "shouldn't" like "shouldn't" in school. I would never say, "You *shouldn't* want to sleep with her." I would say, "You are not in love with me," and it would be a statement of fact. It needn't be a reproach or anything.'

And Asya had imagined being at a dinner party with Saif. She had conjured up a table resplendent with silver and cut glass. Saif sat opposite her and at his right was a beautiful woman in a black velvet dress, very low-cut, with no jewellery but with diamond combs sparkling in her chignon. They were talking and laughing and a knife twisted in Asya's heart as she watched him lean back in his chair and turn and look into his companion's smiling eyes. Later, as they drive home in silence, he reaches up and pulls impatiently at his neck-tie. And later still, he stands, still in silence, at the open window staring out into the blackness. He has done nothing. But he has broken her heart. She lies in their bed, trying to decide to leave him.

So now it is in vain for her to lie in her bed at the Signora's – that same bed where she had cried for him on her first two nights here – and plead that she had 'done' nothing when she had wanted – oh, she would never ever be able to talk about this to anyone, not to her mother, not to Chrissie, not even to Dada Zeina.

Next morning Asya is too ill to go to class. She cannot bear to see Eva and Bobba. She cannot bear to sit through the Soggiuntivo. She cannot bear to climb the thousand steps to the university. She lies in bed, and the Signora, coming with her baby on her hip to do the room, finds her. She feels her head with her cool, moist palm and finds her 'un po' calda, poverina' and makes her a large jug of iced lemonade which she places on the marble-topped table by the bed together with a pretty etched glass which makes Asya think of her grandmother's display cabinet.

The Signora likes Asya although she thinks her a bit strange. She knows she is on a scholarship – an award of some kind. And she had of

168

course paid all of her ten thousand lire rent in advance; the Signora is strict about that. She had arrived on Monday afternoon – not with a rucksack like all the other students, but with one very big suitcase and a small beauty-case made of white leather. And she had exclaimed that her room was very pretty and then she had come out and asked for more hangers, and when the Signora had taken them in she found the Signorina was unpacking everything properly, pressing things with a little iron and putting them in the wardrobe. And she had looked so sad. And she had made no fuss about paying the ten thousand lire right there on the spot. Then she had said that she would not be wanting any meals but would need the kitchen just twice in the four weeks to make what she seemed to be saying was some beauty preparation.

She had gone out that first evening and then the Signora had heard her come in after hardly one hour. Hardly long enough even to climb all the way up to the centre and then all the way down again. At midnight the Signora had opened the door of the room and looked in. She was ready with an excuse if challenged: an emergency jar of puréed fruit for the baby which she had judiciously forgotten in the corner of the bottom left-hand drawer of the wardrobe. But she had to look in to make sure. Sometimes you thought you had only one lodger and then it turned out you had had two for the month only you did not know it. The Signora has no moral views on this matter. Young people are young people and the world is not what it used to be, and the girls, after all, are not Italian, but ten thousand lire is the rent for one person in the room. The rent for two people is seventeen thousand lire. However, when the Signora had opened the door and looked in, there was no doubt that the Signorina was alone in the bed. There was no doubt also that she was in some sort of distress. She was speaking, and as it was a language the Signora did not recognise and had never heard before she had concluded that it was Egyptian. The Signora had called her softly, 'Signorina Asya! Signorina Asya!' And when she got no reply even though the talking continued, she had approached the bed and seen that the Signorina was fast asleep. And in her sleep she talked so sadly – and she kept saying 'se' and the Signora listened to find out 'se' what, but she could not make out anything else. Well, what could the Signora do? She considered shaking her awake and then thought, 'Poor soul, why is it better to be miserable awake than asleep? At least the dream will end.' And of course the Signora's husband was already in bed waiting for her, and the baby was asleep but could wake up at any moment –

And the Signorina had not been out in the evening since. Not one single time. It cannot be that she was not asked because she is bellissima and in fact there is a very nice Swiss boy staying with the Signora Farinata in the apartment across the hall and he is always hanging about the Signorina and walking her back from the university – he is in her same class – but the Signorina did not seem to think of him at all. She just came and went looking sad and hardly ate anything; the Signora only found biscuit wrappers and peach stones wrapped in tissue in her waste-paper basket, and in the bin in the bathroom she had over the Signorina's first three days in the house found several sanitary pads – used and very politely wrapped up – so she was, fortunately, not in that sort of trouble. No, she is merely old-fashioned and love-sick for her fidanzato in an old-fashioned way, and now today she is ill, la poverina, and staying in bed, and so the Signora will not be able to clean the room.

Next day, however, Asya feels better. For no reason at all. She simply wakes up feeling better and gets dressed and goes to class. And she looks at Eva and Bobba and sees them sitting at their desks taking notes and looking ordinary and studious and giving her casual smiles. And the young Swiss with the sunburnt nose from across the hall sits there smiling and the Professor talks of the achievement of Perugino, and at four o'clock, as she walks out of the university gates wondering what she will do with the rest of this gorgeous day, she sees the dark blue car and Umberto in a beige linen jacket leaning against the bonnet. He opens the passenger door and she notices that the car is an Alfa-Romeo and slides in.

Outside the Signora's he turns round to face her. His eyes are very blue.
'Seven o'clock? I pick you up? We have dinner?'
And Asya says, 'Yes.'

Gamberetti and pecattine and insalata. Then zabaglione and espresso. The conversation has to stay very simple. But the great windows look down the dark slope of the mountain where occasionally you can see the gleaming cluster of lights that is a villa. What would they be like, the people who live down there? Asya tries to imagine the family within one particular cluster of lights: people reading, talking, eating, getting dressed. She tries to imagine them, and in her mind they begin to move, although rather stiffly. She can see what they look like and what they're doing but she cannot imagine their – their *real* lives. The girl sitting on the bed, half undressed, with one pink sock in her hand – what is she thinking of? What does she want? What –

'Andiamo ballare,' says Umberto, and they streak off into the night.

For Asya the hillside is now full of wonderful places: restaurants, bars, discothèques, and Umberto knows them all. They could go into any one of them but the one they do go into is the Conca del Sole, where they are greeted as they walk in and it seems that he knows everybody and he introduces her and suddenly it is fun and even a bit exotic being herself –

'Io non ti conosco,
Io non so chi sei.

170

Sono nata ieri,
Nei pensieri tuoi –'

And he really likes dancing. Just for its own sake. Not to put his hands all over her or to show off but just for its own sake. So they dance and he drinks his gin and tonics and she drinks Coca-Cola senza limone, and they dance again, and then he takes her out into the garden, and as they lean over the parapet and look down the dark hillside he cups his hands gently around her head and starts to kiss her. He kisses her brow and her temples and her neck and her mouth. His lips feel slighter, thinner than Saif's, in fact his whole physical presence seems altogether lighter, less substantial. But he is sweet and comforting and his scent is delicious and she lets him kiss her. Then he puts his hand on her breast and she pushes it away, and when he puts it there again she pulls her head back and steps away from him.

'Ma perchè?'

Her explanation has to be short and to the point.

'There is someone at home. I am a fiancée.'

'Va bene,' he agrees with a smile, 'ma adesso siamo qui!'

'No,' she says. 'No,' and shakes her head. Then she adds, 'I should tell you: sono vergine.'

'Ah!' He runs his fingers through her hair and looks closely into her face. Then he smiles and shrugs. 'Allora! Andiamo ballare.'

At the Signora's door he kisses her upturned palm and drives away. It is just after midnight, and as she turns into the front garden she sees the Swiss boy sitting on the steps of the house. 'Buona sera!' she calls out happily, and stops as he lifts his face.

'Oh, Jean-Luc!' she says softly. He is weeping. 'What is the matter?'

But she knows what the matter is, and somewhere deep in her heart a small flame of pleasure flickers into life: a man sits weeping on her doorstep because she has been out till midnight! But he is not really a man. Just a boy. And very miserable. And she is very very sorry for him. So she sits down beside him on the step and doesn't say anything but pats his hand and whispers, 'Please don't be unhappy,' and he lays his head on her shoulder and weeps some more and says something in what she thinks is probably Romansh because it isn't Italian or French or German. But he smells of beer and sweat and she really wants him to take his head away and get up, although she reminds herself that there is no need to panic because it doesn't matter who comes across them sitting ridiculously on the step like this, only now his head has slipped down and it is lying on her breast, and he turns his face and is nuzzling into her neckline so she pushes him away, but his head comes back so she pushes it and keeps her hand on it and says, 'Jean-Luc, I have to go in now,' but he reaches up and starts placing kisses like wet moths on the underside of her chin and she feels herself getting cross: so she has chatted to him; listened, mainly, really, walked back from college a couple of times, shared a potato pizza once, but what business did he have curling up against her in this baby-like posture, all red and raw and chapped and pushing his wet face into her neck and breathing beer-fumes all over her hair at half past twelve in the morning? So she pushes him determinedly to one side and stands up and says, 'Jean-Luc, I'm going in.'

And he stays on the step like a supplicant and asks, 'Tomorrow? In the evening? We eat together?'

'No,' she says, but it sounds so naked that she adds, 'I'll see you in class.'

'I wait here? We walk together?'

'No. Only in class. Goodnight, Jean-Luc.'

Next day, throughout l'Architettura Etruscana, Jean-Luc's sorrowful eyes are upon her, but that doesn't stop her thinking about Umberto. Black-haired, blue-eyed Umberto who would now, of course, not want to go out with her again. She can see that that is the deal. And fair enough. If you want to feel you are part of the scene – to meet people, to go out on yachts, to get 'the Italy experience' – you have to play the game. You have to *really* become part of the scene. She can see it all clearly now. There are the Italian Girls and the Foreign Girls. The Italian Girls stay in (much like at home) and behave themselves and wait to get married. The Foreign Girls come here for the summer, for the courses, and for the men. There are the Italian Men and the Foreign Men. The Italian Men spend the summer with the Straniere. They drive them around in their sports cars and take them places and sleep with them as they cannot do with the Italian Girls. It mostly works out fine. The Foreign Men are at a disadvantage. Even if they are not quite as weedy as Jean-Luc, they are still at a disadvantage: they have no local know-how, they are only just learning the language and they don't have much money. They take what they can get. This is the system. And what is Asya to do? In this system Umberto is probably a terrific catch. In most systems, really. It is true he is not very big, not much taller than she is, but he *acts* big. He has a way of standing with his legs apart as though he was braced for a gunfight. In the garden – but no, in the Conca he was such fun to be with. They'd seemed to be having such an uncomplicatedly good time. And she didn't have to worry about what he was thinking or whether he was liking what they were doing. She didn't even have to worry about whether they were talking or silent since they could only say the most basic things. And yes, she'd liked his smell and his hands and his jacket, and is she expected to just go from college to the Signora's and back and not do anything else at all? She's already been to the Chiesa and to the museum and there isn't much else left to do on her own. None of the girls will want to go out with just another girl. Going out with a man *is* the only way to be here, and she had probably picked up more Italian yesterday than in a week of classes. But now it isn't even up to her. She has told him the truth and he won't want to see her again and that is that. There isn't anything she can do about it.

At four o'clock, when classes are over for the day, she collects her books and bag and, intent on avoiding Jean-Luc's company, she runs down the university steps and out into the street. And there, just round the corner, the blue Alfa-Romeo stands shining and waiting.

Outside the Signora's he takes her hand and says, 'At seven?'

Asya picks at a piece of black fluff that has found its way on to her white skirt. 'But Umberto, I already told you –'

'Sì. I know. Dunque' – he makes a face – 'I want to be with you.'

Asya turns to him. 'But –'

She looks so troubled that he smiles and pats her hand: 'It is OK. Però, I still want to be with you.'

Over dinner he reaches out and strokes her face: 'You are – come si dice? It is serious, this engagement?'

'Yes.'

'But you like me?'

'Yes, but –'

'But?'

Asya shrugs, frowns at her plate, glances briefly at him, then stares out of the window.

'You like me but you love him?'

Asya nods.

'And you want to remain vergine?'

'Yes,' whispers Asya, feeling her neck, her arms, her breasts ache as his fingers stroke her collar-bone.

'Va bene! Io sono ragazzo bravo. You stay vergine. But there is condition –'

'Yes?'

'You must say to no one. You understand? Nessuno. If someone know che io – that I see you but I am not sleep with you, is very bad for me. You understand? OK?'

Asya nods slowly. 'OK.' Then she laughs and takes his hand away from her neck and holds it tight in both her own as she smiles at him from across the table. She is delighted. This is so wonderful. So much the opposite of everything she's ever known: people sleeping with each other but pretending not to. People suspecting people of sleeping with each other. Hiding. Covering up tracks. Here it's all the other way round. She loves it. And she can go on seeing him and listening to him and going places with him. Oh, it is perfect. It is like a fantasy and he is making it possible: sweet, delicious, gallant Umberto – she hangs on to his arm as they walk out to the car, and when he stops and turns to look

173

at her she puts both hands on his shoulders and gently kisses his mouth.

Eighteen days. Eighteen days of yachting and sailing and dancing and driving to Padua, Siena, Florence; of sunshine and laughing and warm nights and kissing and stroking and holding hands, of not caring what anyone thinks or thinks about. What does it matter if Carlo thinks they are fighting the Israelis because they are Jews or that Nasser is 'un buon fascista'? Asya tries, 'Non è fascista,' and gets, 'Ma certo è fascista, è un uomo molto bravo.' What does it matter what Carlo thinks? Or Eva? Or Paolo? Or even – for that matter – Umberto? She doesn't care. She doesn't care, and how wonderful not to care. Care? She does not even *know* what anyone around her thinks, really. The language sees to that. If she'd wanted to, Asya could have imagined exactly what Saif would have had to say about the whole lot of them. Or her father. Or even, really, Chrissie. But she does not want to. Time enough. Soon she would go back. Back to all that. To the people she really loves and cares about. But for now, how wonderful to think her own thoughts – not to have her mother's or her father's or Saif's superimposed over her own so that she cannot truly tell which is which. So that she cannot tell if the thoughts she manages to have are arrived at freely or in sympathy – or in reaction. How wonderful to simply do things instead of wondering if they are worth doing or discussing whether to do them or being told not to do them or listening to somebody else describe doing them. Maybe there *is* no point to dancing till three then driving to the top of a mountain to watch the sunrise, then having breakfast in the railway café before going off to class. No point, except that it is fun and she enjoys it and she demands the right to get bored with it herself instead of being continually told that it is boring.

Asya and Umberto drop into parties at the villas on the hillside. Umberto drinks gin and tonic and Asya drinks Coca-Cola because alcohol makes her ill. They dance and sing and play cards for kisses and watch couples vanish into rooms, and cigarettes are passed around which at first smell funny but which she learns to recognise and which do not make her ill. Then Carlo offers her a line of white powder on the back of his hand and shows her how, and first she sneezes but then she gets it and learns what freedom really is, for now she realises that all her life she has had a headache and her mind had been pressed and cramped and confined in a tiny space, and at last it is being set free and the headache is lifting and lifting so her mind can stretch itself out and out and out.

'Oh happy day
Oh happy da-ay
When Jesus walked
Oh when he wa-a-alked
To wipe my sins away

174

Oh happy day
He taught me how . . .'

Later, Umberto takes her arm and leads her into a room where there is
a very big bed and he closes the door. She looks at him. 'We will share,'
he says, 'with Eva and Carlo. I think it is better we come in first.'

She still looks at him.

'Then they think already we make love.'

Asya nods. She undresses to nothing but her slip and he to his pants
and they get into bed and kiss and lick and feel and eventually fall asleep.

Asya wakes to semi-darkness. The bed is heaving. Eva's right knee is
banging into Asya's left hip as Carlo screws her. Eva's right arm is flung
across Asya's face and she pants out one phrase over and over again.

'Un diavolo, Carlo, sei un diavolo, Carlo, sei un –' while Carlo grunts
as he labours over her.

Asya wakes again to loud music and lights. Carlo now towers above her. He
has pulled on Eva's green tube dress and is dancing on the bed. Lots of people
are standing around the bed watching and clapping in time. To her left,
leaning against a wall, Asya sees a man she had noticed earlier. He is tall and
broad-shouldered and square-jawed. His hair is dark. His nose looks as if it
had been broken. He has the look of a boxer. A blonde girl is burrowing into
his chest. His hands are moving on her waist and hips but over her head he is
watching Carlo dance, and for a moment Asya finds herself staring into his
eyes. She turns away: Umberto is lying on his face, his arms cradling his head;
he is fast asleep. Carlo is attempting a belly-dance: the dress reaches to the
middle of his hairy, muscular thighs and curves around his tight buttocks. But
the unmistakable focal point is the fisted bulge of his penis pushing out the
tight stretchy cloth at the base of his flat belly.

Later Asya wakes again. A heavy, warm weight lies on top of her. The
room is dark. Eva is no longer there. At her side Umberto sleeps. The
man on top of her is kissing her throat and her ears, sucking them, biting
them, eating them. 'Bella,' he whispers. 'Bellissima. Sei bella bella bella
tanto bella.' His tongue pushes into her ear. She knows it is the man with
the broken nose. He smells of leather and fresh sweat and her arms are
around his back and she is kissing him. The fingers of his left hand are
wound tightly in her hair. His right hand is between her legs and she is
kissing him and arching her back and moving to get his hand to the spot
where she wants it to be; where now, for the first time, she knows she
wants to be touched. She feels a burning, liquid, simple need, intensely
specific but radiating out to every finger tip. She whispers, 'No,' but his
fingers continue their slow, gentle, teasing search. She had never known

there was so much scope for searching down there: a miniature maze where you could wander for a lifetime, a maze of soft, shaded paths and a hundred hiding-places all longing to be discovered. She wants him to go on for ever, for ever – but there, there in the centre, *there*, is where she most wants him to be. A terrible, terrible urge to spread her legs as far as they will go and strain towards him so that he can push his fingers inside her – and even as she clutches him with one hand she pulls at Umberto with the other. She tugs and pinches and he rouses and rolls over and pushes at the man on top of her. The boxer raises his head and his voice sounds hoarse.

'Ma che cosa c'è? Perchè?'

'È la mia. La voglio io,' says Umberto and gathers her into his arms.

'Cazzone!' says the boxer, and gets up and walks off naked.

In Umberto's arms she weeps. Her heart is beating as if she'd almost fallen off a great height. She is relieved and miserable and between her legs she is in pain. If she could only put her hand down there and press the pain away – but she can't because Umberto is holding her and comforting her and making soothing noises to her, and soon she can feel him growing against her, and though she does not want to be stroked or kissed any more he is her friend and she does not want to hurt his feelings, and he rolls on top of her and kisses her lightly and looks into her face.

'Facciamo l'amore.'

'But Umberto –'

'Sì, sì, I know: una vergine!'

'So?'

'Facciamo l'amore!'

'And then?'

'And then you are no longer vergine!'

'No.'

'Va bene: sposami.'

'Scherzi –'

He traces her lips with his fingers. 'I joke?'

'Yes.'

'And if I not joke? You marry me?'

Asya looks into his blue eyes and winds a lock of his soft black hair round her finger. She smells his Eau Sauvage and strokes the back of his right leg with the sole of her left foot.

'Caro 'Berto. No.'

Scene 6

Saturday, 13 September 1969

London

She stands in the window of their flat. She has learned to stand concealed behind the thin curtain. The neon light on the building facing her goes on and off. It flashes red and green, red and green. To the left, the doors of the Piccadilly Theatre are still closed. Behind her she can hear Saif tearing open a bag of crisps. Then she hears the crisps patter into a bowl. He has put Bob Dylan on the record-player and the sound fills the room. The sound is fantastic, but then the flat belongs to a disc jockey.

'No no no it ain't me, Babe,
It ain't me you're looking for, Babe –'

She looks up at the clear sky; they've been lucky with the weather so far: no rain, no drizzle, no yellow fog. She stands on tiptoe and looks down at the pavement. The man standing there is an unhappy sort of man: thinning brownish hair, unsteady on his feet. He looks up at the windows of the house and sways a little. A plastic carrier bag is slung over his arm and both his hands are in the pockets of his raincoat. It isn't raining and doesn't look as if it's going to. Maybe after dinner they can go for a walk. It's pleasant walking down the Haymarket to Trafalgar Square late at night then walking on down Whitehall to the river. Amazing to have found a flat in the very heart of London. Amazing the speed with which she has left Italy behind her; a few hours on an aeroplane. Umberto at Fiumicino, Saif at Heathrow. On the plane she had wondered what would happen when she met him; something dramatic had to happen. He would look at her and know. Or she would look at him and be overwhelmed by regret, remorse, guilt. Or she would find she did not love him. Something would happen. But he had met her and she had felt the same old love and relief welling up in her heart when she saw him, and they had hugged, happy to be able to hug immediately without having to wait to be in a closed room, and he had commented, as she had known he would, on the size of her suitcase, and then pushed her trolley with his right hand keeping his left arm round her shoulders. And soon they had settled into a pattern. In the morning she wakes as he is leaving. He has a long journey every day to his training centre and on the first few days Asya – in a sort of make-believe domesticity – had woken up and put Corn Flakes and milk and boiled eggs and toast and butter on the table and sat in sleepy silence and watched him eat. But then he'd said that it really would be much better if she slept on and let him sort himself

177

out on his own. So now he just comes back into the bedroom with his briefcase in his hand to kiss her goodbye. Two hours later Asya is dressed and riding the number fourteen bus up Shaftesbury Avenue. Up the Charing Cross Road, where the bookshop man had given her *Pinocchio* when she was six because she'd stood quietly and let her father browse, and halfway up the Tottenham Court Road. She cuts through Torrington Place and gets to the university, where she is doing a course called Perspectives in Modern Literature. She ponders why modern literature seems to be so exclusively about disappointment, disillusionment, alienation – misery. She carries *The Whitsun Weddings* in her bag and repeats chunks of it to herself although she thinks that if you really believed all the time that that was all there was to everything you'd just have to sit down wherever you happened to be and not get up again – and yet, just to be able to say it like that, 'Our almost-instinct almost true –'

In the evening they would both be back in Denman Street. They shopped together. They cooked spaghetti and goulash soup and salads. They went out for drinks and walks and apple pie at the Swiss Centre and dinner at Schmidt's. They went to the cinema (*The Longest Day* and *The Wild Bunch* for him, *Cat on a Hot Tin Roof* and *The Lion in Winter* for her), read the papers and chatted. And tonight they are expecting guests. This seems to set a kind of seal on their arrangements: to somehow legitimise them. Even though their guests are not, of course, Egyptian. She has never met these people before and she is nervous. She is always nervous when she meets friends of his for the first time. She stands on tiptoe again to see if the chap in the street has got his nerve together and rung the bell. Red and green, red and green. No, he's still there. They should be here soon. Her hand in her pocket is twisting and crumpling a piece of paper. Saif has gone to the kitchen. She pulls the paper out: Chrissie's letter.

Dear Asya,

I got your letter just after we came back from Alex. We were at the club and I said I was going to the bathroom and hurried off before my ma could say I'll come with you. I ran to the Lido and asked if there were any letters for Miss Mona Afifi. It's always horrible to do that, I am always expecting someone to ask me to prove I am Mona Afifi. Or if someone comes in who really knows me or my family it would be a calamity. But it didn't happen yet thank God.

I am glad that you are well and having a nice time with Saif in London. I was very happy to get your letter you can imagine. I only got one letter from you which you wrote just after you arrived in Perugia and since then I heard nothing. I don't know if you wrote and your letter never arrived or if you didn't write. I wrote to you but I don't know if you got my letter. I am dying to know how it was being on your own. Was it frightening? Your letter did not sound very happy but I guess you must have been lonely at the beginning. Did you collect any new 'admirers'? What nationality? You will have to tell me everything when you come home.

It is very strange to think of you and Saif living together in a flat as though you are already married (although not in every way I hope!). Aren't you terrified of meeting someone who knows you in the street? (Asya, you must burn this letter after you read it – I have destroyed yours.) I can't imagine you learning to cook as you say you're doing, and Asya, be careful: don't let him quickly get used to things you're not going to want to do for ever like picking his clothes up off the floor.

This summer here has been so boring without you. We went, as you know, to Alex for half of July and all of August but it was not like it used to be. It never can be again I guess. Being there makes us all think about Issam even more than usual because all the family is together and everything brings back memories and it is very difficult. Tante Rita (his ma) is really not well. I don't think she will ever accept what has happened. Sometimes I think if she knew for sure that she had lost him, that he was, you know – that something had happened to him, maybe her heart would find some peace. But as long as she thinks that he is somewhere she is also thinking that he must be in prison or ill or in pain and it is very bad for her. There is nothing anyone can say because of course it is true. If he were OK he would be back here with us. She is always trying to get his father to do something but he has done everything he can and there is nothing left for him to do. He is as much destroyed by this as she is but of course he is a man (and an officer) and he can't even show it. Anyway my mother started to tell me, 'Look, it's over, he's not coming back. Run your eye among your cousins, you will find one that you like.' I think she worried that seeing Tante Rita so unhappy was going to make me too depressed. So she started, 'Issam was my nephew and you know how dear he was to me but he's gone. No one comes back after going missing for two years and you have to think of yourself, Chrissie, and of your future. You weren't married to him, only engaged, and you were very young and you mustn't close your heart: you have five other cousins and they are all fine young men and you can choose one of them –' But all my five cousins have been in front of me since I was born and I have never been interested in any of them. Not in that way. They are all like my brothers. And I keep thinking how Issam would feel. I mean, I know he's not coming back but sometimes I think he might. I don't really know. I don't even know what I feel any more. When I think about him I am unhappy for *him* – but not really for myself any more.

179

And I forgot to tell you. Something that made Alex even worse. Do you remember the gazelle that Tante Rita kept as a pet? You saw it last summer when you came and visited and you thought it was very pretty but looked very odd in the flat, and Tante Rita was making a little plaster statue of him and was feeding him out of a bottle? Well, he threw himself off the balcony. They said he'd had some sort of nervous breakdown and couldn't be allowed into the flat any more and they kept him locked out on the balcony and he went mad and killed himself. Just threw himself off. It happened while we were there. Not in the house, thank God, but in Alex, and Tante Rita was hysterical and my uncle was not very sympathetic because he had never liked having the gazelle in the house anyway, he said it was too highly strung and was always starting and twitching and made him (my uncle) nervous in his own home. Anyway, that of course made it all more miserable –

Asya smooths out the letter and folds it properly and puts it back in her pocket. She will get rid of it before she goes back to Cairo. Chrissie seems so far away. And what can she tell her about Italy? *Can* she tell her about Italy? No, of course not, how totally stupid; what could she possibly say? I was in bed with this guy – no no, it's OK, nothing happened; we had an agreement, but then there was this other guy, I'd seen him earlier but I didn't know his name or anything but there he was on top of me and I really really wanted –

The doorbell rings and Saif talks into the entryphone. The man with the plastic bag is no longer on the pavement. Asya stands in the window talking down her panic. Saif had said that Nicola was only a couple of years older than her (but she's been married for more than a year and that makes her older, Asya had thought) and Leon had been on the course at the Omar Khayyam last year so they could talk about Egypt. And now they are in and walking towards her smiling and Asya too is smiling and shaking hands and saying, 'Yes, isn't it just perfect?'

'It's great. It's really great. How brilliant of you to find it.'

Asya smiles and looks at Saif and carefully waits for his account of how they'd found it.

'It was in the *Evening News*, and we phoned and came round and made the deal. That was it.'

'But to live right on top of a –'

'Asya is adventurous.'

'It doesn't worry you?'

'No,' says Asya. 'It's fun standing behind the curtains watching the customers on the pavement –'

'A chap rang the bell up here the other day –'

'What are the girls like?'

'We've never seen them. They don't seem to go out –'

It's going well: the goulash soup has been eaten, the sound system has been commented on and so has Dylan's odd desertion of his fans. Nicola is friendly and not too pretty, Leon and Saif are easy and comradely – from across the table she loves him. His teeth flash white under his moustache, the blue sleeves of his shirt are rolled up to the elbow and his arms are solid and brown and covered with fine black hair. He keeps the conversation going and teases Nicola gently as though she were his kid sister. It will be nice entertaining with him when they are married. In a way he's at his best at a dinner party. With an audience. They must have lots of dinner parties. As long as they're *his* friends so she doesn't have to worry about whether he likes them. Asya can see Nicola liking him. Can see her feel attracted to him and she doesn't mind. She has seen this happen now several times and she does not mind – because he doesn't seem to even notice. She certainly sees nothing to make her jealous. She is jealous only of the past; of Didi Hashim whom he had deflowered and wished to marry and would never talk about. But he's good with women: he treats them like friends, sort of junior friends. He should have daughters. He should have many children and a massive table and sit always at the head. Asya is proud to belong to him. He is cleverer and quicker and funnier than anybody she knows. She will walk with him into any room in the whole world and be proud to belong to him –

'Saif says you're doing a course at the university here?' asks Leon.

He is trying to draw her into the conversation but all Asya can think of to say is, 'Yes. It's only a summer course.'

'What's it on?'

'Well, it's kind of about how modern writers see the world – or how they present the world in their work, anyway.'

'Which writers are you doing?'

'Well, there are general lectures, but then you have to choose two writers for your papers: one poet and one prose writer. I've taken Philip Larkin and Sartre.'

'Oh, Nicola's doing a course in French literature.'

'It's nothing really,' says Nicola quickly. 'It's just to keep me busy for the moment.'

'But you're very good,' says Leon. 'You're always getting A's and B's. I keep telling her,' he turns back to Asya, 'she ought to go back to university. She stopped when she met me. But I really think she should go back.'

Nicola shrugs and smiles. She looks at Asya. 'Which of Sartre's things are you doing?'

'A collection of stories. *Le Mur.* I thought the plays had probably been done often enough.'

181

'She really ought to go back. I mean, she speaks French and everything and I'm away so often –'

Asya wonders: Leon is telling his wife something and she is pretending
not to understand. But what if he told her straight out? Why was that
somehow never an option? *She* should talk; why doesn't *she* tell Saif
straight out? Tell him what? Tell him how worried she is. Tell him about
Italy. What does that have to do with anything? It had nothing at all to do
with him. It would be gratuitously hurting him. He had not asked her
anything. Not one single question which would have forced her either to
lie or to tell him. So why should she suddenly volunteer something that
could only be hurtful and pointless?

'It's all going the way I said it would: there's only a very limited scope
for giants and that's probably ninety per cent used up already. It'll all
have to get smaller and more diverse.'

'Well, I don't know,' Leon objects mildly. 'They're going ahead with
Project Fifty-two.'

'And when's it scheduled for?' Saif supplies the answer himself.
'Seventy-three. That's four years from now. It'll be scrapped. By next
summer they'll have scrapped it just as they've scrapped the 1908A now.
What did I tell you in Cairo?'

'Yeah, I know you said everybody'll have their own mini-computer; but
that isn't exactly what's happening. Just because they've terminated one
project –'

'But it was their biggest project –'

'Well, we seem to be on the right track anyhow; working in the systems
end: did you see the news about Hambros and Schroder Wragg?'

'Yes. And Rothschilds and Industrial Commercial.'

'What? I didn't see that –'

'Half a million into software: Computeraid Holdings.'

Leon nods slowly. 'You should get out, you know. Set up on your own.
A systems house, in the Middle East –'

Saif smiles. ' "First Arabian". I'm going to. But not yet. It's too soon.'

They have been together in London for thirteen days and they have
still seventeen to go. On the first of October Asya will fly back to Cairo,
and he will follow a week later, and then again it will be the walks in the
club, the Sunday afternoons in his room, the seven-thirty curfew. Asya
hopes that they can get engaged next summer. She has pointed out to her
mother that since they are going to get married in the summer of 1971 –
as soon as Asya graduates – they ought to get engaged at least a year
before. They would need time to get a flat, buy furniture and do all the
things that go with a wedding – and the family would have to be involved.
How could Uncle Hamid and Tante Soraya and Grandfather get involved in preparations for a marriage if there was no formal engagement?
Now *that* is a reasonable argument, and it did carry weight, and Asya

knows that her father will be receptive to it when her mother puts it to him. But of course it hinges on the assumption that they will be married in the summer of 1971. But she will fight for that. They had said wait till you graduate. Well, she would graduate in June and they would have no reasons then for postponement; there was nothing to stop her marrying in July. July 1971. Can things really go on like this for another two years, though? Maybe the year after they were engaged would not be too bad. It would certainly be busy. And her father couldn't possibly still insist on her coming home at seven-thirty when she was *officially* out with Saif. But even the thought of the months stretching ahead just to next summer, to next July, seems barely tolerable. Nine months. Nine months of tip-toeing around being careful. Nine months of losing ground. Asya now feels that this time, this time spent in less than total intimacy, is actually pushing them apart. They are not drawing gradually closer; they are solidifying in their positions. And their positions are separate. She looks at him and she is afraid. He seems somehow more inaccessible now than he did when she first met him. And what about *her*? What about Italy? Italy would never have happened if they had been married.

'He's gone to Greece. That's the first place they head for when they're thrown out.'

'What about this new lot? Do you know anything about them?'

Saif shakes his head. 'Nobody knows anything about them –'

'Nobody knows who they are, even,' says Asya. 'The papers started off calling their leader "Colonel Bushweir" and now they're calling him "Colonel Shweireb" – and they're not sure he's really the leader.'

'They say the Crown Prince is with them –'

'He would be.' Saif grins.

'I can't help feeling sorry for the old man, though,' says Leon. 'Old King Idrisi. I mean, he was a religious old bloke, wasn't he? And stable. This lot sound a bit like communists to me.'

'They're socialists,' says Asya, 'and nationalists. They sound like they were inspired by '52.'

'Well, Egypt was certainly quick to recognise them,' says Leon.

'And Iraq and Syria and Sudan,' Saif points out.

'It will mean more chaos, though,' reflects Leon. 'Another revolution-ary régime. The old King –'

'It isn't the Arab countries that are causing the chaos –' Asya says.

'Well, no, it's the war,' Leon agrees.

'It's Israel,' she continues.

'Well, it takes two – at least – to wage war,' Leon argues.

'You can't talk about "two" as though all things were equal. Israel is fighting an expansionist war. The Arabs are fighting a defensive one.'

'I should have thought it's the other way round: all the Israelis want is to live in peace –'

'On land which isn't theirs. On land from which people have been thrown out into refugee camps just a hundred miles down the road –'

'Yes, but you can't change history. You have to accept the status quo and take it from there –'

'I don't agree; I mean, I don't agree that one ever has to accept the status quo. But even if I did – even if we only speak about the present: why won't Israel accept Resolution 242? Why do they carry on bombing Lebanon?'

'Because that's where the terrorists are. Do you approve of terrorism?'

'No, I don't. But terrorism wasn't invented by the Palestinians. The Israelis themselves used it long ago: in Deir Yassin, for example, and nobody's dragging their elder statesmen up – people who were involved in the Stern and Irgun – in front of a court –'

'We're talking about the present –'

'Well at present, I'm ready for coffee.' Saif smiles at her and then at Leon.

Asya pushes her seat back and stands up.

'OK, who else would like coffee?' she asks.

On Wednesday, when they'd seen the reports of the landing at Za'farana, they had almost quarrelled.

'But shouldn't we try to call Cairo?' Asya had insisted.

'It was only a local thing,' Saif had objected, 'there's no point in calling Cairo.'

'How can you say "*only* a local thing"? They land tanks in our country, massacre the entire personnel of a border post –'

'Asya, it's in Za'farana –'

'I know it's in Za'farana. I've *been* there. The last time was just before the war. You said you'd gone diving there –'

'Why are you getting angry? Did I say the Israelis were right to land in Za'farana?'

'No, but you're talking as if it doesn't matter.'

'I'm saying there's no point in going through a whole business of phoning Cairo because nothing has happened in or near Cairo –'

'Well then, do you think maybe we should go to the Embassy?'

'The Embassy? The Embassy probably won't have even heard about it yet. They won't have got around to reading the papers. Look, there's nothing to be done. This was an incident and now it's over.'

'How do you know? Might it not be the beginning of something bigger?'

'No.'

'But why not? Why not?'

'The beginning of what? The invasion of Egypt? You think they want to take Cairo over? They've got exactly what they want and now all they have to do is keep up the pressure – and that's what they're doing. So if

184

you're going to go rushing off to embassies every time some soldier on an outpost is killed –'

'So you're saying everybody should sit around and do nothing?'

'Not everybody, no.'

'But *I* should sit around and do nothing.'

'Asya! What can *you* do?'

Prowl and sulk and stand in the window and nibble at a not-very-sweet bunch of grapes and eventually sit down to work on her poetry paper and wonder why the sadness in Larkin is sadder than the sadness in Eliot.

And now she stands in the kitchen. No, she is not Jameela Bohreid, nor was meant to be – but at least one thing she can do is to say what she thinks . . . Should she have, though? It was only a dinner, not some political meeting, and besides Leon was a guest – well, she hadn't done anything dreadful or been unpleasant or anything, she'd only disagreed, and she'd been right to disagree, you can't just sit there and nod and smile at whatever people choose to say – she does enough nodding and smiling as it is already. Saif comes in with the empty ice-cream dishes. He puts them down by the sink and turns to her. 'Come here.' Leaning against the sink he pulls her into his arms and kisses her. He kisses her hard. When his glasses get misty he takes them off and puts them on the pile of plates waiting to be washed and carries on kissing her. Oh, how she loves him and how she loves being in his arms. And now it all comes back: the hot flickerings in her thighs and her breasts, the dissolving in the pit of the stomach, is it because they're in the kitchen, not in bed? Is it because Leon and Nicola are next door? What does it matter? It's here. It's all here and how wonderful to feel it and feel it to be right, not to be having to think of someone else at the same time, not to be thinking that she shouldn't –

He holds her head away from him and looks into her face. 'That's better.'

'What?' She smiles at him.

'The cross look: it's gone. Now you look like a pussycat again. Shall we take them out for a walk after coffee? The pubs will still be open.'

'Yes,' says Asya. 'Yes, let's.'

She has to hold on to this. She has to. Forget Italy. It didn't matter. It didn't count. This is what counts: here, right here. She loves him and she knows he loves her. Where would she ever find someone she could love as completely as this? His walk, his smile, his hands, his room, his mother, his jokes, their Sundays – why, they already have a history – and her brother likes him and she knows that, next summer, her father will like him too. They all will. She follows him back into the dining-room. Leon is saying something about Ho Chi Minh, but he stops as she comes in with the coffee tray and in the silence they all hear Dylan wail, 'All I really wanna do-o-o-o-o/is, baby, be friends with you'.

'Saif told us all about how you two met.' Nicola is smiling at her. 'It's so romantic!'

Asya is pouring out coffee and smiles back. She pours cream in over the back of a silver spoon.

'Did you know straight away?' Nicola asks.

Asya looks up at her. Freckles. Blue eyes candid and wide. OK. Even if she is making sure they didn't get back into politics, she is right. She looks at Saif: he is looking at her attentively and – with love. 'Yes,' she says. 'Yes. I knew straight away.' She hands Nicola the sugar and considers, once again, the scene outside the library: the January light, the stillness, the man standing on the sunlit steps as she comes down with her armful of books. The bandage on her knee. The look on his face –

'Were you frightened?' asks Nicola.

'Frightened? Well, no, not frightened –'

'Not even when the police charged and you fell and hurt your knee?'

Asya keeps her eyes fixed on the full coffee cup she is handing to Saif, and when she sees it steady in his hand she shrugs and finds she can say nothing except, 'Well . . .' She hopes something will come after it, but nothing does, and Nicola says, 'I think it's so brave of you to go out on demonstrations like that. I've never even been *near* a demonstration. I'd be terrified.'

Asya says, 'It's not that bad,' and hears her voice sounding artificial and strained and rather high. She stirs her coffee and wonders how her face must look. She hears Saif say, 'I told you she's adventurous,' and glances up at him. He smiles at her and she looks down again into her coffee. 'She made us go to a service at the Rama Krishna Temple thing last week,' he adds.

'No!' Nicola exclaims.

'She did.'

'But why?'

'That's what I said. Ask her!'

They are all looking at her.

'Well,' says Asya, 'well – I like their song.' They are still silent, waiting for more. 'And they seem to care. I mean, enough to shave their heads and wear those clothes and all that. So I thought, why not go and see? I mean, it's not as if we had to go all the way to Tibet or anything –'

'How was it?'

'Bloody awful,' Saif laughs. He looks at Asya. 'You can't deny that.'

'No. No. It was dreadful,' she says.

'Tell them.'

'We stood and chanted for hours, then they served us some horrible messy stuff in paper dishes and we didn't dare not eat it. No, it was –'

'They're perverts,' said Leon.

'Leon thinks everything is down to sex,' Nicola explains.

186

'It didn't feel perverted,' says Asya. She is very, very tired. 'Just sort of boring.'

'They're all on drugs and they all sleep together and they have all these kids,' Leon continues.

'What's perverted about having kids?' Nicola asks, and Leon looks at her.

Saif stands up. 'How about a walk?' he says. 'It's not closing time yet.'

Why? Why this? What was wrong with how they had really met? What was wrong with the library steps and the tranquillity and the voices of their friends far away in the cafeteria? She looks at his back as he walks ahead with Leon: he holds himself erect and strides with that bounce to every step. He was the reason she hadn't been in the demonstrations. When she had gone on the very first march he had disapproved. He had added his disapproval to that of her parents and against him she could not level the charges she levelled against them. She could not accuse him of being pompous or past it or frightened on his own behalf. He had argued that the demonstrations were absurd, pointless, would change nothing, and how did she even know they were spontaneous? How did she know they were not being engineered and the student body manipulated towards ends she was ignorant of and would almost certainly not like? He had made it sound like a rather dim thing to do, to be in there shouting and singing and writing out demands. She had not felt it to be so, but she had found no arguments except ones that she knew would sound young and naïve. And she'd been flattered that he cared that nothing should happen to her. So why? Why tell these people that they'd met during a demonstration? She glances at Nicola walking beside her. But Nicola has been silent and downcast ever since they left the dinner-table. And he had *smiled* at her. When she had managed to look at him he had looked at her as though nothing at all strange was happening and he had smiled at her. But of course if he hadn't wanted her to know he'd told Leon and Nicola they'd met during the demonstrations he'd have just kept them away from her. He would not have invited them to dinner. He had just looked at her and smiled. Did he think she'd forgotten how they met? Or did he think she'd think she'd got it wrong? Or had *he* forgotten? Did he really, now, think they'd met during a demonstration? And what if she'd been someone else? Someone who could just look up and say, 'What police? We were on the steps of the college library and everything was perfectly peaceful.' What would he have done then? Perhaps it would have been better if she were like that. But she isn't. She couldn't do that. And she knows she will not be able to ask him afterwards. The men had reached the river and were standing leaning against the stone wall and waiting for them. As they come up Saif reaches out and takes her hand and pulls her to stand close to him. He pulls her hair a little so that she looks up at him.

'A BMW or a Lancia?' he asks.

'Lancia,' says Asya.

'Good girl,' he says, and hugs her.

'I tell you,' says Leon, 'the new 2800 is something else –'

Why? He can't know what he's doing. It would be too wicked. Too cruel. If he would tell her she'd go along with whatever he wanted. 'Look, sweetie. This couple who're coming to dinner. I've told them we met during a battle with the police. OK?' What would she say? Well, of course it sounded strange, and maybe at first she'd feel a bit odd, but she'd go along with it. And she would never make him feel bad about it. It might even be quite fun changing things around – just as a game. But that can't be how it is for him because he'd have said something. He can't *know* he's lying and look at her across the table like that. So what should she do? What should she do? But what's the point of asking that? She knows what she *will* do: hold on to him. Protect him. Make sure no one finds out –

'Right,' says Leon. 'How about we dive back into Soho and do a club?' He looks around. They are back in Trafalgar Square, standing somewhat aimlessly by one of the big fountains. The pigeons are all asleep on top of South Africa House. Asya has a photograph of herself feeding them when she was six years old. She is crouching down, elegant in a fur-trimmed high-waisted coat and a soft mohair bonnet, her hand held out to the birds, her eyes laughing into the camera. Behind her a black marble lion snarls.

'I'm tired,' says Nicola.

'You're sulking,' says Leon.

'I'm not,' says Nicola. 'I'm tired.'

'I guess we've all had it,' says Saif.

Perversely, Asya feels that yes, she would like to go to a club. She's never been to one. And she knows Saif will never suggest it. And of course *she* can't. And she can't go on her own. But his arm is around her shoulders and he's looking down at her.

'And Princess here has a paper to hand in on Monday; so I guess we'll call it a night.'

Leon kisses Asya and Saif kisses Nicola, and Leon and Saif clap each other on the shoulder, and Nicola and Asya smile at each other a little awkwardly, and they all say they must do it again soon, and Leon and Saif say, 'See you Monday,' to each other, and Saif and Asya head for the little street west of the National Gallery. As they pass the Pastoria Hotel Asya says, 'Nicola wants to have children and Leon doesn't?'

Saif shrugs. 'Yeah, I guess.'

'How come people don't sort out that kind of thing before they're married?' asks Asya. She hears herself sounding a bit aggressive. Saif glances at her, then shrugs again. 'I suppose,' she goes on, 'that this is what this modern stuff is all about: people not communicating with each other. One of these stories I'm doing is about a man who's sort of mad. He's locked up in a room and his wife looks after him and – have you read it? It's Sartre.'

'No.'

'He thinks he sees statues flying into his room to attack him. And everyone wants his wife to leave him because he's mad. But she won't. She loves him and she says she doesn't want to be "normal", she says to him, "It is like you that I want to think," but of course he doesn't even notice that she's said that. Anyway, she stays. She sits there with him as he screams that the statues are buzzing around the room and she grips the arms of her chair and *wills* herself to see the statues too. Even though he calls her "Agathe" and her name is "Eve". She tries to see the statues with him.'

'You know, I don't think his stories are much good,' says Saif. 'I think his plays are better. Although, even there, he's more interested in preaching his philosophy than in plot and character and whatever writers are supposed to be interested in.'

'Are you saying I shouldn't have picked his stories for my topic?'

'No. But I think it's a waste of time looking in them for anything except his own philosophy.'

She came back from the bathroom and sat on my knee and looked out of the window. The neon sign had at last gone off and it was dark outside. She sat silently on my knee and I could feel the softness and heat of her cunt through her cotton skirt. When she went into the bathroom the first thing she'd done was turn the tap on – loud. She did this so that no one outside could hear the sound of her pee hitting the water in the loo. It could be that she even did it when she was alone in the house – I don't know. Leon had said he would not let Nicola even close the bathroom door. He said, 'You let them lock themselves into the bathroom and then they'll lock themselves into the bedroom and then there'll be some bloke in there with them.' I thought of Leon and Nicola probably slugging it out in the car right then while she sat on my knee, staring out into the darkness, looking sad. I had just lit a cigarette and I blew the smoke carefully away from her: I knew she didn't like it in her hair. Her hair took hours to wash and dry but it was beautiful. It was much longer then than when I'd first met her and one of the things I liked in bed was to lie with it all black covering my face and think of nothing. I put my hand up to stroke it and pulled it to see how far down her back it would stretch. She moved her head and shifted slightly and I put the cigarette-end in the ashtray and pushed her skirt up and looked down at her smooth, tanned thighs and pushed her knees apart with my hand. The truth is that what I wanted to do was push her down on to the floor and do something violent to her. I don't know. Hurt her. But I stroked the cool insides of her thighs and she twisted and put her arms round my neck and bent and started to kiss me. After a bit I reached for her breast. Her left breast. My favourite. I always had to remind myself of the other one. I brought my hand up under it and felt again its weight and how it seemed to push against my fingers, and then her hand was on the bulge of my prick through the denim and she whispered, 'You want me?' I didn't answer, since it seemed to me she had all the evidence she needed, but I undid a button on her skirt and suddenly she stood up. She reached up under her skirt and pulled off her panties. She dropped them on the floor and knelt down in front of me with her hand on my flies.

'Please,' she said. 'Please, Saif, take them off.'

I held her hands and bent to kiss her but she broke free and fumbled at the zip. 'Please, Saif, I want you so –'

'I want you too, Princess, but –'

'No. Please. Please I want you inside me –'

'One day I'll come inside you –'

'No. Not one day, Saif. Now. Please. You want me. I know you do. And I want you so much. And it's right, I know it's right –'

'No, it isn't.'

She sat back. 'Why? Why isn't it?'

'Because we're not married.'

'What does that matter? We're only not married because they won't let us get married. But we know we want to and we know we will –'

'And supposing we don't?' I felt her withdraw.

'What do you mean?'

'I love you and I want to spend my life with you, but supposing I fell under a bus tomorrow?'

'Then I'd die anyway so it wouldn't matter.'

'Now you're talking silly,' I said. 'Come on, get up.'

She got up, but she was crying, and I pulled her to me and she sat down astride my knees and I kept thinking how wide open she was like that, and I just had to put my hand down to feel her, and then she was licking my nostrils and sucking on the ends of my moustache and kissing my ears and please, please, oh please, Saif, let's do it now, I can't go on like this any longer, let's make love tonight, I want you so to be inside me and we'll get married when they let us but I want us to be together properly now now – and in the end I said all right, but it'll have to be tomorrow.

'Why tomorrow?'

'Because we'll need a few things.'

'What things? What sort of things?'

'Something to make the first time easier on you –'

'I don't care, I don't care that it should be easy –'

'And also you don't want to get pregnant right away, do you?'

I held her away and she got up off my knee and stood and looked at me as though she was going to ask me something else but then thought better of it. She *tilted her head and tried to smile at me a little and said, 'Tomorrow then.' She bent and picked her panties up off the floor and went into the bedroom. When I went in she was way over on her side of the bed with her eyes closed. I didn't touch her again that night.*

V

July 1970 - January 1971

Listen, my heart, and bewail the fortune of thy land. Weep, O Heart, alone; for there is none to comfort you. Look, my heart, at the sun which is neither rising nor setting but hidden by clouds. Look at Egypt's Nile, its waters shrinking. Look at the cattle roaming without a shepherd, and the ships no longer speed to the Phoenician shore. The scales of justice have been thrown out on the road to be trodden under the heel of every passer-by. Nothing remains of justice but the name, and in that name crimes are committed. The ululations of weddings have died down and in their place are wails and screams to be heard.

Is this not the land of Ra? When will the Good Shepherd rise to its rescue? He whose heart knows no desolation, He who spends His day gathering His stray cattle and leading them to water? When will He come to tear out evil by the root? To annihilate the seed of evil even before it takes root? Where is He? Where is He today?

— AB-U-OR (2030 BC)

Scene 1

Thursday, 6 August 1970
Cairo

'Do you really like it?'

'It's beautiful. Really, really beautiful. It's a lovely idea using the silver embroidery on the high waist like that. And your aunt is doing it beautifully.'

'You weren't just being polite to Tante Soraya?'

'No, of course not. She's really got a talent for that kind of thing.'

'She doesn't like it, though; doesn't like doing it. It's such a shame. Chrissie, do you think the embroidery will be all right with the pendant?'

'Yes. You're using platinum for the pendant aren't you?'

'Yes.'

'So they'll both be silvery. It'll be very nice. When will it be ready?'

Asya almost misses a step and grabs at Chrissie's arm. Chrissie steadies her.

'These steps are getting so worn,' she says.

'Oh yes, but they're beautiful,' says Asya, coming to a stop and turning round to look back up the stairs. 'See how rounded their edges are and how smoothly they curve into each corner? They just need to be scrubbed and polished up a bit.'

'Where *is* the doorman here?' asks Chrissie. 'We call the lift and clap and bang and nothing happens. And the stairs and landings aren't washed –'

'He's getting old. He used to be everywhere. He had three wives at a time living on the roof. But he's getting old.'

They walk carefully down the last, the most worn, flight of steps.

'So when will the jewellery be ready?'

'He's promised it for the eighteenth.'

'Isn't that cutting it a bit fine? Your party's on the twenty-seventh –'

They round the last corner and come to the large, marble-floored hall. The black and white tiles have not been washed for days. The outer doors of the lift stand wide open and in between them, stretched out on a brown blanket in the sawdust, 'Am Abdu, the doorman, lies sleeping. Asya and Chrissie look at him. 'And he can't sleep except in the lift doorway?' asks Chrissie.

'He doesn't like anyone using the lift without him.'

'And what'll happen when your grandfather comes home?'

Asya shrugs. 'He'll kick him awake.'

Outside the large glass and wrought-iron house-gates, the protective brick wall, built just after June 1967, blocks out the sunlight.

'These things are just so ugly,' says Asya, 'and they're everywhere.'

'It's been three years,' says Chrissie. 'Three years and two months.'

'They're going to stay for ever. Nobody's ever going to take them down.'

'We're still in a state of war.'

'That's what I mean. And we'll stay in a state of war for ever. I can't see how anything is going to change.'

The afternoon sun blazes on to the sweating back of a chestnut horse which is trying to drag a cart across the four tramway tracks running down the centre of the street. Two trams curl on either side, clanging as they wait. The drivers lean out of their windows and abuse the cart-man while he curses the horse and flicks at him with his whip. The horse, head flung back, mouth open, eyes rolling, sweats and strains and pulls and eventually yanks the wooden wheels over the iron tracks. Asya thinks of Gerald in *Women in Love*. Chrissie and Asya split up to negotiate the crossing. First the crowd of workmen outside the *koshari* shop eating a late lunch out of blue and white tin dishes, then the small mob waiting for the buses, then the big red and white buses themselves, choking and keeling over on their near-sides with the weight of their passengers, then the stream of private cars and black and white taxis and the odd cart and bicycle, then the tram, then the tram going the other way, then everything again in turn.

Asya steps forward confidently. This street could get as crowded and pot-holed and dirty as it is possible for a street to be and she would still thread her way effortlessly across it.

On the other side, walking past the clothes shops, they make their way under a floating ceiling of bright dresses. Outside the doorway of one shop a rack of nighties stands on the pavement and Asya nudges Chrissie. Chrissie follows the direction of her friend's eyes and grins.

'But they're so horrible,' whispers Asya, not taking her eyes off the row of Baby Dolls: all transparent, all nylon, all with plunging necklines, some with a little modesty bow across the chest, and all in glowing phosphorescent colours: lime green, candyfloss pink, flame red . . .

'*They* don't think so,' Chrissie murmurs, indicating two women who have stopped and are leafing through the nylon, their expressions serious.

'They can't wear those,' Asya objects. 'They can't possibly. They'll look ridiculous.'

'Their husbands will be really happy. Come on –'

Asya has come to a standstill and Chrissie tugs at her arm. They walk on but Asya glances back. One of the women is studious-looking, with round glasses and her hair in an untidy bun. Asya thinks of her arriving home with a small brown-paper parcel which she hides in her crammed

196

cupboard with the creaking doors. She'd like to take it out and hang it so that it loses its creases but she doesn't have time. The children are at home. Three of them. She gets busy in the kitchen. Fade out. Evening. The family have had supper. The children are asleep. The husband is sitting on the balcony in his pyjama-trousers and vest. He yawns and stretches. He stands up slowly. He throws one last look down at the quiet street and goes through into the bedroom. A look of surprise fastens itself on to his face: his wife's hair is loose and she is brushing and arranging it over her shoulders. Her legs, thighs and arms are bare and she is wearing some see-through thing in bright pink. She smiles at him in the mirror. How does he see her? Does he see that her hair is stringy and thinning? That her flesh is dull and flabby? Or does he see a woman: provocative and desirable? Or does he – worst of all – see his companion of fifteen years, the mother of his children, got up in a ridiculous outfit in expectation of actions which he has not the slightest wish to perform?

'Chrissie?' asks Asya. 'How long do you think people can go on wanting each other? A particular couple, I mean? What do you think?'

'I think it varies –'

A boy on a bicycle balancing a great pallet of round loaves on top of his head swerves past them as they cross Shari' al-Azhar. They start to walk down Morgan Street. Watermelons, grapes, red dates and figs are piled high in baskets on either side of the road. Today is one of the three days on which slaughtering is permitted and the butchers' shops are open. A man staggers backwards from a parked van embracing a large carcass stamped all over in red.

'Do you think it's possible for a couple to go on wanting each other for years and years after they're together?'

'I think so. Especially if they loved each other to begin with. But I think it's different for men than for women. I think women get tired –'

'Welcome, welcome. Welcome, Sett Asya. Go inside. Your grand-father and your uncle are both here –'

'Am Farrag, Ismail Mursi's foreman, rises from his seat in the doorway of the shop. A retired sergeant, even his greetings have the gruffness of a command. When she was small Asya had used to share his bench and sit with him outside the shop in the winter sunshine, but for years now he has not permitted this. As soon as she appears he jumps up and ushers her off the street and into the privacy of the shop. Asya would like to sit out on the street but she loves the shop. It never changes. It is cool and quiet and clean after the heat and noise and dust outside. It smells of washed tiles and sawdust and wood polish and her grandfather's *shisha*. On one wall hangs a photograph of her Uncle Hamid, young, serious and intent, and on another a photograph of his father Ismail Mursi, taken at about the time he married his wife, Fadeela al-Nabulsi. His face is strong and heavy-jowled and his eyes are dark and determined. His fez is set

197

squarely on his head with the tassel falling in a straight line down the left-hand side. The fez has gone now and the eyes have dimmed a little, but that same pugnacious thrust of the head is there, even as he sits in a side chair smoking his *shisha*. He rises slowly to his feet to greet Chrissie, who is shy and awkward as she shakes hands with him and with Sheikh Zayid who stands beside him, and then with Hamid, who has stood up also behind his desk, his left hand tucked into his pocket.

'El-'Ataba has filled with light, Sett Chrissie. Welcome. Sit down, Asya, and tell your friend to sit down. You came at just the right moment; we were ordering lunch. You'll eat with us.'

'Geddu, we were on our way to the shops –'

'The shops are all closed now. They won't open for another hour,' says Hamid. 'Have some lunch, then go.'

The shop is full of new furniture. Wardrobes stand in stately rows, swivelling desk-chairs perch heavily on top of their desks, the footboard of each bed presses up against its headboard, and parading in front of the plate-glass windows are the rows of French-style gilt drawing-room sofas and chairs. When she was small, Asya would climb on to a crimson or a turquoise moiré Louis XVI and sit for hours, cross-legged, watching the world outside: the boys from the coffee-shops and restaurants weaving through the busy street with *shishas* and trays of tea and coffee and cold drinks, the butcher's shop across the road with the fat old father at the cash-desk and his son in the bloodstained apron standing behind the block, chopping great hunks of meat and keeping a suspicious eye on the world from behind his great waxed moustache in case a better object for his hatchet presented itself, the greengrocer next door building great pyramids of green and gold, slapping each watermelon and bouncing it in his hands before he laid it down, handling each mango and turning it this way and that to find the most enticing of its smooth sides, the three women in black sitting on the narrow pavement next to their piled-high cages of pigeons and chickens, laughing and smoking and fighting in the street, and when a customer came, reaching for a squawking, terrified bird, weighing and slaughtering and tossing it into a barrel to thrash out its last moments within its darkness, then lifting out the warm, plump little mass of feathers and wrapping it in an old sheet of newspaper. The gutter would run with blood, and small monuments of entrails and yellow feet would form on the pavement throughout the day. Asya used to watch and wonder whether the birds in the cages knew – whether each one of them watched that barrel with dread, knowing that the time would come when it too would beat out its last blood-choked breaths against its walls.

'What are you going to the shops for?'

'I need some satin shoes, Grandfather.'

Ismail Mursi removes the *shisha* from his mouth and goes into a fit of coughing.

When he has finished Asya says, 'Pink.'

'For the engagement,' Chrissie says.

'Or they could be silver,' says Asya.

'You're all set for the twenty-seventh?' Hamid smiles. Asya smiles back at him and shrugs lightly.

'If Tante Soraya finishes the embroidery and Ali Agha finishes the jewellery.'

'Embroidery and jewellery and pink shoes – what is all this? The Princess Qatr el-Nada?' Ismail Mursi says gruffly.

'Hardly, Geddu. It's only a tiny party –'

He makes the slight backward movement of his head his family knows so well. It comes when Soraya presses more food on him. Or when Hamid suggests a different way of keeping the books. Asya can imagine it happening years ago – when one of his children asked him for money.

'Let the young people have their day, 'Am Mursi,' says Sheikh Zayid comfortably as he fingers his prayer-beads. 'We've had ours. Now it's their turn.'

'Ours?' Ismail Mursi puffs at his *shisha*. 'Our days were nothing but misery and hard work. Now things come right up to them as they sit there.'

Asya sees Hamid's mouth tighten while Sheikh Zayid coughs and murmurs, 'And why did we work so hard and put up with so much? It was for them. Let them enjoy it.'

Mursi makes the dismissive movement of the head again. 'In any case,' he says, 'thank God it has only come to this.'

Then he puffs at his *shisha* again. Chrissie glances at Asya questioningly and the boy from the restaurant comes in with a large covered round tray which he puts down on the desk in front of Hamid.

'Was your grandfather annoyed by something?' Chrissie asks. 'He was all welcoming at first –'

'Maybe it was the pink shoes. I don't know. He's very – careful. With money, I mean. He always gives us lots at the festivals but he hates doing it. Always leaves it to the last moment. And Mummy says when they were small he'd send baskets of fruit and loads of meat and things to the house every day but he'd never give my grandmother any cash. I don't know. No, I think it's just a strain for him and Uncle Hamid being together in the shop. He must feel that Khalu is only there because there's not much else he can do. And he won't really let him have a say in anything or change anything. I don't know.'

Asya holds Chrissie's arm as they cross Midan el-Opera and start up Qasr el-Nil Street.

'It must be a difficult situation for your uncle,' says Chrissie.

'Yes it is. Absolutely. Everybody thinks he could do lots with the business but Grandfather won't give him a chance. And he sees Grandfather doing things like walking round with thousands of pounds in his pocket and taking days before he gets it to the bank – he doesn't like banks – and if Khalu says anything they have a row.'

'What did he mean by 'Thank God it has only come to this' though?' asks Chrissie. 'Come to what?'

'Oh, it's all right. He approves of Saif. He didn't tell *me*, of course, but he told Tante Soraya that he'd been sure I'd want to marry some "long-haired Beatle". He was surprised when I came up with a "real man" – with a moustache.'

'It's good Tante Soraya told you.'

'Yes.'

'Is your father happy with him? Saif?'

'Yes. Yes, they're getting on OK. And Mummy has quite warmed to him too. And of course Kareem has always liked him a lot – more than a lot, really. They can talk about cars and aeroplanes and computers for hours –'

'Shall we try here?' says Chrissie. They go into Desirée and Asya tries on shoes. Then into La Belle Jardinière. Then Hamid Mahmoud. It is six o'clock and soon the streets will be full of Thursday-nighters: newly married couples out for a walk, engaged couples out shopping, courting couples meeting in secret in cinema doorways, bands of young men, arms linked, looking for action – but now it is still too hot and too light and Asya and Chrissie walk slowly up Soliman Pasha Street looking in the shop windows.

'You know what, Chrissie? I do like Sheikh Zayid.'

'Sheikh Zayid?'

'Yes, really. I do. All the family talks about how strong he was when he was young, and how he taught them all to swim, and how far he could jump and how many kids he could carry. And then he fell in love with this half-Moroccan woman who's incredibly beautiful in a barbaric sort of way, and she wouldn't have him because he didn't wear European clothes, so he took off his Sa'idi clothes and put on a suit for her sake and – I don't know, he just seems very romantic. And now he's got this grey beard and the prayer-mark on his forehead, and he's so gentle, but I think he's probably still terrifically strong –'

'Oh, Asya! You're going to stay nutty like this all your life. He's a really old man and you're going on about strong and gentle and how *romantic* he is?'

'Well, it's true. Anyway, a man can be old *and* strong and gentle –'

They try Bahari and Bellina, and finally in Gadallah they find the perfect pair of satin court shoes in dusty pink. They cost twenty-nine pounds, so Asya borrows four from Chrissie. Then they double back and treat themselves to a 'trois petits cochons' each at l'Américaine.

Scene 2

Monday, 24 August 1970
Amman
King Hussein of Jordan proclaims the necessity of protecting and pre-serving the Palestinian Revolution.

Wednesday, 26 August
Baghdad
Thousands of Iraqi nationalists are arrested.

Thursday, 27 August
Amman
The Palestine National Council convenes.

Cairo
In the elegant apartment of the Egyptian-French Club the families of Asya al-Ulama (twenty) and Saif Madi (twenty-eight) celebrate the engagement of their two children. The toes of Asya's pink satin shoes peep out from underneath her pink and silver lace dress; the bespoke jewels which Saif has presented her with gleam at her throat and her ears and on her fingers. Saif is in a dark grey suit cut by Abbas the Mute. He wears a plain midnight-blue silk tie. The two drawing-rooms are full of flowers and guests, and a tall black waiter in a white jacket serves glasses of sherbet off a round silver tray. The windows are wide open and Asya and Saif stand for a moment in one of them. Down below them the southern tip of Gezira, thick with trees, rises out of the Nile. They see the Exhibition Grounds to the left, then the straight, well-lit road that spans the island and joins the two bridges of Gala' and Qasr el-Nil, then the Mukhtar Museum and its gardens, then the small Municipal Club, then the Headquarters of the Command Council of the Revolution half hidden by trees, and then the river: one wide gleaming mass until it is split by the island. Forced apart from itself for a two-mile interruption, its dark waters lap at the land and ripple back a reflection of the globed lights from Gala' Bridge. The fountain at its centre is a useless black stump jutting out of the water.

'The flowers are beautiful,' Asya says. 'Thank you, darling. It felt terribly special having them arrive in the morning.'

Saif looks at her and smiles.

'Happy, Princess? Really happy?' He puts his hand on her upper arm as she rests her elbow on the window-sill. She can feel the cold

201

smoothness of the wedding band she has just slipped on to his finger. Looking out at the river and the late August night she nods quietly then glances up at him. Together. Openly. No more catching of the breath at the sight of a familiar face in the car next to you at the traffic lights. No more sinking of the heart at seven o'clock and frantic dashing home for seven-thirty. No more lingering partings outside Simmonds before she crosses 26th July Street alone. Together. Framed in a dark window, his hand on her arm, their new rings shining in the lamp-light.

Tuesday, 1 September
Amman

Representatives of the Jordanian government meet with representatives of the Palestinian Resistance.

Wednesday, 2 September
Tel Aviv

General Moshe Dayan threatens to resign if he is not given free rein in the Occupied Territories.

Thursday, 3 September
Cairo

Asya al-Ulama and Chrissie al-Tarabulsi are in Heliopolis to meet Adeela Hanim Madi's dressmaker. Asya is not really happy about this for fear of what Tante Soraya will say. But Tante Adeela has bought Asya a beautiful piece of fuchsia silk from Hong Kong and has suggested that Asya talk to her own dressmaker about it, so Asya feels she ought to at least go once. But she won't go alone, so Chrissie accompanies her. When they drive Tante Adeela back to her villa – with the issue of the fuchsia silk still unresolved – she insists that they come in for a short visit. It is five o'clock and too early for any of the men to be home. Tante Adeela goes into the kitchen and puts on the kettle. It is the first time Chrissie has been to Saif's home. She and Asya stand in the hall. As Tante Adeela walks towards her bedroom to take off her jacket and her high-heeled black vernis shoes there is a knock at the front door. She changes direction and goes to open it. Outside stands a young man. He is tall and thin and he is wearing army fatigues and carrying a knapsack.

'Darling! Where have you been this long while?' cries Adeela Hanim.

The soldier steps forward to hug her and kisses her on both cheeks and on her brow.

'Tante Adeela! I'm sorry to drop in on you like this. I know Saif can't possibly be here now.'

'It's your home, my darling, it's your home. Come in, come in.' She draws him in and shuts the door behind him. 'How are you? And how are your mother and your father?'

202

'I haven't seen them, Tante. You see, I was able to get a one-day leave suddenly so I came down without warning anyone and I've found the house all shut down and the neighbours say they've gone to the country. I haven't even got my key.'

'Well then, you'll stay with us. Saif will be so happy to see you. Come, let me introduce you. This is Asya, Saif's fiancée; I know he's told you about her. And this is Chrissie al-Tarabulsi, Asya's friend –'

'Saif told me about her too.' The young man grins.

'And this is Engineer Fuad el-Sinnari, Saif's friend since they were that high,' says Adeela Hanim, measuring with her hand a height up to her knee. 'He finished his engineering degree last year and is doing his army service up in the Canal and we haven't seen him for months. Sit down, sit down, my darling, would you like a shower? Or will you have some tea first? And something to eat. You're probably hungry. Look how thin you've become.'

'I've always been thin, Tante,' he laughs. 'You always say, "Look how thin you've become," every time you see me.'

'The kettle must have boiled, Tante. I'll make the tea,' Asya says, and moves towards the kitchen. Chrissie immediately follows her. In the kitchen Chrissie, who would normally be reaching for a tray and finding the glasses and the spoons, simply sits down on a chair. Asya puts the tea-leaves into the everyday white and blue pot and pours the water over them. She puts the lid on the pot and turns to her friend. Chrissie is huddled up on her chair – crying.

'What's up? Chrissie? *Chrissie*, what's *up?*' Asya runs over to her friend.

'I thought it was Issam,' Chrissie whispers. 'He was standing with the light behind him and all I could see was a tall, thin shape and the army clothes and the knapsack, and Tante said, "Where have you been all this time?" and I thought it was Issam.'

'Oh, Chrissie!' Asya bends to hug her friend and presses Chrissie's head to her chest. 'Oh, Chrissie, darling!'

After a few moments Chrissie straightens up and pats Asya's arm.

'Come on. You'd better take out the tea. I'll follow straight after you.'

'Are you really putting up a "wall of missiles"?' Adeela Hanim is asking incredulously. 'Have you seen them with your own eyes?'

'Seen them? I've touched them, Tante. I touch them every day. That's what we're doing: installing SAM Three's along the western bank of the Canal. Everybody knows that.'

'It's supposed to be a big secret,' says Asya as she pours out the tea. Chrissie comes out of the kitchen and sits next to Asya on the big sofa.

'Everybody knows it. The *New York Times* in March reported their arrival. And the Israelis of course are the first to know exactly what's happening.'

'But then how are they letting you go ahead?' asks Tante Adeela.

'They're not. They're raiding the installations. They're mounting at least five hundred raids a week – that's not counting all the raids on the interior. It's practically a war out there. The figures for the first four months of this year say that four thousand of our construction workers were killed. If we go on like this we'll match the twenty thousand killed in the original excavation of the Canal.'

He has black eyes with long eyelashes; eyes that are piercing and deep and have humour but no softness in them. He has straight black eyebrows and short black hair and a strong nose, chin and jaw. He speaks lightly and smiles at the three women ranged opposite, but there is an intensity about him, and when he is not speaking his face settles into an anxious look with what is already a deep furrow between the eyebrows.

To break a silence Asya says, 'Saif told me a lot about you.'

'He told me a lot about you too,' he replies, and Asya feels the return of that familiar terror. What if, right now, in front of Chrissie – Tante wasn't too bad, maybe she even knows already, but Asya has never said anything to Chrissie about all that, and if suddenly now this friend of his said something – something that was obviously and unadaptably untrue –

Fuad smiles. 'He told me that Asya al-Ulama and Chrissie al-Tarabulsi are inseparable. I see it's true.'

Friday, 4 September
Amman

Palestinian commando groups and units from the Jordanian army are positioned near the entrance to the Royal Palace and near Broadcasting House on the Amman Heights.

The Palestine Liberation Organisation asks the Council of the Arab League to convene an urgent meeting next day.

The people of Amman are stocking up on food and supplies.

Saturday, 5 September
Amman

A close relative of King Hussein of Jordan, an important government official in the Occupied Territories, is jailed for eight years on a charge of spying for the PLO.

Sunday, 6 September
Zarqa, Jordan

Serious clashes between Jordanian government forces and Palestinian Resistance. Preliminary reports: thirty dead.

Cairo

President Wild-Dada, Archbishop Makarios and Mr Kamal Jumblatt arrive on official visits.

Monday, 7 September
Worldwide
Within one hour Arab commandos hijack four planes with a total of six hundred passengers on board.

Cairo
The Arab League calls for peace in Jordan.

Tel Aviv
The Israeli government declares its withdrawal from negotiations with United Nations Representative Gunar Jareng.

Washington, DC
The United States expresses anxiety at the results of the elections in Chile in which Salvador Allende won by a clear margin.

Tuesday, 8 September
Cairo
One of the hijacked planes, a Pan Am Jumbo, is blown up at Cairo Airport.

Thursday, 10 September
Washington, DC
The United States government announces the approval of ten new Phantom jets for Israel.

Amman
Fierce fighting breaks out between the forces of the Jordanian government and the men of the Palestinian Resistance.

Bombay–London
A British Airways flight carrying one hundred and twenty-eight passengers is hijacked.

Saturday, 12 September
Amman
Reports say one hundred and fifty dead and five hundred wounded in the clashes in Jordan.

Monday, 14 September
Occupied Territories
Israeli forces detain four hundred and fifty Arabs.

Thursday, 17 September

Amman

King Hussein forms a military cabinet and imposes martial law in Jordan.

4.30 p.m.

Cairo

The phone rings in the Tarabulsis' living-room. Chrissie picks it up.

'Hello?' It is a very crackly line and a voice comes from far away.

'Good afternoon. This is Fuad el-Sinnari.'

'Oh!' Chrissie drops her voice. 'Good afternoon.'

'Chrissie?'

'Yes.'

Chrissie picks up the black telephone and starts to move away. Away from the inner part of the flat where her parents and brothers are resting, through the corridor and out into the drawing-room.

'Can you talk? Are you alone?'

'Yes.'

'Is everybody having a siesta?'

'Yes.'

'Don't *you* sleep in the afternoon?'

'Pardon? I can't really hear you —'

'It's a very bad line. But I daren't hang up and try again. I might lose it altogether.'

'Are you in — still up there?'

'Yes. Chrissie. I know I shouldn't really call you like this. But I had to speak to you. Chrissie?'

'Yes?'

'I've been thinking about you since we met. I don't know when I'll be able to come down again, but when I do, I want to see you.'

'. . .'

'Chrissie?'

'Yes.'

'Can you hear me?'

'Yes.'

'Will I be able to see you?'

'. . .'

'Chrissie. Please. I know that this is sudden for you but — it's been on my mind for two weeks. I had to speak to you —'

'Yes. Yes, all right. When you come to Cairo. I have to go now.'

'Take care of yourself.'

'And you too,' Chrissie says softly before she hangs up.

Friday, 18 September

Amman

Thick smoke covers the city as street battles are fought between the Jordanian army and the Palestine Liberation Organisation. PLO leader Yassir Arafat asks President Nasser to intervene to prevent the annihilation of the Palestinian Resistance.

Cairo

President Gamal 'Abd el-Nasser decides to break off a short holiday in Marsa Matrouh which had been recommended by his doctors. He returns to Cairo.

Saturday, 19 September

Amman

Reports estimate five thousand dead and wounded.

The Mediterranean

The Sixth Fleet patrols in the Eastern Mediterranean.

Cyprus

British troops are put on the alert.

Sunday, 20 September

Cairo

His Majesty King Hussein Bin Tallal:

My envoy, General Muhammad Sadeq, was unable to meet with Yassir Arafat . . . in an attempt to end this bloody conflict between brothers in Jordan.

Carrying the burden of responsibility, we are unable to leave the situation as it is, and therefore, I address you directly, with a straightforward Arab appeal that there should be a ceasefire as soon as possible even if only for twenty-four hours to give our nation the chance it needs at the national and patriotic and human levels.

The information we have of the losses is terrifying, and the consequences of what is happening now can be immensely dangerous. Thousands of innocent people are at the mercy of gunfire or simply bleeding to death on the streets.

This is a situation which our nation cannot tolerate – and it is a situation which shames us all in front of our consciences and in front of the coming generations and in front of the world; both our friends and our enemies.

I repeat my request to you . . . and I am confident that my appeal will find with you an immediate response: let us end the tragedy that is now taking place. We must block the international conspiracy which is indicated by the suspicious movements of the Sixth Fleet in the Mediterranean; a conspiracy which will attempt to use the sad events in Jordan in order to interfere in our region. If this happens it will have terrible consequences which our nation will find insupportable. Your historic responsibility in these hours is decisive. May God help us all to perform our duty.

Gamal 'Abd el-Nasser

Gaza
Israeli forces shoot at Arabs who break the curfew.

Monday, 21 September
Amman

In response to President Gamal 'Abd el-Nasser's call for a ceasefire, the Palestinian Revolution declares that it is ready to take the necessary steps to implement a ceasefire so that the envoy of the three Presidents, General Muhammad Sadeq, may perform his mission.

We ask the authorities in return to hold their fire, to stop the shedding of innocent blood and to prevent our country from the danger of entering into a long civil war and from the danger of foreign interference. And also to save the land from the danger of plagues as there are thousands of corpses lying unburied under the rubble.

We shall adhere to a ceasefire the moment it is declared and we are informed of it.

Your brother, the Commander General of the Revolution, salutes you, brave fighters, for your heroism in defence of the Revolution and in defence of the right of our people to live and to return and to liberate our country, and in defence of the honour of the Arab nation. Revolution unto victory.

Your brother,
Yassir Arafat

6 p.m.
Amman
King Hussein orders a ceasefire.

Baghdad
The Broadcasting Service of the Central Revolutionary Committee announces that the Palestinians have refused the ceasefire 'until the throne in Amman is destroyed'.

Amman

Some units of the Jordanian army continue to open fire in the streets.

Cairo

His Majesty King Hussein Bin Tallal:

The latest reports I have received from General Muhammad Sadeq indicate that there are huge dangers involved in what is happening now in Amman. And that these dangers will affect the progress, the struggle and the hopes of our nation to an immense degree.

Some elements in the Jordanian army continue to open fire despite the assurances I have received from Your Majesty and despite what I know of the leadership of the Central Committee for the Liberation of Palestine's acceptance of the ceasefire.

I will not hide from Your Majesty the fact that I feel that General Sadeq is not being given the opportunity to accomplish his mission in Jordan as I had hoped and that this is causing us all the gravest anxiety.

I ask, in the name of every national and historic right, that you should now take a firm stand on the side of the unity and security of our nation – and our struggle against the enemy, a struggle which must continue.

Gamal 'Abd el-Nasser

Tuesday, 22 September: dawn

Amman

The fighting starts up again. The Jordanian army deploys tanks in the streets.

Cairo

His Majesty King Hussein Bin Tallal:

. . . I ask you once again to help us to get past this crisis with all the pain and the disaster that it has brought.

The smallest miscalculation now can drag us all into regions where we do not want to be – where our nation does not want to be . . . We must all consider our steps carefully before the development of events pushes us into critical complications.

I hope with all my heart that you will make the immediate decisions that will put an end to what is happening. This nation has endured enough torture during the last days.

May God guide your steps and give you success,

Gamal 'Abd el-Nasser

209

Amman

The Military Governor declares an end to the ceasefire.

A unit of the Iraqi peace-keeping force leaves its position between the army and the Palestinian Resistance in Jabal Amman.

Palestinian refugee camps come under heavy fire.

Cairo

Al-Bahi al-Adgham, Prime Minister of Tunis, Nur ed-Din al-Atasi, President of Syria, Moamer Qaddafi, leader of the Revolutionary Council in Libya, and Ja'far Numeiri, President of Sudan, arrive in Cairo.

Hussein el-Shaf'i, member of the Supreme Executive, carries a message from President Gamal 'Abd el-Nasser to King Faisal of Saudi Arabia.

Wednesday, 23 September
Cairo

Charles Helu, President of Lebanon, Al-Qadi 'Abd el-Rahman al-Iriani, President of Yemen, Salim Rabi', President of South Yemen, and Prince Sabbah al-Salim al-Sabbah, ruler of Kuwait, arrive in Cairo.

Amman

King Hussein asks Iraq to protect him in the event of Syrian military intervention.

Yassir Arafat estimates twenty thousand buried under the rubble.

Cairo

King Faisal Al Saud arrives in Cairo. The meetings are moved from the Qubba Palace to the Nile Hilton where the leaders are staying. President Nasser moves into a suite on the thirteenth floor of the Hilton.

Friday, 25 September
Cairo

Al-Za'im Muhammad Daoud, Prime Minister in the Jordanian military cabinet, goes to the Embassy of Jordan where he meets Ambassador Hazim Nusaibah. Afterwards, he dismisses his official car and goes for a walk in downtown Cairo. He then sends his ADC to his suite in the Hilton with instructions to pick up a letter that he will find there and deliver it to the Kings and Heads of State meeting at the hotel. In this letter he declares his resignation from the Jordanian cabinet. He also declares that:

1. His government has been made to bear the blame for deeds of which it is innocent.

2. He wishes to clear the way for a patriotic civilian cabinet which would re-establish peace in Jordan and create a climate within which the ceasefire can be respected.

3. He will not make any further statements because of his concern for Jordanian–Palestinian relations, and for the Palestinian Resistance, and for the stability of the government in a country that has the most extensive borders with the enemy.

11 p.m.

Prime Minister Daoud is tracked down by the media. All he will say is that he wishes to be alone and that 'the glare of unnecessary publicity should not be trained upon him as he needs to be by himself at this time when he has taken a decision so important to his conscience as a human being and a citizen of the Arab nation'.

Cairo

During the meeting of Kings and Heads of State a proposal is put forward that Egypt should send in troops to occupy Jordan. Nasser states, 'I have once before sent troops into Yemen. We lost more than ten thousand men there and Israel still occupies our lands. I am not prepared to send Egyptian soldiers to be killed in Jordan.' It is noticed that a muscle in the President's jaw is working almost continuously and that he often leaves his chair to walk about the room.

Saturday, 26 September
Amman

The Jordanian army attacks the Ashrafiyyah Hospital, killing the wounded and kidnapping staff in an attempt to force the commandos out of the area.

Sunday, 27 September: 1 p.m.
Cairo, The Nile Hilton

King Hussein joins the meeting of Kings and Heads of State. During the stormy two and a half hour session in the Grand Conference Hall, King Hussein, Yassir Arafat and Colonel Moamer Qaddafi are all seen to be carrying guns.

5.45 p.m.

In President Nasser's suite Arafat explodes. 'How can we trust them? We are here negotiating while in Amman they are intent on annihilating the

211

Movement. Nothing remains but to pull the whole thing down upon our heads and theirs.'

'I,' says 'Abd el-Nasser, 'have burnt up my blood in these last days to protect you. I could have come out with some strong rhetoric in your support and then given you a radio station from which you could say what you liked about the King and then sat back and watched you all. But my conscience would not let me.

'Numeiri went into Jordan and came back with four of your commanders.

'He went in again and came back with you.

'We have issued a report in which the whole truth is stated.

'Our aim has been to obtain a ceasefire. Shall we try? Or shall we stop trying? My position from the start has been to protect you and to protect all those people who have committed no wrong and who are now being killed and can't even find anyone to bury them –'

Colonel Qaddafi enters and says that the meeting has convened.

Nasser: 'Shall we go?'

Numeiri: 'We go – with God's blessing.'

Arafat: 'God be with us.'

6 p.m.

A meeting is held *in camera* in the Grand Conference Hall in which resolutions are reached to:

declare a cease fire;

permit relief agencies to begin their work in Jordan immediately;

implement supervision of the ceasefire;

work out a peaceful basis for all parties to continue living in Jordan.

The resolutions are signed, in order of precedence, by King Faisal, King Hussein, President Gamal 'Abd el-Nasser, Mr Yassir Arafat, Colonel Moamer Qaddafi, President Ja'far Numeiri, Mr al-Bahi al-Adgham and the others.

Mr Arafat then issues an appeal to Arab youth to join the Palestinian Resistance and all countries present agree to open recruitment centres and start lists of volunteers.

Later that evening

President 'Abd el-Nasser receives a message from the British Prime Minister, Mr Edward Heath, through Ambassador Sir Charles Beaumont that the six Arab commandos responsible for the plane hijackings have been set free.

President 'Abd el-Nasser sends a message to President Nixon (who has arrived in Italy to watch the Sixth Fleet manoeuvres due to take place on the 29th) through Donald Burgess to say that the fuss Israel is making about the alleged installation of SAM Three missiles on the western bank of the Suez Canal is getting out of hand and is without logic: 'either they intend to leave the Occupied Territories, in which case the SAMs should not matter to them, or they do not intend to leave, in which case we would be right to install the missiles – if indeed we are installing them.'

Later yet that evening

President Nasser steps out on to the balcony of his bedroom at the Hilton and looks down at the Nile with the lights from Qasr el-Nil Bridge and the banks of Gezira glittering in the water. He smiles at 'Abd el-Megid Farid, the Secretary-General of the Presidency, who stands beside him.

'How come I've never seen this wonderful view before? Look at this! I'm buried alive out there in Heliopolis.'

President 'Abd el-Nasser learns that Colonel Moamer Qaddafi has left for the airport sending him his greetings and his congratulations and saying that he did not wish to disturb him with the formalities of leave-taking. 'Abd el-Nasser orders Qaddafi's plane to be held while he goes to the airport to thank him for his efforts over the last few days. 'There is no further need for me here,' he tells his staff. 'I shall sleep at home tonight.'

Monday, 28 September: 9.10 a.m.
Cairo

President 'Abd el-Nasser is at Cairo Airport. He sees off President Suleiman Frinjieh, then King Hussein, then King Faisal, then President Numeiri. The President then goes home for a brief rest. His wife tells him that four of his children and his two grandchildren will be lunching with him later. She notices that instead of walking the two flights downstairs as he usually does, he takes the lift.

2 p.m.
Cairo

Prince Sabbah al-Salim al-Sabbah is last to leave. While President 'Abd el-Nasser and the Prince stand to attention during the playing of the two national anthems, it is noticed that the President is perspiring a great deal.

As the plane roars on the tarmac, 'Abd el-Nasser, contrary to habit, asks for his car to be brought to him. He gets into the car and is driven home.

3.40 p.m.

'Abd el-Nasser returns home. He speaks for a moment to his grandchildren, then goes to his bedroom. His wife asks when he would like lunch and he replies that he does not feel he can eat anything. He changes into pyjamas and lies down on his bed. Soon his physician, Dr Al-Sawi Habeeb, arrives. Dr Habeeb asks the President's wife to prepare a glass of fruit juice and then he calls four more of the President's physicians and consultants: Dr Mansour Fayez, Dr Zaki al-Ramli, Dr Taha 'Abd el-Aziz and Dr Rifa'i Muhammad Kamel. Mrs Tahiyya 'Abd el-Nasser comes back with two glasses: one of orange juice, and one of lemon.

4.50 p.m.

Three of the other doctors arrive. They decide that the President has suffered a massive stroke which, together with his acute diabetes, has brought on a severe heart attack. He seems perfectly calm and insists that he wishes to visit the front in the early evening. He warns the doctors that he cannot be made to stay in bed as he has a great deal of work to do in the coming days. He listens to the headlines on the five o'clock news then switches off the radio.

'Nixon is having a circus out there in Napoli, but there's nothing new,' he smiles.

Dr Al-Sawi Habeeb approaches the bed.

'You should rest, sir. You have switched the radio on and then off. You really must not make any effort at all.'

'It's all right, Sawi. I feel fine now.'

His heart is beating regularly again and Dr Mansour Fayez leaves the room. Outside he lights a cigarette and tells the President's wife, who is standing behind the door, that she can go in to him. She hesitates; her husband has never liked her to be in his bedroom when there are other men there.

5.05 p.m.

On television all programmes stop and the Qur'an is broadcast on both channels.

All army units at the front are placed on full alert. All other army units are confined to barracks.

The BBC in English is the first to announce the news:

President Gamal 'Abd el-Nasser is dead.

11.45 p.m.

The body of the President is moved by ambulance from his house to the Qubbah presidential palace.

Tuesday, 29 September
Amman

. . . and if the last task of that great man was to bandage the wounds

214

inflicted on our nation by the tragedy of Jordan, a country so dear to his heart, yet the wounds inflicted on Jordan and on the nation by his loss are proof against all healing and are beyond all comfort . . .

Al-Hussein Bin Tallal

The Arab World
All countries declare a forty-day period of mourning.

The Mediterranean
The manoeuvres of the Sixth Fleet are cancelled.

The Occupied Territories
Israeli forces open fire on massive demonstrations in Gaza, Jerusalem and other cities.

Cairo
Hundreds of thousands of mourners surround the Qubbah Palace.

Thursday, 1 October
Cairo
The President's body is moved by helicopter from the Qubbah palace to the Gezirah Sporting Club and then by ambulance to the headquarters of the Command Council of the Revolution where the funeral is planned to begin.

Lebanon
No newspapers come out.

The Arab World
Prayers are said for Gamal 'Abd el-Nasser in every mosque and every church.

Jordan
Jordanian artillery attacks Resistance bases in Irbid.

Jerusalem
Forty thousand Arabs walk in a funeral for 'Abd el-Nasser.

Cairo
The President's personal secretary, Mr Muhammad Ahmad, collapses and needs medical attention before returning to the funeral.
    Acting President Muhammad Anwar al-Sadat turns a weeping face to the media:

'I hope you are recording these terrible moments.'

Mrs Tahiyya 'Abd el-Nasser and the President's two daughters watch the funeral from the windows of the Arab Socialist Union building. Mrs 'Abd el-Nasser faints as the procession reaches the middle of Qasr el-Nil Bridge.

Mr Yassir Arafat, President Nur ed-Din al-Atasi, Mrs Bandaranaika, Emperor Bocasa, President Huari Boumédienne, M. Jacques Chaban Delmas, President Suleiman Frinjieh, Emperor Haile Selassie, President Charles Helu, Sir Alec Douglas-Home, Prime Minister Rashid Karami, Prime Minister Alexei Kosygin, Pope Kyrolos the Third, Archbishop Makarios, President Ja'far Numeiri, President Hirdan al-Takriti, President Wild-Dada and Marshal Zhakharov walk in the funeral as far as the Nile Hilton.

At the Mosque of Gamal 'Abd el-Nasser in Manshiat al-Bakri, the President's coffin is laid on a green carpet with his head towards Makkah. Prayers are said. The President's eldest son, Khalid 'Abd el-Nasser, accompanies his father's body into the tomb. The President's private secretary Mr Muhammad Ahmad goes with him. A MIG formation growls in the sky. The cannon fire twenty-one shots. The bugles play 'Sunset' and then a 'Reveille'.

'O ye confident and reassured soul, return contented unto thy Lord, to enter among My children and enter into My paradise. And verily God hath spoken.'

Scene 3

Saturday, 15 November 1970

Cairo

One o'clock but the sun is pale and weak. Cold gusts of wind rise occasionally, rustling the students' papers and making them reach out for heavy books and folders with which to weigh them down. There are no parasols now above the tables and the coarse check tablecloths are knotted at the corners to keep them in place. Chrissie, Asya, Noora and Mimi choose a table close to the wall of the coffee-shop and put their books down.

'I'll get tea,' Chrissie volunteers.

Asya follows her and Mimi and Noora sit down. Inside the coffee-shop Chrissie and Asya queue at the counter.

'What time is Saif coming?' Chrissie asks.

'Two-ish.'

'Are you skipping Drama?'

'I don't know. I don't think so.'

'Have you quarrelled?'

'No, not at all.' Asya picks up the tray and carries it out into the garden.

'Well, then? Why are you so quiet?'

'Nothing, really. Nothing particular, anyway.' She puts a glass of tea in front of each of them and hands out the sugar.

'Your heart is changing so soon?' Chrissie is only half joking.

'No, it isn't. But *he's* different.' Asya sits down. 'Since the first time he came to our house we haven't been alone once. He comes round and – well, basically, he visits my father or Kareem –'

'But that's what an engagement is for: it's for him and your family to get to know each other –'

'But he doesn't try to see me alone. Now that it would be so easy. We're supposed to be in love –'

'Of course you are. You *are* in love. And you ought to know that he loves you very much –'

'It's very obvious,' confirms Mimi.

Asya looks at Noora, but Noora smiles and shrugs. 'You've always been – what? Irked, by his – thoughtfulness.'

'It's just that he's not impulsive, that's all,' says Chrissie.

'Since when do you defend him so?' Asya asks.

'You're engaged to him. You've been in love with him for three and a half years and refused to look at anybody else. And now you're engaged. And I don't see anything wrong with his behaviour. He knows he should win your family over. And when you're married you'll have all the time in the world to be alone.'

'So you would be quite delighted if Fuad never tried to see you alone?'

'Asya! We're at the very beginning. We hardly know each other yet. And anyway, there he is, pushing for an engagement straight away –'

'Don't you want to get engaged?'

'I know what my father will say; he'll go on about his four pounds a month army pay. I think we should wait until he's out of the army and sorted out what he's going to do – and *then* talk to my father.'

'I suppose that *would* be wiser.'

'Of course. But tell *him* that. He's impatient. You're angry because Saif isn't impulsive. But impulsiveness brings a lot of troubles, I can tell you.'

'Well, *I* think it's more fun *not* to be engaged. So hang on to it.' Asya looks at Noora. 'You too.'

'I don't have much choice,' Noora says quietly. 'There wouldn't be any

217

point to an engagement. Next summer I'll leave home and Bassam and I will get married.'

'Will your father really never come round?'

Noora shakes her head.

'Never. I got my mother to sound him out slightly. Nothing direct. He said, "She would not be my daughter. I would have nothing to do with her." That's it.'

'But will your whole family follow your father? Your mother and your brothers?' Chrissie asks.

'They always do as he says.'

'But how can you manage without your family, Noora?' says Mimi. 'Bassam is very nice, mais enfin, you will always be your family's daughter –'

'That's a tautology,' Saif's voice says.

Mimi turns to look behind her.

'And you've brought Fuad with you! Well done!' cries Asya as Saif grins down at Mimi.

'Hello, Princess,' Saif says to Asya, and pulls a seat over from the next table. They all shift so that Saif sits next to Asya and Fuad sits next to Chrissie.

'How did you get away?' asks Chrissie. 'I thought you were on full alert?'

'Didn't you want to see me then?'

'Yes, but seriously,' Chrissie insists.

'I said I had to sign a legal document. I'll report back tonight. They're loosening up a bit anyway.'

'It's a new era,' Saif says, shaking out a Rothmans.

'It does feel like it a bit,' Fuad agrees.

Bassam and Hani and two other students join the group and the circle widens.

'We're going to get cosy with the Americans now –'

'Did you see the picture in the paper?'

'What picture?'

'A couple of days after the funeral. The American delegation offering their condolences. Eliot Richardson and Robert Murphy and Sadat. All three with big grins on their faces.'

'I noticed that. And Mahmoud Riadh was there too. Only he wasn't smiling.'

'Well, Sadat's been smiling ever since the funeral.'

'Elected by a majority of 90.04 per cent.'

'At least it wasn't 99.999 –'

'And photographs of Mona and Khalid 'Abd el-Nasser voting. Poor guys.'

'I can't stand all that "Gamal" this and "Gamal" that. I bet he never called him "Gamal" to his face.'

'And all the photographs of him praying. Down in his village.'

'It's all so phoney.'

'You've heard the joke about Sadat in the Qubbah palace?'

'Yeah, we've all heard it –'

'No we haven't. Go on, go on.'

'Well, they'd just transported the President over from his house and got him down the stairs and stuffed him into the kitchen fridge –'

'Look, come on –'

'When Hussein el-Shaf'i noticed that Sadat was nowhere to be seen. He went looking for him. He looked everywhere, then he opened the door to the main drawing-room and found him dancing in front of the mirror singing, "I've become a *Pre*-si-dent, I've become a *Pre*-si-dent –" '

'Have you heard the one about the chap screaming at the Chief's funeral?'

'Look, forty-six people died in that funeral. De Gaulle's funeral was nothing beside –'

'Well, this chap was going crazy, screaming and wailing, "Let me *see-ee* him, let me *see-ee* him," and they thought he was mad, but he went on clutching at the coffin and yelling, "I need to *see-ee* him, I need to *see-ee* him," and they said OK, he's a poor fellow, let him see him. So they opened the coffin lid and he looked in and he said, "That's the son of a bitch. Bury him." '

They are all silent for a bit, then Chrissie says, 'Well, God have mercy on his soul.'

'It was Jordan that killed him,' says Bassam.

'It was sixty-seven that killed him –'

'The defeat. And then everything that came out about his Intelligence Services and 'Abd el-Hakim 'Amer –'

'He set them up in the first place. He gave them power –'

'That must have made it worse. He must have been so disappointed –' Asya says.

'He's had many disappointments. Starting with Syria.'

'But even after that it still looked like it might all come together. Him and Nehru and Sukarno, the non-aligned world realising its potential. The whole African thing: Patrice Lumumba and Jomo Kenyatta and Nkrumah –'

Asya leans over to Saif. 'Are you free for the afternoon?'

'No, sweetie, I'm sorry. I've got to go back to work. I'm giving an extra class at four. I'll pass by you later.'

'Well, it's all fallen apart rapido. Every bit of it.'

'He did try, to the end, to hold it together. Remember in Tripoli in June? He warned the Iraqis then that it was no time for playing games –'

'Those appeals he sent to Hussein –'

'*He's* a dirty double-dealer.'

'Look, guys, don't you think you're talking a bit too –'

'Hussein's a survivor.'

'The man is still warm in his grave and Hussein's got his Patons blasting the Ashrafiyya Hospital –'

'And next day the British agree to supply him with fresh arms.'

'It stinks.'

'What do you mean it stinks? It's politics. They all play it.'

'The people in the camps don't play it. The soldiers who get blown to bits aren't playing –'

Chrissie leans over to Asya. 'We're going to slip away. You'll cover for me? And if you do attend Drama please take notes.'

'Sure,' says Asya.

'Even some leaders seem clean. Allende seems OK.'

'He sounds like he's got it right: "Socialism within Liberty".'

'I guess the Chief didn't concentrate too well on the "Liberty".'

'And socialism can't work. Ever.'

'Why? Why not? It's only its application –'

'Oh no, not that again.'

'But it's true –'

'Have you been following the lists of visitors to the grave?' says Saif. 'It's wonderful. It could be straight out of the fourteenth century: "The Merchants of Sudan, The Clergy of Lebanon, Palestinian Women, The Musicians, The Priests Led by Pope Kyrolos, The Peasants and Workers of the Land, The Sixteen Tribes of the Sinai . . ." '

Scene 4

January 1971
Alexandria

It was cold as we walked through the 'Attareen. The winds of Amsheer had not yet started to blow but the air was thin and crisp. The sun was out but it was not strong enough to dry the puddles left by yesterday's rain; it lit up the grey asphalt and the tired houses with that dark, indirect light that warns of storms to come. Each time we passed a coffee-house a warm breath gusted out at us, loaded with the smell of charcoal and sweet tobacco, and we could hear the clatter of saucers and trays landing on marble table-tops and the voice of Ummu Kulthoum trailed us from doorway to doorway:

'How can I forget her while my heart
Continues to beat in my side?
This is the story of my love —'

Sometimes we walked together, although of course we could not touch or laugh
or even look at each other for too long. But mostly she walked ahead and I
watched her ankles as her polished black shoes delicately avoided the puddles, the
orange-peel and the treacherously solid-seeming paving-tiles that could suddenly give way under your weight. I watched the flow of her soft, blue woollen
skirt and her hands clasped behind her with my gold band shining on the third
finger of her right hand.

Her grandfather led the way in a quick shuffle, never bothering to really lift
his feet off the ground; keeping his head down but sometimes half lifting his
hand to acknowledge the greetings of shopkeepers who knew him. Hamid Mursi,
his son, walked next to me, holding himself rigidly upright, the steel rims of his
spectacles glinting, his crushed left hand removed from its glove and pushed into
the pocket of his trousers.

It was a Friday, just after prayers, and the streets were almost empty. A small
boy from an ironing shop kicked at a stone as he carried his load of pressed
washing on the cardboard sheet and eyed three other small boys playing with bits
of scrap near a garage. The shopkeepers sat in the doorways of shops, huddled in
their overcoats, drinking hot tea and swatting at lazy, insistent winter flies.

There was still good stuff to be picked up in those days. The latest big exodus
had been just over three years before and things that had been left behind were
now being sold off. The antique shops in 'Attareen were crammed with beds and
dining-tables that had stood for three generations in the homes of Greek or
Italian – or even well-off Egyptian – families: large, ornate, self-conscious pieces
that were doomed to look out of place in any setting they were now likely to
occupy. Straight chairs separated from their carvers, tables that had lost their
sideboards; stacked without dignity, they loomed sullenly at us out of shadowy
corners. 'Les choses'. I kept expecting to see my furniture there: mine and Didi's.
And when it wasn't there I imagined it still shrouded under white sheets in the
darkened spare room of the flat in Ibrahimiyya.

In one shop she pushed her sunglasses to the top of her head and bent to look
inside a sideboard. She closed the door and cupped her hand around the carved
nose of the wooden lion that served as a handle and stroked it twice with her
thumb. She looked up at me. It was an oak dining-room. Intact. A massive
draw-leaf table, two sideboards, a drinks cabinet and twelve chairs. It was dark
with age and roaring lions burst out of its every surface. The chairs needed re-
upholstering. We walked out of the shop and when we had walked maybe twenty
paces she said, 'What do you think?' I said, 'I like it.' She plucked at her
grandfather's sleeve. 'The dining-room, Geddu; the heavy, dark one.' Her uncle
said, 'Yes. It is a good room.' He looked strained and the perspiration was
standing out on his forehead in spite of the cold. Her grandfather said nothing,

but after a few more steps he turned around. We all sauntered back past the shop and we walked on while he went inside. In a window full of junk I saw a beautiful enamelled pistol. I pointed it out to her and she went in. She had to touch it. 'It's so smooth,' she said, looking at me wonderingly, 'and so heavy.' But she was content to leave it there. We saw her grandfather walking down the street towards us and the dining-room was ours.

It felt like the end of something. 'Yesterday all the past.' It felt like another part of a closing chapter that had started in 1967 – before I had even met her. That whole autumn and winter. 'Abd el-Nasser dead. Sinai captured. The opera house burnt down. I have the photos I took on that early morning: the dove-white building a scorched ruin, three slim white chairs covered in red velvet lying on their sides in the drive, the marble staircase intact.

I thought that she understood.

That day in Alexandria we also bought a carved desk and some sofas and chairs with feather cushions and inlaid work and a couple of screens. We did not see a bed that we liked.

VĬ

May - July 1971

The head of his instrument was no sooner fixed in the opening, when by four or five sudden shoves he contrived to insert the head entirely. At this moment his penetration was not deep enough to cause me great pain, but he, well knowing what was coming, forcibly secured one of his arms around my body. Everything was now prepared and favourable. He began to improve his advantage by forcibly deepening his penetration; his prodigious stiffness and size gave me such dreadful anguish that I could not refrain from screaming. In my agony I strove to escape, but the Dey easily foiled me by his able thrusts, and quickly buried his tremendous instrument far within me. He followed up his movements with fury until at length one merciless, violent thrust broke in and carried all before him, and sent it imbued, reeking with the blood of my virginity, up to its utmost length in my body. The piercing shriek I gave proclaimed that I felt it up to the very quick; in short, his victory was complete.

— THE LUSTFUL TURK

Scene 1

Wednesday, 19 May 1971
Cairo

'What happened?' asks Chrissie.

Chrissie and Asya are sitting in Asya's mother's car. They can use the car all the time right now because Asya's parents are in Europe. The car is parked in Falaki Square.

'But what happened?' Chrissie asks again. Asya had come out of the doctor's office looking pale and drawn. She had put the ten pounds down in front of the receptionist and just motioned to Chrissie, who sat in the waiting-room. Then she had walked stiffly but hurriedly down the worn old stairs and out into the street. They had walked in silence to the car and got in. And now, although the car was absolutely sweltering, she just sat there with the key in the ignition and stared through the windscreen. Chrissie winds down her window and fans herself with today's *al-Ahram*.

'Well? Tell me,' she says. 'Tell me what happened.'

Chrissie's mind is quickly going through every possible reason for Asya to be upset. The doctor couldn't have made a pass at her; he is an old man, respected and grand and known to both their families. Could he have found something that would prevent Asya marrying Saif in two months' time? But what could that be? Incompatibilities were found through blood tests, not through twenty minutes in the surgery. Chrissie could only think that the doctor had examined Asya and found she wasn't a virgin and said he would tell her parents. But that would mean that Asya had been lying to Chrissie and that was just not possible.

'Look,' she says, 'let's at least go and sit somewhere and have a cold drink; I'm going to die.'

'Oh, I'm sorry, Chrissie, I'm sorry,' says Asya, and winds down her window, starts the car and eases it out into the rush-hour traffic. Fiats, NSUs and the odd Austin crawl around the oval square. She switches on the ventilator and it blows out clouds of hot dust. A beige 1300 has broken down in the middle of the road and the driver stands in front of the open bonnet mopping his face with a handkerchief. The steam from his boiling radiator breaks up the air in front of him into zigzags of pale blue and pink. As the other cars inch past him men lean out with advice and jokes and instructions.

'She's a bitch, the thirteen hundred. Can't stand the heat.'

'Don't come near her lest she burn out the whole engine for you. Wait till she's cooled down.'

'How's she going to cool down in this sun of hell? Push her into the shade.'

'Get her out of the way, man, people want to get home.'

A tram crawls slowly out of Shari' Mazloum and clangs its way into the middle of the square. A small crowd of pedestrians gather round the broken-down car and two men transform themselves into traffic police and hold up the already almost stationary cars while others help the driver to push the Fiat towards the kerb.

'I went to him for contraceptives,' says Asya. 'For the pill. Right?'

'Yes.'

'Why does he have to examine me?'

'Did he examine you?'

'Yes.'

'And?'

'And nothing. He said, "Well, that all seems fine. Of course I can't really get in there because of the hymen. But everything seems perfectly fine." Well, I *knew* that everything was fine. I mean, I didn't go to him with a complaint or anything. Just to get started on the pill. And I don't know why we needed to go through all this.'

Chrissie waits. The car is inching along again now. They are round the southern point of the square and Asya sees a break in the traffic and makes for Shari' Hoda Sha'rawi, which is usually not too bad, but as they turn into it they find that that too is at a standstill.

'Look!' says Chrissie. 'There's a space. Why don't you park and we'll walk to AUC for a drink?'

Chrissie sticks her arm out of the window and Asya edges the car across the hooting traffic and backs into the empty space outside a mechanic's workshop. She gets out and looks around but there's no one in the shop. She looks at Chrissie. Chrissie pulls a face.

'I didn't see the workshop. We'd better not.'

'They've gone to lunch.'

'They'll come back.'

'You think we might come back and find the tyres emptied?'

'It's possible.'

Asya looks at the traffic. 'Come on, Chrissie. We won't be long.'

It is just after half past two. They turn the corner and walk up Falaki Square. As they pass the coffee-shop the news blares out at them from the radio: '– masked gunmen forced their way into the home of the Israeli Consul-General. They tied up everybody in the house, then took the Consul in their car and fled through the streets of Istanbul –' Chrissie and Asya pause. '– Sources say the men are members of the Turkish "People's Liberation Army". In Jerusalem, Israeli Mayor Teddy Kolech admitted that Israel has expelled thousands of Arabs from Arab Jerusalem since it took control of the city after the aggression of 1967.

He declared that more Arabs would be expelled in implementation of Israel's Zionist decision to transform Jerusalem into a completely Jewish city –'

They cross the square again. The wind is hot and dusty and their skirts stick to their legs.

'Aren't the Khamaseen supposed to be over now?'

'They're getting longer and longer every year.'

'You need to spend the whole day under the shower in this weather.'

'Or in the pool.'

In Jawad Husni Street they have to walk in the narrow road because of the cars parked nose to bumper on the pavement. A van goes past and they flatten themselves against a parked car and burn the backs of their arms against the metal. Outside the huge wooden doors of the second campus of the American University they squeeze between two cars and enter. Although they are not students here, the Nubian doorman can't be bothered with questions and waves them through with a gentle smile. In the marble hall the air is immediately cooler and free of dust. They find two cane chairs in the cloister and Asya goes to fetch two bottles of fizzy orange and two slices of English cake.

'He didn't *need* to examine me,' says Asya, when she comes back.

'How do you know?' says Chrissie.

'Well, what might he have found? He said from the start that I couldn't have an IUD until after I'd had a baby. And he couldn't fit me with a diaphragm until at least three months after I was married. So that just leaves the pill. What could he have found in there that would have told him I shouldn't take the pill?'

'*I* don't know,' says Chrissie. 'But he's a doctor. Maybe there are things that he can see –'

'He didn't even want to put me *on* the pill. Gave me this sermon about how it was best to have a baby right away, for God's sake.'

'Well you know –'

'Yes, I know that's what you think too. And of course that's what Tante Soraya thinks and Dada Zeina and everybody. And Tante Adeela too if she weren't too frightened of Saif to say anything about it.'

'What I was going to say,' says Chrissie patiently, 'was: you know he doesn't have any children. The doctor. It's a big tragedy in his life.'

'It's still no reason to want *me* to have one right away. It won't make any difference to him.'

Chrissie looks at Asya, who has thrown her head against the back of her chair and closed her eyes behind her sunglasses. Her hair is gathered into a long ponytail to keep it away from her face and neck in the heat. She is in her loose beige skirt and white shirt with the brown leather belt she brought back from Italy. Her clothes have become much more subdued in the last two years. She hardly ever wears patterns any more;

227

just plain colours, with very occasionally the odd tiny flower. Saif's engagement ring is on her right hand and the Omega he gave her on her left wrist. Her nails are the matt beige which he prefers. Her bare legs are stretched out and her toenails in the open brown shoes are the same beige. Chrissie raises her drink to her mouth. Asya opens her eyes.

'You and Fuad are going to start a baby the minute you get married, aren't you?'

'Asya. What *is* the matter?'

Asya leans forward and picks a crumb from her plate. She frowns at it, then dusts it off the tip of her finger back on to the plate. Her slice of cake lies untouched.

'I hated it. I hated lying there and being poked at. And I hated being lectured. And Chrissie, it's all meant to be spontaneous. People are supposed not to be able to *help* it, you know, Hetty Sorrel and all that, can't *stop* themselves. And this is just so – so – *deliberate*. And then to be talking about babies – before we've even done it –'

'Well, you'll do it soon enough.'

'I know, I know, but – I do so wish it were different.'

'This is marriage. It can't be any other way.'

'I know – but if we could have just moved in together straight after we'd met. When I used to sit across the table from him at the Omar Khayyam and watch his hands and long for them to touch me. Or even got married – since we live in this country. But *then* – straight away.'

'Well, you're getting married now. You're still you and he's still him and you're getting married soon, so why are you so upset?'

'It isn't even going to be soon.'

'What do you mean? Why not?'

'Everything's taking for ever to get ready.'

'I thought you'd got most of your things.'

'We got a lot of things in Alexandria but we couldn't find a bedroom we liked so Grandfather is making one for us – to Saif's design. I don't know when that will be finished. And then there's all the embroidery and stuff, and Chrissie, I didn't tell you – you know Tante Soraya is having this silk bedspread crocheted for us?'

'Yes. You said it was all separate flowers and then they're joined together.'

'Well, I went with her to see the lady who's making it and it was dreadful.'

'What, the bedspread?'

'No. No. The – everything. She's got no legs. Can you imagine? The lady who's making it. We went through a hundred alleys in Darb el-Barabra – all muddy with sewage – and we went up the most evil staircase and into this nasty flat and there she was. And she's got no legs. She's plump and smiling and looks like Dada Zeina – except she's got

228

both eyes – but she's got no legs. No legs *at all*: two short fat stumps under her bottom, and she's got this tiny gilded drawing-room we had to sit in, and she propelled herself around with her hands and made us tea. And we sat there and all around us were little mounds of creamy silk flowers.'

'But Asya –'

'Wait. And she had six children. And her husband is old and senile: he was sitting in a corner being fed rice pudding by one of his daughters and his eyes were all watery and he was drooling on to his chest – I swear, you could see the dribble in one thin continuous line from his lips to his *galabiyya*, and the kid was shovelling the food in for him. And the smallest child – listen – is five months old. He was lying there with a bare bottom.'

'Asya.'

'*And* she's pregnant.'

'Asya –'

'Well, it's all *true*. She has no legs. She lives in this *awful* squalor but with this – this *travesty* of a drawing-room. She has to sleep with the most disgusting old man I've ever seen – ever *imagined*. She has to somehow deliver herself of his children. And she spends her days crocheting silk flowers for my bedspread.'

'She must be glad of the work. How would she live without it?'

'That's what Tante Soraya said. She wasn't fazed by it at all. But, Chrissie, it's not right.'

'What isn't right?'

'Chrissie, it shouldn't *be* like this.'

'But *what* shouldn't be like this? That's how the world *is*. This is her lot. She's putting up with it and God comes to her help. He sends her your aunt to help her. He sends her your bedspread –'

'I don't even *want* it any more.'

'So you'll take the job away from her?'

'No, of course not.' Asya looks down and kicks the leg of the table.

'Well then, what? What's the use of not having it when it's made? How will that help her? How do you know the circumstances of all the people who make your other things? You just happened to see this one.'

'I know.' Asya has put her head on the back of the seat again and closed her eyes. 'Chrissie, it seems to me there's not very much one can do about anything.'

'You were perfectly fine an hour ago. Why are you so upset? Just because the doctor examined you?'

'Yes. It was horrible. He even had a light shining on – me.'

'Well, it's over now and you won't need to do that again until you have your first baby. Asya, you do want children, don't you?'

'Yes. I guess I do. Of course I do. I mean, I can't imagine being forty and not having had a child. But I don't want one right now and neither does Saif. In fact *he* doesn't want children at all. Ever. He says they frighten him.'

'He'll want them. Men always do.'

'Does Fuad?'

'My dear, he wants five!'

'Chrissie!'

'He does, it's true.'

Asya looks at Chrissie, comfortable in her green shirt-waister, her sunglasses pushed to the top of her head, her large handbag bulging with neatly written notes for last-minute studying.

'Well, you'll be a brilliant mother: very practical and down-to-earth and you'll see they get their homework done neatly and –'

'Oh, I won't have five.' Chrissie smiles. 'Two will be enough. Maybe three. Fuad, as long as he gets one boy, he'll be OK. Anyway, I don't even know how he's going to afford to feed them. He won't do it on his army pay.'

'He's only got another three months in the army.'

'And then what? A junior engineer in some company or some factory. He can't hope to earn very much –'

'I've heard him and Saif talk about setting up something together –'

'They're in completely different areas.'

'But they're good friends and they trust each other. And it's all technical stuff –'

'Projects!' Chrissie says with a smile.

'Chrissie, what's wrong with projects? The biggest things start with two people talking or one person dreaming –'

'Dreaming is right. Well, they'll both have to do more than dream.'

'I know. Saif already behaves as if he's got millions. You know, when we were shopping for furniture in Alexandria he saw this fantastic gun – did I tell you?'

Chrissie shakes her head.

'It was beautiful: all inlaid with mother-of-pearl and really beautiful – and very old. He went back to Alex next week and bought it.'

'How much did he spend?'

'I don't know. He wouldn't tell me. But it can't have been less than a hundred.'

Chrissie raises her eyebrows and speaks in what Asya has come to think of as her 'Tante Soraya' manner. 'You'll have to put a stop to all that, my dear, and to his smoking. He smokes far too much.' She looks at her watch. 'Come on, we ought to go. The traffic should be better now and we've got poetry tomorrow, remember?'

'Oh, Chrissie, Chrissie, it's the last exam,' sings Asya as she jumps up. She pulls at the strap of her friend's handbag:

'Let's go to a movie tomorrow. Let's see *Borsalino*.'

That night

O my America! my new-found-land,
My kingdome, safeliest when with one man man'd,
My Myne of precious stones, My Emperie –

'Asya!' says Mimi. 'You're looking at the wrong book.'

Chrissie and Noora both look up. Bassam is working alone in a far corner of Asya's father's study. His notes are on a table in front of him. On the floor by his chair lies a folded copy of today's *al-Ahram*. He is able to be there because of Asya's parents being away. 'That book was for the second year,' Mimi goes on.

'Leave Asya alone,' says Chrissie. 'She doesn't even need to study this stuff.'

'I thought,' says Asya, 'we might get a question on influences and all that.'

'Influences?'

'Well, you know, how Eliot was influenced by the seventeenth century –'

Mimi looks anxiously at Chrissie, who sucks on her pencil and gives Asya a warning look.

'He wouldn't do that, would he?' asks Mimi. 'We've only done the twentieth century this year –'

'You're supposed to remember *all* of it,' says Asya. 'Not just what we did this year. And it's a completely obvious question' – ignoring Chrissie's look – ' "T. S. Eliot states that the body of poetry is organic, discuss with reference to his own poems." '

'Chrissie, Chrissie, do you think he'll do this?'

'It's all right,' says Chrissie. 'You'll have a choice. You'll be asked to answer only three questions out of at least five.'

'But I haven't even looked at what we've done in the other years and if he gives us anything from outside –'

Asya has picked up her twentieth-century anthology: 'Her hair over her arms and her arms full of flowers.' If she were to stop them. If she were to stop them and read this to them aloud. To say forget the exam and the essay questions and the unseen text. Just listen. Listen:

She turned away, but with the autumn weather
Compelled my imagination many days,
Many days and many hours:
Her hair over her arms and her arms full of flowers.

She takes a deep breath. This *has* to be what matters. Or a large part of what matters. How can people read it and just go on as though they'd been reading the newspaper or some geography lesson that they had to memorise? But if they said, well, what's so great about that? If they

231

couldn't feel it for themselves? Then how would you tell them? Asya looks at Chrissie. Chrissie at least has preferences. She'll say she likes one poem more than another, but she won't read a poem for the pleasure of it. She might read a novel for pleasure. But not a poem. Mimi is just waiting till she's got her degree so she can stop reading altogether. Asya isn't being unkind or bitchy. Mimi had said it herself: after the exams she doesn't want ever to see another book again. Noora will read. Even now, with Bassam in the same room, Noora sits lost in her books. She sits well back in the armchair with one ankle comfortably over her knee like a man. When her mother objects she says, 'But I'm wearing trousers – what does it matter how I cross my legs?' She has taken to wearing trousers all the time because she never can remember to sit politely with her legs together. Beige gabardines mostly, loose and going-into-the-desert type. She still has her long braid flung over her shoulder and still has to be roused from her dreams every time you want to speak to her. She possesses eight different editions of the *Seven Pillars of Wisdom* and has read *Arabia Deserta* through, and one day a policeman had come upon her sitting on a boulder gazing up at the middle pyramid after dark. The word 'boulder' always makes Asya think of a joke that puzzles her. Saif had told it to her. It was a cartoon he'd seen some-where in which a Stone Age man speaks to this big stone and says, 'Boulder, boulder on the ground, tell me something most profound' – only it's not 'most' it's something else which Asya has forgotten, and she puts 'most' in there for the rhythm – and the boulder says, 'What's to tell?' He thinks it is very funny and she can see it is sort of funny but not that funny. She's tried it out on a couple of people, and both times they laughed a lot so she knows she is missing the point – unless they were being extra polite – but she can't at all find any point beyond the obvious one that even the speaking boulder didn't think anything was profound . . .

Noora stretches and yawns. Bassam glances up and smiles at her across the room. No one knows what's going to happen to them after the exams. Her father has now specifically said that if she marries Bassam al-Husseini he will disown her. Both Asya's mother and Tante Muneera think he won't really; can't. She's his only daughter. He has three sons but only one daughter. How can he disown her? And how can her mother possibly let him?

'Tante Saliha isn't that strong, Mummy, and Noora's father is a very powerful man. Noora herself thinks he might do it. She says if he forbids her mother to see her, her mother will be too frightened to disobey him.'

'And still she is going to marry Bassam?'

Asya nods. Lateefa had pushed her glasses back on to her nose. 'Well, he is a good boy. Even though he's not an "A" student like her.'

'He writes these wonderful sad poems. And he's already published.'

'If she gets an "A" this year as well she'll get a job in the university. But what will he do?'

'He's told her he's going to work with the Organisation.'

'He's going to work with the PLO?'

'Not fighting. In their broadcasting service.'

'No wonder Manesterli Bey is going up the wall.'

'What can Bassam do? No, really. The way he sees it, if he takes any ordinary job – even if anybody would give him an ordinary job – then it's like pretending he's not Palestinian; as though none of what's happening over there is anything to do with him –'

'His brothers are working in Kuwait.'

'But he's different. He would have gone back to Nablus and lived with his mother in their old house and hung on and tried to build a life there writing and all that – but because of Noora he'll stay here, but he has to stay involved –'

'Noora's letting herself in for a lifeful of problems.'

'She says she can't side with Israel and King Hussein against him. She was joking but it's also kind of true –'

Noora looks up and sees Asya looking at her. 'I hope we get a question about the poetry of war. Some of it is amazing,' she says. She pushes her open book over to Asya:

Are limbs, so dear achieved, are sides,
Full-nerved – still warm – too hard to stir?
Was it for this the clay grew tall?

Asya closes the book gently and glances at Bassam. She had wondered since she had met him – what was it *really* like to be him? To be so displaced? He was born in 1949; one year after the partition and the war. He'd grown up in Nablus and since 1967 his family – and he in the summer holidays – had been living under occupation. Actual physical occupation. What would that be like? To have people, Norwegians, say, or Iraqis or Chinese, or, indeed – why go far? the Israelis themselves, stop you, say, at the gate of the Gezira Club, and say, 'Sorry. You can't come in here any more. You are banned.' Because taking over the Gezira Club would be the first thing anyone would do if they took over Cairo. You would just have to turn around and walk back home. And you would never even be sure of home anyway because any day, any minute, they might knock on the door and say, 'We are taking over this house. You have one hour to pack.' Like in *Dr Zhivago*. So where would we go? To Grandfather's, I suppose. But it would be really weird. And he was living with it. There was no place that he could assume he would be in ten, five, one year's time. If he went back to Nablus and walked down a street to buy a newspaper he could not assume that he would be able to walk down that same street again the next day. And that was why when you looked at him it seemed, despite the good looks, the mixture of French and Turkish with curly black hair, green eyes and a slightish build, he appeared almost – maimed. One of a bruised people. All those bruised people: Palestinians, Armenians, Kurds, and of course the Jews themselves – and who knows what others would be added to the list; what others were in the making right now. Amazing, really, and frightening, so frightening, to think of all the things that are happening right now. Right now as they sit here studying for their poetry exam: secret deals being arranged in government departments, counterdeals in secret service meetings, ignorant armies moving silently by night, people being thrown out of their houses, babies being born, people being tortured – this is the point where Asya's mind starts to do a loop. People being tortured. Right now. As we sit here. Tortured. And what do we do? We go on studying for our exams. And millions of others. They must think of this once in a while – and they go on doing what they're doing. But what else is to be done? What *can* be done? Can you get up right now and rush off to some prison – assuming you know where one is – and hammer at the door? 'Let them out, let them out' – or at least, 'Stop what you're doing.' No. No, well, of course not, that's stupid – and yet how can you just go on sitting here while someone somewhere is having live wires pushed up his rectum, his teeth pulled out of his head, her vagina stuffed with hungry rats, or having to watch her baby's head being smashed against the –

Asya jumps up. She always jumps up when she gets to this bit. Now she goes out on to the balcony and stands holding on to the stone balustrade and breathing fast and looking at the lights of the Officers' Club. She daren't look up at the sky because the darkness and the stars will make her think of how the earth is a tiny ball spinning round and round in space, and space is something that she cannot even begin to imagine. The lights of the Officers' Club always make her think of Khalu Hamid's accident; of how she watched him cut through the petrol station on the corner and closed her shutters and lay down on her bed while at that very moment his life was being ruined by an army truck that stopped a second too late. Across the road, on the second floor of the Pharmacie Nouvelle Victoria building, she can see a boy sitting at a table with a book lying open under the light of a desk-lamp – 'something amazing – a boy falling out of the sky' – so right, so *right*, it said it all, but apart from poetry – what? What did you actually *do*? Campaign? Where and how and who would permit it, and even if anything worked, by the time it did the people to whom it was happening right now would be dead – or if they weren't dead they would have suffered that much more. Suffered. How odd it is, this word. 'Suffer' the little children to come unto me. You also 'suffered' from headaches, from disappointments, from delusions. And people under torture 'suffered' too. When Savak forced you down on to a hot steel grid you 'suffered'. When the Israeli police broke your arms and legs you 'suffered'. And here? She'd heard that in 1954 men from the Muslim Brotherhood had been pumped up, blown full of water and then guys had jumped on their stomachs and exploded them. She'd heard that 'Abd el-Nasser had known what was being done even if he hadn't ordered it. And as for the Communists – her father had not been tortured in jail in 1942, but Khalu Hamid had a few years later. Who dreamed up these things? Not the knocking about, the punching, anyone could do that. But the advanced stuff. Who sat there and drew up a blueprint for a nifty little machine that would make pulling out finger-nails more efficient: slower perhaps and jerky – oh oh oh. She bends over her stomach then straightens up again. How could you *be* someone who actually does it? Asya can imagine doing anything – or almost anything – in the heat of the moment or under terrible immediate pressure. She can imagine killing in anger; or cutting up a body and eating it if you were on a desert island and starving to death. But this? You would be a perfectly normal person, eat your breakfast in the morning and drink your tea with two spoonfuls of sugar, see your kids off to school, choose what you were going to wear – 'I'll wear the blue and white shirt today; the thin stripes' – shave and get dressed – maybe even say your morning prayers – and set off for work. And when you got there you would take off your jacket, roll up your thin-striped sleeves and go into a bare windowless room where you started stripping a guy and blindfolding him, cursing and abusing him of course as you went along –

'Asya! Is something the matter? Do you have a tummy-ache?'

Asya lets her arms drop to her sides as she turns to face Deena who is standing in the lit doorway of the balcony. Behind her she can see her father's desk with the big empty swivelling captain's chair and in front of the desk Mimi, Noora and Chrissie each in her armchair grouped around the big coffee-table. On the table in the middle of all the books and papers is the polished silver tray on which Deena has brought them tea and breadsticks and yoghurt and honey. In the far corner Bassam is heavily underscoring some passage in his notebook. As the light falls on Asya's face Deena moves forward.

'Asya, what is it? You look awful. You've gone green.'

Asya can tell Deena anything – almost anything. Deena has been comforting her sister through her panics since she was seven and Asya was thirteen. Asya would wake up in the night and her first thought as she lay in the dark would be that she mustn't think about death. Not now. This would be a bad moment to think about death. Everything was so still and quiet. There would be nothing to distract her. Nothing to stop her. So she mustn't think about it. Because if she did she would not be able to stop, to skirt it in some way, to get round it. There would be no escape. Absolutely no escape. She would have to come face to face with the fact that one day she would speak to her mother and her mother would not answer. One day Lateefa wouldn't rouse herself from the book she was reading and push her glasses back on to her nose and say, 'What do you want now?' No. She would never, ever, answer. Never never never *never*. And there would be a stretch of Asya's life, days and weeks and years of her life, when she would want her mother, *need* her mother, and her mother would not be found. Her mother would be – nowhere. *Nowhere*. For ever. It would be a state that had no end. No possibility – not the tiniest little tiny crack through which a possibility of comfort could come through. And it would end only when Asya herself was dead. And now terror. Terror of being under the octagonal marble *shahid* that stands in the centre of the family mausoleum. Of being carried there and then being taken out of the coffin and taken through the trapdoor and left down there in the dark for ever and ever and ever. That is the end of it. The end of it all. And it *must* come – it *will* come. Asya does not speak about this. It is too terrible to speak about. Once she had spoken to her father. She had been fourteen and she had gone into his study and asked him seriously whether he thought there was anything afterwards and he had said no. So she had asked him how he could bear to go from one minute to the next knowing that it would all end, and he had said that that was the only choice he had. And she had asked, but how could he get it out of his mind? How come he was not constantly thinking of the dreadfulness of it all? And her father had eventually had no answer, and she had seen his eyes go red, and that was the only time she had ever seen that, and he would not look at her any more, so she knew that there really was no answer and no secret comfort and that it was indeed as terrible as she thought it was and she didn't speak about it any more. Except to Deena when she woke up in the middle of the night and her sister heard her and crept into her bed, and Asya would shake with fear and with a sort of terrible 'missing her parents in advance' kind of feeling, but after a while it would seem quite funny to her: both of them sitting in their nighties on the single bed in the middle of the night with books on the desk and tomorrow's school clothes hanging neatly behind the door and Mummy and Daddy asleep next door, and Deena listening patiently to Asya for the hundredth time, and then she would start to giggle and it would be over. But she cannot imagine what she would have done if Deena hadn't been there.

Asya stretches out her hand to Deena's face.

'Why are you looking so worried? There's nothing the matter at all. It was just really hot in there. You've brought us some tea, darling, thank you.'

As Asya and Deena walk back into the room the doorbell rings. They are expecting Fuad to come and pick up Chrissie. Deena goes to the door and with her hand on the knob looks casually through the spy-hole. Then she turns, her face transformed, and waves urgently at Bassam with one hand, the index finger of the other placed warningly on her lips. Bassam leaps up and starts collecting his papers. Deena is pointing at Chrissie and then stretching her arm upwards to indicate a great height above her head, and the girls understand that it is Chrissie's father at the door. Asya moves over to Bassam and whispers, 'Leave the books. Quick.' Mimi whispers, 'Go into the bathroom and lock the door.' 'No,' whispers Chrissie, 'supposing he needs the bathroom?' 'Go into Kareem's room,' whispers Asya. 'Quick. Turn out the light and close the door.'

Deena is hopping up and down with one hand on the doorknob. The doorbell goes again. She hears Kareem's door shut softly and turns the knob. Sidki al-Tarabulsi is standing in the vestibule outside. Asya approaches the door.

'Uncle Sidki! What a nice surprise! This is a precious step! Welcome, welcome! Please come in.'

As he comes through the door, Chrissie rises.

'Father! Good evening!' And then, 'Is something the matter?'

'No, no.' Sidki al-Tarabulsi stands large in the middle of the room. He shakes hands with Mimi and Noora who have both come forward to greet him. After each handshake he places his hand on his heart and makes a slight bow. 'Fuad phoned at home and said they've cancelled all leave for two weeks. They've even got orders not to allow phone-calls, but he managed. Anyway, your mother started to fret and phoned me at the office so I said I'd come and get you.'

'I wish Mama wouldn't fret so,' says Chrissie. 'I'm at Asya's after all.'

'In any case, it gives us an opportunity to see you,' says Asya quickly. 'Do sit down, Uncle. I'll make you some tea. The kettle was just boiling.'

'There's no need, Asya –'

'So you will come and go like this without my offering you anything? Please sit. I won't be a minute.'

In the kitchen Asya makes a pot of tea and pours out two glasses. She puts two spoonfuls of sugar into each one, stirs it, then puts the glasses on to a small tray and carries them into the interior of the flat. At Kareem's room she stops and knocks, then turns the handle quietly and puts her head round the door. Kareem is sitting on his bed and Bassam is in the armchair. Deena has joined them and is sitting at Kareem's desk. Only the desk-lamp is lit, and it is turned towards the wall. They are talking, but stop when the door opens.

'Are you all right?' whispers Asya, offering Bassam a glass of tea.

'Perfectly,' he whispers back. He smiles. 'Don't look so worried; I'm perfectly happy here.'

Asya offers the second glass to Kareem and says to Deena, 'I didn't know you were here.'

'It's all right,' Deena says. 'I don't want any tea.'

Asya goes back to the kitchen and pours out a third glass of tea. She places it on a small silver tray and puts the silver sugar-bowl next to it. She puts a spoon in the sugar-bowl and another on the tray next to the glass and goes back to her father's study.

Chrissie's father has sat down in the chair now empty of Bassam and picked up the newspaper that has been lying on the floor.

'Look at this: it's three times its normal size and there's nothing in it. Messages of support and pictures of the rabble they've picked up from the streets and deposited in front of Qubba palace: "The masses continue to pour upon Qubba palace from every corner of the Republic to express unconditional approval of all President Muhammad Anwar el-Sadat's latest measures and pledge etc. etc." Fifty piastres is what each of these beggars is worth. And tomorrow we'll get another instalment of The Mystery of the Tapes.'

Asya places the tray on the table near him. He folds the paper and puts it back on the floor.

'So, what exam have you got tomorrow?' He leans back in his chair; big and genial and relaxed, his syllables fractionally drawn out, a little heavy. Asya thinks that all traditional, older, upper-class men speak like this, then finds she can only think of Uncle Sidki and Great-Uncle Nabulsi as examples.

'Poetry,' Chrissie says, and shrugs.

'Ah!' Her father picks up one of the copy-books lying next to him and leafs through it. Then he closes it and glances idly at the cover. 'Bassam al-Husseini? Who is this Bassam al-Husseini?'

'One of our colleagues,' Asya says casually.

Asya and Chrissie look straight at Sidki al-Tarabulsi. Noora continues to gaze out into the blackness beyond the balcony door. Only Mimi flutters little nervous glances from Asya to Chrissie and then back to Chrissie's father.

'But he's Palestinian. This is a Palestinian name,' Chrissie's father says.

'Yes, he is Palestinian.' Asya remembers Tante Muneera's reaction when she had learnt that the man Chrissie had been seen walking with in the street was Palestinian. Yes, but Uncle Sidki hadn't known that; hadn't known it was Bassam. And he'd probably forgotten all about that scene anyway. 'We've borrowed his notes.'

'He lends you his notes on the eve of the exam? What's *he* studying from then?'

'They're just his *rough* notes,' says Asya, and while she speaks she marvels at the inspiration that has descended upon her. 'He copies everything out very neatly. You should see his proper copy-book where he makes the fair copy. So he said he didn't need this and all we want is just a few dates –'

'Shall I phone Mother before she starts fretting again?' Chrissie cuts in.

'No, no,' says her father, putting down his glass. 'There's no need. We're going home.' He pushes with his two hands against the arms of the chair and rises to his feet. 'Shall we give anyone a lift? Mimi? Noora?'

'No, thank you very much, Uncle; I'm just across the road, you know,' says Mimi.

'Noora?'

'No, thank you, Uncle. I'll be all right.'

'How are you going to get home? Will one of your brothers come for you?'

'Yes, Uncle.'

'Well, why don't you save them the trip and Chrissie and I can take you home now?'

'Thank you very much, Uncle. It's just that I haven't quite finished and I still need to check a couple of things in Asya's books.'

'All right, then. But you shouldn't stay up very late, you know. Being rested and fresh in the exam is much more useful than this last-minute cramming. Are you ready, Chrissie?'

Chrissie gives her friends a quick wave and a grin before she disappears out of the door behind her father. Asya waits till the lights of the lift have disappeared down the shaft, then closes the door and bolts it and leans back against it.

Noora laughs. 'You don't have to lock it. He won't come bursting back in.'

'Goodness, I thought I was going to die!' exclaims Mimi, collapsing in her chair and fanning herself with a sheaf of papers. Asya runs out to the balcony and leans over until she sees Chrissie and her father emerge from the building. She sees Chrissie throw a quick look upwards, then her father opens the car door and she gets in. When the black Mercedes moves away from the kerb Asya runs inside and flings open the door of Kareem's room.

'He's gone?' Bassam asks.

'Yes, and he wanted to take Noora with him. Offered her a lift.'

They all walk back into the study. Mimi is collecting her things. 'I had better go home now,' she says.

'But if you're going now why didn't you go down with them?' asks Asya.

'No no no, chérie. I would have said something wrong and made a big problem. I know myself. It would not have taken long: while we were still in the lift I would have said something I shouldn't.'

'Kareem will walk you back,' says Asya.

'Sure,' says Kareem, and wanders back to his room to find some shoes.

'Why don't you call your mother and ask her if you can stay over?' Asya asks Noora. 'Then you two can sit here all night if you want.'

'No. No, I won't. It'll only make her miserable. She thinks that since my father is away she doesn't need to tell him that I've been out at your place studying. But if I spend the night she'll feel he ought to know and that'll make problems for her. No, I'll go home.'

Alone in the flat, Asya and Deena clear up the tea-trays and the papers and tidy up their father's study.

'Bassam is very nice, you know,' Deena says.

'I know,' says Asya. 'He is.'

'Do you really think Noora's father will carry out his threat? Even Uncle Sidki allowed Chrissie to get engaged to Fuad.'

'Uncle Sidki always listens to Tante Muneera in the end. I don't know about Noora's father. *She* thinks he'll cut her off.'

'That's horrible. Daddy wouldn't do that.'

'I don't know. I don't know if any of us would dare push him that far. No, I suppose he wouldn't.'

'Noora's very brave.'

'Yes, OK. Don't go getting ideas.'

'If I loved someone I'd marry him whatever happened.' Deena looks defiant as she puts the glasses carefully in the sink.

'You're fourteen.'

'Asya, if Daddy said he'd never speak to you again if you married Saif, would you give him up?'

Asya pulls on her pink rubber gloves and starts soaping the glasses. 'I don't know.'

'Asya!'

'No, really. It's very hard to say.'

'You wouldn't have spoken like this a year ago. Is it because of what you told me? About his dog and all that?'

'What? Oh no, of course not.'

'You never said anything about it again.'

'There really wasn't anything to say.' Asya concentrates on the washing-up.

'It hasn't happened again?'

'No.'

'So why don't you know if you'd still marry him if Daddy said he'd never speak to you again?'

'Deena! How *can* I know?' She looks up from the sink. 'OK, I suppose I *would* go ahead – I guess I – yes, I'm sure I would.'

Thursday, 20 May

The tent is extremely hot. The students are allowed water because 'Am 'Ali is there to administer it. 'Am 'Ali is beyond any suspicion of passing notes or helping anyone to cheat. Indeed, as he sits at the front of the tent watching the students for the sign that will beckon him towards one of them with his big enamelled jug and his one glass, he looks fiercer and more hawkish than any of the invigilators. In this hot weather his thinning grey hair is revealed and, without the shawl he wears most of the year, his nose, his chin, his cheekbones – all lines and angles and not a curve to be seen – seem even sharper and more defined than usual. His long, bony feet are bare in brown plastic sandals but he still wears his brown jacket buttoned carefully over his beige *galabiyya*. It is said that he has a son studying medicine but no one knows for sure. Asya is chewing her pencil and watching him absently. It is almost three o'clock in the afternoon and they have been in the tent for ten minutes. Usually the professor of the subject is on hand when the paper is opened. Some of them even insist on personally reading out the questions to their students. But the professor has not yet arrived. Why is he not here? The new wife, probably. He has a new wife. The last one had stayed with him twelve years. Then one day he'd gone home and found her gone. Together with all her furniture and her books and her clothes and her carpets. Neat. She had made him divorce her and then he'd had to marry the mistress he'd kept for four years in a small apartment downtown. That was about the time Asya had got engaged and she had felt pangs of jealousy. Strong. Until she'd seen the new wife. She couldn't believe anyone would voluntarily make themselves look so ridiculous: big hats, purple eyelids, crimson cheeks. The lot. Asya had privately dubbed her 'Satyricon' and the name had stuck. Everybody used it and it seemed only a matter of time before someone actually called her that to her face – innocently. And yet – and yet it was said that he doted on her. The story was that the first time he'd made love to her she had fallen to her knees at his feet and kissed his hands and given vociferous thanks to God who had finally sent her a real man –

The university clock strikes three and Dr Mary Tadros calls out in her refined, clipped voice, 'We turn over the papers.'

One 'unseen', one 'comment' made up of five extracts, and three essays from which you had to choose one. Asya looks across at Chrissie who gives her a faint smile. Exam-time is the only time when Asya is more confident than Chrissie. Chrissie hates exams. She trembles and runs high temperatures and once during Latin her legs had become paralysed – temporarily. Asya likes exams. They are defined. They are finite. They last three hours and then they are over.

Yet when all's done you'll keep the emerald
I placed upon your finger in the street;
And I will keep the patches that you sewed
On my old battledress tonight, my sweet.

In this final stanza –

The students are seated at single desks placed in rows. Between each student and their neighbour is one metre in each direction. The tent seems to stretch on for ever although of course it really only takes up the space bordered on four sides by the Departments of English and History, the Cafeteria, the Library and the main college building. The space is mostly garden and now some desks are on grass and some on gravel and some are perilously near the step that leads down to the asphalt path. Throughout the year the old gardener carefully tends this space. He waters it every day and coaxes marigolds and sweetpeas from the two flowerbeds. The students are never allowed on the grass and once, when Ronald Hedges, the new British Council funded ESL instructor, tried to conduct a small conversation class there on a quiet, sunny winter morning the entire administration rose up in arms against him. Every May, however, the trucks carrying the big tent roll up. Thick, wooden poles are driven deep into the earth, iron pegs are hammered down among the flowers, and chairs and tables are dragged into position across the grass. Heaven knew what the garden would look like when the exams were over: when the poles were uprooted, the chairs stacked away and the tent dismantled. Only Heaven and the old gardener. None of the students would see it till the following October, and by then it would be struggling back to life.

– the poem, in the end, then, is about 'objects', about 'things'; things which depend for their significance on what people – on what the lovers – invest them with, but which ultimately outlast both the lovers and their love.

Saif. Saif right now is sitting his 'History of the Arab World in the Twentieth Century' exam. He'd get a B plus with no trouble. An A if he tried. Together they had stood outside till two forty-five and he had teased Chrissie about the bits of paper she was insisting on reading till the very last minute.

'And why should *you* care?' she'd answered. 'What you're doing is a hobby. A sideline. It makes no difference to you whether you pass or fail.'

'Of course it does,' he'd laughed. 'I'd have to keep coming back here next year when you had all gone.'

'Yes, that's right. You really used to attend. Never missed a class. Now tell me truly: have you even *read* the books?'

'Which books?'

242

'There! You see? The course books, of course. For the exam you're just about to walk into.'

'My dear Chrissie: this course in particular is practically general knowledge. Current affairs. You want me to stand here trying to read today's newspaper very quickly?'

'He's impossible.'

'There'll be one essay on Palestine. And one on neo-colonialism for the smart-asses who want to exhibit their thoughts on the shape of things to come –'

Asya had watched him and loved him. The confidence. The friendly arrogance. The charm. The mischief. The light, light way he had of standing as though he were about to take off. Even when he was talking to someone else he always included her: an arm on her shoulder when possible. When not, the odd glance and the flash of a smile. And yet. More and more she felt distanced. Peripheral. Easy, easy, she had told herself. Take it easy. Soon you'll be married. Seventy-one days and you'll be married and you'll be really together and everything will fall into place.

We live in an old chaos of the sun,
Or old dependency of day and night,
Or island solitude, unsponsored, free,
Of that wide water, inescapable.

Dr Mostanser creeps stealthily down the aisles on his spotless white sneakers. Silently he pauses behind unsuspecting students. His face is getting ever more drained of colour and each day draws the skin more tightly over the bone. His eyes burn. He is waiting for a slip. The slightest slip: a crumpled fragment of chewing-gum wrapper, perhaps, a whisper, a few characters scratched on to a table. Behind Mahrous he pauses longer and more frequently. And across the rows of bent heads 'Am 'Ali's gaunt features watch him with contempt.

Scene 2

Thursday, 29 July 1971
Cairo
'Shall we have some juice?'

'Yes, please. Sugar-cane,' says Asya.

Fuad pulls up in front of the shop.

'Or maybe I'll have mango,' says Asya.

The young waiter in the white jacket reaches the car as Chrissie winds down the window. He bends down to take the order and his face breaks into a grin when he sees Asya's white dress and veil, the bouquet on Chrissie's knee.

'You all in a play or what?' he asks.

Fuad turns to look at him. Chrissie and Asya giggle quietly. Saif is lighting a cigarette. He had pulled off his tie as he walked down the steps of the Semiramis. He had stuffed it into his jacket pocket and then taken off the jacket and flung it on to the back seat of Chrissie's father's car. He had held the door open for Asya and shut it carefully after her, then he had walked round to the other side and climbed in while he undid his cuffs and rolled up his shirtsleeves. His jacket now lay on the seat between them.

'No, it's not a play,' Fuad says curtly. 'Fetch the bride a large mango juice, and . . .' He looks at Chrissie.

'Strawberries with milk, please,' says Chrissie.

'And a large strawberries with milk here, and I'll have mango as well –'

'And the bridegroom?' The waiter smiles broadly at Saif.

'Get me a lemon juice,' Saif says, 'and put ice in it.'

'Yes, sir. Congratulations, sir.' The waiter beams and hurries off.

'It's the first time in his life he sees a bride stopping at a juice shop.' Chrissie laughs.

Saif looks at Asya. 'You could take off the veil,' he says.

'I can't,' says Asya. 'It's put on in a really complicated way.' She nudges Chrissie's back with her knee. 'Chrissie will have to help me with it later.'

Saif glances at her, then drags on his cigarette.

'It was a really good idea, though: getting out,' says Asya. 'Otherwise we'd have had to sit there and wait for everybody to go home.'

'Or gone upstairs with everybody watching you,' says Chrissie.

'Are you sure you don't want to go somewhere for supper?' Fuad asks.

'No, no. I had hundreds of canapés,' Asya says.

'The food was really good,' says Chrissie.

'Could we drive up to the pyramids?' asks Asya.

Fuad shrugs. 'Yes, why not?' He glances at Saif in the rear-view mirror.

The waiter comes back with four tall glasses on a tray: one pink, one green and two orange. Round the bottom of each is wrapped a white paper napkin. They look cool and delicious. Asya secretly wonders at Saif ordering lemon. You can have lemon all the year round but it's only in the summer that you can have mango and strawberries. She thinks lemon always looks attractive and tastes horrid. It looks creamy and thick with a crown of white foam and then you find it tastes thin and bitter with the sugar in a sort of parenthesis that never quite blends in.

When they've finished Fuad taps the horn and the waiter hurries back, still smiling. Saif puts some money on his tray.

'Thank you, sir. Congratulations, sir. May God give you all happiness.'

So many wishes for their happiness. On the cards that came with the flowers that started arriving four days ago: 'With Happiness and Progeny', 'With Happiness and Joy', 'Our Wishes for Your Permanent Happiness . . .'

'OK. Let's go,' says Fuad, starting up the car.

'Let's have some music,' says Chrissie. She pushes in a tape, and Ummu Kulthoum's latest song fills the car.

'Shall I meet you tomorrow?
Ah! How my heart fears the morrow –'

'Does it have to be this wailing?' Saif asks.

'I'm looking for something else,' says Chrissie as she rummages through the glove compartment.

'Why the hell do you have this shit sitting in the cassette anyway?' he asks.

'I'm sorry, Majesty. But it's my father's Mercedes, not mine, Majesty,' says Chrissie.

'I can't believe how it's all back as though nothing had happened,' says Asya. 'Ten months ago they were all acting like it was the end of the world and she cancelled her season and everything, and now it's back to the Thursday night concerts and all the Arab countries tuning in and it's as if nothing had happened. And nobody mentions the Chief any more except Sadat himself when he wants to claim that 'Abd el-Nasser had approved of something he is now about to do. And it's always "The Immortal Leader" –'

'That's what the world is like,' says Chrissie.

'It's so – trite,' says Asya.

Chrissie finds a tape and holds it up to the window to see the title. 'There, that should please His Excellency.'

The 'Aranjuez' Guitar Concerto bursts into the car and Saif settles back against his seat and lights another cigarette. When Asya catches his eye he smiles at her and reaches over to pat her hand. The bouquet of white orchids he had sent her in the morning lies on the rear window shelf. Tante Adeela and Uncle Madi had sent a large basket of iris and pink carnations. And the Professor had sent a dozen birds of paradise.

They have gone round Falaki and up again through Tahrir and they are passing the Semiramis where their wedding party is even now continuing. Except that Khalu Hamid has probably gone home. His friend, 'Abd el-Khaliq Mahjoub, the leader of the Sudanese Communist Party, was yesterday executed in Khartoum. Asya thinks – although nobody says so – that they'd probably been comrades long ago when Khalu had been politically active. Mahjoub had been in Cairo last summer and Khalu had seen him a few times; he'd even come to Friday lunch at Grandfather's once. He'd been very quiet; dignified and graceful in the way the Sudanese have, and pleasant: praised Tante Soraya's *mulukhiyya* to the skies and had second helpings and now he was dead. And when Khalu had come into Asya's bedroom with Grandfather earlier today, and Asya had been in her dressing-gown waiting for Hassan to come and dress her hair and Monsieur Ma'moulian to bring her dress, and she had seen him look – not sad, because he would not let himself look sad on her wedding-day, and he had smiled and congratulated her – but tired and sort of older, she had felt so sorry and she had put her arms around him and said, 'I'm so sorry about 'Abd el-Khaliq Mahjoub, Khalu,' and he had hugged her and said, 'It's all right, Asya, it's all right. This isn't what you should be thinking about on your wedding day. Greet your grandfather.' And Asya had taken Geddu's hand and kissed him and as he had kissed her head and said, 'Congratulations, my daughter,' two *zaghroudas* one after the other had rung out from behind the closed door and she had felt ashamed and glanced at Khalu, and he'd patted her shoulder and said, 'We have come as witnesses to take your statement.' And she had asked, 'Is Saif outside?'

'Yes. With his father and the *ma'thoun.*'

'Whom do you appoint as your proxy, Asya, my child?' Geddu had asked.

And Asya had answered – as she had been taught, 'I have appointed my father as my proxy.'

And outside she had heard the *zaghroudas* rise to the sky as Saif and her father signed her marriage contract, and then her father and her mother and Geddu and Sheikh Zayid and Uncle Madi had come in one after the other to kiss and congratulate her, and Khalu Hamid had come in and looked at her and said, 'Don't think of anything sad. Think of your wedding and of Saif. This is *your* night, my dear.'

Asya looks out of her window. They have crossed Qasr el-Nil Bridge and Gezira and – although it is almost midnight, Fuad is respecting the traffic signals – they are sitting in a red light on Gala' Bridge. Just in front of them the new Giza Sheraton rises and dwarfs the building where they had had their engagement party and which until this year had been the tallest along this stretch of the river. It had used to be an impressive yellow-stone block and now it looks rather dainty and outmoded and bijoux. Just below it is the almost derelict boat which houses the Egyptian Rowing Club where Saif – and now Kareem – train, and beyond that the Nile stretches and glitters and opens up and she can see the tip of Roda Island, which used to have the Casino Fontana where her parents had taken her so often when she was a child. It used to have a lighthouse slide and a merry-go-round but they're not there any more.

'Imagine if we went into the rowing club now. We'd just sit at a table and call, "Ghazali! Four orders of white cheese and watermelon!" ' Asya says.

'Ghazali would think he was seeing visions,' Saif laughs.

Chrissie glances backwards. 'Ghazali wouldn't be surprised at anything coming from you two.'

The light turns green and Asya sits back in her corner. Her white lace gloves which she had taken off to drink her mango juice are lying in her lap. Her hands are folded on top of them. Her nails are a soft pearl and her wedding ring has been moved from her right hand to her left. Asya has no problems with her hands; she likes her hands. She has reservations about various bits of her, but her hands and her eyes and her mouth are OK. She'd had to think about the various bits of her quite a lot the last few days. And right now all the bits of her are at their best. Her hair has the right degree of wave and falls just exactly to her shoulders, her arms and legs are burnished gold, her feet are scraped and scrubbed and pedicured. Even down there feels special; nicer. It doesn't *look* nicer; she prefers how it looked with the triangle of curly black hair rather than like this, all plucked and naked and sort of – rude. But it does *feel* nicer; soft and smooth and – padded. You can feel all the different bits of it much better like this. What is *he* going to think, though? She had thought of asking him what he would prefer but they hadn't been talking about stuff like that very much lately and she hadn't been able to. She had had to decide, and both Chrissie and Dada Zeina had thought she should do it. Chrissie had said, 'Even if it's not what he wants it's what he expects. He knows that's what a girl does before her wedding.'

'But what if he doesn't want me to?'

'He knows you're going to do it. If he doesn't want you to he should ask you not to.'

'What? Say, "I say, Asya, you know your – er, whatsit? Could you please not do *halawa* on it?" Is that possible, Chrissie?'

'You complicate everything for yourself. You can choose what you want to do. Nobody's forcing you to do anything. But this is what people

247

do before a wedding and Saif knows that. He's not a foreigner.'

And Dada Zeina had said, 'What do you mean you're thinking this and thinking that? You want to get married with hair on your underneath? What a scandal! What shame! You want to put a hex on your bridegroom? What would he say of you?'

'But, Dada, he knows –'

'Never mind what he knows. You're his bride now. You want to embarrass him? You want to insult him?'

'Is it going to hurt very much?'

'Everything hurts the first time. You'll get used to it. Be grateful you've got sugar and lemon and don't have to make do with the grit from the oven.'

So Asya had asked her mother – who had just come back two weeks before the wedding and was having to go away again on Saturday – had asked her to send for the Mashta, and Lateefa had said, 'But you'd better be quite sure you've made up your mind because you can't bring the woman here and then tell her just to do your arms and legs and go away; she knows you're a bride.'

The Mashta had come on Wednesday morning at ten o'clock and Asya's father had been very correct and gone off at nine saying he was going to have breakfast at the club, and Lateefa said he'd fixed up several things for himself so he would stay out all day but he had asked whether they would be through with all their women's stuff by seven in the evening and Lateefa had said yes. And Asya was glad that she was going to have a proper Henna Day, and Dada Sayyida came from Grandfather's house, and Hasna, the half-blind washerwoman, was there, and so were her mother and her daughter. Her mother, Ummu Hasna, was practically a bedouin and had the three blue lines tattooed on her chin and used to wander with a herd of goats. Now that she is over seventy she has to stay in a corner of Hasna's house and depend on her, but she still wears a silver nose-ring and four heavy silver bangles, one on each wrist and ankle, and constantly accuses her granddaughter, Toota, Hasna's daughter, of having her eye on them. Toota was born three months before Asya and when they were small and Hasna came to do the washing either at Grandfather's or at the Ulamas' the two girls would play together. When they were about twelve Asya had envied Toota terribly; she was so much more sophisticated and knew everything and could dress as tight and as short as she chose because her father was dead and she had no uncles or brothers. And when she was sixteen Toota had married an ironing-man. It was a good match because he had his own shop and he was only in his thirties, and his wife was dead and he didn't have any children, and within two weeks Toota had come home to her mother after her first beating. Her husband had come round and kissed her head, of course, and begged her to come back, and the women

248

had told her that a husband who didn't beat his wife didn't love her, and she had gone. Now she had three children and was missing two front teeth and there was a wide scar down her neck and her left arm where he had thrown a saucepan full of boiling water at her when she didn't hand it to him quickly enough in the bath. Dada Zeina said whatever happened to her served her right because she went with men for money and she was having a thing with the greengrocer downstairs and fleecing him, but Asya thinks that can't be true because the greengrocer is always sitting in a corner in a hashish trance and because his wife watches him ferociously and because Toota would surely be as terrified of her as everybody else was – but Toota is still a natty dresser, and she loves to sing and dance, and her *zaghrouda* is the best and the loudest and the one with the curviest tail.

And sure enough one *zaghrouda* after another had risen in a relay from the normally sedate house in Zamalek once Mukhtar al-Ulama's car was seen to drive away and turn the corner into Hassan Sabri Street. That, thinks Asya now, was probably about the time that 'Abd el-Khaliq Mahjoub was being led from his cell to be executed. And trays of sherbet were carried down to the doormen and the men in the ironing shop and the florist and the greengrocer and Ghattas's ironing shop, and to all the various men who sat around on benches in the shade and jumped up to call a taxi or to guide a car into or out of a parking-space or to carry the shopping or a child or just to salaam as you went by. And Kareem woke up and said see you later and grabbed his swimsuit and a towel and went off to the club, and Toota put a tape of wedding songs into the cassette player in the hall and the music rang through the flat, and the Mashta cooked the candy and drank her coffee while the mixture cooled, and when she started kneading the candy it clicked loudly several times and all the women said that meant the groom was desperately in love with the bride, and Saif phoned to say good morning and what on earth is that racket? And Asya said it was the maids celebrating and he asked did Asya need anything? And she said he mustn't come round today because it was bad luck, so he said OK, I'll give you a ring later.

'Oh you who love the Prophet
Praise his beauty.
This is the bride of the handsome one
Let's hold her up for him.
This is her wedding day
Its crescent has revealed itself.
What happiness for him who wins her!
What happiness is in store for him –'

Asya lay on a folded white sheet on the floor of her room with a pillow under her head. She wore a pair of white panties and a camisole. The

Mashta sat cross-legged on the floor beside her. She was in a green smock and her hair was tightly wrapped in a black kerchief. She had the smoothest face that Asya had ever seen. She worked quickly and silently except to tell Asya what to do. One leg and then the other and now stand up and turn around. Sit down. One arm and then the other, now raise your arms. And now take off your knickers, pretty one, and let's clean you up and polish you and turn you into a bride. She spreads the paste and names the Name of God, and when she pulls Asya scrambles to her feet and jumps up and down a couple of times then lies down again. At the second pull Asya sits up and draws her knees to her chest and holds on to them tight and breathes hard. Her eyes are full of tears. The Mashta waits a bit then pats the sheet, come on, bride, come on. 'No, no, it's over,' says Asya.

'What do you mean it's over? We haven't even done half.'

'It's over. I don't want any more. I can't.'

'Sweetheart, there's nothing called I can't. Look at yourself and see. You'll go to your bridegroom with one half clean and the other half as it is? You're going to make him laugh at you? Come on, darling, let's get it done.'

When Asya lies down the Mashta says, 'No more getting up and I'll lighten my hand as much as I can.'

Asya bites her lips and clenches her hands but after the next three pulls when she begs for a minute, just a minute, to get her breath back the Mashta holds on to her knee and says, 'No, no, there's no minute. Like this quickly it's better. Like this you'll go numb and not feel anything. Come on, come on. Just open for me. Open for me as wide as you can. Look, why don't you put this foot on top of the bed like this so I can get at you. Yes. Now we've just got this little bit to do. There. There. And there. Congratulations, bride.'

'Who has ever seen such people?
You had to turn out beautiful:
The mother is a sprig of jasmine,
And the father is broad and fat.
Oh you little bit of sugar
You perfumed distilled syrup
And her bridegroom
Is the handsomest I've seen –'

She had spread a big bath towel over Asya and left her alone to recover. And Dada Zeina had brought her a damp flannel to cool herself down with and a glass of red sherbet to drink, and as Asya had slipped the flannel under the towel and held it against herself and trembled she had patted her shoulder and said, 'Congratulations, bride. May God give you happiness and not change your fortune or that of your groom. May

250

he be your man and your partner and above you in this world and the next.'

And Asya had said, 'Where's my mother?'

'She's gone to the what's-its-name, the hotel. To see to the food. An expense for which there was no need. What would have happened if you'd had it here?'

'Oh, Dada. Three hundred guests and we would have had them here?'

'Three hundred guests and no dancer to entertain them,' Dada Zeina had said, and curled her lip.

Asya was silent. Saif had said OK he'd get dressed up in a monkey suit and sit on a fake throne to be stared at if he had to, but there was no way he'd walk in a procession of tambourines and screeching women. He'd said, why didn't they get a string quartet, at least that would be pleasant to listen to. Asya had secretly wanted the dancer and the drums and the tambourines, but of course she couldn't say so, but she did say a string quartet would be too weird and people would think it was pretentious and in the end he'd agreed to a band.

'Like this you'll go to him, without a *zaffa*?' Dada Zeina had gone on. 'Why? Is there something wrong with you, God forbid? How many times does a woman get married? It's once only in a whole lifetime.'

'Never mind, Dada. You know Saif. And Daddy wouldn't have liked it either. You can all drum and dance here today as much as you like.'

'And her groom God's name bless him,
Generous and open-handed,
Flings out a thousand pounds
You'd say they were farthings in his hands.
May he always be pleasure-loving
Under your influence little flower –'

Asya had lain on the black marble tiles in the bathroom and the Mashta, with her hand in a black cloth bag, had rubbed her and rubbed her and rubbed her. Every bit of her. Her back and her belly and her breasts and her neck and her shoulders. And out of her skin had come hundreds of tiny black pellets like you get when you use an eraser on a pencil mark. And then in the bath she had rubbed her again with a soapy loofah, and then she had showered her off and dried her and Asya had walked across the hall wrapped in her white fluffy towel and then slipped it off and got into bed, and the Mashta had rubbed her body all over with rosewater and jasmine oil and she had remembered a Chinese story that told of how the concubines prepared themselves for bedding the emperor and one of the things they had to do was make sure their seven orifices were perfumed, and once again Asya tried to think of seven orifices but could only come up with six unless you counted the nostrils separately, because of course your wee-wee hole didn't count because

251

you couldn't possibly get at it and it would hurt so dreadfully if you did. Then she had fallen asleep –

'Did you see Noora introducing Bassam to her father?' asks Chrissie.

'She's really brave,' Asya says. 'But her father did shake hands with him.'

'What else could he do? A wedding and people around; he doesn't want to make a scandal for himself.'

'Tante Saliha looked so terrified.'

'She knows he'll yell at her when they get home.'

'He won't wait till they get home: he'll start in the car.'

'He does have a point, you know,' Fuad says. 'She's his daughter. It's natural that he wouldn't want her to marry a Palestinian.'

'Oh Fuad, *why*?' pleads Asya. 'Has he committed a crime by being Palestinian?'

'No, he hasn't committed a crime. But he'll bring with him a lot of problems.'

'Everybody has problems.'

'But there are problems that have solutions and problems that don't,' Saif says.

'I thought you were his friend.'

'I *am* his friend. But friendship is one thing and marriage is another.'

Fuad sweeps the car into a half-circle and pulls to a stop on the escarpment halfway along the road to Sahara City. He switches off the engine and there is complete silence. Saif is the first to open his door and get out. He stands in the darkness with his back to the car. From where he stands he can see the three pyramids along one line – just like on the postcards: Khofo and Khafra' massive and solid and together, Manqara' infant-like and tousled beside them. Way beyond, the glare of Cairo rises in a white haze into the night sky. He thinks of this new tomb they say they've just discovered. Imhutub – then he hears the car door shut. Asya comes to stand beside him and he puts his arm across her shoulders and pulls her close.

'You OK, Princess?'

She nods and smiles up at him, snuggling herself closer under his arm. She tries to put her head against his shoulder but her veil prickles at her face. She moves away and turns around, looking upwards and searching through the sky. 'Ah, there it is! It's only half a moon though.' She considers it for a while, then comes back to him. She stands in front of him and raises her arms to take his face in her hands. 'Are *you* all right?'

They hear the cough of the soldier approaching. Asya drops her arms. The soldier has climbed the escarpment and is walking towards them muffled against the warm night in a thick grey shawl which he wears over his head and shoulders on top of his uniform. He has the usual bow-legged, bent-backed gait of the peasant in soldier's clothing and his gun is slung over his back. Already as he approaches the Mercedes and the moonlit white dress he seems hesitant.

'Salamu aleikum!'

'Aleikum es-salam!' Saif responds.

'Excuse me, sir. It is forbidden to be here, sir, after sunset.'

'Why, Sergeant? Why is it forbidden?' asks Saif pleasantly although he knows perfectly well why it is forbidden and that the man is not a sergeant.

'Excuse me, sir. This is a military area.'

'You're protecting the pyramids, eh?' Saif gives him his big grin and the man smiles back. Fuad opens the door of the car and steps out. His tie has been pulled down and his top shirt button is undone. His hair is ruffled.

'What is it? What's up, soldier?'

The soldier recognises an officer's tone and pulls himself up a bit straighter, although as Fuad is in civilian gear he does not salute.

'It is forbidden to be here, sir, after sunset.'

'This is what you've come all the way up here to say? Go and attend to your duties, soldier! Go!'

'Sir, this is a military area. And it is forbidden –'

'Soldier!'

'Listen, Sergeant,' Saif cuts in. 'The lady wants to visit the pyramids on the night of her wedding and you are a man of discernment.' He puts his hand in his pocket and draws out a wad of notes. He selects two. 'Now you go and buy yourself a glass of tea to warm you up, and we'll be leaving in a couple of minutes.'

'Congratulations, sir,' the soldier mumbles, and moves away, ignoring Fuad and salaaming with the fist into which the notes are crumpled. 'May God complete it well for you tonight.'

They listen to his footsteps crunching the pebbles. Fuad kicks a stone off the escarpment and they hear it rattle and bounce all the way down the steep side. Saif strolls over to him. 'A poor man,' he says. 'Why take it out on him?' When Asya gets back into the car Chrissie is brushing her hair.

In the Bridal Suite of the Semiramis Hotel Chrissie carefully unpins the Juliet's cap. As she takes out the last pin and lifts the cap and the veil off Asya's head a small black padded cushion tumbles out from underneath them and on to the floor.

'See!' says Asya as she rubs her scalp with her fingertips and shakes her hair free in the big dressing-table mirror. 'He'd have thought it was a mouse.'

Chrissie picks up the little cushion and turns it over.

'It was at the last minute,' says Asya. 'Hassan decided that the cap was sitting too flat and needed height so he put this in under it.'

'It's clever,' says Chrissie. 'You'd never have known there was anything there; it all looked completely natural.'

'Yes, well, that was the end of any idea I might have had of Saif gently taking off my veil or anything like that. Imagine. A fat little hairy black cushion leaping out at him.'

'Asya, where are the scissors?'

'Scissors?'

'Never mind. I've got some in my bag.' Chrissie opens her gold net evening bag and produces a tiny pair of nail scissors. 'I knew you would forget. You're going to have to stand up now.'

'Oh, sorry.' Asya lifts her long skirt and gets to her feet and Chrissie takes her place on the small armchair in front of the dressing-table. She pulls Asya so that she stands directly in front of her with her back turned. Asya is looking out through the open french windows. 'I love rooms that look out on water. Our room in Beirut looked out over the sea. But the Nile is better. It's more – ornamented – can you say "ornamented"? The bridges and the lights and the trees on the other side. Although the sea of course makes you –'

'You're going to have to hold very still,' says Chrissie, 'otherwise I'll cut the lace and the dress will be ruined.'

'I'm not going to wear it again, am I?'

'Asya, hold still.'

'This is quite sad, you know; I've done something I'm never ever going to do again. And it isn't like I imagined it: I'd always thought that he'd undress me: ease the dress off my shoulders and kiss them kind of thing.' Asya does a little wriggle.

'Please hold still. The girl has done this in such tiny stitches; they're hard enough to cut without you jumping around. Ouf. Did you have to go and lose three kilos in two days and ruin the fit of the dress?'

'I didn't mean to. You should have seen Monsieur Ma'moulian's face when he came to put it on. "But it was purr-fect, purr-fect," he wailed. "Mademoiselle just had a fitting three days ago." So then he grabbed it and rushed off to his atelier to "create" two new seams, as he said, and when he rushed back the lace wouldn't lie down over the zip.'

'That's when you phoned me. There's hardly any light in here.' Chrissie is squinting at the tiny stitching that she snips with the points of her scissors.

'Well I thought I'd better warn you that you would have to come up and undo me. Oh, Chrissie, what am I to do now?'

'What are you to do about what?'

'Well I'd always thought we'd walk in here together and then it would all be up to him, you know, he'd take care of everything. And now it's all different.'

'Hold *still*. Why is it all different?'

'Because I'm here first. I mean, do I undress or what?'

'You could still wait for him to undress you if that's what you've had in your mind.'

'But he knows that we're up here because of the stitches. I mean, he doesn't know about the cushion but he does know about the stitches.'

'So?'

'So it'll look like we undid the stitches and then I sat down and waited for him to come and undress me.'

'What's wrong with that?' Chrissie is snipping repeatedly at a particularly tight stitch.

'He'll walk in and see me sitting here, still in my wedding dress after all this time with you, and he'll think, she kept it on so I would take it off. I couldn't bear that. Oh, I wanted it all to just happen naturally.'

'Then just start undressing. He can come in and find you in the middle of undressing –'

'Just like it was any old night.'

'There, it's done. Now you do what you want. I'm going, otherwise both Saif and Fuad will kill me.'

'Chrissie, wait.'

Chrissie picks up her bag and slips the scissors into it. She steps up to her friend and puts her hands on Asya's shoulders. 'Congratulations, darling. Just remember how long you've waited for this day. Everything will be fine. If you can, give me a quick ring tomorrow. Just to tell me you're OK.'

As they hug each other their eyes fill with tears.

'Oh no, oh no,' says Asya, 'my mascara,' and she pinches her lower lids and holds them out like pockets to receive the tears.

Chrissie laughs. 'You look horrible when you do that.' She peers into the mirror and wipes her own eyes with her fingertips, looks at Asya one more time, blows her a kiss and hurries out of the room.

Asya stands holding out her lower eyelids for a moment and then lets go and pats them lightly back into shape. She likes this room. It is not quite the room in which whatever-her-name-was is ravished by the Dey of Algiers; that was: 'a small room every side of which was covered in glass. In the centre of the room was a low dark crimson velvet couch, with one large cushion at the head. In the centre of the couch was fastened, properly extended, a beautiful white damask cloth.' But this room is fine; it's a good setting for what is about to happen: she likes the big, dark, old-fashioned, ornate furniture, the mosquito-net curtains with the beaded hems, the veranda with the stone balustrade, the polished wooden floor and the high ceiling. How strange that soon they will be in this room, in this bed, with everybody knowing and thinking it's OK. The bouquet of iris and carnations sent by her in-laws stands on a small table near the open doors of the french windows. At the foot of the massive bed her nightdress lies where Tante Soraya had carefully arranged it six hours ago. Perhaps she should put it on? 'I was stripped in an instant by the eunuchs of every particle of my dress; they even untied the fillets which fastened up my hair; when, having reduced me to a complete state of nature, they retired, taking away my clothes.' It looked so very bridal – the nightdress. But he would be coming up soon and she ought to decide. 'He took me in his arms, after kissing me . . . "You quickly shall taste such joys as your beauties so well deserve you should partake of." So drawing me to his bosom, he gently forced me on my back. "There, that's right; now open your soft thighs!" ' Asya turns to the window. The lights gleam on Qasr el-Nil Bridge – 'Earth has not anything to show more fair . . .' She ought to take a shower. Why is she just standing here like this? There is really nothing at all to be afraid of. Even if it does hurt a bit at first, it is bound to be an OK sort of pain – 'While he was fixing its head between the lips of my virgin sheath, he tried by every kind of endearment and kisses to soothe me, assuring me the pain would be nothing – that my fears were all; besides, it was a sacrifice which Nature had decreed, and once over the sweetest joys would be my reward; then why these foolish fears? Thus did he soften me to his desires.' And she has wanted him for three and a half years, and it's true that nothing very much had been happening lately, but that was just a whole configuration of circumstances and of course they want each other as much as ever and now it could all begin. Life – *their* life – could begin – but now she hears his footsteps, yes, she hears his footsteps coming down the marble corridor.

When I walked into our room she wasn't there. I guess I'd imagined her sitting at the dressing-table, or maybe out on the balcony. Anyhow, I know I'd imagined her in her wedding dress, in a half-light, and very still.

Chrissie had stayed up there with her for a long time. Sinnari and I had sat in the hotel bar with the ice melting in our whiskies and talked projects. As I stubbed out my third cigarette Chrissie had come down. Her eyes had looked a bit red and she'd said something about the stitches being tiny and not wanting to ruin the lace – and then they'd gone.

Our room was on the second floor but I hadn't taken the lift upstairs. I'd walked. And I'd walked down the long corridor and I'd found the door pushed to, but not shut properly. I'd walked in and found that – she wasn't there. I locked the door behind me. After a moment I lit a cigarette. I could hear the shower going full blast behind the bathroom door. Her veil was hanging from the top of the mirror and billowed out over the dressing-table and on to the rug.

Standing in the desert I had heard the car door open and shut and she had come towards me. Her dress was white and silver and shimmered in the moonlight. The ends of her sleeves just touched the backs of her bare, perfect hands. On the third finger of her left hand my gold wedding band had shone steadily out from under the big diamond ring I had given her for our engagement. My diamond earrings were in her ears and my pendant at her throat. She had cut her long hair so that it just curled into her shoulders and from the little embroidered cap her long white veil came floating down. Her face was luminous but I thought tired. And there in the emptiness of the desert, with the pyramids for a backdrop, she had seemed smaller and more fragile than I knew. Was she aware of the figure she was cutting, the image she was creating as she came towards me across the stones and the sand? I think she was.

There on the dressing-table was all her gear. Neatly laid out. In Beirut and in London, the first thing she'd do in a strange room was lay all her stuff out on the dressing-table: the perfume, the creams, the colours, the silver-backed magnifying mirror, the various brushes. I thought it was a sweet home-making instinct. She'd annex an ashtray for her rings and an ashtray for her hairpins. She'd always leave two ashtrays for me: one on a table somewhere, and one by the bed.

Her shoes were just outside the bathroom door. Plain white satin with a small heel. I always liked her style in shoes; plain and classy, no buckles or bows or fancy trimmings. The right shoe pointed at the bathroom door, the left lay on its side at an angle. She must have kicked them off in a hurry or they'd be sitting side by side with their backs against the wall and their toes pointing into the room.

Across the foot of the bed I saw what had to be her wedding nightdress. I went over and looked at it. A modest neckline and long sleeves and so much pale embroidery that at first I thought it must be part of the cloth itself. But then I thought of her many trips with her Tante Soraya to 'check on the stuff that's being embroidered' and I lifted the neckline and turned it over, and there sure enough were all the lines and knots stretched and crisscrossing like some primitive electronic circuit, and then I saw that the ash on my cigarette had got dangerously long so I dropped the nightdress and walked over to the balcony and flicked the ash over the balustrade. It was two in the morning. I watched the lights from the bridge flicker on the river. Moored against the near shore I could make out the shapes of a couple of boatmen rolled up in blankets asleep in their feluccas.

I heard the bathroom door open. When I turned she was sitting at the dressing-table wrapped in one of the hotel towels, unpinning her hair. The dress was lying on the armchair just outside the bathroom door. I went and stood behind her. I started to stroke her neck and her shoulders. But when she looked up at me in the mirror I ruffled her hair and said, 'I'm going into the shower.' She smiled and said, 'OK.' On my way to the bathroom I stopped and touched the dress. In the heart of each lace flower, a small pearl had been secured.

When I kissed her she kissed me back. When I held her breasts she put her arms around me. When I lay between her legs she went very quiet and still. I put

257

my hand on her face and said, 'Don't worry. It'll be all right.' And she said, 'Yes, I know,' but I felt her tense and stiffen until she was lying under me like a statue. I put my hand on her and it was odd and somehow unreal. I'd known, I guess, or just assumed that she'd have it done. But it was disorienting to slide my hand downwards and not come upon a soft bush of hair. Nothing to run my fingers through. Nothing to toy with along the way, but just a smooth curve and then the bald lips. She whispered anxiously, 'Is it – I mean, I didn't know whether – is it OK?' and I said, 'Of course it's OK. It's very nice,' and slipped my fingers between her lips, and when I felt her soften I tried her again, and again I felt her grow rigid and I said, 'Don't you want to?' and she said, 'Yes, of course I do,' but when I pushed she cried out. I stopped and pulled back and after a bit her breath evened out and I tried again, and she cried out, but then she said, 'No, do it do it please let's get it done,' when I pushed hard she bucked under me trying to get away and cried that it hurt too much and that she'd never thought it would hurt so much, and then from behind our headboard I heard someone in the next room sneeze and blow his nose, and I'd thought the walls of these old hotels were supposed to be thick and solid, and she must have heard it too for she became very quiet and even stopped wriggling. I was surprised that my hard-on was still there. It was, but it was no longer part of me; it had become like some instrument I could decide whether or not to use. And I thought right, let's do it. I braced myself and gave two strong shoves, and I felt her tremble all over, and she started pushing with her heels against the bed to try and unhook herself, and she was whispering frantically that she couldn't bear it and she couldn't breathe and could I please stop just for a moment for one moment – and I lifted myself off and let her go and she rolled over on her side away from me and curled up into a little ball and pulled the sheet over herself and lay there trembling. I lit a cigarette and lay on my back smoking and after a bit she uncurled herself and came to lie against my side and I knew that she was crying so I stroked her hair and she said she was sorry oh she was so sorry. And after a bit, with her face against my arm, she asked do you want to – do you think we – I just really didn't know – and I said hush, it doesn't matter, it doesn't have to be tonight.

VII

August 1972 - May 1973

Scene 1

7 August, 1972
Cairo

Asya is pregnant – and hot. This is probably the first time ever that she has spent August in Cairo. She lies on the sofa in their living-room. The cushions underneath her are pale green velvet filled with down. The sunshine falls through the slats of the closed blinds tracing bright lines across the patterns of the Turkish kelim and striping the swollen white underside of the grey cat who has adopted Asya: white on white like the little settee on Saif's old veranda. The cat lies on her side; four legs stretched out, one ear twitching, panting gently. She too is pregnant. Across the room, the record-player and large tape-deck sit on a long, elaborately inlaid chest. Above them hangs her portrait wearing her gold lamé evening dress with Saif's first gift – the antique Persian silver collar – at her throat. None of this is giving her any pleasure right now for she has a backache and another, dull, ache in the lower part of her tummy. Thirteen months married and four months pregnant. But how could it have happened? Until this day she does not know how it could have happened. And when she had asked her doctor he had looked at her as though she were mad.

'You are pregnant. You're a married woman and you are pregnant.'

'Yes, but we've hardly – I mean nothing much has really – I mean I can't possibly be.'

He had looked at her coldly. He had come to disapprove of her very much in the last few months.

'You are not on the pill and both you and your husband are young and healthy. The strange thing would be if you were not pregnant.'

'But I only came off the pill because it made me feel so sick and you said I shouldn't use an IUD until I'd had at least one baby and you said – you *promised* – I couldn't get pregnant. You said I was too tense, too nervous –'

He shook his head. 'Go home, child. Go home and give thanks to God. There are women who live out their lives praying for what you've got. Look after yourself carefully and come and see me in four weeks. Look after your husband but avoid intercourse for three months.'

Intercourse. Avoid it. Have it. Want it. Do you want it? Don't want it? Shit!

So Asya had gone. Not home. But to Chrissie. Asya sat down in front of a table in the British Council Library and pulled a book towards her and waited for her friend to be free. She opened the book at page one:

261

The boy's name was Said Mohammed. If he had had a family they would have called him Said; but he had no family and the people with whom he associated called him, simply and affectionately, Sinbad –

Asya has always liked this room. It had been the ballroom of the British Embassy back when they had a use for such things. Well before her time. It was long and high-ceilinged. One end opened on to the gardens – which they say used to run right down to the river before the Corniche Road was cut through – and at the other end, above the wide, pillared entrance, was a minstrels' gallery. Down both sides a series of discreet alcoves were scooped out – for filling out a card or sitting out a dance, for slipping a foot out of a satin slipper, for whispering behind a fan. In years to come this room – a faithful reflector of current British interest in Egypt – will be turned into the Visa Section. It will have a guarded turnstile at the door and be filled with rows of straight-backed grey plastic chairs. And the alcoves would become interviewing cubicles where pale clerks would exercise what remained of the white man's power over native visa applicants. But this was still to come. For the moment the alcoves were filled with elegantly bound books, the air was hushed and the chandeliers were still reasonably well polished. Asya looked around her at the powder-blue walls and scolded herself for thinking childish thoughts of fans and satin slippers, and when Chrissie finally came over she found her friend staring resolutely at the first page of a small, brown book:

The camp was called Sohag and it was just too far from Cairo for the men to get there and back in a day and too far from the nearest lake for them to get there and back in an afternoon, and there were no girls and only a garrison cinema that broke down at critical points in the story –

They had gone out into the garden.
'What's the matter?' Chrissie had asked. 'You look awful.'
'I'm pregnant.'
'Oh, darling! That's great. Terrific. A thousand congratulations.'
'Chrissie!' Asya pushes away Chrissie who is trying to hug her. 'I know you adore babies but this isn't possible.'
'Why? Why isn't it possible?'
'Chrissie. We were married last July. This is April. But you know what things have been like. You know everything. We haven't even really made love properly yet. I don't *feel* married – it's just far too soon. Saif doesn't even *want* children –'
'Men are like that. Don't pay any attention. He'll want it once it's there.'
'But *I* don't want it.'

262

'OK. Have it and give it to me.'

'*Chrissie!* Don't joke.'

'Well what can I say? You mustn't talk like that. What's wrong with having a baby now? This is Saif, isn't it? Saif whom you've loved for more than four years? And now you'll bear him a child. I know this last bit hasn't been easy but, believe me, a baby will put everything right. Be reasonable.'

Asya had waited for her friend, and when Chrissie had finished work the two girls had hailed a taxi, driven across Qasr el-Nil Bridge and into the Gezira Club and there, in a green cane chair in the mellow sunshine of the now hardly used race-course, Asya had buried her face in her hands and wept with anger.

'It's too soon. The timing's wrong. Everything is just always being ruined. First we have to wait four years – *four years* – before we can marry. And in four years – well, who knows what one ends up wanting? I know I don't feel now as I would have if they'd let us marry then. And maybe we wouldn't have had all these beastly problems. But anyway here we *are* and we're *trying* to make a go of it and then *this* happens. It isn't the right time.'

'It's never the "right time". This is life not a novel; you can't time things in life. This is how things happen.'

'And Chrissie, I'm frightened.'

'Frightened?'

'Of looking absolutely horrible while I'm pregnant. And then – really – of giving birth.'

'But everybody has babies all the time.'

'Yes, and everybody does it all the time too.'

'Does what?'

'Chrissie! Makes love.'

'So?'

'So if I'm finding even that so painful and horrid – and that's meant to be nice – then how about something that's actually *supposed* to be painful and horrid, like having a whole baby coming out of there?'

Chrissie had put a hand on her friend's knee.

'You're not going to find it horrid for ever. It's just been – circumstances. Look. Think of all the women who've had babies. Even my mother had five and you know how delicate she is. How come you've grown so silly all of a sudden? Although,' she had added, smiling, 'why should I say "all of a sudden"? You've always been a little bit silly –'

Yes, she had known that she sounded silly. But she had also known that Chrissie wouldn't understand. Wouldn't understand about being not ready. Chrissie has always cooed over babies; has sometimes even volunteered to look after her cousin's four-month-old son. And now that Chrissie is married to Fuad she is waiting every day to conceive, to transform herself into a 'family'.

*

Now Asya shifts on her sofa in the August heat. The cat raises her head and blinks at her then lays it lazily back on the kelim. Asya's feelings haven't really changed, but over the last week – since she's been ordered to rest because of her backache and the few drops of blood that she had lost – she has come to think more about the baby and less about what the baby would do to *her*. She hadn't really thought of it as a baby before; just as something that was going to affect her life enormously. Now she tries to think of it as it is now – inside her – and wonders at how little she knows. In adolescent afternoons she had stolen into her father's empty study and sat on the floor staring at table after table in Kinsey's two volumes until she'd practically learnt them by heart. But she knows nothing. She has the standard image of the curled-up foetus in her mind but she has no idea, for example, how big the actual baby inside her is now, this minute. She puts a hand on her slightly rounded belly. Has it already decided whether it will be a girl or a boy? Could she tell if she saw it? There is so much that she doesn't know. As well as not knowing how to make love. If her mother had been here. She could have told her. About the baby, that is. Or got her a book or something. But her mother, father, sister, brother are all in London till school starts again in October. And Nadia too is in England. Dada Sayyida is good on some things but hugely unspecific. Asya smiles at the thought of trying to pin Dada Sayyida down to the measurements of a four-month-old foetus. And Chrissie and Tante Soraya, for all that they adore babies, wouldn't really know. Not in detail. Saif? Well. He can get her a book from the AUC Library.

Saif. She still cannot tell how he feels about it. When she had told him he hadn't been particularly jubilant. Or particularly miserable. Or even surprised. It was like it was some totally normal, everyday thing that had happened. She hadn't thought it would be a good idea to go on about how she didn't want the baby and all that, but she had asked what he thought they'd do about the practical problems and he had shrugged.

'We'll manage. Everybody does.'

'And the doctor said we mustn't – mustn't, you know, do anything for three months –'

'OK.'

And that was that. He had gone on treating her with that kind, amused, almost brotherly affection that he had adopted since their engagement, and it was left to Shahir and their other men friends to be all excited about the baby: to jump up and push chairs forward and arrange cushions and dream up nice things to eat. She no longer knows how to reach him. No, that isn't quite right. She has always been the same, but he had been – accessible – and now he isn't. Since when? Since they had married? Since they had become engaged? Was it because

264

things had gone wrong in bed that he had sort of retreated from her? Or had things gone wrong, in part, because they were already separate? Were they really, finally, irrevocably separate, or can she still do something about it? She'd used to. No, she hadn't used to. He had always gone in and out of moods as it suited *him*. Had he ever been truly accessible to her? Think of the best times: think of Beirut, think of the Omar Khayyam, think of London – well, apart from that one thing – but think of all those Sunday afternoons, three years of Sunday afternoons. Yes. Yes, he *had* been. And she had been happy. But when she'd been *un*happy – when *they'd* been unhappy – had she ever been able to do anything about it? Had she ever been able to influence how he was? She could make him angry. But could she make him *not* angry? Could she make him smile if he was cross? Could she make him melt and love her? No. No, she had never been able to do that. And why should she think she could do it now after things had got so tangled up between them. Because she loves him. Because they love each other. Because they are friends and have good times and he wants to be married to her otherwise why is he here?

The doorbell rings briefly and a key turns in the lock.

'Hello, pussycat. I've brought you some kebab and this.'

He puts the little parcel and the copy of *House Beautiful* on the desk and throws his key-chain – his gold key-chain with the entwined initials of his name that had been her first gift to him – next to them. He puts his hands in his pockets and stands looking down at her – smiling. He does not come over and kiss her or sit beside her on the sofa and touch her face, but maybe he just doesn't know she wants him to. But shouldn't *he* want to? Maybe it just hasn't occurred to him. But it's not a matter of 'occurring'; why does he not want to? Maybe he *does* want to. Well, if he does then why doesn't he just do it? Maybe he thinks *she* doesn't want him to –

'Well? How d'you feel? Are you OK?'

'Yes. I've been fine.'

'She's still here, is she?'

The cat has padded up and is rubbing her head and her sides in turns against his trouser leg.

Asya shrugs. 'I guess she'll stay. Until she's had her babies anyway. Dada Sayyida gave me a whole epic about omens and affinities and how it was a kind of natural honour that she should choose us. She threatened to tell me all about how a cat played some definitive role in her life.'

'Shall I get you a plate and something to drink?'

'Won't *you* eat?'

'No. I had some sandwiches earlier. Shahir's coming round later and one of us can go and get something then if we need it.'

He goes to the kitchen and comes back with the black lacquered tray his mother had brought them from Hong Kong. On it he had placed one of the plates with the smudged blue bird they had bought together in Beirut, a knife and fork they had bought there as well, a paper napkin and a glass from the everyday set Tante Soraya had given them.

'What do you want to drink? There's Sport Cola or water.'

'Water, please.'

He takes the glass to the kitchen and comes back with it full of iced water. He opens the parcel and places the meat and salad on the plate. He puts the tray on the coffee-table and carries the table over close to the sofa where she lies. She passes a finger over the black hairs on the back of his hand.

'OK, pussycat?' He pats her hand and moves to switch on the lamp behind her head. 'I'm going to have a shower.'

He walks out of the room and disappears behind the arabesque screen that stands at the mouth of the corridor. She still loves the way he walks; rising ever so slightly with each step as though he were walking on water.

'I'm pregnant,' Asya had told Tante Soraya.

'Congratulations. And what are you looking like that for?'

'Nothing. I just think it's a bit too early, that's all.'

'Early in your life! Why? Early for what?'

'Well, for a start, our flat has only one bedroom —'

'Is this a way to talk? A tiny baby and you won't find a corner to put him in?'

'Well, where?'

'With you at first, and then you move the dining-table into the hall and turn the dining-room into a nursery.'

'Oh, but I don't want to do that. It'll all look crowded and horrible. We've only had two proper dinner parties and already we're talking about dismantling the dining-room.'

'Dinner party? What's more important? A dinner party or a child?'

Dada Sayyida, sitting under the window, picking out bits of grit and chaff from a trayful of white rice, nods her head in affirmation of Tante Soraya's words. Asya tries her usually winning card.

'And I'm supposed to finish my MA this coming year and then go abroad to do a Ph.D. How am I going to do that?'

'You'll do it. Your mother did it, didn't she? And towards the end she had not only you to look after but your sister as well. And no money. And your father is a hundred times more difficult to manage than your husband. *She* did it.'

'I'm not *like* Mummy. You can say I'm spoilt. Say it as much as you like. And maybe I *am*. But you've all brought me up that way. Mummy actually doesn't *mind* not having money and working terribly hard all the time. And besides she – well, she's exceptional.'

266

'And you're exceptional too, Asya.' Tante Soraya had leaned over and hugged her niece's shoulders.

Dada Sayyida said, 'Certainly. Exceptional. The name of God protect you and keep you safe,' without taking her eye off a minute piece of grit she was examining carefully before adding it to the pile in the ashtray. 'You've always been clever and sweet,' Tante Soraya said, 'and now you'll give us a beautiful clever sweet little girl just like you and she'll be the first grandchild in the family just as you were the first child.'

Asya had known there was no more to be said. Dada Sayyida filled the little silence.

' "Children are the ornament of life," truly it was said.'

Asya had shrugged. Dada Sayyida had seven children, two of them blind. Tante Soraya glanced at Asya's face.

'Smooth it out now and stop frowning. This is the greatest gift God can give a human being, and you receive it like this?'

The sharpness of her tone had taken Asya by surprise, but then Tante Soraya had willingly spent nine months lying flat on her back in order to incubate and deliver, with huge trouble, her beloved Meedo. And after she had produced him she had been told he would always be her one and only because having another would surely kill her. The 'Diamond Baby' they had called him at the hospital. He was almost seven now, and in years to come Tante Soraya would complain bitterly of him; of his bad grades at school, of his profligacy with money, of his lack of concern for her and his father, of his refusal to perform the simplest of tasks, like buying yoghurt on his way home, and all these failings she would ascribe to a common cause: that he was an only child. Better to have died attempting to provide him with a sister or a brother to instil in him the knowledge that he was not the only person in the world than to have lived to see such monstrous egotism and bad behaviour. But that was in years to come and for now Tante Soraya was concerned that Asya should be grateful for her lot – which after all, let's face it, was nothing to grumble about – and get on with the true and central business of life: raising a family.

In May Asya had gone to see her Professor. She had written the proposal for her MA dissertation and wanted him to approve it before the summer holidays began. It is a hot day and he is mopping his face with the usual fastidious white handkerchief.

'What's the matter, Asya? Why do you look so changed?'

Asya is conscious of her puffy face and her pallor. She is so sorry for herself. Her eyes fill with tears.

'I'm pregnant.'

'Congratulations.'

She looks up but he is not mocking her.

'I don't want to be pregnant.'

'Why not?'

'It's much too soon.'

'Too soon for what? It's natural.'

'It's horrid. And frightening.'

'Ah, frightening! *That's* natural too. Listen, I get pregnant every year. And each time I'm frightened.'

Asya frowns at him.

'Yes. Every year I get pregnant, and then, with varying degrees of difficulty, I give birth to a new play. It is Nature.'

Ah! A metaphor.

'Nothing good – nothing natural – comes without difficulty and without a period of gestation.'

'Yes. Well. If it was *your* kind of pregnancy, Professor, I shouldn't mind at all – but I feel that I haven't had – time, that all my decisions are being taken for me. That I can't catch up with my own life.'

'You chose your husband, didn't you?'

'Yes, I did.'

'And you are happy with him?'

'Yes, I am.'

'Then everything else will fall into place. And you will make a very beautiful mother.'

'Thank you, Professor.'

'So, what was your title?'

' "Romeo as the Embodiment of the Platonic Ideals of Courtly Love".'

15 August

Asya shifts on the sofa. She thinks she would like to go to the bathroom but decides to wait. If she were really behaving as the doctor had advised, she would be in her bed with a bedpan at her side. Of course she is concerned about the baby – and frightened. But still she cheats. What difference will it make if she lies all day on the sofa instead of on the bed? And it can't matter *that* much if she very very carefully walks to the loo twice a day – not counting stopping there on her way in the morning from bed to sofa and in the evening from sofa to bed – and lies absolutely still the rest of the time.

Their telephone had been applied for last year when they signed the contract for the flat but, of course, it hasn't arrived yet. So Dada Sayyida has to come and sit with Asya every day in case 'something happens' and then (may evil stay far away from us and may we never need to do this) she would run – or trot, rather, for Dada Sayyida is plump and heavy – to the grocer round the corner and phone Grandfather or Uncle Hamid and then come back. They (or one of them) would phone the doctor and find out what to do, then phone Saif and tackle the intricacies of the AUC switchboard. In the event, when the dreaded thing finally hap-

pened, they had no need of any of this, for Saif was on the spot, but still –
it had been right to have a plan.

Dada Sayyida rings the bell politely to signal her arrival, then turns
the key in the lock. Dada Sayyida is on loan to Asya during her illness.
Dada Zeina had left in a big huff when Asya had permitted Saif's old
nanny, Dada Wageeda, to be the one to clean up the flat when the
builders had finally left and Saif and Asya had at long last taken
delivery of the keys. Dada Zeina had collected her clothes and gone.
Tante Soraya said she had just used the incident as an excuse to leave
because she had already been negotiating with a Saudi family who were
offering her three times what she made with the Ulama – and besides
Asya was married. Her sister was sixteen and her brother fourteen.
There were no longer any children to be looked after. (Well, now there
are – is – will be, thinks Asya.) And Dada Wageeda can come only once
a week because she is looking after her own daughter who drank a
bottle of gasoline when she found out that her husband had taken
another wife and is now very ill and cannot manage anything for herself. So every morning Dada Sayyida makes her way from behind the
railway tracks in Giza to Midan El-'Ataba and does what needs to be
done at Grandfather's house. Then she crosses the city again to
Mohandesseen, rings the bell politely and opens the door with the key
that Saif had had cut for her, naming the Name of God as she steps
over the threshold.

'On the sofa? Still?'

'What's wrong with the sofa?'

'Didn't the doctor say bed?'

'And what's the difference between the sofa and the bed?'

'But the doctor said bed. Bed is more comfortable, Sett Asya.'

'OK, Dada. Don't preach. I've been lying on my back for two weeks
now. Come and sit with me and chat to me.'

Sayyida has taken off her black silk outer smock and unwrapped the
black *tarha* from around her head. Her shoes she has taken off at the
door and is carrying under her arm. She laughs and takes her outer
clothes to the servants' bathroom and hangs them there behind the door.
Now, in her flowered house smock and with a flowered peasant kerchief
on her head, she pads barefoot back into the living-room.

'Where is she, the name of the Prophet guard her?'

Asya looks at her. How old is she? My mother's age? Younger? Her
face is very smooth with wonderful skin – but working-class women's
often are and Asya has heard that it's because they depilate them
regularly along with their arms and legs and everything else. Asya
shudders at the thought of the candy ripping the tiny hairs away from her
own brow. Dada Zeina once, stroking her forehead as she lay with her
head on her knee, had said, 'And didn't they wipe your brow for you

when you were born, poor child?' Asya, sensing criticism, had remained silent, then had confronted her mother.

'Why do you wipe a baby's brow when it's born?'

Lateefa had looked up from some huge volume with tiny print and no pictures and Asya had had to repeat her question.

'Wipe their – oh, with milk you mean? It's just a habit.'

'Why do people do it?'

'It's supposed to stop hair from growing on your forehead.'

'Why didn't you do it to me?'

'We did. At least, my mother did. With cotton-wool dipped in goat's milk. She had to do it in secret, though, so your father wouldn't know.'

'Well, why didn't it work? Was she *supposed* to use goat's milk?'

'Asya, what is all this about?'

'I've got hair on my forehead.'

'You haven't got hair on your forehead.'

'I *have* got hair on my forehead. Look.'

And Asya had come close and stood in front of her mother looking tortured. Lateefa had examined her forehead.

'You haven't got "hair". Just normal down. Everyone has that. I have that. They only do that stupid thing with the milk because they think very broad foreheads are beautiful. But that's just one opinion.'

'Maybe the goat's milk made it grow.'

'*You haven't got hair on your forehead.* Now stop being silly and go away and read or something. Who told you about all this?'

But Asya wasn't going to get Dada Zeina into trouble, so she just went away. She didn't have hair on her forehead, of course, not really. But she was miserable enough about it for a while –

'Where *is* the cat?'

Dada Sayyida had come back from looking under the bed and in the wardrobe and in various places where a cat might hide.

'She went out this morning when Saif opened the door.'

'It will be her time soon.' Dada Sayyida looks worried. 'I'm going to prepare a comfortable corner for her today, Sett Asya –'

'Dada Sayyida. Why don't you make us some tea and come and sit down.'

'What? I haven't even started my work yet and I'm going to sit and behave like a guest? I'll make tea for *you*, Sett Asya –'

'No, no. I don't want any right now. Dada, how old is Osta Mohammad? He's your eldest, isn't he?'

Dada Sayyida doesn't need time to think.

'Twenty-five in the face of the enemy. But he's a poor lad.'

Twenty-five. If she had him when she was twenty, say, that would make her forty-five: exactly Asya's mother's age.

'How old were you when you married, Dada Sayyida?'

270

'Fifteen – but that's a long story and I've got to get on with my work now. What can I get you, Sett Asya?'

'Nothing, thank you.'

Asya goes to the bathroom, keeping her body as still and stiff as she can. Dada Sayyida, busy at the kitchen sink, does not see her. In the bathroom Asya locks the door and switches on the light. Sitting on the loo she examines the gusset of her panties carefully for any spots, streaks, signs of any description, any colour. Nothing. She tries to merely release the pee, not make any effort, any pushing movements, creating the least possible disturbance down there. At the end, though, she does push just the tiniest bit. Otherwise she would have to come back again soon. She dries herself and examines the tissue carefully. Nothing. Then she stands up and scans the loo. All clear. She throws the tissue in and pulls the chain. She daren't use the douche in the bidet so she just uses some water in a cupped hand, then dries herself carefully, examines the towel, stares in the mirror at her face, which does not seem so swollen any more – in fact it's not looking too bad. In the corridor she meets Dada Sayyida.

'And why are you walking like Khosheshban? Aren't you feeling well?'

'I'm just trying not to move – as much as possible, that is.'

Dada Sayyida follows her stiff progress with raised eyebrows and pursed lips. Down the corridor, across the hall – and as she starts through the living-room a small miaow is heard, together with a scratching at the door. Dada Sayyida hurries past Asya and opens the door and the slim grey cat saunters in, with her pronounced belly, tail held high, the merest crook at the tip.

'Where have you been, Lady? We've been asking after you.'

But the cat ignores Sayyida. She wanders through to the living-room, leaps on to Asya as she lies on the sofa, and stands there, her back legs on Asya's thighs, her front on her tummy. She stretches and paces gently, claws slightly out, picking up some of Asya's dressing-gown with every step. Asya puts her hand on the soft fur under her chin and the cat lies down with her, belly to belly, and closes her eyes.

'A blessing, Sett Asya. This is a blessing and a good omen.'

Asya strokes the cat's side and feels the vibration of her purr. She runs her hand down her front legs and holds her paws and fingers the velvet pads. To come and go as you please. To vanish for a day and miaow at the door and be let in. To leap with such grace on to a friendly lap, and stretch and purr and settle lazily into sleep.

'I've put a cardboard box for her in the second bathroom, Sett Asya. I've put some fresh rags in it and I'll show it to her when she wakes up.'

'Dada Sayyida, if you don't come and sit down and talk to me I'll – I'll get up and jump about.'

Scene 2

1944

A village in the Nile Delta

When Sayyida turned twelve the talk of the women of her household began to turn towards her marriage. There were three or four young men in the village who could be thought of as possible bridegrooms; nothing very fancy, it was true, but then what was she bringing to a husband? Good looks, yes, for she was fair for a village girl, and rounded, though she had only had her 'habit' four times and so was later than all but one of her girlfriends, and that one did not count as she had caught polio when she was little and it had left her stunted and crooked, poor thing, and unless she could be found a blind boy or a fool she stood no chance at all of getting married in this life. But Sayyida had had her habit four times and already she was rounded out and pushing against her child's smock, and even though she was a bit short she had a healthy, rosy colouring, and who wanted to have to stand on tiptoe to reach his wife? But best of all was her disposition, for she was open and cheerful; she could be trusted to look after small children and livestock and not to let them wander away or sicken – (A few months ago, as they carried armfuls of plants from the car upstairs to the second-floor balcony, Asya had turned and laughed to see Sayyida walking along, arms full, balancing a potted dragon-tree on her head. 'Dada Sayyida, you look like a tree.'

'I *am* a tree,' Sayyida had replied. 'See how many souls I shade and bear fruit for –') – could be trusted not to answer sharply or be impatient with the great-grandmother who sat against the wall in the sunshine shelling peas or dozingly rocking a baby on her knee. So if she would not bring a bit of land or much of a dowry to her husband, she would put her sturdy health and her steady character to his service and the service of his children, and as for money, with a good woman in his home a man can sort himself out and put one piastre on top of another and may God bless him.

So the talk went in Sayyida's hearing, and no doubt out of it. And in a short while this talk of women would have curved its way along the dusty lanes of the village, stopping for a while at each house, and would have settled one dusk at the cardboard and tin shack which served for the village coffee-house where the men sat between sunset and evening prayers on straight-backed wooden chairs held together with twine. And talk of the marriage of Sayyida would have made some small place for itself amongst the murmurings over crops and taxes, the smokers' coughs

272

and spit, the slamming of backgammon counters and the crackle of the wireless placed high on a shelf and turned up loud to catch what could be caught of the news of the spreading war in far-away and hard-to-imagine Europe.

And soon one of the possible bridegrooms would have sent a father, brother, uncle or friend to single out Sayyida's father; perhaps to walk home with him in the evening along the bank of their streamlet and break open the now ripe question of marriage to his daughter. And what would have happened then? Ah! Knowledge of what might have been is the privilege of God alone. For in this life Man sees only what has been written down for him, and it was written that Sayyida, having prepared the food and collected the small brothers and sisters, nephews and nieces left in her care – Sayyida, just as she was gathering the skirt of her *galabiyya* into her plump lap, and as she lowered herself on to the floor in front of the low table spread with supper in the doorway of her father's house – Sayyida paused. She paused and looked around her to make sure that the children were all there. She paused, still holding her bunched-up skirts in her left hand and leaning on the earthen floor with her right. And at that moment a cat – one of the many strays who roamed the village and tried to raid the chicken-coops – a cat sprang on to the low table and off it again, but now with a piece of meat in her mouth. As the cat leapt Sayyida struck at it with her right hand.

'Well, Dada? Did you get the cat?'

No. The cat had run away unharmed with the piece of meat still in its mouth and had probably gone and enjoyed it up a tree somewhere away from everybody. Meanwhile Sayyida leaned on her elbow and levered herself upright on the floor. She put both hands up to adjust her clothes and found that her right hand could grip neither her neckline nor her kerchief. She looked at her hand, and all the children looked at it with her: the fingers had curled inward on themselves, the formed fist was shaking. She put it on the table in front of her – in front of them all – among the dishes of still untouched food, and it jumped about and would not be still. She knew what had happened. Even as her voice rose in a wail calling for her mother, she knew. Her hand was rebelling against the act she had made it commit: it shrank into itself; revolted, it jumped about; to escape.

'But you hadn't sat there *planning* on getting the cat. It was a reflex.'

Indeed it was. For had she not used her right hand, the hand that was supporting her as she sat herself down on the floor, so that without it she fell on her bottom and then on to her side at the very moment that she had struck the cat? And who could blame her, for was the stolen meat not one of the four pieces that were to be divided among eight open mouths that had not tasted meat for a week?

'Well, then?'

Well, then? What use is it arguing with your fate? The talk of marriage disappeared and was replaced by talk of this novel obstacle to marriage: the jumping hand. And this new talk, more vigorous and fresh-blooded than the old, sped into the neighbouring villages so that as Sayyida was taken round by her mother and aunts to attend a *zar* in one place or consult with a holy man in another, that talk raced ahead of her, and everyone they met had words of advice and words of reproach: how could she have forgotten, even for an instant, that the cat is a blessed animal, that the Prophet – the praise and blessings of God be upon him – had allowed kittens to nestle and play in the sleeves of his robes, why, that he had even put his own pure lips to a vessel of water from which a cat had just been lapping?

For two years Sayyida's womenfolk asked leave of husbands, left children with neighbours and saved small and secret sums to travel on foot, on carts and on buses, taking the girl to wherever anyone had heard of someone who could maybe by the will of God work a cure. As for Sayyida, she did everything that was asked of her: she wore amulets with sacred words and names of Jinn tied to bits of string around her neck, she held out her hand to be purified with incense, pricked with needles, burnt with hot irons; she wore her *galabiyya* back to front for a week, during which she uttered no sound from the rising of the sun to its setting. And all to no avail. The only change that took place was that Sayyida learned to control the jumping hand by gripping it tightly in the other; that she even learned to work with it; so she would press it hard, say, against the chicken she was plucking, wedging the bird into her bosom and tearing off its feathers with her free and functioning left hand. This Sayyida had learnt for herself without the help either of the Jinn or the holy people and she had learnt it in the early days of her trouble.

But Sayyida's trouble continued for many months. And after a time, when the surrounding and reasonably far places and people of holiness had been exhausted, when the women grew tired of leaving their children and their poultry and the men grew cross and restive to come home so often to houses empty of wives, when also the village had grown to regard the jumping hand as part of Sayyida – as though it were an unfortunate feature that had been with her from birth, and when the possibility of subduing the hand had become remote and unreal, Sayyida, now familiar to everyone's consciousness as constantly clutching one hand with another, was left to get on with her life as best she might.

And there it might all have ended had Sayyida's father not had a sister who lived in a place as remote and unreal to the village as the possibility of ending his daughter's plight. Cairo. Sayyida's aunt lived in Cairo, and in Cairo – the Mother of the World – there was a very very big hospital called the Qasr where every illness you'd ever heard of, and others – may evil remain far from us – that would never cross your mind could, by the command of God, be cured. So when the hardest work was done for the season, Sayyida's father rose early. He put on his good woollen *galabiyya*, he threw his long brown scarf with the tasselled ends over his linen turban and pushed his feet into his deerskin slippers. Sayyida's mother lifted a cage, in which six laying chicken were clucking, on to her daughter's head, and on top of it she balanced the bundle of Sayyida's clothing. She hung a basket full of country butter and homemade cakes on her left arm and tucked some silver money knotted in a clean white rag into her bosom. Then she kissed her and wept. Her father reached for his cudgel and Sayyida held her right hand tightly in her left, and they set off at dawn on the long walk to the nearest small town and the macadamed road and the bus stop.

Sayyida was welcomed in her aunt's house with joy, for she was a pretty and pleasant girl despite her misfortune – why, even the misfortune was in the nature of an asset for it was an original curiosity and would give her aunt a new topic and new prominence among her neighbours – and besides the girl bore it so well that it was not likely to prove a hindrance to her usefulness with the housework. So Sayyida took her place in her aunt's household: the daughter that the woman did not have, for she was mother to three sons. Three – in the face of the enemy – three young men like roses except that the youngest – oh apple of his mother's eye – who was sixteen and like the moon in every other respect, had had his legs severed when he was nine years old and playing with his friends on the trams as all boys do, jumping on and then jumping off when the conductor came for the tickets. But he had jumped off into the path of another tram. Everyone had thought he would die, but good people had rushed him to the Qasr and there they'd saved him – but his legs were gone. From just above the knee. His brothers had fashioned him a little platform on four wheels and he propelled himself along with two blocks of wood he held in his hands and could also use as brakes. He did not go very far. And he did not work. But his brothers, one a plumber and one a car-body worker, were good boys and would support him as long as God put it in their power to do so.

After a month of silently weeping in the night for her mother and the little brothers and sisters whose soft bodies had warmed her while they slept, Sayyida woke up one morning, wiped away her tears and put on her best black *galabiyya* and followed her cousin the plumber through the crowded Cairo streets, on to a bus and off it again and into a building bigger than anything she had ever imagined or dreamed of. They walked and walked, one corridor handing them over to another, one office to another, one set of people to another, until at the end of the day they sat in front of a kind, white-coated man who looked at Sayyida's jumping hand, touched it, ran little black machines over it and put it inside other big chrome-coloured machines and asked Sayyida and her cousin to

275

come back tomorrow. Tomorrow and the day after and the day after that the plumber turned his work over to a friend while he took his cousin to the Qasr, where her hand was looked at, prodded, examined, its story listened to by more and more people, some in white coats and others not. But such things cannot go on for ever and a man who has a mother and a crippled brother to feed as well as a future to think about has, eventually, to attend to his work.

And so the months passed one after another until it was the year of the big war in Palestine and the hot season came round again and Salih, Sayyida's youngest cousin, was on his platform fighting with his mother about a shirt he wanted to wear, and why was it not clean? The mother was short-tempered. Her eldest had been called up to fight and her spirit was constrained, and should she cut herself up into a hundred pieces to do all the things that they were constantly demanding of her? Sayyida quietly took the shirt and went over to the washing tub. She poured the water, then sat down and pushed the shirt against the bottom of the tub with her jumping right hand. She took the little cake of soap in her left and started to scrub – and slowly, slowly, as she scrubbed, her hand quietened down until it was quite still.

When her aunt saw this miracle she knew that Sayyida had been destined for her son. She sent for her brother, who came and saw for himself and testified that there is no God but God and that Muhammad is his Messenger and that His wisdom is beyond the comprehension of man, and upon that he gave his daughter in marriage to her crippled cousin who had been the instrument of the beneficial will of the Almighty.

'But, Dada, when he had no legs – could he, I mean, could he – marry?'

'I bore him eleven children to put shame in the eye of the Evil One – and seven of them lived.'

'But how – I mean how – with no legs – ?'

Sayyida laughs.

'With a little help, Sett Asya. With a little help.'

She nudges Asya's side as she lies on the sofa, then she laughs so much that she has to throw the pillowcase she has been folding over her face.

Scene 3

21 August, 1972
Cairo

The cat is having her babies – kittens. At least, that must be what she's doing, even though she is not doing it in the cardboard box Sayyida set up so carefully. She has chosen to go into labour in a pile of freshly laundered napkins left in the middle of the dining-room table. On her halting, robot-like way from the bathroom to the living-room, just before midday, Asya notices the movement in the heap of linen. She circles the table slowly and peers. The cat has made herself a nest. She is lying stretched out on her side and she is trembling violently. Her head is thrown back and her eyes stare straight into Asya's but she does not make a single sound. Asya sits down in Saif's chair at the head of the table. She watches the cat. It seems odd that a creature who miaows for the smallest thing and sometimes for pleasure should now, in extremity, fall so silent. For this is an extremity, and no doubt about it. All this terrible shivering and shaking – and yet she lies there, four legs stretched out, front paws folded neatly over each other. She is not trying to do anything; she is merely suffering what is happening to her. This is her first time, Dada Sayyida had said so. A primagravida. Asya grimaces. The pain in her back is worse this morning – she straightens against the back of the chair. But it is probably nothing compared to what the cat is going through. Maybe she doesn't know what she is doing: what is happening to her. Since it's her first time. Or has she seen it happen to other cats? Can cats learn from other cats' experiences? Yes – no, that was monkeys. The monkey trainer would tie the novice monkey to a stake and fetch a cat. 'Jump,' he'd tell the cat. 'Dance.' And of course the cat neither jumped nor danced. 'Sit,' he would command it. 'Sleep.' And when the cat failed to respond to his commands he would take out a sharp knife and slit its throat under the monkey's nose. The monkey, chattering with terror, would then learn his moves with skill and speed: 'Knead the dough like a peasant-woman,' 'Sleep like a restless bachelor' – for the rest of his days he would never fail to respond with desperate alacrity to the commands of his master. Amazing how harmless it had all seemed in the days when hearing the tambourine of the monkey-man coming down the street meant rushing to the balcony to watch the show for a few moments before throwing down a silver coin. Or had it? She supposes, really, that she had always been made a bit uneasy by the sight of the muzzled beast with its peculiarly prominent lumpy red buttocks throwing itself around at the end of a rope to the laughter and jeers of the crowd. Still: uneasy

277

merely. With no knowledge of some dim, dank room – Asya imagines it made of concrete, with no windows, like a cell – in which captive cats were slaughtered to produce the show. But this cat is in pain, there is no doubt about it. Her eyes have rolled back, half closed, and she is no longer aware of Asya's presence. What can Asya do for her? What can she do? If she could go out she would have phoned someone – Chrissie or Noora or someone. But she can't go out – and her back hurts so much. Asya gets up and walks slowly, pressing her hands into the small of her back, over to the sofa. She can do nothing for the cat.

When Sayyida arrives she complains.

'She had to do it in the middle of the fresh napkins?'

'She's in trouble, Dada.'

'No trouble at all. She's had three.'

Asya braves Sayyida's displeasure and hobbles over to look. Her stomach turns; they are not kittens at all. They are hairless slimy red rats. And the cat is curled up around one of them and nibbling it; actually eating bits of it up. Asya looks at Sayyida with horror but Sayyida only smiles.

'What's she doing?'

'She's cleaning them up.'

'Does she have to do it like that?'

'What else? Should she leave them in their bags and let them die?'

The cat is nibbling, chewing, licking.

'You said it was her first time.'

'It is.'

'How does she know what to do?'

'God, my daughter,' Sayyida sighs. 'God. It is God's wisdom: He looks after all His servants.'

When Asya next dares to leave her sofa and look it is four o'clock. The cat has left the soiled napkins and is lying on her side in a patch of afternoon sunshine on the burnished oak of the dining-table. Snuggled into her belly, wriggling and reaching and nuzzling blindly at her nipples, are three pointy-eared kittens. One is grey. One is grey and white. And one is black. The cat yawns and closes her eyes, then opens them wide and stares steadily at Asya, and makes no move as Asya puts out a tentative finger and feels the softness of the kittens. Sayyida puts a saucer of milk near the cat's head.

'She won't leave them now for a while. We'll have to feed her where she is.'

She scoops up the napkins.

'We'll boil these and see what happens. Maybe I can get them clean.'

'Dada Sayyida. You know the cardboard box you fixed up for her? Put it in the middle of the bedroom floor. She wants her kittens to be in the sunshine.'

*

278

It is six o'clock. Dada Sayyida has gone and Saif has not yet come home. Asya has had a sudden and terrible pain. It had taken hold of her tummy and squeezed it as though with the powerful hands of a washerwoman. It had pressed itself into her then gone round and round inside her like a grinding-stone. It had doubled her over, and when she'd got her breath back it had sent her whimpering and cradling herself with both arms from the sofa to her bed. Now she lies in bed and waits for the next thing that is to happen and for Saif to come home. The pain has not come back but the ache in the lower part of her back is more acute than ever, and from time to time she feels another brief, corkscrew-like pain flashing upwards between her legs. As she lies on her bed she cranes her neck – just her neck – to look into her dressing-table mirror. She looks all right. Nothing really bad can be happening to her; this odd assortment of pains would pass and she would be fine. And the baby would be fine. Lately she had taken to seeing him as a little boy; a little boy in black velvet pants. About two years old. With Saif's face, round and solemn and dark-eyed like in the photos of Saif as a baby Tante Adeela had given her. She sees him in soft black trousers and a loose white shirt and bare feet climbing over her as she lies on her back in the middle of the living-room carpet –

She hears Saif's key in the lock, and he comes in, surprised to find her in bed.

'What's up, sweetie?'

She tells him about the pain, and without waiting to eat or have a shower or anything he turns and goes straight out to fetch Tante Soraya and phone the doctor. Thinking back later, she will wonder why they both thought it so imperative to fetch Tante Soraya from way across town. Why had he not phoned the doctor from the neighbours' or from the grocer's shop nearby and come back to her? Some dim notion of 'things only a woman can do', probably. Would it have changed anything if he had come back to her? Probably not. He is gone for an hour and a half. As Asya lies in bed waiting she feels a sudden rushing wetness between her legs. She pushes back the covers, pulls up her nightie, and braces herself for the sight of the blood she knows she will find. But there is no blood. Only water, and she breathes in relief. That's all right, then. It's not blood. But why should water be coming out of her suddenly? Her first thought is that this is pee somehow escaping. But as she looks she feels more coming out, and more. And she cannot hold it back. And it has no colour and no smell. So it's not pee. Should she get up and get some towels with which to stem this flood? Or should she lie still? The sheets are being ruined. They can be washed. But the mattress is getting ruined. But is she going to get up and flood the carpets? And who knows what more will come out of her if she stands up? She lies very still, and after a while when she looks again it seems to have stopped. So,

279

very carefully, she gets up. She puts on a pair of fresh white cotton panties and stuffs them with small face-towels. She changes her nightie. Then, very slowly, she strips the sheet from the bed, mops up the wet patch on the mattress as much as possible, and lays a fresh towel over it, puts a fresh sheet on the bed and transports the wet one, together with her discarded clothes, to the bathroom, where she stuffs them into the laundry basket. She brushes her teeth and hair and puts on a little mascara and lip-gloss. When Saif comes back she is lying arranged and pretty in the fresh bed. He looks tired and ragged.

'Come on. We've got to get you to hospital. Tante Soraya's in the car. Can you walk?'

'Did you phone the doctor?'

'Of course I did. He said to get you to hospital as quickly as possible. So come on, sweetie, come on.'

'Should I change?'

'No. Dressing-gown and slippers. If you need anything else I'll fetch it for you later. Come on.'

Down in the car, Tante Soraya's face is grim.

'Good evening, Tante Soraya. I'm so sorry we got you out like this.'

'What have you done to yourself?'

'I don't know, Tante, I don't know what's happening.'

This is the hospital where she was supposed to come five months later. A small, private maternity hospital in Shari' Finney. Asya thinks that hospital receptions – even private hospital receptions – always look horrid at night: the lights, neon but dim, the smudged, dirty green walls, the grey linoleum floor, the unwilling night-staff – Saif takes care of the formalities with Tante Soraya standing at his elbow while Asya sits against a wall on a wooden bench. Then she is taken, alone, into a small dim room with a screen and a patients' trolley. She is given a white hospital smock and told to put it on and lie on the trolley. She wonders what she should do with the nightie and dressing-gown she has taken off, then she decides to fold them up and put them at the foot of the trolley. At the last moment she remembers to retrieve the face-towels from her panties. She feels suddenly relieved, as though she has been spared a huge embarrassment. The towels are dry. Good. She folds them up and hides them in the dressing-gown pocket. Then she climbs up on to the trolley and lies down. She folds her hands over her tummy and crosses her ankles. As she does this the pain returns: taking her by surprise, grinding her tummy and beating at her back. A nurse comes in and puts a thermometer in her mouth and a finger and thumb on her pulse. She writes some figures down on a piece of paper attached to a clip-board, then she measures Asya's blood-pressure and writes that down too. Then she ties a rubber tube tight around her upper left arm and gives her an injection in the purple vein that pulses hesitantly in the crook of her elbow. She asks her to count backward from a hundred – aloud.

22 August

Asya feels something heavy weighing her down. She tries to move and finds she cannot shift her lower half at all. When she opens her eyes she sees streaks of sunshine on a green wall. She sees the shape of Tante Soraya seated beside her. She can remember saying ninety-six, ninety-five. She says, 'Tante Soraya, I can't move my legs.'

Tante Soraya's face is even grimmer than it was the night before. She says, 'You're not supposed to move your legs.'

Asya raises herself on both elbows. She feels sick, and waits for a moment and tries to take a deep breath. She lifts the sheet covering her and looks under it. Her legs are wide open, and between them and on the tops of her thighs lie several little bags covered in grey cloth. She balances on one elbow and reaches out and picks up one of the bags. A sandbag. They've put sandbags between her legs. They've barricaded the baby. She feels sick with the effort of leaning on her elbow and drops the sandbag. Her head is so heavy, so heavy and so hazy. As she lies back on the pillow with her eyes closed she hears a baby crying: a frail, sad quaver; brief but insistent. She opens her eyes and turns her head to look at Tante Soraya. She knows that if she speaks she'll throw up but she questions her with her eyes. Tante Soraya's tone is bitter.

'A baby girl. Born in the night.'

A girl after all. But then Asya is struck with doubt.

'Mine?'

'Are you raving?'

'Then what –'

'It's finished. It's gone.'

'But the baby –'

'It's over. There's no more baby.'

'But –'

'But what? Isn't this what you wanted?'

'No. No,' Asya says faintly. 'It isn't –'

'You didn't want it. You didn't know where to put it. You wanted to keep your dining-room for your dinner parties.'

'But I didn't. I didn't. I didn't want it to go –'

Asya suddenly leans over the side of the bed, and Tante Soraya reaches for the bowl that has been lying in readiness. When she has finished throwing up, and rinsed out her mouth with the water Tante Soraya brings her, Asya lies back, wiping her eyes. Silence. And the baby's desolate cry.

'Where's Saif?' Asya whispers.

'At work.'

281

'When did he go?'

'At half past seven.'

'He was here all night?'

'Yes. I told him there was no need. I was staying. But he wouldn't go. We both sat in chairs all night.'

'I'm very sorry.'

He hadn't left her. All night he hadn't left her. He had stayed. Of course, though, when it was morning he had to go to work. But he had stayed all night. Had he known what was happening? What they were doing to her? How did he feel? Was he relieved? Or sad? How did *she* feel? *Not* relieved, no, oh no: lonely. Terribly lonely. She puts her hands on her tummy: there's no baby in there any more. What have they done with it? Where is it now? An image of a curled foetus floating in a soiled hospital toilet unfurls itself in her mind. Someone is trying to flush it away but it won't go. Every time the turbulence of the water dies down, there it is, rising once more to the surface. Then she sees it surrounded by yellow fluid in a knotted plastic bag: it lies on a sunny, clean kitchen counter next to a lidless dustbin. And now it is on a shelf on top of the counter, already sealed and floating in a brown jar full of formaldehyde. They are going to give it to her. She can take it away. Take *him* away. Could they tell if it was a boy or a girl? Had they looked? Did they know?

'Was it a boy or a girl?' she says to Tante Soraya.

'What's the use of this talk now?'

'But do you know? Was it a boy or a girl?'

'A boy.'

A boy. A son. Her son. She feels so lonely. And empty. And all cold inside. And she is starting to shiver and to feel a horrid pain down there where she is all wadded up so she can't get her legs together. And all the joints of her thighs are aching. But mostly her heart is aching. She is sorry. Oh, so sorry for the poor little baby lying now in some plastic bag. The little baby whom she hadn't welcomed. Hadn't wanted. Had he known as he lay curled up inside her that she didn't want him? She, his mother? But she did. She *did*. She had *started* to want him. To think of what he would be like.

Soraya sees the tears falling through the closed eyelids. She sees the bitten lip and the hand that grips the iron side of the bed, and she goes and stands on the little balcony and blows her nose loudly several times.

At eleven Asya drinks some hot tea with milk and sugar and eats a biscuit. At two the doctor comes. He looks at her chart, takes her pulse and measures her blood pressure. The nurse removes the sandbags and he feels her tummy and looks at the bloodied napkins the nurse extracts from between her legs.

'You can take out the catheter. She can go home today, and no intercourse for two months.'

He does not look at her face. Tante Soraya follows him out of the room. Asya suddenly realises: they think I did it on purpose. They think I actually did something to myself to make this happen. What could I have done? Knitting needles? She'd heard you could do something with knitting needles. She turns her head to face the wall and keeps her eyes closed. Soon the patch of pillow under her cheek is wet through and she has to move her head slightly. Other than that she does not move except twice to be sick into the bowl that Tante Soraya holds out.

At six o'clock Saif comes into the room. He is still wearing the clothes he was wearing yesterday. He greets Tante Soraya and stands near the bed. His face looks haggard and sagging and he hasn't shaved. He looks kind and friendly. And worried. She is so relieved he is here. He bends over her and puts his hand on her hair.

'I want to come home,' she whispers.

He looks at Tante Soraya.

'The doctor said she can go.'

Saif waits outside the closed door while Tante Soraya helps her back into her own nightie and dressing-gown. Asya walks slowly, moving her legs with great care until she gets into the car.

'I'll come with you and settle her in.'

Tante Soraya climbs into the back of the car.

At home, curious faces hang out of windows as she walks slowly, leaning on her aunt, into the building. The two flights of stairs take a long time to climb, but finally she is there, back in her own bedroom where, when she switches on the light, the mother cat looks up, nose and ears all alert. Then she leaps away from her sleeping mass of kittens to come and rub herself against Asya's leg.

'What are all these cats?'

'Didn't Dada Sayyida tell you?'

'No, she didn't tell me anything.'

'It was one cat. Then she had three kittens.'

'And what do you want them in your bedroom for? If you have to have cats at least put them into the servant's bathroom.'

Asya goes into her bathroom to clean herself up. No need to move slowly now. No need to keep checking. What has happened has happened and there's nothing more to fear. She sits astride the bidet, then puts on fresh clothes. She is too tired to take a shower. She washes her face and brushes her hair and by the time she comes out Tante Soraya has finished fussing around and has checked the kitchen to see if they have food, and is sitting silently with Saif in the living-room. Asya gets into bed. Then she hears Tante Soraya walk up the long corridor to her bedroom.

'Take care of yourself. Sleep early. I'll come and see you tomorrow.'

Tante Soraya permits herself to pat her niece's hand.

'I'll drive Tante home,' Saif says.

'It really isn't necessary. I'll find a taxi –'

'No, no. Of course Saif will drive you home. And thank you, Tante, for everything.'

When he comes back and comes into the bedroom her face is all wet. She has been thinking about the poor, dead little baby. But she can't talk to him about that.

'They think I did it on purpose.'

'Who does?'

'Tante Soraya and the doctor and everyone.'

'Nonsense. Of course they don't.'

'They do. I know they do. But I didn't. I didn't do anything.'

'I know you didn't, sweetie.'

As she continues to weep he sits on the bed and holds her hands.

'Come on, Princess. Stop crying. We'll make another one.'

She looks at him. She wants to ask, will we really? But I don't even know how we made this one. She wants to weep over the little piece of her flesh – their flesh – floating in the hospital loo. She wants to tell him it was a boy. To ask if he had wanted him. To ask what he feels now. To ask what he really, really, thinks is going to happen to them. To ask if he thinks she lost the baby because she'd wanted to lose it. To ask if he knows what they do with little dead babies. To throw herself into his arms and cry and cry and cry until something happens – but what can happen now? She holds on to his hand and knows he is just waiting for her to say she is all right so that it can be over. It *is* over. She leans back against the mahogany bedhead and manages a small smile and he lets go of her hands and stands up.

'Do you want to stay here or come to the living-room?' he asks. 'You can have a tiny Drambuie while I have a shower –'

Scene 4

Wednesday, 9 May 1973
Cairo

The flat is unrecognisable. All the furniture has been moved, and the drawing-room, the sitting-room and the hall look ill at ease with the hired straight-backed wooden chairs wedged into stiff circles against the walls.

The walls were redecorated last year and are still a soft, eye-engulfing cream, contained and bordered by the twirls and rosettes of the elaborate cornice.

The floor is bare and the parquet glows with a deep honey colour that testifies to the energy that has been expended on it over the years by many servants and – in servantless times – by the daughters of the house. The morning sunshine comes streaming in through the tall, wide-open hall window and flecks each wooden strand with gold. Asya turns to look out of the window. She looks at the globe on top of the Averino Building in 'Ataba Square: the earth, still held aloft by three draped angels, but dusty now, a section of it shattered and jagged-edged. From the market-place down below familiar noises float up and nothing out there seems different. Nothing at all to testify that Ismail Mursi, who has spent the last sixty-three years in that marketplace, is now dead. Asya wonders at herself that she does not feel more sad. That her quarrel with Saif still seems more real to her than the fact that her grandfather died early this morning, the fact that even now, in some green-walled room, Uncle Hamid is supervising the washing and the laying out of his father's body. She looks around for some way in which to make herself useful.

Soraya sits on the side of her bed. She has put on a straight black skirt over her black slip and bra. She is forty-three now, still good-looking but growing plump: her flesh swells on either side of the bra-straps and she grimaces slightly as she bends down to carefully roll a black stocking up her left leg. Everything is prepared and as it should be: there are five kilograms of spiced coffee in the kitchen and she had taken out and polished all her mother's old silver trays. Half an hour ago, a man had delivered five dozen demi-tasses, and now Ne'ma had washed them and they were drying in the kitchen. Meedo is at school; she has arranged for Kareem to collect him and he will stay with the Ulama for the coming three days. Both bathrooms have been given a good scrub. There is nothing else she can think of. She straightens up. Yes. She should lock her father's bedroom. She should lock it before people start arriving. It's a terrible mess in there, but when the three days are over she will start sorting it out. All the old medicines will have to go: capsules and tablets and syrups and heaven knows what. Some dating from twenty years ago, and if anyone so much as touched them he would find out and raise hell. She will have to look through the clothes before giving them away; even though she knows there will be nothing there worth keeping. For years he had refused to buy himself so much as a new shirt, and there had been days when he would put on an old, torn sweater and insist on wearing it to the shop. She would follow him through the hall remonstrating and holding out a fresh ironed shirt and a good cashmere cardigan. 'Father, please, what will people say?'

'Let them say whatever they say. Am I an ambassador or a prime minister?'

'They'll say, " 'Am Mursi's daughter doesn't look after her father." '

'They'll be right.'

'Father! After all these years –'

With a backward wave of his arm and a shake of his head the old man would stoop out of the door, shuffling down the marble corridor between the pots of ivy and jasmine till he turned the corner and started down the stairs. And yet she *had* looked after him. When Nadia finished Medical School and had to go and work in Alexandria, *she*, Soraya, had left her own home a short while after her marriage, had brought her husband and her furniture and given up her flat to come and live here and look after her father –

Muhammad al-Fadl pushes the door open and walks in, a newspaper in his hand.

'Aren't you ready yet? You'd better hurry up: people will be arriving soon.'

Soraya does not look at him but bends down to put on her other stocking.

'In any case,' he continues, 'everything's almost ready downstairs: the marquee is up and they're arranging the chairs and wiring up the lights and the microphones. The announcement's come out. We just caught the second edition. Even for that they tried to pretend it was too late – I had to give them something. A dirty bitch of a country! Even in this –'

'You told me all this last night.'

'They don't consider that these are special circumstances and that the dead are owed respect. Here, I'll read it to you.' He takes the paper from under his arm and shakes it open.

Soraya walks over to her wardrobe and takes down the black cotton blouse that is hanging neatly ready on the door. She starts to put it on.

' "Into the mercy of God: Ismail Mursi, well-known merchant and furniture manufacturer. Father of Hamid, previously of the Italian Eastern Company, Lateefa of Cairo University, Soraya of the Ministry for Social Affairs and Nadia of Alexandria University. Related by marriage to the families of al-Nabulsi, al-Ulama, al-Fadl, Madi".'

Soraya finishes buttoning up her blouse, opens the shutters and walks out on to the balcony. She is married to a fool; a loud, talkative fool. She looks down and sees the red, blue and white marquee in front of the house. A truck is parked next to it and several men are unloading chairs. She leans out over the railings and sees a man come out of the entrance to their own building. He is wearing a striped *galabiyya* which he has gathered up around his waist and on his feet there are wooden bathroom clogs. He carries a bucket of soapy water which he empties into the street in a wide, practised arc. As the soap bubbles burst on the asphalt he turns and walks back into the building with the empty bucket, his back straight. She comes back into the room. Her husband is standing in front of the dressing-table carefully brushing the sparse, greying hair at the sides and back of his head with her silver hairbrush.

'I shouldn't have let them lay him out downstairs. I should have insisted –' she begins.

'Insisted on what?' her husband interrupts. 'The lift isn't working. Who was going to carry him up four flights of stairs?'

'Hamid and Sheikh Zayid could have carried –'

'Sheikh Zayid is sixty-five and Hamid can barely carry himself. Wake up, lady. Up four flights of stairs and down them again? *And* the coffin?'

'It still isn't right.'

He gives his moustache a quick flick with the comb. 'They've almost finished now anyhow and there's no need –'

A slight knock and Asya puts her head around the door.

'Uncle? Tante?' She walks in, and she and Soraya hug each other. 'May the rest be in your life, Tante.'

'Your life be long, child,' her aunt responds, and pats her cheek. 'It grieves me to see you in black, Asya. Have you been here long, darling?'

'Not long. The door was wide open and I thought you might be resting so I sat outside. Tell me what to do, Tante.'

'Everything is ready, dear, but, look, here's the key to your grandfather's room. I think it's better if you go and lock it up. Lock it and bring me back the key.'

In her grandfather's bedroom Asya finds the missing furniture: the two massive mirrored sideboards, the dining-table he used to boast you could build a house on, it was that solid, the twelve chairs that went with it, the two sofas and four armchairs in Fadeela al-Nabulsi's favourite embossed grey velvet, all made of solid, dark, carved oak. They are huddled together with the modern, less substantial furniture in light beech: armchairs upholstered in bridal brocaded pale blue satin, now a bit faded and frayed, dining-chairs in red imitation leather, coffee-tables with their glass tops stacked away. Chair-legs stick up in the air and the rolled-up Persian carpets lie heavily between them.

Beyond the mountain of furniture stands her grandfather's bed: the bed he had shared with her grandmother for twenty years, banished her from for eleven, then continued to sleep alone in for a further seventeen. These figures seem almost incomprehensible to Asya, who still counts out happiness and sorrow in days and hours. The tall mahogany headboard has a garland of roses carved round its edges and the sides into which the mattress sinks are curved and inlaid and have always made Asya think of a boat. The cream quilt is drawn across the bed and the four pillows are in place. On the two-tiered bedside table there is a large old wireless set, a tray heaped with medicines and several newspapers and magazines. How strange to think that she will never again find her grandfather here, endlessly twiddling the knob on the radio, pausing at every station just long enough to recognise it, then moving on. He would fall asleep to the whistles and shrieks of interference and if anyone switched the radio off he would wake up and be angry. He loved the jokes and always commented on Jaheen's daily cartoon in *al-Ahram* – always *used* to comment. She should have visited him, should have sat with him. But it had been so quick. She hadn't even known he had gone into hospital – and the phone-call this morning at Mimi's was a complete surprise. Asya imagines him in the bed, then finds herself trying to imagine him now, right now, one arm is lifted and washed, and then – no, no, she thinks, don't do that.

Asya walks over to her grandmother's wardrobe. She hasn't opened it for ages but it used to be one of her favourite pieces of furniture. She hadn't really been allowed to play with it, but Mama Deela had often turned a blind eye to her only granddaughter's posing in front of its mirrors. She opens the central door and there they are: the ingenious triple mirrors that can show her every single bit of herself from every possible angle. Asya positions the mirrors and stares. She prefers the three-quarter rear view: the thick black hair, the strong curve of the back, the small round bump of the bottom, then the good, long legs. Her back view she can admire impersonally, as it were, without vanity. She turns slightly to profile. Still OK. The miscarriage had not left its mark. She pulls herself up straight. Mimi's sister's skirt is fine on her and Mimi's little knitted cotton jumper is really quite fetching. Thank goodness she'd had black shoes on since their feet were all so tiny. She turns round and adjusts the line of the jumper below her waist. When she meets her own eyes she stares into them for a moment then makes a face and shuts the door. She stands still for a moment with her back to the wardrobe and thinks of the Elizabethans who used to keep a skull: a *memento mori*. She had often wondered that they thought they needed reminding. But now she thinks maybe it was to familiarise themselves with the idea rather than to remind themselves of it. To blunt their feelings so that that wide, noseless, black-eyed grin would not strike terror into the heart at every turn – no, but Geddu does not look like that, not yet. Not *yet*, no. What are you comforting yourself with, fool? He *will* look like this, *everybody* will look like this, and looking like this isn't so terrible; it's how you get to look like this that's bad: the flesh decaying in the damp earth, the worms crawling blindly out to feed: worms that you refuse even to look at because you think they're so slimy the sight of them will make you sick, will take their time to crawl over your face, will burrow into the corners of your eyes – she puts her hand to her stomach, bends over and retches and gasps and then she straightens up and with closed eyes draws in several deep breaths: think of something ordinary. Quick. Not something happy that you will regret losing. Just something ordinary, boring, annoying even: the exam papers you will have to begin correcting next week. One hundred and fifty terrible translation papers, maybe three good ones. She tries to imagine herself sitting down with a red pen in her hand and the papers in front of her. Where will she be sitting? At the dining-room table, of course. But will she have gone home by then? Oh yes, of course she will. How? How is she going to go home? Does she *want* to go home? She sighs and turns towards the door. She walks out and remembers to lock the door behind her. Then she walks down the long corridor towards Tante Soraya's room.

Lateefa hurries in looking red-eyed and pale. She meets Soraya in the corridor and suddenly and with uncharacteristic drama cries out, 'We're orphans now, Soraya! Orphans!'

The two sisters throw themselves into each other's arms and weep. Muhammad al-Fadl comes down the corridor.

'May the rest be in your life, Dr Lateefa,' he says.

The women separate and Lateefa says, 'May your life be long, Muhammad.' Then, to her sister, 'I'm sorry I couldn't come earlier –'

'It's all right, Teefa. Nobody'll get here before eleven and Asya's here. Everything is ready –'

'Asya's here?'

'Yes. She came a little while ago. Poor child, I so hate to see her in black.'

'Where is she? I didn't see her.'

'She's here somewhere. Teefa, did you see what we had to – I'm so unhappy about Father being down there.'

'I know, I know. I met Hamid downstairs.'

'The lift isn't working,' says Muhammad al-Fadl, 'and that son of a bitch who calls himself a doorman was a grain of salt that had dissolved –'

'Please, Muhammad, please,' says his wife, 'go and find him. Get him to do something about the lift. People can't walk up and down the stairs all day.'

'Right. I'll go and see.'

'Let's go inside.' Soraya pats her sister's back. 'We'll hear if someone comes.'

In Soraya's bedroom Lateefa sits in the armchair by the dressing-table.

'What shall we do about Nadia?'

'Hamid says there's no need for a cable or anything like that. She can't come back now, it's too late.' Soraya sits heavily on the bed. 'He'll write her a letter tonight and we'll send it express.'

'But supposing she sees *al-Ahram*? Or someone sees it and says something to her?'

'Can they get *al-Ahram* there?'

'Of course they can. It'll be in the shops tomorrow.'

'Then we'll have to let her know today. Perhaps we should arrange to phone her.'

'Yes, I think that would be better.'

'She's going to take it hard.'

Lateefa nods. They sit silently together. Nadia is the youngest. The youngest by a long way. She had been seven when the rift had opened up between Ismail Mursi and his wife and she had not felt it as keenly as the older children. Nadia had grown up accepting the separate rooms, the weeks of unbroken silence, the hostile messages delivered through Lateefa and Soraya, the ill-health of her mother and the unexplained absences of her father. Besides, she had always been his favourite child. He had done things with her that he had never done with the others: sat her on his knee, carried her on his shoulders, bought her unsolicited treats, allowed her pinches of snuff and puffs at his *shisha* and even taken her with him to see the shows and plays he had been so fond of. He had been proud of her studying medicine – 'something useful' – and gener-ous in subsidising her first lonely months in Alexandria. She would take it hard.

'It's better if Hamid speaks to her,' Soraya says, and Lateefa nods.

'Have you sent word to our aunt?'

'We told her he was ill two days ago. She's bound to come.'

'Of course. She wouldn't let an occasion like this pass. How long is it since we've seen her? Ten years?'

'Oh, more. More.'

Asya appears in the doorway.

'Oh! Good morning, Mummy. Here are the keys, Tante.'

'What keys?' Lateefa asks.

'The keys to Father's room,' Soraya explains. 'I thought it would be better to lock it up. You know.'

'Oh yes. Yes, of course. We'll have to sort it all out later. Asya –' A loud scream rings through the house.

'Aunt Farhana!'

Both sisters jump to their feet and head for the door. The scream turns into a wail, and another, and another.

'My bro–ther, my brother!'

Asya follows her mother and aunt down the corridor and into the hall. In the sunlit passageway a woman in a black silk peasant smock is standing squarely outside the front door; both her arms are raised, her two index fingers are pointing at the sky.

'My bro–ther, my brother!'

The suitcase at her feet has knocked over a pot of jasmine and Uncle Muhammad has one eye on the plant as he tries to urge her indoors.

'Look at your chil–dren, Brother, look at your children!' She claps her hands then raises them to the sky again.

'Come inside, Aunt Farhana, come inside.'

'You carried them on your shou–lders and they don't find it in their hearts to carry you–ou–ou!'

'Sett Farhana, there is no need for this talk. Please to go inside.'

'My bro–ther, my brother!'

'Come inside and rest a bit, Aunt, before people start to arrive.'

Soraya pulls the old lady in by the arm and her husband rights the pot of jasmine carefully, then picks up the suitcase and carries it inside. Asya has never seen her before but she has heard about her. Her grandfather's elder and only sister whom he couldn't stand. She figures she must be seventy-five. But she has an amazingly strong voice.

'*Rest*? Is there any rest left in the world? You wash him downstairs? In the stairwell? In the doorman's room? Your father? The flesh on your shoulders is from his bounty and you don't shelter him in his death? You wash him in the street?'

The back of the right hand she raises to her black-veiled head is covered in an intricate blue tattoo.

'Not in the street, Aunt, and it's good we managed to get him out of the hospital. It's against the law, you know.'

'Law? What law? Is there a law that says a man can't be buried from his own home? My brother! My bro–ther –'

Lateefa motions to Asya. 'I want to talk to you.'

Asya follows her mother away from the wailing, down the corridor and into Tante Soraya's bedroom.

Lateefa closes the door. 'What is this whole story, then?'

'What does she mean "wash him on the stairs"? Is Grandfather downstairs?' Asya asks.

'Yes. But it's finished. It's done now. Your uncle couldn't carry him up four flights of stairs and Sheikh Zayid is out at the cemetery –'

'I thought Geddu was still in the hospital.'

'You can't do this in a hospital. It's a good job they allowed him out.'

'Mummy, when did he actually . . .?'

'Five o'clock this morning.'

'You weren't there, were you?'

'No, I'd left at one. We thought he was all right for the night. Then they called your uncle at half past four, but by the time he got there it was over.'

So he died alone. Died Alone. Died Alone. No, there would have been a nurse with him. Still. Had he known he was dying?

'He just went into hospital last night?'

'At ten. It was very sudden.'

'I didn't know he was ill. More ill than usual, I mean.'

'It was very sudden.'

Why wasn't her mother terror-struck? Destroyed? Her father had just died. And apart from that first outburst and looking very pale Lateefa seems almost normal. *She* wouldn't be like that if *her* father died. Or her mother –

'Asya, what's this business of you not being home? And what are these clothes?'

'I borrowed them from Mimi.'

'But what's going on? Why did you stay the night at Mimi's?'

'Because I don't want to be at home,' Asya says quietly.

Lateefa sits down. She sits on the small, pink, damask-covered stool in front of Soraya's dressing-table. Asya can see her mother's broad back in the mirror.

'Don't want to be at home? Why, child, what happened?'

Asya shrugs slightly. 'He doesn't love me, Mummy.'

'Asya! What *are* you saying? Have you gone mad?'

'It's true.'

'True that Saif doesn't love you? How can you say that? What happened?'

'We had an argument. I know it's going to sound silly, but it isn't.'

'An argument about what? What sort of an argument?'

'The night we were at your place –'

'But that was three nights ago!'

'Yes.'

'Well?'

'Well, you remember he left alone?'

'You said he was just going to pick up some papers from Shahir and you were going to follow him. You left almost immediately after.'

'Yes, well, that wasn't true.'

'You mean you had already quarrelled?'

'Yes.'

'At *our* place?'

292

A fresh bout of wailing starts in the hall.

'Yes. Oh, goodness! It really makes my heart jump, this screaming.'

'But why? What about? You mean you haven't been home for three nights?'

'Yes. Look, Mummy, I didn't want you to know any of this. I was going to –'

'How can I not know? You left home three days ago and you don't want me to *know*? Why didn't you come to me? Why didn't you tell me?'

'Because you would have tried to make me go back.'

The door opens and Hamid walks in. 'Asya.' He puts his right arm round his niece's shoulder and hugs her, then he sits down heavily on the bed.

'May the rest be in your life, Khalu,' she says.

'May your life be long, darling,' he says. 'When is your viva?'

'Oh it's not till next week, Khalu.'

'You should be preparing. Don't stay here long.'

'You look very tired, Hamid,' Lateefa says. 'Come and sit here in the armchair and rest your back for a moment. Asya, make your uncle some tea.'

'No, no. I'm all right. I'll have to go downstairs again in a minute.'

'Is the lift working now?'

'No, not yet.'

Asya leaves the room.

In the kitchen Ne'ma, the servant girl, jumps up and takes the kettle out of Asya's hand.

'I'll do it, Sett Asya, I'll do it.'

'Where's Dada Sayyida?' Asya asks.

'She'll be on her way,' says Ne'ma. 'She doesn't know what's waiting for her.'

She starts to cry as she fills the kettle. Asya sits on the low stool in the corner and watches her. She is dressed in a black *galabiyya* with her hair tied up in a black kerchief. Her eyes are red and swollen. She probably is genuinely sad, for Grandfather had been quite kind to her. Through the barred window Asya can see the marble passage outside the front door, sunny and silent. On the iron servants' staircase immediately outside, a black cat has found one patch of sooty sunshine and has curled itself up in it to sleep. Saif will probably come to the evening session. If he wants an excuse to see her he will come upstairs to offer his condolences to Tante Soraya. If he doesn't he'll stay with the men in the marquee downstairs. And what *is* she going to do? She can't stay at Mimi's for ever. Mimi's mother will be back in a couple of days and Asya won't be able to stay there then. She doesn't want her to know – she hadn't wanted any of the grown-ups to know anything at all about this, and now her mother knows – and of course she'll tell her father and they won't leave it alone. She

293

can't tell them everything, and without everything – viewed on its own – this quarrel looks like a total triviality; certainly not enough to leave home over. Asya sneezes, once, twice, four times, then frowns angrily and stands up. Ne'ma had said bless you after the first two, then stopped. It gives her a headache all this sneezing, and it's getting worse and worse. The other day she'd had a sneezing fit while driving her mother's car down Gabalaya Street, and had sneezed so much and so hard that she must have blacked out for a few seconds, and when she came to the car had rolled to a stop just short of hitting a tree. She hears the creak of the lift and sees it come to a faltering halt at their landing. The doors open and Sheikh Zayid gets out and pulls them carefully closed behind him before walking down the passage. Although the front door stands wide open he rings the bell and waits outside. He takes a white handkerchief from his pocket and wipes his face. He looks sad and stooped. Asya looks back towards the closed gates of the lift, then realises that he is alone and that this is the first time she has seen him without her grandfather.

'Shall I take it in, Sett Asya?'

'Put another glass there, Ne'ma, 'Am el-Sheikh is here. I'll take it.'

Asya takes the tray and walks with it to Tante Soraya's room. Soraya opens the door.

'Sheikh Zayid is here, Teefa.'

Lateefa stands up and Sheikh Zayid takes her hand. 'May the rest be in your life, Lateefa my daughter.'

'And your life be long, 'Am el-Sheikh. Is everything ready?'

Sheikh Zayid nods. 'Yes. It's all ready. I told them we'd be there after the noon prayers.'

'Sit down, 'Am el-Sheikh. Sit down and have some tea.'

'No, child, no. I'll go downstairs now.'

'I'll come with you,' Hamid says, standing up. He pats the older man on the back to make him go first and then follows him through the doorway.

'Hamid looks very tired,' Lateefa says.

'He can only have slept for three hours.'

'But he's been looking more and more tired lately.'

'I wish Nadia were here. He won't go to a doctor, says he's fine.'

'I wish he wouldn't drive with that hand.'

'He wouldn't be able to manage at all, Teefa, if he didn't drive.'

Lateefa is silent for a minute, then she asks, 'Where's Aunt Farhana?'

'In Meedo's room. I made her lie down and she's fallen asleep. She's been travelling all night.'

'Do you think she'll stay?'

'Definitely. At least for the three days.'

Asya leaves the room before her mother can start questioning her again. She goes out into the hall and sits on the chair nearest the front door. Her grandfather is dead. When she goes to the shop he won't be there. Never again will she say, 'I've come to have lunch with you, Geddu.' Never again will she – what? She tries to think of things they've done together. Every year for the festival of al-Sayyid al-Badawi they had all gone up to Tanta. They had visited the mosque of al-Sayyid and they had visited the shrine of Sheikha Sabah and then had a big lunch and driven back to Cairo loaded with sweets and special festival candy. Every year during Ramadan they'd broken the fast one evening at al-Dahhan in the Azhar. They'd eaten kebab and grilled goat and Grandfather would always drink a large glassful of straight pickle juice. Then she remembers a beach: a table and two chairs under a parasol; she'd been six when he taught her how to play backgammon. He'd taught her seriously, with all the proper Persian names for the different throws of the dice, and he'd never let her win. She'd liked that. It made her feel grown-up. And in Alexandria he'd always take them – the children – to the Trianon and ordered croissants and tea. He'd bang on his glass with his teaspoon to call the waiter and Asya and Kareem would always giggle. Something else came back to her. Once, two years ago, she had driven him back from Alexandria. He'd been clearly unwilling at first, but he had had to get back to Cairo and eventually he'd climbed into the Fiat and they had set off. At first she'd been very cautious, but as the kilometres slipped by and he seemed relaxed she'd started to drive in her usual style. The desert road had been closed because of the war and they'd used the Delta road, and there was, of course, a lot of traffic and lots and lots of trucks. They had hardly talked, but they had stopped twice for tea and coffee and she'd felt completely comfortable and companionable with him. They had arrived in Cairo after the three-hour drive and she'd headed for 'Ataba and Morgan Street and pulled up neatly outside his shop. 'Am Farrag had snapped to attention and Sheikh Zayid had come out from the inside of the shop, and as they'd stood on the pavement Grandfather had put a hand briefly on her shoulder and said to them, 'This girl, she drives like a man.' Then he'd gone inside. Asya feels again that sudden rush of pride she'd felt then as she had stood on the pavement in the marketplace. And now the tears rise to her eyes.

Asya hears the clang of the lift-gates and wipes her eyes. Tante Sunny, Khalu Hamid's wife, is coming up the passage. She looks immaculate in a black linen suit with very high-heeled shiny black shoes and her short chestnut hair feathered with gold. Asya stands up and they kiss.

'May the rest be in your life, Asya.'

'And your life be long, Tante Sunny. Please come in.'

'How is Soraya doing?'

'She's all right. She and Mummy are inside. Do you want to go to them?'

'No. No, I won't disturb them. I'll sit here.'

She chooses a chair opposite Asya and sits elegantly with her long legs angled sideways and crossed at the ankles, her hands resting on the soft black purse on her knee. She appears so tranquil. Hard to look at her and imagine the rumoured rages, the shredded curtains and the broken furniture, and Khalu Hamid in a white and silent fury watching it all. And yet, well, how are you really to know anything about anybody? Soraya and Lateefa come into the hall. They both kiss their sister-in-law and then all three women take seats near the door. Asya goes inside to ask Ne'ma to make one black coffee. Then she continues to Tante Soraya's bedroom. She sits at the dressing-table. Tante Soraya's heavy silver toilet set – Mama Deela's really – is still there: the mirror, the brush and the antimone pot. So are the pink crystal poudrière and the perfume-flask with its golden tassel. When Asya was eight and Tante Soraya was a bride living in her own flat near Falaki, Asya had used to spend hours with this toilet set. She would sit in front of this dressing-table rimming her eyes with kohl, powdering her face and spraying perfume on her neck. Sometimes she even painted her nails. And before she went home Tante Soraya would wipe it all off for her so Daddy wouldn't get cross. She picks up the perfume-flask and gives the silk pump an experimental squeeze. Nothing. The poudrière too is empty, and so is the antimone pot. There are no bottles of nail varnish lying around. Asya sighs. She looks up as the marquisette curtains billow in towards her. This is the north-facing balcony and on it there is always a fresh breeze. Asya steps out. A tram is grinding slowly by and there are the usual small crowds standing around in the street. There too are the pharmacy, the calligrapher's shop and the kebab restaurant, but at the entrance to the building a big red, blue and white marquee has gone up. It will stand there for three days and three nights and then be taken down – to be set up again somewhere else. People die but the world goes on. The world didn't stop for Picasso or for LBJ. It almost stopped for 'Abd el-Nasser but it didn't quite –

'Asya!'

Asya turns around and hugs Chrissie. Chrissie is in a loose black cotton dress and her hair is gathered into a small pony-tail held by a black elastic band.

'I came as soon as I could. I've apologised to Tante Lateefa for my mother; she couldn't come with me but she'll come this afternoon.'

'You shouldn't have taken time off from work.'

'It's OK. Mimi's covering for me. She'll come in the afternoon too.'

'Do you want to sit down? How are you feeling?'

'I'm fine. I wasn't sick this morning.'

'Well done!' Asya smiles at her friend. Chrissie is pregnant: four months pregnant and very happy. 'Let's sit down anyway. Shall I get you a cold drink?'

296

'No, really, not yet. I don't want anything. Did it happen last night?'

'No. This morning. At dawn.'

'Was someone with him?'

'No.' Asya shakes her head 'They'd all left at one. The hospital phoned my uncle at half past four but by the time he got there it was over.'

'Had they known he was that bad?'

'No. Not at all. He's been not terribly well for years, but he's old. Then last night they rushed him to hospital, I don't really know why. Then later they must have thought it was all under control.'

'It's his time. God have mercy on him. When you're old it's better if it's over quickly.'

They sit silently for a few minutes, then Chrissie asks, 'Asya, has anything happened? With Saif, I mean.'

Asya shakes her head.

'Well, what are you going to do?'

'Don't know. I'm not going back, though.'

'You can't camp out for ever. Remember you've got your viva in five days. You've got to be in good shape.'

'I'm having a good time. I went to see *Z* last night.'

'Ah! Jean-Louis Trintignthing!'

'I preferred Yves Montand.'

'Oh, Asya! You always go for the old men!'

'He's not old. You'll be telling me Ahmad Mazhar is old. He's my favourite.'

'You shouldn't have done this, you know. Left home. You can fight with Saif, yes. But not leave home.'

'I couldn't have done anything else. I couldn't have just followed him tamely back.'

'Well, what are you going to do?'

'I don't know. I could go home – to my parents, I mean. Except that's the classic upset wife thing and I don't want to do it. Besides, they'd keep on and on at me.'

'You're not doing the right thing, you know. You should have it out with him. Tell him everything that's bothering you. *Fight* it out, even –'

'Chrissie, he won't fight. He won't argue. He won't talk if it gets heavy. He'll put on a record, light a cigarette and open a book. He thinks I'm stupid – and hysterical. And of course I sound stupid and hysterical. I can hear myself. But that's because . . .'

'Because what?'

'Because I can't say everything I mean.'

'Why not?'

Asya shrugs.

'Why *not*, Asya?'

'Because – I suppose because I believe that he knows it all already. There is no new information I'd be giving him. He knows everything I know and he wants it all left alone. So I'd be forcing him to not leave it alone. So it's not like we'd be having a conversation –'

'Asya, you always complicate things. Why do you think out his thoughts for him. *You* say *your* bit and let *him* say *his*.'

'I can't and he won't. It won't work –'

'What won't work? What's this business with your friend, Chrissie? My dear, shouldn't you have told me? You let her sleep outside her home for three nights, Chrissie, and you don't tell me?' Lateefa looks at Chrissie reproachfully.

'I thought they would sort it out, Tante. I promised her I wouldn't tell and I thought they would sort it out before it got too big.'

'But what is *it*? I don't yet know what actually happened.'

Chrissie glances at Asya. 'Well, they had an argument over something at your place and Saif said he was going and Asya said she didn't want to go just yet, and he said he was going and she could go with him or not as she chose, and Asya said if he left without her she wouldn't follow him home – and he left.'

'Is that it? But what was the argument *about*?'

Chrissie looks at Asya again, but Asya stares out of the window.

'What was it about, Chrissie?' Lateefa asks.

'It was about George Eliot, Tante.'

'George Eliot?'

Chrissie shrugs.

'But why were they arguing about George Eliot?'

'I think Asya was saying she was a great writer and he was saying she wasn't.'

'So she gets up and leaves home?'

'I thought you were supposed to care about literature,' Asya bursts out. 'And anyway that *wasn't* what it was about, it was about *him*. He hasn't read her and yet he can sit there and say she's not worth reading. If it's not Sartre or the Spanish Civil War or Camus or someone he already knows then it's worth nothing. I know he knows about plenty but he makes fun of things he doesn't know anything about. I thought he was adventurous, I thought he was – he was – *available* to – to *life*. But he's got a closed mind. He actually makes me think of that passage where she says Mr Casaubon's mind is like a – an enclosed basin. And he's so completely sure of himself – he's, he's like *Gradgrind*: he wants *facts* –'

'All right, darling, all right. But you didn't have to push it this far –'

'We were having this argument – or rather *I* was – and he stood up and said, "Right, we're going." I was supposed to just shut up and go? I didn't even *want* to be with him –'

298

'But, Asya, you gave him an ultimatum.'

'He could have got round it. *He* wasn't out of control. He's *never* out of control. He wasn't even *angry*. Just pissed off. He didn't care. He didn't care whether I went with him or not. He'd rather talk to Kareem or to Daddy than to me *any* time and it's been like this since we got engaged –'

'Are you jealous of your own brother?'

'No, I'm *not* jealous of my own brother, and you know Kareem is practically my favourite person in the world, but Saif isn't bothered about my – company. He just didn't care whether we made up or not. And he wanted to make that clear. Well, it *is* clear. Clear to *me*, anyhow.'

'Asya, dear, you always get on so well –'

'Yes, we do. As long as I behave the way he wants me to behave.'

'Yes, but darling, he's not unreasonable. And he loves you. We all *know* how much he loves you –'

'And how do you know that?'

'Asya, come on –'

'He waited for you for four years –'

'Yes, well maybe he didn't mind waiting.'

'What do you mean?'

'Oh, *Mummy*! And anyway, *you* always want to minimise things. When I was desperately in love with him and terribly wanted to marry him it was, "Oh, it can't be that bad. What's wrong with waiting till you graduate?" and now I'm angry it's, "Oh, it can't be that bad. Why don't you trot off home like a good girl?" '

'Well, you *will* have to go home.'

'I won't.'

'Asya, if everybody behaved like you, every home in the world would be ruined.'

'Yes, that's always been your policy: minimise, appease, avoid confrontation, peace at any price – why shouldn't homes be ruined if they're ripe for ruining?'

'I'll go and see if Tante Soraya needs anything.' Chrissie slips out of the room and closes the door.

'It's as if nothing matters but a peaceful life. Even though it's only *outwardly* peaceful, mind you. You've *never* stood up to Daddy. Not *once*. We were supposed to believe you had this wonderfully happy marriage, but it was all at *your* expense.'

'Asya!'

'Well, it's true. I remember hearing you argue once when I was seven and I thought *then* he was being beastly and I thought, why doesn't she walk out and slam the door? And later I saw you crying in the kitchen while he sat around inside thinking everything was just fine – and that's how it's always been, and I'm *not* going to let it be like that for me. I'm *not*.'

Lateefa sits down on the bed and takes off her glasses.

'Oh, Mummy, I'm sorry.' Asya sits down quickly next to her mother and puts her head on her shoulder. 'I'm sorry, *really* I am. But I knew this would be the line you'd take and I can see how you can't take any other, but that was why I didn't want you to know. And you *wouldn't* have known. It was only because Grandfather died that you found out.'

Lateefa wipes her glasses and puts them back on.

'So how were you proposing to end this situation?'

'I don't know.'

Soraya comes in.

'You know who has arrived?'

'Who?'

'Zahra.'

'Zahra? Zahra who used to work for you?'

'Yes.'

'She has a cheek.'

As Asya walks down the corridor she looks into the kitchen. Hasna and her mother and Toota sit on a small rug on the floor with their hands on their cheeks. Toota nudges her mother as she gets up to greet Asya. No *zagharid* or wedding songs today, Toota, Asya thinks as they kiss on both cheeks. But Toota is a fighter; her black skirt is cut too tight and her black mercurised cotton sweater reveals two centimetres of cleavage as she bends to sit down again.

'Don't get up, Ummu Hasna, for my sake,' Asya urges, and squats down by the old woman to be hugged and kissed and condoled with. Ummu Hasna always smells of spice and incense and her hands are like smooth polished pieces of hard dark wood.

'A man, Sett Asya, he was a real man,' Toota says as she helps Asya up and out of her mother's embrace. 'May God forgive his transgressions and lighten for him the torment of the grave.'

The door to the servants' staircase is pushed open and Sayyida comes in.

'May the rest be in your life, Sett Asya,' she says as she hugs Asya and pats her back.

'Where have you been, Dada Sayyida? I was looking for you.'

'I had to go up to the roof, Sett Asya. Who was going to feed the chickens and the rabbits? They're souls too, and it's a sin to forget them.' Dada Sayyida wipes her brow with a corner of her *galabiyya*. 'Ne'ma,' she orders. 'Put some cups out and let's make coffee. The hall outside is filling up.'

Asya sits on the small stool and watches Sayyida; Sayyida, who had overcome the jumping hand, who had borne eleven children to a legless man and watched four of them die, who had gone out to work in people's

300

houses after watching her husband rejoice unto death in 1967.

'The first day of the war, Sett Asya, the first day. It was a Monday. He kept listening to the radio and they tell him about the planes. Fifty-six. Eighty-three. One hundred. He kept pushing himself along and shouting and crying, "We've won, we've won." He was patriotic. It was patriotism. Yes, his blood was hot, but I'd never seen him like that before. I kept trying to run after him, stop him, calm him down – but never. Well, anyway, I was watching, and suddenly he stopped and I saw him jerk once like he'd been touched by electricity (far from you), and he called out for me one time with a voice like the voice of an ox, and by the time I ran over he was gone. May God never show you, they told me I was bouncing up and down like a rubber ball. I screamed and slapped my face and everything. What else? Wasn't he my man and the father of my children?'

Sayyida measures out the coffee and Toota pours cold water into glasses. What would Toota do if she were in Asya's position? When Toota leaves her husband she never goes back until he comes and begs her. But then he throws boiling water at her, knocks out her teeth. Asya tries to imagine Saif advancing upon her, arm pulled back in readiness to deliver a blow that would knock out her teeth. She cannot imagine it. She cannot imagine him caring about her enough to hit her.

The house is full of women now. In the hall and in the drawing-room they sit patiently by the walls on the hard chairs. Sheikh Zayid has led the blind reciter into the drawing-room and he sits in the centre, cross-legged on the only armchair, rolling the whites of his eyes that show through a narrow slit in the almost-sealed eyelids, clearing his throat and sipping at a glass of water. Asya looks around. It's terrible what black does to women. It dries up their skin and robs their hair of life. They all look so old. But black is also for seduction, for dinner-gowns, for the femme fatale. So what's the difference between mourning black and good-time black?

'I seek protection from God against Satan who is to be stoned. In the name of God the Compassionate, the Merciful.'

The voice of the blind reciter rises in the high rooms and the women murmur their responses and settle themselves on their chairs.

'The Compassionate. He revealed the Qur'an. He created Man. He taught him eloquence. He created the sun and the moon with precision –'

The chant floods the house. All else is silence. Next to Asya sits Chrissie and across from her sits Sheikh Zayid's wife. Asya revises her theory about black. Even in black Sheikh Zayid's wife is beautiful. And she must be – what? Fifty? She sits straight and tall and the way she holds her head always looks so proud. And there is something about her face that is different from all the other women. Something – she had described it to Chrissie as 'barbaric'. Where does it come from? The Moroccan mother?

'The stars and the trees bow down and praise Him. And the skies He raised and established all measures –'

What would *she* have done if Sheikh Zayid had said to her – before the second year of their marriage was out – if he'd said to her, 'I love you well enough to live with you like a sister'? She'd have probably screamed in his face – maybe even hit him. She'd have run home to her mother and told her. Told the world. Asya almost starts to laugh as she imagines the Moroccan mother striking her breast with her hand amid a great clamour of bracelets. 'O black day! He said *that* to you?' But then Sheikh Zayid's wife wouldn't have given him reason to say this to her in the first place. She wouldn't have gone all frozen on him, wouldn't have sneezed every time he came near her. If it weren't so awful it would be funny. But she hadn't started out like that. She had wanted him so terribly in the beginning. But it all seems to have – to have vanished. Well, then, what *does* she expect from him? Asya sighs and shifts slightly. She's gone over this so many times. She had expected him to make it work. After all, *he* was supposed to be the one who'd wanted to wait. If only they had done it ages ago, on one of those Sunday afternoons in Heliopolis, or in their little flat in London; she could have put up with any amount of pain then – maybe even liked it. But later it was all so – so *expected*. Well, what had she wanted? She had wanted him, she supposes, to romance her, to seduce her, to *make* her want him, not simply to assume that they were going to bed together. And she can imagine what Chrissie or her mother or Dada Zeina or anyone would say to that. 'But he's your *husband*!' Well, he *isn't*. Not really. Goodness, how he must be regretting having married her.

'OK, Princess,' he'd said. 'Let's just leave it. I love you. I love you well enough to live with you like a sister.'

'But that isn't what I want.'

'It is.'

'It isn't. I *know* it isn't. I want us to be together properly. I *do*. I want –'

'No you don't. Not really. It's all right, Princess, don't worry. We'll do it the way you want it.' He'd given her head a quick pat and got out of bed. He'd put on his dressing-gown and she'd heard his lighter click as he walked down the corridor. But I don't. I don't I don't I don't. I *want* us to make love. I want us to *want* to make love. I want us to be in love like we used to be. I want to watch his hands and long for them to touch me. I want to look at his mouth and need it on my lips and on my breasts. I want our eyes to meet across a room and both of us to know that we're just waiting for the moment when we can be alone together – *that's* what I want –

'He created man out of clay like pottery. And He made the jinn out of the flames of fire. What then of thy Lord's favours do ye deny? Lord of the two sunrises and Lord of the two sunsets. What then of thy Lord's favours do ye deny?'

But then, of course, that can't be what everybody has all of the time. Some people maybe don't ever have it. Maybe *most* people don't ever have it; she doesn't care. She doesn't care what most people have or don't have –

'All that dwells upon earth shall perish. And nought shall remain but the Face of thy Lord, honoured and majestic. What then of thy Lord's favours do ye deny?'

Was that it, then? The answer? What is the answer? Renunciation? A la Maggie Tulliver and Dorothea Brooke? But it is so hard. Maybe it would be easier to renounce something you'd already had. Something you had had your fill of. But to renounce something you had been promised – something you had only imagined – but isn't that the point of renunciation: that it's not easy? But why? What was it like this *for*? Why *should* it be like this? Well, what are you going to do, then? You've tried: twice when you felt particularly brave you've tried to seduce him, and twice you got the friendly pat on the head, the 'You ought to go to sleep, Princess. You'll be really tired tomorrow.' There's *nothing* you can do. What would any of these people say, she wonders, if they knew? They'd probably, she thinks, start talking about manhood and conjugal duties and that would be awful. She shudders. Duties. That's not it; that's not it at all.

'Are you all right?' Chrissie whispers.

'Yes. Are *you*?'

'Yes.'

'He will send against thee fragments of fire and molten brass and thou shalt not be the victor. What then of thy Lord's favours do ye deny? And when the sky shall be cleft open and show itself rosy as red hide. What then of thy Lord's favours do ye deny? On that day neither man nor jinn shall be asked of their misdeeds –'

Who knows what situations people are living with? In the drawing-room, framed against the big folding doors made up of a hundred panels of English glass that separate the drawing-room from the dining-room, sits Tante Rasmiyyah the Knife-Sharpener, enormously fat and comfortable. She isn't a knife-sharpener, of course; only married to a man who'd made a fortune from starting out on a tool-sharpening stall. Does he still make love to her? Does she want him to? He had been a good friend of Grandfather's until Geddu had forbidden Tante Rasmiyyah the house. He'd said she turned Mama Deela against him. Mama Deela and then Tante Soraya had stayed good friends with Tante Rasmiyyah, though. But this must be the first time she's been in this flat for – maybe twenty, twenty-five years. All these lifetimes!

'This is Hell which the criminals deny. They are driven between its stations and tortured with boiling water. What then of thy Lord's favours do ye deny?'

It was – how many? – seventeen? Seventeen years since Mama Deela had died. They had been in London then and Mukhtar al-Ulama had gravely told a six-year-old Asya that Mama Deela had died and that Mummy was upset and Asya had to be very careful and very good for a while. And Asya had jumped up and down on her parents' big bed that she'd never been allowed to sleep in and chanted, 'Mama Deela's dead, dead; Mama Deela's dead.' Why had she done that? She had always loved Mama Deela. She loves her still. She remembers her every time she goes into the big room that is now Meedo's and had used to be Mama Deela's sitting-room. Every time she sees the sunshine hit the wooden floor and the corner of the wine-red Persian carpet she remembers Mama Deela kneeling in prayer wrapped in the light white cotton veil that always smelled of soap and of the wind, and she sees herself, a small, dark child, using her grandmother's body in the various postures of prayer as a climbing-frame: hanging on to her knees as she bends over, climbing on to her back as she prostrates herself, lying with her head in her lap as she settles into the salutations, and never ever being pushed away, but always caught up and kissed and hugged and mock-smacked as soon as the prayers were over. And yet she had jumped up and down on the bed and celebrated – *celebrated* in the face of her mother's tear-shrunk eyes and pale, trembling mouth. And then she had started to have nightmares: nightmares about her own mother dying. About begging her and begging her not to die and Mummy quietly saying, 'But I must,' about octopuses – octopi? – barring her way to her mother whom she can see at the end of a dark corridor and, worst of all, about speaking to her, shaking her, pleading with her – and never getting a reply. She had spent weeks, months, in a panic, hanging about her mother, questioning her, tugging at her, watching her, preventing her from dying. And when she stopped it was out of exhaustion, not because the reason for her panic had gone. She looks over at her mother.

They are not panicking now, Mummy and Tante Soraya. They are not having these thoughts about their father. And he is still downstairs. Lying wrapped in his shroud on the doorman's narrow brown-blanketed bed with his coffin placed close by. They could race downstairs and throw themselves upon him if they wanted. How would that feel? Asya sees the shrouded figure jolt with the impact of Lateefa and Soraya's bodies, but then it is still; the hand does not lift to push the sheet away from the face, the arm does not rise to rest on his daughters' shoulders. Just one jolt – and then it lies still again. Oh, stop, stop.

Grandfather's sister sits near the door of Meedo's room. Her long

304

black dress covers her feet. Asya can see a line of white hair beneath her black veil. Her eyes are closed and her face is creased and sorrowful. Probably permanently sorrowful. She mourns the brother she has not seen for ten years or more. The brother she has probably never really known since he left their village sixty-three years ago to seek his fortune in Cairo. Asya wonders now at how sketchy her own knowledge is of her grandfather's life. He'd always been there, in the shop, sitting in front of the big desk, never behind it, smoking his *shisha* and reading the papers. She knew he was interested in politics. She knew he loved the theatre. She knew he had an eye for women, especially plump, fair-skinned ones. What else? Over the years she'd learnt that he'd left home when he was ten. That his parents had died and his uncles had done him out of his share of the family land. So he had left. Ten years old, he had arrived in Cairo and headed for the marketplace because that was where all the Sa'idis from Upper Egypt went. And his fellow-Sa'idis had looked after him and given him work, and a few years later his childhood friend, Zayid, had followed him to Cairo and to the central marketplace. And then? And then he was twenty-five and had a thriving furniture business and married Fadeela al-Nabulsi, who was fifteen and came from Alexandria and who had no womenfolk but only a father who had come from Palestine and who soon died – and two brothers who loved her dearly. And Grandfather too had loved her dearly, and they had been very happy, and then – some time in the 1940s, after Nadia was born – he had stopped loving her and had formed some liaison with a married woman, and Mama Deela had spent the rest of her life in misery, and that was why his children were not too bothered that he was now dead –

'And for him who feareth the station of his Lord there are two Heavens. What then of thy Lord's favours do ye deny? Two Heavens of many colours. What then of thy Lord's favours do ye deny? In them run two clear springs. What then of thy Lord's favours do ye deny?'

Asya notices Tante Soraya looking steadily at a particular corner. Her face is carefully impassive but Asya knows that this is the furthest she will go to show disapproval – except towards Uncle Muhammad al-Fadl. She follows the look, and there, of course, is Zahra. Ten years older, but still Zahra: the amazingly milky face, the soft black eyes always half hidden by lids with long, curved lashes. Her hair is completely covered by the tightly wrapped black veil but Asya knows it is long and brown and fine and abundant. Her hands, loosely folded on her knee, are coarse and chapped – but still white. Her body has thickened, but there is still an air of yieldingness about her; of non-resistance. Holding her would be like holding a soft, down-filled pillow. You could make her do whatever you wanted. Yet there must be a hard core to her somewhere: a core that makes her choose to sit here defiantly among the guests rather than in the kitchen with the other servants –

'And women who lower their gaze, untouched before him by man or by jinn. What then of thy Lord's favours do ye deny? Women like rubies and like coral. What then of thy Lord's favours do ye deny? Can the reward for good be other than good? What then of thy Lord's favours do ye deny?'

She had been divorced when she came to work in this house. Divorced and with a small child. And Asya still remembers half-heard conversations, arguments that came to a sudden halt when one of the children walked into the room, and she remembers herself asking her mother, 'Does Geddu want to marry Zahra?' and Lateefa faltering and hesitating and finally saying, 'My dear, a whim that will pass.'

'But Mummy, why shouldn't he?'

And Lateefa casting around. 'Well, he's sixty-three.'

'So what?'

'She's about twenty-five.'

'But she wants to marry him, doesn't she? Then she can stop being a servant.'

'Ah, yes, but that's it. She only wants to marry him because of that.'

'But she'll probably be nice to him. And she'll look after him and do all his things. Tante Soraya doesn't really want to look after him.'

'It won't do, Asya.'

'Why not?'

'It's – it's insulting.'

'Who is it insulting to?'

'To – to Mama Deela's memory –'

'But Mama Deela's dead.'

'And to his children.'

'I don't think Khalu Hamid minds.'

'Your uncle is a generous man. Too generous.'

'Anyway, why should it be "insulting" to his children? It's his life.'

'It won't do.'

'If I wanted to marry someone I'd marry him no matter what.'

But of course it wouldn't have done. It might have made him happy for the last ten years of his life. Might. But it still wouldn't have done. Asya suddenly realises that even now, at this very moment, her mother and her aunt are probably dreading some terrible revelation. 'I have been married to your father for ten years. Here is the marriage certificate and here' – as five grubby little urchins come marching in – 'are your brothers.' It had happened when Mama Deela's brother had died, so why not now? But Zahra is holding her peace. She doesn't look as though she has anything to say, and if she had she would have said it to Khalu Hamid downstairs. He'd be a softer touch and she must know it –

306

'Untouched before him by man or by jinn. What then of thy Lord's favours do ye deny? Reclining upon green grass and beautiful carpets. What then of thy Lord's favours do ye deny? Blessed be the Name of thy Lord, honoured and majestic.'

The women mutter, 'Verily God hath spoken truth,' and shift and wipe their eyes and blow their noses. Ne'ma comes in from the kitchen with a trayful of glasses of cold water. Soraya puts one in the hand of the reciter and Ne'ma goes round the women with the rest. A quiet hum of conversation rises from the room.

Sheikh Zayid appears outside the door. He makes a small sign and steps back so as not to have the women inside the flat in his view. Soraya crosses the hall and steps outside to speak to him. Asya sees her nod, and nod again with lowered eyes. Her face is set and her mouth is a tight, straight line. He walks away and Asya watches her aunt as she makes her way towards her sister. She bends over Lateefa. Lateefa gets up and follows Soraya down the corridor. Aunt Farhana uncrosses her legs and raises both hands to her head and screams. Asya looks at Chrissie sitting beside her. Chrissie whispers, 'He's going.' Aunt Farhana slaps her face with both hands, then tears the veil from her head. Asya watches as the long white hair springs to life.

'My bro—ther, my *brother*. You died far awa—ay, far away from home.'

Tante Sunny places a hand on the old woman's back and tries to whisper something in her ear. Aunt Farhana shakes her off.

'Nobody screamed in the hospital. Nobody screamed over you in the hospital, my dar—ling. They brought you home in si—lence, in silence.' She pulls at her hair and slaps her face.

Chrissie whispers, 'You should go to your mother,' and Asya stands up and heads for Tante Soraya's bedroom.

Soraya and Lateefa are both leaning out of the balcony and sobbing. They press handkerchiefs to their mouths and clutch at the railings and at each other. Asya joins them and puts an arm around each. Down in the street she sees her grandfather's coffin leave the marquee. Hamid and Sheikh Zayid carry the front end, 'Am Farrag and Sobhi, the old french-polisher, are in the middle, 'Am Mahmoud the knife-sharpener and Muhammad Bismark the upholsterer bring up the rear. Other men follow the coffin out of the marquee: Mukhtar al-Ulama and Saif, both wiping their faces in the May heat, Hassan Bey, her grandfather's solicitor, Ustaz Abdul-Ghani, the accountant, and others and others. The coffin, covered in its green pall, progresses slowly and jerkily past the pharmacy, and now Asya feels truly that her grandfather is dead. She finds herself sobbing with her mother and her aunt as they all lean over the railings, unmindful of the passers-by who make way for the procession, mutter a prayer for mercy and forgiveness and then

307

look up at the balconies for a glimpse of the mourning womenfolk.

'My bro–ther, my *brother.*'

Aunt Farhana pulls them aside as she bends low over the railings. Her white hair is completely dishevelled, her black dress torn at the neck and her face lacerated with red scratches.

'He doesn't want to go, he doesn't want to go,' she screams. 'See how slow–ly he's going. He hasn't had enough, he hasn't had his fill of the world *I tell you.* My brother. Dying before your day had come, my brother.'

The coffin and the procession disappear slowly round the corner, heading north. Soraya elbows her way past Aunt Farhana and collapses on the armchair in her room and Lateefa rounds on the old woman.

'Stop it, Aunt, stop it. Instead of consoling us you've come to fan our grief into a blaze? By God, this is sinful even.'

That afternoon

The house is silent now. The women have gone home and will come back in the evening. The blind reciter has gone home to rest. Aunt Farhana is in Meedo's room and Lateefa and Soraya are lying down in Soraya's room. Tante Sunny has said she will go to work for a couple of hours and come back. The servants have gone upstairs to the roof and the men are at the cemetery. Asya, Chrissie, Noora and Mimi sit by an open window in the corner of the dining-room. A tray of mint tea is on the table beside them and they nurse the hot glasses in their hands.

'Is Fuad going to come, Chrissie?'

'Yes. He'll come on his way to work. He's on night-shift – again.'

'I don't think he likes it in that factory, does he?'

'You know Fuad: he's always quick to see what other people are doing wrong. He wants to start something on his own. He's going on about "building up something for this child" already.' She smiles and shakes her head.

'Maybe it would be better for him,' Mimi says.

'Maybe,' Chrissie concedes. 'But it's risky.'

'It's a good moment for that,' says Asya. 'Sadat seems bent on taking us back into the world of private enterprise. Fuad can become a capitalist –'

'Well, you've always got your job, Chrissie,' Noora cuts in. 'You *are* going to carry on, aren't you?'

'Oh yes, goodness. Six weeks' maternity leave and then back to the library.'

'You'll leave the baby with Tante?' asks Mimi.

Chrissie nods. 'She can't wait.' She turns to Noora. 'Have you done anything about *your* mother?'

Noora shakes her head. 'Do I dare to smoke?' she asks, and when Asya nods and points at the open window she reaches in her bag and digs out a pack of Cleopatras. 'I called her twice in the last week – since I heard she was ill. And both times she said, "You've got a wrong number," and put the phone down.'

'What did she sound like?'

'Terrible!' Noora blows the smoke out through her nostrils. 'Terrible.'

'Maybe your father was in the room?'

'Maybe. It's possible, I suppose. But she'd be frightened of him even if he weren't around. After all, he hasn't been constantly with her for two years. She could have contacted me if she'd wanted. If she'd dared.'

They are all silent, then Mimi asks, 'Bassam, comment va-t-il?'

'He's fine. He's been on night-shift for six weeks.'

'I heard him the other night,' says Asya. ' "Voice of Palestine: The News", and then "Poetry of the Resistance". He sounds terribly impressive. A couple of the poems were OK, too.'

'He likes it. The job, I mean. He doesn't partculary like the news he has tꞈ read.'

'No, I know, it's really terrible. It's like Jordan all over again.'

'It can't be like Jordan: Lebanon is too democratic. And they don't have King Hussein there –'

'Still, they don't want the Palestinians there. Frinjieh more or less said so.'

'Did he?'

'He said they are the "Palestinian Resistance"; they should resist from within their occupied homeland, not from Arab capitals.'

'You can see his point,' says Chrissie. 'How can a government rule a country where there is a standing army – with weapons – that doesn't owe allegiance to it? Where there are areas that the government's police and security can't enter?'

'Oh, I know. Absolutely. But the Palestinians won't give up their arms. Arafat has said that that would reduce them once again to the status of simple refugees, and would be tantamount to wiping out the Resistance. He's demanding that the Lebanese stick to the Cairo Agreement of '69.'

'But the Palestinians aren't behaving as –'

'I'm sure there's something else going on,' Asya interrupts. 'Yesterday they arrested some Jordanians who were firing on both sides. And the bombing of the Governor's office in Saida; the Resistance has declared it didn't do that. And what about the weird broadcasts they've found using the name of Voice of Palestine? Somebody's in there stirring things up.'

'And of course Golda Meir has declared that Israel will intervene in "self-defence" if any Arab countries step in to help the Palestinians.'

'They're celebrating their twenty-fifth anniversary. Of course she'd come on strong.'

'We need 'Abd el-Nasser now.'

'Poor man. Leave him alone: he's better off not knowing what's happening.'

'At least we'd have been sure nothing would happen to the Palestinians in Egypt.'

'But nothing *is* going to happen to them. Why should it?'

'There are rumours Sadat's going to close down their radio station. Maybe even throw them all out. I don't know.' Noora crosses her long legs and pulls her skirt down over her knees. Even though she teaches in the department now, Noora still mostly wears her gabardine trousers and her abstracted air. Today, though, she is in a black dress, but her hair still hangs in its long braid, tied at the end with a narrow black velvet ribbon. She and Bassam have found a small ground-floor flat with a garden. All they have is a bed and two armchairs but their kitchen is always stocked with supplies sent over by his mother from Nablus and his sister from Jerusalem. Crates of oranges give off a delicious smell in their hall. Noora is a little paler than she used to be but they seem very happy. Mimi gazes at her speculatively.

'Noora, isn't it time you had a little surprise for us?'

For a moment Noora looks vague, then she understands.

'Mimi, darling, shouldn't we know where we're going to be this time next year first?'

'Will you *ever* know where you're going to be this time next year?' Asya asks.

'And you're a fine one to talk.' Chrissie turns on Mimi. 'Are you exempt or something? Why don't you hurry up and find yourself a bridegroom?'

'Ouf. Don't talk to me of bridegrooms. I'm fed up with the sight of them.'

'That's because you won't choose. So they keep bringing you more. Your poor mother is going mad, she's so worried.'

'Chrissie, it's impossible. You should see the specimens they're bringing me.'

'I saw the last one. Tall and broad with a Mercedes waiting in the street. What was wrong with him?'

'He sat, chérie, in the middle of the sofa, and said, "I would like to tell you, Mademoiselle Mimi, that I am a home-loving kind of man. I don't mean I don't believe in recreation. Not at all. Occasionally I even go to the cinema. But, on the whole, I'm a home-loving kind of man." '

'Oh do stop, stop,' whispers Asya. 'If one of the grown-ups should come in and find us laughing –'

'Well, pity the poor man,' says Chrissie. 'He's never spoken to you before. He has to present himself in your house and sit there and give an account of himself. And of course your mother was there, wasn't she?'

Mimi nods.

'And Father Boulos?'

Mimi nods.

'Well, what do you want? You want the man to come in and say, "I'm a spendthrift and a gadabout and I love drink and women"?'

'Oh, stop, please,' pleads Asya. 'I can just see Tante Safi's face: "In any case, my son, we have to consult her uncles and we do need time to think" –'

'No but seriously, Mimi. You've got to be careful. There aren't that many eligible young Christian men around; they've all been going off to Canada and the States for years. You know that. I'm not saying marry someone you don't want. But you must give people a chance. Don't say no from the first meeting –'

'Mimi,' asks Asya, 'who is this Saint Athanasius that Pope Shenoda is bringing home after he's been in Rome sixteen hundred years?'

'Well, I think –'

'A lot of good Saint Athanasius is going to do *her* –'

The telephone, sitting on the floor beside them, rings, and Asya picks it up.

'Hello? Hello, Tante Adeela . . . And may your life be long, Tante . . . Last night, Tante . . . No, no, Tante . . . God will give them patience . . . Yes, she's here but she's resting. Do you want me to wake her? . . . I'll tell her . . . No, of course not, Tante. I'm sure she'll understand . . . Yes, I'll tell her . . . No, he's not.' She raises her eyebrows at Chrissie. '. . . Yes, he came to the funeral in the morning . . . Yes, I will, Tante, I will . . . And you, Tante. With safety.'

'Your mother-in-law isn't coming?' Chrissie asks.

'No. She'll come tomorrow.'

'Does she know?'

'Know what?'

'About you and Saif.'

'No.'

'Maybe you should tell her. She'd tell him off.'

' "Tante Adeela, I've no idea where your son is or what he's doing. We had a quarrel and I haven't been home for three days and he hasn't bothered to even find out where I am." I couldn't do that to her.'

'Well, what *are* you going to do?'

'You keep asking me that. I don't *know*. I swear I don't know. But I do know that if he doesn't come looking for me I'm not going back.'

'She has a point,' says Mimi.

'The thing is,' says Noora, 'you see going back as a defeat. And he probably sees looking for you as a defeat. But he also thinks that the situation is of your making. And maybe from your side there's a lot more that you're angry about than just that argument. You should tell him.'

'He won't listen. He won't permit a conversation about anything that – matters.'

'Asya, is there still any – particular problem between you?'

'No. No, there isn't. I told you everything's – OK.'

'Then what is it that's upsetting you with him?' Chrissie asks. 'Just that he's not exactly how you imagined he'd be?'

Asya looks at Chrissie. After a moment she nods.

'Yes. Yes, I suppose so.'

'Well then, surely you know about life – or at least you've read enough novels to know that people never turn out *exactly* the way you expect? *And* I don't understand how you can have a viva in five days and stay away from your home where all your books and papers are. Don't you want to prepare?'

Asya shrugs. 'I *wrote* the stuff. I just have to defend it. And the Professor said it was very good. Right now, of course, I can't remember anything except "Death is my son-in-law; death is my heir".'

'Oh, Asya, don't be morbid.'

'Well, think of Beirut. Everybody talks about the Resistance all the time. But the people who got bombed in the camps – in Burj al Barajneh and Sabra – were women. Women and children. And here we are, and my grandfather's dead, and it seems to me that's the only reality that –'

'On parlait de toi at the Council today,' Mimi says.

'Who?' asks Asya.

'The Representative was telling John Munro what a fine scholar you are and how they expect you to do great things in your Ph.D.'

Asya pulls a face.

'I didn't tell you,' says Chrissie. 'They're all surprised that you chose the north of England rather than Oxford. He even said to me on – what was it? – Saturday, he said, "Your friend is making rather an eccentric choice, is she not?" I tried to tell him your stuff about doing something that's never been done before, but I don't think I got it right.'

'What *I* don't understand,' Noora says, 'is why you're choosing linguistics. You've never liked linguistics. Why aren't you going to do poetry or fiction or something you actually enjoy?'

'It's not linguistics. It's stylistics. And it *is* poetry. It's using linguistics to approach poetry. And it's really just an extension of the New Criticism. Concentrating on the text and all that. It makes sense. Since poetry is a specific use of language then the most sensible approach to it – not to appreciating or enjoying it, just to being able to analyse and explain passages – is through the science of language. Then, when some student says, "But why are those lines so special?" instead of talking loosely about "effects" and stuff you can demonstrate your point clearly in a way that he'll understand, and also –'

'You'll still have to do linguistics.'

'Yes, but that's like a surgeon learning about instruments: the instruments aren't his job.'

'He's got to know how to handle them.'

'I'll learn.'

That evening

In the evening session the women sat in the drawing-room and the dining-room; the hall was left free for men who wanted to come and pay their condolences to the daughters of Ismail Mursi. All the men from the shop and the workshops have been, and so have Sheikh Zayid's sons and some colleagues of Soraya's. The Professor has been, accompanied by Dr Minyawi. Saif has been and gone and with him came Fuad al-Sinnari and Bassam al-Husseini. Several of the Mursis' cousins from Alexandria have been, and now, at nine o'clock, the hall is empty save for Sheikh Zayid who sits telling his prayer-beads in the corner by the window. Asya brings him a glass of mint tea without sugar. He is the one to be pitied most of all: her grandfather's lifelong friend. As he raises his eyes to hers for a moment she thinks, 'The theatre of all my actions is gone.'

The blind reciter has finished and gone home to return tomorrow morning, and in the drawing-room Lateefa tries to persuade Aunt Farhana to go to bed while Sunny sits quietly sipping at a last cup of black coffee.

In the bedroom Hamid has stretched out to ease his back for a moment and fallen asleep on Soraya's bed. Soraya sits quietly next to him – watching him. He looks so tired. She has undone the top button of his shirt for him and in the soft lamp-light his loosened tie rises and falls gently on his chest. His left arm is flung out on the satin coverlet: the crumpled, clenched hand for once exposed. She thinks it looks different, swollen, but she can't be sure. She feels so sorry for him. Now he will have everything to sort out and the business to run. There are bound to be long and complicated procedures with tax and duties and inheritance, and he would let himself in for a lot of trouble because he would refuse to take double each girl's share, as was his right, and it would all get very difficult with trying to go against the *shari'a* and split everything up four ways equally. Although, really, they probably wouldn't split anything up after all. He would continue to run the business and that was that. If he wanted to, of course. But he would want to. What else was there for him to do? As he sleeps he softens once again into the young brother she had looked after all those years ago. Until he'd shot up and grown a moustache and fallen in love with a fancy lady who didn't know a thing about loving him. Soraya sighs. God gives earrings to those who are without ears. Her husband would come up soon, no doubt, full of loud talk about every trivial thing that had had the misfortune to pass across his vision. Still, she reminds herself, he is a good man and can always be counted

313

on to do his duty: he will sit down there in the marquee till the last guest has gone and no more are expected; he will make sure the lights are out and the men's reciter has eaten and has someone to take him home. He will not come near her until the forty days of mourning at least are over. She remembers her father's jibes at her husband; once, in the first year of their marriage, Muhammad had arrived at the shop tired and sweating and had told them all how difficult he'd always found it to get shoes his size – 'Sometimes I even have to look in the boys' department.' Her father had taken his *shisha* out of his mouth, pointed it at him, and asked her, 'Is he child-size all over, then?' Muhammad hadn't even noticed, and Hamid, who had thank God been there, had deflected his father from pursuing the joke. She watches her sleeping brother.

Noora has gone home with Bassam but Asya, Chrissie and Mimi are back in the dining-room by the window. Mimi is getting restless.

'Asya, dear, I have to go soon. Every one of my cousins will have rung my doorbell by now. They know I'm here but they will still worry. Are you coming with me?'

'I don't know what to do. If I get up and leave with you my mother will start making a fuss straight away.'

'So you're hoping if you sit here quietly she'll forget you?' asks Chrissie.

'Oh, Chrissie! No. I thought maybe I'd just sleep here tonight.'

'And share a bed with Aunt Farhana? It must be better to share with Saif. Asya. Go home.'

'He came here twice today. In the morning to the funeral and in the evening to condole with Tante Soraya and Mummy. He didn't speak to me.'

'Did he see you?'

'Well, of course I didn't rush out to see him. But if he'd wanted to he could have come inside. He knew I was here. He's making a point.'

The telephone rings and Asya picks it up.

'Hello? . . . Hello, Tante.' She makes a face at Chrissie. 'Yes. Yes, she's here. No, she's fine, nothing's wrong, and Mummy says to thank you very much for coming earlier, Tante . . . Yes, here she is.'

Chrissie takes the phone.

'Mama . . . No, I'm fine . . . There's nothing wrong . . . I'm just staying with Asya for a bit then I'll go home . . . No, Mama, you know he's on the night-shift . . . Asya will drop me off . . . No, Saif isn't here . . . We'll come with Uncle Ulama and Tante Lateefa . . . There's nothing to worry about, I'll phone you . . . Oh, Mama, no, I won't do that . . . Yes, I know he is but . . . My clothes for the morning are in my flat . . . All right, Mama, I will. Now please stop worrying. When Asya leaves

I'll come with her . . . Yes, yes, I will . . . I will. Goodbye.' She looks at Asya. ' "The heart of the mother".'

'You're sleeping at your mother's tonight?'

'Yes. So what about you? Where are *you* sleeping tonight? Put Mimi out of her misery.'

Mukhtar al-Ulama appears in the doorway. He is wearing his most formal dark grey suit and a mourning tie.

'Good evening, ladies. Chrissie, congratulations, you look well. Hello, Mimi. Will you permit me to have a word with your friend?'

'Of course, Uncle, of course. Please come in.'

Both girls hurry out of the room and Asya stands alone by the window. Her father joins her.

'Well, Asya?' he says quietly. 'What's all this I hear from your mother?'

Asya takes a deep breath.

'This isn't right, my daughter. This is not the behaviour of an adult.'

Asya says nothing. Once when she was two, Deena had thrown a pile of fresh laundry out of this window. Their mother had screamed and Dada Zeina had smacked her hand but Daddy had shushed them all. He had picked Deena up and, holding her in his arms and standing next to the window, he had explained to her reasonably and at length that that was a bad thing to do: that clothes were for wearing and nothing was to be gained by throwing them out of windows. Deena had looked into his eyes the whole time, and when he had finished she had quietly reached out for the two blouses that were still lying there, ironed and folded, and she had thrown those out too –

'Asya? Are you listening to me? There are problems in every marriage, in fact there are problems in every relationship. But the thing to do is to solve them, not to run away.'

'I'm not running away, Daddy.'

'Then why have you left home? Why are you hiding out at Mimi's?'

'I'm not hiding out. He could have found me with two phone-calls. He didn't choose to find me.'

'Asya, this is childish. This is no way to conduct married life. You will go home tonight. If it will make it any easier for you I'm prepared to come with you and smooth things over. This situation cannot be allowed to continue any longer.'

'Daddy, I don't want to go home. And *he* doesn't want me to go home either.'

'What makes you say that? Has he told you that he doesn't want you?'

'No.'

'Then what right have you to say that?'

'If he'd wanted me he would have looked for me. He would at least have *spoken* to me tonight.'

'Here? This is a funeral. Saif is a decent man; he has a strong sense of what is proper. He wouldn't make your grandfather's funeral the occasion for a scene.'

'There wouldn't have *been* a scene —'

'Asya. This is enough. As I understand it the man hasn't done anything to you. You had an argument and — whatever the rights and wrongs of that — you chose to leave home. Now you have to go back —'

Lateefa opens the door and comes in.

'Let's go. It's getting late, and we should drop Chrissie and Mimi off on the way.'

On the stairs Lateefa says, 'You're crazy.'

'I'm not. I'm *right*. I'm coming with you because of Daddy. But I'm right.'

'You're just crazy.'

'Quand même, Tante,' Mimi begins as she negotiates the dark stairs carefully. 'He should have looked for her —' then Chrissie pinches her and she falls silent.

In the car Lateefa says, 'I don't believe this. Isn't this Saif whom you were dying to marry for four years?'

'Are you going to keep telling me four years four years? Is it *my* fault it was four years?'

'There is no point to this talk,' Mukhtar al-Ulama says quietly. 'And Lateefa, I think it would be best if you stayed in Zamalek and I'll go with Asya.'

At the door of the flat Asya says, 'I haven't got my key.'

Her father rings the doorbell and Saif opens the door.

'Dr Mukhtar,' he says, 'this is a nice surprise, welcome. Please come in.' To Asya he says, 'Hello.'

They walk in and her father settles himself comfortably in one of the large armchairs and reaches into his pocket for his pipe. Saif pours out one whisky and asks Asya if she would like a drink. She says no, thank you. Her father finds his tobacco pouch and is busy filling his pipe. In here all is serenity. Saif turns down the Simon and Garfunkel record he's been playing. *Motor* magazine lies face-down on the floor. Around it there are some sheets of his blue squared paper covered in his neat black writing and next to them there is a half-full ashtray and a large mug with some coffee left in it and a tall crystal glass with some whisky at the bottom. The light from the two lamps shaded with antiqued parchment makes everything soft and golden. The french windows to the two balconies stand wide open but no breeze moves the heavy Akhmeem curtains.

Asya cannot decide what to do. She can't just join them on an armchair as though they were having a pleasant visit. But neither can she go inside and make herself comfortable as though she belonged here.

316

But she can't keep standing in the middle of the hall either. She sits down on the furthest corner of the kelim – next to one of the speakers.

'Lateefa tells me it's all set?' Mukhtar says pleasantly.

Saif looks at him questioningly.

'You've got the UNDP job,' his father-in-law says.

'Oh, yes. Yes.'

'Where will you be based?'

'The first installation I'll work on will be in Damascus, but I'll be mainly based in Beirut –'

'Beirut? And all this fighting that's going on there? What do you think? Is it going to quieten down?'

'Who knows?' Saif shrugs. 'They've lifted the curfew, though, and that's a good sign. In any case, the UNDP has no plans to move its regional office. So they must think things will probably quieten down. Lebanon has always been adaptable. What's one more militia to the Lebanese?'

> 'Home, where my music's playing,
> Home, where my love lies waiting
> Silently for me.'

'I hope they can agree on some policy. The last thing the area needs now is a civil war in Lebanon.'

'I think the area could do without a great many of the things that are happening in it.'

'That's true,' Mukhtar al-Ulama puffs on his pipe, then says, 'It's a pity you two can't stay together.'

Saif spreads his hands in a gesture of helplessness. 'I'm not clever enough to get a grant like Asya. Still, with the money this job is paying me, Asya can come over to Beirut or Damascus every time she has a holiday.'

'When do you begin?'

'I've fixed it for the same day she leaves: first of October.'

'Well, it needn't be for long. Her mother finished her Ph.D in two years, and she had a home to run and *her* to look after as well.'

Mukhtar al-Ulama stands up with his glass in his hand.

Saif says, 'Let me get us something to eat. I think we've got biscuits and some cold meats and cheeses?' He looks at Asya who looks away. How would *she* know what 'we've' got? She hasn't been here for three days. Only he hasn't noticed.

'No, no, thank you. I'm not staying much longer.' Her father steps up to the desk to put down his glass and sees the slim, inlaid gun lying on the lacquered tray. 'Ah! Is this the gun you were telling me about? Your grandfather's gun?'

'Yes,' says Saif.

Asya leaps to her feet. 'I'm going to pack a few things, then I'm going home with you, Daddy.'

'Asya! what is this, child?'

'I'm going with you.'

'I thought you had come to your senses.'

'I'm going home with you, Daddy.'

Mukhtar al-Ulama looks at Saif, but he has walked back to the other end of the room and is shaking out a Rothmans. He turns back to Asya.

'Asya. Come, come, my dear. *This* is your home.'

'No. No, it's not. I don't *want* it to be.'

'Asya, this is not reasonable.'

'I don't care. I'm not staying here.'

'Asya. Your home is here: with your husband.'

'My *husband*? He doesn't *want* me to be here. He doesn't *care* if I'm here or not –' Asya has started to cry.

'Asya, my dear. We don't want to get emotional now –'

'Why not? Why *not*? He doesn't care, Daddy, he doesn't care –'

'Now, you said there wouldn't be a scene.'

'He doesn't *care*.'

'Of course he does.'

'He doesn't. He isn't pleased to see me. He –'

'Of course he is. Saif?'

'Of course I am,' Saif says quietly from the other end of the room.

'There, you see?'

'Oh Daddy, he isn't. I know he isn't. All he wants is peace and quiet and –'

Mukhtar al-Ulama steps forward and takes his daughter in his arms. He pats her back and smiles. 'What's so bad about peace and quiet?' he asks.

'Daddy, he doesn't care. He doesn't love me –' she sobs on to his shirt.

'How can you say that, darling? The whole world knows how Saif loves you.'

Saif is looking at Asya. Watching her.

'Well, *look* at him. *Ask* him. Ask him if he loves me –'

'This really is – juvenile. My child, nobody can do this' – he pushes her gently away – 'unless there's something radically wrong between you –'

Asya sneezes.

'But if there are just – differences, you have to sort them out together. Isn't that right, Saif?'

Saif nods.

'We won't sort out anything. Nothing *can* be sorted out. He won't *want* to sort anything out. When you've gone he'll just turn back to his books and –'

'Asya! What is this? Are you a philistine? Since when have books become a bad thing?'

'Daddy, I don't want to stay –'

'Come, my dear, come. This is all no use. What's the matter with you? You've always been so positive –'

When her father leaves Asya goes into the bathroom and cries some more. Then she has a shower and bathes her eyes in cold water to stop them looking puffy next day. She brushes her teeth and her hair and puts on a white cotton nightdress. As she lies in bed she remembers a photograph in the back of the newspaper: a home in Beirut, a wall, and two formal photographs of a man and a woman. Lodged neatly between them is a missile. Then she remembers a small item she had read: a security guard counting the corpses in the morgue of the Quarantine Hospital in Beirut sees the hand of one of the bodies twitch. He takes the body out of the fridge and rushes it to the doctors. It is alive: a young Palestinian man named Anton Credli. He is recovering. He was in the fridge. Was he trying to signal? Supposing he was? Supposing he was just conscious enough to try to signal? And supposing the security guard had just happened not to be looking? And supposing he was still conscious when they buried him? When they put him in the earth and heaped dust on to him? No. No. Don't think about that. Think about something else. Saif. No. Something else. She looks around her. At her pretty bedroom: the pink embossed wallpaper, the full curtains that shine with gold and pink in the morning, the embroidered sheets. She reflects that the furniture – her bed, her dressing-table and her chiffonier – will be there after both she and Saif are dead. Then she reflects that they are among the last things to come out of her grandfather's workshop. Then she realises that Geddu was her last grandparent, and now he is dead: she has no grandparents left.

VIII

October 1973 -
August 1974

Scene 1

Tuesday, 2 October 1973

The North of England

In the darkness outside the glass the rain comes steadily down. Inside, neon strips light up the white walls, the grey linoleum floor, the darker grey plastic chairs and the empty pigeon-holes. Asya's two large suitcases stand at her feet. She waits. The white clock on the wall says half past eight.

She had taken the train from Euston at four o'clock and watched the fields and villages go by till darkness came and all she could see was the lit interior of the carriage reflected in the glass of the window-pane, herself a shadowy silhouette – an obstruction – in the foreground. She looks around: there is no one.

The taxi driver had been a graduate of this university. And when he'd learnt she had come to do English he'd told her there were no jobs to be had at the end; that was why he was driving a taxi. She'd said, 'But in the end I'm going home. I've got a job at home. I'm only here on study leave.' And he'd said, 'You're lucky then.'

She presses her nose to the glass wall and makes out an open space and then a low brick building – and another. The taxi had driven out of town, up a hill, and then round what must have been the perimeter of the university. 'That's the Chaplaincy Centre,' the graduate had told her, 'and down there goes to the Medical Centre and your college is round this way.' He'd carried her bags in and left her. 'You wait here by the porters' lodge.'

She walks over to the pigeon-holes. Of course they're empty – but she looks in the 'U' and then in the 'A', just in case. She walks back to her bags. Then she has a thought and walks back to the pigeon-holes and looks in the 'M'. Empty. Chrissie will write to her soon. When they had hugged at the airport for the last time Chrissie had whispered, 'I'll write to you tomorrow.' It was a funny hug because Chrissie has almost finished her ninth month and is enormous. When Asya was crying, Chrissie – who was crying too – had shown her the newspaper. Under Aries it had said: 'A good start or a change that will please you.' She thinks of sitting down. But she does not want to sit down. She's not tired. Not the slightest bit tired. Where *is* everybody? You wouldn't think this was the first day of term.

The fire-door swings open and an elderly, whiskered, kind-looking man carrying a huge bunch of keys walks in. He is dressed in a blue uniform. He looks at the luggage and smiles and nods. He is followed by a very tall young man with straggly long hair wearing jeans and a loose pullover. The whiskered man unlocks the door of the porters' cubicle, checks out Asya's name and gives her a key. 'He'll help you,' he says. The young man picks up one of her bags and Asya follows him out of the door dragging the other and carrying her white beauty-case. They labour across the grass of the open space and squeeze through a small door into the building she had peered at while she waited. 'Second floor,' he says. He hesitates a moment, then picks up the bag again and goes through a swing-door. Asya thinks they must be going up some emergency stairs because the walls are unpainted brick and concrete with big red fire extinguishers and sand-buckets on every landing.

On the last landing the young man pushes through the swing-doors, turns right and right again and stops in front of the first door on the left. 'This is you,' he says, and puts her bag down. Asya says, 'Thank you,' and watches him as he goes back round the corner, down the corridor and through the swing-doors.

It is very quiet. The floor is beige linoleum tiles and the walls are white. The doors too are white. There are two doors beyond hers on the left and three doors facing them on the right. Straight ahead there is a blank wall. On the wall beside her door, and three of the other doors, there are electricity meters. The two remaining doors have no electricity meters – and no locks. She tries one of them very gently: a bathroom – a toilet, a bath-tub and a wash-basin. No bidet and no shower. She tries the next door: two showers, each in a cubicle with a curtain across the front. She goes back to her own door. She puts the key the porter had given her into the lock and opens the door. This is her room. A rectangle. On the wall facing her there is a window with a blue and brown striped curtain that reaches only to the sill. Seven paces take her to it. The door slams shut behind her. She puts her beauty-case down on the floor and opens the curtains wide. Outside there is that same empty space and beyond it the perimeter road, and then the dark outline of a hedge, and then the sky. She opens the window and leans out, holding a scarf over her head against the rain. On the right there is a brick wall, on the left the lit glass of the porters' lodge. But it is very cold. She pulls her head in and closes the window. She takes the seven paces back to the door and pushes the light-switch. A neon circle on the ceiling flickers to life. On the left there is a brown single wardrobe and a single bed. Next to the bed there is a small bedside unit with one drawer. On the bed there is a brown bedspread in a sort of tufty material. Against the right-hand wall there is a grey metal desk with a work-lamp and a brown desk-chair, and above it a noticeboard and two wooden bookshelves. Two paces separate the bed from the desk. There is a brown armchair, and behind the door a wash-basin with a white shelf, a chrome towel-rail and a small mirror. On the floor there is a brown rug of the same texture as the bedspread, only thicker. The wall by the bed is white. The wall by the desk is bare brick. Asya walks to the desk and switches on the reading-light, then back to the door and switches off the neon in the ceiling. In the black glass of the window she can see dim reflections. She looks at the room again, then she takes two paces and bends down. Using the tips of her fingers she folds up the rug and pushes it under the bed. She lifts the bedspread a tiny bit and peeps: white cotton sheets and a beige blanket. She peels back the bedspread, folds it up and pushes it under the bed next to the rug. She straightens up.

After she has stood for a while in the middle of the room, Asya decides that she is hungry. She looks at her watch. Nine o'clock. It is eleven o'clock in Cairo and in Beirut. They will all have eaten by now. Deena and Kareem are probably in their rooms. Her parents are in her father's study, drinking tea and talking about her. Maybe. Even if they're not, she knows her mother is thinking about her. And Saif? Is he in the restaurant of the hotel? The Hôtel Martinez? Eating french onion soup? Or in the bar? Or in his room? Tomorrow he is supposed to leave Beirut for Damascus. She decides to go and look for somewhere to eat. That's where everybody will be, of course: in the campus buttery, or tuckhouse, or canteen or whatever they call it here. She opens her door and drags her two bags inside. She picks up her beauty-case, puts it on the desk and opens it. In the small mirror above the basin she quickly brushes her hair and freshens her lip-gloss. She digs out her purse and puts it, together with her key, in her coat pocket.

And now she is lost. She walks down corridors and pushes through heavy swing-doors to come out into more corridors. And they all look the same: grey linoleum floors, white walls and closed doors on either side. There are no people. She thinks she's been down this particular corridor before but she can't be sure. She walks down some more corridors, opens a door and finds herself in a broad open passage that runs between the buildings. This must be what the prospectus called the 'spine'. She steps out on to it and a cold wind smashes into her. Taken by surprise, she cowers for a moment against the wall, drawing her coat close around her. The 'spine' is covered and open to the sky in alternate blocks. Now that it's raining Asya has to walk in a zigzag so as not to get wet. Still, she can see the sky – except right now it's completely black. She digs her hands into her pockets and sets off. This has got to lead somewhere. She zigzags quickly down the spine propelled by the wind, which pushes at her back until it pushes her into a great, paved, rectangular square. This must be it: the centre of the university. There are street-lights and some shops but they are all closed. And there is still no one about. Asya stands by the wall in the entrance to the square. What now? Now she is very hungry – and very cold. The wind is whipping her legs in their sheer stockings and the coat that had been so warm at home does nothing for her here. She turns back. She walks up the spine. This time the wind is against her and she lowers her head and braces herself against it. As she walks she hears a sound: a rhythmic thud. It comes from the left. She follows the sound through a door, down another corridor and through another door and comes into a large hall. The music is very, very loud. It is nothing she has ever heard before. There is no song, just the loud wailing of electric guitars and the thud of percussion. It is dark except for some white lights on a sort of tripod that flash on and off. Eventually she can make out figures. They seem to be running slowly round the hall. Round and round they go. Occasionally one of them takes a slow run across the middle of the floor. Whether they are men or women she does not know. Then she sees in the far corner a number of people standing around a table. She makes her way there along the sides of the room. When she looks closely at the table she can make out some carrot sticks, bits of cheese and empty glasses. She picks up a piece of carrot and a piece of cheese and starts to nibble at them. Someone near her shouts, 'Quit farting around, will you?' and someone else drawls, 'Shut your fucking mouth!' 'He's pissed, he's pissed,' a laughing voice says. She moves slowly away.

She is trying to find her way back to her room. She keeps walking down corridors and coming back to the spine. She doesn't want to go on the spine because it is so windy. Then, mounted on a brick wall, she sees a chocolate machine. She hunts in her purse. Please. Please let there be – yes. She puts her coins into the machine, pulls out a drawer and now she has a large bar of Cadbury's Milk Chocolate. Chocolate makes her come out in spots but never mind; she can buy Clearasil at the pharmacy – she doesn't have to wait for it to come all the way from the States. With the chocolate bar safely in her pocket she navigates the corridors again until – by pure chance – she comes upon her building. She climbs the two flights of stairs, fits her key into the lock and goes into her room. She is so very cold she can hardly bear to move her arms from her sides. She sits in her coat on the bed and unwraps the bar of chocolate. It would have been nice to have some tea – or a glass of milk. She bites off half a brick. In Cairo it is almost midnight. They're probably asleep by now. Her grandfather would have been awake, listening to the interference. But her grandfather is dead. Last Thursday they had had the usual First of Ramadan breakfast at Tante Soraya's. Without him for the first time. Around the table they had all sat in their usual places, but no one had sat at the head in front of the big glass doors. And just after they had begun to eat Nadia, who had come back in August, had left the table. She had vanished for a while and come back with red eyes and a faint hiccup. It had all been pretty sad.

She has finished half the chocolate and now she really needs some water. There must be a kitchen here. She checks that her key is in her pocket. This time she walks down the other corridor and at the end there is a door standing ajar – and there is a light. She pushes the door open a fraction: a steel sink and a drainer and some cupboards. A little more: a cooker and a fridge. She walks in. At a table by a window a woman with short curly brown hair sits reading a book. Asya says, 'Hi!' The woman looks up, says, 'Hi!' and looks down again at her book. Asya looks at the sink. There are three taps: one hot, two cold. One of the cold taps is for drinking. But which one? Asya decides on the one furthest from the hot tap. There are no cups or glasses. Not a single one. A teaspoon sits on the drainer. Asya turns on the tap and drinks out of her hand. Let her think I'm a barbarian then, I don't care. She turns off the tap, shakes her hand which is now freezing, and leaves the kitchen without looking at the other woman.

Back in her room she sees the wall-heater mounted above the bed. A string dangles from it. She pulls the string and after a moment the heater starts to glow. She kneels on the bed and raises her hands to it to warm them. OK, she thinks, OK. Let's unpack. She jumps up, takes her coat off and hangs it from the hook on the back of the door. She kicks her shoes off but the cold tiles of the floor sting her feet, so she puts the shoes on again. She starts with the beauty-case. The red ruffles are as fresh as ever, and the mirror is polished. But the Opera House is gone. Burnt down, and what was left had been razed to the ground. Before they had gone to a single performance together. Maybe he would not have wanted to go. He'd been there and taken photos. Broken chairs lying in a heap. A couple of marble busts rolling in the dust. Of course, the government had said they'd build another one. Bigger and better. And of course, they'd had the official ceremony, the Laying of the Foundation Stone. But there was still nothing there. Just a piece of waste land. And anyway, who wanted a bigger and better one? The old one had been so pretty. When she was small Nadia had taken her there when the Cairo Symphony Orchestra were rehearsing. And once she'd seen Khatchaturian conduct – she puts her passport in the top drawer of the desk. She has no return ticket. She would not have one until she had finished her Ph.D. She has the cash they had given her yesterday at the Council. She counts it – fifty-four pounds – and puts it in the drawer too. In the pocket of the case she finds the slip of paper Chrissie had given her. At the airport Chrissie had written quickly and torn the paper in half. She had kept the half that said 'There is no god but God' and given Asya the half that said 'Muhammad is the Messenger of God'. Chrissie had said the two bits of paper would one day have to come together again. She folds her bit and puts it inside her passport. She looks at the shelf beside the basin. It really is very small. She puts out her toothbrush and her toothpaste, a cake of Johnson's Baby Soap, a spray deodorant and a bottle of Ma Griffe eau de toilette. She thinks she should keep the rest of the things in the case for the moment. She puts the case on the floor by the basin and opens up the two big suitcases on the floor, then she opens the cupboard. There are shelves and drawers on one side and on the other there are no hangers. None at all.

She is not going to cry, no she isn't. She is going to sit down and sort out her clothes. There are lots of things that don't need to be hung up. She can put them on the shelves and in the drawers. And tomorrow she can go shopping. Yes, that's what she'll do. In the morning she has to meet her supervisor and then she'll go and explore the town. She should have done that tonight but she can't go down now and get lost all over again so tomorrow she'll go into town and buy clothes-hangers, a key-chain and some cups, check out what cinemas they have, the cafés, the restaurants . . .

Wednesday, 3 October

When she wakes up she has no moment of disorientation; before she opens her eyes she knows exactly where she is: she is in a small bed in a rectangular room with a linoleum floor on which her suitcases are still open. But she is not cold any more. Even her head, outside the covers, is not cold. She opens her eyes. It is still almost dark. The thin curtains are lit up but the light that filters through them is pale and weak. Her wall-heater is still glowing. She unwinds her left arm from around herself, pushes it out from under the cover and pulls at the curtain. It opens slightly, but no light floods in. She looks at her watch: ten past seven. In Cairo and Beirut it is ten past nine. Maybe she should stay in bed. *Cosmopolitan* lies open face-down on the floor. But she does not feel like starting to read it again now. Her father and mother are already at college and Deena and Kareem are in their first lesson at school. Saif too must be already at work. But her appointment with her supervisor is not till eleven. She turns on to her side and closes her eyes. Why not stay in bed a little longer? Try to go back to sleep. She had not thought loneliness could come like this; like a sudden big black wave out of nowhere. She had thought it would take time, be cumulative, so to speak; that by the time it was getting bad it would be almost Christmas and time to go to Beirut. On the train she had read the papers that the Council had given her, and they said that students were not allowed to leave the UK until their studies were completed. But they could not possibly mean that. They were just covering themselves so as not to pay for tickets. But she isn't going to ask them for a ticket. Saif will send her the ticket, so it's got to be all right. She'll have to ask her supervisor. Not today, of course. You can't go in for your first tutorial and ask if you can go away for a holiday. But later she will ask him. When her work is well under way and he can see that there would be no harm in letting her go for a few days. Just while there was a holiday at the university. Well, the sooner she gets started on her work the better. He is bound to be brilliant, her supervisor. His book is brilliant. It was his book that had brought her here; made her choose this university rather than any other. A quarter past seven. Saif is going to Damascus today. But she doesn't know when.

She sits up. She didn't have a shower last night. She'll have one now. Have a shower and sort herself out. She puts on her dressing-gown and starts collecting her things. Loofah, backbrush, soap and shower-gel, shower-cap, towel – how is she going to carry all this? And the key to her room. This is why people have what they call 'sponge-bags'. She'll have to get herself one of those too.

The moment she opens her door she is struck by the cold. She runs quickly across the corridor in her thin dressing-gown and slippers. She turns on the water in one of the shower cubicles and waits for it to heat up. It needs courage to take off her dressing-gown and nightdress but after a moment as she stands under the hot water she feels good for the first time since getting off the plane. She lets the muscles of her shoulders and her back relax and turns to let the hot water stroke and warm up every bit of her. This will last her till she's dressed. She will wear her prettiest dress, the dark blue one with the tiny red flowers, and make herself look really good. She'll go and find some breakfast, there must be somewhere to have breakfast. Then she'll go check out the library. Then she'll open a bank account and by then it will be time to go and see her supervisor. This time she won't get lost. She'll run across that open space and ask the porter where she should go. And besides, it's daylight. Things are bound to be clearer in daylight. Even if the daylight is weak.

She waits until it is one minute past eleven, then knocks.

'Come in!'

She opens the door. A room with modern furniture. Teak effect. But then, she was silly to expect anything else here. To expect deep leather armchairs, an enormous nineteenth-century desk, books piled up on the floor, a silver tray with drinks and biscuits, a window-seat looking out over a quiet sunny quad – with cloisters. The professor is at the far end of the room and now comes forward to greet her. A tall, big man with green eyes and a lot of grey hair short at the back and long in front. They shake hands and he retreats behind his desk. Asya sits in a chair facing him.

'Did you – have – a good journey?' he asks, glancing up then quickly down again at the papers he is arranging on his desk.

'Yes, thank you,' Asya says.

'Good.'

There is silence.

'You've – sorted out your – your accommodation – and everything?'

'Oh, yes, thank you.'

Another silence.

'Well – your – record is certainly most – very impressive. Both at Cairo University and in the – umm – Graduate Record Exam.' He shuffles some papers in front of him. 'The Council recommends you highly and your – references – are most – most friendly –' He seems almost more ill at ease than she is. 'Do you – did you have a – particular – topic in mind?'

'Well – I – I would like to do something with poetry, Professor. Modern poetry.'

'Ah! Poetry – Ah! – you mustn't call me Professor, you know –' He gives her a quick, shy smile. 'You can call me Bill.'

'Oh! Right. Thank you.'

Of course, she can't possibly call him 'Bill'. But now she can't call him anything else either. She glances at him. He has a way of moving his lips soundlessly between words, biting his lower lip, looking as if he is about to say something, and then moving his lips again in silence.

'I would very much like to work on Philip Larkin,' Asya says.

'Ah!'

'Or if you think that's too modern then maybe Yeats?'

'Yeats – yes – but – what *linguistic* aspect in particular?'

'Oh! I hadn't really thought – I don't really know. I'm sorry.'

There is a silence. Goodness, what a complete fool. Of course, she should have been prepared for that question.

'Well, perhaps – there is a list – let me see if I can find – you might find it helpful – why don't you look through these – see if they give you any ideas – then we can talk – make an appointment –'

'Yes. Yes, of course. Thank you very much. When should I . . .?'

She is already on her feet and heading for the door.

'Two weeks?'

He smiles at her cheerily, encouragingly.

'Yes. Thank you.'

She hurries out and closes the door gently behind her. Oh, how stupid. How very stupid. She should have been prepared with 'the structure of sentences' or 'musical repetitions' or something. Now he is going to think her a total idiot. Right. She'll sit down somewhere right now and go through this list. Maybe she could talk to some other student who's working with him. See what sort of thing they're doing. Eleven-fifteen. She stops at the door of the department secretary.

'Hi! Excuse me. Could you tell me where the graduate common room is?'

'The – oh, sorry, dear. There isn't one. There used to be but the JCR voted to abolish it.'

330

The secretary is very smiley and comfortable with lots and lots of papers on her desk.

'The JCR?'

'The Junior Common Room.'

'Is there a room for department students? Or a small department library?'

'No, dear, there isn't. There'll be the Linguistic Circle, but they meet every two weeks in a different room. Depends what they can get. There'll be a notice up on the board in a couple of weeks.'

'Thank you.'

Visions of a big warm room with deep chairs: the sunshine pours through open curtains, newspapers and periodicals are scattered on the tables. There is a smell of fresh coffee. From a sofa by a window a woman smiles up at her. She wears glasses and a long loose skirt and has one leg tucked up comfortably beneath her. 'Oh, you're the new student who's come to work with Bill Murray. Listen, what you should do is –' But it's no use thinking like this. No use at all. Obviously she'll have to go back to the main library. Yes. She'll go there and work for an hour and then go into town and explore. Have lunch – have something really nice – and then do her shopping. That should be fun; setting up a mini-house, her very own, all over again.

She stands in the underpass waiting for the bus. The notice says there is a bus every half-hour but she does not know when the last one went. It is not windy down here, but it is very cold. Cold and damp. The cold seeps up through the soles of her shoes. She stamps her feet and pushes her hands into her pockets and shivers. She will have to go back to the library in the evening. She had looked up two items in the list the professor had given her: one an article in *Poetics* and the other in *Linguistic Inquiry*. And she had understood nothing. Nothing at all. It was as if they were in a different language. A different idiom, anyway. The list was all articles and she had read it through and not recognised a single name. She would have to go back to the library and really get down to it. She waits. It's almost one o'clock. At home it's three o'clock and everybody is having a siesta.

There are three people on the bus. As they emerge from the underpass and roll down the hill and on to the main road Asya looks back at the university. Red brick with broad white bands round the top. It is true that it makes you think of a ship, as the brochure says. But what is the point of looking like a ship if you are on top of a hill? Marooned. It takes twenty minutes to get from the university into the town. Asya gets off at the terminal. She expects it to be at the centre of the town but it appears to be on the edge. She follows the notices that say 'To Town Centre' and finds herself in an enormous, mostly empty, car-park. She follows the notices that say 'Way Out' and finds herself in a paved shopping precinct made of concrete. Woolworth's, Boots the Chemist, Curry. But no people about. She shivers. If she breathes out she can see her breath floating upwards. She walks up to Woolworth's. They would have clothes-hangers. As she approaches she realises that she can see no one at all inside. But the lights are on. She tries one of the doors. It is locked. She tries one more. That's locked too. She looks in the windows of Boots. It is closed. All the shops are closed. Even a little pretend-Tyrolean tea-shop. All closed. But there will be places outside the precinct. And of course she'll find her way to the bus-stop when she wants to go back. She can always ask someone.

She pulls her coat tighter around her and walks quickly up a street outside the precinct. It is narrow but not picturesque. It doesn't even feel particularly old. She comes to Marks and Spencer's but it is closed. She follows a sign that says 'Market Hall' and arrives at a small glass-panelled door. Through it she can see shops with no lights and stalls with sheets thrown over them. What is the matter with this place? She's never seen a town so definitely shut down before. It's like a town in a Western when the baddies are heard thundering along the mountain pass. Are there people behind these curtains? How is she going to unpack? She can't start working properly until she's sorted out her room and hung up her clothes. She can't live for ever stepping over two suitcases. How *come* the whole town is shut down? They don't close for siestas here. And she hasn't seen any notice that says 'Closed for Lunch' or 'Open at Four' or anything. What is she going to do? There must be *some* place here where you can buy a few hangers . . .

An old woman is walking down the other side of the street. Asya crosses over.

'Excuse me, can you tell me what time the shops will open?'

'They won't be opening no more today, love. They close at twelve.'

'Do they always close at twelve?'

'It's Wednesday, love. Early Closing Day.'

'Oh. Thank you.'

When she's walked a couple of paces Asya thinks of something and hurries back after the old woman.

'Excuse me, can you tell me the way to the castle?'

The woman gives her what Asya thinks is an odd look. 'It's over there,' she says.

Well, if she can't shop, she'll explore. Even if she's freezing. She can't just get on the bus and go back to the underpass.

And there it is. On top of a green hill. Smallish for a castle, but impressive all the same. All grey stone and battlements, with a great, barred oak gateway and a portcullis. That's better. She starts walking up the hill and sees a security guard in a blue uniform. Maybe the castle too closes at twelve on Wednesday. She walks up to the guard.

'Excuse me. Is the castle open to visitors?'

'Not unless you've got someone here,' he says, 'and not today anyway.'

'Sorry?'

'This is a prison, love.'

'A prison?'

'If you want to look at something there's the cathedral over there.'

The old door yields slightly to her hand and Asya squeezes through the narrow opening and into the shadowy vastness of the cathedral. It must be all right to come in here; the door was not locked, and besides, anybody can enter a house of God at any time. Any reasonable time. She thinks of all the churches she's visited in Italy: the flamboyant paintings, the colourful Madonnas, the dramatically suffering Christs – the light. This is very different. And yet, she is glad to be here. She slips quietly into a pew and sits very still. She has the cathedral all to herself. Here the dimness does not oppress her and what light there is outside gently illuminates the huge stained-glass window at the bottom of the nave. She touches the smooth wood, worn edgeless by so many fingers before hers, and lets her eyes wander up the contours of the arches to the high vaults above. The stone-flagged floor too is worn and beautiful, and even the cold here is not too bad. The peace that passeth all understanding. What is she going to do? The two articles she'd looked at were full of words like 'variable', 'parameter', 'formation rules', 'singulary operator', 'n-nary operator'. If she had to sit down and tell someone what either article aimed to prove or disprove she would not be able to do it. In front of her lies the Book of Common Prayer. She opens it:

They smite down thy people, O Lord: and trouble thine heritage. They murder the widow, and the stranger: and put the fatherless to death. And yet they say, Tush, the Lord shall not see: neither shall the God of Jacob regard it. Take heed, ye unwise among the people: O ye fools, when will ye understand? He that planted the ear, shall He not hear: or He that made the eye, shall He not see? Or He that nurtureth the heathen: it is He that teacheth man knowledge, shall not He punish? The Lord knoweth the thoughts of man: that they are but vain.

She half smiles. Thank you. That takes care of the hangers and a lot else besides. For shame. Think of the things that people come in here to pray for. She remembers women in Egypt: in Tanta at the shrine of al-Sayyid al-Badawi and in Cairo at the shrine of St George the Martyr; women hanging on to the grille, kissing the cold metal, weeping, putting coins they had saved into the collection and begging, begging, for health to be given back to a bread-winning husband, for the return from the desert of a beloved son, for eyesight, for feeling in paralysed limbs, for the womb to bear once a child: once, once only God, dear God, and I will spend the rest of my life thanking you and praising you and I will never ask for anything again. Think. You feel lost because you could not buy hangers, but you have clothes to hang up; you are afraid because you could not understand an article in *Poetics*, but you are being paid eighty-four pounds a month to sit and learn to understand it; you are lonely and homesick, but you have a home and a family to long for. You are not a Palestinian woman living in a camp in south Lebanon, nor are you a Polish Jewess in 1939. You are not an Ethiopian mother hearing her baby scream with hunger and knowing that her milk is running dry, nor a Chilean communist being tortured right now in some jail. You are not even Khalu Hamid, looking at the world out of one eye, driving with one arm and struggling to make up for areas of burnt-out brain. Work. Work hard. You don't want to be here but this is what you've chosen and you won't be here for ever. You can do it in two years. It's all up to you. And the time will be broken up. There's another thing: how many women starting their theses today will be able to go off and see their husbands after three months? And he loves you. Of course he does. Why else was he so upset on Monday and kissed every bit of your face and the palms of your hands in the car on the way to the airport? Why else will he spend his money flying you over at Christmas to be with him? She buries her face in her hands. Oh God. Make it right, please, please make it right. I'll work hard. I'll be good and not complain. I'll be no trouble when I go to Beirut; I'll be just the way he wants me to be. Only make it all right. Please. After a moment she takes her hands away and looks up. There are the great golden pipes of the organ. How magnificent it must be when the music plays. It would be nice to come here when there is a service and hear it, and hear the hymns and the synchronised rustle of paper. She looks around. The walls are covered with plaques comme-morating people who have died. So many. I had not thought – oh yes I had. From here she can read several. The most recent date is 1958: the year Kareem was born. And suddenly she thinks, I am thinking about death. But it is not catching at my heart. The thought is gentle, like an old, well-worn sadness. Not immediately terrifying. But don't push it. Stop while you can. She opens the Prayer Book again:

Though I speak with the tongues of men and of angels, and have not charity, I am become as sounding brass, or a tinkling cymbal. And though I have the gift of prophecy, and understand all mysteries, and all knowledge; and though I have all faith, so that I could remove mountains, and have not charity, I am nothing. And though I bestow all my goods to feed the poor, and though I give my body to be burned, and have not charity, it profiteth me nothing.

334

Outside the cathedral Asya looks at her watch. It is almost four o'clock. The light has the same dusky, end-of-day feel it has had since the morning. To her left is the castle and below her feet lie the grey streets of the town. Beyond the town there are fields and wooded hills. And rising out of a dense wood she can see a white, ornate dome. She's read something about it somewhere: it's someone's 'Folly', built as a memorial to his wife who died young. Its centrepiece is an aviary of dead birds.

Sunday, 7 October: 7 p.m.

Dear Chrissie,

I'm beginning to think your people were right to look doubtful about this place. It's so cold, oh Chrissie it's *so* cold. I'm always cold. They gave me a cold clothes allowance when I got to London (I must say, they *are* generous and I *do* feel grateful – you can tell them that at your end – here there's nobody to tell), but I have to live on it till my first grant comes through. I did buy myself a heavy coat and a scarf though the day before yesterday.

They've got this thing here called the 'spine' which is a passage that runs from the beginning of the university to the end and you can't get anywhere without going through it, only it acts as a wind tunnel. Even when it isn't partcularly windy in other places it's windy down the spine and you're either blown down it or you have to fight your way up, and sometimes it feels as though it's blowing from both directions at once. Also bits of it are covered and bits aren't so as you're being blown down you have to run in a zigzag like you're crossing a minefield to stay dry if it's raining, and it's raining most of the time. My hair gets wet here even when it isn't raining: it's so damp. If I put my hand under it near my neck it's all cold inside. And you know how it curls and how long it takes to dry, so I've had to buy myself a woolly hat – don't laugh or even smile: it's *horrid* – it really is – I look so *ugly* in it. I put it on behind the door, then run to wherever I'm going, and as soon as I get inside somewhere I whip it off and stuff it into my bag. Vanity, of course, and pointless, since no one looks at anyone here. Crazy.

They've also put the university on top of a hill, just to make sure it's as windy and cold as possible. And it's quite a way from the town, and the only way you can go into town is on a bus, and the busstop is underground, and I can't tell you how horrid it is down there – Oh dear. I stopped just now and tried to find something nice to say about this place but I swear I can't. I was pretty excited at first to see up-to-date periodicals instead of everything coming to a stop in 1967, and

335

the library is 'well-stocked' I suppose, but then every university library must be well-stocked – so?

It really *is* a weird place. This is my sixth day here and I haven't talked to anybody except my supervisor for fifteen minutes on Wednesday. I think he's OK, but it wasn't a particularly comfortable meeting and it's beginning to look like Noora was right and I'll have to do a lot more linguistics than I'd thought. I've started, but I don't recognise any of the stuff I'm supposed to read – still, I suppose it will all fall into place.

The house I live in has three floors: nine rooms on each floor. The ground and first floors are for men and the second for girls. I think all the people on my floor are on courses together because they all seem to know each other. We say 'Hi' politely in the kitchen and that's about it. I don't really see how I'm going to actually *meet* anyone – there's no senior common room and what they call the junior common room is really the TV room: dark, with rows of chairs and people just slumping with beer-cans in their hands. And of course you can't choose what to watch because it's on one channel only. In my college it's on ITV which is the commercial channel and always has things that are supposed to be funny and aren't, and the students make such a noise and yell and fight that you just can't be there unless you're one of them.

Today is Sunday so I took my time getting up and getting dressed. I lingered over my breakfast. I tried to make it feel like a holiday. Then I wrapped myself up in my coat, scarf and gloves and braved the wind on the spine to get the papers – and found that the newsagent was closed. It closes at ten on a Sunday. Things here are always in a great rush to close. Now I've been in my room all day and at least I'm not cold with the heater on. We've each got our own meter and we pay for the electricity at the end of each month. I'm sure I'll have an enormous bill. I've been trying to read a horrid article (Listen: 'If there are no restrictions on occurrence of spondees, and if juncture is not reckoned with, I see no way of distinguishing this system from the sequence-of-positions-stress-maximum theory, supported only by lexically based stress rules . . . the constraint which states that a trochee may not follow another trochee appears to be simply a variant way of saying that the first syllable of a given trochee, if it follows another trochee or a pyrrhic, will be a stress maximum in an odd position, but that neutralisation between abutting strong stresses will occur if a trochee follows an iamb or a spondee' – this is about Keats – except I don't think it is *really*) and taking breaks to read *Cosmopolitan* and bits of *Anna Karenina* for a treat. I've decided to buy a radio, it'll help me not feel so terribly cut off.

I think about you all a great deal. In fact Cairo is *always* on my mind. And of course I think about *you* in particular – and miss you. Chrissie, you will let me know as soon as the baby comes, won't you? And please, could you give Mummy a ring and say –

Monday, 8 October

Sinai

Egyptian Chief of Staff General Shazli visits the Third Army as it advances across the desert capturing 'Uyun Musa and other important positions. *The Times* of London reports: 'Four hundred tanks of the Egyptian Third Army trapped in the desert.'

Israel claims that nine of the ten bridges the Egyptians had thrown across the Suez Canal to effect their crossing have been destroyed. It claims that it has cut Egypt's lines of retreat and is now consolidating its forces for an offensive.

Damascus

'The mood of the Syrian capital is quiet but expectant. The war seems very close. People in the streets stop to watch a dogfight in the skies just south of the city. One jet crashed into a village about ten miles from the city centre. The closest point of battle is in Qatana – fifteen miles south of Damascus – and the thud of artillery can be heard clearly in the city. A total blackout has been imposed.' (*The Times*)

Beirut

'People are out enjoying a normal fine day but an air of expectancy pervades the city.' (*The Times*)

Cairo

'Cairo radio has been broadcasting martial music and patriotic songs interrupted by military communiqués on the progress of the fighting. A total blackout has been imposed and all car headlights have been painted blue. Civil defence and popular resistance training centres have been opened for students and members of youth organisations. Fuel, meat, sugar and other foodstuffs have been rationed. President Muhammad Anwar al-Sadat has moved to military headquarters and assumed personal command of operations.' (*The Times*)

The North of England

Asya wakes up relieved that it is Monday and that Sunday is over. She gets dressed, has breakfast and goes first to the post office and then to the library. She tries to read an article on the analysis of 'ed-adjectives' but gives up at ten past twelve. She decides to have lunch; to buy a newspaper and have lunch – even though she hasn't earned a hot lunch she can have a salad – what is she going to do? She can't go back to the

337

Professor and say, 'I don't quite see what all this has to do with what I want, I don't understand these articles, I hate reading them, they seem to be assuming things that I know nothing about and making a huge fuss about others which are quite obvious. What shall I do?' She stops at the newsagent. As she picks the top copy of *The Times* off the pile on the floor she sees the headlines.

Tuesday, 9 October 1973
Sinai
'After fierce street fighting Egyptian troops recaptured el-Qantara, capital of occupied Sinai, and hoisted the Egyptian flag there for the first time since June 1967.' (*The Times*)

> We had to climb the wall and help the engineers to cut through the barbed wire – I could not wait so I climbed over the wire and ran through the minefield and climbed Fortified Point Number One in the middle of flames and gunshot and a squadron of fighters blotting the sun out from the sky. We fired at the Israeli soldiers as they fled and someone put the flag in my hand. I wrote on it in my blood 'All Pride to Egypt' and hoisted it. Some of the men were kissing the ground and some were putting the dust on their heads or in their pockets and some were rolling over in it and yelling for joy and I swear on the heads of my children that I looked up and saw the words 'Allahu Akbar' written on the sky at that moment in black smoke and that that evening we looked around us and saw that the desert had come out in white blossoms with fresh green leaves.

> Muhammad al Abbasi, soldier
> (*al-Ahram*)

Damascus
'Thousands take to air-raid shelters after Israeli air strikes on military airfields near the city. Israeli and Syrian jets continuously streak over the city.' (*The Times*)
'The Beirut–Damascus highway remains open and traffic on it is normal.' (*The Times*)

Jerusalem
'Anti-Zionists refusing to serve in the army have gone into hiding. The Israeli Revolutionary Action Committee Abroad (IRACA) and the Israel–Palestine Socialist Action Group (IPSAG) have issued a statement: ". . . whatever the circumstances surrounding the opening of hostilities, the basic responsibility for the war lies with the leaders of the Zionist State . . . the present fighting is taking place over territories seized by Israel in 1967 . . . Egypt and Syria aim only at creating

338

conditions for the imposition of a diplomatic settlement under the auspices of Imperialism . . . at the expense of the Palestinians' interests . . . Only a thoroughgoing social revolution, which will overthrow both Zionism and Arab régimes, can solve the problems of the Arab East including the Palestinian problem'. (*The Times*)

The North of England

For the second night Asya sits in University House reading the newspaper and waiting for the phone-call she has placed to Cairo to come through. She cannot call Saif; she doesn't even know where he is. Over and over she tries to picture him running to a shelter and can't. He'll stay in his flat or in his hotel room reading or working with the TV on. Anyway, his flat would probably be in the posh section of the city; that's where UN and embassy people are always housed. Nothing would happen there. And maybe he hasn't even gone to Damascus yet; maybe he's still in Beirut. Things there are not bad – yet. At home she can imagine exactly what it's like now: the blackout, her mother quarrelling with Deena and Kareem to stay in the inner hall, the martial music on the radio, the Qur'an and footage of past military parades and Sadat in an invented uniform on television. Poor Chrissie, oh poor, poor Chrissie. Fuad must be out there in the thick of it. They must have called up all the reserve officers, particularly the engineers. And Noora – what about Bassam? Things are bound to change for them now –

She turns the page and sees a blurred photograph of a thin-faced dark-haired young man: there is a bandage around his forehead and over his right eye; the other eye is steady and sharp. The text says 'captured Israeli David Ben Rahim' but he looks terribly like that old photograph of Chrissie's fiancé, Issam al-Uthmanli – The telephone rings in the operator's room and Asya jumps up. The operator speaks into the phone then turns to her.

'There's a five-hour delay on calls to Egypt, dear. I wouldn't wait, you know.'

Back in her room Asya switches on her new transistor radio and is just in time to catch the tail-end of the news: '– in the centre of Damascus. Three members of the Norwegian embassy have been reported dead. An eye-witness said, "It was horrifying. There were so many dead and wounded lying around in the streets –"' That was Mrs Marta Servic, the wife of a Polish embassy official.

'In New York the Soviet representative, Yakov Malik, walked out of a Security Council meeting when Israeli representative Yosef Tekoah expressed his country's condolences for the loss of life in the air strike on Damascus.

'A radar station in neutral Lebanon has been destroyed in a bombing run by two Israeli Phantoms. Columns of smoke were seen rising above the cedars of Barouk, a picnic spot twenty-five miles south-east of Beirut, and Israeli armoured border troops have been reported to have raked Blida, a village in southern Lebanon, with machine-gun fire for fifteen minutes.

'There have also been Israeli air strikes at airfields north and south of Cairo –'

She switches the radio off. The wall-heater glows behind her but the room takes hours to warm up. She sits on the bed in her coat and scarf. Nothing will have happened to him. Of course not. Why *him?* But why anyone? That must be what everybody thinks: nothing will have happened to him – and yet it's happened to *someone.* Well, nothing *has* happened. She would have known. They would have reached her somehow. It is twenty past eight but it feels like midnight. At home it is twenty past ten. She wants to be there. She *has* to be there. She would stay in the inner hall and not quarrel with her mother. Not talk about nursing or civil defence or anything; just stay in the inner hall with Deena and Kareem. What would happen if she went? Just packed one small bag – which bag? Well, just her beauty case, even – oh, don't be silly. Cairo Airport is closed, and how would she get out when it was over? Imagine all that exit visa procedure all over again. They would all be furious with her. It would only be self-indulgence, and besides she has only fifteen pounds; that wouldn't pay for a ticket. Well, what is she to –

A quick knock on her door and a man's voice calls out, 'Telephone.' She jumps up and opens the door but he has gone. She races down the corridor and catches the door as it swings to. Down the stairs to the first floor, and there in the corner by the window is the wall-mounted incoming calls only extension with the receiver dangling from its lead. She grabs the receiver and says, 'Hello, hello.' But there is nothing. She waits a moment and says, 'Hello,' again. Still nothing. It is dead. She tries twice more and then hangs up. She stands by the phone for a little while. Maybe they will call back. A door opens and shuts and a young man walks by. 'There was a call for you yesterday but you weren't there.' He carries on walking and goes into the kitchen. She stands and stares out of the dark window. She can hear the odd door slam and see the occasional shadow moving in the glass in front of her. But she can't go on standing like this in the men's corridor. She will have to go back to her room. She starts to cry before she is out of the corridor and hurries up the stairs with her head down. At her door she finds that she has not got her key. Of course, it is lying on the desk inside. The bathroom door is not locked. She goes inside and finishes crying as quickly as she can, dries her face with toilet-paper and sets off down the stairs again. She runs across the frozen grass to the porter's lodge.

'I'm afraid I've locked myself out.' As she speaks she can feel the tears start to well up again.

340

'You don't have to look so miserable over it,' the whiskered old porter says kindly. 'Here.' He hands over a key. 'But mind you bring it straight back. And don't forget *your* key this time.'

When she is finally back in her room there is nothing for it except to go to bed. She puts on a pair of woollen socks and fills her hot-water bottle at the tap in the basin. She puts her key in the pocket of her dressing-gown and lays it over the chair. She gets into bed and switches off the light and stares at the red bar of the heater.

She is woken by a loud knock on her door and hears a voice call, 'Telephone.' She snatches up her dressing-gown and runs down the stairs in her socks. When she hears Saif's voice say, 'Asya,' she starts to cry.

'It's all right, sweetie. It's all right.'

'Oh, Saif, Saif —'

'It's all right. You've been worried?'

'Oh yes, yes.'

'Everything's OK. Listen. I tried to call you yesterday and Sunday but I couldn't get you —'

'They've got the most *stupid* system —'

'It's very hard to get lines out of here —'

'Have you got a telephone where I —'

'No. I'm leaving Damascus tomorrow. The whole place is shut down anyhow. I'll be in Beirut and I'll call you whenever I can. Look, stop crying. I've just spoken to your father and they're all telling you not to worry. OK? Just sit tight and —'

'Do you have any news of Fuad?'

'No. But Chrissie had her baby yesterday. A girl. They're calling her Ranya. Don't cry, Princess, come on. It's all going to be all right. You just get on with what you're doing. How is it there?'

'Oh, Saif, it's *horrid*. I can't begin — Saif? Hello? Hello? Oh —'

She waits a few seconds then says, 'Hello?' tentatively and softly. When there is no reply she puts the phone down and presses her hand to her mouth. If only she could stay here beside it —

A door opens and a man puts his head out.

'Do they know this phone isn't in your room? It's one o'clock, you know. In the fucking *morning*.'

Sunday, 4 November

Dear Mummy,

It's Sunday again and everything is very firmly closed. I've been working in my room all day except from four to five when a girl called Esmeralda came round and I made her some tea. She's nothing like

341

an Esmeralda really: she's short and stubby with cropped brown hair and she doesn't wear any make-up. She goes on, in fact, about how make-up is bad for you and how she only puts baby oil or something on her face every morning. She's from Chile and you would (or *I* would, I suppose) expect her to have some impassioned stance of one type or another. But she doesn't. All she'll say is that the government of President Allende had reduced Chile to economic ruin. So I said, but he was only in government for less than three years, and she shrugged, and that was that. I suppose you're thinking she's 'prudent'. Well, she's jolly *boring*. She's doing maths and she's decided (I don't know why) to be my friend. This means a cup of tea twice a week in my room while she goes on about vegetarian diets and liquid diets and banana diets and yoga and types of exercise (how some are harmful and others beneficial) until I feel cramp pains in my legs with boredom. Still, I'm always terrifically pleased to be alone when she's gone, so I suppose she's good for me.

I can't tell you how relieved I am that things are back to normal (well, normalish) – I suppose it's too early yet to have news of Fuad? Please let me know anything you hear. I've written to Chrissie and to Noora but I guess letters will be held up. I don't know when you're going to get *this*. It's been fairly rough here and made me think of what it must have been like for you when we were in London during Suez. Not that anything's actually happened, but there is this hostility in the air. The papers report things pretty even-handedly, I think, but still – they always have photographs of individual Israeli soldiers – girls too – looking, of course, like perfectly normal sympathetic people, while the Egyptians are always a dusty rabble swarming over tanks or something; you can never see any of their faces. And a public opinion poll showed that support for Israel is ten times – *ten times* – greater than for the Arabs. And this stuff with the oil isn't going to help our popularity. Still, I'm glad of it. I saw this Sheikh Yamani on TV. I like him.

I'm OK. I've fixed up my room so it's not too horrid: put a shawl over the chair and some posters up, stuff like that. And I'm getting on with the work as well as I can, although so far I don't actually like it. I'm due to meet Prof. Murray for the third time on Wednesday and that's quite an ordeal. He's so unrelaxed – and of course I am too, but maybe it will get better when I get more into the work; so far I've not really had much to say and he's had to just give me stuff to read.

I went to this Linguistic Circle meeting last week and didn't understand anything anybody said. Except every once in a while someone mentioned love and pain. I sat there thinking that was pretty weird until I realised they were co-editors of a book: I looked it up next day: Love & Payne! But nobody seemed the slightest bit aware of the oddity of it. I suppose it's because they know it so well.

342

Saif called me again yesterday. He called me twice while the war was on. He's still in Beirut but says he'll be going to Damascus some time next week. I always start to cry when I hear his voice and he must think it's dreadfully stupid. It's pretty embarrassing, too: the phone is on the men's corridor and I stand there blubbing into the phone, and they walk by and pretend not to see me –

Scene 2

December 1973
Beirut

She came out of Customs trying to look cool. Trying not to look as if she was expecting anyone but looking lost all the same. She looked good, though. I hadn't forgotten, but it struck me all over again. The mass of black hair, the long legs in the short skirt. Guys turned to look at her. I took her in my arms and she held on like she was a kid. She buried her face in my neck. I'd borrowed a red Ferrari Dino for her to drive and booked us into the Phoenicia with a balcony right out on the bay. She was happy. She kept saying, 'Oh, this is wonderful! Wonderful!' She had french onion soup for dinner. She was wearing some silky blue thing and she practically shone – blazed – across the table. She licked the cheese off the spoon and said, 'Don't you notice anything about me? About my hair?'

I said, 'No. It looks great. What?'

'I've dyed it. Well, not dyed it exactly, but I've put a colour rinse in it.'

'It looks exactly the same.'

She looked downcast. 'I know. I used a black rinse.' Then she looked at me and grinned. 'Well, I couldn't imagine it any other colour. But I thought it might make a bit of difference all the same.'

When we went up to the room she went into the bathroom and turned all the taps on. Then the shower. Then she came out in her nightdress and dressing-gown looking uncomfortable. I thought she was going to start sneezing but she went straight out on to the balcony and stood there looking at the sea.

After a bit she came in and sat on the floor beside my chair. She said, 'There's no moon.' She laid her head against my knee and I stroked her hair, then I pulled her around and took her face in my hands. She was beautiful. She knelt between my legs, and when I bent down to her I felt her hands light on my shoulders and she kissed me. Kissed me like she used to in the Omar Khayyam:

343

deep and sweet but with a touch of uncertainty; a slight tremor beneath the surface. I stood up. I looked at her kneeling there in her long white nightdress as innocent and absolute and unseeing as Desdemona – and I wanted her. But more, I wanted to protect her.

In bed she put her hand on my face and whispered, 'I've missed you. Oh, I've missed you so much. It's been so awful being away from you.' I smelled her hair and I pushed my hand into it. I ran it through my fingers. I twisted it round my hand and she winced and I saw her mouth open. I put my mouth to hers and kissed her until she fought for breath. I bit her lips and licked her teeth and sucked on her tongue and crushed her until she almost disappeared, vanished underneath my weight, and all there was under me was a yielding, silky, hot softness. I pulled her clothes up and heard a small, startled, bird-like cry, and when I put my hand on her I felt her stiffen and she whispered, 'Do you – is it OK? I've stopped – it just hurt so much I couldn't do it on my own.' I said, 'Hush, it's OK. It's lovely. Hush.' I tried not to look at her but her eyes were enormous and – more than anxious: terrified. I could hear her breath coming in quick, short gasps, and she parted her thighs a fraction as though by a tremendous effort of will, and when I pushed my hand into her she was dry, dry with fear. A far cry from that 'enormous yes' she'd quoted at me in London. I sat up and looked at her as she lay there with her pretty silk nightie pushed up to her waist and her legs stiff with her resolve not to pull them together and the moonless Beirut night behind her in the window and I felt like weeping and I was afraid.

I pulled her nightdress down and took her in my arms and heard her cry, 'No, oh no, oh, please,' but when I reached for her breast she pushed my hand away and said fiercely, 'I don't want it like that. It can't just be that.' I lit a cigarette and went out on to the balcony. It was getting cold and the sea was choppy and loud. Thirty kilometres to our left the Palestinians were firing Katyusha rockets into Israeli settlements and Lebanese women were barricading their houses against Israeli border troops. After a bit she went into the bathroom and locked the door.

She stayed in the bathroom for about forty minutes, then she came and climbed slowly into bed. She lay very still on her own side for a while, then she curled up and snuggled silently into my back. I felt tears on my shoulder-blades but I did not move.

In the morning she was very quiet so I said, 'Let's go visit Ba'albek.' She drove through Beirut and I took over when we got outside the city. The mountain road is narrow. It goes straight and smooth for a while, then you find yourself on a treacherous hairpin bend with an army truck roaring up at you from the other side. To the left the mountain rises, almost perpendicular, with wire mesh at the bottom: to the right it's a sheer drop. I was concentrating on driving and we had Cat Stevens on the cassette player: Tea for the Tillerman. *It was the fourth track and I had just lit a cigarette when she said, 'You don't really see any connection between things, do you?'*

'What things?'

'Well, say, between this song and anything.'

'What are you talking about?'

'Or books. Even the ones you like. You know, I've been thinking: all the women in the books you like – Sartre and Camus and all that – they don't really exist. Not as people. They're only there to wait for the men. To love them and be loved back or not – mostly not; to be beaten up or killed; to appear as a face on the wall of Meurseault's cell –'

I said 'Look. This is a dangerous road. You gonna let me drive and lecture me on women's lib another time?'

'It's nothing to do with women's lib.'

'I said this is a dangerous road.'

'I can see it's a dangerous road.'

'If you want to get to Ba'albek –'

'What does it matter if we get to Ba'albek? What does it matter where we go? We're just killing time and everything –'

I pulled up. The tyres screeched and she threw her arm out to stop herself going into the windscreen.

'If you don't care where we go then we won't go,' I said.

'OK then. Let's not go.'

I pulled the car into a U-turn and felt a couple of stones give beneath the wheels and heard them bouncing off down the cliff as I headed back for Beirut. She had her hands clenched in her lap and was saying over and over again, with great dry sobs. 'It doesn't matter, it doesn't matter, it doesn't matter,' then she threw herself at me. I thought, we'll either go off the road or straight into an oncoming truck, and I put my foot down hard on the accelerator. She hung on to my arm, crying, 'Don't do this to me, please don't do this –' But after a while she was just weeping quietly and said, 'I'm sorry. Please can we go to Ba'albek?' I thought of just carrying on – but I did another U-turn and we went and spent the morning in the sunshine among the ruins.

Things kind of settled after that. We stayed in Beirut until the New Year. She loved the huge Christmas tree in Jounieh and she pretended to be spooked in the caves of J'eita and she marvelled at the ceramics in Beit ed-Din and she shopped for clothes. I noticed she didn't sneeze any more and I told her that, and she shrugged and said, 'It must have been the dust in Cairo.' She was great when she was happy and I loved to spoil her and give her things. We went to a couple of parties and I took her to the Casino du Liban for New Year's Eve. I thought that should be dramatic enough for her. She was a bit uncertain when all the girls with the tassels hanging from their nipples came on, but I thought she was prettier than any of them and told her so and she was OK.

We drove to Damascus on the second day of January and she enjoyed that like a kid on a trip: the waking up at dawn, the Beirut–Damascus highway, the stopping at Chtoura for a breakfast of labneh and olives – even the armed soldiers and the queueing at the checkpoint.

She didn't seem particularly happy in Damascus, but then Damascus is not

Beirut, and also I had to leave her alone a bit when I went to work. She was ill there for a couple of days and she was starting to worry about going back to England. She was pretty miserable about that and I felt really sorry for her, but I knew it was out of the question that she should give up on her thesis so I just said, 'You'll come back at Easter, Princess. And till then I'll write to you every day.' And I did.

Sunday, 13 January 1974

Dear Chrissie,

Thank you, *thank* you for your long letter and the photographs. Your baby looks very cute; she reminds me a bit of Uncle Sidki, is that very silly? But really there's something about her face – I loved what you said about him spoiling her terribly. I'm sure she won't get any of that dreadful strict stuff there was with you; she'll have him completely round her little finger – well, there you are, I'm sure you can't get enough of cuddling and feeding and all that – you won't need to borrow your cousins' children to look after any more.

I found your letter waiting in my pigeon-hole when I got back from Damascus – as well as a letter from Saif, written – would you believe it – while we were together in Beirut so that it would cheer me up when I got here! He's really been very sweet: borrowed a Ferrari for me to drive and took me to all sorts of places. Lebanon is wonderful, Chrissie – I would really like to live in Beirut sometime, maybe after I've finished if Saif is still there – then you could come and visit. You'd never think the war was so close. I kept looking south along the coast and thinking, it's all just over there: Israel, the war, the shelling, but you can't actually *feel* it in Beirut. It feels like a sort of Arab Europe – I suppose it doesn't feel that wonderful if you're in a refugee camp. But it isn't *all* to do with having money. I mean *here*, for example, however much money you had, it still wouldn't be a good place to be; you'd still want to get out.

We went to Ba'albek and I saw the poppy fields again: amazing. I mean, it's supposed to be illegal and everything, but there it is, green and flourishing as far as the eye can see. We didn't pick any, of course, in fact I remembered that Saif had looked a bit disapproving at my interest last time we were there so I kept quiet.

We spent New Year's Eve at the Casino du Liban and I wanted to make myself look extra special so he booked me into this beautician's who's supposed to be famous: Margaret Rose. Well, I didn't trust them to do my hair – nobody can do that except Hassan – but I lay on a table for an hour while they made up my face. They padded around all discreet and murmuring and when they handed me the mirror at the end – well, I didn't actually *cry* because that would have been terrible, but I got so depressed I couldn't speak. I cried outside, though. I washed it all off the moment I got to our room. I practically ran through the hotel. Oh, Chrissie, you should have seen it. It was somehow tarty and old and boring all together – they'd drawn this line round my lips and – oh, it was awful. I had always thought how wonderful and transforming it would be to have a professional make-up put on – what a shame.

Oh, and I think I've got an ulcer. I was pretty ill in Damascus. I got this terrible stomach pain and then I started to throw up. Saif was wonderful. He sat right next to me, holding my hair back with one hand and holding the bowl with the other – is this very yukky? – but really, I don't know how he stood it, I mean, I have to keep my eyes closed so I don't see the stuff, and if I even hear the sound of somebody throwing up I feel my stomach turn over – I kept trying to tell him it was OK, he could leave me, but he just said, 'Stop worrying,' and sat there holding me. Anyway, he called the doctor and he thought I was starting an ulcer. It made me feel fantastically grown up.

Well, I'm back here now and trying to settle into a routine. I really haven't made much headway in this work so far. I don't even know yet quite what I'm supposed to be doing. But I'm carrying on reading these horrid articles and trying to apply some of their ideas to poems – it really seems pointless, but I guess that's because I don't know enough about it. I've got this system where I can only eat something hot if I do a piece of work that I think is OK. So far I've been living on salads.

Oh, and Chrissie, I must tell you the funniest thing: I learned that there was a room set aside for graduate students to work in so I went. It was a small room with three desks and there were already two people there. Two men. So I asked politely if I could use the third desk and they said of course of course and I sat down and got out my papers and started to try and work. We'd introduced ourselves, and one was an Irani and the other a Turk. The Irani was a tiny, dainty little chap, very pleased with himself in a buttoned-up sort of way, and I think he's married to an Irani girl who sometimes works in one of the refectories. The Turk was tall and brown-haired and leather-jacketed, and after I'd been there half an hour he left his desk, came up to mine, and said, 'Come on, we go for a coffee.' No, I didn't, Chrissie. I thought of you and I could *see* you giving me one of your warning looks, and I thought this could be the beginning of trouble, and besides I didn't like his manner, so I said, 'No, thank you, I really want to carry on.' He went out but came back pretty soon. After a bit the Irani left, smiling and bowing, and from then on I knew the Turk was staring at me. I didn't look at him at all and I carried on reading my stuff, or trying to, and I kind of put my left hand on the desk where he couldn't miss the wedding ring, but every time I *breathed* I knew he was looking at me so I thought I'd better leave. The moment I started collecting my things he came up and said, 'Tonight I buy dinner for you.' So I said, 'No, thank you,' again, only I was getting cross because I knew I wouldn't be able to come back to the room any more and I thought he was being tremendously pushy, and he said, 'Oh yes. I buy dinner for you. You are very nice.' 'No, thank you. I don't want to have dinner.' So would you believe, he comes right up and bangs his fist on my desk and demands, 'Why you are despising me? Why?' I said, 'I don't despise you. I don't even *know* you. I just don't want to have dinner with you.' 'I know you despising me,' he said. I picked up my things and went. So now not only do I have no friends; I have an enemy. Oh, Chrissie, Chrissie, I wish you were here. Baby and all. I would be all right if you were here, I *know* I would –

Scene 3

March 1974

London

There is the road of safety. There is the road of regret. And there is the road that permits of no return.

Sidki al-Tarabulsi's road has led him to a bare oblong room in a red-brick hospital in a pleasant street in London where he looks too large for his white iron bedstead. His voice is still deep and loud, with the same curious heaviness on the longer syllables, but under his bed they've hung a plastic bag to collect the urine his bladder is no longer able to cope with. The tubes looped up under and around the bed all end up in his body: in orifices both natural and man-made. He lies on the bed all day. The only variety permitted him is in the angle of the backrest. A few days ago he was in his office: three secretaries and a chef du bureau. Doctors, dieticians, translators, conferences, every hospital in the country running by his command. Yet he does not seem angry, or even particularly concerned. Resigned, amused, and the most sweet-tempered that Asya has ever seen him.

He tells Asya the latest political jokes and roars at them himself: '. . . so five hours pass and still the two head donkeys are inside the presidential palace with Sadat, and eventually they come out on to the balcony

348

and they shake their heads at their waiting friends and bray' – he shakes his head sadly – ' "We're *still* trying to explain it to him." ' He laughs loudly and looks at Tante Muneera, who smiles without looking up.

He is full of tenderness and solicitude for his wife. 'Muneera, you're sitting in a draught. Move your chair over here a bit.' 'Muneera, have you eaten? Here. You have this peach. It's ripe, look. Peaches in London in the winter, hey? How about that?' 'Muneera, you must go and get some rest. Go on, go. I'm fine. I don't need anything. I'll make eyes at the nurses while you're not here. Go and rest. Asya, make your aunt go to the hotel.'

Once Tante Muneera drops her spectacle case, and he starts to rise to get it for her. But the tubes tug at him and for a moment he looks at her with surprised eyes in a suddenly young face. 'I swear to God I forgot.' Then he lies back and stares at the ceiling while she fusses around his pillows and tucks the sheets in around his feet.

Tante Muneera sits in his room and serves him and looks after him all day. Twenty-nine years of watching him and anticipating him now stand her in good stead, and she has the newspaper, the glass of water, the painkiller, the damp towel ready before he even thinks to ask. She rarely meets his eye. She busies herself around him. She knits or sews or writes letters to the children at home. He watches her constantly. His eyes follow her around the room. Sometimes he looks at nurses passing his door or the grey sky outside his window, but when his eyes rest they rest on her.

When she absolutely has to weep she stands outside in the corridor for five minutes. Once, in their second week in the hospital and on Asya's third day with them, Asya finds her crying into the wall in the corridor outside his room. Asya hugs her and kisses her but Chrissie's mother holds on to her, whispering over and over again that she is losing him. 'I'm losing him, Asya. We're losing him.' Inside, Uncle Sidki does look grey and somehow smaller, but next day he is better, and two days after that the doctors are talking about a remission and an early release, and the next day Asya has to go back to the north to show herself to her supervisor so she won't be missed, and the day after that she comes back but his room is empty and Tante Muneera has flown back home with the body of her husband.

Scene 4

Sunday, 19 May 1974
The North of England

Dear Mummy,

Here I am back again and I can't believe how cold it still is. It was pretty warm in Damascus. Not like Cairo, of course – I can imagine it all now: the exam tent and the heat and 'Am 'Ali with his jug of water and Dr (is he Professor yet?) Mostanser creeping up behind the students, and the Control room and the red wax and you and Daddy going home with stacks of exam papers. I must say, *that* is something I don't envy you. Deena must be in the middle of exams too – and Kareem, goodness, the run-up to the Thanawiyya 'Ama and all the staying up nights and the lights on in other windows and the news-papers whipping it up. I miss them both – I miss you *all* – so much. It feels terribly odd not to be on a count-down to vacation now. I have to keep reminding myself that it doesn't matter that we're in May and that we might as well be in February or October, there *is* no holiday. Or maybe that's not fair, since I've just come back from one. But it didn't feel like a holiday, Mummy. Maybe it never will any more until I've actually finished. That is a depressing thought.

Damascus reminds me so much of how Cairo used to be thirty, forty years ago. (Is 'remind' the right word? I mean it is just like what I imagine Cairo to have been then.) It's sort of a miniature Cairo as well: one bazaar, one main mosque, even their much-poemed Barada is just a tiny little trickle, like an irrigation ditch almost. It's all very clean and it's quiet, and remember what you used to tell me about Grandfather taking Mama Deela to the ice-cream parlour and walk-ing quite separately from her lest someone should think they'd had the satisfaction of setting eyes on Ismail Mursi's wife? Well, it's just like that. The men and the women are completely separate as far as I can see. And the women are all addressed as Ummu someone – I mean even the sort of upper-middle-class ones. So you would be Ummu Kareem, I guess.

The wife of Saif's Syrian counterpart called on me and took me out twice: once to a café where we sat with some other women and ate ice-creams and drank coffee and they laughed and joked a lot, and once to a sort of tea-party at someone's house. It was quite odd: it was all women and children, and after tea and loads of delicious sticky cakes they put the music on, girdled themselves up and danced. Each one

350

got up and did a little number. They were horrified that I couldn't dance – not really. They totally believed that all Egyptians were born belly-dancers, and of course I couldn't possibly have sat there and explained how Daddy would freak out if I just shook my head in front of the mirror. Remember the day he saw me tossing my hair around when I was ten and I had to go the same day and have it cut? And I had to wear it short for seven years after that until I went to university? And how he came home one day and heard me practising the *zagh-rouda* and almost sacked Dada Zeina on the spot?

Anyway, this lady can't be much more than thirty and she's exceedingly soignée, and she's got this daughter (Salma) who's fifteen and taller than her, and she seems perfectly content and happy with her life. And there does seem to be this settled feel about all the people I've met there. They still have cafés that only do ice-cream and they have thousands of different types and, Mummy, you should see their pistachios: mountains of them; they sell them by the kilo. It's very much a case of rags to riches for me when I visit Saif: suddenly it's all big beds and private bathrooms and warm weather and wonderful food and he's really tremendously generous; he's given me the most extravagant long Turkish earrings, all tiny diamonds and emeralds in the most delicate filigree gold setting, and he is always trying to make me buy clothes. Normally, I guess, I'd go mad, but now I would just have to bring them back here and there isn't a lot of point in that, and my cupboard is already too small for the clothes I've got, I have to fight to pull a dress out and I mostly just wear jeans and pullovers.

Oh, and I must tell you, Mummy, the funniest thing. Ever since I'd got here I'd heard people mention the 'wreck' and I've wondered about it. You'd be in the refectory and you'd hear someone say, 'I'll see you at the wreck.' At first I thought it was a ship; a wrecked ship. I suppose because they go on about this place looking like a ship. And I couldn't think why there should be a shipwreck here on top of a hill just off a motorway, then I thought maybe it was to do with Environmental Studies in some way, a simulation of some kind. And I couldn't find any reference to it in the brochure. Then I thought it was maybe some dilapidated building; something they'd started and given up on because of some fault or lack of funds or something. Anyway, I finally asked one of the Egyptians.

'What is this wreck they keep talking about?'

'The indoor wreck.'

'Indoor wreck?'

'Indoor Recreation Centre.'

Imagine!

They're a really funny lot, the Egyptians. There are three of them. All men. One of them, Hisham Badran (who is very handsome and

351

classy and really fancies himself), is having a thing with one of the lecturers who is miles older than him. Anyone can see it's just a thing and that he's heading for some dynastic marriage at home, but she seems to have thought they were going to get married, and when he didn't make moves in that direction (he's almost finished his Ph.D) she tried to spur him on by making him jealous and she went and actually spent the night with an Iraqi! Well, of course now the Iraqis are one up on the Egyptians and Hisham won't have anything to do with her any more and I'm sure she hasn't a clue why. The other two are married. One is quite old – in his late thirties maybe – and his eyes squint outward in opposite directions so you're never sure he's actually speaking to *you*, and he speaks very very slowly so it's totally nerve-racking having to stand there. The other is young and has a beard and does his prayers at the right times but he also seems a bit to the left so I can't make him out. Their wives are firmly set in their supportive roles and work in the sandwich bars to help out, and the only time I went to one of their meetings they spent the whole time talking about where you could get 'fool', and the exact recipe for *ta'miyya*, and what schools they were going to send their kids to when they got back home, and how you could use leftover scraps of soap to make one whole brand-new bar of soap. They've all got their radios propped up at an angle with the aerials sticking out of the window (in this cold!) so they can listen to 'Voice of the Arabs' – through horrendous crackling, of course – and contrive to pass the days as though they were not really here. I mean, of course here is completely deadly, but still – they're sort of so *insistent* on their Egyptianness –

Mummy, dear, do you see Chrissie at all? Did you go to Uncle Sidki's funeral and fortieth day and all that? How is Tante Muneera? I'm sure she must be taking it very hard. It was so awful how they'd been talking about a remission and then I came back from university and they just weren't there. I peeped in the room and there was someone else in the bed – another man, and another wife sitting in the chair –

Wednesday, 22 May

And this is what it all boils down to? All of life reduced to this? A small rectangular room with a curtain that doesn't reach to the floor covering a window looking out over nothing. Work: a series of articles that she cannot understand and that read like eating gravel, her mentor a man who hides behind his desk and tells her that at twenty-four perhaps her mind is not mature enough to deal with a Ph.D. Friendship: a plain South American girl balancing on her head in the space between the basin and the door, explaining how being upside-down is good for the

352

system, and farting to prove her point. Love: a quarterly visit to a husband who treats her like a pet; to be indulged and given treats as long as she behaves – a husband who turns his back on her every night, who speaks of looking forward to the day when, in the courtesy of advancing years, they will address each other as 'Asya Hanim' and 'Saif Bey' and take gentle strolls round the garden of the house he will build for them in the desert – and wait to die.

And what about life? What about all the years that still have to pass? Emptiness. And then age, and then the only end of age.

How will she bear it? What can she do? She cannot claim coercion. No one forced her to do anything. She chose. She chose English Literature, she chose Saif Madi, she chose the north of England.

A couple of days ago the phonetics lecturer had stopped by her table at lunch-time in the refectory.

'You are Asya Ulama, aren't you?'

'Yes.'

Why hadn't she said, 'Could be,' and looked mysterious? 'Who's asking?' Why does she always have to be so boring?

'I wanted to ask you, do you think you could come and do a demonstration for the MAs on Wednesday?'

'A demonstration?'

'We need to listen to new sounds – non-English – to plot them on the Universal Phonetic Alphabet. I thought perhaps you could demonstrate some Arabic sounds.'

'Yes, of course. What time and where?'

And today she had gone. There were more than twenty of them. Some she saw at Linguistic Circle. Some were in her building. She sat down and waited. After a while the lecturer turned to her.

'There is a sound in Arabic that is like an "h" only from lower down in the throat, isn't there?'

'Yes.'

'Could you say a word that has it?'

'Haraam.'

'Ah! Did you hear that? Say it again.'

'Haraam.'

'And listen to that second vowel sound. Again.'

'Haraam.'

'Thank you. You hear that vowel? The closest we get to that in English is in the first vowel of "father". We never get it on a final syllable except in words that come from French like "boulevard", and then we tend to eat it or even anglicise it as in "garage". Now, Asya, please, the sound that in English is represented as "kh". Could you say a word that has that in it?'

'Khiyana.'

'Again. Clearly.'

Asya can hear her voice in the silence of the classroom.

'Khiyana.'

The sounds she makes start to seem odd to her. Odd sounds without meaning. Nobody is writing or doing anything. Just listening. Some of them are looking at her.

'Now there is a sound that non-Arab speakers find impossible. The one that is sometimes represented by an "ain". Could we have a word with that?'

"Antar.'

She tells herself that a lot of the MAs have funny sounds in their own languages. There's a lady from Malaysia and three men from Pakistan and –

'Again, please.'

Her mouth is very dry.

"Antar.'

'And there is the sound represented by "q" which involves the same process as the "k" but further down the throat?'

Asya tries 'Qur'an' but the word won't come. The class is waiting. She tries 'qaf', but her voice just won't come.

The lecturer thinks she can't find a word, or can't pronounce the difficult consonant. He says, 'Well, can you say your name? For the vowels and stresses?'

But that is the most difficult of all. She knows it will be impossible. She shakes her head.

'Just your name?' he coaxes.

She opens her mouth, but the sounds won't come. She closes it again and shakes her head. Then she whispers, 'I can't.'

He looks at her for a moment, then smiles. 'Never mind. Another time. Thank you.'

She cannot get up and have everybody look at her as she walks out, so she sits upright and still until the end of the class, then leaves quickly while the others are collecting their things.

Everything is absurd. She wakes up every morning at four, and instead of enjoying staying in bed, or getting up and working, or making herself tea and reading something, she lies there shaking with fear at the thought of the hours that lie ahead, wishing that it was evening and that it was possible to go to sleep. Ridiculous. How can you dread age and fear death and lament the brevity of life and yet wish for the passing of each day? Where can we live but days? Ah! But *these* days, *these* days – she goes to the library for somewhere to go. She stares at the pages of a journal, reads, 'We can so determine the relation of these texts to the other elements of the communicational diagram (sender, code, channel, receiver etc.) and the synchronic and diachronic aspects of these relations. This approach makes it possible, on the one hand, to take into consideration those claims which are made towards the co-textual analysis by the con-textual analysis –' and watches a tear plop on to the print. She goes to the Linguistic Circle and has to fidget and stretch and cross and uncross her legs to ward off sleep and cramps. She lives on carrots and bran and hot water as a punishment for not evolving a theory or at least getting to like the stuff she has to work with. She has banished fiction from her room because she knows she will not withstand the temptation and she isn't here to read novels. She has got to get into the work. This is her eighth month here and she is no closer to formulating a thesis proposal than she was when she started. In fact she's probably further off. At least at the beginning she had enthusiasm and confidence and now they've both vanished. What on earth has happened to her? It's OK to not like the stuff, but to not *understand* it? What would her mother say? What would her father say? What would the people at the Council – what would *everybody* say? Of course, she's not going to tell them; she can't tell anyone, not ever. It's just completely idiotic – and shameful.

She comes back to her room at six o'clock. She switches on the heater and the desk-lamp and sits on the bed in her coat waiting to warm up. Often she sits for an hour or longer thinking about things. She knows she should get out of her coat and sit at her desk, and she intends to, but she carries on sitting on the bed and thinking. She thinks about the stairs in Grandfather's house and how the sun used to fall on to the marble long ago when it was polished and smooth, and she sees herself when she was eight creeping along with a half-open empty matchbox, hunting for baby cockroaches – she was afraid of the big ones – for Nadia's anatomy class. She thinks of Mama Deela and Tante Soraya sitting up all night, making her the little bridal gown in pink tulle she wore for her fourth birthday. Mama Deela's life already more or less ruined by the stray bullet that had blown a hole through her window in 1945. She thinks of Zio Philippe in the flat next door, living with his mother, and spending his days in the room with the beautiful faded wallpaper – all ribbons and bows and fantastic birds; the room in which he had been born – burning awkward drawings into wood, while above him his mother's bridal wreath sits yellow and withered in a glass-fronted corner cabinet on the wall. She thinks of Tante Soraya and how she used to take her to watch the big youth parades in the late 1950s and how beautiful she used to be and how tiny her waist had looked in her great-grandmother's belt of silver fish-scale sequins the night she got married. She thinks of Khalu Hamid when he had a moustache and rolled out Italian songs at the top of his voice and could drink three Sinalcos and eat seven *ta'miyya* sandwiches in a sitting. She thinks of the flat opposite Grandfather's, and Madame Biba, the widowed lady who lived there with her four sons, and how she had gone away one day to be with her only daughter who was being delivered of her first child. It was the only time she had slept away from her flat since she had gone there on her wedding-night and when she got back next day all her sons were dead. She had got back at midday, happy and a grandmother for the first time, and all her sons were dead. Four young men. Tall, well-built, handsome young men. Two in the army, one in the police and one in the navy. She'd opened the front door and found the policeman on his face in the hall. The others were in their beds. The smell of gas when she opened the door was so strong it could knock you off your feet, but these flats were old and solid and the thick doors and windows fitted well. Asya remembers her screams, and how she had stumbled and reeled along the corridor, and how they had to hold her down and call the pharmacist from downstairs to inject her with something so she wouldn't hurl herself off the balcony there and then. And she remembers later when the four coffins came out of the door one after the other, each heavy with young limbs, with blood, with muscle that was now no use to anyone except the receiving earth –

Asya sits on her bed under the heater and weeps for them and for their mother. They'd buried them that same day before sunset, and when Tante Biba came to they were gone and she had become a crazed old woman whose daughter had to move in with her and look after her. All those lives, ruined – and then lived out – lived *through* in the knowledge of that ruin. And now she shivers with dread: has it already happened to her? Has she, without knowing, crossed that line; crossed from the land where everything is yet to come into the land from which you look back and think it *might* have come – but didn't? But then she thinks of summers in Alexandria and the songs of 'Abd el-Halim Hafez marking the passage of the years:

'Over the thorns my road led me
Saying: come, let's go to love.
After years it said: turn back
You'll only live there with a broken heart –'

Kareem aged four standing on a chair to sing:

'There is no "I"
Only "us" my friend:
Me and you and him and her:
It's up to us to build socialism.
A pleasant meal, a happy song
A house, a dress and people living –'

It had all been so simple. Now she cries when she thinks of Kareem or Deena – or her mother. Or 'Abd el-Nasser. Poor 'Abd el-Nasser. It must have all seemed so black and difficult for him in the last three years. Ill and in pain and keeping it secret. Finding out about the men close to

356

him. Suspecting, maybe, but refusing to believe that his glorious dream had been aborted, that what he had thought of as a prelude was really all there was to be. 'The children of '48: the commandoes of '68,' hunted and homeless and bringing destruction wherever they go.

She thinks of Noora and Bassam, and how Noora can bear to be so completely cut off from her mother and her brothers though she lives fifteen minutes from them. What happens – how does she feel when she quarrels with Bassam – even some silly little tiff – and her mind says, 'For this you defied your family, and now you are alone'?

She thinks of the night of the 'Eid at Grandfather's and chestnuts roasting on the stove, and being allowed to play outside after dark, and fireworks and sparklers and the smell of burning sulphur, and staying up to watch the Fuad el-Muhandess play on TV, and then all the children sleeping together on mattresses on the floor with hot-water bottles and feather quilts.

She thinks of Tante Adeela, busy in her kitchen. If you opened any cupboard in her house it would be neat and fragrant. The linens snowy and soft and folded, the socks paired and turned so that the job of putting them on was made as easy as possible for the men, the shirts in crisp piles of five, the collars alternating so they would not get crumpled.

She thinks of Dada Zeina taking her head on her knee on Wednesday evenings when her parents went out, and rocking gently to the sound of the Qur'an or Ummu Kulthoum while she absently stroked Asya's head until she slept.

She thinks of school and cheering the boys at away matches and the big party for Mothers' Day, the stage and the marquee and the coloured lights set up in the playground, and the national anthem that had changed when she was eight and Egypt had united with Syria, and the prize-givings and the erect, lilac-haired, widowed headmistress she had adored, and Hilal whom she had watched on the football field and secretly and privately loved and wondered whether perhaps he . . . until he had followed her into an empty classroom and said her name and shyly kissed her right cheek and made it tingle for days, and how they had, without ever declaring anything, taken to walking alone together hand in hand in the race-track at the club every Thursday afternoon.

She thinks of Saif and that first evening at the Omar Khayyam when he had taken her into the rock maze and kissed her till her lip bled – she had thought they would come together again in Beirut: *really* come together. That that first eighty-three-day separation would break the deadlock between them. That everything that had been buried and hidden would break out in the joy and the relief of their being together again, and again it had all gone wrong. And now a new pattern has been set. That was what it had felt like this time in Damascus: that every three months they would meet and settle into a new deadlock. She tries to pinpoint the things he does not like, the things about her that put him off. She makes a list of them: she can get rid of them – or at least keep them away from him. He does not like:

1. Her tendency towards abstract discussion, e.g. 'How do you know *absolutely for sure* there is no reincarnation?'
2. Her enthusiasms, e.g. for sit-ins, demonstrations, dancing etc.
3. When she takes too long to tell a story.
4. When she points out things to him: 'Oh gosh! Look at that moon!'
5. Her not liking judgments, e.g. 'But if you look at it from *his* point of view –'
6. Her wish to *do* things. He finds it juvenile.

But what about in bed? What *about* in bed? Well, in Cairo, with the pain and the miscarriage and the sneezing, he had decided she had stopped wanting him. But he can't have thought that in Beirut. He can't have been in any doubt at all that first night that she wanted him. And she had been absolutely determined that, however much it hurt, she would not complain. It would not hurt for ever. It would get better and then it would stop hurting and be just wonderful. That's what everybody and all the books said. And the miscarriage had taken care of the hymen and all that. And she had wanted him – so very much. And she had thought if they made love, if they came together – really – if they could be in love again as they had been before, then everything else would adjust itself, would fall into place. On the road to Ba'albek on that first visit she had thought, why am I doing this? Why am I picking arguments with him? I know he doesn't like arguments or scenes or crying or making a fuss. I know he can go away inside himself and wait till it's over – and then some. He's taken days off work, he's got this car, he's glad to see me, so why am I doing this to him? And she had forced herself to quieten down. And she had resolved not to do the things he didn't like and to try to be the way he wanted her to be. It was no use thinking, But he *used* to ask me to talk to him, I *believed* he wanted to know what I thought about things and would tell me what he thought too, I *believed* he wanted us to do lots of things – to explore everything – together. No use at all. The only thing to be done now is to adapt, to be the person he wants her to be; the person he probably believes she is – apart from the odd aberration. And if she does that, and gives him what he wants, maybe he'll love her again. She had seen all that on the road to Ba'albek. But what about last night, she had then thought: she hadn't done anything – yet. And she knows he had been about to make love to her. It had been something about her that put him off. Something about the way she was *then*. What was it? It wasn't that she didn't want him. Maybe he thought she wanted him too much? Maybe he was repelled by that? No. He'd liked her to want him – in the Omar Khayyam and on those Sunday afternoons in Heliopolis. Maybe she was too passive, lying there waiting for something to happen? But that couldn't be it. She'd always been fairly passive. That was how he'd liked it. That was how he'd *made* it. He would be completely amazed – aghast – if she started climbing all over him. Maybe it was – maybe she was too serious about it? Maybe he thought that was phoney? Or maybe he thought she was making too much of a deal out of things? And maybe indeed she was. And then a few days later, when they'd had lunch at the Tamraz's, and she'd had some white wine and braved his displeasure by taking a few puffs at the joints that were going round, and they'd gone back to their room for a siesta and the sun was coming in through the blinds and every move hadn't seemed portentous and fraught with a thousand perilous possibilities, she'd walked up to him and sat next to him on the bed and rubbed his shoulders and nibbled at his ears and kissed him, and felt a sweet hazy desire welling up inside her, and she'd knelt in front of him and rubbed her face against his strong thighs and felt him hard and hot against her lips and her cheeks, and then he'd pulled her head back and looked at her and said, 'You have to be doped up to the eyeballs to do this?' He'd said it with contempt – it wasn't too strong a word. He *had*. He had said it with contempt and he had put her away. So what then? After the anger had died down, as anger always does, what then? She has no more cards to play, no more moves to make. Leave him? 'Your Honour, my husband won't perform his conjugal –' Absurd. She might as well talk of leaving her father, or her country. She might as well talk of leaving herself. And when she woke up feeling terrible he was so sweet to her, and nursed her through her hangover and her sickness, and fed her room-service consommé and melba toast and massaged her temples till her headache had gone away, and put her to bed early and held her hand until she slept.

And this time in Damascus she had managed it. Fairly well. There had been the ulcer and a couple of tricky moments but on the whole she had been good and they had been chummy and happy and – friends. Oh, if only he were here, this place would not be so unbearable. She would give him what he wanted. She would give him peace and quiet and she would be serene and cool and easy to be with. If only he were here.

Every day she waits for night-time. She goes to bed at half past eight because that is the earliest time she can imagine going to bed and because that means the day is officially over and she doesn't have to do anything more about it. About anything.

Scene 5

August 1974
Cairo

It is so *so* hot. So wonderfully hot. The sun beats down on her face, on her breasts, on her tummy, on her legs. The heat rises into her shoulders and her back from the ever so slightly rough paving-stones, and behind her closed eyelids there is a warm, golden glow. She sighs softly and lets her hand dangle into the cool water of the pool. Soon, soon, when she's really really hot all through, she'll get up and ease herself in. What pleasure. Swim slow and easy across and back, climb out, lie down and start heating up all over again. Maybe go over and eat a piece of watermelon with Chrissie and Mimi first and *then* come back and lie down. She opens her eyes and raises her head slightly to look at her friends where they sit at a white table on the Lido terrace. Chrissie is in a bright blue dress with giant pink butterflies, and Mimi is in a long yellow cotton shirt with maybe twenty coloured bangles on her arm. She lies back and closes her eyes. Bliss. The heat is making her all nice and dozy. It's a shame she can't dive today; diving is so much more fun, so much more effective: to feel the cool water on your scalp, tickling the roots of your hair, and somehow you're in the water much more suddenly than if you just jump. But her hair is freshly washed and pinned up in a loose knot at the top of her head to keep it dry – so she can't dive. She sighs again. It's so wonderful just to be able to walk into Hassan's salon and sit back and chat and read the papers and have your head and neck massaged, and walk out again in three hours with fresh, soft, sweet-smelling hair and pink feet and perfect shiny nails. That's probably what is meant by being spoilt, but it's really such a drag doing it all yourself, and it makes her arms ache so, all that putting the hair in rollers, and the hand-dryer takes more than three hours, and even then it's not completely –

'Aren't you afraid of falling in?'

She blinks in the sudden glare and shades her eyes with her hand.

'Hilal!'

Suddenly she is conscious of lying on the ground stretched out in a yellow bikini, but he settles himself comfortably cross-legged on the ground beside her and it would be awkward to spring up, and she'd be just as undressed anyway, and besides she's looking good –

'Asya!'

She pulls her sunglasses down over her eyes and smiles at him.

He is brown all over, and round his neck there is a delicate gold chain

360

with a small gold plate hanging from it, and there are those great shoulders and the longish brown hair and the surprisingly soft brown eyes.

'I thought you were in England?' he asks.

'I had to come back. My mother was ill.'

'Oh.' He looks concerned. 'Was it serious?'

'She had a heart attack –'

She remembers that *his* mother is dead and that that had been the first thing that had given him a special place in her thoughts; that he was sixteen and his mother had died in the summer vacation, and yet there he was: getting top grades in maths and science and things she had stopped understanding, and playing football and scoring goals. She'd thought maybe that was what made his eyes look so soft. She'd never been able to ask him about it; she'd been afraid just mentioning it might make something terrible happen to him.

'– but she's OK. It wasn't major. Now she has to stay in bed for a while, but she's fine.'

'So when are you going back? *Are* you going back?'

'Of course. Mid-September.'

'Are you having a good time there?'

'No.'

'Why? I thought you liked England?'

'I do, but that isn't England – I mean, I suppose it is really, but I only knew London and Oxford and I guess that was what I liked. The university I'm at is three miles outside a little country town in the north where it's bitterly cold and every single thing closes down at five. There are two cinemas and one is being turned into a bingo hall.'

'You don't look like you're suffering; in fact you –'

'I'm not suffering *now*. I've been here three weeks. You should have seen me when I first got here. Anyway, how about you? Are you still with – what was it you were with?'

'No. I've gone in with my father.'

'Ah! You've surrendered!'

He laughs. 'No, not quite. We've – divided the responsibilities.'

'But how do you get on with him? I mean, you refused to join him in the first place, so what's changed?'

'He got married.'

'Hilal!'

'No, seriously. They've even had a baby; a little girl, just a month ago. I suppose he got something to think about other than the business and he was willing to hand over a bit of it.'

'A bit of it – does that mean it's pretty big? The business?'

'It's getting big.'

'What do *you* actually do?'

361

'Contracts. Agency contracts. Import/export. Mainly import right now.'

'But Hilal, what do *you* have to do with agencies? You are an engineer and your father's company used to reclaim land, to plant it –'

And that was another thing that had attracted her: that his father was involved in 'Abd el-Nasser's big land reclamation project in Mudiriyat el-Tahrir, frontier stuff, turning the desert green – well, part of the desert anyway; it would be a shame if it all turned green and there was no more desert –

'This is bigger. Much bigger. Now with the door wide open to trade and foreign investment it makes much more sense.'

'So you're mainly wining and dining, really? You've got no more to do with engineering?'

'Hey, you're not being fair: how would I make the right choices without the engineering background?'

'"Background", you see, just "background".'

'Eventually we might start making our own machinery.'

'But won't there always be more profit in importing it? Who did your father marry?'

'Since when have you turned into a pessimist? He married, in fact, a cousin of my mother's. A distant cousin.'

'And that was OK by you?'

He shrugs. 'He's forty-eight. He was forty-one when my mother died. Why shouldn't he have a life?'

Asya smiles. 'You've always been reasonable.'

'I've – got married too.'

She pushes up her glasses to look at him, then pulls them down again. 'Congratulations. When?'

'Eight months ago. There wasn't much point in waiting any more, was there?'

'What *are* you talking about?'

'Asya, you know I've always been in love with you. You know I've always wanted to marry you.' His voice has dropped very low and he looks intently at her.

'I don't know that at all, and, Hilal' – she sits up to face him – 'no one marries their first sweetheart –'

'Why not?'

'We were only at school.'

'I was in love with you.'

'You went off to – somewhere.'

'I *had* to go to Switzerland after school because of my father. I broke off my studies there and came back because of you, but you had –'

'Hilal, we'd already drifted apart. We were in different –'

'I came to see you at your college, at that cafeteria.'

362

'Yes, but that was just friendship.'

'Yes. For you it was.' Suddenly he smiles at her. An old friend's smile: full of kindness. 'Don't worry. It's all right. Come on, I'll race you to the other side.'

'No, no, I can't. And I can't be splashed either. I don't want my hair to get wet.'

He dives straight and deep, hitting the water with hardly a splash, but still not as elegantly as Saif. She lowers herself in and breast-strokes slowly across the pool to join him.

'You swim like a *hanim*,' he says.

She rests her back against the smooth ceramic wall and stretches her arms out on either side to hold on to the ledge.

'It's only because of my hair. If it weren't just washed I'd take you on.'

'You'd take me on, would you?'

He is treading water very close to her. There aren't many people around the pool. It's August and most people have left Cairo. At the edge of the Lido she can see Chrissie and Mimi sitting in the shade, chatting and studiously not watching her.

'Come on, let's go back to the other side. It's not so warm here.'

'Asya —' He takes her left hand off the ledge. He looks into her face for a moment, then down at her hand. 'That's new.'

'What?' She is holding tightly to the ledge with her right hand.

'That scar. That wasn't there before.'

'Oh. I was crossing the road and walked into a car mirror.'

'You should have had it stitched.' He is still holding on to her hand. Examining it.

'It's only a small scar,' she says defensively.

'Oh, I don't mean it makes your hand any less beautiful. I really loved your hands.'

'Will you let go now? Please? My arm is aching. Thank you. Come on, let's get into the sun.'

At the other side she turns to him.

'Hilal, who did you marry?'

'A friend. Someone who was with me in college.'

'Do you still play football?'

'Only here at the club.'

'I'd love to watch you again some time.'

'We play every Thursday afternoon. But not in August, of course, because everybody's away —'

'How come you're in Cairo?'

'Mona, my wife, is three months pregnant and having a hard time. She can't travel. Is Saif still in Beirut?'

'He is right now. But he's joining me. We'll meet somewhere and go to England together.'

'He's going to stay there with you?'

'Yes.'

'But what about his work?'

'He's resigned from the UN.'

'Resigned? Just to be with you?'

Asya laughs. '"Just" to be with me? Yes. Don't look so surprised. He won't be doing the dusting and the cooking. He'll do a Ph.D too.'

'Is that a good move?'

'He says he can always get back in. There aren't that many Egyptian computer men around and he's been into it since '66. *And* he's terribly good at it.' She smiles at him. 'You look so doubtful. I suppose you wouldn't give up your work to follow your wife to some –'

'Mona left her job when we got engaged. She's staying home.'

'I guess you need her to do your entertaining and all that?'

'Well –'

'Well, there you are then. Look, I've got to get back to Chrissie now. Do you want to come over and say hello?'

'No. No, I don't think I will.'

'OK. Well, I'm getting out. I'll see you, yes?'

'Yes,' he says slowly.

When she looks back he is leaning on the ledge, watching her. She waves.

Asya wraps her big blue towel round her, sits down, reaches for a piece of watermelon and stretches her feet out on another chair before biting into it. Chrissie sings softly, '"And they called it –"'

'"Puppy lo-o-ove",' Asya continues with her mouth full.

'He doesn't look like a puppy to me,' says Mimi, glancing round to the pool. Hilal is climbing out on the ladder at the deep end.

'A full grown German Shepherd,' Asya says.

'Il est beau!' says Mimi.

'You should have seen him on the football field.' Asya reaches out for another piece of watermelon. 'And all of us on the sidelines yelling out his name.'

'Is he not married yet?' asks Chrissie.

'He got married eight months ago and his wife is three months pregnant.' Asya turns to Mimi. 'May you follow in her footsteps.'

'This time next year,' Chrissie adds.

'I don't know if my mother will put up with babies as well as yours does,' says Mimi.

'Tante Safi will do anything. Just as long as you get married.'

'I'm so unhappy you're going to miss the wedding,' Mimi says to Asya.

'Yes, dear, and so am I. But I've got to get back by the middle of

September, latest. I'm not even supposed to be here now. You'll send me lots of photos?'

'Of course. You haven't even *seen* Wageeh.'

'No, but you've described him. And so has Chrissie.'

'Chrissie doesn't like him.'

'I'm not marrying him,' says Chrissie. 'And besides, I didn't say I didn't like him.'

'No. But you said, "You've turned down twenty suitors and accepted *him?*"'

'I just couldn't see why he was different.'

Mimi shrugs. 'I'm twenty-five. Everybody was getting terribly anxious. They kept having these family – conferences. Wageeh gets on very well with my uncles. And he *is* romantic – a bit, anyway.'

'Everybody's "romantic" at the beginning,' says Chrissie.

'But I suppose you *will* have babies.'

Asya laughs. 'Chrissie! You don't get married just for babies. Otherwise why didn't you marry one of your cousins? They all asked you.'

'Well, they *are* important. Babies, I mean. Maybe they *are* the most important thing.'

'Where's Ranya? Why didn't you bring her?'

'Mama wouldn't let me,' Chrissie says. Asya looks at her. 'It's true. In the morning I said I'd go home after work and pick her up and bring her, and Mama phoned me later saying why did I want to take her and surely I would like some free time with my friends, and she thought she had a bit of a temperature and the sun wouldn't be good for her and so on and so on, so I gave up. She doesn't like to let her out of her sight.'

'God give her good health,' says Mimi. 'She removes all burdens from you.'

'Yes, of course, may God preserve her always, but still – she does tie me down. I can hardly ever get hold of the baby and she gets very upset if I sleep in my flat when Fuad is away. Sometimes when I've finished work I feel I'd like to collect Ranya and go up to my flat and just be alone with her till next morning. But . . .' She shrugs.

'You won't consider going to Suez?' Asya asks.

'No, of course not, how can I? For a start I'd have to leave my job. We've been living on my salary –'

'Yes, but Fuad is doing OK –'

'It's risky. It's all – speculation. He's got big plans and he's very clever and he knows the work but – it's not at all secure. He's got huge loans –'

'It sounds tremendously exciting: being out there on the Canal, dragging up sunken ships and salvaging –'

'It's exciting for *him*. But I'd be staying in a tiny flat looking after Ranya and cooking his dinner full stop. You should see Suez now. Have you been there since '67?'

'No.'

'It's *nothing*. There's nothing there except rubble and government housing estates. It's not possible. And besides, there's Mama. She's completely dependent on me now that Father's gone. The boys don't do anything. They're good to her, of course, but they all live their own lives and only show up for meals. They don't even ask who shopped for the food they're eating. And she'd die if I took Ranya away from her.'

'What about Fuad?'

'I don't know. Of course, he's not happy. He thinks I should drop everything and go with him. But I can't. And it was his choice. I don't blame him. His family is from there, and all their land and their connections are there, and the scope is wide open for him. For him it's logical. But for me it isn't.'

'So how often do you actually see him?'

'He's in Cairo at least twice a week, and I have to rush around and pretend I'm always living at the flat and Ranya's only sleeping at my mother's so that we can be alone together. Thank God I don't have a telephone.'

'But when you leave him alone like this,' says Mimi, 'enfin, aren't you afraid he might look here or there?'

'I don't know. I've thought of that. I suppose he might. But what's he going to find out there? There's *no one* there.'

'I'm going back into the sun,' says Asya.

'You'll get sunstroke.'

'No I won't. I love it.'

'She's become like the foreigners. Mad. Nobody's out in the sun except the foreigners.'

Lateefa is lying in her bed. She has only one pillow under her head and her eyes are closed. Her left hand is holding the light green coverlet close to her neck. The window is wide open and the gentle light of the setting sun falls on the bed. The room faces north and a pleasant gust of breeze occasionally blows in. Asya looks at her mother: she's not – no, of course not, don't be silly: the cover is rising and falling gently as Lateefa sleeps. Asya settles herself with her glass of iced mango juice into the armchair by the bed. She crosses her legs, sips at her juice and watches her mother. Asya had gone swimming, she had walked home from the club, she had stopped at Simmonds to buy some petit fours, and all the time she had known that when she got home her mother would be here, in this bed. She does not want her to be ill, of course she doesn't. If she were really, really ill she would be distraught, terrified. As she was when Saif had phoned her and next morning she had rushed off to find her supervisor and tell him she had to – absolutely *had* to go to Cairo because her mother had had a heart attack and she had to be with her. But now

366

she is much, much better and they are only keeping her in bed as a precaution, and meanwhile it is wonderful to know that she can't go anywhere, can't read or work or be too busy – it isn't so terrible to feel that way; Lateefa herself wouldn't mind if Asya told her.

It was, in fact, as though her mother had given her a gift, worked a little miracle for her, by falling ill enough to make Asya come home, and then getting better. And at home, Asya had got her self back. Sitting barefoot in her old nightie at her old desk, with the window open to the night air and the sounds of the street, and Deena lying on her bed behind her reading, everything had fallen into place. Well, perhaps not everything, but enough. He should have given her books in the first place, not all those articles. But of course he didn't know. When she said, 'I don't under-stand,' he must have thought she didn't understand specific points, not all the underlying assumptions: the givens. It would never have occurred to him that she didn't know what TG stood for; that she had never even heard of Chomsky before going there. They should do something about that at the department here. It's probably not too dreadful if the latest novel they read is twenty years old. But you can't do that with linguistics. She still doesn't *like* it. If she could decide all over again she would never choose it. But she can see how it's done and she'll be able to do it. Area of interest: semantics. Specific area of interest: metaphor (define). Best-known text on metaphor: Brooke-Rose. But Brooke-Rose classifies metaphor by syntactic criteria. Metaphor is a semantic phenomenon (prove and prove and prove) and therefore a semantic classification is more appropriate. And there we are: choose an existing and sympathetic semantic model, select a population of metaphors, apply the model to the population. It is almost a question of wording.

Asya had once flung her pencil down, put her head in her hands and said aloud, 'I can't bear it,' and Deena from behind her had said, 'Can't bear what?'

'All this stuff. The words vanish into formulas – formulae, and I just – it's like doing maths all over again. *You* ought to be doing this, not me –'

Deena had leaned over her shoulder.

'Ya-ya, it's nothing –'

'Well what the hell does "pi-phrase" mean?'

' "Pi" just means an unspecified number.'

'Well why don't they use "x" then?'

'Because "x" is specific. Look –'

For a couple of days she had been suspicious; it couldn't all be that basic. That simple. But then she had had her idea and started writing it up. She'd go back with her proposal all ready and show him her brains were not immature. He might still shoot it down. There might still be something – she may have got some essential thing wrong – but this time Saif would be there –

Lateefa draws a deep breath and opens her eyes. Asya leans forward. 'Mummy. How do you feel?'

'Asya. You've come back? Did you have a nice day, dear?'

'Umm, lovely. How do you feel?'

'Where are your sister and brother?'

'Kareem went out half an hour ago; he's got rowing practice. Deena's in the living-room; she's got a friend with her, I've forgotten her name.'

'Iffat?'

'That's right.'

'Is your father here?'

'No, he had to go out. He's got some committee meeting. He said he'd phone at nine. Mummy, how are you feeling?'

'I'm fine. A bit thirsty.'

'I'll get you a drink. You haven't got any pains, have you?'

Lateefa shakes her head. When Asya stands up she says, 'Close the shutters, darling, and switch on the light. No, not just the table-lamp –'

'You can't have the big light, Mummy; Daddy said so. You know he did. Too much stimulation.'

'Ouf. Your father wants to turn me into a vegetable.'

'No he doesn't; he's just very worried. Nadia said he was really frightened when it happened.'

'I could be up and about now if it weren't for him.'

'Come on, Mumsy, be reasonable. The doctors said two more weeks' rest in bed. And it doesn't count as rest if you're lying there fretting and being rebellious. What would you like to drink? Juice or tea? And remember you can't have the tea too hot or the juice too cold.'

'I'll have some juice. I can't bear luke-warm tea. And could you give me the comb and the mirror before you go?'

When Asya comes back with the juice she helps her mother to a half-sitting position and wedges two more pillows behind her back.

'Noora phoned. She and Bassam send their love, and they want to come and see you as soon as you're up.'

'That's nice. I haven't seen Noora for a while. She went on maternity leave from the department in April and of course I went to her when she had the baby but I haven't seen them since.'

'The baby's very pretty.'

'He was only two days old when I saw him.'

'Very Levantine: huge black eyes and a fair skin. And her mother's sold on him. Noora says she visits them secretly practically every day.'

'El-Manesterli Bey still hasn't come round then?'

Asya shakes her head. 'No. And now she thinks he never will. If the baby didn't make him – his first grandchild –'

'Well, he's the loser, really,' Lateefa says.

'Yes. But of course Noora – she wrote him a letter telling him about the baby and asking if she could bring it over to see him and he never even replied. Are things more difficult for Bassam now? I didn't see her alone and I didn't feel I could ask in front of him.'

'Why not? You're old friends. Yes, they seem to be. And they're expecting things to really change now because of the rapprochement with America.'

'Their flat is very sweet. They're still on boxes, practically, but the baby's room is all complete, with bluebells painted on the furniture.'

Lateefa puts the half-empty glass down on the bedside table.

'Have you heard from Saif?'

'I got a letter this morning. He's fine.'

'He's going through with this?'

'He says he's handed in his resignation. And he suggests we meet in Paris and travel to England together.'

'Why doesn't he just join you there?'

'Because I said I didn't want to go there on my own any more. Not for one day.'

'It's a very generous thing he's doing. You do know that, don't you? Not a lot of men would have done it. Of course, he'll get a Ph.D too –'

'Oh, Mummy, you and your Ph.Ds!'

'Well. It's very important, and if he can get one he should. But it is still very generous to give up a job like that because *you* are miserable.'

'I know. I do know that.'

'Well. Remember this next time you fly into a temper and moan, "He doesn't love me." '

'Mummy – I think you'd better rest now. Daddy said I wasn't to –'

There is a light tap on the open door and Hamid Mursi looks in.

'Good evening.'

'Khalu Hamid!'

Asya jumps up to kiss him and Lateefa sits upright in bed pulling her bedjacket round her.

'Hamid! Welcome, welcome, come on in. I didn't hear the doorbell.'

He is wearing a pale beige suit with a white shirt open at the neck and he keeps his left hand in the pocket of his trousers. His hair is receding just a little. He hugs Asya with his right arm, kisses her on both cheeks and goes over to sit by his sister on the bed.

'Deena heard the lift doors and let me in before I could ring the bell in case you were asleep.' He pats the cover over Lateefa's knee. 'How are you feeling, Teefa?'

'I'm fine, perfectly fine.'

'She shouldn't be sitting up.'

'Well, lie down then. Come on, let's sort out your pillows.' He bends down, but straightens up again with a slight grimace. 'Asya, come and help your mother.'

'What is it? Is it your back?' Lateefa asks anxiously.

'Yes, yes. It's nothing, just a twinge. I went to bed for a bit this afternoon. That's always a mistake. I can't get straight again. It's better to have my siesta in a chair.'

'Just like Grandfather – all you'll need is the towel over your head,' Asya laughs. 'Come on, Mummy, I'll get these pillows out from behind you and you lie down. Otherwise I'll tell Daddy when he phones. I'll say, "She's sitting bolt upright in bed talking to her brother and she wants the big light on." '

'Of course,' says Lateefa, 'it's your chance to boss me around.' But she lies down. 'How are you, Hamid? How is your hand?'

'It's fine.'

'Has the swelling stopped? Show it to me.'

'You've taken up medicine all of a sudden? You're the one who's ill. Now calm down and tell me: did the doctor come today?'

'Yes. He comes every day.'

'And?'

'Nothing. There's no more sign of anything wrong but they want me to stay in bed for another two weeks.'

'Shall I get you a drink, Khalu? We've got some fresh mango juice. Or would you rather have a cup of coffee?'

'A coffee would be very nice, Asya. And you know about the sugar.'

'I know.'

As she leaves the room Asya hears her mother say, 'You're going to stay up playing chess again tonight?'

In the kitchen Asya measures the water into the coffee-pot and prepares the tray. She cannot be in the kitchen without thinking of Dada Zeina. Yesterday she had gone looking for her. She had gone into the kitchen in the afternoon and found Hasna drinking a cup of coffee while she folded the sheets fresh gathered from the line.

'You're still washing, Hasna?'

The old washerwoman had squinted up at her, her eyes covered by the pale blue mists of a cataract.

'Who? Sett Asya? Praise God for your safe return.' She had got up and hugged Asya and kissed her. 'I heard you were back but you weren't here when I came last week.'

'Hasna, you can hardly see.'

'I don't need my eyes for the washing, Sett Asya. My hands are still strong, praise God.'

'How are you and how is Toota? And your mother?'

'Praise God. All well. We thank Him in any case. How is Sett Teefa today?'

And then it had come to her.

'Hasna, you know where Dada Zeina lives, don't you?'

'I know their street, but I don't know if she –'

'Will you take me there?'

'What, now?'

'Yes. Is there any washing still upstairs?'

'No, it's finished. This was the last lot.'

'Well, look: I'll fold these up while you finish your coffee and get your dress on. We'll go visit Dada Zeina and then I'll drive you home. OK?'

'Whatever you say, Sett Asya.'

Her mother had been asleep and her father in his study with the door closed. A quick word with Deena and they were off.

They had parked in Giza Square and set off on foot through the narrow lanes branching south, one lane following another, until Hasna had said, 'This is the street, Sett Asya, but I don't know the house.' Dada Zeina had always said that her people were butchers, and there, indeed, was a butcher's shop on the corner. Hasna had sat down in a doorway and Asya had gone into the shop and enquired for the whereabouts of Sett Um Sobhi. 'Sett Um Sobhi?' the butcher had said. 'The one with the honoured eye? She's gone away but her sister lives here.' He'd called a young boy and Asya had followed him to a house where he had knocked on the door. 'The lady here is asking for Sett Um Sobhi.' In the doorway a fat woman had stood. She was wearing the usual flowered smock with a white kerchief round her head.

'Who's asking for her?'

'My name is Asya al-Ulama, I wanted –'.

'You're Sett Asya? An embrace, my darling, an embrace!' The woman had pulled her into her bosom, then held her away to look at her. 'By God, they spoke the truth, my sister never lied. A moon, by God, a moon. She used to always tell us about you. I named my third daughter after you –'

'You must be Sett So'ad –'

'That's true, my darling, true. A *zaghrouda* for joy, my darling. Sett Asya has come to visit us at last –'

'The butcher said Dada – Sett Um Sobhi had gone?'

'She went away with her Saudi family, my darling. They had to go and they couldn't do without her, the children loved her so. So she left her kids in safe keeping with me – they're big kids now, may God protect them – and went. She sends me a hundred pounds a month for their expenses. The Saudis value her so much –'

'She is truly to be valued. I valued her too.'

'She was that heart-broken when she left you, but after all –'

'It's our fate and our lot. Sett So'ad, please, will you tell her I asked after her? I'm studying abroad now, otherwise I would have come sooner. And would you give these to the children?' She handed over the box of chocolates she'd bought. 'It's only a small thing –'

'By God, you won't go like that. You have to come in and eat with us. We know how to honour a guest –'

'I really can't –'

'You'll shame us like this? You'll go away from the door?'

'I can't, Sett So'ad; my mother is not well and I've got to get back to her. But please remember me to your sister – give her my salaam –'

She had been ready with her little speech: 'Dada Zeina, I will be back in two years. Will you come back to me? If I have children I want you to look after them. No housework. Just look after my children . . .'

She takes Khalu Hamid his coffee. She leaves him alone with her mother and goes to phone Nadia before the phone has to be left free for her father's call.

When she hears her uncle leave she comes out to meet him in the hall. 'Khalu. I've just spoken to Nadia. She's told me.'

'Well, and why do you look so stricken?'

'Aren't you?'

'Hush, come outside.'

Out in the vestibule by the lift Khalu Hamid says warningly, 'Asya, I don't want your mother worried by any of this right now. All right? I know she hates things being hidden from her, but this really *is* for the best. We'll tell her when she's better, yes? For the moment, I've said I'm going up to Damietta about some furniture and then on to Alexandria for a few days. When I come back and she sees me well, then she can know.'

'But Khalu, you're going in tomorrow?'

'Yes. And by the day after it will all be over.'

'But aren't you – upset?'

'Asya, darling, look. What am I losing? What has this hand done for me in the last seven years? Nothing. Nothing at all. And recently it's been a source of pain. The way I see it, I thank God they only need to cut below the elbow. It could have been worse. I could have lost the whole arm.'

'But Khalu –'

'What, dear?'

'If there's a – malignancy there, might there not be – others?'

'They've checked. There's nothing. You think Nadia wouldn't have thought of that? There's nothing. Everything else is perfect. So they'll take away the hand and then I'll be a hundred per cent. Right? So now stop looking like that –' He pats her cheek. 'Smile for me and go in and look after your mother.'

'I'll come to the hospital tomorrow.'

'I'll be under sedation. Come the day after – in the evening.'

Later, much later, Asya is out on the balcony. The night air is cool and pleasant. No lit windows signal young people studying. It is August and all exams are finished. In the house everyone sleeps. Another day is over. One less day for her mother to be kept in bed. Soon she will be completely well. Soon she will be up and about, doing a million things, creating a chaos of books, tea-cups and little scraps of paper; making them all search for her glasses, her shoes, her handbag. Asya smiles. She is right, of course, about its being terrifically generous of Saif to resign and go with her. Giving up a job with the UN – the blue passport, the salary in dollars, the cachet – to go to the north of England and become a student again. And everybody is so surprised. Tante Adeela, sitting in the big sunny kitchen with Dada Wageeda, heaping little mounds of rice and mince on to moistened vine-leaves and then rolling them into delicate parcels.

'He loves you very much, my dear. He said you were very unhappy there.'

'I was, Tante.'

'He said, "She has to have a Ph.D; she can't have a career in the university without a Ph.D." We all know that, of course.'

Asya had been silent.

'But he's leaving a good job. A job that people would have worn their shoes out running after for years.'

'I know that, Tante. I didn't ask him – in fact, I never even thought –'

'Oh, I know that, my dear, I know. Saif has always been generous –'

'Generous and big-hearted, God's Name protect him,' Dada Wageeda had put in.

'And, as I say, he loves you. His father was a bit doubtful –'

'I'm sure Uncle Madi can't be happy –'

'No. But Saif is a man now and he must know what he's doing. And it *is* better that you two should be together. Nobody knows what the world may bring.'

Asya is grateful, yes; immensely grateful. In her heart there lurks the guilt of knowing that she would not have done the same for him. Indeed, *had* not done the same for him. 'Be but sworn, my love, and I'll no longer – do a Ph.D.' But seriously, what would she have done in Damascus? Sat around developing ulcers? She had got a grant. You get a grant only once in a lifetime. And his job? He says he can always get it back. And anyway, it isn't what he really, ultimately wants. What he wants is to set up on his own; the first computer consultancy in the Middle East – the Arab Middle East, anyway. And the Ph.D, the title at least, would be useful there. But she is grateful. If he hadn't been coming with her the thought of going back would have filled her with dread. As it is, it is just not pleasant. But they would be together. And when they'd had a chance to settle in, to build up their friendship again, everything would come right between them.

She looks down into the street. The shops are closed and shuttered, but the baker's door is open and the greengrocer's big gas-lamp burns on. It was odd how she'd had no urge to go and see her flat. *Here* was still home. Here and her grandfather's – Tante Soraya's. And tomorrow Khalu Hamid goes into hospital. She thinks of a story her father had told her when she was small. It had become one of her favourites and she'd ask him to tell it again and again. It told how Epictetus was being tortured. He was supposed to say something to make the torture stop but he wouldn't. And the chap who was torturing him was twisting his leg and Epictetus said, 'I think you're going to break it.' And the chap twisted some more, and more, and – crack! And Epictetus said, 'I told you you would break it.' Is that how one should be? To take whatever is thrown at you with equanimity, with cool? But from there it is only a step to turning the other cheek. What about an eye for an eye and a tooth for a tooth and he who started it is the more evil? That appeals to her more. Why had Epictetus not kicked his torturer? Why had he not sprung up and – because he was probably surrounded, by armed men, or imprisoned. He was probably tied down. He could not exact an eye – or a leg. So the cool was the only form his courage, his anger, his defiance could take. What can Khalu Hamid do? Rant and rave about the soldier who had crashed into him seven years ago? About the army that was still haggling over his 'compensation'? No. The way he is is the way he ought to be.

She yawns and stretches and looks up at the sky. The stars are brilliant flickering pinpricks and all around her the houses are asleep. But it is not night everywhere. In Australia and America –

Go to bed, she tells herself. Go to bed.

IX

December 1974 – December 1975

Permanent rebellion, the disorder of a life without some loving, reverent resolve, was not possible to her; but she was now in an interval when the very force of her nature heightened its confusion.

—GEORGE ELIOT
Middlemarch

Scene 1

31 December 1974

The North of England

Saif and Mario have stolen some chairs from the Maths department downstairs. The dining-table, both its leaves spread, has been moved to the centre of the sitting-room in the small flat on top of the college which, as a couple, Asya and Saif are allowed to rent for seven pounds a week. The sofa has been banished to the landing they share with an elderly Israeli couple. They also share a mouse, which is the only thing they've talked about in their infrequent meetings on the landing. Asya is always terrified when the mouse suddenly appears on top of the sofa-back or streaking across the floor. Mercifully, however, he only comes in the evenings when Saif is there and she cowers on the landing until he's chased it away. They've set a trap for it, with cheese spiked with what Asya has been assured is a painless poison, but he hasn't come near it. Once, in primary school, Dada Nazeema – a kindly Sudanese cleaning-woman whom Asya had liked – had caught a mouse in the girls' toilets. She had held it in her hand and quickly snapped its arms and legs from their sockets as you do with a boiled chicken. Asya feels sick when she remembers that and the high-pitched screaming of the mouse. She doesn't want to kill this mouse, or to catch it. She just wants it to go away. To *choose* to go away. And these days he has. The Israelis have gone home for Christmas and he seems to be happy having the run of their flat.

'He'll probably come in later,' says Mario. He waves at the table. 'He'll smell all this food and sneak in while you're asleep.'

'Don't tell her that,' Saif warns. 'She'll stay up all night.'

Asya smiles at Mario. He'd done an exaggerated double-take when he'd come in earlier tonight and seen the bare shoulders, the dangly Turkish earrings and the purple silk camisole.

'My God!' he had exclaimed, laying on a heavy Italian accent. 'But you are beautiful! Bellissima! My compliments!'

'Mario!' she had cried. 'Tiger-lilies! Where on earth did you get them, up here, in December?' and reached up to kiss him, her arms full of flowers, her hair piled on top of her head in a loose chignon.

'For you – Mrs Madi' – he had shrugged – 'all things are possible.'

Now Olympia looks fearfully around her. She starts to lift the corner of the tablecloth. 'You do not think maybe he is –'

'Relax, Olympia.' Saif laughs. 'He's hiding next door, terrified at all this noise.'

'It's good your neighbours aren't here,' says Mina. 'You would have had to invite them.'

'I don't think they'd have enjoyed themselves very much,' Saif says.

'They're terribly timid,' Asya says. 'They back off and close their door if they hear us coming.'

'They probably think you'll assassinate them –' William begins, but Asya is on her guard.

'I wonder if *she's* afraid of the mouse?' she says lightly.

'Women are funny about mice,' Leon observes.

'I'm not,' says Nicola. 'I'm not afraid of mice.'

She turns her head, and her expensive bob swings, rises to display earrings of coiled gold, and settles again as she stares at her husband belligerently, continuing a long argument even though these are the first words she has uttered since she sat down.

'But you're afraid of spiders,' Leon says with a smile.

'Everybody's afraid of spiders,' she retorts, and looks away.

Once again, the blonde hair swings, then settles.

'You should see the spiders we have in South Africa,' Frederick puts in. 'They are so big' – he holds out his hand, fingers spread wide – 'and they are furry –'

'Yeah, and they're squashy: they can get in anywhere –'

'Please stop.' Asya shudders, and frowns at Mario. 'A mouse is bad enough –'

Mario puts up his hands in a briefly surrendering gesture, and as he reaches for the salad bowl she thinks again how dramatic he appears – not intentionally, or even actively dramatic, but dramatic as a painting is dramatic. The first time she'd seen him coming out of Saif's department, a tall, broad-shouldered man with lots of curly brown hair, amused eyes, and a thick moustache half covered by the long multi-coloured scarf he'd thrown around his neck, she'd thought of David's *Horatii*. Saif had said he was 'just some South African on the MA course'.

'He doesn't look South African –'

'His family's from Italy. I haven't spoken to him.'

A week later Saif and Mario were friends, and now the three of them do everything together. They meet for lunch in the Salad Bar. They play squash in the Indoor Rec. They scour the countryside for good restaurants and quaint pubs; in the white Morris Saif has bought for three hundred pounds they drive ten, thirty, fifty miles for roast duckling, perfectly sautéed carrots with rosemary, and upside-down pudding – and when the two men spend hours talking computers or projects or cars or sport she doesn't mind at all but sits and watches them both and thinks how lucky she is to be with them, and how different life is now that Saif is with her: her thesis proposal has been accepted by her supervisor; she is officially enrolled in the Ph.D programme and she has started to do the

378

work: one hundred and sixty poems selected at carefully worked-out random from the Oxford Books of Sixteenth, Seventeenth, Eighteenth, Nineteenth and Twentieth Century Verse. And now she has to comb them for metaphors. Thousands of blank record cards are stacked up in readiness. Also a row of empty blue card-boxes. They all sit on the table of their tiny sitting-room – except when, as tonight, the university cutlery and glasses, polished and gleaming, shine there on the white tablecloth. Tonight the room is aglow with candle-light and Mario's golden lilies. On the table three bottles of red wine stand in the green lacquered dishes Leon and Nicola have brought with them as a gift. The music plays softly in the background and Asya has lit two of her special incense sticks.

'This is fantastic,' Mario says as Asya pours more sauce over his third helping of roast duck. 'How did you do all this with that little cooker?'

'She's a great cook, better even than my mother.' Saif smiles at Asya. 'How's that?'

'Not true.' Asya laughs. 'I can't stuff vine-leaves.'

'But it is easy,' Olympia protests seriously. 'First, you have to be certain that the vine-leaves themselves are completely – how do say? Sound – you know, not torn. You have to check –'

Olympia is a fair, plump Greek born in Alexandria and she is always serious. When she smiles she smiles regretfully – as though she were giving something up. Once when she had had a cold Asya had dropped in on her with a present of oranges and had found her wearing beige flannel pyjamas with pink piping round the edges of the jacket, the cuffs and the collar, and she had told Asya – sadly – that her mother had bought them in Cicurel in Cairo back before they had left Egypt in 1956. All things seem to her to be occasions for sadness, but then, thinks Asya, she is homesick. She thinks of Olympia as enduring now what she herself had been almost unable to endure last year – but she also looks at her and wonders why the Greeks are supposed to be a boisterous, fun-loving people (wild *sirtakis* amid the debris of plates and all that); she has not yet met one who was not basically melancholy: Mariana with her defeated jealousies; Monsieur Philippe; Nina's son, who lives next door to Tante Soraya and spends his days in the bedroom of his childhood painstakingly burning elaborately hideous drawings into wood – even Milou, sensible and massive behind her cash-desk in her restaurant on Shari' Sarwat seems to hide a secret unhappiness – and now Olympia, who never sleeps without bed-socks and weeps every time she hears Demis Roussos, not out of homesickness, or (thank goodness) because he moves her, but because he had started out in Alexandria in the same band as her cousin, and her cousin had been better than him, and more musical, and look where Demis is now, while her cousin is – where? Olympia would fix you with reproachful eyes and ask, 'And where is my cousin now?' –

379

well, where, I ask you, is Olympia's cousin? Asya assumes that he is occupying the dim spot allocated to him by an unjust world: entertaining the tourists in some 'authentic' kebab house in a small Mediterranean resort – if he is lucky – but faced with Olympia's reproachful face she averts her eyes and shakes her head sadly.

'I didn't make it all, anyway,' Asya says when Olympia has finished. 'Olympia made this huge salad. And Mina made the nut rissoles and the vegetarian lasagne –'

'William did, actually,' Mina says, drawing on her cigarette. 'He cooks everything.'

'I have to,' says William, 'otherwise we wouldn't eat.'

Mina blows out her smoke and looks at him. She is Persian and beautiful and Asya is slightly in awe of her. She seems so strong, so sure of herself. She lives with William in a small house in the town where she makes small silver, oriental-looking trinkets, and sells them to the stall-holders in the market and at craft fairs. She is waiting for William to finish his Ph.D in the Department of Social Sciences so that they can move down to London and she can hit the big time. Although she despises the big time – they both do – still, there's no sense in selling your talent for less than it's worth or hiding away from the recognition you deserve. And meanwhile she does what she likes. She makes her own clothes and she wears her nails square and clean like a man's, and six weeks ago she had cut her hair, which had been longer and blacker even than Asya's, to a short, soft brush just covering her scalp. When William had tried to object, had tried to stop her, she had asked him if he would wash and dry it for her twice a week while she used her time to do the things that mattered to her. But although none of the men likes it, Asya thinks the haircut has revealed the appeal – the perfection – of the small round skull, as it has brought out the depth of the large black eyes under their heavy eyebrows and the delicate strength of the cheekbones on which tonight she wears the merest hint of silvery blusher. Asya, whose recurrent nightmares include one in which she looks in a mirror and finds that her hair is cut short, admires her, not just for looking like this, but for looking like this by doing what she wants; by *knowing* what she wants and not being afraid to do it – and she puzzles over what her family back in Iran must think she's doing now. They can't know she is living with a man –

'I thought oriental women were – paragons of all that stuff,' Mario grins at Mina.

'You thought wrong, mate,' William says. 'She won't lift a finger. *And* she doesn't like kids.'

'Why do you put up with it? You're not even married –'

'Mario,' Asya chides, 'you're making mischief.'

'Let's see what *you* come up with, Mario,' says Mina. 'You'll be one of

380

those blokes with a baby in a metal frame on his back and two carrier-bags full of nappies.'

'Me?' Mario leans back in his chair and stretches his legs out. 'I'm a bachelor for ever. All the best women are married. To my friends.'

'Well, Jenny MacRae's after you. And she always gets what she wants.'

'Nah.' He waves a dismissive hand and reaches for a cigarette. 'I'm not into that kind of scene.'

'This is a good tape,' Nicola says suddenly. 'What is it?'

'Asya al-Ulama's All-Time Personal Greats.' Saif reaches over and pats Asya's bare shoulders. 'She's done it very cleverly, with fade-outs and volume changes and everything.'

Asya makes him a little bow, then, serious, turns to Mario.

'Mario,' she asks, 'if we were in South Africa, could we have this dinner party?'

Frederick, Mario's childhood buddy who has come up from London for Christmas, stiffens, but Mario says easily, 'Sure. Some of my best friends are black.'

'No, but seriously,' Asya insists, 'could we? I mean, would *we* be black and have to live in another part of town and all that?'

'It is very complicated,' Frederick says.

Frederick is very German. South Africa doesn't seem to wipe out original national differences, Asya thinks. When he had followed Mario into the apartment earlier tonight he had clicked his heels as he bowed over Asya's hand. And he wasn't being funny.

'Of course you would,' William says, 'Mina would be black anyway. I'm not sure about Olympia.'

'No,' Mario says slowly, 'you would be Coloured. Whites, Coloureds and Indians can mix at a private party. But not Africans. At least, they can't drink. The Africans can't. Unless they bring their own booze. And they have to buy it in a segregated liquor store. But if you have a police raid you can't prove that the Africans were drinking their own drinks and not drinks they had been served at the party. It's all very stupid.'

'It is very complicated,' Frederick says again.

'But surely Egyptians *are* Africans?' Asya says.

'They're not,' Saif says.

'I thought you were supposed to be Arabs?' Leon says.

'But how come? Egypt is in Africa, isn't it?' says Asya.

'Yes, but you're not the same race as the – Zulus, say, or the Bantu. You are – more white. I told you it was stupid.'

'Well, at least you've got multi-racial sport now,' says Leon. 'That's something.'

Leon is being nice to Frederick. Because they are both strangers; outsiders to this circle. Or is it because he's smelt out a possible South

African business connection? Asya had been worried about having him and William round the same table; William with his unchanging loose sweater and tight jeans – she looks across the table at Leon's Cardin suit and his diamond tie-pin and the gold signet ring on his little finger; you could look at Saif or Mario and not know whether they were left or right, but these guys are in uniform. Asya had been worried that they might quarrel but Saif had been surprised she'd even thought that. 'No,' he'd assured her, 'they'll be fine.' She looks at Nicola's tense face and decides that, yes, she really does not like Leon. What right does he have to make her so unhappy? Steady on, she tells herself – maybe she makes *him* unhappy, too, only he's better at hiding it, how do *you* know what goes on between them? Well, on the evidence, she argues, as though she were arguing with Saif – although she tries not to do that because he's been so kind to her and without him she would have still been catatonic in her dreadful little room with no friends, even if her work had been going all right – on the evidence, he seems to be perfectly OK and at ease with himself and doing successful stuff with his work, while she seems to be unhappy and kind of held in –

'Maybe she's just a neurotic bitch. What do *you* know?'

'You know, you never use the term "neurotic" about a man – ever; it's always women who are "neurotic". I know she wants children and he won't let her have any –'

'If he doesn't want kids that's his right. That's no reason for her to spend her time – and his money – on one stupid idea after another and then complain she isn't "fulfilled" or "realised" or whatever holy term –'

'But he married her from school. She was seventeen. She hasn't had a chance to find out what matters to her except she knows she wants children. She was *brought up* to be "fulfilled" by having children and he must have known that – *plus* I don't see why you need to be scornful of –'

Hold on, Asya thinks: it's not even fair arguing with him in your mind. At least if you say it out loud he knows what's going on. Look at him; he's like a little boy enjoying his own party while you dream words into his mouth and then hold him responsible for them. How can you have such a black heart?

'They'd be bloody fools not to have it,' says Mina. 'There wouldn't *be* sports if it weren't for the blacks.'

'That is somewhat strong,' Frederick objects.

'Did you see the squash?' asks Saif, and Mario turns to him with relief. 'That's going to be a hell of a final. I wouldn't mind going to it.'

'Let's,' says Saif. 'Why not?'

'They have such wonderful names,' says Asya. 'Muhibullah Khan and Qamar Zaman; straight out of the *Arabian Nights*. Do you think they were born with them?'

'Yeah, and a silver spoon each,' William says.

'William, you always think everything pivots around class.'

'It does.'

'It does not.'

'Be fair, Asya,' Saif says. 'Do you think your average Pakistani street-sweeper grows up playing squash?'

'No, but they all know about squash over there, and surely if some impoverished kid showed promise –'

'Where would he show promise?'

'I don't know, playing against some wall somewhere with a warped racket –'

'Sure. Just like in *Andy Pandy* or whatever it is you still read. She's just romantic –'

'What's wrong with romantic?' Asya says.

'What's wrong with class?' asks Nicola, tapping the ash off her cigarette with a long finger on which a large grey pearl shivers in the light of the candle.

'Are you *serious?*' William leans over. His long hair falls in a straight line down the sides of his pale face and his frameless glasses glint in the candle-light. 'Are you seriously asking what's *wrong* with *class?*' More than ever tonight he looks like Strelnikov in the film of *Doctor Zhivago*; Sasha with his hair grown long.

'For God's sake don't start him on that,' Mina groans. 'He'll give you a complete rundown of all the Marxist-Leninist-Trotskyist theories of everything and –'

'I don't know how' – William turns to her – 'coming from your part of the world you can be so ignorant of politics.'

'What do you know of my "part of the world"? Tell me that? Have you ever been there? What do you –'

'I know you're always at each other's throats, that's one thing I know.'

'And who's responsible for that? Who set it up to be that way?'

'What you're saying is, you are unable to outgrow your past,' Leon says.

'We are not *allowed* to outgrow our past –'

'That's just an easy answer –'

'What about what was done to Mussadaq?'

'And what about what's happening in Lebanon?' Asya adds.

'But that's the Palestinians –'

'Right now it's the Palestinians – but why are they there? And why does Israel continue to bomb the Lebanese south? To raid villages in a country that isn't even at war –'

'Because of Qiryat Shemona and Ma'alot. Is *that* something you approve of?'

'No. Of course I don't. But I could say to you, "What about Bahr el

383

Baqar and 'Abu Za'bal?" and you wouldn't know what I was talking about. Would you?'

'No.'

'A primary school and a factory. In Egypt. Both bombed by the Israelis, who pride themselves on their precision. But somehow nobody knows about *them* and the world is full of Qiryat Shemona. Just because an act of terrorism is committed by a *state* –'

'That's a question of publicity,' says Saif, 'and the Arabs have only themselves to blame for that –'

'*Our*selves –' interjects Asya.

'Ourselves, sure.' Saif smiles and looks at Asya, and she remembers that this is her table and that these people are her guests and it will not do to quarrel with them, so she stands up and offers the salad bowl to Leon.

'Leon – have some salad. It's delicious. Olympia made it.'

'This tape gets better and better, hey?' Mario says. He claps Frederick on the shoulder. 'Your glass is empty, man.' He pours more wine into everybody's glasses.

'In any case,' Leon says, cutting a quarter of a tomato carefully into two-eighths, 'you're well out of it now.'

'How are we out of it?' Asya asks.

'Well, you're going to sign a peace treaty and get the Sinai back, aren't you?'

'That's all meaningless. There can never *be* a separate peace, not really.'

'Your President seems to think there can.'

'Our President mainly wants to be friends with Mr Kissinger.' Saif smiles.

'How can there be peace, actual *peace*, when the problem is still there? This agreement can only harm the Palestinian cause and it's going to be seen as a piece of treachery.'

'So what would the solution be according to you, Asya?'

'I don't know what the *solution* would be – but I do think it has to be an overall solution, not a bitty one.'

'But you guys can't even agree among yourselves, let alone with the Israelis! Look at this Abu Iyad guy today declaring they've got Hussein of Jordan on some hit-list –'

'You're right,' Saif agrees.

'Yes,' Asya admits. 'That *is* our tragedy. And that's what Nasser saw and – for all his faults – what he tried so hard to correct. But maybe it's impossible –'

'So what's the answer?'

'I don't know. Nothing. Maybe we've had our day.'

'You're giving up?' asks Mina. 'This isn't like you.'

'I'm not, really.' Asya smiles at her. 'It's just for the moment.'

'Oh no!' Saif groans. 'Let's turn the music up.'

'Just what the *truth* is –
I can't tell any mo-ore'

'William,' asks Asya, 'what's that badge you're wearing?'

'What? This? It's CAMRA.'

'What's CAMRA?'

'Asya, you *are* ignorant. It's the Campaign for Real Ale.'

'And what is that?'

'What do you mean, "What is that?" '

'She doesn't drink beer,' Saif says.

'I know that "ale" is beer. But what is "*real* ale"?'

'It's beer brewed in the traditional way, the old way, without all the modern synthetic –'

'Is it supposed to be healthier? Or does it taste better?'

'Both.'

'Would anyone be able to recognise the difference?'

'Not someone who didn't drink beer in the first place.'

'What is this? An interrogation?'

'I'm just trying to find out –'

'C A M R A started three years ago and we now have twenty-seven thousand members –'

'And it's another of his hobby-horses.' Mina smiles at him – but gently.

'Hey –' William turns to her, 'I'm not the only one with fads, you know.' He turns to the company. 'I became a vegetarian because of her –'

'You didn't have to,' Mina says. 'No one forced you –'

'You don't force people when you live with them; you just make other options impossible –'

Asya suddenly sees the remains of the duck through Mina's eyes: a corpse; a dead bird lying on its back, legs and wings torn off, ribcage picked clean –

She stands up.

'Well, if no one wants more of this, I'll clear it up and we can move on to pudding.'

'Pudding! Oh, goodie!' Leon smiles up at her. Olympia and Nicola start to get up.

'You mustn't, really,' Asya protests, and waves them down again. 'There's no room, anyway. I'm going to have to dump everything on the landing and clear it up later.'

On the landing she blinks at the bright light. She bends and puts the serving plate with the remains of the duck on the floor by the wall. She straightens up, then bends again to look out of the window beyond the first flight of stairs. She can see nothing outside. She places her hands against the banisters and leans all her weight upon them. She studies her watch. Eleven o'clock. At least another two hours to go. It's not that they're horrid or anything. It's just that she can't see why she should be spending this evening with them. Mario, yes. If she were just with Saif and Mario she would be all right. She wouldn't sound as dreadful as she's been sounding in there. Whatever she does – she picks up their topics, she asks questions – but whatever she does, she sounds fraudulent. She'll have to go in. She can't really just stay out here like this. She glances at the door of the other apartment. Thank goodness they're away. They would have been tripping over sofas and dirty plates – a little refugee camp out here – *he* seems nice, though: very old-fashioned and East European and like some secondary character out of Philip Roth; as if he has a sense of humour somewhere underneath all the caution. He had actually raised his hat to her. 'Madame, I believe we share a mouse?' Well, the mouse would definitely venture forth now to check out these plates. What *had* made Dada Nazeema do that? And so automatically; without a moment's thought, as though it was something she'd known for ever: 'This Is What You Do To Mice'. And as for the mouse, there he was scampering around the loos simply being a mouse when suddenly he is seized by a mighty power: seized and scooped up to the sky and before he knows it – snap snap snap snap his arms and legs are off, and his life is no use to him any more – worse than no use –

Nicola comes out on to the landing, a cigarette in her hand.

'Do you need help?'

'No, no, I'm fine. I was just – well, I suppose it won't do any harm to leave them here for a couple of hours, will it?'

'I shouldn't think so. You said there was no one here anyway.'

'Nicola, is your room OK? It's terribly sweet of you to come all the way up from London like this –'

'No, it's very nice for us: it meant we didn't have to go to either of our sets of parents.'

'Was that what you'd have done?'

'Leon thought we might go off somewhere alone, but –' She breaks off and shrugs. But she has stopped in the middle of a sentence. It would be rude to leave it there –'

'Did you not want to?'

Nicola shrugs again. She is slim and elegant in her soft grey sweater-dress. 'We are always alone –'

Olympia puts her head around the door. 'What are you doing?' she asks. 'Why are you standing out here? It is very cold.'

'We were just coming in,' Asya says.

386

'I'll use your loo,' Nicola says, and disappears into the bathroom as Asya goes back into the living-room.

'Where is this pudding you promised us?' William asks.

'It's coming, it's coming,' Asya promises, lifting the lid off a saucepan and backing away from the steam.

'What *do* you think, then?' Mina continues. 'Do you think it's Stonehouse?'

'No, it's Lord Lucan.'

'I think it's Stonehouse –'

'His wife doesn't seem to think so.'

'What would she know?'

'No, but she seemed pretty certain he'd been drowned –'

'It would be weird, wouldn't it,' says Asya, 'if it turned out she didn't know the first thing about him.'

'Not that weird,' Saif says.

Asya turns to him –

'Can I use your loo?' Mina says, standing up and shaking out the loose, flowered trousers she's chosen to wear gathered at her waist with one of William's ties.

Let it pass, Asya tells herself. They would only end up arguing if she asks him what he means. But can he mean what he appears to mean?

'It is time for toasts!' Frederick cries, leaning back in his chair, happy and flushed with food and wine. 'We will each one propose a toast!'

'Oh no, I can't –' Olympia begins.

'Come on, Olympia, be brave,' Mario says.

'You can drink to the Colonels,' Saif says.

'Oh, but I would *not* –'

'A toast to Bangladesh,' William proposes loudly, raising his glass. They all look at him.

'Surely not,' says Asya.

'Why the hell not? Just because we're sitting here eating and drinking it doesn't mean we shouldn't spare a thought for those poor buggers.'

'But it seems so – cosmetic; it's almost insulting.'

'I'm sure they wouldn't agree. But then, they can't afford abstract qualms –'

'Asya, you've even put a candle in the *bathroom*! Honestly!' Mina has come back.

'Well, I just –'

'It's nice,' says Nicola.

'It's just that the walls are so *purple*,' Asya begins again.

'To Bangladesh!' William says loudly, and raises his glass.

'What?' Mina asks.

387

They all raise their glasses. 'To Bangladesh!'

'Nicola now,' says Asya. 'Nicola.'

Nicola looks into her glass, then she raises it and keeps her eyes fixed on it. 'The Dying Year!' she says.

'That is sad,' Frederick says.

They all raise their glasses. 'The Dying Year!'

'I will now propose a toast,' Frederick says. 'I propose a toast to nineteen seventy-five!'

'Nineteen seventy-five!' they all say, and raise their glasses.

'Olympia's turn now,' says Asya.

'Oh, I can't,' Olympia says.

'Yes you can. Think of something. Anything you like.'

'But I can't, I can't think of anything –'

'Go on. Try,' Mina urges her. 'Close your eyes and think.'

Olympia closes her eyes and they wait. She opens them and curls her fingers round the stem of her glass, anchoring it firmly to the table. Holding it down she says, deprecatingly, 'Success?'

'Hear, hear!' cries Mario. 'See? You did it.'

'Success!' they cry, and raise their glasses.

'What?' asks Leon, as Asya looks at him. 'Me? Right. I'll drink to Absent Friends!'

'Absent Friends!' They raise their glasses, but Asya watches Nicola push hers away and pretend to hunt in her bag for something.

'OK, Mina. It's you.'

'Right. I'll drink to Women!' She raises her glass, and as she smiles her strong white teeth shine in the candle-light.

'I'll say,' says Leon, and bangs on the table.

'Yes, that is good,' Olympia nods. 'It is, after all, the Year of the Woman.'

'Women!' they shout, and raise their glasses.

'I'll complete that,' Saif says, raising his glass to Mina. 'Wine – and Song!'

'Good one, good one,' laughs Mario, punching him.

They raise their glasses. 'Wine and Song!'

Asya has been considering her options. As everyone looks towards her, she raises her glass. 'Home!' she says.

'Home!' they shout, and drink.

'And now,' says Mario, 'I have the last toast.' He pauses. 'It has to be to Asya and Saif who have brought us all together.' He raises his glass. 'Asya and Saif!'

'Asya and Saif!'

'And now, we will dance,' Frederick cries, standing up.

'But there is no room,' Olympia says.

'Yes, yes, if we move the table – it is all right, Asya?'

'Oh, of course. Absolutely. Let's,' says Asya, looking at Saif, knowing he won't want to dance, knowing that he will know *she* wants to dance; that he will think she wants *him* to dance if only so that she does not look like The Woman With Whom Her Husband Will Not Dance – among other things, but they don't know about the 'other things'. She resolves to not want him to dance –

'Saif, it is all right to move the table?'

'Sure. I'll help you.'

'Right, let's go –'

And of course he moves the table and rolls up the rug, and when they're all jumping about in the middle of the room – even Olympia, putting aside for the moment her cousin's wasted promise and the hundred other sadnesses that claim her attention – he retires to the window with a cigarette and responds to all the men's urgings and Mina's attempts to pull him by the hand with a smile and a shake of the head.

'Doesn't he ever dance?' Nicola asks Asya.

'He'll only dance in Paris.'

'In Paris? Why?'

'I don't know. He just said that to me once.'

'Come on, Asya, dance with me,' William takes her arm.

William breathes into her ear, and Asya holds herself as rigid and as far from him as she can. Take it easy, she thinks. It's nothing personal. He'll do the same to Olympia and to Nicola. But how ridiculous it is to be going through this while Saif stands gazing into the middle distance and thinks she's enjoying herself. How can he just stand there – well, if he doesn't want to dance he doesn't want to dance. It's his right, after all. But to just *stand* there – but what else can he do that would not seem even more pointed? Go into the bedroom and close the door? Go and sit on the landing with the dirty dishes? Go for a drive? She keeps her hand wedged firmly against William's chest so she can hold him away from her. She wants to go and stand next to Saif, link her arm through his and be his friend. She frees herself from William.

'But it isn't finished yet –'

'I just need Saif for a moment –'

And she goes and stands next to Saif and puts her arm through his. He pats her hand.

'You having a good time, Princess?'

'Ummm. You?'

'Uh-huh. The food was great. The bits *you* made.'

'Thank you.'

They stand together looking out at the blackness, the perimeter hedge, and the few lights of the parking lot. The music quickens and the Beatles start on 'Ob-la-di ob-la-da'.

'Come on, you two!' cries Mina, but Saif shakes his head. She pulls Asya's hand. 'Come on, Asya, leave him behind!'

How wonderful to be Mina – to be so certain of what you're doing, so sure of yourself, to know what you want and feel what you feel . . . Olympia's dropped out – without reference to anyone else – she can imagine William going into long sulks . . . Nicola's dropped out, but Mina never will – and her just carrying on with her normal things until he came round – Leon would rather die than drop out – perhaps he will – he looks terrible – how wonderful to be Molly – a singer with a band – with the frank, and simple, Desmond – and no lines except: 'Ob-la-di ob-la-da –'

Panting and laughing and pressing her hand to her side, she looks at Mario, who is breathing in deep and breathing out loud, and who gives her a wide smile and, as the next tune starts up, holds his arms out to her, and she walks into them and feels for the first time what she has suspected for three months: that his hands are strong and gentle –

'Something in the way she moves
Attracts me like no other lover –'

– that he smells of spice and tobacco and leather, that her forehead comes to just above his shoulder and her face would just fit into his neck. The way he holds her is perfect, he does not breathe in her ear or try to press her close, he holds her with all the innocence there can be and her body yearns to draw closer to him . . .

But it is New Year's Eve, and it's the music, and the wine – and when the last high note fades and he stands with his hands still circling her waist, looking at her, she gives him a little smile and pats his chest and pulls herself away. As she makes for the bathroom she sees him cross the floor towards the only chair that's been left in the room.

And in the candle-lit bathroom she talks to the face she sees in the mirror; the face whose eyes have grown bigger and darker, whose lips have grown fuller and softer, whose whole aspect is more flushed and curved and smooth than she's seen it for a long, long time. She says 'Why?' and she says, 'It isn't fair,' and she whispers, 'Stop it, oh, stop it,' and presses her hot forehead to the mirror. Then she sits on the edge of the bathtub. She braces her feet against the floor and presses herself down on the hard plastic, willing her body to stop pulsing, to subside. They tell you – all your life they tell you – that a woman's sexuality is responsive, a woman's sexuality is tied up with her emotions. Her mother says she's never even thought of any man that way except her father. Dada Zeina claims she had never desired any man but her husband – and then only because he had taught her. But Asya had seen a letter in one of Saif's magazines in which a housewife had described how, feeling lustful after her husband has gone to work, she undresses and makes love with candles, broomsticks, soup-ladle handles, vegetables, the cylinders from toilet-roll holders – and Asya had told her mother, who'd said that the letter hadn't been written by a woman at all but by some sub-editor on the magazine and that all it was was another male fantasy. Is she a freak, then? But it isn't like that; she doesn't want to make love with *things*. If she did, well, there's a candle right here. At the thought of pulling up her velvet skirt and making love to the candle – she'd have to snuff it out first, of course, and then the bathroom would be completely black – Asya starts to giggle. Then she tells herself that she's got nothing to laugh about; that she's an even worse freak than the *Penthouse* housewife, real or imagined. Look at her: in Italy she is friends with Umberto but desires some unknown man with a broken nose who is handling a blonde in a corner – even while she is in love, *in love*, with Saif; and tonight, to want to press up against Mario, to want his hand to slide down from her waist – oh, but she had used to want Saif, she had used to want him so much. Oh, to feel again the passion that had made her force the rickety thirteen hundred from Zamalek to Heliopolis through the mid-town traffic in twelve minutes flat. Oh, to exchange a few words with his mother in her sweet-smelling kitchen, then fall into his bed and into his arms. The whole afternoon on top of his quilted red eiderdown lost and lost and lost again while the shadow of the pear tree quivers and lengthens on the floor of the open balcony. She rests her arms on the basin and her face on her arms. Tonight, when Mario and the others all go away, and this dreadful party has come to an end, she and Saif will tidy up and bring in the sofa and the dirty plates, and then he'll come in here for a shower, and then come to bed with a copy of *Road and Track* or *Amateur Photographer*, and she would be there under their king-size duvet in a silk nightie with her pearls still round her neck and her face scrubbed clean of make-up but her lashes and lips subtly touched up and her neck and shoulders and wrists painted with Capricci, and she would be patient while he read, and she would count her blessings, for here he is with her – oh, it isn't fair though, it isn't *fair* –

'Asya!' Mina knocks at the door. 'It's almost midnight. Come on out.'

'I'm coming.'

Her hair has slipped loose from the grips she had put into it before the evening began, and she brushes it quickly, then pushes it back from her face as she unlocks the door. She makes her way past the dancing couples to where Saif and Mario are standing at the window.

'We thought you'd moved in,' Saif says, as he puts his arm around her shoulders. 'You haven't been puking, have you?'

'No, of course not, silly.'

Mario drags on his cigarette and continues to look out of the window.

'I should have told him I'd do anything
If I could hold him –'

Yes, she would be patient while he read, and she would count her blessings, for here he is with her. No longer alone. No longer shivering under a thin blanket in a narrow bed in a brick-walled room listening to footsteps go by, and never ever, not once, stopping at her door; but here, cosy with central heating and feather-filled bedding, luxurious by the side of her husband. Her husband whom she loves and who loves her – for she knows he loves her, otherwise why is he here? And so she would wait. And eventually Saif would throw the magazines to the floor and put his glasses down on top of them and reach to switch off the bedside light and, turning over, would say, 'Goodnight, Princess.' And in a rush of loneliness she would touch his back with the tips of her fingers and say, 'Could you? Please? Turn around and hold me?'

'Oh, sweetie, sweetie. Go to sleep.'

'Please? Just for a minute?'

And he would turn round, and big and solid and sweet-smelling would hold her close for maybe five minutes, then he'd ask lightly, 'Is that enough? Can I go to sleep now?' And patting her hip or arm or whatever was nearest he would murmur, 'Goodnight, Princess,' and he would turn over, and in minutes he would be asleep. And she would lie awake and hold down the loneliness that threatened to turn into a full-blown panic. Instantly, like the magic trees you can buy in supermarkets that flower while you watch. And finally she would sit up in bed and, in the light that filtered through from the living-room, would watch him as he slept. He sleeps curled on his side away from her. The quilt is at his waist. She does not need to look to see the smooth buttocks, the sturdy legs, the feet with their even, moderate toes and their still uncallused soles. He is dreaming, no doubt, of planes or cars or computers. Or of nothing at all. And why not? What should he dream of? Of her? Does she want him to call out her name in his sleep? Why should he? She is here, right here beside him – if he wants her. But he does not want her. She is his wife, his friend and his companion. But he does not *want* her. When he was away from her he wrote to her every day. But he does not want her. He wrote that he loved her and that he missed her. He drew her little pictures: pictures of houses with whitewashed walls and fountained courtyards and prowling cats; houses which they will build and live in together on the edge of the desert beyond the Pyramids on the road to Memphis. For ever and ever. Until they die. Until they die.

Now she watches him. I know you love me. But you don't want me. You did once, but you don't any more. But stop. Stop, she tells herself. Be grateful. You *are* grateful. Grateful that he loves you enough to come and live here with you. Think what it was like just four months ago and be grateful. She looks at his hands lying still and half open on the quilt. Amazing to think that there was a time when she was powerless not to touch them. When watching his hands across the table as he lit a Rothmans she would imagine them on her breasts and grow weak with desire. But to be repulsed, turned away so many times – but that's what he thinks *you* did to *him* – at first. But she *wants* to want him. She badly wants to want him. She wants him to *make* her want him; make her want him like she used to. But he won't. He will have nothing to do with it at all. So what's the answer, then – *what*? Wait. There *will* be an answer, of course there will. Just wait. One thing at a time. Because of him you are yourself again. You can do your work. You have friends – well, acquaintances anyway. You have a life. You don't have to lie here trembling at the thought of the hours that lie ahead. He has *saved* you. Remember that. And remember all your resolutions and your promises to yourself. Remember how good you said you'd be. And how you would be content and ask for nothing, absolutely nothing, if only you could get yourself back again. If only you could do your work. If only you did not have to feel so desperately alone. It has all happened. He has made it happen.

Scene 2

4 February 1975
The North of England

> 'Touch me in the mo-o-orning,
> Then just walk away –'

Saif swings the car into the parking bay, pulls up the handbrake and turns off the engine – and then the sound.

'Let's go for a walk. Come on, Princess. Wrap up.'

Asya is reluctant, but he stands on the pavement and waits for her as she winds a big shawl around her head and Mina's scarf around her neck and then fastens up her coat. She pulls on her woollen gloves. Outside, she can see the breath steaming from his mouth, and he bounces a couple of times on the balls of his feet. He keeps his hands in his pockets.

393

She gets out of the car, slams the door, pulls her head down between her shoulders and shivers in the cold.

'Let's walk,' he says. 'Come on.'

She has seen this place several times now but she does not stop wondering at it. *This* is a seaside town? *This* is the sea? In the worst of the winter months Alexandria doesn't look like this. Alexandria looks graciously ruined, bravely keeping up appearances – well, of course, that isn't fair: Alexandria isn't some small provincial resort that has nothing in it except a few horrible bed and breakfast places. But this is the *sea*? This dreary expanse of mud and stones? And the weirdest thing is that there are three people in boots and jumpers down there on the – what *could* you call it? You would probably have to call it the 'beach' – down there, scrabbling about in the mud looking as if there was something down there to enjoy. They have a dog with them, only he's sitting rather miserably on the edge of things with his head on his front paws. They were probably 'whelking', she'd heard of that –

'Don't hunch up like that,' Saif says. 'You'll feel less cold if you straighten up. No, no. Stop. Straighten up. Completely. That's better. Now walk.'

'Don't we have tides in the Mediterranean, then?' Her teeth chatter when she speaks and she has to make an effort to hold herself straight.

'Every sea has tides, but in the Mediterranean they're not as pronounced. You can see them more in the Red Sea.' He stops and looks out across the bay. 'You can walk across this, you know. All you need is a pair of wellingtons.'

Asya shudders at the thought of trudging across that damp and windblown waste into the bleak, shadowy hills beyond.

'Let's go on the pier,' he says. 'Come on, Princess. Be brave. At least it isn't raining.'

She tucks her gloved hand into his arm and they walk towards the pier. Apart from the figures down on the beach, the whole town appears deserted. No cars pass along the corniche and everything along the seafront seems unequivocally closed. Yet people must go on living here all the year round. And some students board out here. She shudders again at the thought of some dank little room with an evil-smelling gas-fire, a soiled rug and a complaining landlady. But how do you know it's like that? she rebukes herself. Can't it be warm and cosy with embroidered antimacassars on faded red velvet armchairs, a smell of baking coming from the kitchen and *David Copperfield* lying open on the coffee-table in front of the fire? Can't it? As they step out on to the rickety wooden planks she glances back at the town. It is hard to imagine pleasant lives being lived out behind those grim barricaded façades, and yet –

A quick, high yelp breaks the silence. Down on the beach the dog is chasing madly after something one of the walkers has thrown. The figure's arm is just descending from the throw and the dog takes off in great, flying bounds towards an unseen ball or stick lying in the mud. He picks it up, races back and drops it at his master's – or mistress's, Asya can't make out which – feet. Then, unable to contain himself, he leaps up at the figure, stabbing at its face with the point of his nose before wheeling out to describe great circles around it. Up comes the arm again. Throw – and with a high yelp the dog shoots off – *Da*badabadab *da*badabadab *da*rara-*da*-ra – Asya thinks of *Un Homme et une Femme*. How she had admired the sculpted cheekbones and winged eyebrows of Anouk Aimée; her expression serene and almost unchanging, but the serenity itself conveying such depth of feeling, such turmoil –

Saif picks up a pebble that had strayed on to the pier and spins it forcefully, disc-like, down on to the beach below where it skims and bounces for a few yards then tumbles to a stop.

'You think he might bring it back?' Asya smiles and with a movement of her head indicates the yelping dog.

'No.' Saif gives a rueful half-smile and shakes his head. 'He'll only bring back what his owner throws. If he's well trained.'

'Otherwise he'd go leaping off after everything, right?'

He nods. 'Right.' And then, 'Are you really terribly cold, sweetie? Shall we go and find some tea somewhere?'

'Yes. In a minute.'

They lean on the wooden railings and stare westward through the mist at the setting sun and the fading outlines of the distant hills. No fiery disc, no apocalyptic sky, no straight, shining path blazing upon the water. Just a pale, cold sun edging its way cautiously below a grey horizon. Asya shivers, and Saif puts an arm round her shoulders. She moves closer into his side for warmth and says, 'I know.'

'What?'

'What we need to talk about.'

He pulls her close and rests his brow for a moment on her temple.

'It's up to you, sweetie. Honestly.'

She nods. 'Of course, you must go.'

'I won't if you don't want me to.'

'Saif. It's what you've always wanted.'

'. . .'

'Isn't that true? I've listened to you talking to Shahir, to Fuad, to Mario, to Kareem, even. You've always wanted to start your own company: to work for yourself and do things the way you think they should be done.'

'Yes.'

'And you've got all sorts of ideas for systems and configurations and mixing components and things –'

He smiles.

'Well, at least as far as I understand it,' she continues.

'Yes, yes, that's quite true.' He tightens his arm around her.

'And your chance to try them out can really only come if you're working on your own?'

'Well, it's a better chance –'

'You should take it.'

'Asya, I've been thinking about this for more than three months now –'

'Since the first phone-call.'

'Yes.'

'You've turned down what? Four offers?'

'Yes. It's the Syrians who keep coming back.' He moves away from her and stamps his feet on the ground as he looks out to sea.

She looks at him. 'It's been really weird sitting in our little flat watching you get phone-calls from across the world –'

He shrugs and kicks half-heartedly at the wooden railings.

'I don't think it was wrong to turn them down to begin with.'

'It's probably made them want you more.'

'They're very keen. It's the first government installation and of course it's the army –'

'And there's no one better or more suitable than you – and by a happy coincidence, you are now independent and free to take on any job you like.' He gives her a quick, suspicious look, and Asya smiles and draws nearer and puts up a gloved hand to stroke his head. 'No, I'm serious. Really. Darling, don't look so worried. You must have been hoping this would happen –'

'Yes, of course I have. But I thought I could stall for longer. I don't want to leave you alone again.'

'It isn't the same, now. Not any more. I'm not afraid of this place any more. And as long as I'm doing the work – as long as nothing goes wrong there, I'll be all right.'

'And you've got friends now.'

'*We've* got friends.'

'But I mean, you won't be lonely any more.'

'I'll still miss you.'

'I know, and I'll miss you too, sweetie. But we won't be apart for long.'

'No. How long?'

'Well, I can't tell exactly, but maybe this first time it would be two or three weeks.'

'But then you'd have to go again?'

'Yes.'

'And again and again.'

'It's a big project.'

'And there'll be others.'

He walks a few paces away from her, then comes back.

'Asya. If we go into this we're doing it for *us* – not just for me.'

'I know. It'll be lots and lots of money, won't it?'

'Probably. Probably in a few years I could make enough to last us for life.'

'With everything you want? The Lagonda and the antique guns and the white Hassan Fat'hi house and all the rest of it?'

He smiles. 'Possibly. I don't know whether the Lagonda isn't well and truly dead though.'

'All they needed was sixty thousand –'

'They needed sixty thousand straight away. Then they needed time. They needed money to buy time.'

'How long do you really think you would be away?'

'I think I could probably keep it down to around three weeks each time.'

'And how long would you be here in between?'

'I'd aim at a couple of months. But, sweetie, it's hard to say. Look, maybe it won't work out and I'll come back and that'll be it.'

'Oh no. That definitely won't happen.'

'It might.'

'No it won't. You're brilliant and they know it already, and they'll get to know it more and more and ask you to do more and more, and of course that's what we want, really. We just thought it would happen after we'd finished here, so it's just come a bit early, that's all. But I'm sure we'll make it work.'

'Sweetie, I'm sorry.'

'Don't be. Really really really don't be. I mean, it was already wonderful of you to come here and hold my hand in the first place, and now I'm OK. Only, these separations, you know, I mean, do you think we'll be all right? We, together, I mean?'

'Of course we will, Princess. We've been separated before.'

'Yes, but really. I mean, it kind of could become the way things are, and you know how people are always afraid of – of growing apart – I mean, even the reason your mother wasn't completely against your giving up your job was because she said, "At least you'll be together," and I'm just worried – I mean maybe we were starting to get used to – maybe we might have –'

'Everything will get sorted out. And when we're together we'll be really together.'

'Yes?'

'It really isn't a big deal, you know. We'll still be basically living here, with me just making the odd trip. And we'll take it slow. Let it build up slowly and speed up on the studying –'

'I think if we made sure that when we're together we're really really together. That we'd – do things, and – talk, and stuff – you know, we should be all right, really.'

'Of course we'll be all right.'

'Because it would be such a shame . . .' Asya looks down at the worn planks. 'I mean, I know it's not a "grande amour" any more, or anything –'

'Who says it isn't?'

She looks up at him for a moment, but his eyes meet hers unwaveringly; he looks surprised and hurt.

'Anyway,' she resumes, looking away. 'We've still got a lot to lose; we're such good friends.'

'But of course, sweetie. We're best chums, aren't we?'

Bulky in overcoats and scarves and gloves, they hug each other at the end of the pier. The last edge of the white sun has vanished from the horizon and the grey mist is closing in.

Scene 3

25 March 1975
Paris

'But you said you only dance in Paris –'

'Only *danced* in Paris.'

'Do you only ever do anything once? Even things you enjoy?'

Asya keeps her tone deliberately light. For one thing she doesn't want to upset either him or herself; they haven't met in Paris in order to quarrel. And for another, she had found – the moment she'd turned to look at him, and he, correctly interpreting her look as an invitation, had leaned back in his chair and shaken his head – she had found that she did not want to dance with him. She still wanted to dance – because the music made her feel like dancing – but she did not particularly want to dance with *him*. Which was just as well, since he did not want to dance with her.

'Who said I enjoyed dancing?'

'Et pourtant, pourtant,
Je n'aime que toi –'

'You said that when you lived with Danielle here for six months you went dancing almost every night.'

398

'That was different.'

Mario has stopped for a chat with the barman on his way to the men's room. Mina and William are swaying on the floor with their arms around each other. William is in his regulation jeans and baggy brown sweater – it is as though wearing anything else would mean he'd betrayed his principles. But Mina has made a concession: this is the first time Asya has seen her in a dress; her legs are surprisingly muscular and sturdy, but the rest of her – for once without a chunky pullover – is slender and graceful, and she moves well on the floor. Her hair is still very short, and tonight she wears in her ears little golden drops that shine against her dark skin.

'Why was it different? I'm not arguing or trying to make you do anything. I don't even want to dance any more. I'm really just trying to understand.'

'It was another – time. Another era.' He shrugs.

So that was the arty living-in-Paris-with-a-Frenchwoman era, and this is the respectable travelling-with-the-wife era. Or does he mean he's older? He's thirty-three. Asya tries to imagine being thirty-three. What does it feel like to be thirty-three? She knows she should not go on asking him questions. Whatever she says now he will interpret as an attack – because he knows that for a moment she had wanted to get up and dance.

'Don't you feel like looking her up? Since you're in Paris, I mean?' She surprises herself as much as she does Saif by the question. The last time she had thought of Danielle she had had to fight down her jealousy: the pale, sad Parisienne living in the Latin Quarter, ill-treated by her Algerian boyfriend and comforting herself with Saif for the six months he'd stayed with her – she had seemed to embody all the romance of *La Bohème*. 'I mean, doesn't it feel at all odd to be here? With the rue de la Huchette just round the corner?'

He shakes his head. 'I don't think going back – to anything – is ever a good idea.'

Why are they here? Asya asks herself. Since the moment they met they have behaved like strangers – and why is she not jealous? She thinks back; she examines her jealousy. Maybe she hadn't been jealous of Danielle personally. She had seen her almost as a girl in a story. She had, come to think of it, always imagined her in period clothes, in costume: something pert and nostalgic and elegant; something out of Colette, or Katherine Mansfield. Very beautiful, fragile, with a simple chignon and a melodious voice. She'd even imagined her in a hat: black and velvety with a narrow brim which she wore tilted over her face. She had wanted to be her. That was it, she had envied her – not Saif – but her life; her life above a jazz joint in the rue de la Huchette, with her simplest action coloured by the notes of the clarinet escaping from the windows downstairs and spiralling up into the darkness. She hadn't really felt about her

399

as she'd felt about Didi Hashim –

Mario has come back. He pulls out the chair facing her and sits next to Saif. Since Saif had gone away there had been a slight shift in her relationship with Mario. It had really started after New Year's Eve – nothing big or noticeable from the outside; just that they only felt completely at ease together when Saif was there. If he left them for a few moments at a restaurant table they would lapse into silence until he returned, when they would both come back to life and resume the jokey, arguing banter his absence had interrupted. And then Saif had gone away. Gone away and left Mario clearly *in loco* – *in loco* what? *'maritus'*? And their reaction had been to draw further away from each other – to leave, for example, an empty seat between them when they went to the cinema. And yet, they sought each other out. If a day passed when they did not bump into each other in the library or in the coffee-bar, Asya would be likely to get a phone-call in the early evening saying, 'Let's have a drink,' or, 'Let's go eat somewhere,' and they would go, alone or with the others – but mostly alone. And they would talk about everything – everything in the whole world – except, of course, their own present selves. And Mario would walk her back to the college, or she would drop him off at his room, and their, 'Night!' was as casual as casual could be, and not once had either of them made an excuse to be alone with the other in a closed room.

Now Mario punches Saif on the shoulder as he sits down, and the two men grin – delighted to see each other again. Both are wearing jackets and woollen open-necked shirts with no tie. Saif's jacket is a beige tweed and Mario's is a grey corduroy. He leans over to take Saif's lighter, which is lying on the table, and lights a cigarette. Saif turns to Asya and brings his arm up to clap Mario on the shoulder.

'Mario'll dance with you,' he says.

Mario looks up at her, but Asya shakes her head.

'I don't want to dance. Not right now.'

William and Mina are threading their way back to the table.

'Why didn't you come out and dance?' asks Mina.

'Asya prefers to sit and look beautiful,' William says, sitting down next to her.

'She can still look beautiful out there,' Mina says, 'she's not a bloody statue.'

Mario turns to Saif. 'What do you think is going to happen in Saudi now?'

'Nothing at all,' Saif says. 'Prince Khalid has taken over. Nothing will happen.'

'Poor King Faisal, though,' says Asya.

'The less there are of those chaps the better,' William says.

'Why?' asks Asya.

400

'They're no good. They run the country like it's their private business. They're reactionary –'

'William, you simplify everything so. He wasn't particularly reactionary; he started girls' education, schools and –'

'Big deal. It was wrong that there was no education for girls in the first place –'

'You're sitting here in a Paris restaurant saying that. You have to judge him by the standards of his own country, and in those terms he was progressive. And it isn't like the populace was crying out for their women to be educated; he ran into a lot of opposition but he saw it through. And his wife has always been active in social affairs –'

'Which wife? Presumably he has several?'

'His main wife: Queen 'Iffat –'

'How easily you say that,' cries Mina. ' "His main wife". I'm surprised at you –'

'Well, it *is* the fact –'

'This is interesting,' says William. 'Asya believes in polygamy. You're OK then, mate.' He smiles at Saif.

'I don't "believe" in polygamy,' Asya says. 'But I don't condemn it out of hand, and –'

'What *do* you believe in, then?'

'What kind of a question is that?' Asya objects.

'It's a straightforward question. You're always sitting on the fence, saying "from *her* point of view" and "in *his* terms". What about *your* point of view? You'll have to come down on one side some time –'

'What on earth is the use of *me* coming down on one side or another about this? We're not talking about *me*. We're talking about an old king, born and bred in a country where it is the norm –'

'So if it's the norm, it's OK?'

'Come on, William,' Saif says.

'What about personal choice?' says William.

'If it's the norm, then I think we should start by accepting that it's the norm and not sneer at people for – for being part of it. Then, if we want, we can consider *why* it is the norm, what are the circumstances under which it became the norm, how come it continues to be –'

'So under certain circumstances you find polygamy acceptable?'

'Yes, of course.'

'But what about *you*? What about *your* feelings? You can't really be that indifferent. What about cannibalism?' Mina asks. 'Why shouldn't –'

'Hey, guys –' says Mario.

'I wouldn't judge a cannibal by criteria other than those of his own society.'

'Look, William,' says Saif, smiling, 'by Saudi lights you guys are guilty of one of the worst crimes possible: you're living together without being married. You could get a hundred lashes for that.'

'Except, of course,' puts in Asya, 'they would give you the option of getting married instead. Righting the wrong, you know.'

'It's not just Saudi lights,' Mina says. 'At home, in Iran, it would not be possible. But I made a choice, I made a decision –'

'Fine. Nobody's quarrelling with that.'

'But *you* don't make choices, Asya –'

'This is ridiculous –'

'Well, what choices have you made?'

Asya hesitates. Why *should* she trot out snippets of her life for them?

'I've made whatever choices I had to –'

'Like what?'

'Well, to go to the north of England, for example.'

'But that's not a choice –'

'Why not?'

'Because it's in line with your whole life. It isn't as though you'd suddenly decided to join Greenpeace, or go to an ashram –'

'A what?'

'An ashram.'

'It's a kind of transcendental commune – in India,' Saif explains to Asya, with a small smile.

'Oh. So for a decision to count in your book it has to be completely disruptive of whatever one has been doing up to then?'

'It's interesting that you use "disruptive". You see, you place such a high value on order that you unconsciously only take decisions which allow your life to continue along a particular path –'

'You are making a whole grand theory out of nothing. Most people's lives *do* go along a particular path, especially if they happen to start off doing what they want anyway.'

'But you don't like the work you're doing.'

'No, but I'd already undertaken to do it, and –'

' "Undertaken", you see, it's all duty –'

'But I had *chosen* it. Nobody had *forced* it on me –'

'You don't have to live with your choices for ever.'

'And by the time I'd found out why I don't like it, by the time I'd have been able to formulate some reasonable case for not wanting to do it, I'd already used up a year of my grant.'

'You could still have quit.'

'And *then* what? I'd have had two options: to start looking around for another project and another university – and think of all the explaining I'd have had to do, to my supervisor, to the Council, to the university at home – and besides, there's nothing else that I desperately want to do –'

'So you're carrying on with this by default.'

'*Or*, the second option would have been to go home, and that would have meant forgetting about a university career after having wasted a grant that somebody else could have had. The obvious thing is to carry on and get it done.'

'And that's what you really want, is it? A university career?'

'Yes, of course it is.'

'She's a wonderful teacher.' Saif smiles at Asya. 'All her students say so.'

'I can imagine,' laughs Mina. 'The big black eyes seeing into their souls.'

'I would have thought you knew more about eyes and souls than I do.' Asya smiles and reaches over for a piece of cheese.

There *had* been no other option. There still *is* no other option. And there is nothing wrong with finishing something you've begun. She can see Dada Zeina regarding her sceptically out of her one eye as Asya enthusiastically takes up a new piece of knitting or embroidery. 'You'll ruin your eyes over it for a couple of days and then you'll forget all about it. I know you.' And sure enough, after months of being moved off the dining-table for every meal, or being retrieved from under various seat cushions, the bit of fabric would find its way to the kitchen and a useful though short life as a polishing cloth or a shoe rag. And the violin lessons – but her teacher had been so awful; bending down till his thick dark glasses almost touched the music sheets and giving instructions out of a mouth round the corners of which residues of spittle gathered and foamed and assumed new shapes, till she could bear it no longer and stopped trying to learn the violin. But once when she was struggling through an incredibly dry book that her father had given her – *A History of the Arabs in the Land of Israel* – her mother had come upon her still on page eleven, miserably re-reading a particularly convoluted paragraph, and had gently taken the book from her and closed it. 'You don't *have* to finish it, you know. It's not a duty.' And she had been so relieved. It had seemed that her life and her leisure had been restored to her, spread before her, free and untrammelled. But work is different. Work *is* a duty. True, it had never seemed so before, but that was because she had been lucky. This time she had made a wrong choice and she was paying for it. There is no other way. And one day it will be over. And it's up to her to make that day come quickly. She had already extracted almost a thousand metaphors from a hundred poems, and maybe things will get more interesting when she starts to analyse them. The only problem she's had to face so far has been the metaphors that don't seem to deserve to be classed as 'imaginative fusions' but have not yet faded completely into 'normal' speech. She's sat for hours staring at them: '*Youth's the Season* made for joys,' 'Happy, thrice happy times in *silver age*', 'What time *soft Night* had silently begun', 'He disappeared in the *dead of winter*' – but

403

now she has created a category of 'moribund' metaphors, and into this she places them and lets them sleep –

'So you see,' says Mina, 'she was living in a dream world.'

'Who?' asks Asya.

'Barbara Stonehouse. Remember at New Year when you were convinced she had believed he was dead?'

'She *had* believed he was dead.'

'Yes, and you said how weird it would be if she'd been living with him and had no idea at all that he was planning to vanish – that he wanted to get out of their life completely?'

'She didn't know him at all, did she? She'd lost sight of him.'

'He was having it off with Sheila Buckley the whole time,' says William. 'It was obvious the minute you saw her picture in the paper.'

'And then there was this whole business of her flying out to Australia.'

'It must have been the last thing he wanted.'

Asya toys with Saif's lighter until he holds out his hand for it.

'Hey, hey!' says Mina catching Asya's hand. 'I haven't seen *this* before. Is it new?'

Asya looks down at her ring: little diamonds, emeralds, rubies and sapphires set in a curving branch of gold.

'Saif just got it for me.'

'And Asya, you've gone and changed your nail polish specially. I don't believe it.'

Mina shakes her head sorrowfully, then turns to Saif.

'It's fantastic. Wherever did you find it?'

'In Beirut – an old Armenian . . .'

He had thrown the ring into her lap. She had looked up and seen that wide boyish grin she so loves. The grin that says he is pleased with himself and waiting for her to be pleased too. And she had been. She had held the ring up and stared at it and exclaimed over every stone and asked for its story. It was old and bound to have a story. And he had told her about the Armenian and about how, somewhere in Beirut, there were the bracelet and the collar to go with it, and how it would take time to track them down but he would do it. For her. And he had said, 'Go on, put it on. Let's see.' And she had slipped it on to her finger, just above her wedding ring, and spread out her hand, and they'd both admired it, but her nail varnish was all wrong for it so she'd said she'd better change it. And she'd gone into the bathroom for her nail-varnish remover and the deep red varnish that would go with the rubies and the whole flamboyance of the ring, and then she'd come back and sat at the dressing-table and wondered whether when she'd finished her nails there would still be time – if they were going to – kiss, or anything, and then he'd switched on the television and she'd looked up and seen the picture of King Faisal Al-Saud and learnt that he'd been shot by his nephew Prince Musa'id. And she hadn't particularly cared for King Faisal – she had hardly thought about him since Black September – but she still felt it was terrible to be shot by your own nephew just as you were stepping forward to take him in your arms – imagine if she walked in on Khalu Hamid or Tante Soraya, and just as their faces were breaking into a smile of greeting she'd pulled a gun: look what would happen to their faces then – and then to die, without ever understanding or even quite realising what had happened. But after a few minutes she'd carried on wiping off the pink varnish she had put on in England yesterday, and then she'd painted on two coats of the red and one of the transparent gloss and sprayed them with the instant drying stuff that Mina had thought was so funny when she'd seen it in her bathroom but which was immensely practical. And now the ring was set off perfectly on her hand. She glances down at it again, and as she looks up she meets Mario's eye and he smiles. She smiles back and takes her hand off the table and hides it on her knee. Mario's smile is so wonderfully straightforward. Mina's smile says, I like you against my better judgment, which tells me you are a frivolous, conventional woman. William's smile says, I see through you – which of course he doesn't – and I fancy you, which is too horrid to be thought about. And Olympia, Olympia's smile says, I am smiling at you because that's what you expect and because I am brave but it's an effort because all the time what I'm really thinking about is the sadness of all things. But Mario's smile carries not a hint of mockery or irony or hidden meaning. Just a smile that says, it's OK. I like you and I'm smiling at you. Since Christmas she's been telling herself that behind the laughing eyes, the exuberant hair, the big, solid build, the ever so faint aroma of Italian in his English, there is just an ordinary, perhaps even potentially boring, guy – but she doesn't believe it. She prefers to believe that he is subtle and understanding and that the reason they have both steered clear of personal topics is precisely because he is subtle and understanding. She prefers to credit him with sympathetic perception – although it would be terrible if he perceived too much. Had it seemed odd to him that, after forty-four days apart, she and Saif should choose to meet, and spend their entire time, in the company of their friends? Nobody seemed to think it was odd. Saif had phoned and said, 'I'm going to have to be in Paris for about a week and then I'll come on to England. Why don't you come over?'

'Oh, yes, I'd love to. When –'

'I'm going to be very busy, Princess, so perhaps you could just come for a couple of days. Get Mario and come over. We can have two days together and then you go back and I'll follow you.'

'Oh. OK. I'll ask him.'

'Don't you want to come?'

'Oh, yes. Of course I do. It'll be fun.'

And she had asked Mario, and Mina and William had said they would come too, and they had all driven over in William's car and nobody thought there was anything odd about it. And maybe there isn't –

'Come on, come on, let's dance –' Mina jumps up. 'Come on, Asya. Come out.'

'No, really, I –'

'Come on, Asya, dance with me –'

William leans over her, and she leans back, away from him.

'No, I don't want –'

'OK. Come on, William.' Mina pulls William on to the floor.

Asya looks around the restaurant and avoids looking at Saif. Saif says, 'Go on, Mario, be a pal and dance with Asya.'

Asya turns to glare at Saif, but before she can say anything about why he should volunteer both of them like this, Mario has stood up. He stands waiting to pull her seat out for her and Asya stands up, smiles at him quickly and walks to the floor.

She is only grateful that Saif's seat faces the other way. For a moment on the floor she feels awkward. Hopping about to monkey music, he would be thinking. He's never liked the Stones. But she does. Not everything they've done, of course – but this is good. To dance to, anyway. Then she sees that he makes no attempt to turn or even look around. He leans back in his chair, and she can see the cigarette in the hand he raises; he is probably staring out of the small-paned window with the red curtains that had been behind her and thinking – what? Well, not of her – and not of this music – so what's the harm in dancing and enjoying it?

When the music changes Mario stops and she moves quickly into his arms before William can come over – and being in his arms is everything that she has remembered it, for three months, to be. She feels his hands settle gently on her back, and feels his warmth, and breathes in his scent of leather and tobacco and a hint of aftershave. She feels the soft ribbed corduroy under her fingertips . . .

Oh, now *this* would be something worth preparing for: the backbreaking two hours that she has spent over the *halawa*, the three hours on her hair, the mud-mask and the thirty minutes at the living-room table with her elbows planted in two halves of a lemon to make them silky soft, the careful pedicure, the nail varnish, the conditioner and perfume on the soft triangle of hair, the pretty underwear, the stockings – even while she was doing it all she'd told herself that it wasn't a waste of time, that she wasn't being ridiculous, that she was doing it for herself, because she gets miserable when she isn't pretty, that the most raddled of old women goes on doing these things out of self-respect and in case she dies suddenly – but still she'd felt absurd. What was the point of furnishing a room, of lighting candles and burning incense, if you were going to close the door and lock it until the candles had melted and the dust had settled once again over everything? Once she glances up at Mario and sees a face she does not know, a face stern and still like a statue's. She does not know what her own face looks like, but she does not let her cheek rest on his jacket or graze the roughness of his chin. She does not let her eyes close but keeps them firmly open and her head upright.

Later, as Saif reads and she, not feeling like going straight to bed, sits in the armchair by the window, she thinks of him. Is he thinking about her now? And if he is, what does he imagine she is doing, here, in her room, with his friend: her husband? She looks at Saif. He had not minded at all. Of course, there was nothing to mind – as far as anyone could see. They'd danced just that once and gone back to the table and Saif had looked up and said, 'Had enough, Princess?' and they had sat down and refused to get up again until it was time to leave. But there *was* a time when he would have minded. A time when even her just wearing a low-cut dress was guaranteed to make him miserable and beastly. But then *she* would have minded too. But she *still* minds. Even if she is no longer jealous of Danielle she is jealous of Didi Hashim. Didi Hashim – she thinks the name again and waits for the familiar pang that is sure to accompany it. It comes, but it is insubstantial and passing like a shadow. She calls it back and probes it: Didi Hashim who had deflowered herself astride him on a Queen Anne chair in her father's library; she imagines the scene in the darkened room and does not feel the sharp stab that used to make her spring up and stop imagining. She waits, but it does not come. She jabs at it, willing it to sting her: Didi leans forward, eyes closed, neck arching to be kissed. Saif takes off his glasses and feels for a nearby surface to put them on. His hand finds a mahogany wine-table and his knuckles scrape against a crystal ashtray as he puts the glasses down. He bends his head and puts his open lips to her neck. His hand comes round and slips under Didi's skirt to caress her smooth, braced bottom. Nothing. Nothing at all. They might as well be a Rodin statue.

Saif turns the page and looks up and into her eyes.

'What are you staring at, Princess?'

Asya shakes her head quickly. 'I'm not. Not really. I was just – thinking.'

'Ah.'

He turns back to his magazine and she turns to the window. She is no longer jealous of Didi Hashim.

Across the road the old walls of Cluny are bathed in golden flood-lights. When they had first checked into the hotel Saif had not yet arrived and she had gone up to her room and opened the window and seen these mellow square buildings – and she had not waited to unpack but had walked straight out again. In the clear spring day she had crossed the Boulevard Saint-Germain and wandered for a while through the ancient rooms of the abbey. Then, in one great hall, she had come upon the tapestries. She had not even known that they were here. It was as though somebody had prepared the most marvellous surprise for her, and she had felt her heart opening up in recognition and thanks. She had spent more than an hour in that dimly lit room and no one else had come in – no one at all. The tapestries were so much more faded, so much more subtle than any reproduction she had ever seen. The lady's face was so calm; pale and unseeing and tranquil, she knew exactly where she was and what she was doing. Or she did not know and did not care. The unicorn looked up at her tenderly. He must have been a baby unicorn; he was so small. Or were unicorns supposed to be small? No, because you are supposed to be able to ride them. He must have been a baby then. He looks up at the lady and lays his head in her lap, and her long white fingers caress him absently. A slim, white dog with a feathered tail and a wide embroidered collar sits self-consciously upright. A leopard with pointed ears elegantly turns a grinning face towards a bird standing motionless on a tree. A tethered monkey places his hand on his heart. All is serenity and order. She had thought of the fingers that wove these tapestries. Somebody – somebod*ies* – had spent a lifetime working on this. Somebody who'd known his place in the order of things. Somebody who, when the daylight had petered out, had gone home to a dark, cold cottage, to a loved or hated spouse and a brood of not particularly thriving children and a daily ration of soup and bread and longing and affection and despair and dreams, and had come back next morning to weave some more figures into this lastingly breathtaking model of harmony and decorum. But the rabbits: the rabbits are playful. They conduct their happy, fragile little lives in the corners of the tapestry; they frolic heedlessly between the paws of great, shield-bearing lions. One rabbit sits up on his hindquarters, his tail bobbed neatly under him, rubbing his soft nose and considering a nibble at a lion's tail which lies temptingly near. The rabbits are subversive. But they are only rabbits, when all is said and done –

'Sweetie, this is the fifth time you've hummed that tune.'

Asya stops, but it carries on in her head – 'no way to treat a lady, no, no way to treat your baby – your woman – your friend – That ain't no way to treat a lady, no, no way to treat your baby –' She turns to Saif.

'Let's go across to the abbey tomorrow. I want to show you something.'

'Sure,' he says. 'That's where the Lady and the Unicorn tapestries are, isn't it? I wouldn't mind seeing them.'

'Let's not go with everyone else, shall we? I don't really want to hear William going on about the society of privilege that made it possible for them to be woven, or Mina discoursing on the types of dye they used.'

Saif smiles. 'No. OK. We'll sneak off on our own.' He yawns and throws his magazine down on the floor. 'I'm going to get some sleep now. Do you want this light?'

'No. No, turn it off. I'll come to bed soon.'

When he switches off the light she turns back to the view outside. She knows that if she goes to bed nothing will happen, so she will wait until he knows that she knows it too so that he should not think that she is lying there waiting for him to touch her – so that she wouldn't, in fact, *be* lying there waiting for him to have a change of heart and reach out for her – so that she wouldn't, in a moment of despair, whisper to him to hold her, 'just for a moment'. She will never do that again.

One street-lamp shines outside their window. Across the road, the gardens of the abbey are deep, dark spaces between the lit-up walls. A yellow municipality car passes slowly through the empty street, spewing water and rotating its giant brushes.

Scene 4

Friday, 6 June 1975
Cairo

Dear Asya,

I got your postcard a few days ago – you certainly seem to be living it up: Paris in March, Vienna in May – you can't possibly be complaining that 'nothing is happening' in your life any more. Or can you? I remember the first time you complained that nothing 'interesting' happened in your life. You were eight. We had just settled into the Zamalek flat after the three years in London and you had just started at your new school and were making new friends and learning to read Arabic, and I found you sitting on your bed looking glum, and when I asked you what was the matter you said, 'I'm so bored. Nothing interesting ever happens in my life.' And how often since then have I heard you say that – oh dear! Well I suppose you should be all right now.

You don't say anything about what you actually did in Vienna. I

409

know Saif was at a conference, but what about you? Did you go to the Prater or the Woods or the Opera? You're right, the university building there is beautiful, and there *is* something different about a university with a dome – although you shouldn't judge where you are now by that: nobody is going to build universities with domes any more, probably mosques are the only things that will be built with domes from now on.

And Asya, dear, what about your work? You say it is going well but how far have you actually got with it? And what does Professor Murray think of it so far? I wish you would write to me about that in more detail. Are you aware that your grant runs out in September? I'm sure we can get you an Egyptian government grant to carry on but I really don't think you should take more than three years or so over a Ph.D. It will get stale on you – and besides, there is no need.

Here, we are knee-deep in exam papers. We are having to take in more and more students each year and the load is becoming really heavy – to say nothing of the standards, which are, needless to say, dropping fast. Since your father has left the Ministry he has put down a new set of criteria to limit the students coming into *his* department, but of course not every head of department is able – or willing – to do that, and we now have a situation where some classes are too big for the room in which they're held and some students have to sit outside and listen to the lecture over a loudspeaker. It is completely ridiculous.

Everybody is well and sends you their love. We had Meedo's birthday the other day and we were all there and we all remembered you and missed you. Tante Soraya is well and your uncle is very well, thank God: you would never think, to look at him and see the way he works, that he had gone through all these traumas. Nadia says he is in excellent shape, all things considered, and there is no particular reason to fear a recurrence of the disease.

Nadia herself is well and her baby son is great – although she and her husband are having some problems. I gather he wanted them to stay in the States – for ever. And of course she wouldn't, but now he blames her every time the lift doesn't work or a drain in the street overflows or he bumps his car in a pot-hole. Kareem has just started his first-year exams in college and of course he's going to do brilliantly well – although like all of you he hardly studies. Deena is fine and doing very well at college. She has, however, taken up with a young man whom I am not at all sure about. He is nice enough and genuine and all that but he is politically involved in a left-wing organisation and devotes all his time and energies to that, with the result that he is taking every year of college in two although he seems quite bright. And of course there is no reasoning with your sister; she can argue anyone into the ground. Do you remember when she was quite small how she used to take up impossible positions and argue vehemently for them? Do you remember when she was five and we asked her who had moved Daddy's pen (his *favourite* pen) from its usual place on his desk to the dining-room table, and she said, 'God.' And when your father pressed her she said, 'God is able to do anything, isn't He?'

'But why should God want to move my pen from the desk to the dining-table?'

'You should not question His motives. He knows best.'

He almost told her then and there that there was no God but he managed to keep hold of his temper. We're having lots of that kind of argument now, about how both Daddy and Khalu Hamid were active on the left. In a way she is right. And in a way I suppose when you are a parent you become more concerned about your children's welfare than about the general welfare. You become more limited. But I cannot help feeling that it will not be Muhsin Nur-el-Din and his friends who change the course of Egyptian history. They are too nice, too decent, too civilised. So, then, why don't I particularly welcome him as a son-in-law, she would ask. And the answer is that I foresee a lot of problems and hardships coming her way through being married to him. But she would say that problems and hardships of one sort or another come anyway – and so we would go on arguing round and round. However, Deena will have her own way, as you have done, and as Kareem will eventually do, and we shall have to help her as best we can and see what happens.

Speaking of sons-in-law, Saif (I'm sure you know) was in Cairo last week. He really looks flourishing. This has been a very good move for him: independence (together with success, of course) really suits him. He took me out to dinner at the Sheraton and was at his best: charming, witty, expansive and so on. Of course, he always knows best about everything, but I suppose he can be forgiven that for the present. I saw his mother at Groppi's the other day – she had come down from Heliopolis for some of their special clotted cream – and she sends her love and thanks you for the card you sent her on Mother's Day. She is worried about Saif being in Lebanon so often with all the fighting breaking out so frequently now, but he brushes it aside and seems to think that nothing can really affect life in Beirut – that the Lebanese will always do business.

I really ought to close now: I have hundreds of exam papers to get through. Chrissie came to see me the other day. She seems well enough but she's very tied down to her mother now – feels very responsible for her after Dr Sidki's death. She says Fuad is doing very well and that he expects, of course, to be busier than ever after the Canal is opened for shipping – although *I* understand there are quite a

411

few doubts about how profitable it will actually be now that world trade has been used to doing without it for eight years. However, they opened (re-opened) it yesterday amid much fanfare as you can imagine – on the anniversary of sixty-seven: *that* is supposed to be quite wiped out by the Heroic Crossing, and now this – never mind that Jerusalem, the West Bank, the Golan Heights and Sinai are still under occupation! However, at least the Canal is really there and not just a phantom like the New Opera House.

I saw Mimi the other day and she's pregnant again, and very happy and full of hope. Noora sends her love – she's looking quite strained these days and I gather Bassam is under a fair amount of pressure: they never know what will happen to them from one day to the next. You see, *that* is what I mean by opening yourself up to a particular type of problem – she has had to turn down the offer of a grant to do her Ph.D in England because he has been refused an entry visa and she does not want to separate him and the baby. But by the time he had been refused the visa it was too late for anyone else to make use of the grant, so that's a year's hard currency wasted for the department. Next year, though, we shall probably send two candidates, and one of them will be – guess who – your old friend Mahrous! He is so keen, that boy, and it must be said he is a very hard worker. He is already in correspondence with your university and might end up there and prove a great addition to your social life!

I really have to stop now, I'm giving this to the son of a friend who's travelling to London and he's just arrived to collect it. Write to me soon, darling, and keep well, and above all tell me what is happening with your WORK – much love,

Mummy

Scene 5

Sunday, 17 August 1975
London

It is a summer of flowered cotton dresses worn tight and low across the breasts, of wide-brimmed sun hats and pink and purple sandals, and temperatures in the thirties, and money and fast cars – Asya kisses Saif's cheek and climbs into the white Lancia next to Mario. Saif leans down to the open window.

'Bye, Princess. See you probably Friday.'

He raises his hand to Mario and stands back. The car moves away from the kerb. At the end of the road, as they wait for a break in the Sloane Street traffic, Asya turns round to look back: Saif is still standing on the pavement outside the hotel; his hands are in his pockets and he is looking after them. She waves at him one last time, and he waves back.

On Park Lane Mario glances round at her.

'Cheer up. It's only four days.'

'Oh, it's all right.' She smiles at him.

Asya looks – as she always does – at Victory in her chariot. She has always meant to come here on foot – to cross to the island and really look at this statue – but so far she never has. The tree outside the Dorchester is bright with fairy lights.

'Are you going to take the cottage?' Mario asks.

'I don't know . . .'

'It *is* a bit isolated.'

'It's not that. The flat is pretty isolated too.'

'Why not, then? You've admired it every time you've been there.'

And what about when *you've* been there, Asya wonders. Mina had teased him once: 'I thought you said you didn't fancy Jenny MacRae; what were you doing leaving her cottage at four in the morning? You were spotted.' He'd frowned and looked gloomy and eventually said, shortly, that he'd been drunk, and then he wouldn't be drawn further – and she'd noticed him politely avoiding Jenny after that –

'Oh, it's beautiful,' she says, 'but –'

He waits a little, then urges, 'But?'

'Well, it's a bit expensive – renting a whole cottage for just one person.'

'You're not one person.'

She looks at him quickly, but he is watching the road ahead.

'But Saif is hardly ever around. You know that. In the last six months he's only been up twice. Once for ten days and once for four.'

A short silence, and then he says, 'When he does come it will be more pleasant for him. He was saying he might get his mother to visit.'

'Yes, well, that *would* be nice.' Asya thinks of Tante Adeela in the cottage. The whole of the upstairs is one huge room, with a high, sloping, beamed roof and a wooden floor. One end is the living-room with a stove, a big black leather sofa and two armchairs and a fluffy cream rug, and the other end is the kitchen, all pine, with a long dining-table and two benches. Tante Adeela would take over the kitchen. They would light a fire and Asya would sit and listen to Tante Adeela and help her while she cooked. She could spread her work over half of the kitchen table. 'You would like my mother-in-law, Mario. Except –' She remembers. 'Mario, when do you get your results?'

'In two weeks.'

'And then?'

He spreads his hands for a moment, then closes them again over the steering-wheel.

'I don't know yet.'

'Will you go back to South Africa?'

'My father wants me to. This car, you see' – he makes a face – 'it's really a bribe.'

'You don't want to, do you?'

'I've taken the car.'

'No, seriously.'

'No. I don't want to.'

'Where *do* you want to be?'

He pauses.

'I think I might feel better living in Italy.'

Italy. Italy with Mario. That would be something. Sunshine, piazzas, statues, warm nights, fountains, this car – it would be like tonight, except that they would be driving towards some room where she would spend the night in his arms – except that at any moment she could reach out and touch his hand as it rests on the steering-wheel . . .

'You've lived in Italy quite a bit, haven't you?' she asks.

'Yes. But he has a right to want me to go back. There's the farm – the business. I'm his only son.'

'Of course.'

How can she think that so easily? '*Spend the night in his arms*'? Apart from everything else, what about the reason why it never worked out with Saif? What about the pain? What about being afraid of the pain? The only reason she doesn't think of the pain is that it's been almost twenty months since anything has happened to give her reason to think about it. She imagines herself in a strange bed, lying very still, rigid with fear, as Mario leans over her; his hand is on her breast – she sits up straight. Just thinking the words is enough to make the warm blood rush pulsing into

414

her breasts, her neck, her thighs; a delicious chaos. Where on earth does it all come from? One minute there is nothing, nothing at all, the next this torrent appears out of nowhere, no, not out of nowhere, but out of some kind of central depot that must be so vast and so deep that it can contain all this and even hide it for weeks at a time. She focuses on the world outside and finds that they've stopped. This is it: the last traffic-light in Finchley.

She looks at the clock and says, 'Shall we get the news?'

They both move forward and their fingers meet on the knob of the radio. They say, 'Oh, sorry,' and pull back. Then Mario leans forward again and switches the radio on. As he tunes in to Radio Four Asya sits well back in her corner, holding the back of her left hand which he has just touched. She is wearing a light cotton dress with wide shoulder-straps, and the leather of the seat feels smooth against her bare back and her arms. The night is so warm. Everyone keeps saying how hot the weather is, and how impossible it is to do any work, but she loves it. She had almost forgotten what it felt like to walk freely, not always tensing her whole self up against the cold. She tries to stop thinking about Mario, to stop thinking about how nice and warm she feels, and how the back of her left hand that he has just touched still feels – alive. On the radio there is more news about the killing of Sheikh Mujibur-Rahman. How terrible to be poor and in Bangladesh now . . . But her heart isn't in it. Her seat is pushed back as far as it will go and she stretches her legs out slowly. Her right knee is still a bit stiff with yesterday's bruise. She had tripped. Stupidly. Inexplicably – except maybe it was because she was still tired and shaky after the scene they'd had earlier in the day. But whatever the reason, getting out of the car on Long Acre she had found herself pitching forward. She had flung out her arms and landed on two hands and a knee at the feet of the two men waiting for her on the pavement. When she knew she was falling she had thought a great big oh no! of shame and embarrassment, but when her knee and her hands had touched the ground and she had felt the cuts start to burn into her she had mainly thought about the pain. She had instantly looked up and met Mario's eyes and seen in them an enormous tenderness, and looking into her eyes he had stepped back and put his hands behind his back – just like Rudolph Rassendyl had done, thus giving Rupert of Hentzau the perfect opportunity to stab him – and she had felt the tears rise to her eyes, and Saif, already bending over her leg, with a fresh white cotton handkerchief, had looked at her and said, 'You're not going to cry over a cut knee, Princess?' and as the tears had spilled over she'd held out her hands all hot and red and grazed and he'd said, 'Oh, it's your hands too. Poor Princess. Come on then, let's find you somewhere where you can wash.' And he'd helped her up, and as she'd limped down the street towards La Bussola where they were going to have dinner she'd hidden her face in his neck and sobbed for just a moment, and he'd turned to Mario and smiled. 'The first time I saw her she was coming down the library steps at Cairo University with a bandage on her knee.'

She leans her head back against the head-rest. At least that was the real version. So she'd known then that he remembered. But what if Mario meets Leon and Nicola again? What if they start talking about how they'd all met each other? She glances at Mario. Maybe he wouldn't remember. Maybe no one would remember – except her. She is stretched out comfortably, one foot crossed over the other, pretty in white sandals. But what does it matter? What's the use of being pretty anyway? So Professor Murray pays her the odd compliment out of Keats – stammers it out from the safety of his big desk – and then what? When she had gone to pick Saif up from some meeting on Friday and he'd been in the middle of a group of people whom she didn't know, he had said, 'You look great,' and stepped forward to kiss her, and she had been so startled she had stepped back, and outside he had been angry.

'What the hell did you do that for? What will they all think?'

'Nobody noticed. I was surprised, that's all.'

'You made me look stupid, going up to kiss my wife –'

'You only kiss me in front of people and then you're surprised when I'm surprised?'

She had ended up apologising, of course, but it was true. He only sees her when he sees other people seeing her – not for himself – not any more –

'They're amazing in this country,' says Mario. 'Every time they find out somebody has been ill-treated in jail everybody acts so surprised.'

'I'm sorry?'

'The Birmingham Six –'

'Oh, of course it will turn out they've done dreadful things to them –'

'But here people generally assume this doesn't happen. It's not part of their –'

'Do you think they actually torture people here, though?'

He shrugs.

'I mean – I guess there has to be a difference between kicking someone around when you've just caught him and systematically torturing him, you know, at a set hour every day?'

'I don't think they just kick them around when they've caught them.'

'But do you think they torture them? Actually *torture* them?'

'Maybe they don't use advanced technology, but they probably don't let them sleep, keep them in dark cells – things like that.'

'Yes. Oh, it's terrible –'

She looks out of the window. Even now, as they drive along this motorway, watching the red tail-lights of the cars in front of them, keeping their distance from the steel barrier that could in a second send them flying in a million scattered burning pieces all over these black fields, even now someone, somewhere, many people in many places – in Iran, for example, Mina's home – poor Mina, coming through the door all weeping and dishevelled. 'I'm leaving him, the bastard, I can't bear it, oh, I can't bear it!' Metamorphosing from a pale, composed, sorrowing lady in a Persian miniature into a screaming, distorted fury out of Greek theatre and back again. 'He's actually going to do it, the bastard, he's going to make his move tonight! Aaaaaaah!' She had screamed and thrown herself on the sofa while Asya, horrified, had sat beside her and held her hands –

'Why are you shaking your head?'

'Was I? Oh, I was just thinking of Mina.'

'She's having a bad time – but she seems to have agreed to William's proposal in the first place.'

'Yes, but now she thinks he made that proposal not out of some general idea that an "open" relationship was better for them, but because he fancied this particular woman.'

'Isn't that natural? I mean, isn't that when the need for an "open" relationship would become pressing?' Mario is smiling into his moustache.

'Yes. I suppose. And I don't know what he or they should do or anything – but I feel sorry for her, because normally she's so strong and together and – it's horrid to see her now –'

'What made you start thinking of her suddenly?'

'Well, I was thinking of torture, and so I thought of Iran and Savak, and so – Mario –'

What she had been about to ask was, is that part of why you would rather live in Italy than in South Africa, to be further away from all that? But then she feels it would be somehow indelicate, asking him to say something particularly horrible about his own country, and so she falls silent – but now, when she does not go on, he says, 'Yes?'

'I – I was wondering if we could have some music?'

He looks around at her in surprise. 'Music? Sure. Was that what you were going to say?'

If she had been with Saif he would have just been glad she had decided not to say what she had been going to say. He would have switched on the tape –

'Yes. No. I was going to ask if your preferring to live in Italy, you know, had something to do with – I mean, in South Africa you probably always have to be thinking of – things, don't you?'

'Yes. Yes, life in Italy would be simpler.'

'But one can't stop being involved with one's country just because one is living abroad, do you think?'

'I don't know. I have family in Italy. I've lived there for long stretches. I don't know. I'll probably go back, though. To South Africa.' After a moment he says, 'Do you want to choose a tape?'

'Can we have the radio?' she asks. 'That way we won't know what we're going to get.'

He'll probably go back and that'll be it and she'll never see him again. In two weeks. In two weeks he'll go back and she'll be all on her own again. She can't really count Mina and William as proper friends – friends she can feel comfortable with – and that was so even before this thing they're having now which is making it all so terrible. And even Olympia is finishing her course and leaving. But Mario – she leans on her door, even though she shouldn't, and looks at him. Mario has always been there. Even if days passed when they didn't meet she'd always known he was there. She watches his profile, lit only by the muted light from the dashboard. She looks for a word to describe his profile and she can only come up with 'rugged' which she can't use because it is so Mills and Boonish. Would she never, ever, hold that face in her hands? Trace the vein that she can't see now but that she knows is gently throbbing in his right temple? Feel those hands on her body once again? At Jenny's party, when everyone was dancing and they were the only ones sitting on the leather sofa with their drinks in their hands, she – made bold by red wine – had asked, 'Can't we just have *one*, just one dance?' And he'd looked into his glass and shaken his head and said, 'No.' Then he'd looked up and looked at her and said, 'No. Nothing, Asya. We're having nothing.' And he was right. Of course he is right.

'Sailing, we are sailing,
far awa-ay, across the sea,
We are sailing, stormy waters,
To be wi-ith you, to be free.
Can you hear me? Can you he-ear me –'

He is Saif's friend. They play squash and drink and talk and laugh together. And even though he saw what he saw yesterday, it would probably make him, as an honourable man, and he *is* an honourable man, step even further away. Of course, he would back off even further if he thought she was unhappy with his friend. They've bought identical cars, except Saif's is red and Mario's is white. Mario had already been in London, giving Frederick some things to take back to South Africa, and Asya and Saif had driven down in the red car and played tapes and stopped for Cokes and ice-creams, and at the Corby stop he'd said, 'You know, I think Ummu Salma is trying to seduce me.'

'How do you mean?'

'Well, she's always coming round. They've got a key, of course, and she's decided to do the cleaning for me. But she'll contrive to do it while I'm there. Or I'll come back at my normal time and find her washing the floor with her dress hitched up around her waist, and she'll just smile up at me and say, "No offence, brother Saif. I'll be finished in a minute." '

Asya had smiled, imagining the soignée Ummu Salma, perfectly made-up and coiffed, kneeling on the floor, barefoot, with a scrubbing-brush in her hand, her white knees surrounded by soapy water, Saif standing in the still open doorway with his key in one hand and his briefcase in the other: a scene from an Arabic film. In an Arabic film the camera would zoom in on his face, it would travel between the bare, spread knees on the floor, the woman's inviting smile and the man's eyes moving over her until, his face contorted with lust, he would step forward and kick the door shut as the camera closed in on it.

'So what do you do?'

'I either turn around and walk out again or I go and sit on the terrace with a book.'

'And then?'

'Nothing. She finishes and comes out and asks, "Is there anything else I can do for you, Mr Saif?" and I say, "You've left nothing undone, Sett Ummu Salma, may your bounty be increased, but there really is no need for this." And she goes.'

'Does her husband know?'

'Of course he does. I've asked him not to let her: "There is no need, Abu Salma. It pains me to see your wife washing my floor," but he twirls his moustache and says, "It is our duty, brother Saif. You are our guest. We are doing no more than our duty. After all, a man on his own" etc. etc. I'm going to have to move into a hotel. But I'll have to do it without offending them.'

'Aren't you tempted?'

'What?'

He'd stared at her.

'Well, she's very pretty and blonde.'

'She's enormous –'

'She's not enormous at all; she's attractively plump.'

He'd flashed her the grin. ' "If you can't lift it, don't screw it." '

'But hasn't it even crossed your mind to –'

'No,' he'd answered briefly, and she had known she shouldn't go on. But she'd wanted to ask, why not? Why hadn't he been tempted? She believed that he hadn't, but why? What is he doing about all that anyway? And how could he tell her a story like that, as though everything was normal between them? What was the sub-text? Some husbands don't mind their wives screwing other men? Is that what he's up to with her and Mario? Mario will dance with you, you go with Mario, bring Mario down and we'll have a weekend in Paris, we'll drive down together and then you go back with Mario – no. He'd been contemptuous of Abu Salma in the story, exaggerating the expansiveness and the Syrian accent – either

because he thought Abu Salma didn't suspect or because he thought he
did. Whichever. What, then? What was the unspoken message? Women
find me attractive? But she knows that. She's known it for seven years.
And why should he need to tell her? *She* isn't the reason they're not
sleeping together. Not any more. She can't be blamed for that any more.
She's done everything she could possibly do to show that she wants to –
wanted to – and she's stopped because he doesn't want to know. So what
was the point of that story? Could it be just a story – told on impulse,
signifying nothing? Couldn't it even be untrue? But what would be the
point of *that*? Wouldn't he know that it would set her thinking? And what
does he imagine *she* is doing about all that? Doesn't he realise that it's
been five years since she – to put it crudely – last came in his arms. She,
who used to want him every day, who used to describe the starbursts to
him four times in a row – what the hell does he think she's doing? Doing
it on her own? But she can't do it on her own; she's never learnt, nothing
happens for her when she tries except she feels a little bit ill. But what's
the use of putting it like that? Put it like that and it becomes a right,
something she can demand, something he is supposed to provide her
with, but that's not it. Sir, you and I have loved, but there's not it –

    '*Love*! Love will keep us toge-ther!
    Think of me Babe when-ever –'

    'Asya, are you all right?'
    'Yes. Why?'
    'You were shivering.'
    'I'm just getting a bit cold. No, don't close your window, it's still nice.
I've got something –' She reaches for the soft white cardigan lying on the
back seat and drapes it round her shoulders. 'There. That's fine now.'

    '*You*
    You belong to me, girl.
    Ain't gonna set you free –'

    'Mario, does Frederick mind about going back?'
    'No. I don't think so. He's never questioned it, anyway. There's a
Services coming up. Do you want to stop?'
    'No, I'm all right. Unless you want a break?'
    'No, I'm fine.'
    They speed on. She looks at the dashboard. He's doing a hundred.
Amazing how you can drive on these roads knowing for sure that you're
safe; that a pot-hole won't suddenly send you spinning off or a great big
rock wipe out your chassis. And this car is so smooth you don't even
know you're going fast. These Lancias are so different from her little
Morris. She'll take her on a run tomorrow just so she doesn't feel

420

neglected. Poor little car. Only gets taken out to do the shopping nowadays. And there isn't that much shopping when Saif's not around.'

'When do you think *you'll* finish?' Mario asks suddenly.

'Me? Another year and a half at least. I've really only been working properly since September and – things keep slowing me down.'

'It must be very hard working on a Ph.D. I could never do it.'

'It's not difficult. It's just weird – working all on your own on one little thing all the time. It's – you kind of have to think it's terribly important.'

'Isn't it?'

'No. Not really. I mean, if I were trying to discover a new vaccine, or invent something, or write a book, then I guess it would feel OK. But I'm going to sit there working on my metaphors day after day for three years, and then I'll finish and do the viva and the world will be just the same.'

She can see him smile in the darkness.

'Asya. You want the *world* to change?'

'Well, you know what I mean. I'm not mad or anything, but the world *does* change through the act of one person –'

'Napoleon?'

'Your Dr Christian Barnard, for example.'

'True. But behind him there are teams and teams of back-up guys. People who –'

'I know. But I don't want to *be* a back-up guy. Is that terrible? It's why I didn't go to another university and do yet another literary thesis on Milton's Lucifer or something. I wanted to do something radically new.'

'But this *is* new, what you're doing, isn't it?'

'Yes, it's new. But it just doesn't feel important. Maybe it's because I'm working so completely on my own –'

'But you see your supervisor –'

'Yes, I do. Every two weeks. And he is totally conscientious and goes through every single sentence I write – but I don't feel we're embarked upon a perilous voyage of discovery exactly.' She smiles, thinking of the now familiar awkwardness of those fortnightly tutorials and how it always feels as if she *has* arrived at the end of a perilous voyage when she walks out of the office and closes the door quietly behind her. 'If Mina could hear me now, she'd really despise me.'

Mario smiles, discounting Mina with a gesture of his hand.

'She's OK though, really,' Asya says. 'It's William I don't think I like. Not because of now – from before.'

'He's a smart-ass.'

'He walks around with this ready-made framework and he's always trying to fit everything into it.'

'Isn't that Marxism?'

'I don't think so. It could be anything. It's just the way his mind works –"

421

'Lay your head
Upon my pillow
Lay your warm and gentle body –'

The sad voice fills the car. This is the song that was on when she and
Saif had started to quarrel yesterday – the only quarrel they've had in
front of Mario. She glances at him. But he hadn't been in their car so he
wouldn't know about the song, and he hadn't, of course, mentioned what
he'd seen or heard. And he wouldn't. Not the roundabout with Victory
gleaming in the sunlight, nor the scene under the gazes of the stately
white Belgravia houses. He had been in his car, following behind, when
their quarrel broke out, but he can't have known anything was wrong
until the roundabout – and even then he couldn't have been sure. It must
have been only when he came up to them in Belgrave Terrace that he'd
realised they were fighting. But they had started earlier.

On Shaftesbury Avenue Saif had said, 'Leon told me the oddest thing
today. He said he and Nicola were involved in wife-swapping.'

Asya's first thought had been to wonder if this was true.

'No! Really?' she'd said.

'Yeah. They seem to have been doing it for a while: two or three years.'

Asya had reflected on this. 'Well, I suppose it's not so surprising
really.'

'No?'

'No. I think, since we met them together in London six years ago –
well, I've always thought they were dissatisfied with each other –'

Watch it there, just watch it, she'd thought, and then he'd said lightly,
'Leon asked today if we'd be interested.'

He hadn't looked at her; he was concentrating on the road but she'd
forgotten all about her navigation.

'And?' she had prompted him.

'And what?'

'And what did *you* say?'

'I said no, of course – nicely. That you'd never be interested in a thing
like that.'

'I wouldn't?'

'Of course you wouldn't.'

'How do you know?' She had said it as gently and non-combatively as
she could; trying to make it sound like a simple question rather than a
statement and a challenge.

'What do you mean, "How do you know"?'

'Well, how *do* you, in fact, know? We've never talked about anything
like that –'

Oh, she should stop this, she had thought: it will lead nowhere at all
except to anger and silence, and they have to stay together for the rest of

422

today and most of tomorrow, and anyway she wouldn't want to go anywhere *near* Leon –

'You want me to ask you if you're interested in wife-swapping? Are you serious? I don't believe you. I'm to come home and say "Would you be interested in a bit of *wife-swapping*"?'

His voice had risen on the compound noun and Asya's voice in response had become more reasonable, more measured.

'Well, you could say, "Leon and Nicola were wondering whether we might want to exchange partners for a few hours. I said no. You wouldn't, would you?" ' She is goading him now, and he is silent at the wheel and she daren't look at him, but she goes on, 'And anyway, why should it be called "*wife*-swapping"? I think the presuppositions underlying that term –'

'Which road?'

'Pardon?'

'Which road should I take?'

His voice had been clipped and cold and furious.

'Oh' – she had looked around her: they were on the Hyde Park Corner roundabout – 'I don't know . . .'

'You're navigating.'

'But we hadn't decided where we're going – where *are* we going?'

'You tell me.'

'Saif, don't go round again –'

'Tell me which road then –'

'But I don't know where you want to go –'

'. . .'

'Saif, will you *answer* me?'

'Which road?'

'I don't *know* – please don't go round again –'

'I'm going round this roundabout till you tell me which road to take.'

He'd put out his hand and switched on the radio.

'– to count the bridges,
That we're burning.
Lay your head –'

'This is *stupid*,' she'd shouted, and then sat back. OK. If he could drive round and round Hyde Park Corner like this she was going to sit there and let him. What did it matter? He was bound to stop at some point. He was the one who was driving. She could easily outsit him.

'And just pretend you love me,
One more time,
For the good times –'

On their fourth time round she had said, 'Mario is behind us, remember?'

He had not answered.

Trying to back off, she'd said, 'Why are you so angry with me anyway? I didn't say I *wanted* to do anything; only that I couldn't see how you would know whether I wanted to or not. Saif?'

'. . .'

'Saif, will you answer me please?'

'. . .'

'Saif, you know I hate it, *hate it*, when you do this. It's like you're *dead*. Saif, I don't want to fight with you, but if we *are* fighting, let's *fight* –'

Even now the tears come to her eyes as she thinks of how he can sit like a statue and be completely closed to her. She leans back in her seat and closes her eyes.

'– if you're angry, tell me *why* you're angry, don't just – oh *please* stop going round this lousy roundabout –'

'Which road?'

Mario had left the roundabout; she had seen him take a left and seen his rear lights turn red as he had braked. He must have parked. When they'd gone round again, she'd said, 'OK. Left here, *left*,' and as the car swerved she'd started to cry. 'Why do you do this to me? How *can* you do this to me? The only reason you can *do* this is because I love you – I don't go round quarrelling with people or caring what they think; the only reason you can do this to me is because I care –'

Now she turns her face, eyes closed, towards the window, and bites her lip.

'– But *you* don't care. You don't care about me one bit as long as I don't bug you. I could drop dead or take a lover or anything and you wouldn't care –'

'You won't drop dead and you won't take a lover.'

'And that's something else you know, is it? Why *should* you assume you know everything about me? Everything about how I'll react to anything? Particularly given the – given that it isn't something we've ever talked about –'

'You're bloody right we've never talked about it –'

'Well, why not? Why *not*? Why do we never talk about *anything*?'

He had pulled the car in next to the kerb in front of Mario's and turned to look at her.

'There are things that decent people don't talk about.'

She'd stared at him. 'This isn't true – I'm not hearing this – since when do you think in this way? This wasn't even the case at my parents' lunch-table, and I thought *that* was repressive. I thought I was walking out to freedom – you read Jean Genet and Strindberg and you tell me there are things decent people don't talk about?'

424

'I've had enough of this,' he had said, and climbed out of the car, slamming his door shut. But Asya had sprung out of her door and faced him across their red bonnet as Mario walked up from his car, looking puzzled.

'*Wait*, please wait. Are you serious? Are you saying that it isn't just a matter of being busy and preoccupied and wanting things told to you – if they *have* to be told to you at all – in a *nutshell* – are you saying that there are subjects that you and I *cannot* discuss, *ever*?'

'Yes,' he had said, and pushed his hands deep into his pockets. 'And if you *were* to take a lover, I would expect you to at least have the decency not to tell me about it.'

'Oh!' she had whispered. 'Oh!'

'And now I've really had enough. Would you please get into Mario's car and let us go and get some lunch.'

'No,' she'd said, 'I'm not getting into Mario's car.' How rude, how terrible, but Mario was already walking away towards his car, lighting a cigarette.

'Asya, I don't want you with me.'

'*I'm not going.*'

'Then *I* am,' he'd said. And he had walked to the white Lancia and got into the passenger seat and closed the door, and she'd wanted to run after him and pull open his door and pull him out and scream at him and cry and say she was sorry, oh, sorry, but please could he say he hadn't meant it – but she hadn't. She had gone on standing in the road with her hands on the bonnet, and Mario had come over and put his arm around her shoulders and said, 'Hey, take it easy. He doesn't mean any of it.'

'He does, he does,' she'd wept.

'No, he doesn't. How can he? Oh, Asya, you're being so silly –'

And she'd disloyally said, 'He does, he does, it's all he wants, just to skim over the surface of things, never *ever* to *look* –'

Mario had squeezed her shoulders. 'Have you got a handkerchief? Here, take this –' And he had dug out a large, crumpled white handkerchief from his pocket and given it to her and waited. 'You're going to stop now. OK? Yes?'

She'd nodded: after all, what had *he* done to find himself in the middle of this?

'Will you be able to drive?' he had asked.

'Oh, yes.' She'd blown her nose.

'Come on, then. Get in. We'll go to Luba's, OK? We'll see you there. You'll be all right?'

She'd nodded and he'd closed the car door on her and given it two quick pats as though he were urging a horse into a trot. She had driven to Luba's and sat through lunch, but she had felt tired. So tired that after lunch she had gone to their hotel and slept until evening . . .

When she opens her eyes, Mario is leaning back against his door. There is a cigarette between his lips; she sees its tip glow in the darkness, then fade as he moves it away. She knows he is looking at her. Behind him she can see the lights of the porters' lodge.

'Oh, I'm sorry,' she says quietly, without moving. 'I'm sorry.'

'Why? Why are you sorry?' he asks gently.

'I fell asleep. I let you drive all this way alone –' She sits up.

'That was OK –'

'How long have you been sitting here – waiting for me –'

'We've only just arrived. When I switched off the engine you woke up.' Asya smiles. 'I didn't snore, did I?'

'You didn't snore.' He smiles back. 'Do you usually?'

'No. But I talk.'

'In your sleep?'

'Yes. And I answer if you speak to me. What's the time?'

'Eleven.'

'We'd better go.'

'Come on, I'll carry your bag up for you.'

'It isn't heavy –'

'Come on.'

They go up in the lift to the fourth floor. In the dark passage Asya takes out the key to the maths department and unlocks the door. She stands aside to let Mario go through, then follows him, locking the door behind them. He walks ahead through the dark corridor, opening the heavy fire-doors one after the other for her to pass through.

'Don't they have any lights here?'

'They do, but you can't switch them off at the end of the corridor. Oh, I'm so glad you're here. I hate this bit.'

The last door he pulls won't open, and she says, 'This one is locked.'

He stands aside and she unlocks it, and when they've passed she locks it again from the other side and takes a deep breath.

'It's so horrible, especially with all those doors; each one of them I think is going to swing open and something really gross will come through, but the worst is that bit where they have the chairs and the coffee – I always *know* there will be something standing there, just waiting – and of course I've locked myself in *with* it –'

They climb the last flight of stairs.

'Then take the cottage,' he says as she picks out the key to her flat and turns it in the lock.

'Yes, I know. I think I will. I'll talk to Jenny tomorrow.'

He carries her bag through and puts it down just inside the bedroom door. Asya switches on the table-lamp and opens the window. When she turns he is still standing in the middle of the small living-room. She looks around at the room. She'd thrown some shawls over the sofa and the armchair to make them look less institutional. Her work is spread out on the dining-table.

'It's not too bad once you're up here, really –'

'No. Not at all. Are these your metaphors?'

Of course, he's only been here when Saif's been here and the table was used for eating, or when she'd made dinner for him and the others. Otherwise he'd picked her up at the door or downstairs to take her somewhere. He'd never seen these before.

'Yes,' she says, and looks down from the other side of the table at the orderly piles of pink, green and blue record-cards, each covered with her small, uncertain writing – she doesn't have a handwriting, not really; her letters slope sometimes this way and sometimes that; sometimes they slope so much they seem to be lying down on the line and sometimes they stand up stiff and straight like little toy soldiers –

'So you sit up here all day arranging these cards.'

'Well, there's a bit more to it than "arranging these cards",' she smiles, 'but yes. I do. And sometimes after a whole day up here sorting out "soft nights", "bitter words" and "tender looks" I feel I'm the only person in the world.'

When a minute or so has passed in silence, she says, 'Mario, shall I make you some coffee? And there's some cheese and biscuits. Or if you'd like a drink I've got some Martini, I think –'

'No. No, I'm going.'

But he stands and looks out of the window, so she empties the kettle, puts some fresh water into it and switches it on. Its faint hiss covers the silence. What is he waiting for? What is he thinking? She doesn't want him to go. Oh, please, she doesn't want him to go. She wants him to stay, nice and big and strong and warm, to stay here with her. Not – not to – he could just put his arms around her, hold her and make her feel – held, again. What if she were to walk round the table and put her arms around *him* and rest her face against that strong, broad back? Of course, she won't *do* it, but what would –

'You do this to yourself, you know.' He turns to her. He seems almost angry. 'You don't have to be up here all the time. You had a cubicle in the library. Why did you leave it?'

'Oh, Mario!' She laughs. 'I'll tell you: there was a chap in the cubicle next to me and he spat all the time.'

Now the brooding, gloomy look has gone from his face. 'He *what?*'

'He did, honestly. He'd cough and hawk, and then spit. And then sometimes he'd cough and hawk and then – nothing. And I'd find myself sitting there waiting for him to spit. So –'

He's laughing now, throwing back his head and laughing.

'Asya. It's *you*. You would always find something –'

'I know. I know I would.' The kettle switches itself off. 'The kettle's

427

boiled if you want that coffee.'

'No. I'm really going.' He walks round the table and towards the door. Just inside the door he stops and looks at her as she stands with her hand on the steaming kettle. 'Are you going to be all right?'

'Yes, of course.'

He still looks at her.

'Goodnight then.'

'Goodnight, Mario.' He turns to go. 'And Mario –' He turns back to her. 'Thank you.'

He waves a dismissive hand and disappears into her hall. She hears her front door close.

Even though she is not cold she fills a hot-water bottle. She wraps it in a white fluffy towel and takes it to bed and holds it close. If he had stayed – but no – but there's no harm in just *thinking* about it. Lying in bed she remembers Tante Mohga, her father's younger sister. Her husband had died, seven years ago now. They'd been married ten years and had two little girls. He'd got cancer. She'd nursed him at home; there wasn't anything else to be done. And he'd died. It had taken two months. She remembers Tante Mohga the day he died and they took him away. She was – distraught. Not screaming, but sort of gasping – and tearing her hair and slapping her face and being sick all over the place, and they'd given her some injection and put her to bed and Daddy had said sit with her: sit with her and touch her. Keep touching her. And she didn't have any mourning nighties, and they'd just put one of her ordinary nighties on; it was pale blue and very open at the neck, and her chest had been white and cushiony, and she'd tossed and turned and writhed in the big bed that he'd just died in, and moaned and called out for him, and complained that he was alone and she was alone, and Asya had held on to her hands and rubbed her neck and her shoulders and patted her head and cried and cried, even though somewhere in a corner of her heart she was thinking that when Mummy took over she'd be able to get away and meet Saif briefly while her father was occupied here. And later she'd asked her father why he'd said to keep touching Tante Mohga, and he'd said that it was only through touch that we really knew things, that it was only by other people's touching us that we knew we were here at all – and Tante Mohga had to remember, had to know that she was still here or she'd be lost. But Tante Mohga was alone. Really alone. Her husband was dead. But she mustn't think about death. Not death. Think about something else. Metaphors. No. Mario –

When the phone rings she jumps out of bed and runs to it.

'You OK, Princess?'

'Yes, darling, I'm fine.'

'Did I wake you?'

428

'No, I wasn't asleep.'

'I just wanted to know you'd got back OK.'

'Yes. Yes, we got back at eleven. Where did you have dinner?'

'Oh, I just had a sandwich in the bar. I'll see you Friday then, Princess.'

'Yes. You will take care, won't you?'

'Yes, of course. Will you take Jenny's cottage?'

'Yes.'

'Good. How soon can you move in?'

'I don't know. I have to speak to her tomorrow –'

'She was saying she's leaving Friday.'

'Yes –'

'Why don't you move in Friday? Get some delivery men to move your stuff and I'll help you sort it out when I come up.'

'This flat is paid for till the end of the summer vac –'

'Blow that. I don't want you spending the summer locked up there.'

'Well, if you think –'

'Yes. Move in Friday, then we can spend a few days there together before I go.'

'OK.'

'You'll do it?'

'Yes.'

'Good girl. You'll go to bed now?'

'Yes I will.'

'Goodnight, then.'

'Goodnight, darling.'

As she curls up on her side with her hot-water bottle she remembers the princess in the glass case. Yesterday morning, while Saif was at his meeting with Leon and someone from Univac, she'd gone to the British Museum. She'd looked at all the statues she knew so well, then she'd gone upstairs. She'd always hurried past the mummies, just seeing the rigid, bandaged forms out of the corner of her eye – but yesterday she'd decided to look. And she had found her. A woman lying curled up on her left side, her knees drawn up to her chest, her right foot crossed delicately over her left. Her left hand shields her eyes, her right is held up as though to ward off a throng of paparazzi. Next to her are placed what must have been her favourite, her most often worn jewels: a bracelet of turquoises set in gold, a pair of gold-leaf dangly earrings and a golden amulet. Asya had gazed and gazed at her. Despite that raised right hand she does not feel she would have minded her standing there. And she feels none of the distancing terror she'd felt for the mummies glimpsed in passing, but a sympathetic, sorrowing friendliness. My ancestor, my sister. The label said she was an unidentified woman who had died young. But Asya thinks of her as the Princess.

Scene 6

6 October 1975

The North of England

Waking up in the cottage is quite different. The bedroom – even though all it has is the double bed, a small bedside table with a tall mirror on top, and a built-in wardrobe – seems more like a proper room. When she gets up and walks out into the hall she will find letters on the mat. When she wants some air she will simply open her front door, cross the little dirt path and sit on the low wall looking down at the tiny stream that runs not five yards from her door. Even the cold here is more congenial than the campus cold. She takes pleasure in standing on the path in her old coat looking at the fields to right and to left, listening to the little stream burbling over its pebbly bed. She fetches in wood for the stove. She stands outside and washes both the red Lancia and the white Morris without shivering or hunching up. Now she only goes to the university to meet her supervisor or to check something out in the library or to use the sauna or the gym. She parks near the department or the library or the Indoor Rec. and never goes near the spine any more.

She stretches her arms out as far as they will go and straightens out on to her back under the covers. Eight o'clock. She switches on the lamp beside her bed. She could make some tea and bring it back to bed – or she could get up and start working. Her cards and papers are laid out over half the kitchen table and in one corner of the living-room floor. She has been working so much better since she's been in the cottage. All her parameters are now set up and she has started to classify her metaphors. One thousand seven hundred and fifty metaphors. One category is easy: Time. They divide into that by themselves. Today she will start on the 'simple to complex' paradigm. She shouldn't run into too many problems there. One occurrence of a transfer of linguistic features from a vehicle to a tenor: simple metaphor. Another occurrence of a transfer between the same items: extended metaphor. An occurrence of a transfer from a different vehicle on to the same tenor: complex meta-phor. She stretches again. What else? What else today?

She sits up, swings her legs out of bed and strokes as she does every morning the fluffy white carpet with her bare toes. She puts on her woollen dressing-gown and goes into the hall. The carpet in the hall is dark blue, and lying on it, just behind the front door, is a pale blue airmail envelope. Saif always uses grey. Asya picks up the envelope and turns it over. It's from Chrissie. Ah, so *that's* the treat for today. It does not even occur to Asya to sit down and open it and read it straight away

430

as, for instance, her mother would have done. Her mother would not only have read her own letters straight away but would have been annoyed by Asya's refusal to read hers. Asya puts the letter down on the third step of the stairs. She will read it tonight. After she can't possibly work any more; after her warm shower and getting into her nightie and brushing her hair and filling her hot-water bottle, she'll make one last cup of tea and sit down in front of the dying fire and read Chrissie's letter. And even if it's short – she picks it up again and feels it: no, it's not, it's got two, maybe three pages in there – it will have news of everyone and one of the odd little drawings Chrissie always puts in for her. If she reads it now it will be over in ten minutes and the day will empty out again and leave her nothing but metaphors; if she leaves it she will have something to look forward to; something to mark the end of the day.

As she gets dressed she wonders if Mario will come again today. Yes, she is sure he will come back. Tonight. Last night he had knocked on her door just as she had finished work and was arranging her papers for today. Standing in the dark outside her door in his worn brown leather jacket he had asked if she'd eaten yet.

'No.'

'Come on, then. Let's go and eat.'

'I could feed you here. I've got –'

'No, no. Let's go out. Come on. Put on a coat and come.'

And she had put on a coat and shawl and taken two minutes to apply mascara, lip-gloss and perfume, and run out to the waiting car.

They had gone to the big barn-turned-restaurant and sat in front of the huge fire and eaten steaks and apple crumble and not spoken very much, but she had asked if he'd decided yet what he was going to do – she had asked that maybe once a week now since his results had come out at the beginning of September – and again he'd shaken his head silently. But then he'd nodded and said, more to himself than to her, 'Soon.'

Back at the cottage he had simply followed her in, taken off his jacket and his scarf and walked behind her up the stairs to the living-room and sat down in one of the armchairs. She had put a whisky with ice in his hand and stoked up the stove and switched on her tape.

'I kissed you in the morning
Your kisses deep and warm
Your hair upon my pillow –
Like a sleepy golden storm –'

She had made herself a coffee and sat down in the other armchair. She knew that she had deliberately avoided the sofa with its possible implied invitation – but had he? They had both sat and watched the fire crackle to life in the black stove.

431

'But let's not talk of love or change
Or things we can't untie
Hey, that's no way –'

Twice he had seemed to be about to speak. And once he had stood up and walked to the window and leaned on the broad sill looking out straight ahead towards the little rippling stream which he could not see but which he knew was there. And the song had seemed to her suddenly in bad taste, like the sofa, a setting of the scene. So she had switched off the tape, but the sudden silence was worse – was too blatantly expectant, waiting to be filled, so then she had put on one of her four lyric-less records, Mozart's Bassoon Concerto, and then turned it right down, but he had said, 'That's good. I like that,' so she had turned it up again and gone back to her chair and sat there holding her coffee in her hand and watching him and the fire. Watching him as he turned from the dark window and went back to his chair; watching the glow of the fire playing on his face; watching him run his fingers through his thick, springy, untidy hair and bite the end of his moustache and frown at the stove as though he were waiting for it to do something. She too had said nothing. What could she say?

And then, at eleven, the phone had rung, and she had run downstairs to answer it.

'Sweetie!'

'Saif! Hi!'

She knew her voice would carry – up the stairs and into the living-room – but she would not whisper.

'Hi! Are you OK?'

'Yes, I'm fine. Where are you? In Damascus?'

'No. I'm in Athens. Just for one day. How's your work?'

'It's fine. It's OK. How's yours?'

'OK. Pretty good. Were you asleep? I tried you earlier –'

'No. No. I went out – to dinner.'

'Oh. Good. How's the cottage working out?'

'Brilliantly. It's very nice.'

'I'm looking forward to being there again.'

'When do you think –'

'Christmas. If not before. But definitely Christmas. Listen, will you do something for me?'

'Of course.'

'Phone Fred Langley and tell him I'm working on that paper. It's a bit late but he should have it in two weeks. OK?'

'Yes. I'll call him tomorrow. Saif, you're not going to Beirut any more, are you? I've been so worried –'

432

'No. No. It's impossible now. I'm afraid you'll have to wait a while for your bracelet and collar, Princess.'

'Oh, that's all right. I was just worried –'

'No, there's nothing to do there now, anyway. Listen. Is Mario still around?'

'Yes.'

'What the hell's he playing at? He's been finished for over a month now.'

'I don't know.'

'Well, when you see him –'

'He's here, actually.'

'What! Well, tell him I won. He owes me.'

'What? Won what?'

'I told him Niki Lauda would – no, listen, put him on.'

She had called out to Mario, then gone upstairs and listened to him talking and laughing with his friend across all the countries of Europe. 'You win,' he'd said, 'you son-of-a-bitch, you were right.' 'Yeah, I'll think about it,' he said later, 'I'll think about it.' And then, 'I will. Sure. And you.'

He had gone into the bathroom, and then she had heard him walk up the stairs. He had stopped at the kitchen end of the room and put his empty glass down on the table. Across the room he had looked at her and said, 'I'm going,' and she had followed him down the stairs. In the hall, with his jacket on and his scarf over his shoulder, he had turned, and she had found herself in his arms. A great big bear-hug. A hug into which she could gladly have vanished, and then she thought she'd heard him whisper her name, and his mouth was on her forehead and on her temples and on her eyes, and even as she felt his arms tighten around her and her heart accelerate he put her away. Stepped away from her, opened the front door and was gone. And what could she do? Open the door and run out after him? That had been her impulse: to run after him, to open the door, to catch him, to hold on to his arm and beg him to stay, oh, stay, stay, or I'll come with you – but then what? *Then* what? It would have been too ridiculous. But would he come back? Today? But then what, too? Last night she had not let herself sit down on the stairs. She had not let herself lean against the door he had just closed behind him. She had not let herself stand in the dim hall feeling lost and alone and so tiny that she was hardly there. She had climbed the stairs and put his glass and her cup into the sink and lifted the needle off the now silently spinning record and switched off the record-player and done everything she should, and not let herself sit down and think at all until she was safely in bed with her hot-water bottle, and even then she read some more of *Anna Karenina* until she fell asleep. But would he come back today?

She looks up from her metaphors. She is hungry. It must be time for lunch. She looks at her watch. A quarter to twelve. Should she eat now? But then her siesta would be too early and the afternoon would – no, one more. Dip in and take one more:

'A little flower of love
  Is ours without a root
  Without the end of fruit
But take the scent thereof.'

'Here are four primary syntactic units which can be represented as (love is a flower), (love has roots), (love produces fruit) and (love has scent). Putting aside the question of whether we should search for specific tenors for "roots", "fruit" and "scent", it seems evident that the three last units reinforce the first semantic transfer (love:flower) by expressing statements implied by it, e.g. (x:flower) implies (x has roots) etc. This is fairly common in extended metaphor. The rules of implicature determine how we interpret the metaphor
e.g. since Semantic Transfer 1 d (love:flower)
which implies (love has roots)
we interpret Semantic Transfer 2 d (love:ø ‹ø.HAVE.roots›)
as (love:flower‹which has roots›
rather than (love:anything else‹which has roots›) – like a pumpkin or a cabbage –' which isn't so ridiculous anyway: 'my vegetable love would grow / vaster than empires and more slow'. Asya puts down her pencil. Well – what this will do is teach machines how to interpret metaphor. That's about it.

But she still feels good. She stretches and gets up to stand at the kitchen window and think about lunch. She feels good and full of life and waiting for something to happen. Not as energetic as she had felt yesterday, when she had done a few little jumps in the kitchen for no reason and then hopped down the stairs and put on her coat and her furry boots and her thick gloves and run out to get some logs. She is so proud when she surveys the rows of logs she has arranged tidily along the wall in the garage. And yesterday, when she'd looked over at the pile of logs that are too big for her stove, she had decided to start chopping some immediately, and soon she had been hard at work. She'd jammed the log as she has learnt to between the low wall bordering the stream and the conveniently near tree-stump, and, holding it steady with her foot, she'd raised her axe and started to hack it. Within minutes she'd been so hot that she had straightened up, thrown off her coat and, in her best lumberjack manner, wiped her brow with her forearm and filled her lungs with air. Asya smiles at her self of yesterday. She likes it here. While at the university she had always hankered after Cairo, had missed the hot weather, the sounds of the street, the views from the windows,

434

the company of her friends and her family; now that she is out here she delights in the very differences between this set-up and every set-up she has ever known. She likes the cold – as long as her hair is wrapped up so it won't curl. She enjoys all the business with the logs and enjoys carrying a few up at a time to arrange on the large stone hearth. She enjoys the tiny beck which on a still day is the only thing that moves in the whole world around her. She has learnt about the fresh cold smell of the fields and the smell of the wood fire she lights every day. She enjoys, no, she *loves* the little cottage. It is such fun living on two floors like someone in a story-book. She takes to sitting on the stairs, reading or dreaming or sipping at her tea. And she surprises herself by enjoying the solitude – not the loneliness of the campus where she was surrounded by people she did not know and would never know, but *this*, this true solitude, and the sense of occasion it gives rise to when she hears the clip-clopping of a horse and runs to her window to see a rider from the stables two miles away trotting along the path under her window. She notices things she had never seen before: changes in the colour of the sky, in the patterns of clouds, in the little plot that passes for her back garden.

When it is completely dark outside the windows it is time to light the fire. Asya sweeps out yesterday's ashes, lays down some small twigs and breaks a firelighter into three pieces which she inserts delicately between them. She puts her last log on top of the twigs and strikes a match which she holds to each fragment of the firelighter in turn. She should brush her hair and do her face before Mario comes. If he's going to come, of course. But first she must get some more logs. She runs downstairs, puts on her coat and thick gloves to go out to the garage. She opens her front door, and as she steps out she feels her foot kick something light and fragile and she hears a rustle. She looks down: a long bundle of white paper is lying on her doorstep. She picks it up. Flowers. She takes them back into the house, closes the door and switches on the light in the hall. Tulips. A bouquet of white tulips. She sits down on the stairs. She takes off her gloves and starts to unwrap the bouquet and finds the note. She unfolds it. It says: 'Asya – from Mario'.

She sits on the stairs for a long time with the tulips on her knee. She knows what they mean. Before she'd found the note, even, she'd known. Her heart had known – and it had transformed itself into a great big heavy stone inside her. A rock. A boulder – 'boulder, boulder on the ground –' Oh oh oh without saying goodbye – without saying *anything* – oh without saying anything. But this *is* goodbye – what could he say? Oh, Mario – what if she had held him? What if she had thrown herself into his arms last night? Then what? Then he would still have been here today – she lays her head against the wall and weeps. Then she tries to sit up straight again. But *then* what? He would still have had to go, and it would have been worse. Maybe it wouldn't – yes, it would, it would have been

435

bad in the world, now it's only bad in her heart, and it will pass, she knows it will, she wasn't in love with him or anything, he was just – nice – oh, but he's gone, and how could he go just like that? He didn't go 'just like that', he's been trying for six weeks to go, and he had to go in the end, she's known that all along, she's known it would happen and now it has – yes, it has, he's gone, and she doesn't even know where he is. He could be in London, he could have even left the country already. When could he have put these flowers there? It couldn't have been today or she would have heard him. It must have been very early in the morning before she'd woken up, or even last night – oh, she should have heard him, she should have heard him and run out in the dead of night and said, 'What are you doing?' But she didn't. She didn't. She looks down at the tulips: and they've been lying there all this time, poor tulips, they must be frozen to death.

She climbs up to the kitchen and takes the tulips out of their wrapping. She puts some warm water in a vase and stirs a spoonful of sugar into it and arranges them carefully so that the ones that droop lean against the ones that are upright and puts them on the coffee-table in the living-room. In the stove the last log is an intricate cobweb of burning ashes, and she makes herself go downstairs and put her gloves back on and go out to the garage. She comes back carrying seven logs. She throws one into the stove and watches the old log disintegrate immediately into a burning bed for the new. She piles the remaining six on the stone hearth. And stays on her knees next to them. All these arrangements seem pointless now. She had been hoping – all day long hoping that he would come back. Yes, but come back to what? *For* what? Another evening sitting silently in front of her fire, or finding this and that to chat about while his life waited for him outside? Or what? Go to bed with him tonight and let him go tomorrow? Pack up and go with him? To South Africa? To Italy? Darling Saif, I am leaving you to go and live with Mario in Italy? She wipes her eyes and feels the grit from the log on her face.

She goes back to the kitchen table. This is what she has to do.

'This little flower of love –'

It isn't love. Remember that. *Know* that. Anyone this year – anyone kind and funny – and attractive – well, of *course* and attractive – anyone who had liked her and liked talking to her and listening to her stories and didn't say, 'Tell me in a nutshell.' He'd begun saying it in Vienna: 'Could you tell me this in a nutshell?' And of course she couldn't, and wouldn't – but this is beside the point. The point is *this*: this work which she has to do and which is the only reason for her being here. And she is not afraid of it any more. She's OK on her own now. She's fine. Just as long as she carries on with this and gets it finished. Just don't stop. There are still three hours to do tonight before she can stop. And tomorrow? And the day after? And the day after that? Work. Eight hours a day – minimum. And Saif will be here for Christmas – if not before. That's ten weeks – at most. Just concentrate on the work for now. When it is finished she can start thinking about everything else in her life.

'This little flower of love
    Is ours without a root –'

Later that night

Cairo, 25 September 1975

My dear Asya,

I am sorry not to have written to you for so long. I got your last letter just this morning, and believe me I miss you more than I can say. I am having a very bad time here and I needed you beside me because I can't speak to anybody, not even my mother. You will never imagine it – I myself could not believe it, even after I knew it was true – would you believe that Fuad has got married? Married on top of me, Asya, would you believe it? Not having an affair, or keeping some woman, but married – actually *married*.

I had heard a rumour – kind people are plenty in these cases – one of his partners in the business told his wife to tell me to look after my husband better or I would lose him. I heard a word here and a word there and I didn't want to believe it – I didn't even think of marriage, I just didn't want to believe he was going with somebody else – but then it came to me that he has stopped making problems about wanting me to live in Suez and I had thought he had understood why I couldn't but maybe – anyway, at last I couldn't bear it any more and I left Ranya with Mama and took the car and drove up to Suez.

And it was true. He is married. I even saw her. Nothing. A servant. But then, that's what he always wanted. The daughter of a bus driver – one of eleven children whose father can't even keep them properly fed – and then comes mister mighty engineer and marries the daughter and moves her into a flat with a colour TV and a video, and of course every time he goes to his in-laws they all leap to their feet if he walks into a room, and it's Engineer Pasha this and Engineer Pasha that, the bastard, he would never have dared to do this if my father had been alive. I am keeping this from my mother as it would kill her, and of course I am keeping it from Taha because first he would have some psychological crisis and then he'd fight him or do something foolish. And of course you can imagine how I am hiding it all from the rest of the family – my two aunts whose sons proposed to me will be so happy, of course, I can just see them phoning and coming round and pretending to be so concerned for my mother and all the time happy and spiteful because I wouldn't marry their sons and now look what happened to me, can you imagine?

Yes, Asya can imagine. She can see them and hear them.
'My darling, we always told you the near is better than the far and the relative is more worthy than the stranger.'
'No, no, no, it has to be said that Chrissie never deserved this. She's headstrong, yes, but she never deserved *this*. This is too much.'
'May God have mercy on you, Sidki al-Tarabulsi, it's better that you died and didn't see what happened to your daughter.'
'Never mind, Muneera, never mind, it's not the end of the world: "And thou mayest hate that which is good for thee and only God knoweth and thou knowest nothing." '
All this while Tante Muneera sits in a corner of the drawing-room sofa, looking completely crushed and holding her small lace-edged handkerchief to her red eyes; unable to formulate any thought except that if Sidki had been around this could never, ever have happened – where are you, Sidki? Do you see what has become of us?

I had thought, why is he furnishing the flat there like this? You know how it is with him, one week he has hundreds in his pocket and another week he has nothing, but every time he had any money he bought something for the flat in Suez and he never even paid the rent for our flat here. I am only grateful that the flat is in my name, you know when we took it the landlord said he wanted nothing to do with army officers so he wouldn't sign a contract with Fuad and I signed it instead, so at least whatever happens he can't take this flat or bring a new Madame Sinnari here. As I walked away from the flat in Suez I thought to myself, be quiet, be calm, think carefully what you are going to do, think of your daughter – imagine I am sad now that she is a daughter and not a son – I was with his brother, you know, the one who's really in the army full time, in the commando unit, and he said, 'Be wise, Chrissie, you have a share of the responsibility for this situation, remember you're the one who has been refusing to come and live with him here in Suez.' It is so stupid, we keep going round and round the same thing, how can I live with him and leave my job? I would be completely dependent on him – I would actually have to ask him for money to buy food and to put petrol in the car and sometimes he would give it to me and sometimes he wouldn't; sometimes he would have it and sometimes he wouldn't, and anyway what has happened now proves that it was better not to trust him, since he is treacherous enough to do this, he would still have done it even if I'd been sitting on his heart in Suez the whole time, and besides, what would I have *done* in Suez – of course, *she* doesn't have that problem since she does nothing anyway and being the Engineer Pasha's wife is occupation enough for her, and any money he gives her is an improvement on the big fat zero she's got, so it's different, and then his brother tells me, 'You know, Chrissie, in your family he never felt he was anything. Fuad needs to feel respected, needs to feel looked up to, to feel that he's a man.' I didn't know what to say to him – is it my fault I took your brother when he was earning four pounds a month army pay? Is it my fault my father was a cabinet minister while your family was under sequestration? What do you want? Did I deceive you people about anything? Did you want my father to spring to his feet for Mr Fuad al-Sinnari? I never heard anything so mad in my life! He wants to feel like a man so he goes and marries a servant who will be happy washing his shirts all day long and who will kiss her hand palm and back in gratitude to God for every piastre the Pasha throws her way – well, why didn't he do that from the start, he couldn't ever have thought that was how it would be with me, and all that stuff about feeling like a man: every time he's in Cairo I rush to the flat, I leave Ranya with Mama and I cook for him and listen to him and sleep with him, and what else does he want? Oh, Asya, forgive me for going on like this, but Mimi has had a second miscarriage (in the sixth month this time, it is terrible) and Noora and Bassam are under a lot of pressure (financial and political) and I have not been able to talk to anybody at all, I swear I've found myself talking aloud to you sometimes and it seems so strange to me that you are not here.

I asked him for a divorce. I went from the flat to his site office with his brother droning in my ears all the way, and I was telling myself to be wise and to be careful, and when I saw him I forgot everything except that I wanted to attack him, the traitor, I swear I would have gone for his face but – whatever his taste runs to now – *I* was not brought up in the street and his workmen were around so all I said was, I want to talk to you, and I guess he knew, he said, what is it, Chrissie? and I said, I want to talk to you alone, and we went into his own office which isn't very private because they are all just temporary things like portakabins only more primitive, straight on the shore of the Canal, and I couldn't speak for a minute because I did not want to cry in front of him –

She can see it. Asya puts the letter down for a moment. She looks around her quiet living-room; her books and papers are neatly laid out on the kitchen table ready for tomorrow; two small logs are dying in the stove. Mario's tulips are on the table. Outside the windows the night is black. Her heart catches for Chrissie. But it catches for Fuad too. She can feel the blood pounding in Chrissie's head, the unwelcome tears welling up behind her eyes, the cold metal of the chair-back she grips and holds on to, she can feel the automatic affection and the fresh new hatred she feels when she looks at his familiar lean face, the black eyes, the bump on his nose. The two emotions come together in a slow explosion like a chemical reaction and she can also feel the fear that grips Fuad's heart, the sudden clarity that illuminates his mind as he sees the consequences of his string of all too natural actions take form before his eyes, as he sees his two lives come together –

I didn't even know what I was going to say, there were so many things in my mind, but what I said when I opened my mouth was, 'Divorce me.' And of course he said, 'Have you gone mad?' Like you've heard it in a hundred movies, they always say, 'Have you gone mad?' when a woman turns around and asks for a divorce, and I said I have only one thing to say to you: divorce me.
'Chrissie, be reasonable –'

Asya can see them in the grey portakabin facing each other over the grey metal chair Chrissie is gripping. Fuad looks frightened and angry. Chrissie, desperate not to reveal an astounded, wounded, panic-stricken face, has made herself look old and hard.
'*I* be reasonable? *I'm* the one who's gone mad, Engineer Pasha? You think for one minute *I* would have a *dorra*? And what a *dorra*, I wouldn't even have her in my kitchen –'
'There's no need to do wrong by –'
'Wrong? *You* talk about doing wrong? You know what wrong *is*? Today. You will divorce me today.'
'I will *not* divorce –'
'Then you're a coward as well as a traitor – you're a man without honour who would keep a woman against her will –'
'Take care, Chrissie, take care!'
'Go on then, hit me! Hit me, Engineer Pasha! That's what you're used to now, isn't it? That's what you've always wanted – to make you feel like a man! You probably beat her and then she kisses your hand – *I* am telling you –'
'Chrissie, she is nothing. *Nothing*. Understand this –'
'Nothing? How can she be nothing? A human being, a woman living in your flat, sleeping in your bed – I want a divorce and I want it today. Now. I'm not going back to Cairo without a divorce –'
'Chrissie, you had lots of warning – Chrissie, no one could live the way I was living –'
'No? So why didn't *I* go and take a lover? I've fallen out of the bottom of the basket? I'm not a human being? I have no needs?'
'Shut *up*! Don't you dare speak like that!'
'Oh, how stupid I've been –' She sits down suddenly. 'How *stupid*. "Where's your husband, Chrissie?" "In Suez." "He's leaving you alone

all the time like this?" "He's got work." "My dear, this is no life for a young woman." "What can he do? He's not playing there. He's working. Building a future for us." A future. And the Engineer Pasha, God's Name protect him, is courting, getting engaged, buying presents, going for walks on the shore of the Canal —'

'Chrissie — don't torture yourself and torture me —'

'Divorce me.'

'Chrissie, if there's anything left in your heart for —'

'Divorce me. Divorce me. Divorce me.'

In the end he said, 'I'll divorce her. *You* are my wife. I'll divorce her.' I said, 'But I can't stand you. I can't bear to look at you,' and he actually threw himself down on his knees in front of me and held me and kissed my hands, and, Asya, what could I do? I still love him and I have Ranya to think of.

He says now he has divorced her, but he has not shown me the papers so I don't know for sure, and of course the terrible thing is that I am sure it will not end here. What if she is pregnant? She probably is. Even if he really divorced her when he said he did he was married to her for three months and she would have been doing everything to make sure she got pregnant, to tie him down. I tell myself, why think of evil before it befalls you? But I am sure it's just a matter of time. After all, everything is as it was: I am in Cairo and he is in Suez, and he might still be married or at least going with her. I am sure she would still go with him, even if she wasn't married to him, what would someone like her care? And she would always hope to get him back, and even though I try to go up and see him as often as I can it somehow feels all wrong now — everything has been poisoned, even watching him with Ranya, his own daughter —

It would. Of course it would. What would those visits be? Part inspection, part here are your conjugal rights, that should keep you going for another six days? And he would be either resentful or on best behaviour — nothing could come naturally to them any more — oh, Chrissie! She should phone her. But it's one in the morning in Cairo now. She should write to her. Now, straight away. But what can she possibly say to her? It doesn't matter, she should write. She should write to her now.

England, 6 October 1975

My dearest, dearest Chrissie,

I have just read your letter and I feel for you so much — it must be dreadful living with this thing and keeping it from everybody. I feel with you and feel how very hurt you must be — I really don't know what

441

to say to you except that I wish I could be with you now on our sofa with a tray of tea between us so you could tell me all about everything and I could try to make it better or more bearable or, at any rate, bear it *with* you –

But Chrissie – you know – I think Fuad must be having a pretty terrible time too. I mean, for him there is the burden of being the one in the wrong as well as being the one who has to actually make decisions and carry them out and stick by them. In a way it must be easier to be the one who is hurt – can she possibly write *this* to Chrissie? And what use would it be to her now?

Scene 7

Monday 22 December 1975

First I'll say that I know I should not be writing this: if I write anything at all it should be to do with metaphor. But I am writing this because I can't do anything else. I can't work. I can't settle. I can't do anything. I can't concentrate. Every time I sit down to work I keep thinking – I think about everything and I go round and round and then I end up where I began. I used to keep a diary, but I stopped – thank goodness – when I was about eighteen – just after I met Saif. I don't know why I stopped then. Probably because it seemed that real life was beginning and there was no longer any need to yearn for it on the page. I am glad I stopped though: I looked at it when I was in Cairo last year and it is so fervent it made me cringe. It's all perfectly genuine and it isn't even particularly trite, but still – I wouldn't have liked anyone else to see it.

The reason I have started writing this is that I don't know what else to do. Saif phoned me last night.

'Hi, Princess!'

'Hi! Darling!'

I had done nine hours and was feeling pleased with myself. It was just after the ten o'clock news and for a moment I thought that was what he was phoning about: something to do with the OPEC kidnap. Now it sounds absurd, but hearing him on the phone immediately after the news and knowing he's out there working on Syria's Intelligence computer – although he tells everyone it's army – it all seemed to connect. Then I realised, or thought I did, that he was calling to say which day and on which flight he'd be coming over. We were planning to drive up to Edinburgh for Christmas and the New Year. Then I thought he might even be already in London and calling to say he's here. What he said was, 'Listen. I've got bad news.'

'What?'

'I can't come.'

'Saif!'

'I'm sorry. I really am. I left it till the last moment –'

'But you said –'

'I know. I've really tried. I thought I could –'

'But you *can*. Why can't you? You work for yourself; I thought part of the point of working for yourself was that –'

'Asya. These people don't know Christmas. They don't know anything. They want the work done by a particular point and –'

'But you've *been* working –'

'We've run into some problems –'

'But why *now*? Why does it have to be *now*? Oh, Saif –'

'I'm sorry, sweetie, really. If there were any way I could –'

'Can't you come over just for a short while? Just for a week? Just three or four days, even?'

'I can't. I really can't –'

'OK.'

'Come on, don't go all cross on me.'

I said I wasn't going all cross on him and I collected myself and said that of course it was OK and of course I understood, and the thing is I *do* understand. I can just see him there – on site – with all the chaps, piecing the system together – and then a bug comes up – and they're saying we can look at this on Wednesday say, or Thursday and is he supposed to say 'Well, actually I've got to go visit my wife because it's Christmas'? If it had been the 'Eid or some public holiday he could have come over, but nobody stops there for Christmas really – except the Christians, of course. Of course, if he had been in Beirut it would have been perfectly OK to come over and nobody would have minded, but he isn't in Beirut, thank God. Beirut seems to be over – for now, anyway. I can't believe it's for good. But then I can't believe that the Phoenicia and the San Georges have been taken over by Muslim militias –

She looks up from her note-pad. 'Taken over'. She looks at her unlit stove and sees the terrace where they had drunk iced lemonade in the sun: on the edge of the terrace, on the white upright slatted wooden chairs, some men dressed in camouflage fatigues – five men, separately, with large spaces between them – sit, their submachine guns pointing out

443

towards the bay – towards the wooden jetty where she'd lain and asked him about Didi Hashim. If she looks up from the jetty she'll see at the windows of the hotel other men in black glasses with the black and white *kaffiyas* around their necks, pointing more submachine guns at the sea. And back in town – at the Holiday Inn and the unfinished Hilton – more men with machine-guns, this time without *kaffiyas*, the Christian militias. And further in, in Zahlé, where they had sat in the square and she had half envied the Seven-Up-drinking teenagers, five people have just been killed. Killed. And she sits here in the peace of the English countryside wondering what to do with herself –

He phoned and said he couldn't come, and I felt – I really feel – lost. I know it's a cliché, but I stood in the little hall after we'd hung up and I didn't know what to do next. I had been working so well. Racing with time; trying to make up in advance the hours that would be lost as we drove through snowy landscapes and stopped at isolated hotels with roaring fires and genial hosts and roast turkey and mulled wine –

She lays down her biro and rests her elbows on the table and her chin on her cradling palms. It probably would not have been like that anyway. Yes it would. It would have been perfectly nice as long as she was pleasant and said nothing that she shouldn't, and remembered – it didn't even take *remembering*, she always knows in advance what is going to work and what isn't, and all she needs to do is not give in to the fiend that prompts her to say the things that she knows will result in a row, followed by a long, smoky silence. And she needs to leave him alone when he wants to be left alone. But then, do they meet in order for him to be left alone? Do they take trains and aeroplanes and drive for hours so that he should be left alone? If what he wants is to be left alone, then why do they meet at all? Everybody worries so about separation – even *he* had been worried about leaving her – but the problem is not the separations; it is how they are when they're together. If when they were together they were really together, as they'd promised each other that afternoon on the pier, then the separations wouldn't matter. They would hurt, yes, but in themselves they wouldn't matter. But when they're together it's worse than when they're apart – not all the time, of course – but even when they're being pally and chummy and all the rest of it, she always has to be so careful it now seems to her as though she's acting a role: the perfect wife. It is *fraudulent*. And the worst sham of all is how they pretend they're normal people with nothing at all odd about their marriage. Not how they pretend to the world – that is necessary – but how they pretend to each other. This is the worst bit. He is living this lie and forcing her to live it too. *That's* what he's doing – continually. Every time they speak on the phone or go out to dinner or talk about the house they're going to build they're pretending there's nothing between them that is murky

444

and unresolved. Well, it was fine him pretending he had a German Shepherd, but he hadn't asked her to pretend it too. He hadn't sat around saying, 'Down, Fido,' to the air and asking if she'd fed the dog. She starts to smile, but it isn't funny, it really isn't. She puts her face in her hands for a moment then lifts it up again. Oh, of course it doesn't feel like that every single minute. Why, every time she sees him it feels like coming home. It *is* home when he's around: when he's sitting with his blue squared paper or singing in the shower or being funny about something – she only has to look at him to know what he's thinking – she doesn't even have to *look* at him – or be *with* him to know what he's thinking, what he would have thought. When she meets people or watches something on television she thinks what he would have thought – like when she was reading the newspaper earlier and she could see him, could *hear* him, reading out the bit about the Lebanese Melchite Patriarch Maximos V Hakim of Antioch and all the East, not because of what it said or because he was interested in the fate of Monsignor Hilarion Cappuci sentenced to twelve years in an Israeli jail for gun-running – although maybe he was – but because of the title of the Patriarch, saying it out loud and savouring it and laughing and improvising further medieval-sounding titles for Maximos V – yes, but isn't *that* her problem? That she lets his thoughts crowd in on hers – crowd *out* hers –

– and now there was no point. The race wasn't on any more. He wasn't coming. I just kept thinking, what am I going to do, what am I going to do? I knew it was feeble. I also knew – even though I considered it – that I wouldn't get into the car and go for a ten-day drive on my own. I told myself it didn't matter. It *doesn't* matter. These are days like any other days. For me. And I am lucky that it should be so. But I could not settle to anything last night and I just went to bed, although of course I thought I would not be able to sleep. But I did.

But today I feel the same. Displaced. I've tried all morning to do my work. Then I drove into town for the newspaper and tried to think of anything else I wanted, but there was nothing so I came back. And now it is the afternoon and I'm losing today. I'm not going to let myself think that that's OK because of the extra hours I've already clocked up. I'll hold those in reserve. I keep thinking of writing to my mother or to Chrissie. But Chrissie has problems enough of her own – what would she think if I complained that Saif can't come over this Christmas because he's working, really *working*, not going off to marry someone else? And I don't really want to – it would not be possible to go through everything in a letter, and they have no idea, and I don't want to worry Mummy, with her heart and all that, when she's thinking that everything is OK. So then I thought I'd write it all down.

It's not really a waste of time, because I spend time sitting and thinking all the thoughts anyway, and at least like this I can keep track of them all and not just keep covering the same ground over and over again –

Her eye falls on the newspaper carefully folded on the sofa across the room. What is happening to all these people now? *Now*, in a concrete and glass building in Vienna, Carlos 'The Jackal' and three men and a woman stand with their machine-guns around the walls of a big room. At the table in the middle of the room sit some of the world's most influential men – they sit in the same chairs and in the same positions from which a few hours ago their words, their gestures, carried to every corner of the earth and doled out quotas of power and wealth – and now their own power is turned against them, their power is the reason why they are held at gunpoint, having to ask for permission to talk or to go to the loo, having to sit there in the knowledge that at any moment their heads could be blown off. It must be an amazing experience; especially for the Persian chap, Jamshyd something – 'the Courts where Jamshyd gloried and drank deep' – but to be actually *called* Jamshyd: 'Hey Jamshyd, come and get your supper' – well, that probably isn't much comfort to him now: 'I am named Jamshyd. I am Persian. And I am being held hostage by The Arm of the Arab Revolution –' He isn't even an oil minister at all but the Home Office chief; he probably knows all about restraint and detention – but from the other side. And while the world's eyes are directed at the big guys, two families are being told that *their* men, the security chaps, have been killed. Two wives are having to realise that they will never see their husbands again, never, not just this Christmas, and having at the same moment to figure out what they will tell their children, what they will do about their rent, about their food; events, thoughts, feelings affecting so many and all set in motion by a particular man . . . How do you get to be Carlos the Jackal? How do you go from being a dark-haired wide-eyed six-year-old running into his mother's arms after school with his socks around his ankles and his cardigan slipping off one shoulder to being Carlos the Jackal? What is the route, and at what point does it open up in front of you? She can see how you become a PLO fighter. You are simply born in Palestine and choose neither to go away nor to live peaceably under occupation. But this man is Venezuelan. And the woman seems to be German. So how did the route open up to them? How come in her own life she has never so much as glimpsed it, however camouflaged its entrance might have been? Was it street gangs? No, there's a world of difference between kids' gangs and this efficient, trans-world operation. Maybe you're recruited. Someone spots you. A scout with an eye for talent. And then instead of getting a job in the English department – but what would they say? 'Hi! Would you like to join an underground organisation? It's just a few friends. We meet every Saturday night at –' Come on, come on, now she's really wasting time.

What I'll do is this. Work all day as usual, and if I get a thought, instead of letting it gallop off with me I'll pin it down – I'll write it down – quickly – and tell myself I'll follow it through in the evening after I've finished working. I know I won't go on for ever because once it's time for the news it'll be over. Tonight I'll watch *Women in Love*.

Thursday, 25 December

This is Christmas Day. I don't know why it should matter to me or why it should make any difference at all – but it does. I know that I said I'd treat it as just another day in which to put in my minimum eight hours – and I will. I will. But what is it that makes today so different? The 'Eid passed and I felt nothing except homesick thinking of them all at the table at Tante Soraya's, knowing that my uncle will at some point look up from his plate, survey the family seated round the table and say, 'By God, the only one needed to complete us now is Asya,' and then he will remember Grandfather (and what about Mama Deela? how many years does it take when you're dead for you no longer to be 'needed' to complete the circle of family or friends?), and Tante Soraya will shake her head and smile and say, 'Where are you now, darling? The empty space you leave is big!' And my mother will push her glasses back up her nose and eye the rice with nuts she's not supposed to eat and say, 'Well, if she works hard she can be with us next year.' Which is all very well for her to say, since she finished her Ph.D in two years even though she had me to look after etc. But *I* won't. I will work hard but I won't be finished by this time next year. This time 1977 if I keep going well –

Asya puts her biro down and stands up. How can she sit there writing about 'if I keep going well'? Get back to work. She sits down again and pulls her typewriter towards her.

Syntax-independent metaphor, on the other hand, violates rules other than those immediately discernible in the linguistic form. It is, therefore, context-bound, and an awareness of its immediate and/or removed context is necessary for its apprehension as metaphoric, and even more for its full interpretation.

Awake! for Morning in the Bowl of Night
Has flung the Stone that puts the Stars to Flight:
And Lo! the Hunter of the East has caught
The Sultan's Turret in a Noose of Light.

In 'the Hunter of the East' we have an example of the unsignalled metaphoric argument. There is nothing odd about the argument in itself. It is only through the context, and following the principle of maximising the rhetorical coherence of the poem (Mukarovsky in Freeman, 1970), on the grounds that a responsive reader seeks an optimal reading, that a metaphoric utterance is perceived to have occurred. Arrival at the end of the predication with its equative of-construction 'a Noose of Light' confirms the occurrence –

It's true enough, but does it *need* to be stated? Enough just to read it – to read it out loud . . . She stands up again. She walks the length of the room to the window at the right of the stove. What if she went for a walk? Washed the car? She touches the window-pane and quickly pulls back her hand. Oh, it's so cold out there. What if she scrubbed out the bathroom? But it's Christmas. So what? What is Christmas to her? Or if she feels that way, then she should give herself a proper, official holiday. Light the fire. Take out *Heat and Dust*, which she'd sneaked off and bought two weeks ago, and lie on the sofa and read it. No. No, she shouldn't. Because she should work. If only she knew that Chrissie, say, was coming round at, say, seven o'clock, she would work so hard till then. Or even Mina, but Mina's gone to Iran now, pregnant, taking William home to get married. Or Mario – best, best of all – Mario.

The most difficult thing is that nothing happens or will happen. I know that out there in the world plenty is happening: that Pasolini has been murdered by a seventeen-year-old kid and won't be making any more films, that six thousand people have died in Lebanon, that Jewish settlers are camping out near Bassam's mother in Nablus under army protection, that Jehovah's Witnesses are being tortured in Malawi and black guerrillas being killed in South Africa and that Pinochet is claiming that there have been no abuses of human rights in Chile. And I know – in view of all this – that it's a pretty good thing that nothing is happening here: that all I need to think about is right here on this table; I don't *have* to think about the world outside –

But what if she *did* have to. *Have* to. What if there were no food in the fridge and none in the kitchen cupboard and none in the shops? What if there was famine and the baby was hungry and had grown weak beyond screaming and was now silent and listless like the children with big bellies and spindly arms and enormous sad eyes she sees on television? What if that were *her* baby? Her baby would be almost three now. He would be walking. And talking. What if he were with her now? He would be standing, busy with something, at the other end of the room. He has a toy on the sofa and he's standing there in his soft black trousers and a loose white T-shirt – his plump, bare feet planted firmly on the cream rug – playing with it. She can't see the toy because the arm of the sofa is in the way. But she can see him leaning forward to adjust something, concentrating, his soft black hair falling forward over his face, and when he turns to look at her his dark eyes sparkle and his mouth breaks open into Saif's wide grin. What if she had not lost him? If he hadn't been flushed down the hospital loo and left her with sandbags between her legs and a husband no longer in love with her? Is that the reason that Saif does not want her? Because he holds her responsible? But he had not seemed to at the time, and he had been so kind and sweet to her, and besides *he* hadn't wanted the baby either – poor baby, clinging, desperately clinging to the walls of a womb straining to push him out – losing his hold, tumbling out into –

She hadn't wanted that, she really hadn't. Even in the first couple of months when she'd resented him so, she had never, not once, thought of *doing* anything to him. And it couldn't have happened just because she hadn't wanted him at the beginning. She had started to love him. And if he had been with her now she would have had no problems. Her days would have been marked by his needs: his eating, his sleeping, his bath – she had thought that often in her first year here: if she'd had him to take to the crèche, to pick up and bath and feed, if she'd had his small warm body next to her at night – Saif never mentions him. Sometimes she wonders if he ever thinks about him or if he has forgotten him completely. But *she* thinks about him. But maybe that's only because she needs him. Is that it, then? That she sees him only as a prop? As something that would give a point to her days? So that every time she thinks, why am I here, she can answer, because my little boy needs me to be here? Because that is the question that every thought finally leads to:

'Why am I here?'

I am here because I have chosen to do this Ph.D etc.

'Why am I doing this Ph.D?'

Because I have started it. Because it would hurt my mother immensely if I were to walk away from it. Because I myself can't walk away from it. Because without it there would be no possibility of continuing my university career.

'Do I *want* my university career?'

Ah! Now *that's* the question, the truly heretical question. Everybody assumed she did. Everybody except Mina and William; but *their* reasons were all wrong. *She* had assumed she did want it. But had she ever chosen it – really *chosen* it? If the whole world were open to her, if she could be anything at all that she wanted, would she choose to teach English Literature at Cairo University? Even asking the question is betraying her mother and the Professor and all the people who've taught her. But can she *never* ask it? Ever? When had she made that choice? And why? Because what she liked best was reading. And the university had seemed inevitable. It was the only job worth having. Where else would you come and go as you pleased, your own conscience and your own standards dictating what you put into your work? Where else would you be required, *required*, to do research into the topic that interested you more than anything in the world? Where else would you influence generation upon generation so that walking into any office in the country someone would leap up from a far corner and come forward saying, 'I was your student back in whatever. Please sit down, have a coffee, is there anything I can do for you?' To hear her father when he had to give his occupation for some form or other say, 'University professor,' you would know for sure there was no other job in the world worth having. 'Millionaire', 'President of the Republic' would sound as nothing compared to that. It was also the only job she knew about. Who did she know who didn't work in the university? Khalu Hamid was a special case, and she could hardly go and work in Grandfather's shop when 'Am Farrag won't even let her sit on a chair outside the door. And Tante Soraya – Tante Soraya was different, everything that went wrong with her life, even her marrying someone she didn't particularly like, was put down by Asya's mother to her not having gone to university. Her parents, all their friends, Nadia – it was just a fact: if you were clever enough and lucky enough you ended up in the university – preferably in Cairo University because the others didn't really count. The *only* question was what you would teach. Medicine? Architecture? Political science? Psychology? And from that day back in 1956, when her mother, desperate to keep her quiet while they listened to the news, had put into her six-year-old hands an enormous red and gold volume of Lane's *Arabian Nights* with engravings of beautiful long-haired ladies languishing on tasselled cushions, the answer had seemed clear. Well, then, what has changed? Why does it no longer seem so inevitable? Why is she always thinking, somewhere deep down in her mind, underneath the bit that's analysing the metaphors and modifying the theories, why is she always thinking what's the use? She leans back in her chair and stares at her papers. This will be finished. She will sit her viva, get her Ph.D, and then it will be put away. No one will ever look at it again – except perhaps further Ph.D students calling it up on microfilm through inter-library loans. And her whole academic future has been determined. Five years of further research on some aspect of metaphor and an associate professorship. Another five years on, say, psycho-sensory semantic transfers and a professorship. And she would be thirty-five. And she would be teaching this stuff. Well, not this stuff exactly, of course, but linguistics anyway. And supposing she gave two or three courses as well on poetry – or even the novel – would that make any difference? She'd already done two years as an instructor: 'Introduction to Literature'. And what had that been like? A classful of students who didn't give a damn whether the Abbé Marignan recognised the place of love in the scheme of things or the wedding-guest would ever be free of the mariner and the mariner of the albatross. And how could they? They had to look up every other word in the dictionary. She'd liked them and they'd liked her. There had been good will on both sides. She'd gone meticulously through every word of every poem and they'd industriously taken down her every utterance and spewed it all back up at her in their exam papers. Imagine talking to them about 'foregrounding'; how could they respond to foregrounding when they didn't know what the background was? And look at her own class, class of 1971, a good class, how many people there had actually *cared* about what they were doing? How many would have shed one tear if the library across the garden had burnt down to the ground? Three. She and Noora and Mahrous, for all his funny English. The others would have wanted to know if they could be automatically passed now that Fate had taken matters out of their hands and they couldn't look up anything any more. And why *should* they care? If they didn't care they didn't care and that was that. Why should English Literature matter to them if it didn't already? Why should they have to struggle through Swift and Smollett and Pope and Henry James when what they wanted was a BA that would get them a job in a bank? But then, her mother would say, they shouldn't be in the English department; they should be in the School of Languages or taking courses with the British Council. True. But then what would happen to the English department, the department her mother and the Professor had so triumphantly seized from the British in 1952? You'd have a whole department with twelve students in it. If you were lucky. A student for each member of staff. And what is happening is exactly the opposite. The university, designed for six thousand students, is being forced to hold over a hundred thousand. And of course most of the pressure is on the arts. And why? Because they deal in talk and talk is cheap. With arts you don't have to worry about enough labs or chemicals or cadavers or anything to go around. The odd book and pencil and paper and you're there. By the time she gets back seminar groups will have sixty or seventy students in them. And the lectures will have two or three hundred. So is she going to spend her life teaching people things they don't want to learn in conditions that make it impossible for them to learn them? Putting them through the mill for four years, bargaining over whether they will read two novels or four for the twentieth century, so they can put it all behind them, erase it from their minds the moment they enter what will become their real world? And she can't even tell them it's good for them or useful; if she'd been teaching medicine, or how to build bridges or even how to feed cows, she'd feel justified in drilling it into them: 'You know what will happen if you don't attend to this? If you don't put your heart into it? All your cows will be under-nourished, they won't give you any milk, they might even die,

451

and then you'll be left with nothing.' But if you don't open your heart to:

> The glamour
> Of childish days is upon me, my manhood is cast
> Down in the flood of remembrance, I weep like a child for
> The past –

What? What then? You will have missed an opportunity to recognise the power of memory, to see how for every one of us there is no escape from our past, to be conscious of the terrible tenderness that can beset you for things or people lost to you for ever – why should they not learn about all that in Arabic? At least then they wouldn't have to look in the dictionary every two minutes, at least they would recognise for themselves the references to the Qur'an or to Imru' al-Qais, at least they'll know that when a character refers to 1882 he's talking about 'Orabi and the occupation and when he refers to 1919 he's talking about Sa'd Zaghloul's revolution – they'll know how the words *sound*, for heaven's sake. What's English Literature to them or they to English Literature that everyone must live in torment over it?

She stands up. So where do these thoughts lead her? She sits back down again, but on the table, with her feet on the chair, gazing out of the kitchen window. Just beyond her back wall a green hill rises steeply – and above it the sky. The line where they meet is the horizon. There it is, very near, framed by her small window, with not a tree or a fence or anything to break it. The rain drizzles down halfheartedly and hardens into ice on the ground. For her mother it was different. It had been the time of the revolution and everything must have seemed possible. Just getting control of the department must have seemed a mighty achievement. And she was – is – interested in what she does. She believes in the university and she does her work on Byron and Beckford and oriental influences, and she'd had Asya's father whom she was in love with and had married in the face of everybody's opposition, and then she'd had *her*: Asya. Had there been a point when Lateefa Mursi had stopped and thought, why am I here? Asya does not think so. She had been where she wanted to be. But for *her*, Asya, thinking as she thinks, feeling as she feels, it must be that her decision should be to stop. Now. To send a telegram to the university in Cairo, relinquishing her grant, offering her resignation and the last two years' money, to be paid back over a period of time. She would pack up her things and write to Jenny MacRae that she's leaving the cottage and then she'd go to – where? Damascus, to Saif? Or home? Even as she thinks it she knows she won't do it. For a start, no one would believe her reasons. They would all think she simply hadn't been able to complete. Hadn't been up to it. Her parents would believe her – heartbroken and amazed as they would be – but no one else would. And it would be said that the daughter of two eminent professors had dropped out – had failed. And things would never be the same for them in the university again, between some people feeling happy they'd been taken down a peg, and others feeling sorry for them . . .

She finds herself thinking now of Madame Zeinab. If she'd had to sit down and write the names of all the people she knew in the world she surely would never have remembered Madame Zeinab. And yet she sees her so clearly now, thickening and greying in the unchanging black skirt and top as she treads with bowed head between the department and the library carrying folders, papers, books under her arm. Occasionally she lifts her head and smiles at someone: a weak, diffident smile which as it fades seems to address itself more to the stones of the college walls than to the person away from whose face Madame Zeinab's eyes are already sliding. Childless, Madame Zeinab had lost her husband many years back, lost him, in fact, while in the middle of doing her Ph.D. They had been somewhere in England – was it Leeds? And he had died on her. She had brought him home to Cairo and had never gone back. And consequently had never completed her Ph.D. And the only break the university had been able to give her – with the best will in the world and on humanitarian grounds and with all its sympathy for the poor broken creature – was to extend the period during which she could serve as a 'Language Instructor' beyond the statutory ten years. And even that they had not been able to do on a permanent basis, but had to renew her contract every year. And so there she was, year after year, in the limbo of language instructorship, walking slowly round the garden with her files and her notes, and no doubt going into various classes and vaguely stumbling her way through relative clauses and active and passive constructions. And everybody treated her with the careful courtesy with which people – polite people – treat the crippled and the maimed. No, it can't be done. But she, Asya, isn't thinking of staying on in the university; staying on *without* a Ph.D. Well, what else would she do? What else is she qualified for? Sitting on top of the table, Asya considers what job she can get. On a newspaper? How did you get jobs on newspapers? And how many times had she seen her father putting down the phone after someone had asked him for an interview or for his 'opinion as a psychologist' on something or other, how many times had she seen him curl his lip as he put down the phone: 'Just some journalist.' So that would be her ambition? The ambition for which she would walk out on two years' work? To be 'just some journalist'? And what would these two years look like on her CV? How would she explain them: '– and then I had a change of heart. Well, not a change, really, you see, I was living all alone in this cottage and one day I allowed myself to think through something that had been troubling me for almost a year –' They'd think she was mad, or completely phoney. And yet – it is unbearable.

She eases herself off the table and heads for the other side of the room. At the window there she looks down on to the dirt path and then what looks like a slightly hollowed-out space covered in tall nettles, and beyond that the brown fence, and then the dense trees, and above them again the sky. Except that she knows that in that hollow, in the middle of the nettles, is her small hidden stream. She strains her ears for it now but she can hear nothing. After heavy rain she can hear it pass under the window in a murmuring rush. It *is* unbearable. That her life should be so thoroughly mapped out in front of her – that she should know *now* what it was going to – at best – amount to, and that it should be so empty of meaning. Why be alive at all then? Why not be dead now instead of later? How could it have come to this? When she was eighteen she was doing the work she wanted to do and had chosen the man she wanted to marry. Nobody had ever forced anything on her. Every single thing had been her choice. No, no, don't go back over that again – this must be the point where people turn to religion. But what would God think of her if she turned to Him now? Even God would say, 'Finish the task you have undertaken.' He would never recommend breaking her mother's heart, damaging her parents' lives. 'Your mother and then your mother and then your mother,' the Prophet had said, 'and then your father.' But what about her own life? What is to become of that? She goes back to the table and takes up her biro.

All right: what is it that life consists of? She writes down two headings: 'Work' and 'Love'. In front of 'Work' she writes 'Thesis', then she inserts 'Finish' before it and sits back. Is that true? Is there nothing else in life? What about family and friends? Well, they can come under 'Love'. Under 'Love' she makes subdivisions. 'Family', that's OK. She ticks that. 'Friends', that's OK too: Chrissie and Noora would wait for her. And Mario? What about Mario? Does he come under 'friends'? Would that be honest? But if he were here now she would be with him. She wouldn't be sitting here writing this. They would have done something together – as friends. All through last year, until he'd gone away, the knowledge that he was there had made her feel unlonely, befriended. Knowing that Mario was in his room at the other end of the spine had, if the truth be told, sustained her more than knowing that Saif was in Damascus working for their future. Another prop. What is she, then, that she should need the constant flow of feeling from another person in order to live her own life, do her own work? A vampire? Why can she not take her sustenance from – from Nature, for example, like Wordsworth? But Wordsworth had had Dorothy, and besides he was writing poems, *poems*, not some useless treatise on the divisions and subdivisions of metaphor. But she's only writing this because – no. That's been done. Finished. Mario. Was that friendship? It was. But was it *just* friendship? What about the fantasies, the undercurrents? What about Mina saying they were convinced he'd been in love with someone here, otherwise why did he hang on for more than two months after his work was done when his parents were clamouring for him to go back? Why did he disappear so suddenly he didn't even say goodbye? They just couldn't understand it; he'd not been out with anyone, everyone always knew where he was. All the same there must have been someone – but who? Asya had never told anyone about the flowers she had found that night or about how bereft she'd felt in the weeks after he'd gone. He hadn't written, but then she'd known he wouldn't. He hadn't written to anyone. Not even Saif. And what *about* Saif? What had *he* been doing? 'Go with Mario.' How many times during the last year had he said that to her? 'You go with Mario.' 'Mario'll dance with you.' Mario was his stand-in. But how far was he prepared to let him be his stand-in? Or was it some Sir Gawain and the Green Knight deal? Or does he not think like that at all? Is it all much simpler, more immediate – and more unseeing? Oh Trot, blind, blind, blind. But David had seen in the end. Would Saif see? See what? There's nothing left to see. Mario is gone and that's that. Well, does he come under 'Friends'? She throws down her biro and sits back: she doesn't *have* to classify him. He's not a metaphor, and anyway he's gone. Let's say this scheme deals only with current things, not with the past. Especially an *imagined* past, for heaven's sake . . . At the top of the page she writes in big letters, 'The Present'.

'Family' and 'Friends' are dealt with. What about the rest of 'Love'? She picks up her biro again and looks down at her note-pad. She needs another sub-category here. What would she call it? She writes down 'Married Love' then crosses it out because it looks so coy. She draws a rectangle round it and blacks it in. 'Sex', then – but that's not it – or not *only* it. She writes down 'Romance'. But surely the two shouldn't be separate like that. *Weren't* separate like that in those years – those three years when being without him was an ache in her heart and in her body. She draws brackets round both to unite them and sits and looks at her diagram. But that too is the past. What can she put in front of either now? Nothing. Where would she put Saif, then? Well, really he could go under 'Family', or 'Friends'. That would be true. Completely true. She loves him as much as she loves her mother or her father or Kareem or Deena or Khalu Hamid or Nadia or Tante Soraya. And it isn't treachery because it's what he wants. It must be what he wants. But then what? What about this? She traces and retraces the brackets uniting 'Romance' and 'Sex'. Nothing. Empty. For ever? She puts down her biro gently and stands up and walks the two paces to the sink and stands looking again out of the small kitchen window at the unchanging hill. In August she had lain on the sofa in her blue halter top and her white Indian cotton skirt, and he had come over and, smiling, had held a black grape above her mouth, and when she'd opened her mouth for it he'd moved it back, then brought it close and passed its cool smoothness over her lips and her cheeks and looked into her eyes and said, 'You're just a pussycat, aren't you? A real pussycat. You just want to play all the time.' And with her eyes she'd said yes, oh, yes, please; that's all I ever want. And he'd looked at her and whispered, 'My Princess,' and put his cool dry palm on her forehead, then slid it down to close her eyes and held it there. Then she'd heard him get up and walk across the room. She'd lain there with her eyes closed like a statue, like a corpse, like an effigy of herself, and listened to his step on the stairs and then his voice on the phone confirming some dates when components were to be shipped out, and it was only a long while later, after she'd heard the water from the shower drumming on the floor of the bath-tub and his voice rise in the Song of the Volga Boatmen, that she'd got up and walked on unsteady legs over to this kitchen window and stared at the red flowers of the broad beans she'd planted against the back wall and, looking down at the sink, had seen the fresh plump purple grape nestling in the drain.

She looks down into the sink. There is one coffee-cup, one small plate and one teaspoon. She washes and rinses them and puts them face-down on the draining-board. Then she dries her hands and gathers her long black hair and pulls it forward over her left shoulder and twists it into a rope and hangs on to it. Then she gives it a couple of tugs and says, 'Oh,' out loud, and without letting go heads back for the other side of the room and the other window.

'Well, that's all over,' she says, looking out at the nettles and the woods beyond. She had rebelled, she had raged in her heart against him. If he didn't want her, she had cried to herself, he should set her free. They were civilised people, not savages. Why, the whole world knew one could not live like this. Even the government, bureaucratic and ridiculous as it was, could not part a husband from his wife for more than six months – and it wasn't some new thing either: why had the early Muslim campaigns never been allowed to last longer than six months? For precisely this reason: so that the women should not be without their men any longer than that – longer than that and you were asking for trouble. Six months! When he'd loved her a week had been too long to wait, and now it's been – it's been for ever. It's been so long that it doesn't matter any more. It's all gone. Didn't they used to tell her when she looked around, scattily unable to see the thing that was under her nose, 'If you don't use your eyes, God will take them from you'? Well, she hadn't used her desire and God had taken it from her. Relieved her of it. She hadn't felt stirrings of that kind at all – not a hint, not the faintest shadow – since Mario had gone. Even when she lay in her bed at night and remembered the golden Sunday afternoons in Heliopolis, or tried to conjure up the feel of the rocks in the Omar Khayyam maze rough against her back, and his mouth bruising her lips, or the weight of the broken-nosed man's body on hers and his voice in her ear, 'Bellissima, bellissima,' or read the passage in the *Perfumed Garden* where the deluded Chedja el-Temimia, overcome by incense and lust, falls to her knees crying out to Mosailima the Liar, 'I want it all ways, oh Prophet of God' – nothing happened. Gone. All gone. Is it just as well? She turns and, leaning against the window-sill, lets go of her hair and folds her arms as she looks across the room at the table piled with cards and books and papers. And lines of poetry which had made her catch her breath or brought tears to her eyes – gone, too. She can repeat, 'I do not think that they will sing to me', or, 'Dearest, I cannot loiter here / In lather like a polar bear', or 'What has happened to the sturdy knight / the heart breaks loose and he is in flight', or 'Où sont les neiges d'antan?' or, 'You eat out of my hand / Exhausted animal', or 'Timor mortis conturbat me', as often as she likes, and she will still feel cold and feel that nothing matters. Can it be that she has no feelings any more? Only meta-feelings? Meta-feelings about her loss of feeling? What *does* matter to her, then? What? She walks back to the table, sits down and looks at her note-pad. OK, so that's the present. That's how it *is*. She turns the page. Now, how does she *want* it to *be*?

At the top of the new page she writes 'The Future'. When? Well, say, '1980'. She will be thirty then. Thirty! She rewrites the headings of her diagram. In front of 'Work' she writes 'Something that matters' and underlines 'matters' twice. But what *could* matter? Given her training and her self, what could, in the wider sense, *matter*? What could she teach that was worth teaching? What could she do that couldn't be done – and better – by others? She couldn't be Beethoven or Michelangelo or Guevara or Yusif Idris or Tayyib Salih or the Beatles. But does it have to be the heights? Why does she always have to think in such grandiose terms? She could do something that was humble but useful. Something that other people could do just as well – or better – but where she would still be needed. What? When she thinks of being needed she always thinks of medicine – healing people, bending over sickbeds – but even if she did have the training, even if she went back to school and did two years of science, sat another Thanawiyya 'Ama, ludicrous as that would be, then seven years of medical school – that's after finishing the Ph.D, so she would be thirty-six already by then, anyway – does she, quite honestly, have the stomach for that kind of thing? She thinks of the old man in the hospital with his buttock exposed – a buttock into which she had been unable to plunge her hypodermic needle; she thinks of the legless lady up the smelly stairs impregnated by the old idiot drooling in the corner; she thinks of the leprosy-ridden student who had walked into her office like some figure out of Munch and how she'd had to hold on to the arms of her chair to keep herself still and keep herself from racing out of the room and down the corridor and out of the whole university and going home. Home. *There* had been a chance of doing good. And

457

had she embraced it? No. She had dragged her fascinated eyes away from the pink-edged black hole that must once have been the girl's nose, and away from the mass of scar tissue in the middle of her forehead, and forced herself not to think of what further horrors must be concealed beneath the headscarf. To concentrate on the eyes. The eyes were normal. Horribly, obscenely, normal, bearing no trace of the wounds, the decomposing flesh surrounding them. And the girl had wanted help with her composition essays. Her *composition essays*. And all Asya could do was stammer that she was very busy, working on her MA, teaching, a hundred things but – ashamed and collecting herself – of course she would look through her essays and correct them, but what year was she in and how come Asya hadn't seen her before? Because she sure as hell would have remembered her if she –

'I cannot attend class. I have problems.'

She could say *that* again.

'But – we have no external system in the English department?'

'No.' The mouth had smiled – was it beginning to be eaten away at the edges or was it just pale? 'But my teachers are very kind. They allow I work in home and then to come for examination. I am hearing you are very kind, Doctor, and you can help me?'

She had sat and gone through the dreadful essay, conscientiously marking and scribbling and explaining, eyes down, while the shrouded head across the desk had nodded and nodded, and then she had handed over the paper and immediately busied herself with things inside the desk drawers so that the girl, as she voiced her gratitude, would not think to shake her hand. Her hands were encased in white gloves but Asya had dreaded what she would feel if she took one of them in her own: the missing finger, the gnawed palm – and she'd said, yes, of course, if you bring me any more I'll look through them – and then she had lived in dread. She had avoided her office, she had looked right and left as she walked out of each classroom, her heart beating for fear of the hooded noseless figure that was lying in wait for her. So who was *she* to talk about healing the sick? No. Better stay with what she knows. But what good is that? If she were to teach English Literature here, in England, that would be different. She would work with twenty students who would be able, at the very least, to read the language, and among them would be the one or two gifted ones, the ones who really cared, the ones for whom what they read was part of their lives, part of themselves. For them it could be so. But her life and her work are in Egypt. She should have studied Arabic Literature, but that hadn't even crossed her mind. By the time she was seventeen and going into university she was already completely – but what if her mother had thrust *Bein el-Qasrein* into her hands that night instead of Lane? She couldn't have; Asya at six couldn't read Arabic; they were in England and English was what she read. But what if her mother had been a musician, say? What if she'd handed her – what? A violin? But she had, later, and Asya had put it down as soon as she could and gone back to *Sandford and Merton* and her own pathetic rhyming verses. Ah, but the damage was already done then. So was it an accident of fate? Was it simply because her mother, at twelve, had fallen in love with her English teacher – because of Miss Sage, in whom her mother had seen embodied the escape from *her* mother's drudgery, had seen a whole freer way of life and thought than that which prevailed in Ismail Mursi's house – was it because of this that she, Asya al-Ulama, was sitting here today biting her biro and wondering what had happened to her life? She puts down her biro. This is no use. No use at all. Leave it as it is, then: 'something that matters'. She can't start working towards it now, anyway; the thesis has to be finished, and besides, she's not in Egypt, so even if she dreamed up some scheme, like holding literacy classes or helping in government basic health projects or something, she wouldn't be able to do anything about it. So leave it as it is. Finish the thesis and get back home to Cairo and find out *there* how you can do something that is useful.

She picks up her biro again. In front of 'Family' and 'Friends' she writes 'as above' and there she is at 'Love' again. She looks at it for a bit then puts her face in her hands. That can't – *can't* – be 'as above'. Not in 1980. All right. She mustn't panic. She mustn't spiral off into useless thoughts again. What does she *want* it to be like for her when she's thirty? She wants still to be beautiful. She wants to be in love. She wants to be making love, to be wanting to make love and doing it. She wants, she writes down, 'Children'. Yes, it's true she hadn't wanted the baby, not at the beginning – she'd felt cheated – tricked. But she had never, ever, imagined a life without children. A whole *life* without children. And that was what she was heading for. Well, she would not let that happen. She would adopt a child before she would let that happen. The world is full of unwanted, ill-treated, orphaned children. She would adopt two: Ethiopian, Vietnamese – Palestinian children who had no parents, no home, no country, even, and then she would be doing good as well. But never to have a child of her own, her very own? Why shouldn't she? If it had been Fate, if she had been barren – but she isn't; she's been pregnant once – well, that takes her back to 'Sex' and 'Romance'. To Saif. She draws circles round the bracketed words. Maybe it would be easier to treat them separately. More productive. She smiles at her own joke. Well, take 'Sex'. When had it gone wrong? On their wedding-night – no, before that – but radically wrong? On their wedding-night – and after. And why? Because it had hurt so much and she hadn't wanted him enough to not care about the pain, and he had known that and been hurt, and afterwards it had got worse because she had been afraid of the pain before they even started, and eventually he'd got fed up and thought, the hell with it. So surely if he did try now that would just happen again and again? But he should know that she – no, never mind what *he* should know. Why should she expect him to sort that out for her – or even if she does, he is clearly not going to, so maybe she should sort it out for herself. There must be some way in which she can get rid of the pain; know for sure that making love with him is not going to hurt. Yes, hire a lover for a night. Maybe he'd wanted Mario to do *that* too for him – now she's being silly, and bitchy. There must be some medical way. Maybe if she asked Nadia – but she can't tell Nadia, she can't tell anybody, not now, not after all these years. Well, maybe if she just saw a doctor – oh no, not that again. But this is England: it's different here, they won't just pat your shoulder and tell you to be a good girl and go home to your husband. But the doctor might have to examine her – and is it better to be examined once or to live her whole life like this? And maybe he might not, maybe if she just told him all about it – maybe they could just do a little operation on her; put her to sleep and then clear the path there or something. You'd think that would have happened with the miscarriage, but it hadn't. Things had got worse after that, if anything. But that was because they were already so firmly fixed in a pattern – but still, the fact is that there *is* a physical problem which can be sorted out without involving him. And that is what she should do. In front of 'Sex' she writes 'see doctor'. She would go to the campus doctor and ask to be referred – privately – to a gynaecologist. And 'Romance'? Well, maybe they *are* linked: maybe if 'Sex' was all right 'Romance' would follow; that is what happens in arranged marriages, isn't it? Arranged marriages which work. And she and Saif have a head-start because they've *had* 'Romance', they were *engendered* in 'Romance'. And maybe too if she has a child her need for romance would be lessened. Maybe if she didn't *need* it so much – maybe if she laid off him – but she'd never asked for it; you can't *ask* for romance – no, not in so many words, but she asks for it all the same, her whole attitude breathes expectation and, given the state of 'Sex', is he to be blamed for resisting that attitude? For digging his heels in and saying 'No romance'? She should think of what he is saying 'yes' to, of what he wants from her now, and give him that. Then by the time she is ready to make 'Sex' work he will have stopped resisting her; he will have been disarmed. Yes, but even without this scheming type of argument, isn't this something she should do? Be the pebble – 'Love seeketh not itself to please –'? Please him. Please *him*. If she wants to live *for* something, why not live for that? She knows what he wants from her, how he wants her to be, and there's nothing wrong with any of it. He wants her to get on with her work, to be supportive of him and his work – particularly since he's pouring money into their bank account – but she isn't using it, she doesn't *touch* it – so who pays the rent for this cottage, then? Thirty pounds a week. What does that leave from her grant? Twenty-one pounds and forty-three pence if you count every month as thirty days. Is

460

that what she lives on? Yes, but the cottage was his idea – ah, but she's happy here, she's learnt so many things about the sky and the seasons and the different sounds of birds, and she hasn't felt half as trapped or lonely as she used to on campus when there were people all around her, and anyway she does live on her twenty-one pounds a month, and if she doesn't she tries; she *has* no expenses apart from food and petrol and fees for photocopying and inter-library loans – and the bills, and the clothes? But she only buys clothes when she's with him or going to meet him, and besides, can't they be considered legitimate 'business expenses', as it were? If he wants her to look the way he wants her to look, if he wants to be pleased and proud when people see her with him, then she has to dress the part. So that's part of 'pleasing him' – so, to get on with her work, to be supportive, to be intelligently appreciative, tranquilly happy, serene – 'A mind at peace with all below / A heart whose love –' But she doesn't feel like that – yes, but that's what she'll be working on, and where does being cross or hysterical or desperate get her? Think of, for example, Vienna – she had gone to Vienna, and what had she made of it? A misery. Because instead of thinking about *him*, she'd thought only of herself. Instead of thinking how wonderful it was for him to be there, at that conference, reading his paper alongside Stafford Beer whose books have always been on his library shelves and she knows it – instead of thinking how clever he was – she *had* thought he was clever, she'd told him so, she'd been proud of him – yes, but in an abstract, separate sort of way, his success had made no difference to the way she herself had felt, and after she'd done her four hours of metaphors she had roamed the streets while he was at the university asking why she did not feel the 'spirit of Vienna' she had expected to feel, asking as she continually does, 'Is this it, then? Is this all?' Writing postcards home and eating cakes she didn't want in different Konditorei only to sick them up again in the hotel bathroom as he lay sleeping in the huge gilt four-poster. And even going to the Opera, and even in the Hungarian restaurant later, she had sneered in her heart as he leaned back in his chair with his wine-glass in one hand and his Rothmans in the other, enjoying the gypsy music the white-haired violinist with the embroidered waistcoat was serenading them with, enjoying his well-received paper, his well-dressed wife, enjoying the fact of having been able to pull all this off, and why *shouldn't* he enjoy it? He had certainly worked for it and earned it, and she knew that and respected that, and why, then, when he offers it to her, when he tries to share it with her, why should she sit there asking about the meaning of life as though he were required to throw that too into her lap as he did the rings and necklaces and airline tickets? Yes, but if she had known, if as she'd lain on his red eiderdown with him slowly tracing the outline of her lips with his tongue, or as they'd sat on his balcony, he reading Lorca and she *The Blood of Others*, with Cat Stevens on the

461

record-player, or as he taught her about photography on the race-track at the club and showed her how to adjust her lens so that the quivering legs and the stripy, fuzzy body and the transparent wings of the dragon-fly were all captured in absolute focus, and showed her which filter would best bring out the sheen in the drop of dew the creature was drinking from – if then a window had opened in the middle distance and she had seen herself in her silks and jewels sitting at a restaurant table in Vienna, in Paris, in London, and seen her measured movements and heard what she said but heard also what she did not say – what a reduced life she would have deemed it. If she had seen herself, sitting on bathroom floors in hotel suites while he slept because she could not bear the mockery of the ornate double bed, because she would not perform the lie of falling asleep next to him at the end of the day as though there were peace between them – but what about *him* then? She has to think about him too. If that window had opened for him and he had seen himself in London, driving his new car with her, his wife, sitting next to him, priggishly saying, 'And why, pray, is it called *wife*-swapping?' If as she had sat at the table in the Omar Khayyam bar, tongue-tied and adoring and willing to be taught, the window had opened above her head and he'd seen her one moment hostile and cold and bookishly argumentative and the next contemptibly, weakly, hysterical – if he'd been vouchsafed a glance into her heart and seen that for a year she would lust after his best friend – would he have gone right ahead and married her? What does it feel like to him now to have his life tied to hers? Oh, but she tries: she tries to do what he wants, and when he wants nothing she tries to be that too. She tries on her own to do the things that would make her be all right so that when she's with him she can be the way he wants her to be. In every city they've gone to she has tried to do her own things, to find something for herself so that she would not cling to him. Only it hasn't always worked. It worked in Paris but not in Vienna. In Vienna she had gone to the Prater and then hadn't wanted to be there. She had gone to the museum, and even that had felt bland to her, and she had stood and remembered how she had stood in the Uffizi ten years earlier and gazed in wonderment at Botticelli's *Venus*, her long rope of hair curling modestly around her shining hip, at one with the waves from which she was born and the sky towards which she rose – there, *there*, is an image: what is that if not serenity? To aim at that then. To *be* Botticelli's *Venus*. And to do it from within. To use what she has: the love of her family, Saif's support, her security, the fact that she is at least able to do the work she happens to be doing – to value what she *has* instead of longing for what she doesn't have. To be the best she can be; to create meaning in her life by striving to be the best person she can, not in the ways that appeal to her, not by spooning aid porridge into the mouths of rows of starving children or bringing comfort to shrapnelled soldiers or singing

Carmen to a hushed house or writing *Middlemarch*, but in the more difficult way that has been allotted to her – for the moment – and to draw strength from knowing that while she is doing her best for those whose lives most immediately touch her own, she is not at a standstill; she is working towards making her life more the way *she* wants it.

In front of 'Romance', she writes 'ATTAIN IDEAL (Botticelli *Venus?*)'

X

July 1976 – February 1978

It is in these acts called trivialities that the seeds of joy are forever wasted, until men and women look round with haggard faces at the devastation their own waste has made, and say, the earth bears no harvest of sweetness—calling their denial knowledge.

—GEORGE ELIOT
Middlemarch

Scene 1

Tuesday, 20 July 1976
The North of England
'Boy! Am I tired!'

Deena slumps on the sofa, stretches out her legs and rests her joined hands on top of her head. She is wearing old blue jeans, a pair of trainers and a grey sweatshirt. Her black hair is cut very short – like a boy's, Asya thinks, except most boys wear their hair longer than this these days. Asya stirs two spoonfuls of sugar into a mug of coffee, then carries it across from the kitchen end of the room and puts it down on the coaster on the table in front of her sister.

'Thanks,' Deena says. She takes off her glasses and throws them on to the sofa next to her and rubs her eyes. A yawn overtakes her and ends in a long sigh. She picks up the coffee and sits holding it and leaning forward with her elbows on her knees. Asya sits in the armchair closest to the sofa.

'How was it?'

'OK.'

'You look exhausted.'

'I am.'

'Deena,' says Asya, 'Deena, darling. I know you're completely independent and everything – no, listen to me – you *are*. But, please, won't you for my sake stop doing this and let me give you the money?'

'It's just for two weeks and I'll have earned it.'

'You've only done two days and see what you look like: you look completely ragged. What will you be like after two weeks?'

'I know you don't like my working in a restaurant –'

'It isn't because it's waitressing, don't be *silly*. It's because it's so far away. If it were just down the road or something – but you go cycling off *seven* miles –'

'But I *like* cycling.'

'But it's so *far*. And I've been so worried waiting for you tonight and yesterday. All sorts of things could happen to you – and why *should* you do it?'

'Because I need to earn a hundred pounds for the books and reports I want to buy.'

'Yes, I know that, you've told me that –' Asya almost says: but what's a hundred pounds? She stops herself; how can she say that when her whole grant is a hundred and fifty pounds a month? And besides, Deena would then tell her exactly what a hundred pounds – sterling – was; what it

467

would be to some poor family back home. She leans forward and puts her hand on Deena's knee. 'Deena, darling. Let me give you the money. I've *got* a hundred pounds. Do it for *me*, so I don't have to sit here and imagine you flying off your bike lit up by the headlights of a car coming fast round some corner –'

'Ya-ya, dear –' Deena feels on the sofa for her glasses and puts them back on – 'you offered yesterday and I said no. And now I've started. I might as well carry on.'

'OK, well at least let me drive you there –'

'No.'

'*Why* not? Why are you being so completely ridiculous about this?'

'It would disrupt your day. You'd have to take me there, then come back here, then drive out again to collect me. Look, it's all working out very well like this: you're here doing your work and I come back when you've finished. And I *like* cycling. I *enjoy* it.'

'And *I* don't enjoy sitting here imagining you being raped in some ditch by the roadside. So I'm selfish – so humour me –'

'Asya, stop looking so cross. I'm twenty –'

'You could be a hundred and still get knocked off a bike –'

Deena laughs, and after a moment Asya, imagining the hundred-year-old Deena, still in jeans and a sweatshirt, pedalling off to serve sausages in a seaside restaurant, laughs too.

'OK. Do it your way. I give up. Do you want to eat?'

'They fed me. They're going to feed me every night, I told you –'

'OK, OK. What *do* you need then? What can I –'

'Nothing, Ya-ya. After two years I just want to sit here with you. I haven't seen you properly yet.'

Asya sits back in her chair and looks at her sister. She doesn't say, and whose fault is that – that would be a very Tante Soraya-ish thing to say – but it's true nevertheless. Deena had come up on Thursday afternoon, having completed the short course she was doing in Cambridge, and on Friday morning she had gone with Asya into the university. Asya had shown her around the campus and left her in the coffee-shop while she went to collect a book from the library. When she had come back she had found Deena chatting and laughing with a Yemeni student whom Asya had seen around campus but never spoken to.

'This is my sister, Asya al-Ulama –' Deena had begun but the Yemeni had laughingly interrupted her.

'Of course, I know who she is. I am Marzouk el-Ashtal.'

They had shaken hands.

'Marzouk is going to lend me his bicycle,' Deena had said.

'Why?' Asya asked.

'He says he doesn't need it. He can spare it for a couple of weeks –'

'I mean why do you need a bicycle?'

468

'Oh, then I can go around independently – you won't have to drive me everywhere.'

'Oh!' Asya had turned to Marzouk. 'This is very kind of you – are you sure you can do without it?'

'Of course, of course,' he had smiled. 'It just sits there every day. I am happy for Miss Deena to have it.'

'Well, thank you very much,' Asya had said.

'I was telling Miss Deena we are having an Anglo-Arab Friendship evening next Friday in the Chaplaincy Centre –'

'But it's the twenty-third of July,' says Asya.

'Well, that is the reason, really,' says Marzouk, 'but we are combining it with our end of year Anglo-Arab Friendship party. You never come to our evenings –'

'I have done – three years ago –'

'That is too long. It will be nice if you come.'

When Marzouk el-Ashtal had left Asya had said to Deena, 'You know what that's going to be like? Wispies exclaiming over *ta'miyya* and vine-leaves and groupies trying to belly-dance and kids on the rampage and wives huddled suspiciously together in a corner and a few radical Iraqis and Syrians shouting above the music in the middle of the room –'

'You're prejudiced.'

'I'm not. It's a set piece: it can't be any other way.'

'Well, let's go and see.'

'If you like. But we'll have to cook something.'

'It's OK. I'll cook.'

'You can't cook.'

'Of course I can.'

'Since when?'

'Since Dada Zeina left. Asya, who cooked that summer when Mummy was ill? You were there.'

'Oh yes, I'm sorry. Can you stuff vine-leaves though?'

'Yes, of course I can.'

'That's brilliant. I can't.'

'You probably could – if you tried.'

'I can't. Both Tante Adeela and Tante Soraya tried to teach me. I can't do it: they won't stay parcelled up, and when they do they look crooked – deformed.'

'Do you want me to make vine-leaves then?'

'Well, that's the other thing, you see. We'll have to get in touch with the wives and find out what they're making and what's missing that we can provide. We can't just show up with vine-leaves.'

'Well, that's OK. Why is that a problem?'

'I've never done anything with them.'

'I'll ask. I'm new – and transient. I can ask.'

With the bicycle half hanging out of the open boot of the Lancia Asya had negotiated the winding, green-hedged road back to the cottage.

'I'm going to look for a job,' Deena had said.

'A job? What job? You're only here for a couple of weeks.'

'Just a small job. In a restaurant or something.'

'But Deena, why?'

'I need to buy books for about a hundred pounds –'

'I'll buy them for you. A present. You're here to visit me, not to go working in a restaurant.'

'I'd really rather get some work, Asya –'

'But when shall we see each other? I want to take you around and show you all sorts of things –'

'Asya, you've got your thesis. We would still have the evenings and weekends and everything –'

'Please, Deena. I haven't given you anything for ages. It's three years' worth of birthday presents and stuff –'

Deena had patted Asya's shoulder.

'Please? I'd really rather work for this money.'

'What books are they?'

'Well, they're – political stuff, mostly Amnesty reports, really, stuff like that.'

'They're for your – friend? For Muhsin?'

'Yes.' Deena had examined her sister's profile. 'Mummy told you?'

'Yes. She mentioned him in a letter.'

'And she told you she doesn't approve?'

'I gathered that. But you know Mummy. She doesn't approve but she'll help you any way she can.'

'I know. But she'd really like him if she gave him a chance –'

'I think she does already.'

'He's really – nice. He's very very kind. He *helps* people. Kids *love* him. I can really talk to him; he's got the most genuinely open mind of anybody I've ever met –'

'What about the political thing?'

'What about it?' Deena's tone had immediately become defensive.

'I'm just wondering if you can be politically committed and yet have an open mind?'

Asya slowed down as they turned a corner.

'Yes you can if what you're committed to is an ideal of democracy and free speech and all that – what was that line we used to learn at school about, "I may disagree with your opinion –"?'

'– "But I would fight to the death for your right to express that opinion" – approximately. Voltaire.'

'Right.'

'Is that what he's like?'

'Yes.'

'All the way through? At home as well as with his friends?'

'Absolutely. He's one hundred per cent genuine.'

'Can you talk about *anything*? Absolutely *anything*?'

'Yes, of course.'

'And does he want to know what *you* think? I mean, *really* want to know?'

'Yes, he does.'

'Can you make him change his mind?'

'About what?'

'Well, about anything. I mean, can you discuss something you don't agree on and he end up thinking you're the one who's right?'

'Yes – if I *am* the one who's right.'

'He sounds OK.'

'He's more than OK. He's terrific.'

They had crossed the tiny wooden bridge that led to the cottage and Asya had turned and smiled at her sister.

'OK, Doudi. He's terrific.'

Now Asya says, 'Tell me more about Muhsin Nur el-Din. Is there really an "organisation" or is it a group of friends who talk politics, you know, like we used to after '67?'

'Well, what *I* see is a group of friends. But they say there are more of them and that they're not just university people but that they have connections in factories and so on –'

'Would that be the Egyptian Communist Party if it wasn't banned?'

'Sort of. I mean, there isn't *one* thing you could call the CP; there are factions –'

'So it's like it was in the forties, say?'

'Yes, but it's even *more* fractured now, and –'

'Deena?' Asya pulls her legs up on her chair. 'If you did want to join, would you know how? I mean, would you know where to go, for example?'

Deena laughs.

'I wouldn't know where to go, but there are people I could talk to.'

'Apart from Muhsin and his friends?'

'Yes.'

'Where?'

'In college, of course.'

'Well, *why* haven't you joined?'

'Because I see the "comrades" in college and they're all serious and sincere but – as I said – they are all factions, and each faction thinks the others are completely wrong, *completely*, and besides –'

'Besides?'

'Well, I don't know, I'm friendly with some of them, but I think they're isolated from the rest of the student body – I mean, they kind of form a closed circle – several closed circles – and I – I just don't know that they really represent "the people" in the way –'

'But hasn't that always been the case with the left? Apart maybe from 1919? That they're like a sort of club almost –'

'Asya? Why did *you* never join?'

'I wouldn't have known who to approach. And being on the Literary Society taught me – do you remember when we staged *Tartuffe*?'

'Yes.'

'Well, all that committee stuff: I just got tired of it really quickly. Huge discussions and pointless debates and people showing off. I just haven't –'

'I know what you mean. It's exactly right. It's a waste of energy.'

'But then, if you want to be part of changing the world – or the system – then I guess maybe you have to –'

'You have to be part of *something*, but –'

'Well, who *would* represent "the people", then, in your view?'

'Asya, do you know which is the fastest growing grouping in the university now? The Islamic groups.'

'I thought they were outlawed?'

'Not any more. In fact Sadat's encouraging them; he's using them – or thinks he is, anyway – to combat the left. It's part of the rapprochement with the United States. But of course he isn't *making* people join; they're doing that on their own – and it's really growing.'

'But *most* people wouldn't join the Brethren and all that, surely?'

'Well, there are more joining *them* than there are joining anything else – and also of course they can accommodate a left of sorts: an Islamic left – although they wouldn't call it that.'

'It just seems so unlikely. I mean, when I was in college it wouldn't have been an option – I mean, even disregarding the fact that they were so completely underground –'

'But that was 'Abd el-Nasser's time – it was different, it was all opening outward: Pan Arabism, Pan Africanism, non-alignment –'

'Pan-Arabism! Imagine if 'Abd el-Nasser were alive now and had seen Jordan happening all over again in Lebanon. Did you see Frinjieh today calling for "the dispersal of the Palestinians among the Arab countries"?'

'Yes, I read it.'

'Of course they do destabilise the country –'

'They must. Thousands of angry young people, living temporary lives, armed –'

'Do you remember that poster I used to have on my wall: "Children of '48: Commandos of '68"? And two years later it's Black September –'

472

'Lebanon will be worse for them –'

'Lebanon will be worse for everybody –'

'They're all in camps there, like Tel el-Za'tar. They're such easy targets –'

'It's really dreadful. Imagine, in a refugee camp to begin with, and then under siege and under attack –'

'And just across the desert the Kuwaitis are spending millions creating a stock exchange that they don't need.'

'What's that?'

'It's true. They've hired some former stock exchange man from here to make them a modern stock exchange: a fantastic new building with several trading floors. But in the paper it says the Kuwaitis have only thirty quoted companies and only Kuwaitis are permitted to invest in them – and of course you can't charge anything more than seven per cent on money – so your whole investor population amounts to a few hundred, and they've been dealing happily in cafés and things – they don't need a modern stock exchange –'

Friday, 23 July

'Asya,' Deena asks, 'what's a wispy?'

'A wispy?' Asya laughs. She checks her rear-view mirror before swerving out to overtake a blue Escort. 'Oh, it's a Western person – they're mostly English although there are some Germans – who is terrifically interested in all things Arab – interested in a deferential sort of way. It's a variant on the Indian theme – the ashram lot rather than the Empire lot. They're the type, you know, who can go native, grow beards, maybe, who take to sandals – they might even learn some Arabic and a few courtly gestures. It goes with other things too – organic foods, peace –'

Deena is amused. 'Can you apply it further back: was Edward Lane a wispy?'

'Yeah, I guess – except of course he was pretending all the time –'

'T.E. Lawrence?'

'Well, he was an Empire man – although he had at least three agendas, but yes, I suppose he was a wispy – a superior kind of wispy – but don't ever tell Noora I said that –'

'Sir Richard Burton?'

'Oh no. The exception that proves the rule – isn't that what you say in science? Except I suppose you don't. You probably work in a realm where there are no exceptions – or where everything is an exception – where the exception *is* the rule or some such concept. Deena, can you tell me – in language which I can understand – what it is you want to do for your MA, say?'

'Well' – Deena pushes her glasses back up her nose in a gesture which makes Asya think of their mother – 'it's all very abstract really –'

'Is it all formulas – formul*ae* – and things?'

'Yes, mostly.'

'But is it *for* anything, apart from itself? I mean, can you draw a line from something you do to something concrete – like building a bridge?'

'Well, not building a bridge exactly –'

'But something concrete that any chap walking along the street can see and recognise?'

'It would have to be a pretty long line.'

'Will you explain to me?'

'What, now? We're almost there, aren't we?'

'No, not now. But some time while you're here?'

'I'll try.'

'I told you so, I told you so,' Asya croons to her sister.

'They'll hear you.'

'No they won't. I'm *sotto voce* –'

'Shhh!' whispers Deena. 'Let's go and put our stuff down and get a drink.'

'I don't want to walk across the room,' says Asya.

'Well, we can't stand frozen in the doorway carrying two trays. Come on.'

The room in the Chaplaincy Centre is round and high and carpeted in grey. Under a tall window close to a wall stands a black baby grand with its lid closed. At the far side of the room three tables stand end to end covered in white paper tablecloths. Asya and Deena walk across the room and place their offerings down amongst the assortment of food that is already there. Asya pours out orange juice from a carton into two plastic mugs and hands one to Deena. After a moment she says, 'I think I might take up smoking, then I'd always look as if I were doing something – I mean, at least now *you're* here; you see how I couldn't possibly have come on my own?'

'You might have made friends with someone.'

'I doubt it.' Asya looks around the room. 'Come on, Deena, be honest: is it or isn't it exactly as I said it would be?'

Deena smiles as she looks around. 'Yes, you're right – a bit.'

'Why only a bit?'

'Nobody's trying to dance –'

'*Yet*. You just wait. They will.'

'And' – Deena points at the doorway – 'look at him. He doesn't look like a wispy.'

474

Asya looks. Coming through the door is a tall man with a lot of blond hair swept back but curling into his neck. Even from this distance his eyes are very blue. He wears dark brown cowboy boots, faded denims and a loose cotton shirt with faces printed all over it. He pauses in the doorway for a moment, legs apart, thumbs hooked into the pockets of his jeans. A few strands of hair fall over his forehead and he tosses them impatiently away. He looks around the room with a face empty of expression, a rather hard face, Asya thinks, and then he smiles. Asya and Deena watch him walk with long deliberate strides to a group standing by the piano. One man in the group, a lecturer in the Marketing department, has turned towards him. As the stranger walks up, the lecturer introduces him to the other two: Marzouk el-Ashtal and one of the Egyptian students.

'Well?' asks Deena.

'No,' Asya concedes. 'He doesn't look like a wispy – but you never know. Deena, we ought to go over and say hello to the women –'

'OK, let's,' says Deena.

'But I don't want to end up sitting with them,' Asya goes on. She looks towards the end of the long table where a cluster of women sit together. They are all wearing formal two-piece suits or afternoon dresses. Vernis handbags sit on the floor next to feet shod in matching vernis. Set, well made-up faces divide alert attention between fussily dressed children romping around the room and husbands who have detached themselves to stand in groups of threes and fours with other men, smoking, jingling loose change in their pockets, laughing.

'They're so – established,' Asya says. 'If you sit with them you'll see: they won't talk about anything other than their kids and this food on the table – except they're probably talking about *you* now: "Well, of course she can't grow her hair overnight, but she could at least have worn something other than those jeans. Her sister should have told her. This is a party after all" –'

'You're dressed up enough for both of us,' Deena laughs.

'You're joking. I'm not dressed up at all –'

'Asya, come on –'

'This is the simplest dress possible, –' Asya protests. 'Tante Soraya would call it a washing-vest or some such thing – and that's probably what they're all saying now –'

'Sure – with pearls and dangly earrings and velvet stilettos –'

'Well, it *is* supposed to be a party. Is it overdone? You could have told me at home, you know. Should I take the earrings off?'

'No, no. It's OK. You look great.'

'Are you sure?'

'Absolutely.'

'OK. Look, let's go and say hello before it becomes impossible.'

'So this is your sister? You don't look at all alike.'

'Yes, this is my sister Deena –'

'It's because her hair is cut so short –'

'It's nice: *à la garçon* –'

'It would be nicer a bit longer. It would suit her better –'

'But it's true you don't look at all alike –'

'I look like our mother,' Deena says for the thousandth time in her life, 'Asya looks like our father.'

'Oh yes. You can see: she's got the same eyes. A great man, Professor Ulama, a true intellectual –'

'You know him?'

'Know him? Of course I know him. I told Asya when she first came here: I studied with him. Oh yes. He made the whole department walk on dough and not leave a mark – we were so afraid of him. But we loved him too. Your luck is from the sky to have such a father.'

'Yes, indeed,' Asya nods.

'Yes, of course,' Deena says in the same breath.

'And your mother too – a great, great woman –'

'Their mother?'

'Dr Lateefa Mursi.'

'What? Is Professor Ulama married to Dr Lateefa?'

'Yes, of course, didn't you know?'

'No, I swear, it's the first time I hear this –'

'Are you too from the Faculty of Arts?' Asya asks.

'Yes, but from Librarianship. Your mother taught us English Bibliography. A wonderful woman. We all loved her so much. She really influenced us –'

'Were you working before you came here?' Asya asks.

'No. I got married as soon as I graduated, and then the children came. But in sha 'Allah when we go home and the children are older I will work. One has to do something with oneself after all –'

'Of course.'

'You have no children, have you?'

'No.'

'Well done. They hold you up so –'

'You live in Jenny MacRae's cottage, don't you?'

'Yes.'

'Aren't you frightened out there all on your own?'

'But her husband is there, isn't he?'

'No, he isn't. He's in Syria. He's doing his Ph.D as an external. He only comes here once in a while, isn't that right?'

'That's right,' says Asya.

'I didn't know she was married to a Syrian –'

'He isn't Syrian –'

'She isn't married to a Syrian. Her husband is Egyptian. But he's working in Syria –'

'Oh, then it must be very frightening living out there on your own. My dear, there's nobody at all around you; it's all empty –'

'I've got used to it.'

'Got used to it? I'm surprised your husband permits it. Isn't he afraid for you? Don't *you* think it's frightening, Deena?'

'It's a bit strange, but I'm getting used to it,' Deena says.

'How long are you here for?'

'Only another ten days.'

'Are you doing English as well, then?'

'No, Deena is doing Physics,' Asya says.

'Physics? So you've departed from the family tradition?'

'Yes,' says Deena.

'I think the family tradition has ended.' Asya smiles. 'Our brother is doing Engineering.'

'You see?' Asya asks, looking at Deena in the bathroom mirror as they both wash their hands.

'Well, they can only be like that the first time –'

'They would be like that *all* the time.'

'Chrissie and Mimi would probably be like that if you were meeting them for the first time.'

'They wouldn't, Deena, don't be horrid. And Noora definitely wouldn't.'

'No, Noora wouldn't.'

'It's also this business of being our parents' daughter all the time: "You're Professor Ulama's daughter? *And* Dr Lateefa's daughter *too*? How *wonderful*!" Doesn't it get to you?'

'Well, it has its uses.'

'Like what?' Asya shakes her hands out under the dryer.

'When it happens in an airline office or something and then you get things done in minutes instead of days.'

'Yes,' Asya makes room for Deena. 'It's still pretty bugging, though. And in the university – well, they won't even need to *say* it.'

'Yes. It's worse for you, though. I'm in a different college at least.'

'It's awful. I mean, I know it gives me a base and an advantage and everything, but I'll never be able to do anything on my own account. Every single thing I do will always be seen in reference to *them*.'

'Leave Cairo University: transfer to Ain Shams.'

'I can't.'

'Why not?'

'It hasn't got a dome. Deena, what are we going to do now?'

'You mean about going back into the room?'

477

'Yes. I don't want to go back to those women for the rest of the evening, but it'll look rude if we drag two chairs into a corner –'

'We could go and talk to someone else. To Marzouk –'

'Then we'd look as if we prefer to talk to the men.'

'Oh, Asya, don't complicate things.'

'I'm not. They're complicated by themselves.'

'Well, let's go and examine the food and maybe someone will come and talk to us.'

Deena and Asya put some food on to two plates and stand at the edge of the table. Asya looks at Deena.

'Why *do* you wear your hair so short anyway?'

'Do you want the truth?'

'Yes, of course I do.'

'I got so fed up with people saying, "Of course your sister's hair is wonderful" –'

'What are you talking about? What people?'

'Well, at school, mostly. The teachers.'

'The teachers said *that* to you?'

'All the time. It wasn't just the hair, of course, it was everything. Miss Nabeela would shake her head over my copy-book – "Your sister's handwriting was so beautiful" –'

'Miss Nabeela never taught me Arabic; Sheikh Ebeid did, and he always deducted two grades for bad handwriting –'

'Miss Husniyya would always tell me how you *consistently* got top marks for Social Sciences –'

'That was just learning stuff off by heart practically, and she can't have liked me: we locked her up in the classroom once, you know that –'

'I know, but she's forgotten, and all she remembers is what wonderful manners you had and how neat and tidy you were. And even Auntie In'am, our headmistress –'

'*She* had to call Mummy and Daddy in twice to tell them how awful I was –'

'Twice?'

'Yes.'

'I only know about once.'

'Twice.'

'Once was when you led a "revolution" through the playground when you were nine –'

'And I got the giggles when she was imitating me to Daddy: raising a clenched fist and chanting, "*Let – us – revolt*" as she sat behind her desk –'

'What was the second time?'

'When I broke a window-pane over Yassin's head. Do you remember Yassin?'

478

'Of course I do. I thought you were keen on him?'

'I liked him a lot. We were friends. But he was doing this dreadful, supposedly comic routine where he held the door of the french windows open, pretended not to see it, tried to walk through it and bashed his head. Then he'd look surprised, go round the other side, hold it and try again. He went on and on and on and in the end I couldn't bear it.'

'So what did you do? Push him?'

'No. I was holding the door and asking him – *begging* him – to stop; and in the end when he came at the glass one more time I pushed it towards him and he crashed right through.'

'I didn't know about that. You know the thing about you is that you're always so polite to people, so gentle and so sweet, that when you suddenly do something dreadful they're unprepared – or they don't even believe you're doing it –'

'Hi! Did you ladies make any of this?'

Asya and Deena turn: the man in the cowboy boots and the picture-shirt is standing in front of them. He smiles an easy smile and his eyes are indeed very blue. In his hand he holds an empty plate.

'I was hoping you'd advise me . . .' He indicates the table.

'Well,' Asya looks at all the dishes. 'It depends what sort of thing you like.'

'I'll try anything,' he smiles.

'Usually,' says Deena, 'you start with those little things over there – they're called *borek* – and a bit of the – this salad.'

'OK.' He reaches over and picks up one of the small triangular pastry cases. He puts it on his plate and spoons some *tabbouleh* next to it, then he picks up the *borek* and bites it. 'Mmm. You said it's called "*borek*"? It's like a samosa.'

'Samosa?' asks Deena.

'It's a sort of samosa, yes,' says Asya, 'but the filling isn't hot.'

'And what's the salad?'

'It's *tabbouleh*,' says Deena. 'It's made with parsley.'

'It's delicious.'

'Good evening!' Marzouk el-Ashtal greets Asya. 'We have to thank Miss Deena for bringing you to our party.'

'You're very kind,' smiles Asya. 'It's we who have to thank you for telling us about it.'

'Gerald too,' Marzouk says. 'It's the first time he comes.'

'Oh?' says Asya.

'You know each other?' asks Marzouk.

'No, we don't,' the man in the cowboy boots says. 'At least, I've heard of the ladies and I've seen Asya around but we've never met. I'm Gerald Stone.'

479

'I'm Deena. Glad to meet you.' Deena smiles.

'Hi!' says Asya.

'How is the bicycle, Miss Deena, she is behaving?'

'Oh yes, she's great –'

'Is this Egyptian?' Gerald Stone asks Asya as he edges some more *tabbouleh* on to his fork.

'No,' says Asya. 'It's Lebanese.'

'But you are from Egypt, aren't you?'

'Yes.'

'Is it as wonderful as they say it is?'

Asya smiles. 'It's pretty wonderful.'

'I'd love to go one day. Do you miss it?'

'Yes, very much.'

'How long is it since you've been back?'

'I went home in August '74.'

'Two years. That's a long time.'

'Yes.' Asya moves back a step and looks at the table. She picks up a piece of *kofta* and one *borek* and puts them on her plate. He is pleasant enough – apart from the shirt – and friendly. And not *too* friendly. The faces on the shirt are all Warhol's Marilyn Monroe. Already she can sense the eyes of the wives watching them.

'You're doing a Ph.D, aren't you?' He comes a step closer.

'Yes.' She glances up.

'Smart lady!'

'Not particularly, no.' Asya shakes her head. 'What are *you* doing?'

'An MA course. Marketing. When are you planning to finish?'

'I should be through by next summer.'

'And then you'll go home?'

'Yes.'

'Do you know what you'll do then?'

'I've got a job already. In the university. I'm only on study leave.'

'So it's all mapped out.' He smiles.

Asya smiles back. 'Yes. More or less.'

She turns to Deena, but she is deep in conversation with Marzouk; Asya hears her say, 'But look at what Pol Pot is doing –'

'Is your sister staying with you long?'

'Another two weeks maybe.' But she can't just stand here answering questions. 'That's an – interesting shirt,' she says.

'I got it in Jamaica. It's a bit wild – but I thought since this was a party –' He gives her a wide smile.

There is a silence.

'Do you have – brothers and sisters?' Asya asks.

'No.' He smiles. 'I'm an only child.'

'Where do you – where is your home?'

480

'I was brought up in Canterbury. But I've been living in London for a while.'

'Were you working before you came here?'

'Not just before. I took three months off and travelled around a bit.'

'Where? India?'

'No. I went to South America.'

'Oh, sorry, of course: you just mentioned Jamaica. That must have been really interesting.'

'Very, yes. You've never been?'

Asya shakes her head. 'But I'd like to – one day.'

'It's worth going; it's something else.'

'Asya! Hello! I haven't seen you for a long time.'

'Fred! Hi!' Asya turns with relief to Saif's supervisor. 'How're you doing? You look gorgeous. How's Saif?'

'Thank you. He's fine.'

'I haven't heard from him in over a month. Is he due over soon?'

'He's definitely coming next month, yes.'

'Well, his last paper was brilliant.'

'He's a clever man.' Asya smiles. 'I didn't know you came to these dos?'

'Well, once in a while, you know, we've got a lot of your chaps in the school.'

'I'm sorry,' says Asya, 'do you know each other? This is Fred Langley, Gerald Stone, this is my sister, Deena, who's visiting me, and Marzouk el-Ashtal.'

'Hi!' Fred Langley turns to Deena. 'So, are you an academic too?'

'You are not eating,' Marzouk says to Asya. 'And you are not offering food to our guests.' He turns to Gerald Stone. 'You must try the chicken. I am sure you will like it. It is marinaded for a whole night in lemon juice and yoghurt –'

'Excuse me,' Asya says, and makes her way over to the women. She pulls up a chair and sits down. 'The *boreks* are delicious.' She smiles. 'Who made them?'

'Siham did.' One of the women indicates another.

'They're very easy,' Siham says, 'but of course I couldn't get ricotta cheese so I had to use cottage cheese instead and it's not the same –'

Asya glances briefly towards the group at the table. He is good-looking, Gerald Stone – although she generally does not go for blond men: she'd stopped watching James Bond when Sean Connery stopped playing him; her heroes were always the older, darker, more weathered types: Richard Burton, Ahmad Mazhar, Peter Finch, James Mason, Mahmoud Mursi, that sort of thing. But of the type, he's good-looking: tall and well built, the face very angular and masculine and framed by the thick, longish hair – but there's something studied about him; like he's very aware of what impression he might be making. Is that fair? He had behaved easily and naturally, making conversation, being polite, asking about the food, his smile goes right into his eyes – no, he seems natural – natural but not without awareness. That shirt, though, with Marilyn Monroe all over it, that's really vulgar – ah, but from where does she get her notions of vulgar? From her father and Saif – why shouldn't someone wear a fun shirt once in a while – maybe he's wearing it for a joke –

'You're going to remain separatists like this all your lives?'

The women all turn to Hisham Badran, who stands over them laughing.

'You're doing enough mixing for all of us,' one of them says, looking at a group of people standing by one of the windows. Asya follows her glance and sees a young, red-headed girl standing at the edge of the group and looking over towards Hisham.

'Don't put a hex on her now,' he laughs. 'Leave her alone. She's a nice girl.'

'They're all nice girls,' says another woman drily.

'The question is, when are you going to slow down?' adds another.

'I just don't understand what's annoying you,' he protests. 'I'll slow down when I go home. I won't just slow down: I'll *settle* down. Isn't that what's required? What do you say, Asya? Long live he who sees you – what is this? You don't come to the university any more?'

'Yes I do, and here I am,' Asya smiles up at him. 'How are you doing? You must be almost through?'

'I handed it in last week. I'm waiting for them to set a date for the viva.'

'Goodness! So you're really really free now!'

'Yes, my dear. He is free and enjoying his freedom,' Siham says.

'Bear witness, Asya!' cries Hisham. 'Why have they got it in for me? Won't you defend me?'

'Why should Asya defend you? Another few weeks and we'll find that girl sitting by the wall crying.'

'She won't be sitting by any wall. You exaggerate –'

'You'll see – except you won't see because you'll be gone.'

'She knows everything; she knows I'm going –'

'It won't make any difference.'

'I don't understand why you've got this specific girl so much on your mind; you don't see me except you start blaming me –'

'He's right, Siham. After all, she's not a kitten with unopened eyes; she's English, she knows what she's doing.'

'Asya, your sister is visiting you? Yes?' Hisham asks.

'Yes.'

'She's a mathematician?'

'No, a physicist.'

'You must introduce us.'

482

'Sure,' Asya smiles. 'She's over there.'

'Come and introduce me to her,' Hisham turns to the other women. 'Get up. Get up and talk to people and don't sit gossiping in the corner like old women at a wedding.'

'Deena, I want you to meet Hisham Badran who's just finished his Ph.D and is about to go home. The rest of you all know Hisham, I guess.' Marzouk claps Hisham on the arm.

'I thought you'd be stuck to your radio listening to your president?'

'The reception is very bad,' Hisham says. He shakes hands with Gerald Stone.

'We've met in the Indoor Rec,' Gerald Stone says.

' "Voice of the Arabs" usually is clear,' Marzouk says.

'What will he say anyway?' says Deena. 'He'll attack Assad and speak of Palestinian rights – which he's been the first to sell –'

'He's just come back from the Riyadh Summit,' says Hisham. 'He might have something to say about that –'

'Yes. Support for our brother Numeiri and accusations against Qaddafi –'

'The Libyans seem to be trying to patch things up in Lebanon,' Asya begins.

'Everyone wants to interfere in Lebanon,' says Marzouk.

'Is Saif in Lebanon?' Fred Langley asks Asya.

'No, he's in Damascus,' she says.

'Well, I guess that's not too bad right now. Look, I'm going to have to go.' He looks at his watch. 'When Saif is here you must both come out and have dinner with us. OK?'

'We'd love to,' Asya says.

'OK, that's great. I'll hold you to that.'

He steps forward as though to kiss her, but Asya, aware of the watching community, holds out her hand. Fred Langley shakes it, holds up his hand in a general greeting and leaves.

'When *is* Saif coming over?' asks Hisham.

'In a couple of weeks,' Asya says.

'Is that for sure this time?'

'As far as anyone can tell.' Asya shrugs and smiles. 'Look, Hisham, why don't you ask your friend to join us?'

'Sure. Where is she?'

'Over there, looking at you.'

Hisham waves and beckons. Asya watches the girl's face light up, then she walks quickly across the room towards them.

'Let me introduce Lisa,' Hisham begins. 'This is Asya, Deena, Gerald and Marzouk – you can call him Zouki if you like.'

'Hi!'

Everyone smiles at Lisa.

'I haven't seen you eat anything,' Hisham says. He addresses the group. 'She's afraid of our cooking.'

'I'm not,' Lisa begins, and blushes. 'It's just that I don't know what anything is.'

'Come with me.' Asya puts a gentle hand on her arm. 'I'll explain it to you.'

When Lisa has a full plate she and Asya linger by the table.

'What course are you on?' Asya asks.

'I'm not. I mean, it's summer vac now,' Lisa says, and blushes again. 'But I'm doing French.'

'Oh, that's interesting,' says Asya. 'Have you done your junior year abroad yet?'

'I'm supposed to start any time now,' Lisa says, 'but I'm just waiting a bit.'

'Oh,' says Asya, 'I see.' She must be the same age as Deena, this creamy-faced kid with her torn jeans, her unvarnished toenails in brown sandals, her pretty breasts, round and appealing under the big white T-shirt. She looks into candid grey eyes.

'I've – I've seen you before,' Lisa says, 'in the library and once in town. I've wanted to meet you but –'

'But?'

'Well, you look so – so far away,' Lisa laughs, and blushes for the third time. 'That's a silly thing to say. But, I mean, you don't look round you or anything – so one wouldn't dare interrupt your thoughts. Hisham felt so too.'

'Oh!' says Asya. Well, if Hisham felt so too, Hisham the Judge. . . . 'That must be just how I look.' She shrugs. 'I'm never thinking about anything particularly – and I'd have loved to have met you. Anyway, now we *have* met.'

'Yes we have, and I'm very glad,' Lisa smiles at her, a big open smile.

'Listen,' says Asya, on an impulse, 'why don't you come out to where I live? Next Sunday, say. We can just have tea or something to eat –'

'Oh, I'd love to. Can I just check with Hisham?'

'Of course.'

'You still haven't answered my first question.' Gerald Stone is at her shoulder.

'What is that?' Asya looks up guardedly.

'Did *you* make any of this?' He indicates the food on the table.

'Well,' says Asya hesitantly, 'I made that thing over there. In the kind of shallow tray.'

'What is it?'

Lisa smiles at Asya and moves back towards Hisham.

'It's a dessert.'

'Has it got a name?'

'Uh-huh.'

'What is its name?'

'*Basbousa*,' says Asya. She hates exhibiting Arabic words like this: a collection of sounds. And then hearing her interlocuter try out a collection of approximately similar sounds.

'*Basbousa?*' says Gerald Stone.

'Not bad,' says Asya.

'Does it mean anything?'

'It doesn't mean anything in Arabic proper, but in Egyptian dialect it means "that which is patted". Except it's a special type of patting you can only do to pastry – I mean, a specific verb to describe patting pastry. It's like calling something a "crumble", for example.'

'Is Arabic very complicated?'

'You mean I'm making it sound complicated.'

He smiles at her. 'Not at all. I just wondered, really. I mean, one can't get any kind of handle on it because of the different script, you know – and I just wondered if it was as complicated as it seems.'

'Yes, but any language is complicated if you're going to use it properly.'

'I'm going to try some of your – what was it again?'

'It's not very good.'

'I'm sure it's excellent.'

'It isn't – really. It's supposed to be made with a particular flour and I couldn't get it so I used semolina and it isn't the same thing at all.'

'You can't make something and then disclaim responsibility for it.'

'I can in this case.'

'I'll try some anyway.'

Asya shrugs.

'Ah! You're going to try the *basbousa*.' Hisham has come up. 'I am too. Deena says you made it.' He turns to Asya. 'I didn't know you could cook.'

'I can't,' says Asya. 'I used a recipe – and I'm warning you now it's not too good: it's not the right texture.'

'Well' – Hisham chews – 'it's a bit dry and –'

'– a bit grainy,' Asya adds for him. 'I told you –'

'Hisham,' Lisa says, 'Asya has asked us out to her place next Sunday.'

'Is that an open invitation?' Marzouk smiles.

'Of course,' says Asya. 'Do come – everyone – we'll just have tea and improvise. And we'll try not to go on too much about Arab politics.' She smiles at Lisa and Gerald.

'Oh no, they're very interesting,' Lisa says.

'We'll divide the time between the Middle East and Northern Ireland,' Marzouk suggests.

'Asya – hello –'

Asya turns towards the familiar, hesitant voice. 'Oh! Hello! How nice to see you here. Do you know any – let me introduce you. This is Professor Murray, my supervisor –'

'Bill – Bill Murray –'

'We're going,' Hisham says quietly to Asya.

'Sure,' says Asya.

'We'll see you on Sunday.' Lisa smiles at Asya before following Hisham. 'I'm glad we've met at last.'

'You see,' says Marzouk, 'you are meeting all these people. Now are you happy you came?'

'I was telling your sister we have another student from Cairo University coming next term,' Bill Murray says to Asya.

'Mahrous?'

'Mahrous, yes, I believe that's his name. He's on the staff like you.'

'Yes, we were even in the same class,' says Asya.

'That will be nice for you then. To have an old friend here.'

'Yes. Well – we weren't really friends. But he's very nice. He works very hard.'

'You all seem to work hard, I must say. You're very industrious.'

'Ah.' Asya smiles. 'So I don't have to feel guilty about being here tonight instead of curled up with my metaphors?'

'Not at all, no – no. I think – she's doing very well.' Bill Murray addresses Deena. 'She has almost finished, really.'

'I've always wanted to apologise for that first year,' Asya says.

'Oh no, no, you were just – just finding your feet.'

Asya smiles at him. 'Still, it can't have been easy for you.'

'But I admired your determination.' He turns to Deena. 'She didn't miss one tutorial.'

'That's my sister,' says Deena.

'Are you doing graduate studies too?' Gerald Stone asks Deena.

'I've still got my last year to do at college,' Deena says. 'But after that, probably, yes.'

'*She* is brilliant, though,' says Asya. 'Truly. She won't take a year to find her feet.'

When Bill Murray leaves, Asya turns to Deena. 'We should go.'

'Yes,' says Deena. 'OK.'

'That tea on Sunday,' says Gerald. 'Can I take you up on it?'

'Of course,' says Asya.

'But I don't know where you live.'

'Oh, I'll draw you a map.' Asya starts opening her handbag.

'It's all right,' he says, 'give me your phone number and I'll check with you on Sunday.'

'Oh.' Asya looks at him. 'Well, do you want to write it down?'

'No. I'll remember it.' He smiles.

'Well?' says Deena, as Asya puts the car into reverse and pulls out of the car park. 'Was it as dreadful as you thought it would be?'

'No. But that's not to say I couldn't have done without it.'

'You're just too used to being on your own.'

'Well, I had to *get* used to it, didn't I?' Asya's voice is sharp.

'Yes. I suppose so.' Deena is immediately contrite. 'Is it dreadful, Ya-ya?'

Asya shrugs. 'It's *been* dreadful. But it's OK now. Sort of. And it won't be for ever.'

'Are you really going to finish by next summer?'

'Yes. Absolutely.'

'So September seventy-seven you'll be back teaching?'

'I guess so.'

'And the youngest Ph.D in the college. Maybe even in the university. Mummy's going to be so proud.'

'So how did *you* like it tonight?'

'Well, I thought they were quite friendly people, really.'

'Yes. Well, it *was* a Friendship evening.'

'No, but Saif's supervisor seemed really nice.'

'Yes. He's OK. His wife's nice, too; they're very easy to get on with.'

'I didn't think your Professor was as uncomfortable as you made him out to be.'

'He was different tonight. Maybe he's different in company. But, of course, we've got more used to each other now.'

'What about Hisham Badran?'

'Ah! The Crown Prince.'

Deena laughs. 'Yes. He does seem a bit like that. Why?'

'Because that's what he is. He's the son of Dr Nagi Badran, you know, the heart specialist. His family is very big in Alexandria. He's young. handsome. He's got money and class. He's going back to a lectureship and the world is his oyster.'

'That sounds a bit like you.'

'Me?' Asya is surprised. 'But he's free,' she says after a moment. 'He can do absolutely anything he wants. He's getting ready for his life to begin.'

'Do you think he's with the Mabahith?' Deena asks suddenly.

'No.' Asya is taken aback. 'I mean, I never thought of it. Why should you ask that?'

'He's just a bit ready with the official line – and he doesn't look like a dissenter –'

'That's something of a superficial judgment, isn't it? I mean, loads of people would be like that – kind of middle of the road – that doesn't make them Mabahith.'

'Yes. Maybe not,' says Deena.

Sunday, 25 July

'Do you really have to do all this?' asks Deena as Asya goes round the living-room with a duster and a canister of Pledge.

'Of course I do,' says Asya. 'Hisham is Egyptian, remember; he'll be thinking of how his mother would never allow a speck of dust around the place –'

'But you're all students here –'

'He'll think if his mother had been a student here she wouldn't have allowed a speck of dust around the place. Please could you stack up those logs so they don't look too untidy?'

'How would you like them? In a pyramid or –'

'Deena! Just stack them up.'

'You said we'd improvise,' Deena grumbles as she kneels by the logs, 'and you've bought enough food for a banquet; they're only coming to tea.'

'And supposing they stay on? What would we improvise *with*?' asks Asya. She runs downstairs and then comes back with the vacuum cleaner. 'This rug only looks good just after it's been vacuumed,' she says as she starts up the machine. 'The moment it gets trodden on it goes all flat.'

'What do you want me to do now?' Deena asks when Asya switches off the Hoover.

'Do you think you could go out and cut some green stuff to put into a couple of vases? You won't find flowers, but just some – foliage, you know. I'm going to vacuum downstairs.'

'Asya, they won't inspect the bedrooms.'

'Look, it's the first time they've been here. Don't you know what people are like? "Oh, you've got the living-room upstairs! And these are the bedrooms?" and they open the door and peep in. It's natural.'

'What are you doing?'

'I'm building a little fire, just in case.'

'But it's thirty degrees!'

'But in the evening it's nice to have a fire, just to look at.'

When she has finished Asya stands up and looks around. The wooden floor is mellow in the midday light, the black leather sofa and armchairs look soft and inviting, the cream rug is fluffy and the coffee table is gleaming with polish. The hearth looks hospitable, the kitchen table has been cleared of her work and the kitchen counter-tops are tidy and clean. Yes, the room looks charming. The windows stand wide open and the world outside is all greens and blues.

She carries the vacuum cleaner downstairs. As she starts on her bedroom Deena comes in with an armful of greenery.

'Is this all right?'

'Yes, it's lovely. Do you want to go upstairs and arrange them?'

'I think *you'd* better do that. Here, I'll do the vacuuming.'

When Asya comes back down Deena has finished the two bedrooms and is vacuuming the small back room which opens off the hall. Sometimes Asya thinks that this is her favourite room: it is a light, warm room which has no particular function except that it houses the boiler. It is shaped like a crooked 'L', the bottom of which opens out on to the strip of back garden, and when Asya sits or lies on the bedouin rug she has put down on the floor there she feels more free than she does anywhere else in the house. She wonders about that, and decides it must be because while she is in the boiler-room she hasn't used up any of her options; they all remain open: she can go to the living-room and work, or go to the bedroom and sleep. The boiler-room itself is not an option so she can freely be there. Maybe that's why she likes sitting on the stairs as well – but the boiler-room is better because it's got the glass door out on to the back and because you can't lie down on the stairs. If William and Mina were still around they could cite this as one more damning example of her 'sitting on fences'.

Asya goes into the bathroom, drops to her knees and starts scrubbing the bath. She washes the tub, the basin and the toilet, puts a new Blue Loo into the cistern and polishes the mirror. She presses open the pedal-bin: tissue-paper, cotton-wool buds and long, tangled black hairs. She takes out the bin-liner and goes up to the kitchen to get a new one. It isn't that she would claim never to use a cotton-wool bud or that not one hair from her head ever dropped out. But why should people see such personal bits of her – she stops on the stairs: where is it? she thinks. Where has she put the – thing? She'd used to keep it in the bathroom – or, rather, she'd put it in the bathroom and forgotten about it until Deena had come upstairs once holding the long, transparent plastic object and asking, 'What on earth is this?' And it had taken all Asya's duplicitous sang-froid to say, 'What? Oh, I don't know. It was here when I came. Where did you find it?'

'I opened the cabinet in the bathroom to see if you had a fresh tube of toothpaste – and there it was.'

'I must have put it there and forgotten about it. I thought it was maybe a test-tube.'

'It's not a test tube,' Deena had said, holding it up and examining it. 'It's too thick for a test-tube. And a test-tube is a completely regular shape. This has got these ridges – and it swells up at the tip.'

'Oh,' Asya had said. She'd looked at the thing in Deena's hand blankly. And she'd felt like a cheat because she was deceiving her sister – but she'd had another loyalty to consider.

'Do you know what this looks like?' Deena had asked, still holding it up in front of her face.

489

'What?' Asya had asked.

'It looks like a penis.'

'Goodness!' Asya had said. 'You don't think –'

'See, if you hold it like this . . .'

Deena had held the thing from the base and stationed it horizontally in the air – horizontally but with a slightly upward, eager tilt. Asya had stared at it glinting in the sunlight.

'Yes. You're right. Do you think –'

'Well,' Deena had said, lowering her arm and tapping the glans on the table. 'It's some sort of unbreakable material.' She grinned at her sister. 'Maybe it's a sex toy?'

'Oh, Deena!' Asya had jumped up and taken it from her sister. 'Here, give it to me. I'd better put it away.'

'Why don't you send it on to whoever owns this place? She might be missing it?' Deena had laughed.

Asya had run downstairs with it, she remembers *that*, but where had she put it? Deena finding it was bad enough, but if anybody else came across it she'd die. A sex toy, for heaven's sake! What world was that where one would freely, lightly, voluptuously acquire and employ sex toys? She tries to imagine Saif.

'You know what we're doing tonight, Princess?'

'No, what?'

'We're going shopping.'

'Oh? But all the shops are closed.'

'Not the ones we're going to, sweetie.'

'Where are we going then?'

'We're going to buy – a dildo!'

Asya chokes with sudden laughter as she imagines the scene. As she catches her breath, Deena looks round the bottom of the stairs.

'Are you all right?'

'Oh yes, yes, I just – breathed wrong.' Asya goes into the kitchen and puts the plastic bag in the bin. She can't even imagine it. The moment she makes Saif say the words he changes, his face and voice change, he throws his arms out and yells, 'A dildo!' like a game-show host, and the scene turns to farce. Well, what if it came from *her*? Now she sees Saif reclining on a hotel bed reading *Amateur Photographer*. The bathroom door opens and Asya comes through in a white nightie. She holds her hands behind her back. She kneels on the bed next to him and says softly, 'I've got something for you' – except that's not right, because it isn't strictly for him – well, it is for him in the sense that – yes, but he'd be thinking it was the latest Asimov or a first edition of Omar Khayyam or a lighter or a scarf or something – well, what can she say then? 'I've got something for us'? That would be unbearably cloying. OK. Here: Asya

490

kneels on the bed and says softly, 'I've got something to show you.' She holds out her hand, and as he looks up she flings the thing away from her and throws herself back on the bed shrieking with laughter. It's hopeless. It's just completely hopeless. Asya leans on the kitchen window-sill and looks out at the gentle hill behind the house. But if she imagines someone else; not someone particular, just some – stranger: dark, tall, strong, late-thirtyish, she can't see his face very well but he smells good, his voice is low and he has a faint accent. He lifts his mouth from hers and says – whispers, 'Tonight – we are going to do something different.'

'Are we, what?' Her voice is soft and husky. She looks up at him with eyes misted by desire.

'Come.'

He pushes her gently along to a big bed – cushions, tassels, canopies, gold braid – everything – and presses her shoulders so that she sits down. From his pocket he slowly draws out a long strip of black velvet. As his hand approaches her face she shrinks away. He stops. Then he holds it out to her. 'Take it,' he says. 'It is only a cloth. Take it.'

She holds it in her hand and feels its softness. She looks up at him.

'Trust me?' he asks.

'Yes,' she whispers. He pulls at the black velvet and she feels its softness running through her hand.

'Close your eyes,' he says, 'and sit very still.'

She feels the heavy material settling gently on her face, and a deeper darkness envelops her.

'Are you comfortable?' His hands cup her face.

'Yes.'

'You look beautiful like this. Come, lie back on the cushions. I want you to get used to being blind.'

They lie on the bed kissing and stroking for what seems an age, and she feels so comfortable, so at home in her blindfold she wants never to take it off – but she wants – her hands on his chest, on his shoulders, on his arms become more urgent –

'You want me – now?' he whispers into her hair.

'Yes, yes.'

'Yes, what?'

'Yes, please – oh, please –'

He groans as he runs his fingers between her legs.

'Ah, you do, you do.'

She feels a moist touch on her lips . . . She opens her mouth and sucks her own juices off a strong, thick finger.

'What do you want?' he whispers, pulling his finger away, drawing it along the curve of her jaw, 'Tell me.'

'I want you. I want to feel you inside me –'

'Say it, darling, say it –'

'I want you – oh, I want you to fuck me – oh, please –'

'Ah! Brave, so brave.' He kisses her temple. 'Open up for me, then, open for me, there –'

'Oh –'

'Do you feel it?'

'Yes, oh –'

'Be braver now, braver, put your hand on my hand –' His tongue runs over her teeth, licks the corner of her mouth.

'Oh, but what – what –'

'Shhh – you'll see later, what does it feel like?'

'Oh, it's – heavy – as though –'

'As though?'

'Oh, I don't – oh, please –'

'You don't like it?'

'Yes – yes, I like it –'

'Hold it. Hold it. You do it. I want to watch you –'

'Oh, but I can't –'

'Yes, you can – do it – *do* it –'

His hand is tight on her thigh as she gives herself up to the phallus in her left hand; her right hand rests on him until she turns her blind face into his chest with a cry and feels his arms closing round her . . .

OK, Asya, OK, she tells herself as she leans her hot face against the side of the window, you're an intelligent person, a literary person, analyse that. What does it tell you? Come on. It's only in your head, no one will know. A stranger, can't see his face: no reality, no commitment. The accent: what is it? Vaguely European – so, not Arab, not English, further distance, no common ground, so you can't tell – don't need to care what he thinks, how he sees things, what he's *like* outside this room – and the *room*: gold braid and canopies, my God, exoticism run wild, consumerism rampant. The blindfold: further distance, abdication of responsibility; what's happening is nothing to do with me. And then, of course, he doesn't use his own body – his body, as far as we can make out, remains safely clothed throughout. Instead he uses a heavy (ivory? ebony?) object – further distance, further rejection of reality, rejection of the living body in favour of a work of art, further rejection of *him* as anything other than a tool, and in fact at the end he isn't even *using* the tool: he is confined to a watching, cheerleading role – in other words, what you have is a completely masturbatory fantasy – and the language – the chatter – the language is really the point, isn't it? Saying, 'Fuck me,' is the high point of the event – so a repressed, regressive masturbatory fantasy. D.H. Lawrence would have had a field day with you –

'Asya? Do you want me to do anything else?'

Asya turns to her sister.

'Are you all right?' Deena asks.

'Yes, of course I am. Why?'

'You just looked a bit – blank. What should I do now?'

'Nothing, dear. It's all done.'

'What are *you* going to do?'

'I – thought I'd have a shower. Then we can have some lunch. Then I'll just try and do some work until someone comes.'

'OK,' Deena says. 'I'll take a book out into the garden till you're ready.'

'We can eat out there if you like.'

'Yes. That'd be nice.'

Asya collects a new bin-liner from the cupboard under the sink and takes it down to the bathroom. So it's regressive, and pretentious, and masturbatory – and capitalist into the bargain. So she feels more comfortable with art than with life. Where was she supposed to have learned different? And it isn't true that she can't take responsibility for her own actions – she hears Deena go out and starts looking again. She can't have put it back in the bathroom cabinet? No, it isn't there. She goes into her bedroom and searches through her drawers – but she would have come across it any morning while she was getting dressed if it had been there. Where else? She couldn't have gone and put it in Deena's room. And it isn't upstairs because she remembers running downstairs holding it. When their father mislays something, he says, 'I don't know where my hand put it.' There's abdication of responsibility. So where *had* her hand put it? She looks hopelessly into the boiler-room, but there's nowhere there for anything to be: just walls, the boiler, the floor, a rug. She hadn't gone outside –

The phone rings, and Asya steps back into the hall and picks up the receiver.

'Hello?'

'Hello. Is that Asya?'

'Yes.'

'Hi! This is Gerald. Gerald Stone.'

'Oh, hi!'

'This invite for today: is it still on?'

'Yes it is, sure.'

'Will you tell me where you are then?'

'Oh yes, of course. What you do is, when you get out of the university you go right, but before you get into town there's a road – I can never remember its name – it goes right and you have to take it. If you hold on I've got it written down somewhere –'

'Sure.'

Asya rummages with one hand in the top drawer of the chest on which the telephone sits. She knows she has a map with everything clearly marked – but as she reaches into the depths of the drawer her fingers find a hard, smooth, cylindrical object.

'Oh!' she says.

'Sorry?'

'Oh no, it's all right. Sorry. I just – I've got it here. OK. The name of the road is –'

When he rings off Asya pulls out the prosthetic and looks at it. She ought really to throw it away. It's so completely useless and horrible, and she'll just keep forgetting where she's left it and then panicking in case someone finds it. But on the other hand it is such a curious object, she will never in her life have anything like it again. It seems a shame to just throw it away. Anyway, she can't throw it in either the kitchen or the bathroom bin; she'd have to go out to the garage and put it safely in one of the big black bags, and she can't do that now because Deena is in the garden. She takes it into her bedroom. She opens her wardrobe and looks in it, then she takes out the piece of fuchsia silk that Tante Adeela had bought her in Hong Kong. She wraps the prosthetic in the uncut fabric and stuffs it behind a pile of bed-linen in the corner of the top shelf. She closes the wardrobe door.

As Asya undresses for her shower she hears Deena come into the house. She wraps a towel sarong-fashion round her and goes out into the hall.

'Hi!' she says, 'I thought we were eating outside?'

Deena wipes her brow. 'It's too hot out there. Phew.'

'OK. I'll have a shower and then we'll eat.'

'Did I hear the phone? Was it Saif?'

'Yes. No. It was Picture-Shirt.'

'Who?'

'The guy in the Marilyn Monroe picture-shirt. From the party. Gerald Stone.'

'I thought you said it was an interesting shirt?'

'I didn't.'

'You did. I heard you.'

'When?'

'There. That evening.'

'Oh, to *him*. I said it to *him*, yes.'

'It gets even more beautiful here as the light fades,' Lisa enthuses.

'Yes, I'm terribly lucky,' Asya agrees. She looks at Hisham Badran and wonders how well he knows the cottage; how many afternoons, nights, he'd spent here with Jenny MacRae. Lisa obviously doesn't know any of this. She has to know he's been here before because he knew the way –

'But it must be a bit lonely when your husband's not here – and Deena's not here for very long, is she?' says Lisa.

494

'I'm used to it, honestly.' Asya laughs. 'I keep *telling* everybody I'm used to it.'

'They say' – Gerald Stone has kept his sunglasses on throughout the afternoon – 'that if you repeat something often enough you end up believing it.'

Hisham turns from the tapes he has been inspecting and looks at him.

'But it *is* true –' begins Asya.

'What's this?' Hisham interrupts. 'You've got a tape of Sheikh Imam? And you never said?'

'Deena brought it with her.'

'You carried it out of the country? You're very brave.'

'It's not a real tape: just something we recorded when he sang at the university last March.'

'But all his tapes are like that, aren't they? He doesn't sign a contract and go into a recording studio –'

Deena laughs at the unlikeliness of the idea. 'No, of course not. But sometimes people work on the first tape, cutting out extra noise, editing out interruptions – whatever. This is just rough.'

'I have heard of Sheikh Imam,' says Marzouk.

'This is an elderly, blind man, who is a protest singer, more or less banned by the government,' Asya explains to Gerald and Lisa.

'More or less?' Gerald asks.

Asya looks at Deena.

'He isn't officially banned,' Deena explains. 'But the authorities make it difficult for him to perform.'

'How?' Lisa asks.

'Well, for example, we invited him to sing at Cairo University earlier this year and the date was set for March –'

'But the invitation has to be official, doesn't it?' Hisham asks.

'Yes. The Student Union at the Faculty of Science invited him at the request of our society: the Cultural Society. It happens' – Deena turns to Marzouk – 'that the Union this year is run by Nasserite and Independent students, which hasn't been the case in the last two years when it was dominated by students who belonged to the Mabahith –'

'Deena's been in college three years,' Asya puts in.

'So the Sheikh arrives with the poet Ahmad Fuad Nigm and Muhammad Ali the painter, and then we discover that all the big lecture halls in the building have been locked by order of the administration and can only be opened with the permission of the Dean. So we take the Sheikh to the cafeteria and go to see the Dean, but he won't see us and his secretary stalls, and meanwhile crowds of students are gathering round the Sheikh in the cafeteria. And then someone remembered that there's a big hall in the Insects department which is an annex separate from the main college building and might have been overlooked. So we went there and it was open and we had the concert.'

'But there were no repercussions?' Marzouk asks.

'The Dean dissolved our society for "endangering order in the college" and decided to hold an enquiry into the conduct of our chairperson and secretary – and then nothing happened.'

'And was it a good concert?' Gerald asks.

'Wonderful,' says Deena.

'Do you mind if I put the tape on?' asks Hisham. 'I heard him once in Alexandria six years ago but I've been out here since people started making tapes of him –'

'Of course. I'll put it on,' Asya says. 'That is – if Gerald and Lisa won't mind – just briefly?'

'Not as long as you translate it for us,' says Gerald.

'Oh, you really won't find it interesting –' Asya begins.

'But of course we will,' Lisa says, sitting upright and looking attentive.

'And it's so local,' Asya goes on. 'It won't make any sense unless I go into loads of background – and even then it'll sound naïve because that's the style of the song.'

'We'll make allowances for all that. At least give us a chance,' says Gerald.

Asya slots the tape into the machine and presses Play. After the crackling and the whistles and the applause the lute starts up and then the Sheikh's harsh, rasping voice comes on:

'Sharraft ya Nixon Baba,
Ya bta' el-Watergate –'

'What's he saying?' asks Lisa, 'something about Nixon?'

'Well,' says Asya, 'he says, "you've honoured us, Nixon Baba" – "Baba" actually means "father" but it's used here as a title of mock respect – I can't, honestly, he's already passed the next couplet and –'

'Can't we pause it perhaps?' says Gerald.

'But it's the first time Hisham hears it –' Asya says.

Hisham presses the Pause button.

'Let's hear the song through, and then I'll rewind it and pause after every couplet. I'd really like to hear Asya's translation.'

'Sharraft ya Nixon Baba,
Ya bta' el-Watergate –'

Hisham presses pause.

'Well,' says Asya, 'as I said, he says, "You've honoured us, Nixon Baba – "Baba" means "father" but it's also used, as it is used here, as a title of mock respect – as in "Ali Baba", for example – that's probably derived from Muslim Indian use of Arabic – but the thing is you could also address a child as "Baba" as an endearment – a sort of inversion: like calling him Big Chief because he's so little – and so when it's used aggressively – say in an argument between two men – it carries a diminutivising, belittling signification. So here it holds all these meanings. Anyway, "you've honoured us, Nixon Baba" – "You've honoured us" is, by the way, the traditional greeting with which you meet someone coming into your home – it's almost like "come on in" in this country. So it functions merely as a greeting and he uses it in that way but of course he activates – ironically – the meaning of having actually "honoured" us. "You've honoured us, Nixon Baba / O you of Watergate" I suppose would be the closest translation – but the structure "bita' el-whatever" (el – is just the definite article coming before any noun) posits a close but not necessarily defined relationship between the first noun (the person being described) and the second noun. So "bita' el-vegetables", for example, would be someone who sold vegetables, while "bita' el-women" would be someone who pursued women. So Nixon is "bita' el-Watergate", which suggests him selling the idea of Watergate to someone – selling his version of Watergate to the public – and pursuing a Watergate type of policy, but all in a very non-pompous, street vernacular, jokingly abusive kind of way. The use of "el-" to further specify Watergate – a noun which needs no further defining – is necessary for the rhythm and adds comic effect. I'm sure you won't want me to go on like this, so let's stop –'

'Nonsense!' says Gerald.

'It's fascinating,' says Lisa.

'Asya,' says Hisham, 'I swear I'm enjoying this. Come on, I'll play the next couplet.'

"Amaloulak eema w seema
Salateen el-fool wez-zeit –'

'OK, well,' Asya takes a deep breath. ' "Eema" is "worth" or "value". So he says, "They made an eema for you": to make an "eema" for someone is to behave towards them as though they have value when they in fact have none. So, "They've put on a show that gives you value" – "seema" is always used as an idiom with "eema" because of the rhyme. It means appearance. So: "the appearance of a thing of value" – the awful thing, though, is that this is taking all these sentences to translate, and it makes it seem ponderous and convoluted while in fact it's totally direct; it's language that a completely illiterate, uneducated woman would use to her child –'

'*Who* made him appear of value, his press office?' asks Lisa.

'This was on the occasion of Nixon's visit to the Arab world – so he's talking about the Arabs – the Arab leaders,' says Deena.

'It comes in the next line,' says Hisham. 'Asya?'

'Yes. The Sultans of "fool" and "zeit". "Fool" – this is one thing that

497

everybody knows about Egypt – that "fool" is the basic diet of the Egyptians. Particularly those from the more traditional or poorer sectors of society – I suppose they tend to be the same. It's brown beans stewed for a long time over a very low fire. It's the cheapest food you can get, and so to be a "sultan" of "fool" argues massive poverty and backwardness. This "fool" can be dressed in various ways. The simplest and cheapest is with oil – "zeit" – and lemon. So "fool" and "zeit" come together – but "zeit" also, like "oil" in English, means petrol oil. So if you take *that* meaning, then there are two categories of "Sultan" being referred to: the sultans of "fool" and poverty etc. and the sultans of wealth and oil. There is obviously a great disparity between the two categories – but there is also a similarity – underscored by the reading of "fool and zeit" as a unit having only one sultan – a similarity in their attitudes to Nixon and the USA. And "Sultan" in itself is a disparaging title nowadays – except I suppose in folk-tales where the desirable princess continues to be the sultan's daughter – because it's the Ottoman Turkish title for a king and of course these were regarded by the Egyptians and other Arabs as oppressors and parasites – besides which, of course, the later ones had a reputation for weakness and dissipatedness and so on. So to call a ruler now a sultan carries all these overtones. But there's another meaning for "salateen" as well – do you really want this to go on, because I would so much rather –' Asya appeals to Hisham Badran.

'Of course we want you to go on,' Lisa says.

'It's incredible how much there is to it,' says Gerald Stone.

'I'm sure Sheikh Imam himself would be curious to hear this exposition.' Deena laughs.

'OK.' Asya takes a deep breath and pushes her hair back from her face. ' "Salateen" is also the plural of "sultaniyyah" which is a bowl, but which also has to do with madness. You know in a farce where a mad person wears a saucepan on his head? Well, in an Egyptian farce a mad person would wear a "sultaniyyah" on his head. "He put on the sultaniyyah," means "he's gone mad".'

'Farashoulak agda' sekka,
Min Ras et-Tin 'ala 'Akka
We hnak todkhol 'ala Makka
Wiy'oulu 'aleik haggeit –'

' "They laid out the bravest path for you: from the Palace of Ras et-Tin" (that's the palace at the western end of the sea-front in Alexandria – it's the point from which King Farouk sailed into exile) "to 'Akka" – that's in Palestine. It's a city that was notoriously difficult to capture in the time of the Crusades, so someone who's pleased with himself at having performed some feat is asked, mockingly, "So you've opened 'Akka?" "And there you'll enter Makkah –" that's Makkah, the holy city in

498

Saudi Arabia, of course. "And they'll say you've performed the pilgrimage" – you are a "Hajj" – which of course is impossible since only a Muslim can perform the Hajj. This kind of refers back to German propaganda during the Second World War, when Hitler was said to be really the "Hajj Muhammad Hitler" to try and get support for him among the ordinary people.'

'Mahou moulid
Shobash ya's'hab el-beit –'

' "It's a 'moulid'." A "moulid" is strictly a "nativity" of a saint – like Christmas only there are lots of them. But because of how it's celebrated it also means a time of chaos where anything goes. "Shobash" is a kind of really vulgar cry used to attract people's attention: a woman will yell it out in a street fight to signal that she is going all out to destroy the enemy, that she doesn't mind causing a scandal – that in fact she *wants* people to come and watch. So it's used also to signify doing something wrong – shamelessly; not even having the decency to go and do it in a corner but doing it in public. On the other hand, it is used by the belly-dancer in weddings when she starts collecting gifts of money for the bride. "Ya s'hab el-beit" would be the rest of the dancer's cry. "El-beit" is the house, "As'hab el-beit" are the people of the house. So the people of the bride or groom. But the supreme "House" is the Ka'ba in Makkah. And if you ever just say "As'hab el-beit" it is taken automatically to refer to the people of *that* House, of the House of the Prophet, that is the people most honoured among all Muslims – who are now being honoured by the visit of President Nixon. So – well – there's just a lot of structural irony there. And really the rest is repetition. I mean, this really gives you an idea what it's saying and everything. Look, how about some coffee? Oh, excuse me –'

Asya runs down the stairs to answer the telephone.

'That's probably Saif,' says Deena.

'Saif!'

'Hi, sweetie! Are you OK?'

'I'm fine. Are you in Damascus?'

'Yes –'

'Is it all right where you are? The news here is awful.'

'No, it's OK here. Did I stop you working? What were you doing?'

'No, you've saved me. I've got some people visiting and they're making me translate one of Sheikh Imam's songs to them and it's beastly,' Asya whispers.

'I should have thought it'd sound pretty silly in English.'

'It either sounds silly or ponderous. A page of footnotes for every line –'

'So who's there?'

'Well, the ones you know are Hisham Badran and Deena, but there's also –'

'Right. Say hi to them for me. Tell Hisham we must have a game of squash when I come over.'

'I will. Do you know when you're coming?'

'I've got work in London on the tenth which is a Tuesday. I thought if I could get away from here on the Thursday night, I'd come up to the cottage for four days, then drive down to London for Tuesday. What do you think?'

'Oh, that's great. Do you know how long you'll be in London?'

'All through the week. I've even got something on Saturday morning. And then Monday first thing I'd be in Uxbridge. I don't know for how long. Maybe two or three days.'

'OK. So I could follow you to London for the weekend. I mean, you go down for Tuesday and I follow you Friday maybe.'

'Sure. In that case I'll take the train –'

'But I can drive the little car –'

'No you can't. It's not safe. I'll take the train.'

'Well, anyway. We can talk about that when you're here. You're coming here first, aren't you? Do you want me to pick you up?'

'Where from?'

'Heathrow.'

'You're crazy.' He laughs. 'Absolutely not. Don't you dare. I'll call you from Euston and tell you which train I'm on.'

'OK.'

'OK, sweetie?'

'Yes, OK. You'll call me before that, though? I mean, that's still ten days away.'

'Yes, of course I will. Is your work OK?'

'Yes, it's fine. And yours?'

'Yes, it's all right. Deena must be going soon?'

'Yes, on Tuesday.'

'Can't she stay till I come?'

'Her ticket ends.'

'That's no reason; you can take care of that. Get her another.'

'She won't let me. And anyway, I think' – Asya drops her voice – 'she wants to go back.'

'Why?'

'Personal reasons.'

'Oh, the Romance? Our Hero of the Resistance?'

'Yes.'

'Tell her the Egyptian left is good-looking guys and terrific talk and that's about it.'

'Well . . .'

'Well what?'

'People see things differently.'

'You're being overheard?'

'Yes.'

'That's OK. Put her on. *I'll* tell her.'

'Next time, darling.'

'I will. OK. Do you need anything?'

'No, darling, thank you.'

'Are you getting my letters?'

'Yes, every one. The plan of the house is getting very detailed.'

'Well, it shouldn't be too long now.'

'Are you getting mine?'

'Yes. They come in bunches of five.'

'Oh!'

'OK, Princess. I'll call you soon. Yes?'

'Yes, darling.'

'Bye.'

'Bye.'

Upstairs Deena is bending over the cassette-player. As Asya rejoins them she slides in the tape they'd been listening to the night before and starts it. Then she crosses to the kitchen and pours water from the kettle which has just boiled into the coffee jug. The smell of fresh coffee fills the room.

'Do you know
Where you're going to?
Do you like the things that
Life is showing you?'

'How's Saif?' asks Hisham.

'Fine. He says hi and you must have a game of squash when he's here,' Asya says.

'I'm ready,' says Hisham. 'When's he coming?'

'Probably on the fifth.'

'For sure this time?'

Asya smiles: 'Nothing's ever for sure.'

'– When you look behind you
There's no open door,
Do you know –'

'It's so odd,' says Asya. 'Where he is there are armies moving into position and militias rushing around shooting each other and women and children under siege and politicians trading insults across the radio – and we don't mention any of it at all.'

'But the lines are being listened to,' says Marzouk.

'That's what I mean,' says Asya. 'So you impose this silence on yourself and it feels weird.'

'Do you think it will ever be possible for people to live together without war?' Lisa asks, and blushes when everyone looks at her.

Hisham reaches over and pats her hand. 'You can lead them, Lisa. You show them how.'

'It shouldn't *be* beyond humanity, though, should it? I mean, *individuals* will always kill each other,' Asya says, 'but war is different: think of all the preparing that goes into it. You can't wage war in anger, so it must be possible not to do it.'

'It has to be another world,' Marzouk says.

'Mars,' Gerald says.

'If there was life there it's gone,' says Hisham.

'But it can come back, can't it? If conditions are right?'

'Wouldn't that be wonderful! To go to Mars!' Lisa says.

'I don't know,' says Asya.

'Wouldn't you go if you had the chance?' Gerald asks.

'I don't know. I imagine it would be breathtaking to begin with – and then very lonely –'

'But if you had with you the people you cared about?'

Asya thinks for a minute. 'No,' she says, 'I can only imagine it like a film, with me moving in great slow-motion leaps across a red-tinted background. I can't imagine living anywhere except on earth. I would just miss things too much.'

Gerald smiles. 'You're imposing limits on your imagination,' he says. 'Would *you* go?' He turns to Deena.

'I'd go have a look and then decide,' Deena says.

Marzouk stretches and stands up. 'I am going back to the university. I have some work. Or I will not go to Yemen, let alone Mars.'

They all laugh. Hisham stands up and looks at Lisa, who stands up too.

'Asya, thank you very much. It was very nice.'

'It was a pleasure. Really,' Asya says.

'Deena, we'll see you again before you leave?'

'Yes, of course.'

When Asya comes back upstairs from seeing Lisa, Hisham and Marzouk out she finds Gerald and Deena standing at the window. They turn as she walks towards them.

'Your sister was telling me she hasn't been out into the countryside.'

'She hasn't been here long,' Asya says.

'But she's leaving soon, isn't she?'

'In about ten days,' Deena says.

'Well, perhaps you'd let me take you both out for the day next Sunday.

There are some really nice places around and I'd enjoy showing them to you.'

Asya looks at Deena.

'That would be very nice,' says Deena, 'if Asya doesn't have other plans?'

'Well – no. No, I don't. Yes, that *would* be nice. Thank you.'

Scene 2

Monday, 16 August 1976
London

Asya wakes to a knock on the door. The room is dark, but one shaft of light comes through where the curtains fail to meet; it lights a path across the grey carpet then zigzags up on to the white sheets of the bed. She can hear the sound of the shower in the bathroom – and then another knock, politely quiet. She jumps up, covers her shoulders with a white shawl and opens the door. The young man in the black suit walks softly into the room and places the large silver tray he is carrying on the table by the window. Beside it he places a copy of *The Times*. Asya says, 'Thank you,' and waits till the door closes behind him before pushing off her shawl and inspecting the tray: croissants, butter, jam, honey and a large silver coffee-pot. She puts a finger on the croissants: warm. She goes over to the dressing-table and pulls the brush through her hair several times, checks her face, then sees Saif's glasses lying face-down on the wooden top. She picks them up and polishes them carefully with a piece of tissue paper, folds them and lays them down the right way up. The bathroom door opens and Saif, still rubbing his head vigorously with one white towel, another wrapped around his waist, walks into the room.

'Oh, sweetie, I'm sorry. I thought I'd be out before they came. I didn't mean you to be woken. Go back to bed.'

'Oh no,' says Asya. She crosses over to the window and opens the curtains a bit wider. 'Look, it's another beautiful day. What a wonderful summer!'

Saif drops the towel on a chair and pauses in front of the dressing-table mirror. He finds his glasses and puts them on, then he quickly brushes back his still damp hair and flicks the brush over his moustache.

503

He lights a cigarette, then walks over to the window, and she catches a whiff of Monsieur de Givenchy.

'You want some coffee?' he asks.

'Yes, please.'

He pours out two cups of coffee, lifts one out of the tray and puts it on the table near where she is standing. He adds cream and sugar to the other, stirs it quickly, swallows down one mouthful, drags on his cigarette, then balances it on the rim of the ashtray and walks back round the corner to the wardrobe. Asya carries her cup of coffee to the bedside table. She sits on the edge of the bed. Her suitcase is open on the luggage-rack, but it is only half packed. The orange shoes they had bought yesterday are under the dressing-table and the cream silk dress – with some white wrapping-paper still clinging to it – is lying across a chair covered in blue velvet. They are beautiful. Now that she's tanned again they'll look really good when she wears them. She'll have to get some nail varnish in the same orange.

'Shall I butter a croissant for you?' she calls. 'They're nice and hot.'

'It's OK. I'll do it.'

She takes a sip of her coffee and looks at her watch. Eight-fifteen. Saif walks back into view. He is wearing a white shirt and light grey trousers with a sharp crease and holding a dark blue tie with silver-grey spots. In front of the dressing-table he turns up his shirt-collar and starts to knot the tie.

'What time is your meeting?' Asya asks.

'Nine-thirty,' he says.

'Are you driving?'

'Yes. Unless –' He looks at her in the mirror. 'Unless you want the car?'

'Oh no,' she says. 'Thank you. I don't.'

'I can get to Uxbridge by tube,' he says. 'Could even be quicker.'

'No,' she says, 'it's much nicer to drive, and you'll be going against the traffic anyway. If I stay, it'll be a hassle with the car. And if I go Gerald will drive me.'

'Shit!' he says as he finds the narrow end of his tie longer than the broad one. He unknots the tie and starts again.

'Darling, what do you think?' Asya asks after a moment.

'About what?' He gives the tie one last tug, goes back to the wardrobe and returns with a pair of folded black socks. He sits on the chair near the breakfast table, pulls on the cigarette, then stubs it out, swallows down some coffee, crosses his right foot over his left knee and starts putting on a sock.

'About whether I should stay or go.'

He looks up at her, then down again to put on the other sock. 'I thought we'd gone over that last night.'

'We didn't *decide* anything.'

He walks across the room, opens the outer door, then closes it and walks back to the chair carrying his black shoes, polished. He pauses at the dressing-table to pick up his shoe-horn, then sits down and bends to ease both feet into the shoes. He quickly does up the laces.

'It's just that – well, you'll be working practically all the time, won't you? And I really hate that Uxbridge hotel. And you're coming up to the cottage on Thursday anyway. And if I go up today I'd do four days' work which I wouldn't do if I stayed here –'

'Well then, go,' he says. 'I *have* to stay in Uxbridge; otherwise I'd spend all my time travelling into London and out again.'

'Oh, I know,' Asya says quickly. 'I didn't mean *you* shouldn't go there.'

Saif splits open a croissant and spreads some butter inside it. 'Do you want one of these?'

'No thanks, not yet.' She shakes her head.

He drinks the last of the coffee, wipes his mouth with the white napkin and goes over to the wardrobe. He brings out his brown leather case, lays it open and starts quickly putting things into it: a pile of white folded pants and vests, another, smaller, pile of folded black socks, six shirts stiff in their laundry wrappers.

'But on the other hand, if you wanted me to stay –' Asya begins.

'It doesn't make any difference really, does it?' he says, looking into the wardrobe. 'I'll see you on Thursday.'

'Doesn't it? I mean, you'll still have the evenings – or will they all be business dinners?'

He turns and snaps the case shut and looks up at her.

'Princess. I don't know. It depends how things go.'

'Yes, of course. I'm sorry.'

He turns back to the wardrobe and pushes four hangers carrying suits, jackets and trousers into a garment carrier and zips it up. Then he goes into the bathroom and returns with his black sponge-bag. He re-opens the case and throws the sponge-bag into it. He bends down and picks up his soft grey shoes. From the wardrobe he gets the beige flannel shoe-bag and puts the shoes into it, then he throws them down on top of the shirts.

'Saif,' Asya says, 'I just can't decide on my own.'

Again he shuts the case and looks at her. He takes a breath. 'You don't have to decide right now,' he says. 'Have breakfast. Read the paper. I'll pay the bill and tell them we're keeping the room till five. If you're going to stay, just come out to Uxbridge. If you go, I'll see you on Thursday. You've got the card anyway if you need anything –'

'But I have to decide now, because if I'm staying I should put my things in the car so you can take them with you to the other hotel – and besides, I should phone this guy and tell him what I'm doing.'

505

'What guy?'

'Gerald Stone. Saif, I *told* you. I got a lift with him from the university to come down here on Friday. He drove me to this hotel. And I said I didn't know when I was going back and he said he's going back today and if I wanted a lift to let him know.'

'Oh.' He turns away. He opens the wardrobe and takes out a navy blue jacket. He shrugs it on, then he opens the dressing-table drawer and transfers his key chain, his loose change, his wallet, two handkerchiefs, his spectacle case, cigarettes and a lighter to his pockets.

'Would you *like* me to stay?'

'Look' – he turns to her – 'if you aren't packed already then you don't have time to pack. If you want me to leave the car I will. If you don't want it I'll take it. You can spend the whole morning sorting yourself out and deciding what you're going to do. You don't *have* to put your things in the car: you can take a taxi.'

'That would cost at least fifteen pounds.'

'So? Spend fifteen pounds.'

'Instead of getting angry – why don't you simply tell me what you would prefer.'

'Right now I'd prefer to leave here with my brains in one piece. You seem to be incapable of doing anything without turning it into a drama.' He picks up his briefcase from the floor, opens it and leafs quickly through his papers.

'It's only because I get worried about my work when I stay away,' Asya begins.

'How about *my* work?' His voice rises as he puts the briefcase down on top of the suitcase. 'Do you ever consider the effect you're having on my concentration?'

'Saif, I know about your work – but you're perfectly OK doing it. We're not talking about *your* work right now –'

'Well, maybe we should be. You're worried about fifteen pounds? Do you know how much is at stake in this meeting? One million dollars. *One million dollars* of people's money, and it's too much to ask that I should go to it with a clear head –'

'All you needed to say was, "I'd like it if you stayed." '

'Well, I wouldn't. Not if it's going to be like this. It's become impossible –'

'This is just so unfair. How can you say "not if it's going to be like this", as though it's "like this" all the time or even often? As though its being "like this" has *nothing* to do with you? As though I were not *always* being so careful –'

Both their voices are loud now. He takes his right hand out of his pocket and brings it down hard on the briefcase.

'I've had it. Look. I'm leaving.' He walks over to the telephone, picks

506

up the receiver and asks for a porter and his bill to be prepared.

'OK,' says Asya, 'I'm staying in London. How can I go away like this?'

'You do what you like,' Saif says, walking back to the wardrobe and lighting a cigarette. 'Your demands on my time and my emotions have become intolerable.'

Asya gasps. 'My *what*? My *demands*? On your *time*? You're hardly here, we're hardly ever together, and when we are you're not really there – when we are it's as if we'd been face to face for ten years solid until you don't see me any more, and then you tell me my *demands* on your time – and your *emotions*? *I* make demands on your *emotions*? I make more demands on the emotions of – of the bus conductor who sells me a ticket than on *your* emotions – I know better by now than to –'

They both hear the knock, and Saif moves to let the porter in. In the silence he indicates his suitcase and the garment-carrier. The porter carries them out and comes back.

'Anything else, sir?'

'No,' Saif says. And then, 'Just a minute –' as he sees the large green Marks and Spencer bag holding his used clothes. He starts to walk towards it but Asya slides off the bed, runs across the room, picks up the bag and folds her arms around it.

'I'll keep it,' she says. 'I'll take it up to the university and then when you come on Thursday it'll all be washed and ironed.'

Saif advances towards her with his hand outstretched.

'Give me the bag.'

'No. You're coming up on Thursday. I'll keep it till then.'

She starts to cry. The porter walks quietly out of the room.

'Give me this bag.'

Now Saif is pulling at the bag and Asya is holding on to it.

'You don't *need* it. Why should you want to carry a bag of dirty laundry around with you? I'm keeping it. I'm *keeping* it –'

'*Fuck this*,' he says, and steps back. 'Keep it. And if you think you're holding me to ransom with a bag of laundry you're wrong: I'm not coming up on Thursday –'

'When, then? *When*?' she cries, but he's out of the room and the door has slammed behind him. 'Why, why, *why*?' she cries out loud to herself, hugging the green bag tight and digging her nails into it: why does it have to be like this? Oh, but what has she done now? Now he's angry – really angry – but he didn't need to be – it didn't have to be like this – all it needed was one kind word, only he wouldn't say it – she was wrong because she couldn't help herself but she *couldn't help herself*, but he *could*, he simply *wouldn't*, but now he's angry and she can't let him leave like this – what will she *do* if he leaves like this? If he gives her one more chance, just one more chance, she'll show him how reasonable she is really –

She hurries over to the bed and picks up the phone and dials reception.

'Is Mr Madi still there, please?' she asks in a voice which trembles, and when the girl says he's at the cashier's desk she tells her to ask him to come back to the room for a moment. Then she runs and opens the door and hurries back to the bed and sits down again on the edge.

Saif pushes the door open and walks in. The door bounces off the wall and crashes shut. He says, 'What the hell do you want now?'

'I want us to be friends.'

She keeps her voice quiet and steady so that he does not think she is still being hysterical. He is holding a cigarette in one hand and his briefcase in the other. She offers him the bag.

'Take it. I'm not holding you to ransom – with anything.'

He stands and looks at her. In his look she sees a solid refusal to be surprised, to be reconciled – even to be angry; a refusal to have anything to do with the melodrama she is creating. She holds the bag out as far as her arm can stretch.

'Please take it.'

He turns around and walks out of the room.

In months and years to come this image is to stay with Asya: early in the morning on a summer's day she sits in her white nightie – the one with the pale blue ribbons threaded in just below the breasts and the broderie anglaise on the neckline – on the side of the bed in her room in the Howard Hotel on the Embankment in London. Her bare feet are on the floor. Her long hair grazes her bare back. Her toenails against the blue carpet are a muted beige. She presses to her breast a green Marks and Spencer bag which holds all the white vests and underpants, blue shirts and black socks that Saif has used in the last four days. A moment before he had stood at the foot of the bed and looked at her with a closed heart; with more detachment than he would direct at a newspaper photograph of a besieged woman in far-off Tel el-Za'tar, and then he had turned and she had heard the door close and felt overwhelmed by her own power-lessness. Now, sitting on the edge of the bed, she feels panic blossom and spread and unfurl itself inside her. She has no thoughts now. The cold white glare of fear fills her mind and dazzles her view whichever way she turns.

This image will be used to mark the beginning of her descent – of all their descent – into what she was later to call 'the bad bit'. At the moment, of course, she feels it is the end; she believes she has reached – alone – the nadir, the pure distillation of misery, weakness and humilia-tion. Finally one phrase forms itself in her mind. 'No more,' she thinks. 'No more.' She cannot, for one more second, bear to feel what she is feeling. She gets up and crosses the short carpeted space to the window.

She pushes aside the heavy curtains and pulls at the handle. She can only use her right hand because her left is still holding on to the plastic bag. She pushes and pushes at the window but it will only open a fragment and no more. It will let the air in but it will let nothing out. She pushes it again but it will not move. She leans her face against the cool glass, closes her eyes against the light of the sun and moans. Eventually she turns and slides down the wall till she is sitting on the floor. She buries her face in the green plastic and the silent weeping turns into loud, childlike sobs with great shuddering breaths in between. Why should he treat her like this, why? What right does he have to treat her this way? She has tried so hard to be still, to be quiet, to be serene, but she can't do it all the time, she can't, and she can't make him happy, she can't give him what he wants, she'll never be able to, ever –

The door opens and a black maid carrying a vacuum cleaner takes two steps into the room, then stops. Asya raises her face, and for a moment the two women look at each other, then the maid backs off.

'Beg your pardon, Ma'am. I'll come back later.'

Asya starts to giggle. As the door closes behind the woman a great burble of laughter escapes her. Oh my goodness, it must have looked so weird, there she is walking into an empty room with her Hoover and she must have first heard a sound: a sob or a choke or a long inhalation, and then, before she'd even had time to wonder what it was, she must have seen 'Ma'am': beyond the bed, sitting cross-legged on the floor under the window, hugging a great big green Marks and Spencer bag and crying. Asya rocks with laughter but she also doesn't stop crying. Stop it, she tells herself, you'll choke. 'Stop it!' she says out loud. But what if Saif had been there too? What if he'd been standing stony-faced at the foot of the bed pretending nothing was happening – that would have *done* it, that would have *really* done it. Asya laughs so hard that she rolls over on the floor. She lies curled up on her side holding the bag close to her, giving herself up to great hiccuping sobs mixed with yelps of laughter until the waves grow weaker and weaker and finally subside. Then she pushes the bag away and rolls over on to her back. She stretches out and takes several deep breaths and wipes her face with the backs of her hands. Her head feels so fragile she is afraid to move it. 'Your demands on my time and my emotions have become intolerable.' *Intolerable*, no less. His time – he who, as she opens her mouth, says, 'Tell me in a nutshell.' She raises her feet and props them on the edge of the bed. Her nightgown slides down and she finds herself staring at two slim smooth brown legs stretched upwards and crossed elegantly at the ankles. She pulls her feet down again and sits up and feels her headache begin. She should have told him – her demands on his *emotions*, for God's sake – she who had left him alone, who had more or less shut up for five years, who had tried to solve their problems by herself even to the humiliation of that visit to

509

the doctor because her husband wouldn't do what any man taking on a virgin wife, lover, whatever, had to do. *Had* to do? People *paid* to do it, for heaven's sake – 'Find me a virgin,' holding out a purse filled with gold – and *she* had to go to some crappy doctor and tell him that she wanted to stop feeling pain so she might stop putting her husband off. After *five* years. What must he have thought? Asya turns and rests her head against the side of the bed. The nurse who had helped her down from the examination table had asked if she wanted to sit down for a while, she looked so pale. But Asya had just shaken her head and walked into the doctor's office next door. He had stood in his white coat beside a cabinet, and he was looking into a drawer that he had opened, and in the drawer was what looked like a big transparent xylophone: a row of plastic penises of different sizes. He had picked up the second smallest and looked at it, then put it back and picked the next size up. Then he had sat behind his desk and waved her to a chair. He'd held up the penis. 'I think you should begin with this. The nurse will give you some KY jelly. You lubricate and insert. Start with just a couple of minutes and then try to build it up. When you're comfortable with this for, say, twenty minutes, come back and we'll move on to the next size. Are you feeling all right?' Asya had nodded. 'I don't see any reason for you not to overcome this problem. There's nothing wrong down there at all. All right?' Asya had thanked him, paid thirty-five pounds at reception and collected the penis and a tube of KY jelly in a white box. Once she had tried, but she had felt so stupid and so evil lying there coldbloodedly pushing the thing into herself that she had stopped. She had thrown out the KY jelly and hidden the prosthetic and forgotten about it. And he had never known about his surrogate, now wrapped in his mother's fuchsia silk, living among her linen. She massages her temples. The pain in her tummy is starting up again. Her ulcer. She'd better eat a croissant and drink some milk. But she feels so tired. She lies down on the floor again. Out of the window she can see the clear blue sky with not a cloud in sight.

When she looks at her watch it is ten-thirty. Saif is happily into his meeting. Her handbag is on the floor behind her head. She sits up and finds her diary and looks up the number Gerald Stone had given her. She goes into the bathroom and has a drink of water, then she comes back into the room and picks up the telephone.

'Hello, is that Gerald?'

'Asya, hi. How are things?' His voice is friendly and welcoming. He sounds glad to hear from her.

'Things are fine.'

'Did you have a good weekend?'

'Oh yes, thank you. Great. And you?'

'Yeah. I did a few things, saw some wonderful people –'

'Oh good. Are you still going back today?'

'Yes.'

'When were you thinking of going?'

'About four.'

'I thought I might come up with you – if that's still OK?'

'Of course. That's great.'

She takes a deep breath. 'OK. Well, then, perhaps –'

'You know, you don't sound too sure. Asya? Are you all right?'

'What? Oh no, it's just – no, yes, I am.'

'So, do you want me to pick you up?'

'Unless it's too much out of your way – I mean –'

'Of course it isn't. I'll pick you up at four. Is that all right?'

'Yes. Perfectly. Thank you. I'll see you then.'

'See you at four.'

Asya walks slowly along the Embankment feeling the sun on her back and on her arms. Her bags are packed and she has told the hotel that she'll be back at four. Occasionally she stops and looks at the river. Sometimes she stands for a long while, resting her arms against the warm stone of the wall and watching the broken shadows on the brown water. Strange how the Thames seems almost incidental here – incidental to London, even, let alone the whole of England. Well, it *is* incidental, isn't it? It doesn't feed the whole country: 'Great Britain is the gift of the Thames!' If it were to dry up, how many people would be affected? And yet, standing here, seeing just this one section of it, it seems every bit as important, as mighty, as the Nile. Well, it probably is to the people who work on it. She looks at a slow-moving barge with one solitary man seated in the bow. If this were the Nile there would be twenty men at least clambering all over the boat, singing, throwing ropes, shouting to each other, calling out greetings to the people on the shore. Here it is all still and quiet. A pleasure-boat drifts by, its deck packed with sightseers on red seats. The voice of the guide wafts indistinctly across the water. Long ago there would have been rowing-boats with canopies and musicians, carrying kings and queens from Westminster to Windsor to Greenwich – and other boats, dark, silent, covered-up boats carrying Sir Philip Sidney, carrying Sir Thomas More, carrying Anne Boleyn from Hampton Court to the Tower. 'Softly drifts the river –' what was it? 'Other little children, shall bring my boats ashore.' She turns her back to the river and looks again at the solid, grand façades of Whitehall. The statues, the spacious greens where with her parents she used to listen to military bands on sunny afternoons, the great black wrought-iron railings, the intricate tower with the four-faced clock: the accoutrements of Empire. Built of course on Egyptian cotton and debt, on the wealth of India, on the sugar of the West Indies, on centuries of adventure and exploitation ending in the division of the Arab world and the creation of

511

the state of Israel etc.etc.etc. Why then does she not find it in her heart to feel resentment or bitterness or anything but admiration for and pleasure in the beauty, the graciousness, the harmony of this scene? Is it because the action is all in the past; because this is an 'empire in decline' and all this magnificence is only a – monument, rather like the great temples of Abu Simbel or Deir Bahari? Or is it because the thoughts, the words, the poetry that wound their way down the years in parallel with the fortunes of the Empire have touched her so nearly and pulled her in so close that she feels herself a part of all this? Because there *is* a difference between what she feels now and what she has felt when looking with awe at the great sweep of the Champs Elysées, for example – she feels almost *proud* of all this – as though she would be glad to show it all off to some visitor who was new here as she would show off the pyramids or the mosque of Sultan Hassan. It is quite ridiculous, though – as that very English gentleman walking towards her in his grey pinstripe and his hat would tell her if he knew what she was thinking: because of your Empire, sir, a middle-aged spinster from Manchester came out to Cairo in the 1930s to teach English. A small, untidy twelve-year-old girl fell in love with her and lived and breathed English Literature from that day on. That girl was my mother, and here, now, am I. You cannot disclaim responsibility for my existence, nor for my being here – beside your river – today. But I haven't come to you only to take, I haven't come to you empty-handed: I bring you poetry as great as yours but in another tongue, I bring you black eyes and golden skin and curly hair, I bring you Islam and Luxor and Alexandria and lutes and tambourines and date-palms and silk rugs and sunshine and incense and voluptuous ways . . . She smiles, and the man – middle-aged and comfortable, with a florid face and greying bushy eyebrows – glancing up as he passes her, smiles back and walks on.

Or is it not simply ridiculous? Ridiculous and naïve. Is it a sinister, insidious colonialism implanted in her very soul; a form of colonialism that no rebellion can mitigate and no treaty bring to an end? What would happen to her if – as in 1956 – the old lion shook himself awake, growled, and stretched a paw – its claws old and yellow but still sharp – towards Egypt, or Syria, or Iraq, or any other Arab country? How would she feel then standing here among his trappings? Asya turns again to the Thames. A river is a river is a river: water and fish – no, probably not fish, it looks pretty dirty – what, then? Bodies. Oh, stop it, she tells herself: he's right, you know, you *are* melodramatic.

At St Martin-in-the-Fields she sits on a sunny step with a carton of orange juice and reads the newspaper. In Ulster the funeral of a 12-year-old girl killed by bullets. In Svevo several women suffer abortions. She lifts up her head: in the sunshine of Trafalgar Square the pigeons flutter down to be fed. She takes a sip of orange juice and goes back to her paper. In Israel a ten-year-old girl is critically ill after the failed Ankara

512

hijack attempt in which four Turks were killed. In Lebanon the Red Cross estimates two thousand bodies under the rubble in Tel el-Za'tar, the Syrians have closed the borders and the militias are mounting new offensives against Ain Toura, Mtein and Sannin. An old man says when Tel el-Za'tar fell the militias were taking away the surrendering men and shooting them until Pierre Jemayyil's son, Amin, arrived and stopped them. But by then many had been shot. In Italy the Pope and the Communist Party plead for humanity in Lebanon. Asya looks up again: outside the National Gallery a line of people in bright summer clothes form a patient queue all the way down the stairs. In South Africa twenty-seven die in battles with the police. They are all black, so Mario isn't one of them. In Chile, Daniel Vergara Bustos is a prisoner of conscience. In Spain, a nineteen-year-old student is shot dead by the Civil Guard for painting a slogan on a wall. And hopes are rapidly fading for the possibility of life on Mars. She folds up the paper and waits a few minutes. Then she stands up and walks towards the Charing Cross Road. Maybe she can find a couple of the books Deena hadn't managed to get.

On the Charing Cross Road Asya loses herself in a dusty bookshop, and when she looks at her watch it is five minute past two. She hurries out and finds a telephone box. She looks again in her diary and dials:
'Could I speak to Gerald Stone, please?'
'Just a minute,' the woman's voice says, and then he comes on the line:
'Hello?'
'Gerald?'
'Yes.'
'It's Asya.'
'I know.'
'Listen. I think I – I shan't be coming up today.'
'I thought you might not.'
'I'm sorry. Have I messed up your plans at all?'
'No. Why have you changed your mind?'
'Well, I – I thought – it's just that my husband might be finishing early. I'll come up with him.'
'OK. I'll see you at the university.'
'Yes. OK –'
'Since I'm losing the pleasure of your company for the drive, will you make it up to me?'
'Sorry?'
'Can we have dinner some time?'
'Yes. Sure.'
'I'll call you then.'
'Yes, OK. Bye.'   *

Asya sits on a grey plastic chair in one of the long corridors of the Master Brewer Motel. Her tapestried case stands on the floor at her feet. She has had to carry it all the way here because there were no taxis at the station. She hopes no one will come along the corridor and see her, but the place seems completely empty. On the door in front of her hangs the notice that says 'Do not disturb'. Of course, it isn't specifically aimed at *her*, but all the same she obeys it. For a moment when she had first seen it – having checked at reception and been told that Mr Madi was in and that there were no porters, having walked down the corridor still carrying her suitcase, which was growing heavier and heavier, having found the door to his room and been ready to present herself contrite and agreeable – when she had first seen the red notice dangling from the doorknob and saying 'Do not disturb' she had felt rise up in her again an echo of the feelings of the morning. Was the command aimed at her? When he'd left Howard Hotel in the morning he had not known whether she was going to join him. Had he put it up in case she decided to come to him? Or had he put it up believing that she would not come and not wishing to be disturbed by some extra-zealous cleaner? Or had he simply put it up without thinking? Without thinking, 'But what if Asya comes and finds it?' And now she is sorry for herself. He had not tried to phone her at Howard Hotel. She had probably vanished from his thoughts completely by the time he'd turned his car into the Strand. He'd been concentrating on his work. So what is she doing here? If it really *is* all the same to him whether she is here or not here, why should she have sat for an hour on the tube, dragged herself and her suitcase to this place that she hates and sat herself down outside his door to wait for him to wake up? Why is she going to spend the next two days stranded in this dismal hotel looking at brown carpets and orange curtains and ghastly embossed wallpaper and taking long baths to help the hours go by? Because, she reminds herself, *she* could not bear to leave things as they were between them. Because as far as *he* was concerned she had chosen to make a disruptive scene – over something that she could easily and simply have sorted out on her own – at what was for him a particularly bad moment. So how would he read her then going up to the north and leaving him? As further evidence of her insensitivity and selfishness. And because in her heart she knows that what had made the idea of travelling up today attractive was that she would have been driven by Gerald Stone. It was no big deal, only if her options had been to go up by train or to stay here, would she have been so pulled to the idea of going? She knows she wouldn't. And that was dishonest. And so she is here. And why does she sit like this, like a spaniel in disgrace, like the long-dead German Shepherd, outside his door, waiting to hear a sound from within? Why does she not knock on the door? She's his wife, after all, not some minion bearing a message to a tyrant. Because the last thing he knows of her is that scene this

514

morning, so it wouldn't do to follow it up by rousing him from his siesta and so ruining both ends of his working day.

So she sits, and thinks, and listens, until she hears the sounds of movement from within. A drawer opening and shutting, a lighter striking, a curtain being pulled. She waits. She hears a door open and close and then she hears the sound of the shower. When the shower stops and the door opens and closes once again she stands up. She carries her chair away to the little lobby from where she'd got it, then she walks back to the door and knocks. After a moment Saif opens. He is in his dark blue towelling robe; his hair is brushed and his glasses are on.

'Come in.'

He holds the door open and lets her in as though she'd just stepped out to buy a packet of peanuts. He takes her suitcase from her hand and closes the door. She stands just inside the door. He puts her suitcase down on the bed.

'Good timing, I was just about to order tea. Do you want something to eat with it?'

'No, I don't think so, thank you.'

It would be fatal now to start crying. He picks up the phone and orders tea for two.

'I have to have dinner with someone early. Seven-thirtyish. It's supposed to be a pretty good restaurant. Will you come?'

'Yes. If that's all right?'

'Sure it's all right. It'll be dead boring, of course, but –' He makes a face, then grins at her. 'You're allowed to sit down, you know.'

She does not run across the room and throw herself into his arms. She does not collapse weeping on the bed. She does not scream at him and go for his face. She smiles and says, 'I'll just go to the loo first.'

Late that night, as Asya sits in front of the dressing-table taking off her rings, Saif says, 'I did something pretty bad today.'

Asya looks up. He is sitting in an armchair by the TV set, smoking. He has taken off his jacket and hung it on the back of a chair. The discreet pin in his tie gleams dully in the lamp-light.

'What?' she asks.

'There was this young kid at the meeting this morning – and he came up with some point –' He stops.

'And?' she urges.

'Well, he was right. But I shot him down. Made fun of him.'

'What was the point?'

'Oh, something technical.' He shrugs.

'Was it serious? I mean, would it have ruined what you were trying to do?'

'No. Not really. I'm buying, anyway, not selling.'

'Why then?'

'I don't know. Because he was cocksure, I suppose. Showing off.' He stubs out his cigarette.

'Oh!'

'He reminded me of myself ten years ago. I was sorry – immediately, almost.'

'Oh, darling!' Asya runs over, kneels in front of him and hugs his knees. 'Did he come back at you?'

'No. He blushed and shut up for the rest of the morning.'

'Well,' Asya says after a moment, 'it'll be part of his education, won't it? Toughening him up?'

'I suppose so,' he says. 'It was shitty, though.'

She puts her cheek against his knees and he puts his hand on her head. After a bit he says, 'I'm glad you came back, Princess.' Then he holds her shoulders and pushes her gently away. He stands up and loosens his tie. 'We'd better get some sleep.'

Scene 3

Saturday, 28 August 1976

The North of England

'It's not quite what you're used to, of course,' Gerald Stone says as they walk into the restaurant section of the Cock and Crown.

'It's nice,' says Asya, chiding herself for hating – for even noticing – the flock wallpaper and the patterned carpet and the waitresses in black. Who said that waiters had to be men? 'And I did say I wanted to go somewhere I hadn't been before.'

The room is full of northern families, the women with tightly curled hair, the men in check waistcoats. A waitress shows Asya and Gerald to the one empty corner table and hands them two menus.

'You won't get organic rice here,' Asya smiles.

'No. I'll go for the curried chicken,' Gerald says. 'What will you have?'

Asya looks at the menu. What would Saif have chosen – if he'd been here and forced to stay? 'The roast beef salad will be fine.'

'Wine?'

'I don't really. Do you mind? A mineral water, perhaps?'

'They won't do mineral water.'

'Oh, well then, I'd like an orange juice.'

'I'll have a lager then,' he says, as he raises his hand for the waitress, 'and maybe we could get this candle lit.'

'I do like candles,' Asya says when the waitress has gone. She'd never have said that if she was with Saif. He'd have just looked at her. Maybe she'd have said it years ago. The first time he'd taken her out to dinner – her first grown-up dinner was how she'd always described it to herself – they had gone to the Grillon and he had buttered slivers of melba toast and salted them for her. There had been a candle on the table and she might very well have said, 'I do like candles,' and that would have been all right. But last February when he'd been over they had got out of the car outside the cottage and she had noticed the delicate white heads at the base of the tree at the entrance to their garage and said, 'Oh look! The snowdrops are already out!' And he'd said, 'Will you please stop telling me to look at things.' He'd said it as though it was partly a joke, but he'd meant it, and although she would never have said it herself she could see that it could be irritating to have someone at your elbow constantly exclaiming over the flowers or the formations of birds in the sky or the shapes the clouds took or the nearness and colour of the moon –

'Yes,' Gerald says, 'they're the best objects for meditation, you know.'

'Are they? Why?'

'Because a candle is still, but it moves. It's not a living creature, but it's alive. It changes all the time but it's constant until the moment when it's no longer there.'

'Heavens!' says Asya, leaning forward and resting her chin on her hand. 'I never thought of all that. I should have that in my metaphors somewhere. What else can you use? To meditate on?'

'You can use anything, really. And then you can use nothing at all. You can concentrate on your own being.'

Asya can hear Saif saying, '*Sure, till you vanish up your own arsehole –*'

'But you have to be really good at it before you can do that?' she says.

'Yes.'

'Can *you* do it?'

'No, I'm not that good yet.' Gerald smiles.

'Do you have to do it every day? Like exercise?'

'You don't *have* to do it at all. You just do it when you want to.'

'But what does it *feel* like? When you're actually in it, I mean.'

'It feels,' he says slowly, 'it's difficult to describe, but it feels as though you were – infinite. As though all the constraints you normally operate under – take for granted – are lifted off you. Time doesn't exist, nor does the place where you are. You aren't conscious of your body –'

'*You've done it*,' says Saif. '*You've vanished up your own arsehole.*'

517

'That's why people can walk on burning coals and all that?' Asya asks.

'Yes. Your self ceases to exist – or ceases to exist on *this* plane.'

'But then how do you know that you're – there?'

'You know.'

'The chicken curry?'

'Here,' Gerald says.

Asya picks up her fork. 'Uri Geller's been here,' she says. Saif would have thought that was a funny thing to say – unless he'd suspected her of secretly believing in Uri Geller – or of wanting to start a conversation about him.

'We'll change it.' Gerald looks around for the waitress.

'No, no, it's all right. I can do it.' Asya levers the fork against the table and straightens it. 'What do you make of him?'

'Uri Geller? I'm keeping an open mind. He looks a bit too much of this world – but he may have powers.'

'So you believe those powers do exist?'

'Do *you?*'

'Well, I believe there are some things that can't be explained by – normal science – not yet, anyway.'

'But you think one day they might be?'

'Well, somebody in the seventeenth century seeing something to do with electricity might have thought it was supernatural. But now it's explained.'

'But do you believe everything can be explained by "normal" science, as you call it?'

'I don't know.'

'You must know what you believe.'

'Well, part of me thinks, of course everything can be explained by ordinary means – or means which at some point people will regard as ordinary. The other part thinks maybe there *are* things that can only be regarded as "spiritual" in some way. I don't know.'

'You're keeping your options open?'

Asya shrugs, 'I suppose I am.'

That had been a major argument they'd had once, in Mr Chow's. The crispy duck had just arrived and Saif had been pouring the Margaux and – what had started it? It had been something about telepathy –

'What do you mean, "There's no such thing as telepathy"?' she had, of course, objected.

'There's no such thing.' And he'd smiled; the big schoolboy grin that she had loved so.

'How do you *know* there's no such thing? There are people who've – experienced it. There are documented cases –'

'Documented where?'

'Well, in – learned journals; the Russians have done experiments which prove that some people can communicate through their minds –'

518

'What did they communicate?'

'Well, one imagined a hole that a screw makes –'

'A *screw?*'

'A nail with a groove running down it –'

'Princess!'

'And the other had seen it – the hole – and described it.'

'Bullshit –'

'*What's* bullshit?'

'All this: imaginary screws, tables jumping around –'

'I'm not talking about tables jumping around –'

'What *are* you talking about?'

'I'm saying that there are things that happen – that happen to perfectly normal, reasonable people – that can't be explained –'

'Everything that happens can be explained.'

'So how do you explain *that?*'

'What?'

'What I've just been telling you about: the telepathy thing?'

'It didn't happen.'

'So those scientists – and the editors – got together and dreamed up some –'

'Why won't you stand by the tables jumping around then? Or voices from the spirits saying don't eat that duck?'

'All I'm saying is that – while there must be a lot of bullshit and frauds and everything around – there are *possibly* things that happen that can't be explained by the means immediately available to us, and that I don't see how you can say that you know for sure, for sure, *for sure*, that there's nothing.'

'Eat, Princess, eat,' Saif had said, picking up his chop-sticks. 'I don't know what you're talking about – and you don't either.'

'Well,' Gerald says now, picking up a piece of blackcurrant cheesecake on his fork, 'you've gone very silent.'

Asya looks up from her apple crumble. Saif had used to say that too; in the bar of the Omar Khayyam, before the days of the nutshell.

'I thought you said you liked my silences – that it was rare for people to be silent and comfortable – a talent that's been lost in the West, you said.' She smiles.

'But you have to talk sometimes.'

'I do talk sometimes. I've been talking all evening.'

'Then talk now.'

'Well . . .' she says, and is silent.

'There, you see.'

'But what should I talk about?'

He leans back in his seat. His eyes are blue and sharp and fixed on her. His hair curls on the collar of his black shirt. If he smoked he would have lit a cigarette, but he doesn't smoke – except grass, he'd said, when he can get it. He'd said 'grass' so naturally.

'Tell me about you.'

'Me?' Asya toys with her fork. 'You know everything already.'

'No I don't. I don't know any of the important things.'

'Like what?'

'You tell me.'

'Gerald! This isn't fair.'

'All right. Just tell me anything about you. The first thing that comes into your head.'

'Well – well, when I was born' – Asya looks at her plate – 'my uncle, my mother's only brother, was in jail – on a political charge. And as soon as they allowed my mother to get out of bed and go out of the house she wrapped me up – I was fourteen days old – she wrapped me up in the shawls and things that my aunt and grandmother had been embroidering for nine months, and she took me to the jail. It was the season of the Khamaseen – they're sort of hot, dusty winds – and there was a sandstorm brewing, but my uncle wasn't allowed visitors, so she stood outside. The jail is built into the wall of the old Citadel of Cairo, and so she stood below the great wall at a point where she knew he could see her if he looked out of his window, and she drew the shawls back and held up her baby for her brother to see. She stood there for half an hour as the winds started lifting the sands and swirling them around – and then she went home. My uncle was not quite twenty and I was my grandparents' first grandchild; the first child of the next generation. So –' Asya looks at Gerald and ends her story with a shrug.

'Well done.'

'Thank you,' Asya bows slightly.

'And again.'

'Oh, I can't.'

'Yes, you can.'

'No, really –'

'All right, then. Tell me about your marriage.'

'My marriage?'

'Yes, your marriage.'

Asya shrugs. 'Well, we got married in seventy-one. We'd been in love for four years but my parents wanted me to finish college first.'

'Is that all?'

'What else is there?'

'Don't you want children?'

'Yes I do. But I had a miscarriage early on and then –'

'Were you unhappy?'

'Yes I was.' Asya pushes away her plate. 'I was very unhappy.'

Gerald Stone is silent for a moment. Then he says, 'And then?'

'And then I had to come here to do my Ph.D, and it wouldn't have been practical – to have another child.'

'Didn't your husband mind?'

'About what?'

'About your coming here?'

'Of course he did, we both did. But I have a university career and it just – had to be done.'

'What did he do?'

'He took a job with the UN in Lebanon and Syria and I went out to see him every three months.'

'But he's doing a Ph.D here too?'

'Well, my first year here I was very unhappy – I just couldn't seem to – adjust. I couldn't do the work and the weather was so cold and I missed everyone at home. It was horrible. And when he realised what a miserable time I was having, he left his job and came with me.'

'He did?'

'Yes. And it made all the difference, really. We went round all the places that I had hated so and they kind of became OK. And I started working well and we had some friends. It was OK.'

'But he's not here any more?'

'Well, not all the time, no. He got offers of consultancies and things he'd always wanted to do and we decided he should do them but be here as much as he can.'

'He doesn't seem to spend much time here.'

'No. But it's OK. And it's only for a while. I won't be here for ever.'

'But how do you feel about living apart like this?'

'Oh, we hate it, of course. But you see, if one of us were to give up what they're doing in order for us to be together it would have to be me – logically. I mean, he's making more money than I could ever hope to make. But I don't think I could live without doing something that's mine. So really, I'm just trying to finish here as fast as I can and then we'll see.'

'See?'

'Where we'll live, I mean.'

'But you don't feel your marriage is in any danger – living like this?'

'No, of course not. Why should it be?'

'I saw you in the marketplace – together – last weekend.'

'Oh?'

They hadn't been quarrelling, had they? No. She had been careful and Saif had been nice throughout his visit.

'You should have come over and said hello,' she says.

'I didn't think it would be – appropriate. Are you having any more of this?'

'No, I don't think so,' Asya says, looking at her plate.

'Would you like a coffee?'

'Yes, please.'

'So, what about you?' Asya asks as he drives her back to the cottage.

'Me?'

'Yes. You're – twenty-nine. Why aren't you with someone? Or are you?' She smiles.

'No.' He shakes his head. 'I've *been* with someone, for three years – but it's on the way out.'

'Why?'

'Just one of those things.'

It's easy for him to not look at her while he's driving.

'Was that the lady who answered the phone in London?'

'Yes.'

'She didn't sound English.'

'No.'

'Where is she from?'

'Trinidad. Let's have some music, shall we?'

'Sure,' says Asya.

He doesn't like talking about this, she thinks. Loyalty? Or because he wants to present himself as unattached? But why should she care if he's got someone? She's married –

'Do you know this?' he asks as he turns the volume up.

'I'd do anything for you
Your wish is my command
I could move a mountain if your hand is in my hand –'

'No,' says Asya.

'It's "The Real Thing". They're great. They used to be called "Aswad" –'

'You to me are everything
The sweetest love that life can bring
Oh Baby, oh Baby –
To you I guess I'm just a clown
Who picks you up each time you're down
Oh Baby, oh Baby –'

'This isn't the same car you took me down to London in?' Asya asks.

'No,' Gerald says. 'That was borrowed. I've given it back.'

'And this?'

'This is borrowed too. But I've got it for a while.'

Outside the cottage he says, 'You're not going to ask me in for coffee?'

'Oh, of course, if you want,' says Asya. 'But it *is* quite late and I thought –'

'No, it's all right. I think it's best if we leave it.'

'OK. Well. It's been really nice, thank you –'

'Asya?' He turns off the engine and sits back in his seat.

'Yes?' She pauses with her fingers on the door-handle.

'I think you ought to clarify the position.'

'What position?' Asya asks, but her voice sounds false.

'Don't play games with me.'

'I'm not playing games,' she says quickly, and then there is silence.

After a while Gerald says, 'I find you very attractive, you know that.' And when she says nothing he goes on, 'But then I guess you must be used to that.'

'Gerald,' Asya says gently, 'I like you. I like being with you. But –'

'Yes?'

'Well, you hardly know me, really.'

'Oh, I do,' he says, and takes her hand. 'I do know you. Believe me.'

You don't, Asya thinks, but she says nothing. His hand is nice and warm and she ought to take hers away but she doesn't want to.

'I feel there's potential for something really wonderful between us if you'll –'

'Oh no,' she says, and starts to withdraw her hand, but he tightens his grip on it. 'There can't ever be anything between us. Not something real –'

He smiles. 'Ah, there's the problem, you see: I told you, you impose limits on your imagination.'

'No, but seriously,' she insists, 'if that's how you're thinking, then –'

'Yes?' He covers her captive hand with his other hand.

'Then you should – go.'

'All right.' He smiles. 'I'll say goodbye now. Would you like that?'

'No,' she says quietly. 'No, I wouldn't *like* it –'

Why had she said that? Because it preserved the interest of the narrative? Kept her options open? Because it was true? Because he was going in a few weeks anyway?

'But it might be wisest,' she adds.

'It's a bad habit, doing what's wisest,' he says. He lifts her hand to his lips and kisses it: three kisses, one for each of the hollows between her knuckles. 'Can I see you tomorrow?'

'I don't know,' Asya says. 'Maybe we should leave it – for a while, anyway –'

The tremor from his kisses travels up her hand, through her wrist and into her arm. He holds her by the tips of her fingers.

'I've frightened you,' he says.

'Oh no,' says Asya, 'It's not that –'

'Then let me see you tomorrow.'

What is she doing here, sitting with this man, this stranger in cowboy boots and a black shirt, for heaven's sake – sitting with him in a parked car, letting him hold her hand, letting him send currents of electricity through her body –

'Let's – let's not make it tomorrow, Gerald.'

'When then?'

'Well – how about Tuesday?'

He smiles to himself and lets go of her hand.

'If that makes it better for you. Tuesday.'

Sunday, 29 August

We are now at the level of Deep Syntax. As we have seen, the 'detransformation' of syntax-dependent metaphoric expressions results in the isolation of the Primary Syntactic Unit. Our next step is to translate our PSUs into surface semantic predications (SSPNs). As we do this we attempt also to eliminate distracting or irrelevant syntactic factors and approach more closely the essence of the metaphor. To achieve this we make use of the concept of 'expression rules' (Leech:1974). Their function is to filter out irrelevant information from the PSU; to eliminate dummy syntactic constituents and elements of a logical rather than a conceptual character (Leech:69) and to map syntactic units on to their corresponding semantic units.

In the following metaphoric expressions it can be seen that the PSU contains a certain amount of information which is irrelevant to its metaphoric core:

1. I nursed it in my bosom while it lived,
   I hid it in my heart when it was dead.

2. And all the countless things I shall remember
   Lay mummy-cloths of silence round my head

3. But the thoughts we cannot Bridle
   Force their way without the Will

4. As a wind sets in with the autumn that blows
   from the region of stories,
   Blows with a perfume of songs and of memories
   beloved from a boy

Asya lifts her fingers from the typewriter and sits back in her chair. 'Blows with a perfume of songs and of memories –' The voice of Ummu Kulthoum, a whiff of incense, a trick of light, and she is at home, playing on Mama Deela's sunlit carpet, dipping a piece of bread into the heart of a soft-fried egg in Dada Zeina's frying-pan, hurrying home with the touch of Saif's hand fresh on her hand, his mouth on her mouth as the call for sunset prayers echoes distantly through the Zamalek streets. She seems to be more vividly in Cairo, sitting here in her English cottage amid English fields, than she ever was when she was in Egypt. She leans her head on her hand and fingers the keys softly. And yet, for the purposes of this thesis, what we have here is a structure that needs to be defined: 'a perfume of songs and of memories' – is this an 'equative of-construction'? Or a 'genitive construction'? In other words, are the PSUs involved

'song:perfume' and 'memory: perfume' or are they

'song.HAVE.perfume' and 'memory.HAVE.perfume'?

And does it matter? Can't it just be ambiguous? Her hands rest on the keys. Ambiguity, paradox, metaphor; are they not more true, more *real*, than definitions can ever hope to be? Why then does she not let him be? Let him love her and not make love to her, want to be with her and not want to talk to her, let him have met her for the first time in a student demonstration, or walking along a windswept Alexandria street, or standing on the steps of the library in Cairo University? Let him have inherited his inlaid gun from his grandfather, or come across it in a junk shop as he shopped for his wedding bed, or been given it by a Bedu chieftain who had fed and sheltered him during his trek across the Sinai? Why should he not shape his world whichever way he wanted? Why should it be shaped for him in a second, cast in steel by an accident, a chance, once and for all? It *might* have been some other way. Why should she be 'intolerant of ambiguity', as her father would say? Because, she thinks, because this is life, not art. Ah, but there you are, you fall back on the distinction you despised your teachers for making; they discuss Heathcliff and Othello and the Majnoun in the morning and go home to their tidy little lives in the afternoon, insisting that their daughters be home by seven p.m., pushing their sons into medicine and engineering, joining the party of government, making sure the kitchen cupboard is never low on rice and oil and flour. Isn't 'tolerance of ambiguity' one of the mainstays, the founts of 'creativity'? That and 'maintaining your direction', which was just another way of saying that you saw the end in the beginning; the 'designed effect'. And 'flexibility', that was the third thing. Ah, but this is her life: *her life* – not a book he's writing. And they're not writing it together. She has become a spectator merely – waiting to find out what happens next. But can a book be written in tandem? How could that be done? What would the mechanics of it be? Working breakfasts:

'The way I see it' – drawing on his blue-squared notepaper – 'Saif should now become involved with an anti-Asad group. He is very well placed to be of help to them: he is working on the central – the *only* Intelligence computer in the country. He is creating the system that this computer will use. He has freedom of movement and access to information all the way from Kuwait to Athens. The anti-Asads are a motley group of young nationalists with strong Palestinian sympathies – communists, Shi'ites, Islamic reformists, army officers – and they appeal to that part of him which has always been fascinated by the Spanish Civil War, has always regretted that he was born too late to go and fight side by side with Orwell and Hemingway and march to the notes of the Internationale. He will play a dangerous game – and he'll meet a girl, a Palestinian girl with eyes that are sometimes fierce and sometimes gentle and sad. He will go for long walks and talks with her. She will refuse to sit in a restaurant so they will walk the streets eating sandwiches out of a paper bag, stopping briefly at a coffee-shop for tea or at a bar for a glass of cheap wine. They will smoke Gitanes and talk of politics and of history and of poetry, and he will buy her a coat and a scarf to keep out the cold winter of the Levant, and he will take her to his flat and make love to her. And he will tell her of Asya, his beautiful, clever, serene, groomed wife, marooned in the north of England, spinning her web of metaphors eight hours a day and waiting for the time to arrive when she would come to him and they would move into their white, domed, courtyarded and latticed house on the edge of the desert of the pyramids.'

'And Asya? What should she do now?'

'Yes, what do you think Asya should do?'

'Well, she could go into the department and her supervisor could look at her and say, "Asya – I have to tell you the truth: the work you are doing is worth nothing. I thought you would realise on your own how pointless it is. But it is obvious now that your brains have not matured. It is sad; Keats was already dead when he was your age –"

'Or she can go into town and let herself get picked up by a man – a stranger who has parked his Jaguar on a double yellow line and asks her how he can get out of this dead-end town. She takes him home, and in the cottage he murders her. Slowly and exquisitely murders her. No violence, no blood, no mess: he would strangle her gradually and lovingly so that she is never aware of the point where pleasure ends and death begins.

'Or she can run away: close down the cottage and run away and join the theatre – "My dear, do you remember when we took *The Changeling* to Bradford?" '

Your ideas are stupid, she thinks, they're so naïve, so transparent, anger channelled against yourself translated into a *Liebestod* – and then escapism again. If you're going to invent your own life you'd better come up with something better than that. She turns back to her work.

In these extracts we find features of 'tense', 'count', 'negation' and 'definiteness'. In this coming part I shall examine them and argue that they are not essential to the metaphorical nature of the metaphor and that they may be removed by the application of expression rules.

Note first the difference of tense in the extracts above: (1) is in the past, (2) is in the future, (3) and (4) are in the present. None of the examples is more 'metaphoric' than another. Moreover, by changing the tense in the metaphor we do not affect its status as a metaphor. The process suggested here, therefore, consists in 'undoing' the expression rule which incorporates the element of 'time' into the PSU in the form of a tense attached to a verb.

Asya looks at her watch. If she had agreed to see Gerald today she would have had three more hours of work and then it would have been time to get ready. Now she has two more days to wait till Tuesday night. She shakes her head: she is behaving as though she were seventeen all over again; wondering already what to wear on Tuesday night, wanting to look good but wanting it to look as though it had just happened that way – not that she had spent time on making herself pretty. He'd be wearing the same jeans, the same boots, maybe a different shirt. Well, that's good isn't it? Isn't that freedom, to have only one pair of jeans? Not to be burdened by choice? How wonderful to not care that much about money or a career – to walk out of a job, collect whatever money you've got and spend it all on a three-month trip to South America, to have time to talk and look at things and think about things of no immediate consequence – and the way he had kissed her hand – slowly, slowly, his lips barely touching each little dip between her knuckles – the charge in the air in the parked car – how long has it been since she's felt that? With Mario it was different, it was subterranean, she never knew if he felt it too, it was something she had felt on her own and had had to disguise, but with Gerald she knows he feels the – the vibes – as much as she does – maybe even more. And what possible harm can it do to anyone if she goes out – for a short while – with someone who finds her attractive, who wants to know what she thinks about things, someone with whom she can talk about whatever comes into her head, who doesn't think it beneath him to discuss whether there is anything to the Zodiac, or whether primitive societies might not be healthier than developed ones, or whether reincarnation is a possibility? Someone open to chance, to the world, who didn't automatically assume that anybody he hadn't already met was a jerk and wasn't worth meeting? And besides, he was going away soon. Four weeks maximum and he'd be gone, and that would be the end of that. The main thing is to carry on with the work. She has increased her hours to nine a day and is working steadily, covering ground. This time next year it should be over. And then, free at least of that, she would lift up her head and look around her – take her time – breathe – decide what is to happen next.

Tuesday, 31 August

'This meat is delicious,' Gerald says. 'What is it?'

'Veal and lamb – together.'

'And there's fruit there, too.'

'Black cherry.'

'I thought you said you couldn't cook?'

'I can't really. I've got this book by Claudia Roden, *Middle Eastern Food*. And as I follow it I remember odd bits from watching my aunt or my – grandmother in the kitchen.'

'Well, it comes out really well.'

'Thank you. I'm glad you like it.'

'Is this your work?' Gerald points at the papers stacked on a corner of the table.

'Yes.'

'May I look?'

Asya permits him with a movement of her hand.

' "It is the East and Juliet is the sun." The SSPN – what's an SSPN?'

'A surface semantic predication.'

'And what is a surface semantic predication?'

'Well, when you look at an – utterance – one way of looking at an utterance is to see – or to posit – that it has the – the *form* in which it appears, and that at a deeper level it has a – a core of *meaning* – the basic thing it's actually saying. We'll call the form the syntax and the meaning the semantics. And neither the syntax nor the semantics are simple: they're both made up of layers. When we hear or read an utterance – correctly – we decode *all* the layers. When you decode the utterance to its top semantic layer, the one nearest to the surface of the utterance, then what you have is the surface semantic predication. This isn't very accurate –'

' "The SSPN of this utterance is Juliet equals sun. We now apply to the two arguments the analysis that will reveal the semantic clash (incompatibility) between them. This can be seen by subjecting each argument to a 'componential feature analysis' (CFA). The CFA shows that Juliet consists of plus human plus female, while sun consists of heavenly body. But dependency rules show that these features imply other features, so plus human implies plus animate while heavenly body implies minus animate. Hence Juliet equals sun implies plus animate equals minus animate. Thus the incompatibility." '

Tonight he is wearing a plain white heavy cotton shirt with no collar; it's the nicest she's seen him in so far. He always looks so fresh, as if he's just come out from a shower and gone for a long run over the moors – what moors? There are no moors here and this is no Heathcliff –

528

'So you just sit here all day with these?'

'Well, not just *sit* here, but yes. More or less.'

'And you've been doing this for three years?'

'Yes. Sort of.'

'Asya!'

'What?'

'You know what. This is your *life* –'

'What do you mean? This is how Ph.Ds are done. They can't be done any other way –'

'But it's so insulated.'

'From what?'

'From anything real. From life.'

'That's just because it happens to be English Literature and I happen to be Egyptian. If it had been Arabic Literature I'd have been doing it in Cairo with a baby on one arm –'

'No.'

'No what?'

'No, I can't see it.'

'Of course you can't.' She smiles. 'You've only seen me here.'

'Maybe. But I don't think so. I think this is a choice you've made.'

'I don't know what you mean.'

'You choose not to know what I mean.'

'Would you like some more?' Asya indicates his plate.

'You're avoiding the subject.'

'No, I'm not. I really *don't* know what you mean.' Asya looks at him. 'Of course it's a choice I made. But it was a simple choice – not a *life* type of choice. It was simply to do with the topic I wanted to study, and the fact that I'm sitting here – insulated, as you call it – has been a by-product of that. I don't like it and I wouldn't choose it again but I've done three years and I've got one to go and then it'll be over and I'll be living a normal life and working and teaching and all the rest of it –'

'Is it really that simple?'

'Yes, absolutely. *Now* would you like some more?'

'No, thank you.' He smiles. 'It was wonderful.'

Asya stands up. She takes his plate and hers and carries them to the sink. Outside it is completely dark. She turns back. He sits watching her and the lit candle on the table flickers over his face.

'I have some crème caramel for pudding. Is that – would you like some?'

'Did you make that too?'

'No, I'm afraid I bought that.'

'Can I leave it till later?'

'Yes, of course. Would you like coffee now?'

'That would be nice, yes.'

When she has ground the coffee-beans and is pouring the water into the filter over them he says, 'You do everything very properly, don't you?'

Asya smiles at him over her shoulder.

'I might as well; I don't entertain every day.'

And what if Saif were to ring now? Would she say, 'I've got Gerald Stone here for dinner'? Yes, she would, if he asked her. But she wouldn't volunteer? Yes, well, if he said, 'What were you doing, Princess?' she'd say, 'I've got someone here for dinner.' And if he were to say, 'Who?' she'd say, 'Gerald Stone. You remember I told you about him in London?' But that would be reminding him of their quarrel – associating the name with their quarrel. She could say, 'Gerald Stone. I've told you about him before.' He probably wouldn't remember where she'd told him about him before. He wouldn't even remember her telling him before. Would he wonder why she was giving dinner to some bloke he didn't know? Well, if he did he could ask her; he could say, 'Who is this guy?' or, 'How come you're making dinner for this guy?' It would be hard to answer with Gerald sitting upstairs listening, but it would be a real question and she would be glad of it – she could take the phone into the boiler-room and close the door, the flex would reach –

'Shall I put it over there?' she asks when she has prepared the tray with the coffee jug, the two cups, the cream and the brown sugar.

He gets up and moves over to the living-room.

'Do you mind,' he asks, 'if I look through your music?'

Much later, when the coffee has been drunk and the crème caramel eaten and *Caravanserai* played through twice, Gerald Stone lifts himself out of her sofa.

'I'd better go,' he says.

'OK.'

Asya smiles up at him from her chair, and when he does not move she stands up and leads the way down the stairs and into the hall.

Behind the front door he says, 'Thank you for my supper.'

'You're very welcome,' says Asya. 'Come again.'

He pauses. 'You know,' he says, 'I'm feeling all sorts of undercurrents here – but I just can't read them.'

She shrugs, and opens her eyes wide. 'I don't know what you're talking about. I'm not sending any undercurrents.'

'Why do I feel,' he says, looking down into her eyes, 'that with you the shortest route from A to B is not a straight line but a roundabout curve?'

'I don't know,' Asya says. 'I've no idea.'

'Maybe it's me,' he says, stepping back, looking down at his shoes, pushing his hands into his pockets. 'Maybe I have indirect impulses, only it took you to awaken them. I would have said I'm a very direct sort of person.'

'It sounds,' says Asya, 'as though you're accusing me of being devious.'

'Oh no,' he says. 'No. That isn't what I'm saying. I'm sure you're not devious.' He holds out his hand. 'Let's be friends again, please?'

She takes a step forward and puts her hand in his.

'No,' he says again. 'You can't have those eyes, and that look in those eyes, and be devious.'

He slips an almost reluctant arm around her waist and draws her gently to him. Asya puts her right hand against his chest – her left hand is still in his. He bends his head and rests his forehead against her forehead, then after a moment he brings up the hand holding hers and tilts her chin. He kisses her brow and her closed eyes, then holds her head gently against his chest.

'You know,' he says into her hair, 'I said the other night that I'd frightened you – but the truth is I'm the one who's frightened. You must forgive me if sometimes it shows.'

Asya draws away, frees her hand, puts both hands on his shoulders and stands on tiptoe to kiss him once on each cheek.

He stands very still for a moment, and then he says, 'Show me out.'

So where are you going? It's no use sitting there looking flushed and pleased with yourself. This isn't mirror mirror on the wall – this isn't a fairy-tale, Asya. You're dallying with a man in your husband's house. It isn't his house; how much time has he spent here since she's moved in? Twenty days? Not even that. He's paying the rent – oh, so it boils down to that, does it? To who's paying the rent? *She'll* pay the rent: she can pay the rent and have over thirty pounds still to live on for the month. But what's it all *about*? OK, so he's attracted to you, so what? Others have been attracted to you before. What's so special about *him*? Asya shrugs into the mirror. He's cute. I like the feel of his hands and the shape of his body, and I like his eyes and his hair, and his smile when it isn't too weaselly, and I like his *enthusiasm* about things – even if it *can* be called naïve – and the way he talks, and I like his questions when they aren't about how I'm being – and he intrigues me; he could have kissed my mouth, he could have tried to take things even further, but he didn't – and what's Tante Soraya or Daddy or anybody got to do with it? I'm not going to *marry* him; we're only talking about four weeks. She picks up her brush and starts to brush her hair, one hundred strokes. He hadn't said when he would call. But he'll call, he'll call.

Saturday, 4 September

She cannot settle. She sits at her typewriter. She arranges her cards. She re-reads her section on 'expression rules': all it needs is the conclusion.

531

But Wednesday has passed, and Thursday and Friday too. Now Sunday looms ahead empty and silent. Even the birds are more subdued and the beck more sluggish on Sunday. She has never been able to see it as just another day; she has never been able to reason herself into treating it like Tuesday, say, or Wednesday. Friday had never been like that at home. Everything was open on Friday, the club just as busy, friends still there at the other end of the phone, Geddu in his shop ready to offer lunch, Deena and Kareem at home, Daddy relaxed in casual slacks and a grey sweater, ready to light his pipe and talk about the state of the world . . . Where *is* he? Is this it? Has he decided to be 'sensible' and bow out? But what is he afraid of – what does *he* have to lose? He doesn't need to feed her this agonised line, honestly he doesn't; she can see it in simple terms: they can like each other, be friends, be company for each other over the next few weeks – and then? And then they could stay friends but he would go away.

She carries a duster round the house, sorts out her records, re-reads the note from Saif she had found on her hall carpet this morning.

Damascus, 24 August 1976

Dearest Pussycat,

I don't know how long this will take to get to you; things here are pretty disrupted at the moment – but even if you don't get my letters you will know that I am writing to you every day as usual – well, *almost* every day.

I've settled back into my little flat with the over-stuffed armchairs that you disliked so much – I must say the cottage was looking great; you've made it so nice with your odd little things – it's a good place.

Paris on September twenty-ninth is more or less definite, so work hard, Princess, and maybe you'll get to join me there. You can choose which hotel we stay in. I'll be working, but we'll manage dinner at the Tour d'Argent and maybe we can go back to the little restaurant where we had dinner with Mario last year.

I might go to Cairo for a few days before that – but I'll let you know.

lost (!) of love,
Saif

Twenty-five days. Twenty-five days to Paris. But then in Paris, what? She goes into the bathroom and washes her face. The weather is hot and she loves it hot – but it makes her restless. When it's cold she can use her energy just fighting it, huddling in a corner, pushing it away. In the heat she is ready for – for life: for open-air cinemas and strolls through the club and lingering over cold drinks watching the ice melt in them while the smell of jasmine fills the air at dusk and old women sit on street-corners grilling sweetcorn and fanning it with great fans of ostrich feathers. How

532

can she empty her mind of everything and just concentrate on her work – if she works twelve, sixteen hours a day she can cut the time in half – ah, but how will she feel now to leave her cottage? To leave her polished stairs and the great sloping roof and the birds who wake her in the morning and whose song makes her look up from her typewriter at the end of the day and walk to the window to watch the setting sun, the little stream that runs under her window and even the little dirt-path along which no one comes except if they're lost and about to make a U-turn in the field beyond? Now she will miss *this* for ever. She will be sitting at her desk in Cairo and she will dream of this cottage and of the silence and the way the light changed outside her window – she has no discipline, *that* is her problem, she will sit and dream and lose herself in inventions while her work lies in front of her on the table. Maybe she should take up meditation, maybe that would help her to concentrate – she sits down at the table, puts her hands on her typewriter and forces herself to work.

We have now established five main categories of SSPN into which syntax-dependent metaphors fall. The use of semantic analytic procedures suitable for 'standard' language are shown to function for 'deviant' or 'creative' uses of language as well. Through these procedures we have reduced all syntax-dependent metaphor ultimately to one basic predication in which the tenor is one argument and the vehicle is the other; the predication expresses the relationship of identification between them while the analysis of their component features establishes the incompatibility between tenor and vehicle. The predication thus captures all the definitive qualities of linguistic metaphor.

It is seven o'clock when the call comes.
'Asya?'
'Yes?'
'It's me, Gerald.'
'Oh, hi!'
'Are you all right?'
'Yes, I'm fine. And you?'
'OK. What have you been doing?'
'Oh – working – mainly.'
'I had to come down to London.'
'You're phoning from London?'
'Yes.'
' . . . '
'Asya?'
'Yes?'
'Can I see you when I come back?'
'Sure, if you like.'

'I like.'
'. . .'
'Asya?'
'Yes?'
'I'm coming back on Thursday. Shall we go out to dinner?'
'Yes, OK.'
'Are you sure you're all right?'
'Of course I am. Absolutely.'
'I'll pick you up at eight.'

Thursday, 9 September

'I don't really want dinner,' Asya had said. 'Can't we go somewhere where they have music and do pâté or sandwiches or something? Crisps, even?' So they sit on bar-stools in the Golden Grouse, Asya with her tomato juice and Gerald with his lager, and they play the juke-box and get up for the odd dance, and he puts one arm around her, his hand firm on her waist, his other hand holding hers close to his chest –

'Don't go breaking my heart,
I won't go breaking your heart.
Oh don't go breaking my heart –'

He had been to London. He must have seen the woman he'd 'been with' for three years; maybe he'd been 'with' her again – maybe just last night – Asya doesn't mind. She wants him here now, his hand on her back, his thighs against hers, his chin from time to time grazing her face, but she doesn't care where he was yesterday or where he'll be tomorrow –

'You're Aries, aren't you?' he asks.

'Yes,' she says.

He smiles. 'It figures.'

'How do you mean?' she asks.

'Well,' he says, leading her back to her bar-stool, 'it's a fire sign – it's full of contradictions: it's the sign of the leader and the sign of the child; the sign of the egotist and the supremely generous –'

'*Asya, I can't believe this. You disappoint me,*' Saif says. '*You're listening to this horseshit mumbo-jumbo? You're taking this seriously – from a guy who's doing an MA in Marketing? In Marketing, for Christ's sake, and you have to claim you don't want any dinner, and he makes a drink last two hours and cadges a car from a friend to take you out in? What's happened to you?*'

She shrugs.

'What sign are *you*?' she asks.

'Guess.'

'I couldn't possibly.'

534

'Why not?'

'Because I wouldn't begin to know anything about it. Any of the different characteristics or anything.'

'Ah,' he says, 'your education has been sadly neglected. I'll have to take you in hand. I'm Sagittarius, half man, half horse. I'm the communicator.'

At the cottage he follows her in unasked. She puts water on for coffee and he stands and looks out of the dark window.

'I suppose,' he says, 'there is something admirable about living out here all on your own like this.'

'I had the oddest dream last night,' says Asya. 'I've just remembered it –'

If she'd remembered it when she was with Saif she would have said nothing.

'What was it?' Gerald turns to her.

She pours out his coffee.

'I dreamed I looked down at my leg – my left leg – and it was split open. All the way down from the hip to the ankle.' She carries his coffee over to the living-room table and sits in one of the armchairs. He follows her and sits in what has become his place on the sofa. 'And there was blood, lots and lots of blood, only it was black and thick, like it was bad: poisoned or something, and I kind of – recognised it. And I thought, oh, 76 and 77 have come out at last.'

'76 and 77 what?'

'I think it's the years, you know, 1976 –'

'That's a strange dream.'

'Yes.'

'Were you in pain in the dream?'

'No. I even thought how strange it was that there *was* no pain. I was looking down at this leg in a really detached way.'

'Do you often dream?' he asks.

'Oh yes, an awful lot,' says Asya.

'Tell me another of your dreams.'

'Oh, I can't remember. I remember first thing in the morning – but then if I don't think about it, if I just get on with things, then it goes away and I can never remember it again.'

'You should pay attention to them, you know. Dreams tell you all the important things about yourself. They're the language your psyche uses to communicate with you. Like this dream, for instance –'

'Yes.'

'It's telling you there's something in your life that's bad – that's troubling you, festering inside you, and needs to come out. It's also telling you that getting rid of it won't be painful.'

'But why my leg – why is it coming out of my leg?'

'Well, the leg is what you stand on. It provides the basis for whatever else your body does. So it's something basic – something undermining your whole being.'

'And why does it specify 76 and 77? I mean, '77 hasn't even happened yet. So how can I be needing to get rid of it?'

'I don't know. Maybe there's some significance to the numbers – they don't refer to years – maybe they correspond to something specific in your birth chart. We'd have to look into that.'

'Would you like some more coffee?' asks Asya.

Gerald shakes his head. 'I'll be going soon.' Asya says nothing, and after a minute he says, 'You know, I really tried to stop myself phoning you. And I succeeded – for three days. But it got harder and harder – I just kept thinking of you sitting up here with your – metaphors. On the fourth day I cracked.' He runs his hands quickly through his hair. 'Did you think of me? Did you wonder why I didn't call?' He lifts blue eyes to hers.

'I thought maybe you'd decided to be wise.'

'Did you know I *would* call?'

'Well I – I thought you probably would.'

He stands up.

'What do you want from me, Asya?'

'*This guy*,' Saif says, '*is a wanker. And I'm surprised you're bothering with him.*'

She meets Gerald's look steadily. 'Nothing. Nothing at all.'

'What should I do, then? What do you think I should do?'

'Well,' says Asya carefully, 'I think, since you seem to be finding things so – difficult – that perhaps you should go. I don't *want* you to; I'd rather you stayed and we saw each other for the time you have left here – but if it's really making such problems for you, then maybe it isn't worth it – for you.'

He looks at her bleakly.

'Is that all you've got to say?'

'What else *can* I say?' she asks, with a helpless movement of her hands.

'So cold, so cold,' he mutters, and turns to walk out of the room.

Asya thinks of Miss Havisham as she follows him down the stairs. To me, to me-e-e.

At the front door he pauses and turns to look at her.

'When are you next seeing your husband?'

'September twenty-ninth.'

'He's coming here?'

'No. I'm going to meet him.'

'Where?'

'In Paris.'

536

'Very nice,' he says.

Asya shrugs.

'It's where he'll happen to be.'

'I'll have gone by then.'

Asya says nothing.

'All right,' he says. 'All right.' He takes a step forward and puts his arms around her. When she does not move he puts a finger under her chin and tilts her head. Then he bends and places his first kiss on her lips, very dry, very distant.

'Will you see me through my exams, then?'

'Oh yes.' Asya smiles, and puts her arms around his neck, and hugs him.

Sunday, 12 September

He had arrived in the late morning, while she was still in her dressing-gown. But he had gone straight upstairs, and when she had put on her blue cotton dress with the white flowers and followed him he was sitting in his corner of the sofa, with books and papers on the table, a white note-pad on his knee, a psychedelic coloured folder at his side and his white sneakers parked neatly side by side at the edge of the rug. He had looked up and smiled as she came in, accepted her offer of coffee and biscuits, and gone back to his work.

At lunchtime she had prepared sandwiches of roast beef and green olives, a pitcher of iced grape juice and a plate of cheese and biscuits, and they had sat outside leaning against the low sunny wall and listening to the little beck and the odd bird-call and eaten their lunch, and he had told her about his parents; about his mother, mainly, and how difficult a life she had had. He'd said, 'He hasn't made it easy on her, not as easy as he should.'

'Who? Your father?'

'Yes.'

But his father seemed to work terribly hard installing huge water-pipes or something, and he was away from home a lot, and Asya hadn't quite been able to see what he could have done more than he had – but of course she didn't know these people –

She hasn't had her siesta and she feels fuzzy and a little vague without it. But she can't say, 'Excuse me, I'm going to have a little rest,' and leave him sitting in her living-room – she'd sound as though she were inviting him, in a roundabout way, to come with her. So she sits at her table and tries to work.

It's pleasant having him here; it makes Sunday so much easier to get through – there are two more Sundays to go before Paris, and he seems so comfortable, sitting there in his white socks – thank goodness he wears white socks, she couldn't have borne it if he'd worn thin brown ones with an interlocking pattern running down the side, or those kind of diamondy checks in blues and browns – but thick white cotton socks are OK. – Saif couldn't fault those. He couldn't fault the jeans either; just basic worn, faded jeans, and the shirt today is a coarse-ish off-white smock-type thing which has an ethnic look about it. You could imagine a string of beads around the neck but there isn't one. No, there's nothing wrong with the way he looks at all. Tall, well-built, with a handsome, strong face, blue eyes and lots of golden hair. Still, she wouldn't fancy walking with him through the Mousky, for example, taking him into Morgan Street – who said anything about Morgan Street? She shakes her head slightly: we're just talking here, *now*: his legs are crossed under him as though he were about to start reciting the Qur'an and he sits perfectly still except for the hand that writes in the note-pad or turns a page of his book. He doesn't smoke, he doesn't stretch or yawn or put his biro in his mouth or push back his hair, he doesn't appear to get pins and needles or need a drink or the odd nibble or anything at all. He sits there like some Western 1970s version of the Buddha. Does he know it? Is it on purpose? Yes, Asya thinks, it's probably on purpose – not on purpose this very minute but on a sort of long-term purpose: something he's designed, he's cultivated. But isn't that just the same as saying that he's studied meditation and the I Ching and all those things they've been talking about through the evenings they've spent together? Isn't that where this quality of stillness comes from – an alert but relaxed stillness? He would be nice to make love to. Is that *right*? she snaps; you're the great expert, are you? 'He would be nice to make love to' – sitting behind your table surveying him as though you were Colette or Piaf or Cleopatra or even Kushuk Hanim – a vast experience you have, have you? Such a variety of men you've tasted, you've ensnared and bedded: fair ones and dark ones, middle-aged Herculeses and willowy Ganymedes, African warriors and California tycoons, Leons and Rudolphs and love-lorn swains and doublecrossing treacherous bastards, you've had them all, that you can now sit back in your chair and opine that 'he would be nice to make love to'? You are twenty-six and you are more or less a virgin; never mind the lost baby, never mind the laughably pointless IUD, the three years of *carezza*, the plastic penis, the debauchery à la Dolce Vita: the fact is, *you haven't done it* –

'You're not working?'

'Oh, yes, I am,' she says quickly, looking down at her papers, aiming her biro at the top of a blank page. She leafs through the pages she had done in the morning and then starts to write.

In (5.3) it was pointed out that while in syntax-dependent metaphor the PSU is in itself sufficient both for the detection of the deviance/transfer and to provide the warranty for its interpretation, syntax-independent metaphor is context-bound in that the deviance/transfer is neither discernible nor interpretable independently of its wider environment.

The notion of 'environment' or 'context' stands here in need of further clarification –

All through the afternoon and early evening they work, and Asya is vaguely waiting for Saif's call even though he hadn't phoned last Sunday either and she knows it is difficult to get lines out. When Gerald looks up at seven o'clock and suggests they go for a walk Asya thinks, but if Saif phones on a Sunday evening and does not find her he will worry, so she says she's in the middle of a difficult bit and does he mind terribly if she finishes it, and he says no, of course not, and goes back to his writing. Later Asya cooks and they eat lentil soup, and while they are eating the grilled entrecote and green salad that follow it her watch says nine o'clock and she knows that he will not phone her tonight. She serves the bananas spiced with cloves and cinnamon and baked in cream and makes the coffee and puts it on the living-room table.

He sits on the sofa with his coffee and she watches him from her armchair.

'It is so pleasant,' he says, looking into his coffee-cup, 'so deeply peaceful: spending the day with you.'

'Would you like,' says Asya, watching him, 'to spend the night?'

He looks up and meets her eyes. They look at each other seriously, and then he says, 'Yes,' and looks down at his cup.

'Do you disapprove?' she asks, still looking at him.

'No.' He shakes his head, but he still looks down. 'On the contrary: I'm impressed.' Then he puts down his cup, looks up and holds out his hands to her. 'Come to me, baby.'

'*Baby?*' says Saif. '*Baby?*'

And why not? thinks Asya, as she rises and walks the five steps and sinks to the floor between Gerald Stone's denimed knees. Why not? Why *not* 'baby' and 'babe' and 'honey' and 'sugar'? Why should she always be 'sweetie' and 'princess', and never this, never this, never to be kissed and caressed and undressed and looked at and admired, never to feel hot breath on her face and on her neck, never to feel a man's hands on her breasts, on her waist, on her tummy, never to feel strong fingers urgently exploring her, pushing her legs apart, never to feel the weight of another body on hers, the bite of teeth on her shoulder – steady, steady, she tells herself, don't panic, don't panic. He doesn't know, he must *never* know, never even *suspect* – you can't look a man coolly in the eye and say, would you like to spend the night and then start whimpering stop stop – oh, but he must be wondering what the matter *is* with her, why she is so rigid and so stiff, why her hands are braced against him rather than pulling him closer, no, he's not, he's not wondering about anything, he's just doing it, *doing* it: his face above hers is strange and set and pale, his eyes are fixed and staring – as though *he* were the one in terrible pain, as though he were dead and had died in terrible pain and been frozen – except that a great blue vein stands out and throbs on his forehead, but now *her* pain is truly unbearable, and her body bucks and rises to escape, and as Fanny Hill had described the movement brings him driving further in, and a long low moan of pain escapes her, and he covers her mouth with his, but even if she screams her head off from now till morning there is no one around to hear her, not like in the Semiramis with the old chap coughing next door – but the pain doesn't go like the books said it would, and there is no delight, only a new sort of pain, as of a bar of hot sand being driven through her again and again, and she cannot stop her body from shaking, but if he wonders why he'll think it's because she's realised what she's doing; because she, Asya al-Ulama, is committing adultery –

Monday, 13 September

When Asya wakes she surprises herself. She had gone to sleep expecting to wake up to the cold finger on the heart; to the weight of the rock of doom settling on her chest: guilt, fear – confusion would surely coalesce into one mass that would settle inside her and prevent her from even breathing – but there is nothing: she surprises herself by how well and how peacefully she has slept. By how wide awake and full of energy she immediately feels. By the clarity in her head and the lack of pain between her legs: a tenderness, a slight bruising only, enough to remind her of what had happened there. She shifts slightly, and finds that moving doesn't hurt. And she had slept without a nightdress and without sneezing once. She turns her head to look at the man lying beside her. Gerald Stone is asleep.

Asya slips quietly out of bed and crosses the hall into the bathroom. On the loo she bites her lip and concentrates on releasing the pee gradually and carefully so it doesn't hurt. It stings a little, but sitting on the edge of the bathtub she washes the sting away with warm water, then dries herself and stands up and looks in the bathroom mirror. Her face is bright-eyed and rosy and soft – younger, somehow. It reminds her of the face she'd seen in the Contessa's mirror in Beirut eight years ago. But she isn't younger. She is older now, much older, grown-up at last. She starts to brush her teeth. You've committed adultery, you've done it, you've joined Anna and Emma and parted company for ever with Dorothea and Maggie – although Dorothea would have understood – would she? Yes, she would; she would not have approved, she would have urged her to renounce, to stop, to send him away – but she would have understood; she had a great capacity for understanding. And what would she, Asya, have done? Could she have looked into those clear grey eyes and said, 'But he's going away anyway in three weeks – can't I enjoy him for those three weeks and then let him go for ever? And if my body is alive and OK and I'm not frightened any more, might it not happen that Saif senses it, and if *he* loves me again in bed – if that – barrier between us is burst, might not everything else come flooding through so that we can talk to each other, explore things together, have babies together, *love* each other truly, at last?' You know what Dorothea would think? Her mouth frothing over with toothpaste, Asya nods at herself in the mirror: she would think these were the arguments of a whore. She shrugs and rinses out her mouth. Dorothea was, after all, Victorian – and you, what are you, a modern woman? You are an Arab, a Muslim, if the law of your people were applied you would be stoned to death – but would she? You are only stoned to death if you are a *muhasanah*, is she truly a *muhasanah*? What is the fort that protects her within its walls? How has she been made secure? How much care has her husband devoted to making her secure? No, she would not be stoned – and anyway, where are the four witnesses? The birds, the cows two fields away? And besides, the door of repentance is always open.

She pads softly back into the bedroom. He sleeps on his back. He has thrown his pillow on the floor and his head is in perfect alignment with his body. His arms lie straight along his sides, the hands with loosely closed palms facing upwards. Under the sheet, Asya can see his legs form a long and narrow V ending in the two white tents of his feet. Asya creeps into bed and lies on her side facing him, watching him. On his chest there is a pleasing amount of burnished golden hair. She stretches out a finger to a small cluster which bows under her touch then springs upright again. His lips are slightly parted and his chest rises and falls to the rhythm of his soundless breath. Last night, at the end of the final desperate plunging that had made her frantic with pain – had made her dig her heels into the fluffy cream rug and rise up on her elbows in an attempt to escape him – he had thrown his head back and cried, no, *roared* out her name. She had been touched, but she had also wondered how genuine that cry had been. Now she wonders again: to what degree had he actually not been able to help it? To what degree was it deliberate? Had it just occurred to him then and he chose to go ahead and do it rather than not do it? Had he planned it in advance? 'If I get to sleep with her I'll yell her name out at the end'? Was it what he *always* did – only he'd have to be pretty damn certain he'd switched to the appropriate name – it would be much easier to cry out, 'Baby!' or, 'Oh God! God!' – or had he had no choice: had that roar forced itself up his throat and out of his mouth and surprised even him by its volume and its harshness?

541

Either way it was impressive: impressive in its timing and execution if it was planned, in its rawness and power if it was not. Beyond him, the flower-leaves in her curtains shine gold in the morning sunshine, and outside the birds chatter and trill and call. She looks at his face again and finds herself looking into alert deep blue eyes.

'Good morning,' she says, and he places two fingers softly on her lips. He strokes her face slowly and gently with the backs of his fingers.

'You even wake up looking good,' he says.

She lies quiet and still, looking into his eyes and waiting for his hands to slip under the sheets to caress her.

'You are the horniest woman alive,' he says.

'What does that mean?' she whispers.

'You don't know what "horny" means?'

She gives her head one small shake.

'Arousing desire – in your language. It means you make me want you just by looking at you. Touch me, baby, touch me,' he whispers against her lips, 'see what you do to me –'

He guides her hand to where he wants it to be and she gives herself up to the luxury of his strength and his warmth and his hands and his mouth in her early morning sheets with the day stretching ahead and the birds singing outside the window – and when he enters her there is no more pain but intimations of pleasure along with a discomfort which she knows will be eased by the hot bath she plans to take when he's gone.

It is while she is lying in the bath that the call comes. She gets out, wraps her bath-towel quickly round her and, dripping water in a line along the hall carpet, picks up the phone.

'Hello?'

'Is that Asya al-Ulama?'

'Yes?'

'Asya al-Ulama?'

'Yes, speaking, it's me.'

'This is the university operator. We have a telex message for you. Do you want me to read it to you?'

'Yes, please.'

'It says: "Paris trip indefinitely postponed stop See nothing before Xmas stop Sorry Princess stop Will phone when line available stop Love Saif"

'Did you get that?'

'Yes, thank you,' says Asya.

'You can come round and pick it up any time till six o'clock.'

'Thank you,' says Asya.

She puts the phone down and stands in the middle of the small hall wrapped in her towel, not knowing what to do. She sees the damp patches on the carpet at her feet and walks back into the bathroom. She pauses with her hand on the wash-basin: serves you right, she says to herself, serves you right. Maybe last night he'd felt her betrayal – the betrayal of his pal and his chum – but she isn't *only* his pal and his chum – that can't be *all* she is in this world – and anyway, as his pal and his chum she has not betrayed him. Try telling him that. What will she do now? Oh, what will she do now? A slow, rhythmic hammering erupts in her left temple and her eyes lose their focus. She lifts her hand to her head, walks forward and stumbles to her knees by the loo. She raises the plastic seat and bends over the thin china rim and heaves – oh, being sick is so hideous – she'll choke, she'll choke – her face is wet with tears – and again she heaves and retches, and the bathroom is filled with the smell of lentil soup gone acrid, and she presses the flush but she retches again, it's probably those ghastly bananas –

As she rinses out her mouth she catches sight of her face in the mirror, crumpled and pale, the eyes dull and small and red-rimmed. She drapes the towel over the heater and climbs back into the bath. She leans her head against the back of the tub and tries to breathe deep enough to ease the unshifting weight in her chest. Where is the mighty adulteress now, she thinks, the liberated, fulfilled, sensuous woman, the defiant *femme de plaisir*? And then she does not think any more, but just lies quietly and lets the tears roll down the sides of her face and down her neck and eventually into the bath. She stays in the bath until she shivers and sneezes twice and realises how cold the water has become.

7.40 p.m.

Gerald Stone knocks on the door, which is opened by an Asya who seems diminished – who seems shorter and smaller than the woman he left at this door in the morning. She is in her dressing-gown, her feet are bare, her hair is secured carelessly at the back of her head with an elastic band and her face is pale and unmade-up.

'What is it, babe? What happened?'

He moves to take her into his arms but she shakes her head and steps back.

'I thought we'd agreed you wouldn't come today. When you called –'

He closes the door behind him.

'You sounded terrible. I was worried for you –'

'But I asked you – I *asked* you not to come.'

Asya stands in the middle of the hall, holding both arms tightly around herself and shivering.

'You sounded really bad, I couldn't just leave you here –'

He takes a step towards her, but she retreats, putting up both hands as though to fend him off.

'OK, man, OK.' He holds both his hands up in the air. 'Nobody's going to touch you if you don't want to be touched. Can we go upstairs and talk reasonably about this? Or don't you even want me in your living-room?'

Asya turns and walks ahead of him up the stairs. In the kitchen she pauses. 'Would you like a coffee? Or a drink?'

'No, no,' he says, 'you don't have to worry about that.'

In the living-room he stops and looks at her.

'May I sit down?'

'Yes, of course,' Asya says stiffly. She waves him into the sofa and sits down in the armchair furthest away.

'What happened?' he asks again. 'Second thoughts?'

'Gerald,' Asya says, 'I'm sorry,' then she stops. She starts again. 'I'm really, *really* sorry.' Then she stops.

'You're sorry?'

'Last night was my idea. I know.' Asya nods her head. 'I asked you to stay. But now – I think – I don't think this is such a good idea. Really.'

'But you were fine when I left this morning, babe. What happened? Did something happen?'

Asya is silent.

'Come on, man. You owe me that much. Tell me what happened.'

'I got a message that my husband can't come to Paris.'

He is silent, but when she looks up he is watching her. She shrugs and looks away.

'How did you get the message?' he asks.

'Telex. By phone.'

'When? What time?'

'About eleven.' Asya's voice breaks as she starts to cry.

'OK,' he says. 'OK. Look –' He stands up and moves towards her, but when she shrinks back in her seat he stops. 'Let's go out. You've been brooding over this all day. Get dressed and we'll go out.'

Asya shakes her head.

'No?'

'No,' she whispers.

'OK,' he says, 'then I'm going to make you something to eat. Have you eaten anything all day?'

Asya shakes her head as the tears continue to spill over from her eyes. Gerald Stone moves around in her kitchen. He opens cupboards, he opens the fridge, he boils the kettle. He comes back to the living-room with a tray: soup in a cup, toast, butter, cold meat, cheese and grapes. He puts the tray down in front of her and rummages in his hold-all.

'I've got you today's newspaper. I thought you probably wouldn't go out and buy one. Let's see what's on TV while you eat, OK?'

Later he says, 'You have to go to bed now.'

Asya looks at him, watchful again. 'No,' she says. 'I mean, I'll go later –'

'You'll go now, baby. And I'm staying. I'll sleep up here, if you like, but I won't leave you on your own.'

'You've been terribly kind to me,' Asya begins, 'but this really isn't necessary –'

'Do it for me, babe. I'd have a really bad night knowing I'd left you here so unhappy.'

'But I'm not so unhappy any more, honestly.'

'Please,' he says. 'Please?'

He sleeps in Asya's bed. He puts his arms around her and says, 'Relax. Just relax. OK? Nothing will happen that you don't want to happen.'

Asya lies stiffly in his arms until he sleeps and then, relaxing, she rests her face against his chest and, taking comfort from the feel of warm, solid flesh against her own, she falls asleep.

Scene 4

Friday, 12 November 1976

Asya puts the phone down and runs up the stairs. She stands in the middle of the living-room looking around her. What is there here that she should remove? What is there that would tell? She picks up Gerald's four books that sit on the corner of the cream rug and stacks them behind the sofa. She looks along the window-sills: plants. On the hearth the fire is laid ready to be lit. The records, ah, the records – but they wouldn't know, they wouldn't know that the Barry Whites, the Hot Chocolates, the Marvin Gayes had come in over the last six weeks: come in with him. The kitchen table is completely clear. Asya digs out her typewriter and a random batch of papers from inside the kitchen cupboard and spreads them out on the table. Next to the sink stand a bottle of brandy and a tumbler. Asya slips the bottle into the kitchen cupboard and rinses out the tumbler, dries it and puts it away. He doesn't smoke, so the ashtrays are clean. Whatever else he's got is downstairs in her bedroom. She opens the living-room windows, wide, to the chill November air, puts a match to the fire, fills the kettle and switches it on. She lights a stick of incense and balances it on top of the stove. Then she goes downstairs. Does she have time to wash her face and do it up again? She washes her face and peers closely into the mirror: she can see some red blood-vessels appearing like cracks on the whites of her eyes, and underneath the eyes she can detect a darkening and puffiness of her skin. She quickly rubs some tinted moisturiser into her face, flicks a brush dipped in golden blusher over her cheekbones, draws her kohl-stick between her closed eyelids, brushes on one coat of mascara and pulls the neutral lip-gloss stick once over her lips. She drags her hairbrush through her hair several times, gives her neck two sprays of Nina Ricci – and she is ready. No, no, she isn't, she realises, looking at herself in the full-length mirror she has propped up against her bedroom wall. Quickly she peels off her jeans and the thick cotton socks she is wearing. She puts on a garter belt, a pair of sheer tan stockings and a beige woollen skirt that falls to just below her knee. She looks in the mirror again and pulls off her black pullover, holding the neck wide open so that it doesn't mess up her face. She puts on a white bra, a camisole and a loose white cashmere sweater. She clips her strand of pearls round her neck and the matching earrings on to her ears. She brushes her hair again, sweeps it up and secures it with five hairgrips into a loose chignon. Then she finds a white half-slip and pulls it on under her skirt and looks again into the mirror: yes, that will do. She pushes her feet into some high-heeled brown shoes and looks around: one pair of jeans and a black and gold kimono, a pair of sneakers, on the dressing-table the hairbrush and the small dryer, on the bedside table the reading-light has been removed along with *Anna Karenina*, *Middlemarch* and *My Life as a Man*, and their place taken by a candle and an incense-burner. She switches off the overhead light and then leaves, closing the door behind her. She makes sure the door of the spare room – the room she now thinks of as Saif's room – is closed, and then she hears the knock.

'Mahrous! Welcome, welcome. The north is full of light. John, please come in. Mrs Heatherington, it's nice to see you.'

Asya draws her guests in, closes the front door and locks it and ushers them up the stairs. As she follows them up the stairs she checks her watch: five o'clock.

In the living-room John Heatherington and his wife stand around admiring the cottage, admiring the view, acting as if this was just a social call. Mahrous stands in his big grey overcoat and scarf looking at nothing. He does not appear very different from Asya's memory of him: the same crinkly black hair, the surprisingly fair skin, the too wide mouth. The eyes are different: the eyes which used to be at once uncertain and ready for a fight are now carefully, guardedly, blank. Asya guesses that he is in some sort of trouble; John Heatherington over the phone had said, 'Do you think we could bring him over to see you? I think it might help if you talked to him.'

'Of course,' Asya had said, 'but what's the matter? What has happened to him?'

'Oh, he's just finding it hard to adjust. We'll be able to talk better when we see you. Joan might come with me.'

'Of course,' Asya had said again. 'When would you like to come?'

'Well,' John had said, 'it should take us about half an hour to get to you. Is that all right?'

Now Asya offers tea, puts out biscuits and a fruit cake, insists on taking Mahrous's coat. When she asks him how much sugar he would like he says in a low voice, 'But first – I mean, if it's possible – I would like to catch the 'Asr prayers before the sun sets –'

He speaks as though embarrassed, and Asya jumps up.

'Of course, of course. It's better if you go downstairs, then you can be alone.'

She takes him down the stairs. She can't take him into either of the bedrooms so she opens the door of the boiler-room.

'It's quiet here – you won't be disturbed.'

'Thank you,' he says, 'thank you.' He looks around him in a slightly lost way. 'Which way is the Qibla?' he asks.

Oh God! Asya thinks, I should know this, I should know the answer to this like I know my own name. West is that way so –

'It's this way,' she says, selecting a vaguely south-easterly direction. She looks down at her bedouin rug, and by a miracle it is facing in the right direction. 'The way the rug is facing,' she adds. 'Please use it: it's completely clean. And let me show you the bathroom.' She leads him to the bathroom, takes out a towel from the towel basket and balances it on the edge of the bath. 'There's a fresh towel. I'll leave you now. When you've finished you'll come to us upstairs? Yes?'

On the stairs she looks at her watch: twenty past five. She is safe for a while yet. Gerald had said he would be back at seven. But of course he might be early. From six-thirty it will become dangerous. But what if he came back now? What if he just decided to come back now? Maybe he would see the Heatheringtons' car outside her door and drive away –

'He's having a difficult time,' John Heatherington says. 'He's finding it – hard.'

'I feel so sorry for him,' says Joan.

She is, Asya thinks, surprisingly young and good-looking – not *that* surprisingly, she corrects herself: John is quite handsome too, but there is something very pleasant about Joan. 'He was so kind to us when we were in Egypt, and now there seems to be so little we can do to help him –'

'Has something actually happened?' asks Asya.

'Well, there have been two incidents,' John says. 'One was three weeks ago and one was yesterday –'

'It's all quite understandable really,' says Joan.

'You haven't seen him at all since he's been here, have you?' John asks.

Asya shakes her head. 'No, I'm afraid I haven't. I haven't been going into the university much, and – he's staying on campus, isn't he?'

'Yes, he has a room on campus, but apparently he decided to go into town for some shopping and he found the shopping centre and – well, basically, he walked out of Boots without paying for the goods.'

'He must have made a mistake,' says Asya.

'The store detectives followed him and they took him back to the shop and held him there and called the police, and the police took him in. He couldn't make himself understood but he gave them my name and they called me. I went round and we sorted it out.'

'What did he say?' asks Asya. 'I mean, why did he say he had done it?'

'He said he thought the whole shopping centre was one shop and that you paid for everything together.'

'I believe him,' Joan says.

'It *is* pretty confusing the first time,' says Asya.

'Yes,' John says. 'Well, it was all right. They let him go and nothing happened. But this business yesterday wasn't very good –'

'John sorted it out,' says Joan, 'but now I've made it worse.'

'Apparently some girl smiled at him,' says John. 'He was in Market Hall and this girl smiled at him, so he followed her around, and when she left the market he caught her in – you know, those empty entrances with the stairs? Well, he caught up with her there and pushed her against the wall and shouted – she says he shouted and screamed at her, "Why you are smiling at me? Is it sex you want? Is it sex you want?" And, so on.'

Asya bites her lip. Of course, it's terrible, but the idea of poor bewildered Mahrous pushing some equally bewildered English girl against a wall because she'd smiled at him . . .

'So what happened?' she asks.

John shrugs. 'She pushed him off and walked away, but he followed her. So she walked to the police station and he followed her there and they took him in. We managed to get him out again, but –'

'Oh, I *am* sorry,' says Asya, 'this must be horrible for you –'

'Oh no, that's not the point,' John says. 'The thing is, we just don't really know what to do. I took him home and talked to him and explained that she was just being friendly, that the smile was just a – a hospitality signal to someone who was obviously a stranger. But then he started blaming himself terribly, and this morning we thought that Joan –'

'He stayed with you?'

'Well, we couldn't just take him back to his room and leave him there in the state he was in, you see. And today we thought maybe Joan, with the woman's touch –'

'Well, he was blaming himself so much,' Joan says, 'and – you know he's newly married –'

548

'No, I didn't know,' Asya says.

'Yes, he got married about a year ago, and he's left his wife pregnant, you see, which must be a terrible strain on him as well – so he thinks he's a monster because he'd approached this girl, and I was trying to make him feel better about that because obviously he'd fancied her and I said everybody has these feelings and one has to recognise them and then decide what to do about them. And he wouldn't believe that he wasn't the only person in the world to have a – a thought like that, he just really *would* not believe it, so in the end I said I'd had the odd thought now and then about some man but the thing that mattered was to keep it just a thought, and he said, "You?" and I said, "Yes." And he asked if I was telling the truth, and I said yes, and then he asked if John knew, and I said yes, but I was beginning to feel something of a freak so I said that lots of women have these thoughts. And he more or less stood up and said that since he had it on my authority that women have these thoughts he was going to go home and divorce his wife right now.'

'Yes, well, it's all a bit dramatic,' John says, leaning forward, his elbows resting on the knees of his grey corduroys.

'He won't divorce her,' Asya says. 'She won't let him. Nor will her mother or his mother or anyone. Once he's there.'

'Yes, but if he leaves he spoils his chances – *ruins* his chances, maybe, of the Ph.D,' John says.

'Yes,' says Asya.

'You see,' says Joan, 'when we were in Egypt he took us home to his village and they were all very kind and very hospitable to us and made us a banquet, but we saw the – circumstances in which his parents live, and I'm sure it matters a great deal to them to have a son who's making a career in the university –'

'Yes, I'm sure –' says Asya.

'Anyway, we thought you might have a word with him. He was very willing to come to you.'

'Yes, of course,' says Asya, 'I'll do anything I can.'

And what if Gerald comes back now? What if he drives up and parks and – Asya stands up and moves over to the window. Glancing out, she can see as far as the little bridge and it is all clear – for the moment.

'I'll talk to him,' she says, and turns as Mahrous comes up the stairs. 'May you pray in the sacred House!' She smiles at him.

'Together, in sha'Allah!' he responds automatically, his hand placed briefly on his heart.

'Why don't we go for a walk,' Asya suggests. 'Now, before it grows dark. The view from that hill is very pretty.'

It's all right, she tells herself, they don't know how odd a suggestion this is coming from her; they don't know how much she hates the cold.

549

They'll think that it's only because outside she can talk to him alone.

'Do you mind if we stay and wait for you here?' Joan asks, on cue.

'Of course not,' Asya says. 'You'll help yourself to some more tea and cookies? And if Saif, my husband, calls, can you wave at me from the window and I'll run back?'

At least if she's outside and Gerald comes back she can head him off. She can step up to the car window and explain quickly that he has to go away. She can pretend to Mahrous that he's a motorist who's lost his way. And then when he comes back later he'll make a scene – but what can she do? What else can she do now?

Muffled in coats and scarves Mahrous and Asya leave the cottage. Asya locks the door behind her: at least this way he can't just walk in as though he lived there. And why 'as though'? He *is* living there practically, even though she's more or less forced him to rent a guest-room on campus – and he'd argued, she couldn't *believe* how he'd argued, about the waste of money, – seven pounds a week and he'd argued, about the waste of money – never seeing that what he was saying was that he wanted to live for free in a house where the rent was being paid by another man; by an innocent and deceived man; by the man whose wife he was sleeping with, whose wife he was plotting to steal . . .

Asya glances at Mahrous, walking beside her. The last time she'd seen him would probably have been May 1973, when they were both invigilating exams at college. Also, he'd come to offer condolences at her grandfather's funeral, and they'd been members of the Literary Society together, but they had never spoken alone. They trudge in step across the field next to the cottage, leaving footprints in the wet grass, their shoes picking up a layer of mud as they go.

'Dr Heatherington told me what happened,' Asya says.

'I don't know where to put my face,' Mahrous says, staring at the ground as he walks.

'It's something that can happen to anybody,' Asya says.

'No, no,' he says. 'Don't say that. I turned out to be – to be very low; I turned out to be an animal. An animal, merely.' He nods at the grass, confirming to himself what he is saying.

'Mahrous, you misunderstood, that's all: you misunderstood her.'

'Asya.' He stands still. 'If she'd said yes I would have gone with her.' He looks at Asya briefly then down at the ground again. 'I'm sorry. I'm sorry to be telling you such things, but it's the truth. I didn't know that the truth about me was like this.'

'You mustn't torment yourself.' Asya's voice is half angry, half pleading. 'You're on your own, in a strange country, these are factors which have to be taken into consideration. You *must* be feeling lonely –'

'It was the sex impulse,' he says. 'I'm sorry. I should not speak of these things. But you are a married woman –'

550

'Yes,' says Asya. 'It's all right.'

'It was just the sex impulse, that's all. I can't claim it was anything else.'

'I don't think you can draw a complete dividing line between all the different emotions a person feels,' says Asya. 'I mean, would it have happened in your home town? Or even in Cairo?'

'Of course not,' he says.

They have reached the top of the hill. They turn around, and Asya can now scan the cottage and the path that leads to it. Joan Heatherington is not at the window waving. But what would she do if the car turned the corner and started to cross the rickety bridge? She can't just start running wildly down the hill –

'That's what I mean,' she says. 'You are still you, and your impulses are the same, but your circumstances are different.'

They are standing under the solitary tree that marks the top of the hill. The sun has set, and the birds are making their final clamour, saying all they have to say to each other and to the world before they settle for the night . . . She could say, 'Oh, look! They're lost. We'd better warn them before they get stuck.'

'A man should have control over his actions,' Mahrous says. 'Otherwise what's the difference between us and the beasts?'

'I didn't know you'd got married,' Asya says. 'Congratulations.'

Mahrous suddenly sits down on the ground and puts his face in his hands. Maybe she could say, 'Wait here, I'll run and tell them.' He shouldn't sit on the ground: it's all wet.

'Mahrous,' she says gently, 'don't do this to yourself.'

'I'm finished,' he says into his hands. His voice comes out as a groan. 'Finished. I can't stand myself. I can't stand the thoughts that are in my mind.'

'Which thoughts, Mahrous?' she asks.

'I've left my wife pregnant and now I'm thinking – I'm thinking –'

He breaks off and sobs into his hands. Each sob comes out with a deep, rasping sound, as though it were being wrenched from somewhere deep down in his body. I can't just stand over him like this, Asya thinks, but the ground is so wet and my coat will be ruined. She sighs softly and sits down on the ground beside him.

'I'm sorry, I'm sorry,' he manages to say, and then the sobs break out again.

'What's there to be sorry about?' Asya says quietly. She wants to comfort him, to at least put her hand on his shoulder, not just let him sit there separate and weeping on the damp ground. But he would misunderstand and it would make him more unhappy. How can he trust what she says if she's so free and easy as to pat his shoulder?

'Is it because of what Mrs Heatherington said?' she asks.

551

'She opened my eyes,' he weeps, 'she opened my eyes.'

'She was only trying to help you,' Asya says.

'She set a bomb off under my feet. She destroyed my life. I'm thinking I'm a criminal and I don't deserve to live, and she tells me the whole world is like that. The whole world is criminal and corrupt.'

He is angry now. He lifts up his face and looks at Asya fiercely.

'That wasn't what she meant,' Asya says.

'She said all women are like that. She told me of my wife, of my mother –' He jumps to his feet. 'What is a person to live for? How can a man live if his honour isn't guaranteed? What will he build his life on? Can my father imagine that my mother is looking at other men? If a thought like that had crossed his mind he would have strangled her –'

'Mahrous, Mrs Heatherington wasn't talking about your mother –'

'She told me about all women –'

'How can she tell you what she doesn't know?'

'Isn't she a woman? And she told me about women –'

'She told you maybe about herself. Maybe she once had a thought, and now to help you she –'

'She said all women. *All women.*'

'She can't tell you about *all* women. She can only tell you what *she knows* about. How can she *know* about your wife or your mother? She is different; she is a Western woman, everything is different here.'

'I am confused,' he says helplessly, looking out across the sloping ground over which darkness is falling, down to the narrow overgrown ditch where Asya knows her little stream is running, and into the woods beyond. 'This country has confused me. From the moment I set foot in the airport and saw the magazines they put everywhere – they don't even hide them: you can just stand like that and look – it's wrong. It's wrong to do that to women: hang them up to be looked at by everyone coming and going. And then they awaken a person's feelings and what is he to do?'

'They are very worried about you,' Asya says. 'Dr and Mrs Heatherington. And they are good people and their intentions are good.'

Mahrous digs his hands into his pockets and retracts his neck further down into his scarf.

'Dr Heatherington told the police that in my country I live in a mud hut. He was laughing with them.'

Asya can see it: Mahrous, shamed and angry, huddles on a bench while John Heatherington, trying to get him off, jokes with the policemen.

'He was trying to get you away from them.'

'He said, "His family live in a mud hut." '

'Look, what he was trying to do was to make them see that you are not one of them – that they should not judge you –'

'He humiliated me.'

'Mahrous, look, do you believe he meant to insult you?'

'No, but –'

'Wasn't he trying to end the matter and get you out of there?'

'Yes, but –'

'There's no place for but. He dealt with them in the way he saw would work. Maybe there was a better way and he didn't have time to think of it. Don't judge him. He and his wife have been good to you. They are still English people, but they came and went for your sake and they took you into their home, and for English people this is not something small.'

'I know. You are right.' He looks at her. 'Asya, you will catch cold sitting on the damp ground. Do you want to go back? The world has grown dark.'

Asya pushes herself to her feet and stands beside him.

'Mahrous? What are you going to do?'

'I don't know,' he says miserably. 'I don't know. But I can't stay in this country.'

'So you'll go home?' she asks.

'I don't know,' he repeats.

'You've always wanted to work in the university.'

'It was the dream of my life,' he says sadly.

'Then you stay and do your Ph.D.'

'I can't, I can't. I'll go mad.' He shakes his head.

'What if your wife were with you? You haven't told me her name.'

'Maha,' he says, and his voice breaks on the word.

'And when, in sha' Allah, do you expect her to be delivered?'

'The doctor said the beginning of December – but it's her first time –'
He is clenching and unclenching his hands with the effort not to weep.

'Shall I tell you what to do?' Asya asks, looking at him.

'Tell me,' he says, looking into her eyes.

'You write her a letter, you tell her as soon as the doctor says she and the baby are safe to travel she is to bring him and come here.'

'But how? How will I support them? How –'

'You'll manage.' Asya speaks with strength and confidence. 'How much is your grant? A hundred and fifty-two pounds a month, right? You'll get a little flat on campus for thirty, thirty-five pounds a month, and you'll manage on the rest. They have a crèche for babies here. It would cost you nothing and it's a beautiful place. Maybe Maha can do a bit of studying too, or maybe she can take a small part-time job to help you –'

'I would let myself be supported by my wife?' He draws himself up to his full height, his eyes bulging with indignation. 'It's impossible –'

'In any case, you *would* be able to manage. I *know* you would be able to manage. Maybe *you* could work in the coffee-bar for a couple of hours a day and get the Ph.D in four years instead of three. But they would be

four years of *real life* with Maha and your child, not three years cut out –
deducted – lost for ever from your life.' Asya pauses. 'What other
problem remains? The ticket?'

'No. The ticket is not a problem. We can manage that.'

'Well?'

'Will her mother let her go? She will be worried for her.'

'You will write and explain to Maha. *She* will persuade her mother.'

'But how can I tell her in a letter about what happened? How will
she –'

'No, oh no,' says Asya. 'Don't tell her any of that. But tell her how
unhappy you are. Tell her you don't think you will be able to continue
unless she's with you. You are working for the future of both of you – and
she too for sure wants to be with you –'

'But I will have to ask her first,' he says darkly.

'Ask her what?'

'Ask her about what Mrs Heatherington said.'

'Mahrous –' Asya turns to peer into his face in the dusk. 'You're going
to ask her such a question in a letter? You'll confuse her and upset her
when she's about to have a baby? Is this the act of a mature man who
cherishes his wife? Bring her over here, and when she's with you ask her
whatever you like.'

'You have reason,' he says, hanging his head. 'You have reason. I don't
know what to say to you.'

'You'll write to Maha?'

'Yes,' he says. 'This is the solution. I will write to her tonight. Maybe
they can be here before even the year is finished.'

As they walk in the darkness down the hill and towards the lit windows
of the cottage, Mahrous says, 'I am very embarrassed in front of Dr
Heatherington and his wife. I have behaved very badly.'

'You mustn't think like that,' Asya says. 'You just misunderstood a
situation –'

'Yes, but they are civilised people and I behaved like a barbarian.'

'Mahrous,' says Asya, 'would they have known how to behave if they
had gone into your village without you to guide them? They wouldn't.
And they *know* they wouldn't. And because they are civilised people they
make the same allowance for you. Put it out of your mind.'

Later that evening

Gerald Stone pushes away his plate with the quarter of roast chicken
untouched on it. He puts both his hands down on the table and says,
'This is like eating with the bloody Queen.' Then he pushes his chair
back and stands up.

Asya thinks, 'He's going to start again.' But she is also a little, tiny bit
flattered to be compared to the Queen.

'Sure,' he says, standing on the other side of the table, 'just sit there. Don't even look at me.'

She looks up at him.

'What *is* the matter?' she asks.

'You. *You* are the matter: sitting there with your cashmere and your pearls and your – detachment; as though you were beyond it all.'

'All I'm doing,' says Asya, 'is sitting here eating this piece of chicken. How do you want me to behave? What do you want me to do different?'

'That's right,' he says. 'It's always like that. "Give me my cue, Gerald, tell me how you want me to be, Gerald." Some Aries: you're supposed to be an *Aries*, man: a *leader*.'

Asya puts her knife and fork down on her plate and pushes it a few centimetres away from her.

'You *had* to do that, didn't you?' he says.

'Do what?' she asks, puzzled, looking up at him.

'Put your knife and fork exactly side by side and at an angle. You'd never just throw them down –'

'I probably would if I felt like it,' Asya says.

'You wouldn't even *know* if you felt like it –'

'Look, if you're planning to do a Jimmy Porter it's been done –'

'A what? Who's Jimmy Porter?' He looks at her suspiciously.

'A character in some play.' She shrugs. 'It doesn't matter.'

'That's the trouble with you, you see. Your ideas all come from books. You don't know a thing about real life. *Not one thing.* You're not equipped to *handle* real life –'

'Gerald. Something's been wrong ever since you got here tonight. What is it? Did something happen at the university?'

'That's the other thing you're good at: shifting responsibility.'

Asya stands up and starts clearing the table.

'Nothing happened at university,' he says to her back. 'I sat in the library, I worked out in the indoor rec. Nothing happened except I know there's no reason for me to be there.'

Asya presses the pedal of the bin and empties out his uneaten plate. Well then, go, go, go. Just say you'll go, and go.

'And then I come back from there feeling a bit off – a bit like I need reminding of the reason I'm here in the first place – and the woman I love – the woman for whom I'm hanging about and putting my career in the gravest danger – has got her work spread out on the table and treats me like I was – like I was the parish priest come to call.'

'So this is all because I had my work out on the table?'

'No it *isn't* because you had your work out on the table. Don't *do* this to me, man.' He slams his fist down on the back of the chair he had been sitting in. 'It's because of the way you *are*.'

Asya bends to wipe the table with a squeezed-out sponge.

'I'm an hour late coming back: I say I'll be back at seven and I come back at eight and you're sitting in front of your *metaphors*, with some phoney classical stuff filling the room, and you don't even say where the hell were you – not that you'd put it in those terms, God forbid, I mean, one just *wouldn't* do that *would* one –'

Asya straightens up. 'So I should have been sitting behind the front door weeping because you were an hour late? And you should have come up here and found your supper congealing on the table and no evidence of my work –'

' "Congealing"? My supper *congealing* on the table? What's wrong with growing cold?'

Asya looks at him quietly. ' "Congealing" takes it a step further,' she says. 'However . . .' She turns to the sink. 'Your supper growing cold on the table and no evidence of my work.'

'Look, we've had this out about your work before and I've said I've got nothing against your work.'

'No.' Asya drags on her washing-up gloves. 'Except any time you see any sign of it you go off into a huge – state.'

'What I think – what I keep *telling* you – is that you ought to get your priorities straight. You ought to deal first with matters that urgently need to be dealt with. And when I say urgently, I *mean* urgently –'

Asya turns to the sink and starts doing the washing-up.

'And now you're going to turn away and fade into silence as per usual.'

Why 'per', Asya wonders, what's the function of the 'per' in there?

'Will you please answer me? *Answer* me, damn it.'

Asya pauses and half turns from the sink to look at him. He is standing gripping the back of the chair and his knuckles are showing white.

'Answer what?'

'What are you going to do? What – are – you – going – to – do?'

'I don't *know*. I've told you. I don't *know*.'

'You've *got* to know.' His voice changes. He appeals to her. 'No one else can know, baby. It's you who's got to know.'

'I've told you: I can't do *anything* like this. I can't even *think* like this –' Asya grips the edge of the sink with her ugly red rubber-gloved hands.

'So how long am I supposed to wait? How long am I supposed to wait for you to take some action –'

'I don't *want* you to wait. I've told you: I don't want you to wait at *all*.'

'No,' he says bitterly. 'You want me to go away and leave you alone. Leave you in peace to procrastinate for ever.'

Asya bends her head over the kitchen sink. If he says 'procrastinate' one more time she'll throw up. Or 'Aries'. Or 'leader' or 'fire' or 'relationship' or 'do'.

'Please,' Gerald says, 'will you at least look at me?'

Asya turns to face him, keeping her wet-gloved hands behind her over the sink.

556

'How *can* you?' he says. 'How can you *look* at me like this?'

Asya closes her eyes. Please God, she thinks, please God make him stop. Make him suddenly sound normal. Make him say, 'I'm going to have a shower,' make him say, 'Let's leave it,' make him say, 'OK, I understand. You don't want to leave him. You want him to stay your husband and me to be your lover – maybe' –

'I,' he says, 'am standing before you, a soul in torment, and you won't even look at me.'

Asya opens her eyes. He does look terrible: his eyes are red and his face is pale and pinched-looking, with purple patches at the sides of the nostrils. It's not his fault if he says things like 'a soul in torment'; it doesn't invalidate his feelings –

'You won't do anything *about* it –'

'There is nothing I can do,' Asya says again. Her voice sounds dead.

'I can't believe it,' he says. 'I can't believe that this is the same person who knelt by my side and said, "I love you" –'

Asya turns quickly back to the sink. But that was because you were ill, she screams in her mind. Don't you understand anything? Because you were ill, struck down, lying there on the sofa with every bit of colour gone from your face and your hands ice-cold and you not able to breathe and drinking warm brandy and water out of a teaspoon in my hand, and I was so sorry for you because you were suffering so, and the reason you were suffering was that you were going away and leaving me in three days' time. I did love you then; I felt a great wave of tenderness and gratitude washing over me, and I told you, and that same night I wished I hadn't. In three days' time you were going and it's been seven weeks –

'Are you really going to stand there and not say anything?' he asks, and then, in a voice of mild wonder, 'You would, wouldn't you? You'd stand there all night.'

'I've said *everything*,' she says. 'I've said everything again and again. And I want you – *please* – to stop pushing me.'

'This is pushing?' he says. 'I am trying to make contact with you and you call it pushing? I am talking about our lives – our whole lives –'

'Gerald, please, *please*, will you stop, because I can't *bear* it –'

'About this wonderful thing that has been given to us –'

'I cannot *breathe* –'

'OK, OK, baby. Don't go hysterical on me now. Let's just sit down and talk the whole thing over, OK?'

'No. *No.*' Asya hits the sink with a gloved hand. 'Because you won't listen to what I have to say – to what I *really* have to say –'

'I will. I'll listen. What choice have I got? OK? Will you just move away from that sink and come and sit down?'

He stands aside as though to clear her path. Asya takes a deep breath

557

and then dries her gloves on a kitchen towel and peels them off slowly. She lifts her head.

'Would you like some coffee?' she asks.

'Coffee? No, I don't want any *coffee*, thank you.'

There's no need to sneer, Asya thinks. I only offer coffee because you are in my house. I do a lot of things because you're in my house. Oh, I *wish* this were happening somewhere else so I would at least not feel I had to be polite, to be hospitable. She walks round the kitchen table and into the living-room. The fire is dying in the stove and she bends and throws a new log into it before sitting down in an armchair. Gerald sits on the edge of the sofa.

'OK,' he says. 'I'm listening.'

'Do we really have to go through –'

'Yes,' he says. '*Yes.*'

'All right,' she says. She takes a deep breath. 'We started being together two months ago –'

'We started *sleeping* together two months ago. We'd already been seeing each other two months before that.'

'Yes,' she says. 'But if we hadn't slept together those first two months wouldn't have mattered –'

'Wouldn't they? You can *sit* there and say they wouldn't have mattered?'

'All right, that was inaccurate. Nothing doesn't matter. But we'd have seen them as something nice and rather sad – something that maybe had potential but –'

He jumps up from the sofa. 'This is blasphemy. "Nice"? "Potential"? I *despise* these luke-warm terms. This is my *life* we're talking about, man. You're saying because a child has some problems he should have been aborted –'

'What I'm trying to say is that we both went into this thinking that it was – finite –'

'Oh, baby.' He stands by the stove and looks at her sorrowfully. 'How can you say that? How can you describe our love in these terms –'

'You said, "Will you see me through my exams then" –'

'I told you how I felt, I told you how I feared for myself –'

'Yes, but –'

'And I said I loved you and you said you loved me. Admittedly I said it on day two and you said it on day fifteen – but you said it. Were you lying?'

'No, I *wasn't* lying, but –'

'No, you weren't lying, but from the moment you said it you started betraying it. This wonderful, beautiful, *miraculous* thing that we've got, you started dragging it around like a ball and chain, and it's turned into a sorry sight: its feathers are all mangled –'

Asya sees the ball on the end of the chain, a big glossy iron ball . . . Suddenly little downy-white baby feathers start sprouting out all over it . . . She bites her lip.

'What I was going to say,' she says after a moment, 'was that maybe in *your* terms I *was* lying.'

'You weren't, baby. I know you weren't.'

'How do you know?'

'Because I could feel the truth, the truth in you. Because I *know* you.'

'You don't, Gerald,' she says gently. 'Really you don't –'

'Oh, I do,' he says quietly. He moves from the stove and comes and sits down on the coffee-table in front of her. He leans forward and puts his hands on her knees. 'I've known you for ever. You are my soulmate. I knew from our first night together that all my life had been a preparation for this. I felt as if I had already made love to you a hundred times. And now I know that I have found the thing that I was born to serve and to cherish. And that is why it makes me so angry each time you deny it. Don't you see that?'

'But, Gerald, this is all to do with *you* –'

'No, it *isn't*. That's where you're wrong.' He reaches out for one of her hands and holds it. 'It's to do with *us* –'

'Well, on the practical side –'

'That's it, man, that's it.' He throws her hand back into her lap. 'Let's get back to the practical things. We can handle those –'

'Gerald, I can't act under pressure. I just *can't*. And you're putting huge pressure on me. This situation is –'

'I'm only asking you for what is right. I am asking you to give this relationship, this wonderful, unique, precious relationship, a chance to live.' He leans forward again. 'I am asking you not to strangle the newborn baby in its cradle –'

'Would you try – would you *please* try to see it from my side. I've been here for three years working on this thesis. I've persuaded myself – rightly or wrongly – that my life is in abeyance, on hold, until that's done. I've got about six months to go – and then you and I meet. I'm already under pressure because of the work, because of the circumstances under which I'm living, because of the difficulties I've had earlier – I'm kind of just about keeping a grip on things – and you want me, in the middle of all this, to suddenly spring up and make a decision that will change my whole life, a decision the repercussions of which you really have absolutely no way of beginning to fathom –'

'I am asking you to take what's yours. I am asking you to move away from this catatonic state I found you in and which you keep insisting on returning to – to a *real* life – a full life – to be *yourself*, baby –'

'How do you know what *myself* is?' Asya's voice is high and desperate. '*I* don't even know that any more. Maybe my self is catatonic and procrastinating and mendacious –'

'No it isn't, baby. You are beautiful. I know you are. I've felt your fire –'

'Gerald, please. Even if *you* know, *I* have to know. And I *can't* know – I can't know *anything* while we go on like this –'

'So we're back to that?'

'Yes.'

'You want me to go? You're throwing me out?'

'I am not throwing you out. I love being with you, you know I do. But there's a lot that's wrong with this situation –'

'You can sure say that again, man.' He stands up and runs his fingers through his hair as he stands looking down on her.

'You keep saying how I'm gravely jeopardising your career; I don't *want* to do that. And that's putting pressure on me. You need to make a start on what you're going to do next. You can't waste your time with me like this –'

'Baby, what does my career matter when put next to this? How can you say I'm wasting my time when I'm sweating blood every day trying to secure the one thing that will make my life meaningful? And then you tell me to go for my own good –'

'And for mine too: I can't work either. It's been a month since I've been able to do *anything*. I've been putting off my tutorials –'

'We're missing our professor, are we?'

He smiles, but Asya meets his eyes with a blank look.

'I've told you how much finishing this thesis means to me –'

'I leave you alone. I go out every day just so you can get on –'

'But I can't. I can't.'

I can't because when you're not here I sit in his room, touching his things, crying, writing him letters that I won't ever send just in case one day he wants to know – wants to *really* know – about me – about how I feel – about how I want to stop but can't and how sorry I am and how much I love him –

Asya suddenly draws in her breath as if she's been hit and starts to cry. 'I – just – *can't.*'

'Finally,' Gerald says, sitting back. 'Finally we have some emotion. And when? When the lady talks about her Ph.D.'

'It isn't that,' Asya says in the space between two sobs.

'Isn't it?'

'No.' Asya shakes her head. 'I just want this to stop. I am so tired, and there isn't a single night when we go to sleep before four, and I am just exhausted, and I don't want this to be happening here any more.'

'Here?'

'In this house.'

'Why not in this house? This is where you live.'

560

'Gerald, this is my husband's house.'

'We've been through this before and I reminded you that you'd said yourself he'd only been here three times.'

'It's still his house,' Asya insists.

'How come it's still his house?'

'He pays the *rent*, for God's sake.' Now she's done it. Now he'll be so insulted he'll just have to walk out. Oh, she hadn't wanted to insult – Gerald Stone stands up and moves away. He places himself by the window and folds his arms.

'So it finally comes down to money. Now why did I have a feeling it might in the end? That's what's behind it all, really, isn't it?'

'No,' says Asya, wiping her face with her hands. 'No, it isn't actually.'

'That's why you're so afraid. That's why you don't want to leave. That's why you are denying this gift that has been given to us: for the sake of money.'

Asya shakes her head. 'You really *are* wrong,' she says in a low voice.

'Tell him, then. Next time he rings and you take the phone and sneak off into the boiler-room and close the door – tell him.'

'No.'

'Why?'

'I can't tell him.'

'Why?'

'I can't tell him like this.'

'*Why?*'

'I just *can't*.'

'*How* can you tell him?'

'Face to face. And only if he wants to know.'

'If you don't tell him, I will. I don't like hiding out like this. I don't believe this is what we deserve. Our love deserves to be out in the sunlight, to be free, to be given the respect that's owing it –' He punctuates his speech with bangs of his fist on the window-sill.

'I don't think,' says Asya, 'you'll find many people to agree with you.'

'That's because of *you*: *you're* pushing us into a corner, hiding us under veils of lies and deception. You *insult* us. And this has *got* to stop. If *you* won't tell him, *I* will. The next time he phones I'm going to pick up the phone and tell him.'

Asya looks up at him. 'You do that,' she says slowly and quietly, 'you do that and I will be out of here within the hour. You'll never find me. And I'll never, ever have anything to do with you again.'

He looks steadily at her, and then he nods twice. 'OK, baby. You do it your way. But you'll still have to do it.'

As Asya finishes the washing-up, dries the red rubber gloves and peels them off, then washes her hands to get rid of the feel and smell of rubber and massages some cream into her fingers, Gerald Stone says, 'Please will you do something for me?'

'Yes?' Asya says.

'Take off those pearls. Take off those pearls and stop looking like Brenda.'

'Like who?' asks Asya.

'The Queen.'

'Why did you call her Brenda?' asks Asya.

'It's a joke.'

Asya doesn't understand the joke, but she puts her hands up to her neck and unclasps the pearls. She feels them trickle and coil themselves heavily into her right hand and she holds them there, smooth and warm.

'That's better,' Gerald says. 'But I want you to put something else on. One of your silver things.'

'I was going to get into my nightie and have an early – well, early*ish*, night,' Asya says, glancing at her watch. 'I'm so desperately tired.'

'Please, babe, for me? I want to see *you* again. I've been sitting here with this stranger all night.'

Asya leaves the kitchen and goes downstairs. She goes into her bedroom and opens one of the drawers in the wardrobe. The silver jewellery which Saif had bought – each piece of it, and now *he* asks her to go and put it on? He would not be able to buy *one* piece – even if he had the money he wouldn't begin to know where to look. Has *he* been into every corner of Lebanon? Has he been into Kurdish villages on the borders between Iraq and Iran where all their jewellery is made in the shape of pistachio nuts because the one thing they grow is pistachios? But – after all, she suddenly thinks, was that true? Saif had told her that, but might he not after all have simply bought the necklace from a jeweller's on Hamra? She looks at all her necklaces: nothing silver will really go with this sweater. But still, she picks out a filigree choker inlaid with seven crescent moons and goes to the mirror to clip it on. Gerald is standing in the doorway, leaning against the door-frame, looking at her. The now familiar stirring of desire pulses once between her legs, and she turns and keeps her eyes fixed on the dark window as she secures the clasp.

'I'm going to let your hair down,' he says. 'No. *I* want to do it. Sit down.'

He lifts the wooden chair that stands in the corner and carries it over. He puts it down in front of the mirror and Asya sits, her hands folded together on her lap. He fumbles in her hair, drawing out one, two, three, four hairgrips, and her hair tumbles down. But she had put in five. One hairgrip must be lost, still caught somewhere in her hair. He pushes his fingers inside her hair, fanning it out over her shoulders.

'Better,' he says. 'Better. But the pullover's wrong. Let's take it off. Hold up your arms.'

He reaches down and draws her sweater up and over her head. He lets it drop on the floor behind him.

'Oh, yes,' he says. 'Yes. We're getting somewhere.'

He bends and puts his arms around her from behind the chair. He kisses her shoulder – 'Hold up your arms again –' and draws her camisole up over her head. Asya shakes her hair out of her face. He unhooks her bra and Asya closes her eyes as he draws it off.

'You are *beautiful*,' he whispers.

She sits and holds her breath.

'Open your eyes,' he says. 'Look.'

Asya shakes her head.

'Yes,' he says. 'Open your eyes. I want you to see yourself.'

Asya opens her eyes and immediately looks away. He draws his hand lightly over the tip of each breast. She holds on to the arms of the chair.

'Could we – please – at least switch off the light?' she says.

'No.' He shakes his head. He pulls her head round by the hair and holds it so that she has to look into the mirror. 'Look at you, baby. Look at you. I never want you to get dressed when we're married. Be like this for me, babe: naked and perfumed, your hair falling over your shoulders, wearing only your jewels –'

Her jewels that Saif had bought.

'An odalisque you want?' she smiles.

'A what?'

'A concubine. A female slave.'

Holding her head, he bends and puts his mouth to the hollow of her throat. He kisses her chin and her jawbone and her ears and her forehead and her eyes and her lips. With his mouth he presses her head hard against his supporting hands. And if Mahrous should come now? If in despair at the black thoughts in his mind he should come back and climb the wall and look into her bedroom window, he would see her, Asya al-Ulama, who had been walking with him on the hill outside this window just a few hours ago, who had listened to him weep because he'd fancied some girl in the marketplace – he would see her sitting in front of her full-length mirror, her top half bare except for a silver choker, her head, her mouth, her everything surrendered to a strange man – a strange *foreign* man whom she is allowing to – to have his way with her. What would it do to him? Where would he go? She can imagine him stumbling off into the darkness – she would be responsible for whatever happened to him . . . She moves her head, and Gerald's mouth goes down to her neck again, her collarbone, her chest. When it reaches her left breast Asya says, 'No,' and tries to twist away.

'Yes,' he says. 'Yes, yes, *yes*.'

With his hands he clamps her wrists to the arms of the chair and kisses and licks and bites and breathes on her till her head falls helplessly against the back of the chair and she moans. He puts his mouth to hers. 'Moan into my mouth, babe,' he says, 'give it to me. I am going to fuck you, I am going to fuck you like you have never, *never*, been fucked in your life.' He draws his mouth down her cheek and her neck and she feels his teeth on her skin, sharp, and sharper, but when she cries out he lifts his head. 'Oh, baby,' he says, letting go of her wrists, kneeling beside her and taking the arch of her right foot in his hand. 'Oh, baby, baby,' easing one leg away from the other and placing soft kisses on the insides of her thighs. 'I'm the one who's the slave, *your* slave, my beautiful, beautiful Eastern butterfly.'

Later, in bed, with the weight of his body still on hers, but quiet now, breathing deep, she folds her arms loosely around him and marvels again at what his love-making does for her. At times like this, when it's just over, it is as if a great, stormy sea had receded, and in the bed where a moment ago the waves were crashing and seething and foaming, there is space: moist, open sands stretching as far as the eye can reach. Her body is content; actively, consciously content, as when a long and nagging pain suddenly lifts and there is pleasure in simply stretching a leg or moving a finger. But it is her mind that amazes her: where do all those vast spaces come from that open up inside her head? Those great seascapes from which the sea itself is always absent? Sometimes they are like the views here in the north, with a dim and grey sky, wet rock and stones on the seabed, the odd broken bottle, the wagging tail of a leaping dog the only point of hope in the drab, empty scene. Sometimes they are like frames from *Death in Venice*; in pastel colours, with menace in the emptiness, and far away a few blue-striped awnings under which languid, windswept figures pause and shelter. Sometimes they are like the shore at Za'farana, soaked in deep, impossible colours: the revealed sea-bed the colour of rust, the line of sea in the distance shining solid silver with the sun, the sky a Technicolor blue, the mountains rising between the seabed and the sky black and red and rich with ore. She walks through these vistas, weightless, without effort, and thinks that this is what it must be like to be on the moon. Sometimes she has a feeling that she is going to find something, that within the next few steps she will find something in the sand; something that was meant for her. But she hasn't found it yet. Oh, if only, if only 'Sex' and 'Romance' were one – imagine feeling like this and knowing that if she opens her eyes it will be Saif's deep brown eyes that she meets, hazy and tender without their spectacles. Imagine if she were now to hear the click of a lighter and smell the first whiff of a Rothmans floating across her nostrils. She would put her head against his shoulder and say, 'I want the tiles for the fountain in our courtyard –

the ones at the bottom of the fountain – to be the deepest turquoise, with fat little goldfish painted on them –'

Gerald rolls off her and lies on his back. He throws his arm over his forehead and says, 'That was good; too good.' Then he says, 'There's nothing left to do and nowhere left to go.'

'Hush,' whispers Asya, turning and stroking his arm. 'Hush. You are fantastic.'

'I am so miserable, babe,' he says.

'Hush,' she says again. 'Hush. It's always a little sad after. It'll go.'

He sits up in bed and crosses his legs. 'Don't try and smother me in platitudes,' he says. 'You know very well what I'm talking about. You know why I'm miserable. What we have is miraculous and you felt it too – and now how you can –'

Oh, thinks Asya, oh. He can't possibly start again now. Please, please let him not start: it's one-thirty. But if she tells him it's one-thirty she'll get a half-hour sermon on time not mattering and how her noticing the time is a measure of the constraints she places on her existence, how earth-bound she is . . . But how *can* he start on her now? Anyone, *anyone*, would be able to see how tired she is – was this what Saif had been afraid of? That if he gave her an opening she would talk and talk and talk and he would never get any sleep? But she wouldn't have done that. Not like this. She would never have had the energy anyway – Gerald has energy; he has lots of energy. He may not be particularly sensitive to her or particularly strong on logic but he has energy and strength of feeling. And single-mindedness. He ought to put that to good purpose and not waste it on her like this. It could probably make him a millionaire. He would probably be happier if he were a millionaire –

'I don't believe this.' Gerald Stone is shaking her by the shoulder. 'I really would not have believed this if I hadn't seen it with my own eyes. You're sleeping, man. I'm pouring out my soul here and you're sleeping –'

Asya sits up and pulls the sheet around her. She feels she'll die if she doesn't sleep. She looks at Gerald: in his face are both misery and contempt. She focuses on the misery. After all, she knows what it's like to be alone and panic-stricken in the middle of the night while the person you love sleeps soundly beside you – and besides, after what he has just done for her, she ought at least to hear him out. She shakes her head to dispel sleep and feels the first strokes of the headache. She stretches her hand out to his face.

'I'm sorry,' she says. 'I'm sorry. I didn't mean to fall asleep.'

Scene 5

Wednesday, 19 January 1977
Athens

The stone ladies gaze straight ahead. From here they look as if they are standing on the edge of a giant sarcophagus, and on their heads they support its lid. They have supported it for two thousand years. For two thousand years the wind has whistled at them, the rain has lashed them, the sun has beaten down on them, and they have stood here unblinking, uncomplaining. Time has nibbled away at their arms, at their noses, at their lips, but their high breasts and their plump thighs under the transparent, clinging gowns are as rounded as on the day they were brought to this site and made to stand and carry the cover of their sarcophagus on their heads – and women in the same pleated white gowns with girdles round their waists and thonged sandals on their feet came to look at them and admire them and pray to the Goddess for the things that women have always prayed for –

'What am I going to do, Mummy?'

Asya turns to her mother, who has sat down beside her on the big cube of rock facing the temple. Lateefa pushes her spectacles back on to the bridge of her nose, and Asya suddenly realises that her mother's nose has a perfectly smooth slope, that's why her glasses keep slipping off; Daddy's nose on the other hand has a bump – a sort of Roman bump – on the bridge –

'The truth is, darling, I don't see why it has to be right now. Why can't you finish your work first and then –'

'Because I *can't*. I haven't been able to work for almost three months now. Because I found myself terrified of meeting Saif – so terrified that I made him not come to England over Christmas. Imagine that. I have never – *ever* – cancelled a date with him; I mean, I *live* by those dates, I calculate my life as days when we're together and spaces in between – and then I actually couldn't imagine meeting him; meeting him *there* as though nothing were the matter – I just couldn't. And of course I felt so horrible; so evil and wicked saying, I don't think you'd better come over –'

Asya falls miserably silent as she remembers the phone-call. He must have been so surprised, so surprised and *hurt*, but after the briefest of pauses all he'd said was, 'OK, Princess, if that's what you want.'

'It's not what I *want*. But I just think it would be better. I mean, I'm

566

really speeding ahead with the work now, and if you come I'll stop and then when you go I'll be all upset again and – I'll just lose so much *time*.'

'OK. The sooner you finish this work the better.'

'I mean, it isn't a problem for you, is it? I mean, you didn't really *really* want to come, did you? For yourself, I mean?'

'No, it's not a problem. There's no holiday here for Christmas and the New Year. We'll just carry on working.'

How could he have believed her? How *could* he? When had she ever said, don't come? When had she ever said, let's not meet? Let's not meet because of her *work*?

'I'm surprised he let you do that,' Lateefa says.

Asya shrugs. 'He never asks me any questions. However weird I am, he just never asks.'

'But what would you have done with – with this other man if Saif had come?' asks Lateefa.

'He wasn't going to be there anyway; he was going to his parents,' Asya says. 'That's how I know. I mean, that's how I know that the reason I couldn't see Saif was because I had to sort myself out first. I mean, not because it would have meant not seeing Gerald. I mean, I wouldn't do *that* –'

'But you're going to see Saif now –'

'I know, I know –' Asya says.

But that's not till tomorrow. He won't be here till tomorrow, and maybe by then she'll know what it is she's going to say to him –

'Didn't he ask you why you wanted him to come to Athens? Why you wanted me to be here?'

Asya shakes her head. 'No. He just said he'd see if he could get away. Then he called me back next day and said he would get a flight Thursday morning and he would come straight to the Hilton.'

'And how have you left it with – this other man?'

'He thinks I'm going to tell Saif about him. About "us". I haven't actually *said* I would, but I know that's what he thinks.'

All around them the world is white. The ground stretches out in uneven paving-slabs of white rock and pools of white stones where the rocks are broken; white bits of columns, snapped off and jagged-edged, lie untidily together, white stone walls rise into a white sky tinged with blue, and straight ahead, the six white ladies stand . . . 'They are suffering,' the young man who had attached himself to them had said, 'suffering from the pollution. Now there is talk of putting them in glass cases, so –' With his hands he had drawn an imagined glass case from the feet of one of the ladies and up. 'Six: one for every one. They will be protected, but they will not be how they are – they will not be the same.'

'And you've known this man for what? Six months?' Lateefa asks.

Asya nods. 'Yes.'

'And you haven't seen Saif for six months?'

Asya shakes her head. 'Since August. We were supposed to meet in Paris at the end of September, but he cancelled. And then Christmas . . .'

'And you've had this – this *stranger* – living in your house since then? Asya, how could you do that?'

'I don't know, Mummy, I don't know. It just happened that way –'

'But how could you *let* it happen, darling? That's your husband's house –'

'It isn't really. I mean, he's hardly been there – it doesn't really – all the time – feel as if it's my husband's house –'

'Asya –'

'I know: I know it's wrong – and it's the bit I feel worst about.'

'It's the bit you feel *worst* about?'

Asya nods.

'You don't feel worse about – about *sleeping* with this man?'

'No. I don't. I know it's odd, but I don't. It's as if sleeping with him is – private – it's *my* business – but letting him stay in the house when Saif is at least partly financing –'

'What do you mean it's *your* business? Isn't it a matter of concern to your husband if you sleep with another man?'

'But Saif doesn't care about me in that way – any more. If we'd still been having a – *passionate* thing, then I would have felt it *did* concern him – but then it wouldn't have happened – maybe it wouldn't have happened –'

'But you still love Saif?'

Asya smiles: ' "My love for Saif is like the eternal rocks beneath –" '

'Asya –'

'Mummy: "I *am* Saif –" he's always, always in my mind –'

'Asya, stop it. This is not a novel: this is your life –'

'Of course I still love him.'

'I mean, you still – are *together*, when you do meet?'

This is the moment – this is the point at which she should say, well, actually, no, well, actually, we've never really *really* been *together* since we were married. And after I lost the baby he said he loved me well enough to keep me on as his sister and that's what he's done. Should she? It would get her mother firmly on her side. But would it get her *too* firmly on her side?

'Yes,' says Asya, 'we are. But it's just no big deal any more.'

It's better like this – it even feels as if, although it's a falsehood, it's more true – it's a matter of balance –

'But he's still your husband, darling, and he assumes certain –'

'He assumes too much, Mummy. He *assumes* everything and he doesn't want to *know* anything. We had a quarrel once and he said, "If you ever take a lover I hope you'll have the decency to hide it from me." '

Lateefa is silent for a moment, then she says, 'And you took that as *carte blanche* –'

'No. No, I didn't. I mean, he said that a whole *year* before I had anything to do with Gerald. But I mean, that's why when I started the – affair with Gerald I didn't feel like I had to rush to the phone next morning and inform Saif – and that's why I'm not sure even now how much I ought to tell him: I mean, if he doesn't *want* to be told then that's his right, isn't it?'

'Aren't you just trying to make it easy on yourself?'

'No, I don't think so. I don't know. Maybe I am.' Asya bends down and picks up a white stone lying at her feet: it is warm and heavy in her hand but its edges are sharp. 'But I really don't think so. I think in a way it would be easier on me if he knew. Then he'd have to take some action – and I could just *react*. But now I have to think what I *ought* to do.'

'You ought to get rid of this man and finish your Ph.D, and if you have some problems with your husband because you've been apart for so long you'll straighten them out when you're together.'

Lateefa has used her no-nonsense end-of-discussion voice and Asya jumps up from their warm white seat.

'If that's all you're going to say,' she cries, 'then this is useless – *useless*.' Tears of anger rise to her eyes. 'We needn't have bothered to come here *at all*.'

She walks quickly away. But when she comes up against the temple she stops. Where can she go? She looks up at the stone women towering above her. Are they demi-goddesses or just favoured mortals, she wonders. Or are they being punished for something? Made to stand here throughout time, carrying a ton of engraved stone on their heads? She turns and sits on a step at their feet. The minutes pass, and then she is watching her mother walking slowly, slightly stooped, across the vista of white rock towards her. She must be tired, Asya thinks: she just arrived and put her bag in her room and then they went out. She's had nothing to eat or drink. She doesn't like the heat. How old is she now? Fifty. That's not old. But her heart – suddenly Asya is filled with dread: she's not supposed to worry, she's not supposed to be under stress – but what could Asya have done? Who else could she have turned to? Who else knew her well enough to be able to remind her of her self? To be able to tell her what it is she really wants? Lateefa reaches her daughter and stops.

'It's getting very hot,' she says. 'Let's go and find somewhere to have lunch.'

Asya stands up.

'If we go down that way,' Lateefa says, pointing, 'we should find the marketplace. We'll eat there.'

*

A thin, transparent film forms on the cool walls of the jug of water which the old, mustachioed waiter has placed on the table. It shimmers and cracks and fragments into a thousand droplets. From time to time one separates itself, quivers and slides slowly down, gathering speed as it descends to be lost in the narrow pool which is forming itself round the bottom of the jug.

Asya puts her finger into the pool and traces moist squares around the red and white checks of the oilcloth. When the grilled fish arrive, and the slices of lemon, and the dishes of olives and humus, and the basket of warm bread, she lifts her head and says, 'I haven't asked after you or after anybody. How have you been, Mummy?'

'I'm fine,' Lateefa says, reaching for a piece of bread and tearing off a corner.

'Your heart?' Asya asks.

'It's perfectly fine,' Lateefa says, dipping her bread into the humus.

'Has nothing else happened to it? Has it really been all right?' Asya watches her mother carefully.

'It's fine,' Lateefa says. 'I get the odd twinge now and then but I have these tablets I carry around with me. But it's really all right.' She looks up at Asya. 'Don't worry about it. You've got enough to worry about.'

'And my uncle?' Asya asks. 'How is he?'

'He's very well. He's thinking of branching out into aluminium, but your uncle always has projects. He's fine: he works in the shop all day and is up playing chess half the night.'

'I don't know why you and Tante Soraya always sound so disapproving about his chess. Why shouldn't he play chess if he wants to?'

'All right, all right. You needn't leap to his defence. He's perfectly well and happy.'

'When did you last see him?'

'Oh, just the day before yesterday. I was giving him the measurements for the built-in cupboards he's going to make for the new flat.'

'What new flat, Mummy?'

'Don't you know we're moving out of Zamalek?'

'No I don't. Oh, Mummy, that's *terrible* –'

'I'm sure I told you in a letter –'

'But that's *terrible.*'

'Why? Why is it so terrible? It was too small. We're being crowded out by the books. And –'

'But Mummy, it's *home.* How can you just *leave* it?'

'And the street is getting very noisy and there's never anywhere to park. There's no need to look like that. The new flat is really lovely.'

'Where is it?'

'Just across the river. In Mohandesseen.'

'But that's all *new* –'

'The flat is big and the street is very quiet and there are lots of trees –'

'There are lots of trees in Zamalek.'

'And we're only one floor up –'

'What difference does that make? We had three lifts.'

'Yes, but they're often not working now. Since Abd el-Hadi died no one's looking after the building properly –'

'Yes,' says Asya sadly. 'That seems so strange to me: Zamalek without 'Am 'Abd el-Hadi at the door.' After a moment she says, 'Mummy, you're not letting go of the flat are you?'

'No, dear, no. Would anyone let go of a flat in Cairo these days? We'll keep it as a place to put up guests – and for your father to go to when he wants to get away.'

'Is Daddy well?'

'Yes, he's very well.'

'Didn't you think of giving the flat to Deena?'

'She doesn't want it. Zamalek is too posh for them: they want to live close to the Popular Base. We've got them a flat off Pyramid Road.'

'And is she well, Deena? Is she happy?'

'She seems to be. You know she's pregnant?'

Asya looks at her mother in surprise. 'No. No, I didn't know.'

'Yes. She'll be six months pregnant when she sits her finals in May.' Lateefa makes a face. 'But she's happy. Right now, of course, she's pretty worried about Muhsin, but there we are: she's the one who chose him.'

'Why should she be worried about him – right now particularly, I mean?' Asya asks.

'Because of the riots. They're starting to round up people and he'll probably be picked up; he's left home for a while until things quieten down.'

Asya is staring at her mother. 'What riots, Mummy?'

Lateefa frowns at her daughter. 'Don't you know there have been riots in Cairo? Don't you read the newspapers? Don't you watch the news?'

Asya shakes her head.

'Why, child, the world has been upside down for three days now –'

'But why? What about?'

'The government has taken away the subsidies – or reduced them – the subsidies on essential things, of course, and – it's particularly the bread. They doubled the price of bread and people came out into the streets in a rage – how can you *possibly* not know?'

'I just didn't,' says Asya. 'I haven't been – following things – anything, really. But what's going to happen?'

'No one knows. Probably nothing. But Sadat's been yelling his head off on television and he's putting a curfew in force from tonight –'

'Oh, Mummy! Was it extra difficult for you to get out? I mean, apart from the permit from the university and all that?'

'Well, I went to the airport prepared to be turned back. But it was all right. I've made Kareem and Deena both promise to stay at home – but I don't know if they will –' Lateefa sighs: 'I really had thought Deena was the one I was going to worry about; I thought you were settled. I thought you were doing what you want – you've always done what you wanted: you've made your own choices –'

'I know,' Asya says. 'I'm sorry.'

'I thought you were settled and had what you wanted. And now you're going to throw it all away –'

'I don't want to throw *anything* away –'

'You have emotional security, you have financial security –'

'Mummy,' Asya says, 'let's leave financial security out of it; it doesn't count –'

'It doesn't *count*? You don't know anything; you've been sheltered and protected all your life – you don't know what it's like not to have any money – you don't know how the world works. What does your university salary do? It pays the rent on your flat and that's it –'

'So what are you saying?' Asya's voice rises. 'That I should stay married to Saif for the money?'

'Have I ever suggested that you marry for money? Did we say anything when you married Saif and all he had was his salary? And you had already been asked for by other people, people who were already wealthy –'

'Was I?' Asya asks in surprise. 'I didn't know that. Who?'

'Ambassador Faruq Mar'i, for one.'

'Did he? Did he really?'

'Yes he did. He spoke to your father.'

'How come I didn't know?'

'We didn't want an arranged marriage for you. We wanted you to marry for love. And you'd set your heart on Saif when you weren't even eighteen. You *were* in love. That's what I was saying: you have emotional security –'

'I have *no* emotional security, Mummy. I have no emotional *life*. Saif doesn't want to know. He wants me to tell him things in a nutshell. When he's in London and he phones me up in the north he switches on the television first.'

'What do you mean he switches on the television first?'

'Well, he goes into his hotel room. He probably puts down his briefcase and has a shower. Then he switches on the television, sits in front of it and calls me. So while we're speaking he's watching television –'

'Well, he's probably starved of decent television in Damascus.'

'I know. I know *why* he does it. But what it *means* is that I'm just – something on his schedule: call Asya – and when that's over he can get on with what he really wants to do: watch some programme or settle down to some book or magazine –'

'You always read too much into things –'

'No, I don't. *You* always think that what matters is what people *say*; as long as he *says*, "Of course I love Asya, she's my wife, isn't she?" then that's fine –'

'Do you have reason to think he doesn't love you?'

Asya pauses. 'I believe,' she says, 'I believe he believes he loves me. But it's not something he thinks about. He decided back in March '68 that he loved me and he hasn't thought about it since.'

'He's your husband –'

'I believe if you asked him *why* he loves me – what it is *about* me that he loves – he wouldn't be able to say. He wouldn't want to devote a *moment* of his *time* to thinking about it – he'd say, "OK, what are you trying to prove?" or, "We're going to have a metaphysical discussion now, are we?" And as for asking him why *I* love *him* –'

'But, Asya, men are *like* that. They don't spend their time analysing their own and other people's emotions as women do – as *some* women do –'

'They *can't* be, Mummy. That can't be true –'

'And besides, Saif is working terribly hard. He's got a lot on his mind. It's not easy to do what he's doing. He's making a name for himself, building a brilliant career in a very competitive world –'

'I understand that. I have no problem with that. We agreed that he would go away; that he would do whatever he had to to build this brilliant career. I'm *genuinely* not complaining about that: about the separations, about never knowing when we'll meet next, about the broken appointments, all of that can't be helped. What I *am* complaining about is what it's like when we're together. I feel like a stranger, I feel like I'm acting, I know I'm just closing my mouth and suppressing ninety per cent of the things that come into my head. I have nothing to tell me that when he's with me it's *me* he's with; I feel like I could – *should* – slip away and leave some cardboard cutout like those Kodak ladies in my place and he wouldn't notice the difference, or if he did he'd think it was an improvement – and I can't *live* like that. I cannot spend my life like that. What is it? It's glancing at things and naming them and then living blindly on with the name: this is "love", fine, that's settled. Now let's get on with our business. But what *is* our business, in the end, what's it all *for*? What's the point of anything –'

'Oh, Asya. Can't you hear yourself? You're talking like you used to talk when you were fifteen. I thought you had grown up –'

'I *have* grown up but it's all still true. Just because I thought it when I was fifteen doesn't mean it's not true. In fact it means I'm being consistent. I was like this when I fell in love with him and I haven't changed, but he *has*. And besides, not *all* men are like that. Gerald isn't.

573

He really *wants* to look at things, to examine them. He wants to know what I think and how I feel. And he takes time to talk about things. I mean he *believes* in communication.'

Asya falls silent as she considers Gerald's belief in communication. But it is true. It's the situation that is making it so bad. The fact that she can't communicate back to him. She sucks on the stone of a green olive, and Lateefa separates the spine of a fish from its flesh.

'Do you remember,' Asya asks, 'how you used to make me a "banquet" of little pieces of bread with half an olive squashed on each and arranged in circles all fitting inside each other?'

'Yes,' Lateefa says. 'You've always liked olives. Even when we were in England in '56 and they practically hadn't heard of olives there, I had to hunt them down for you in the Greek grocer's in Charlotte Street.'

'Yes,' smiles Asya, 'a banquet of olives on bread would make my day.'

'Asya,' Lateefa says, 'are you – serious – about this man?'

'He's serious about me,' says Asya.

'Of course he's serious about you,' says her mother.

'Why? What's "of course" about it? Just because I'm your daughter and working on a Ph.D doesn't mean I'm a terrific prize, you know –'

'But, darling, you *are* –'

'No I'm not. There's lots and lots that's wrong with me – apart from the things that you would normally be quick to mention –'

'All right.' Lateefa holds up her hand. 'Let's not get into all that now. What I was asking was: are *you* serious about *him*?'

Asya draws circles with the water on the oilcloth. 'I don't seem to be able to – to do without him.'

'But how can you be *serious* about him? In just a few months and in your situation?'

Asya says nothing.

Her mother watches her. Then she says, 'It's probably something that will burn itself out. Why don't you wait? Why do you have to speak to Saif now? If he's not asking you any questions – not forcing you to tell him –'

'Because I can't go on like this. I just can't.'

Lateefa shifts slightly and looks down at her daughter. She checks her watch: it's only half past eight and Asya has been sleeping for an hour.

'Let me just lie down and put my head on your knee, Mummy. Just for five minutes, like I used to. You can put your hand on my hair and read a book over my head like you used to.'

A minute later she had been slapping at Lateefa's hands.

'You don't have to check my hair. I'm twenty-six. I'm not at school any more. Can't you just put your hand on my head without checking my hair or turning my ears over to see if they're clean?'

And a minute later she was asleep. Every time the child sits still for five minutes she falls asleep. She must be exhausted. And all because of that – man. She wishes he would drop dead. What kind of a man could he be to do what he is doing: to move into another man's house the better to persuade his wife to leave him? He must know that he's living on her husband's money; how would a student grant support the house, the bills, the food – unless he thinks *she's* got money? She looks at Asya: from the glossy hair on her mother's knee to the manicured nails of the feet propped up on the arm at the other end of the sofa, she looks – expensive. That's probably part of it. Lateefa hasn't said that, though. She's managed not to say a word against him because she knows her children: any one of them would leap to someone's defence simply because they were being attacked, and anything their mother said after that would be discounted. Just as Asya had got herself into trouble at school by defending Khalid Muhammad Khalid. 'But what on earth do you know of Khalid Muhammad Khalid?' they had questioned her at home later. And Asya nine years old and standing her ground – had said, 'Everybody was attacking him and I liked the sound of his name.' And Lateefa had thought, as she often did when she looked at her impetuous, dark-eyed daughter, she had thought of Maggie Tulliver and what *her* father had said about the long-tailed sheep, and she had been gentle and lenient with her – but this is beyond some school scrape now and she fears that this time she may not be able to help her daughter. Lateefa frowns at the dark television screen: what more can you do for your children? You give them love, you give them confidence, you give them – against all the pressures of the society they were brought up in – the opportunity to think for themselves, to make their own decisions, you give them education and culture – we took her to Luxor, to the Uffizi and the Louvre and the British Museum before she was seven – you give them everything a parent can give and then you give them independence – and they go and mess up their lives.

But Asya had turned to her; had phoned and, even though she knew how difficult it was to get an exit visa, she had asked her mother to meet her.

'I need to talk to you, Mummy. Please, just for the weekend. In whatever place is easiest for you to get to. I don't want to come home, and besides, it would take me a month to get an exit visa. And I don't want to see everybody right now. I just need to talk to *you*.' And now of course everybody at home is worried, wondering why she needs to rush over to Athens to have this – this Summit Meeting with Asya and Saif at two weeks' notice and in the middle of the academic year.

She looks again at her sleeping daughter stretched out so neatly on the sofa. Even her hands are folded tidily over her tummy. No sprawling around for her. How different she and Deena are from each other. When they shared a room you could tell immediately which bit was Asya's and which bit was Deena's. When Asya got up in the morning all she had to do was straighten the quilt and you wouldn't know her bed had been slept in. But they were both headstrong, impulsive, obstinate, and so completely sure they knew what they wanted. And now Asya was even sure of being unsure.

'What is it you expect of Saif?' Lateefa had asked her when they were back in the hotel. 'What do you want him to *do*?'

'I don't know, I've given up wanting him to do anything,' Asya had said. 'Oh, Mummy, I wish *he* would leave *me*.'

'Asya, you're not serious –'

And of course she wasn't, for she had started to cry.

'I do, I do. Then it would be simple. I could just be hurt and miserable but I wouldn't have to *do* anything.'

'But Asya, this is *Saif* you're talking about: Saif Madi whom you've loved for nine years. Why you'd – I don't know *what* you'd do if he left you.'

And Asya had just sat and cried and cried and said, 'I don't know what to do, I don't know what to do.'

'Then do nothing. Finish your work. Wait.'

'I can't. He won't let me.'

'What do you mean he won't let you? He doesn't even know –'

'No, not Saif. Gerald.'

'Him? And are you so weak that he can let you and not let you? You just tell him that's what you're doing. And if you can't deal with him I'll deal with him for you –'

'No no no, Mummy, no. It isn't *like* that. It isn't coercion. It's just that – he has a point. Some of the things he says are things that I think too. And anyway, now it's gone so far *I* feel that I have to do something. I told you: I'm not able to go on meeting Saif as if nothing had happened.' And then she'd looked at her and smiled. 'It's OK, Mummy. Don't look so stricken. I'm going to sort it out, honestly. I really, really don't want to worry you or make you ill or anything – it's just that there's no one, I mean absolutely *no one*' – and she'd started to cry again – 'over there for me to talk to.'

Thursday, 20 January: 11 a.m.

Asya hears the knock on the door. She is sitting at the dressing-table painting her nails. She looks up as the door opens. Saif pauses in the doorway. He is wearing beige suede lace-ups, jeans and a light blue shirt. Over his left shoulder are slung his black leather overnight bag and his camera-case. His eyes look bloodshot. He gives her his big smile, and for one moment Asya hates him; hates him for not knowing, for being normal, for smiling at her – for being Saif. Then she feels a great wave of tenderness rush over her, a protective tenderness as though she had just seen him miss being run over by some huge truck of which he'd been unaware, and she jumps up and runs over to hug him, careful to keep her hands untouched and her fingers spread out so her nail polish doesn't get smudged. He holds her for a minute, then he pats her back and says, 'I'm all sweaty, Princess. Let me have a shower and change and then we can see where you'd like to take your mother for lunch.'

2.15 p.m.

'It was insensitively done as well,' Lateefa says.

'The IMF is sitting on them,' Saif says. 'They're desperate.'

'But for a minister to get up on television,' says Lateefa, 'and say, "We all throw bread away" – to say that when there are people who haven't got enough to eat watching and listening –'

Saif shrugs. 'They're just incredibly stupid,' he says.

Asya pushes a small piece of bread round and round her plate. The taramasalata and humus have been eaten and now the table is loaded with grilled meat, dolmas and salads. A bottle of red wine stands on the white tablecloth. They are the only people in the restaurant. He could have put down his two bags, closed the door and said, 'OK, what's up?' Or if that would have been too melodramatic, he could have had his shower, got dressed, then said, 'Well, Princess, are you going to tell me what this is all about?' And she would have said, 'I've got myself – involved with a man and he won't go away. But I love you. Please can you help me?'

Through the glass behind Saif she can see the stone parapet and then the sea: blue and still as oil. Would that really have been what she'd have said? What *is* she going to say? And when? He isn't going to ask her anything.

'So' – Saif smiles at Lateefa – 'is your other son-in-law going to get into trouble?'

Lateefa makes a 'who knows?' face. 'He's left home and is hiding out for a few days . . .'

He isn't going to ask her. He isn't going to say, 'How come you cancel Christmas because of your work and then you bring us all running over here?'

'Well, they've beaten you two to it,' Lateefa says, 'but never mind: Asya should be through with her Ph.D in six months and you'll have lots of time for babies then.'

Asya looks at her mother, who thinks she's being so subtle. Then she glances at Saif. When he smiles at her she looks away. They are all pretending everything is perfectly normal; like they all just *happened* to be here, having a holiday together –

'And Chrissie's pregnant too, did you know?' Lateefa says.

'Yes, I got a letter from her,' Asya says.

'That's really foolish,' Saif says.

'Why?' asks Asya.

'Because things are so bad between her and Fuad – to the point where they got divorced –'

'But they came back together –'

'And then she lets herself get pregnant.'

'She didn't *let* herself,' Asya says. 'She did it deliberately. She tried for eight months and it didn't work. And then they were divorced. And when she took him back she went and had her tubes blown up, and it was terribly terribly painful but then she got pregnant.'

'It's madness,' Saif says.

'She's always known Fuad wants a son.'

'He's got a son,' Saif says.

'Yes, but by someone else –'

'Has he divorced the other woman?' Lateefa asks.

'So it's just jealousy,' Saif says. 'She's just trying to tie him down –'

'She loves him,' Asya says.

'Has he divorced the other woman?' Lateefa asks.

'Yes,' Asya says.

'Twice,' Saif says. 'He's divorced her twice and Chrissie once. It's a total mess. So Chrissie adds to it by producing yet another child –'

'I don't see why that's adding to it,' Asya says. 'I mean, they've already got a daughter –'

'It's hardly contributing to solving the problem, is it?' asks Saif.

'But what do you think the solution should be?' Asya asks.

'They should live together,' Lateefa says. 'You can't hope to keep a marriage steady if you live apart all the time.'

Asya looks at her mother.

'I mean if you live *permanently* apart,' Lateefa says. 'As far as I can see, Fuad and Chrissie have no plans at all for living together.'

'Do you think it would be a solution if Chrissie gave up her work, left her mother, and went to live with him in Suez?' Asya asks.

'Fuad should decide what he wants,' Saif says.

'He probably wants everything,' Asya says.

'Nobody,' Saif says, 'can have everything. Fuad knows that, he's not three years old.'

'Knowing Fuad,' Asya says, 'I'm sure he is trying to decide what's right and do it. But it must be very difficult – and there are children involved.'

'But he has to,' Lateefa says. 'This is life, not a novel: you can't sit around being in a dilemma. Things move, people change –'

'You keep saying, "This is life, not a novel" ' – Asya turns on Lateefa – 'as though somehow life were more serious – but what it really amounts to is that you don't think people should devote as much time to considering questions of character, circumstances and motivation in real life as you would expect your students to devote to the same questions in a work of fiction –'

'Why are you attacking your mother?' Saif asks. 'You know very well that what she meant was that in life people – real people – suffer as a consequence of action, or inaction, on the part of others, while in a novel you can spin things out as much as you like –'

'I just think,' says Asya, 'that if we could manage to look at real people and real actions with the same interest, the same – generous detachment, that we give to a novel or a play we should – we should understand things better.'

'But books and plays are the product of a conscious imagination,' Lateefa says.

'And so is life,' Asya says.

'Up to a point,' Saif says. 'Now have some wine and something to eat before it all goes cold.'

He will stay two or three days. They will drive around in the hired BMW and eat in restaurants and chat amiably about this and that and then he'll say, 'Goodbye, Princess. I might be going to Brussels – or Paris, or Vienna – in three weeks – or five, or nine – I'll let you know. See if you can join me.' If she lets him. If she doesn't find a way of speaking to him first.

'Was it hard for you to get away?' Asya asks.

'I've left them plenty to do,' he says. 'They should be OK, till I get back.'

There is a silence. Should she say, 'I'm sorry I did this, but I had to see you'? Would he say, 'Why?' No, he'd probably say, 'That's OK. I've always wanted to take you to Greece' –

'Have you seen Mahrous at all?' Lateefa asks Asya. 'He was a bit late getting out. He wasn't happy about leaving his wife –'

'Is that *the* Mahrous?' asks Saif. 'The one who was with Asya in class?'

'Yes,' Lateefa says.

'He's not going *there*, is he?'

'He is,' Lateefa says. 'He's going to do a Ph.D.'

'A Ph.D? He can barely speak English. Boy! He's going to have one lousy time –'

'He's bringing his wife over – and the baby,' Asya says.

'What?' says Lateefa.

'He is,' says Asya. 'They're joining him this month: on the twenty-seventh.'

'How is he going to support them on his grant?' Saif asks.

'He'll manage,' Asya says. 'They'll live on campus and he'll take a part-time job in one of the coffee-shops –'

'That will hold him up badly,' Lateefa says. 'A part-time job and a baby waking him up every night –'

'If they're with him, then he needn't be in a great rush to finish. I mean, it might be a nice part of their lives instead of something they're trying to somehow get through –'

'He should have stuck it out –'

'You're talking about three years, a minimum of three years out of someone's life. Three years of being wretchedly lonely –'

'What is this "lonely" stuff? Aren't there other people on campus? Isn't there a town where –'

'You don't know what it's like there, Mummy. There's nothing. *Nothing*. Unless you're nineteen and like drinking beer –'

'It's not that bad,' says Saif.

'It wasn't that bad when you were there,' Asya says. 'But that's what I mean: if you've got someone with you then it's OK.'

There is a silence, and then Saif says, 'Have you heard from Mario?'

'No,' Asya says. 'Have you?'

He shakes his head.

Even on the paved promenade outside there is no one coming or going. And Mario is in South Africa. If he had stayed this wouldn't be happening – but maybe something else would; something worse. Can there be something worse? Something worse than sitting here waiting to tell your husband you've been sleeping with another man? Is that what she's going to tell him? Is that what matters? The Lady Hamdonna, rising from the couch on which she has just given herself to Bahloul, shrugs off the remonstrances of her black maid. 'On every vulva there is written the name of the man who is destined to enter it,' she says. It's odd how you never see the word 'vulva' except in translations of Arabic erotica –

'How are the metaphors, Princess?' Saif says.

'They're OK,' Asya shrugs. 'Pretty deadly.'

'Deadly?' Lateefa says incredulously.

'Well, they're not deadly in themselves,' Asya says. 'But what I'm doing with them is deadly.'

'I don't know what's got into her,' Lateefa says to Saif. 'You remember how keen she was to go and work with Professor Murray? How it had to be Stylistics? She could have done anything; she could have gone to Oxford – but she was so sure, so *positive*, that this was what she wanted.'

'She's always sure about everything.' Saif gives Asya an indulgent smile and reaches over to ruffle her hair. 'Aren't you, sweetie?'

'That isn't even true –' Asya begins.

'You know when she was six she was sure she'd seen a jinni –' Lateefa says.

'Oh Mummy, please. Not that story again,' Asya says.

'She was,' Lateefa says to Saif. 'Her father and I were going to the theatre, and she was tucked up in bed and the neighbours were going to listen out for her. That was when we were in England, of course, and we couldn't afford baby-sitters – and just as we walked out of the front door we heard a banging – bang bang bang – and we turned round –'

'I'm sure you've told Saif this story before,' says Asya.

'And there she was, in her nightie, banging on the window. She'd climbed up on to the dresser. Of course we went back in, and there she was: screaming and crying, saying she'd seen a jinni –'

'I did,' says Asya. 'The wall opened and he kind of slid in like he was on a conveyor belt –'

'A technological jinni,' says Saif.

'She'd been reading the *Arabian Nights* –'

'I actually saw it,' says Asya.

'And she wouldn't let us go out. We argued, we threatened, her father was furious – but she is just so obstinate –'

'Look,' Asya says leaning forward, 'there's this six-year-old child: she's being left all alone – at night. She's lying in bed, awake – and she sees the walls of her bedroom swing slowly open and out of them this huge, gleaming brown man, with a toga wrapped around his waist, his head shaved except for a pony-tail coming out of the top, his arms folded across his chest, starts to glide out in total silence. She leaps out of bed and on to the dresser by the window, and down in the street she sees her parents. She hammers on the window and they hear her and come back. Is she going to let them go out again?'

'Yes, but Asya, darling, you didn't see him.'

'I did.'

'You couldn't have.'

'I did.'

'She's always imagining things; she lets her imagination run away with her.'

'I saw him. And – while we're about it – I saw the Brownie too.'

'We used to tell her the Brownie brought the sweets she found under her pillow.'

'I saw him.'

'I told you it must have been a mouse.'

'It was the Brownie, and he was running on two legs, not four like a mouse, and he was wearing a little green suit with brass buttons –'

'Like a bell-hop,' Saif says.

'Yes,' says Asya, and starts to laugh.

Her mother smiles, but Asya laughs and laughs.

'It was a good joke but it wasn't that good,' says Saif.

'It – it –' says Asya, and can't speak for laughing. It's too ridiculous.

Just too too ridiculous. She's brought them to Athens so she can fight with her mother over whether she'd seen a jinni on skates and a bell-hop Brownie. She starts to weep.

'I think she's having hysterics,' Lateefa says, seeing the tears come pouring down her daughter's face.

'It's just too –' Asya says, and chokes. She reaches for her napkin.

'Have some water,' Lateefa says, looking worried and pushing a glass towards her. Asya lifts the glass to her lips. Water. A drink of water – that'll take care of everything – a great wave of laughter comes over her and she splutters into the glass and chokes. She leans back in her chair and covers her face with the napkin as she shakes with laughter.

'Come on, Princess. Pull yourself together,' Saif says. He sounds impatient, of course. He's trying not to be angry. Oh, if he knew – Asya cries helplessly into her napkin – if he only knew. He thinks he's come to Athens to watch his wife go nuts in a restaurant. What must the waiters be thinking – as she thinks of what she must look like to the waiters a yelp of laughter forces itself out of her mouth. She pushes her chair back and runs out of the restaurant. She runs round the corner and across the promenade and when she comes to the parapet she climbs on to it and sits facing out to sea and sobbing.

11 p.m.

Asya lies in her bed. The light next to Saif's bed is on but he is in the bathroom. For the first time ever she had taken a room with twin beds – and he hadn't said anything. But then he wouldn't. Just as he hadn't said anything when he and her mother had finally come out of the restaurant and joined her by the sea. She hadn't gone back in, of course; just imagining the two faces looking up at her as she entered, her mother's nakedly questioning, his carefully neutral, had been enough to make whimpers of laughter start up in her again. So she had sat on the wall until they came out. And as they'd walked back to the car she had touched Saif's arm lightly and he'd put his arm around her shoulder to show that she'd been forgiven, and then they'd driven up into the mountains and had tea in a little café place and watched the sun set.

And later they'd all had dinner in the hotel, even though Lateefa had tried to beg off, but Saif wouldn't let her, and Asya had ignored the worried looks her mother kept directing at her and had behaved perfectly and been just the way he liked her and not been argumentative or horrid in any way, and he'd been so nice and so clever, and she loves him so much, but since lunch she feels as if she's all separate, as if – as if she's in a glass case and nothing is really reaching her and what – oh, what is she going to do?

Saif comes out of the bathroom in his dark blue dressing-gown. He walks over to her bed and sits down next to her. Then he leans over, puts one hand on either side of her and puts his mouth to hers. Asya is so surprised that she lies perfectly still as he kisses her. She smells the faintest whiff of the Monsieur de Givenchy that had probably been put on in the morning and had now been showered away twice, and closes her eyes and tries to imagine herself back in the Omar Khayyam. But it is so far away; everything is so far away. When she feels a touch on her breast she flinches and catches his hand. After a moment, when she doesn't let go, he says, 'No?'

She opens her eyes and looks into his. He takes his hand away and stands up.

'Saif –' she says.

'It's OK,' he says.

'Saif –' she says.

He lights a cigarette. Asya sits up.

'I wanted to tell you,' she says. 'I want a break.'

'A break?' he says.

'I have to,' she says. 'I need a break. I have to be my own person for a while. I – I just don't know who I am any more. I don't know what I want. I don't know anything. I think your thoughts instead of my own. And then I have thoughts and I don't know whether they're yours or mine. I've never had a chance to be on my own –'

'I thought the problem was you were too much on your own?'

He knocks his ash off into the ashtray on the dressing-table, then sits down in the chair next to it.

'But I've always been married to you,' Asya says. 'And even before that I belonged to you. You've always been with me.'

'And isn't that a good thing any more, Princess?' he says softly.

'Oh, it is, it is, of course it is. It's just that before that I was basically my parents' daughter and even before I got out of that – as much as one can ever get out – well, there was you. And I really feel that I need to be – free; just for a while. I mean, it's just terribly terribly difficult having so many givens in one's life. Practically everything is given, you see.'

'And this is the one you picked out of the hat to get rid of?'

'Oh, Saif,' she says. She gets out of bed and stands up. Then she sits down again on the edge of the bed. 'It's the most powerful one,' she says.

He drags on his cigarette, watching her. Then he says, 'Why haven't you put your hair up? I thought you put it up every night?'

Asya looks at him. 'I've found I don't need to,' she says. 'Now it's so long it stays OK even when I don't put it up.'

He stubs out his cigarette. He stands up and walks over to the mini-bar and opens it. 'Would you like a drink?' he says.

'No, thank you.'

He breaks off some cubes of ice and puts them into a glass. Then he pours a miniature bottle of whisky over them. He goes back to his seat and lights another cigarette.

'So,' he says, 'what is it you're proposing?'

'I want to think of myself as free – for some time. I need to sort things out and – I might be more able to – if I could think of myself as free – to sort them out.'

'What kind of things are we talking about?' he asks.

Asya looks at him. He swallows down some whisky and looks back at her and he looks – yes, he looks – apprehensive. How much does he really want her to tell him?

'Everything,' she says. 'And – things – things about myself.'

He pulls at his cigarette twice before he says, 'So you want a sabbatical.'

'Yes,' says Asya.

'Does your mother know all this?' he asks.

'Sort of,' says Asya.

'What does she think?'

Asya shrugs. 'She thinks I shouldn't tell you. She thinks I should finish this wretched Ph.D.'

'Aren't you planning on finishing it?'

'Yes, yes, of course I am. But I had to speak to you because –'

'Because?' he says when she stops.

'Because I've felt for so long that we've – we've drifted apart –'

'So you want to give us that final, encouraging shove.'

'No. No, that isn't what I want. That's why I wanted to talk to you: so it could somehow be something we agree rather than something that makes me feel even further away from you.'

He puts out the cigarette.

'How long is this sabbatical going to be, Princess?' he asks.

Asya jumps up and runs over to him. She kneels down at his feet.

'It can be whatever you say, darling,' she says, looking up at him. 'I don't want it to be very long at all.'

'I can't say I like the idea much,' he says.

'Can't I have it then?' Asya asks, hanging on his knee.

'You can have whatever you want,' he says. 'How long?'

Asya stands up. She walks over to the french windows and opens the curtains and stands looking out into the night.

'Six months, then,' she says. 'Till I finish in England.'

After a while he says, 'Does that mean we don't meet for those six months?'

'No it doesn't,' says Asya, still looking out. 'We can meet. We'll just go on as we are. But,' she turns round, 'I won't spend any more of your money.'

'What's money got to do with it?' Saif says.

'I just – it matters to me. I've been trying for three months to live on my grant and I can do it. I won't use your money for the rent or anything –'

'Don't,' he says. 'Don't talk like that, sweetie, please.'

'But it matters,' Asya says fiercely. 'I got this really cheap ticket to come here and you know I said let's not stay in the Hilton –'

'So we'd be having this conversation in some flea-pit – that's really thoughtful –'

'Please listen –'

'No.' He stands up. '*You* listen. Have you ever – *ever* – felt that I was anything other than pleased for you to spend as much money as you want? Pleased that there should be money for you to spend?'

'No,' says Asya.

'Right. When we met I didn't have any money. Whatever I've made is ours – not mine.'

'But you're the one who's been out there making it. I've just sat around being difficult –'

Asya starts to cry.

'Asya,' Saif says, 'the reason I made it – the reason why I was *able* to make it – was because it was for us. If it had been just for me I wouldn't have done it. Are you really so dumb that I have to explain this to you?'

Asya sits down on the floor and hides her face in her hands and weeps. When she looks up again he has put on his jeans and is tying up the laces of his shoes.

'What are you doing?' she asks in a panic. 'Where are you going?'

He pulls on a dark blue polo-neck and puts his wallet in his pocket.

'I'm going for a walk,' he says.

'Oh, please don't,' Asya cries, running to him.

'You want to be grown-up,' he says. 'Now act grown-up.'

'Oh, please, please, Saif. Now you're angry with me –'

'I am not angry with you,' he says, loosening her fingers from his arm, 'so don't push it.'

'But where are you going? Why –'

'I'm going for a walk because I need some air. That's absolutely all there is to it, OK? And when I come back I want you to be asleep.'

'But Saif –'

'You be asleep when I get back,' he says. 'Because there's going to be no more talk tonight. I've had it with talk.'

He walks out and closes the door quietly behind him.

As she gets back into bed Asya remembers that he had approached her. He had actually come to her bed and she had turned him down. How could she have done that? Saif, her husband, had finally come to her bed and she had refused him. Refused him. But why had he come to her bed? That had been the thought in her mind as she felt his lips on hers – that and the realisation that she was feeling nothing – that she was still in her glass case. She had lain there in surprise thinking, How can he think he can do this? Just come to my bed without a word as though the last four years had never happened? If he can do this now why didn't he do it long ago? Is this some sort of a bribe? A bribe so that I shut up and don't say whatever it was I'd come to Athens to say? – until she had felt his hand on her breast and known that she couldn't. It had been as odd as though it were Kareem or her father bending over her, and she couldn't do it. So maybe she had some loyalty after all – or her body did – and her body was loyal to Gerald Stone. But maybe if she and Saif had talked first – maybe if it hadn't been so eerie and so silent – maybe – maybe – maybe – now will she have to wait another four years to find out? She puts out the light. She has to go to sleep. She mustn't cry or get herself into a state. She must go to sleep so she doesn't bug him when he gets back.

Friday, 21 January: 9.30 a.m.

Lateefa arrives at the breakfast table wearing dark glasses.

'I'm going back to Cairo today,' she says. 'I've made a reservation and the flight leaves at twelve.'

'But Mummy, I thought you were staying till tomorrow,' Asya cries.

'I can't, darling. I have to go.'

'Has something happened?' Asya asks. 'In Cairo?'

'No, no,' says Lateefa.

'You're not looking well,' Saif says.

'No. I couldn't sleep. And something has happened to my eye.'

'Take off the glasses, Mummy,' Asya says.

Lateefa takes off the glasses. Her right eye is bright red. Saif stands up.

'We'll get a doctor,' he says.

'No,' says Lateefa. 'Please. Please, Saif, sit down. It'll be all right, I'm sure. I must have just burst a blood-vessel or something. I'll go to my doctor this afternoon in Cairo.'

10 a.m.

'I'm sorry, Mummy,' Asya says. 'I'm really sorry. Are you sure this is all that's happened? You didn't feel any twinges in your heart or anything?'

'Nothing at all has happened,' Lateefa says. 'I didn't even know this eye had happened until I saw it in the mirror.'

'Saif's going away tonight,' says Asya. 'I'll be on my own.'

'I'm sure you'll be all right,' Lateefa says. 'Come and close my bag for me.'

586

While Asya is closing the bag her mother says, 'What happened with Saif last night?'

'I spoke to him,' Asya says.

'Did you tell him?'

'I just told him I want to be free for six months. On sabbatical.'

'And what did he say to that?'

'He said OK.'

'He agreed?'

Lateefa's eyebrows have gone way up and her glasses are sliding down her nose.

'Yes,' says Asya.

'He's giving you too much rope.' Lateefa pushes her glasses up again. 'He should just box your ears and tell you to behave.'

Asya says nothing.

After a moment her mother asks, 'Did you – were you together last night?'

'No,' says Asya.

'Nothing?' asks her mother. 'Not at all?'

'No,' says Asya.

'I really don't understand this,' Lateefa says. 'You've been apart for six months and you meet for one night and nothing happens? Do you think he's having an affair?'

'In Damascus?' says Asya. 'No. I don't think so.'

There is a knock on the door. Asya opens the door and finds a porter outside.

'Mr Madi said I must collect your baggages and he is waiting in the car outside.'

'Your – friend called last night at midnight,' Lateefa says when the porter has gone off with her bag.

'Who? Gerald? What did he say?'

'He just asked for you.'

'And what did *you* say?'

'I said you were with your husband and he wasn't to call you again. Asya, darling,' her mother says, 'please, please, take care.'

'I will, Mummy. I'll try.'

'Remember that Saif loves you, has always loved you –'

'Yes. I remember that. Come on, Mummy.' Asya hugs her mother's shoulders and puts a kiss on her cheek. 'You'll miss your plane.'

6 p.m.

The rock is as warm as Asya remembers it but the colours are different: the sky is a bright blue and the sun, way down near the horizon, is a burning orange. Asya watches Saif walk towards her across the white slabs of rock. Behind him the white ladies rise with their terrible burden.

She would know that walk anywhere, even if he wasn't there; what a silly thought, she thinks: you can't have a walk without a man, a cat without a grin –

'Isn't it just – amazing,' she says when he stands in front of her. 'To think of them standing there all these years –'

'They haven't been,' he says.

'What do you mean?'

'They're not real. Don't you know?'

'What?' says Asya.

'They're fake. The real ones are in the museum.'

'They made them like that? Copies?'

'Yes,' he says.

'And broke off their arms and chiselled away at their faces?'

'Copies,' he says.

'Saif,' says Asya, 'do you really have to go tonight?'

'Yes,' he says.

'But I don't want to stay here alone,' Asya says.

'Why can't you go back tonight?' Saif asks. 'Why do you have to stay till tomorrow?'

'It's this ticket,' Asya says. 'I have to have spent three nights in Greece.'

'Blow the ticket,' he says. 'Buy another one. I'll buy you another one, now.'

'No,' she says.

'Why not?'

'I don't want to.'

'Because of the money?'

'I already told you yesterday. I'm living on my grant.'

'You know,' he says, 'you choose the stupidest things to hang on to.'

'Saif,' says Asya, 'take me with you.'

'Don't be silly,' Saif says.

'I'm not *being* silly,' Asya says. 'It wouldn't be like before. I'd bring my work. I've practically finished. I've just got all the computer stuff to do, counting up the metaphors. I could do it in Damascus, couldn't I? You could show me – no one could show me better than you –'

'It wouldn't work, Princess –'

'Why not? Why not?'

'And it isn't what you want.'

'How do you know what I want? Why are you always telling me what I want?'

'Last night *you* were telling *me* what you want, and it isn't to come to Damascus.'

'But Saif, can't we just *try*? I could come with you and then when you had a few days we could go back together and pack up and get rid of the

cottage and take my work. I'm sure I can talk Bill Murray into letting me
– and he's due to go away for three months soon anyway –'

'No.'

'Why? Why? *Why?*'

'Look, this is just a charade: some sort of flourish you feel compelled
to make. Once you're there –'

'It isn't, oh it isn't. I'm *sure* it isn't –'

'And,' he says, 'I can't have you there.'

'Why?' she says.

'Because,' Saif says, 'I'm working on something fairly sensitive. You
know that –'

'What's that got to do with my being there?'

'And I'm dealing with some pretty ugly people. The only way I can do
that is by being on my own –'

'What on earth do you mean?' asks Asya. 'You're the one who's being
dramatic now.'

'I'm serious,' he says. 'Look: you know I'm setting up their
Intelligence computer. The man in charge of it is very nasty and very
powerful. It would make me completely vulnerable if I had a wife there: if
you were there. What I'm trying to do is finish the job and get the hell
out. And I might even need to get out before I finish the job. And I have
to make sure I get paid *and* get the money out. I can only work it if it's just
me I have to think of.'

Asya is silent. Is it true? Or is he making it up? Making it up so he
wouldn't have to take her with him? So he wouldn't have to handle her
and cope with her and listen to her? What if she just followed him? But it
might be true, and if it were then she would be – doing him harm . . .

'OK,' she says quietly. 'But I just want you to know – in case you
change your mind – and you can change your mind any time – that I
would be good. I wouldn't be sick or hysterical or a drag or anything. I
would just get on with my work and let you get on with yours and I'd just
– just be with you.'

On the way back to the hotel Saif says, 'This "sabbatical" of yours: might
it involve going out with other men?'

'Yes,' says Asya.

They walk silent and apart the rest of the way.

As they collect their key the receptionist hands Asya a piece of paper.

'A telegram for madame.'

Asya glances at it.

'I LOVE YOU STOP I NEED YOU STOP PLEASE COME BACK TO ME
STOP –'

She feels her face burn as she folds it up.

589

'A cable?' Saif says.

'Oh, it's nothing important,' Asya says, her heart beating so hard that she is sure it must be shaking her blouse. She puts the telegram in her handbag and they walk towards the lift.

10.30 p.m.

Asya sits at the dressing-table with some hotel note-paper in front of her and a biro in her hand. She has returned the car, even though Saif had asked her to keep it. 'Give it back at the airport,' he'd said. 'Then you won't have to pay for a taxi out of your grant.' But she had returned it, and tomorrow she would take a bus to the airport. And tonight she hadn't had dinner because she wouldn't put it on the hotel bill and she probably couldn't afford it otherwise. And besides, she doesn't deserve to have dinner.

At nine o'clock – when she had finished crying because Saif had gone – she had thought, well, here I am in Athens. I'm in a strange city where no one knows me. I'm free; he's agreed to let me be free, he even wouldn't take me with him. I can do whatever I want. I can wander round the temples in the moonlight. I can go to a cinema. I can have a drink in the bar. I can pick up a handsome man and spend the night with him and not even know his name or tell him mine. And she had got dressed and walked out into the hotel and as far as the great entrance doors and then turned back. She had walked to the door of the bar and then turned back. She had wandered round the swimming pool then sat in the lobby for five minutes burying her face in a magazine, and when a man in a good grey suit – obviously some type on a business trip – had sat himself down opposite her she had folded up her magazine and come scooting back to her room.

I am going to write this down, she writes, so that I don't ever forget it. This is just for me and nobody else is ever going to see it:

Saif has gone away. He has refused to take me with him – and possibly he was right to refuse. But then again – maybe he wasn't. What he doesn't know is the extent to which I *want* things to be right between us.

This is what I feel: Saif is my husband and I love him. I look at him as he ties up his shoe-laces or lights a cigarette or puts the car into reverse and I know that I love him. I *care* about him. I watch him cross the road and I fear for him: his skull, his limbs, his walk are all precious to me. If he were ill or needed another kidney or another lung or something I should be miserable for him but happy for me because I could give him one of mine.

When I watch Saif walk away from me I feel bereft – lost. Even if I've been miserable while I was with him. I am always waiting for him to come back. When I watch G. walk away I feel – relieved. Not at first: at first when he walked away I used to feel expectant; expectant of his return. But for the last three months when he's gone away I've felt relief – with a bit of almost theoretical sadness at the edge.

I don't really care what becomes of G. I don't even like him much any more. He's cheap. He's envious. He's an opportunist. What he wants is to make money quickly and off other people. He has no particular talent, skill, or knowledge that anyone particularly needs. And he has no desire to have any of these. What he will do is get in between people who are making deals and get a cut. A middleman. He moved into the cottage uninvited. He stayed there knowing that it was Saif's money paying the rent. He would have driven Saif's car if I'd let him. Would have? He yearns, he longs to drive it. So he's living in a man's home and trying to take away his wife. And he can't even see that what he's doing isn't done. *Can't* be done.

I know that over Xmas he had the lady from Trinidad staying at his parents' – I knew that he was planning on seeing her because when I went with him to shop for his Xmas presents he asked me to choose some gloves. And he volunteered that they were for his mother but he had already bought a china dish for his mother and he doesn't have much money and – something in his face told me that they were for his friend. Besides, when once – only once – he had been careless and left his briefcase unlocked on the kitchen table and went out, I looked in it and I found a letter on red – *red* – notepaper and it was from her and it was obvious that he was keeping her hanging on. It was a very sad letter: 'I'm going to be thirty on my next birthday, Gerry, darling, and you still haven't made up your mind –'

When he went away he said the phone at his parents' wasn't working so *he* would call *me*. And he did. He went to a coin-box twice a day and called me. But I called his home number and when his mother answered I hung up, but I knew for sure that he was lying and why.

The thing is, I truly didn't mind – whatever he was doing I didn't mind. I understand that she is from Trinidad, she has no family in England. Xmas is a particularly bad time if you have no family in England, and if she has spent the last three Xmases with him he would naturally feel he had to do something about this one. Particularly when he hasn't told her categorically that it's over between them. And that too I can understand – how can he be sure he has stopped loving someone he has loved for three years? Especially when he is not sure what *I* am going to do in the end? What he is doing to her is not kind, but it makes sense. What I *can't* understand is how he can sound so impassioned and believe himself and what he's saying so completely when he accuses *me* of procrastination, deceptiveness, weakness etc., while he is having the same difficulties himself. Why does he have to present himself as so completely clear-cut and try to force that mode on me when he *knows* that it is false and impossible?

And what am *I* doing? Why am *I* in this? I'm in this because I wanted him to stay one night. And because he made me feel physical again. And because it was a complete novelty to be with a man who wanted to talk and who – I thought – wanted to listen; someone who actually made demands on me – and not just that I should leave him alone. Someone who actually wanted – *needed* to make love to me. Because he is the first man I have really slept with and I like sleeping with him. Not actually sleeping with him. Just screwing with him. I'm sorry. I'm *really* sorry – but what I really want is to occasionally do it with him, then fall asleep and wake up to find he's not there.

He bores me. He is vain. A man shouldn't stand in front of the mirror for hours blow-drying his hair and combing it just so, and staring at himself and getting cross when it doesn't come out right. When we first slept together and he shouted out my name when he came I was impressed. Saif was so silent. In fact, I haven't once known that he has come. Not once – in nine years. I was impressed. But now I'm bored. And sometimes I'm embarrassed. I know he's going to throw his head back and grit his teeth and the veins in his neck will bulge, and then he'll give three mighty shoves and yell out, 'ASYA!' as though I were very very far away when actually I'm right there under him. Now I close my eyes so that when he opens his I won't meet them, and then, when he puts his face in my neck and moans, 'Oh, baby, baby, baby,' I just pat him quietly. The thing is, I don't think he shouts out like that because he can't help it or he doesn't know what he's doing or anything. I think he thinks it's impressive. Or maybe he thinks I expect it.

So what does all this mean? It means that I have to leave him. I have to end this thing with him. What happens to me afterwards, how I sort out my own life, is something else. What I have to remember from this trip is that *I love Saif.* I love him and I'm just too connected to him. I won't ever be able to just walk away. I don't *want* to just walk away. I love listening to him talk. I love his wit, even when it's directed against me. I love going into shops with him. I love spending quiet times with him. I know I'm not actually happy with him all the time; a lot of the time I'm angry or frustrated or conscious that I'm being the way he wants me to be. But I am never ever bored.

Paradox: Since March 1975 I have – apart from certain moments – felt closer to him when we've been separate than when we've been together. So my image of him is getting further and further from the reality. And the same must be happening for him. And what I've done is to try and make myself – when I'm with him – into his image of me.

I have also tried – am trying – to love him as he *is*, not as I imagine him. In other words he is the imagination and I am the execution: he is the author and the director of our drama and I am just the cast. And I have decided to accept that because I care for him. I care that *he* should be happy. I don't want to sleep with him.

I like it when he puts his arm around my shoulders or ruffles my hair. But I don't want to sleep with him. If I imagine him sleeping with someone else I don't mind. But if I imagine him looking after someone else, giving someone else that indulgent, tender smile, then it hurts – it hurts badly.

Saturday, 22 January: 12.30 p.m. London

As Asya pushes the trolley with her one bag on it out of the Customs hall she can see Gerald Stone at the end of the concourse. He is in his jeans and sheepskin coat. His hands are in his pockets. He is unshaven. He is very pale and his eyes are red and bleary. When she reaches him he folds her into his arms, bends to bury his face in her neck and stands very still. They are blocking the path and people have to swerve and wheel their trolleys past them. Gerald breathes heavily into her neck. He looks terrible. He must be ill. If he would move she could get another look at him. Her arms are pinned to her sides so she cannot pat his hair or push his head up. She stands still. What must people be thinking? Thank goodness this was an Athens flight – not a Cairo flight with lots of Egyptians on board. Nobody is paying any attention to them once they've managed to pass – nobody except a beautiful Pakistani woman whose husband is reading the newspaper as they stand and wait for whoever they are waiting for to arrive. She is in yellow silk trousers and a patterned *kurta*, with at least twenty gold bangles on her arms, her hair ripples back from her face and down her back and her velvety, almond-shaped, slightly protruding eyes stare at Asya and Gerald with longing disapproval.

Gerald lifts his face and holds Asya's head in his two hands.

'You've come back to me, baby,' he says.

'Gerald –' Asya begins.

'Hush,' he says, pulling her face into his chest. 'Hush, don't speak. You look worn out, my poor, poor baby.'

The tears rise to Asya's eyes.

'We'll go to the hotel,' he says. 'I am desperate for you, babe; I can't live if I don't make love to you.'

4 p.m.

Asya puts her cup of tea down on the table. Then she sits down.

'Gerald –' she begins.

'Before you say anything,' he interrupts, 'I want you to know what these three days have been like for me. I want you to know this because I have gone through the worst time of my life and I have accepted it – for your sake.'

Just behind Gerald a figure stands swaddled in white. He is bandaged from head to foot and one arm is raised as though he is held in traction by an invisible pulley or hanging on to the handrail in a crowded tram.

'I wrote this for you,' Gerald says, 'and I want you to read it before you say anything.'

He takes a folded sheet of paper from his pocket and hands it to Asya. She opens it.

My Butterfly:
You walked away from
me. I
Sank down admitting:
I am no more than a leaf tossed
    by a wind which has
        temporarily ceased to blow.
And then –
Scything
Through the clouds of my mind – the truth
Returned:
Babe, I would have clawed
    That plane
        Back to earth
Just to hold you, to kiss you,
Just to be
With
You –

Asya imagines an enormous big tabby in a cartoon: it has Gerald's face, it rears up on its hind legs and swipes at a toy aeroplane. She covers her face with her hands, horrified at herself. If she should laugh now that would really be the end; she would never ever forgive herself. It would be no use telling him it was tension, telling him it was those weird bandaged figures around them. He would be just terribly terribly hurt. He *feels* what he has written. You have only to look at him to see how he suffers. He doesn't *know* about poetry. He thinks of himself as a communicator and it would be the worst way she could hurt him now. She reads on.

Thursday night I needed –
I needed you so bad
My hands were shaking –

I picked up
The phone. Three-thirty in the morning.
I got through to your mother –

Asya swallows. She looks at the bandaged figure lying on the floor by
the side of their table. This one has blood on the dressings on his chest
and only half his head is bandaged; his mouth is revealed: open in a
permanent, silent scream of pain.

'Read it,' Gerald says.

Your mother said I couldn't speak to you;
That you were
With *your husband*
In another room.
She said
'Please do not call again.'
I lay awake till dawn
Praying for
The phone to ring. I lay awake
With tears in my eyes
And the grip of the Devil
On my stomach.
Baby I cried out for you.
Her husband!
How can you be married
To another
When you are my twin?

'Gerald –' Asya says, folding the paper.

'No, wait,' Gerald says. He passes his hand over his face then pushes it
through his hair. He leans forward and takes Asya's hands. 'That night I
glimpsed both death and insanity. Death because I didn't know whether I
would survive the darkness. And insanity because I was so afraid of what
you might come back from Athens and say to me. I really felt my mind on
the brink of some very dark precipices that night.'

He looks down at their joined hands.

'There. I've said what I had to say. I don't believe any man can ever
have loved a woman as much as I love you – and I only pray that you don't
kill me with the words you say now.'

'Gerald,' Asya says, 'I'm sorry. I'm really, really sorry about all this.'

'It's all right, babe. It's all right. Tell me now.'

Asya looks into his face. The blue eyes have lost their shine and the
skin under them is yellow and dry. She takes her eyes from his and looks
around the foyer exhibition. There must be at least twenty of those
things: some are standing up, some sitting on the floor, two are on

595

stretchers. All are bandaged, some are spattered with blood, some have a hand or a foot or part of a face showing through: wide-open mouths, horrified eyes –

'Baby, I'm waiting –'

'I know. I – it's just – these things are so weird –'

'Never mind about them now, babe.'

'I just – I didn't know this was on when I suggested we came here –'

'It's all right.'

'When we came in I thought I was seeing things –'

'What did you say to him?'

'I said I wanted to be free.'

'And?'

'I said –' Asya looks at Gerald, 'I said I wanted to think of myself as a free and individual person so that I could sort out my life.'

'And?'

'He agreed.'

'And?'

'That's all.'

Gerald lets go of her hands.

'That's *all?*' he asks.

Asya nods silently.

'I don't believe this.' He sits back in his chair. 'You went all the way to Athens and you told him nothing?'

'I told him I wanted to be free and –'

'You told him nothing about *us?*'

'I told him I had to sort out my life.'

Gerald stands up. 'This is it,' he says. 'This is the end. Even from you I would not have believed it possible. I wait for you here – the victim of the greatest passion I have ever known – and you deny me. How many times – how many more times shall I wait for you to betray me – to betray *us?*'

Gerald paces the foyer. He weaves between the bandaged figures. He stops against one on a stretcher and Asya thinks he is going to kick it – but he turns away. Occasionally he comes back to say something or to bang his fist on the table and make the tea-cups jump.

'I'm giving you one last chance,' he says. 'Write to him. Write to him now and tell him the truth.'

'I *have* told him the truth,' Asya says.

'Tell him that you're leaving him.'

'Even if I leave him,' Asya says, 'it has to be between him and me. It can't be over you.'

'Why?' He grips the back of a chair and leans forward over it. He looks so ill. '*Why?*'

'Gerald,' Asya says, 'please understand. Try to understand this: if I left him over you I would never be able to be with you after that.'

596

'Why?'

'Because it would be too terrible.'

'But why? *Why?* Surely if you know you've paid a high price for something that would only make you value it all the more? Surely –'

'I'm not talking about the price *I'd* pay –'

'What then? What the hell are you talking about?'

'I'm talking about *him*: I would have caused him pain because of you. And I would blame *you* for it. For ever.'

'What about *me*? What about *my* pain? Doesn't *that* count? Can't you see what this is doing to me –'

'Yes, I can. And I am truly, truly sorry. But you knew from the beginning that I was married –'

'Don't say that. Don't say that word –'

'And Gerald, you can feel your pain, you can measure it – after only four months – why can you not imagine his – after eight years?'

'He doesn't love you the way I do. Baby, *no one* can love you the way I do. You saw how it was with us earlier today, when I thought you had done it, when I thought we were together at last. Wasn't it good between us? When I made love to you? Wasn't it good?'

'Yes,' Asya says. 'It was good.'

'That's how it would be, babe. That's how it would always be.'

'If it is to be like that,' says Asya, 'then let it come about in a different way.'

'What do you mean?'

'Let me go back to the university on my own. Let me do my work and sort myself out. You stay in London. Start doing what you're going to do.'

'No.'

'If it's "meant to be", as you keep saying it is, that's the only way it can happen. Let's not burden it with my guilt over leaving my husband.'

'*No.*'

'Why *not?*'

'Because you won't let it happen. You'll go back to your old ways. You'll settle in. You'll always take the easy way.'

'If that's what you really think,' Asya says, 'then you really shouldn't bother. No, I'm serious. Why *should* you bother with a woman you'll have to push and goad and prop up every inch of the way? It wouldn't be worth it.'

'But that's because you're still learning, baby. That's because you're still tied to your earth-bound existence. Once you've tasted freedom, once you're really up there, I know you won't turn back.'

'Gerald, if you want this to have any chance at all, you'll have to let me do it my own way.'

'By being separate now?'

'Yes.'

'*No*. If you go up there on your own, you stay on your own. It'll be over for me. I've already endured more than I would have thought possible. This has to be the end of the line.'

Asya says nothing.

'Well?' asks Gerald.

Asya says nothing.

'Answer me. Are you going up alone? Do you refuse to write to him?'

'Yes,' says Asya.

'You're on your own then, babe,' Gerald says. 'And I only hope for your sake that you never realise what you've done and what you've missed.'

Scene 6

Saturday, 19 February 1977: 8 a.m.

The North of England

The light coming through the curtains is dim and cold. Asya lies in bed and traces with her eyes the outlines of the pink roses and golden-leafed branches all smudged now to the same greyish-beige. She listens to the half-hearted chirping of the birds, so different from their excited welcoming of a summer morning. She scans the plain white walls and wonders that she does not even wonder what she will do with the day. She knows that she will do nothing. That the day will somehow pass and she will sit through it. She knows that thoughts will rise to the surface of her mind and float across it. And each thought will bring something with it: thoughts of metaphors or Professor Murray will bring a tremendous weariness, thoughts of Mama Deela or Khalu Hamid or Saif will bring quiet, sluggish tears which will flow for a while down her face and into the corners of her mouth and then stop. And nothing else will happen for her – nothing at all.

When she hears the metal flap of the letterbox clang back against the door and the flutter and faint thud of letters falling on to the hall carpet, she stiffens. She lies quiet for a few moments more, then gently and slowly picks up Gerald's arm and lifts it a tiny distance off her tummy. She moves a few inches towards the edge of the bed and puts his arm down in the space she has vacated. She starts to push her legs over the edge of the bed but his hand moves and closes on her wrist.

'Where you going, babe?' he says in a sleepy voice.

'Just to the loo,' Asya whispers. 'Go back to sleep.'

'Don't leave me, babe,' he says, and throws his arm around her, forcing her back down into the bed. He moves closer and buries his face in her neck. Asya puts her hand on his hair and strokes it gently.

'Go back to sleep,' she says.

Every morning, if there are letters, she gets them before he wakes. Often there are letters from Saif; short letters that no longer speak of the house on the edge of the desert – no longer say 'I miss you', or mention love even in greeting, or have drawings of prowling cats or fountains. Just letters from a man who'd said he would write and so is putting together a few words about crossing over into Lebanon, or some bit of news from Cairo – just to let her know he is still there. And her letters to him are the same. Although she continues to write him long long letters when Gerald is out of the house. Letters that she will never send, but which one day, if he wants, she might give to him.

But Gerald isn't out of the house much. He doesn't trust her now, doesn't trust her enough to leave her alone. Ever since the day she came back from Athens, when he had walked out of the National Theatre foyer and she had not run after him but had gone up to the north on her own. Ever since then, when she had not called him and he had arrived unannounced on her doorstep, driving his mother's Mini and carrying a big empty brown suitcase and saying he'd come to take his things, and he'd found the living-room with the windows wide open and the fire lit and Mozart's Bassoon Concerto playing and her typewriter and papers back in their place on the table and he had been sick. To think, he'd said, to think that the woman to whom he was devoted – the woman with whom he had proposed to share the highest of worlds, the woman for whom he was suffering as no man had ever suffered – had wiped him out so completely that within one week of leaving him she was able to sit and work at her unreal thesis with her phoney music drifting across the fields – it was just beyond him. It was more than he could have believed possible.

'You didn't even call me, man,' he said. 'You didn't even pick up the phone.'

'How could I?' Asya had asked. 'It would have been unfair on you. If you were able to get away I thought it was better –'

'And to sit here, coldly doing your *work*? What are you? Some sort of *machine*?'

'But it's the only thing I *can* do,' Asya had cried. 'It's what I *have* to do now. It's why I'm *here*. It would be wicked and evil to be here and not to do it.'

But he had been wild and he had been sick. He had banged his head on the wall and Asya had felt the headache for him. He had punched his first through the wall and Asya had felt ashamed that her first thought had been of how she could explain the hole to Jenny MacRae. Then he had rushed down to the bathroom to throw up and had come up and lain on the sofa with stomach cramps and looking completely ghostlike, and Asya had said of course he couldn't drive back to Canterbury when he was so ill, and so he had stayed.

'Where are you, babe?' he whispers into her neck.

'I'm here,' Asya says, stroking his hair. Stroking his hair and comforting him as she had not comforted Saif even though she had seen the fear in his eyes. Even though she had seen beyond the neutral face to the hurt he was feeling. 'But I've always been married to you,' she had cried, as though that were something terrible – oh, that must have cut him deep –

'You feel like you're a million miles away,' Gerald says.

'I'm not,' says Asya. 'I'm right here.'

'I want you, babe,' he says. 'I want you.' He takes her hand and guides it beneath the quilt. 'I always want you. You do it, babe. Do it. I want to wake up and find you making love to me.'

'I need to go to the loo,' Asya says.

'Make love to me. Please make love to me.'

Asya crouches over Gerald and guides him into her. She bends over and places quiet, gentle kisses first on his chest and then on his face. After a moment he opens his eyes. He looks into her eyes and shakes his head.

'You're useless, you know that? Useless.'

He holds her shoulders and rolls them both over so that he is on top. He slides his hand under her head and holds her hair.

'Open your eyes,' he says. 'Keep them open. Look at me. Where *are* you?' he says with every thrust. 'Where *are* you? Come *back* to me, babe, come *back* to me.'

When it is over he rolls away and lies with his face to the wall. Asya wonders if she can get up now, but she does not move. Then Gerald sits up. He sits cross-legged on the bed with his back against the wall and looks down at her.

'Why are you crying?' he asks.

Asya lifts her hand to her face and finds it wet.

'What are you doing, man?' he asks sadly. He puts his hand out and wipes the tears from the side of her face nearest to him. 'You're turning yourself into some kind of a doll; a crying doll: you squeeze her and the water comes out of her eyes. You don't even make a sound.'

600

Asya lies still with her eyes closed.

'I can't bear this,' he says. 'I can't bear to be with you and not with you. I can't bear to see you make yourself fade away like this. Open your eyes. Look at me, babe.'

His voice is kind. Asya opens her eyes and turns her head to look at him. His face is pale and long. His nose looks pinched. His hair is ruffled and sticking out. He looks into her eyes.

'You're planning something,' he says in a sharp voice. 'What are you planning? What's going on in your mind?'

'I'm not planning anything,' Asya says. Her voice is very low.

'You're planning to leave me.'

Asya closes her eyes.

'I want to know what you're thinking,' he says. 'I want to know what you're thinking now.' He holds her shoulder and shakes it.

'I'm thinking,' says Asya, 'that I need to go to the loo.'

She sits up and swings her legs out of bed.

'You're not going to the loo,' he says. 'You're going to collect your letters and hide them. Like you do every morning.'

'I'm going to the loo,' says Asya, 'and I'm going to collect my letters.'

'No,' he says, '*we're* going to collect your letters. We're going to do it together. And we're going to read them together. I am sick and tired of you hiding things from me. Of you planning things behind my back.'

He gets out of bed. Asya stands up and reaches for her dressing-gown. Gerald holds on to it.

'You don't need to get dressed,' he says. 'We're coming back to bed. We're going to work this thing out.'

'Please, Gerald,' she says. 'I can't just walk around like this.'

She pulls at the dressing-gown and he lets go.

'Be a bourgeois then,' he says. 'Stay a prim, repressed bourgeois for the rest of your life.'

Asya shrugs into her lilac cotton dressing-gown while he stands with folded arms and watches her. She ties her belt and pulls her hair free of the neck and throws it down her back.

'Why are you making a fuss about my letters?' she asks.

'Because you sneak off and get them every morning and then they disappear. Because I know you are in correspondence with your husband. Because I have to know what you're planning –'

'What can I be planning –'

'You're planning to leave me.'

'– that you would find out in a letter? I'm master-minding a rescue?'

'I don't know. But there's something wrong. There was always something wrong – but it's been worse since you came back from Athens.'

'I've told you what's wrong. I've told you *everything* –'

'I don't believe you. And I'm going to find out. From now on we're reading your letters together.'

Asya looks at him.

'OK,' she says, 'if there's a letter from my husband I won't read it. It'll stay unopened. And I want you to know that I think your behaviour is appalling.'

'Of course you think so,' he says. 'It isn't cricket, is it? One just doesn't do that sort of thing – not in *your* circle. But I am fighting for my life here, man, and I'll fight with everything I've got.'

From the bedroom door Asya can see the letters on the carpet – and she knows there isn't one from Saif. There is an official one with a window and a franking-machine mark and one in an odd yellowish air-mail envelope and two from Egypt. She stands aside and lets Gerald pick them up. As he looks at them she goes into the bathroom and locks the door.

What is she going to do? Oh, what is she going to do? She sits on the toilet and puts her elbows on her knees and her face in her hands. Walk out and say, 'I don't love you, I don't even care for you, I want you to go away, now, for ever'? How can she do that? She can't. She's looked at him and thought the words and tried to say them but they wouldn't come. And anyway he wouldn't believe her: he'd say he knew her better than she knows herself and that what she wants to do is settle back into a comfortable, earthbound existence, only he won't permit it because he knows of what greatness she is capable and so on and so on and so on. She moans softly into her hands. She can go away herself – just get into the car and drive away – but he would stop her – but what if he wasn't there? What if she went when he wasn't there? But how can she leave him alone in the cottage? What if he opened the door to Saif's room? What if he went through his things – touched them? She can put Saif's things in the car, slowly over a few days: every time he goes out she can put a few things in the car – she can put her work in too – and one day, while he's at the Indoor Rec, she can go. But what if Saif calls? What if Saif calls and the phone just rings and rings? Or what if Saif calls and Gerald answers him? Oh God – no, no, she can do nothing except what she is doing: sitting it out. He can't stay for ever. He can't waste his entire life sitting here with her – he'll have to go and do something about work – about a job – he's bound to at least run out of cash for his petrol – and how can she be thinking about him so cruelly? How *can* she, when she knows that he has it in him to be so tender and sweet? When he has opened up a whole world to her and made her a gift of her own body? When he believes that all his actions stem from the fact of his loving her – his loving her too much? How can she ask of Saif that he be generous with her failings if she is not generous with the failings of this man who is being so tortured because of her?

When she goes back to the bedroom Gerald is sitting in bed with the quilt drawn up to his waist. His hand rests on his knee and in his hand there are her four letters.

'Would you like a coffee?' she asks.

'No,' he says, 'but thank you.'

'Why don't we go up to the living-room?' Asya says.

'Why?' he asks.

'It's just that – we've been here all night,' she says.

'I'm OK here,' he says.

'All right,' Asya says, and sits down on the chair.

'Look, babe,' he says, 'I've never done this before – but I've never been in love before. Normally I wouldn't do this, I hate doing it, but you've forced me to it. You have deceived me and lied to me and you're making plans which I know would destroy me –'

'How have I deceived you?' Asya asks.

'You don't tell me everything. You don't share your innermost thoughts with me. You leave me on the outside.'

'I have tried,' says Asya, 'as much as I possibly –'

'And there's something else.'

'What?' Asya asks.

'This is hard for me to say, babe, and it'll be hard for you to hear: but – you *have* deceived your husband, haven't you?'

Asya stares at him.

'You are saying this to me? You who have been talking about higher levels of existence? About –'

'I know what I've been talking about, babe' – he smiles a weary smile – 'and I stand by everything I've said, and I'd say it to anyone. I'd shout it from the roof-tops. But *you* haven't said anything, and sometimes I haven't known whether you believe in what I'm saying. *You* have found it easier to hide with me in a corner than to face up to your husband and tell him the truth. And I'm not going to let you do that to me.'

Asya takes a deep breath. She feels sick. She feels ashamed. How can she tell him she hadn't felt that she was deceiving her husband – because all she had wanted was to *sleep* with him and her husband hadn't wanted to sleep with *her*?

'Are you going to say anything?' he asks.

'OK,' she says in a very low voice, 'you have a point.'

'All right,' he says. 'Do you want to open them, or shall I?'

'I don't care,' she says.

'OK. Well, this one's a bank statement, addressed to *Mr and Mrs* S. Madi, so I'll leave that. I'm sure you'll enjoy looking at it later.' He throws it on to the quilt. 'Then there are two with Egyptian stamps and one with a South African stamp. I didn't know you knew anyone in South Africa.'

Mario! Mario has written to her at last. After a year and four months he had written to her –

'Will you give me that one, please?' Asya stretches out her hand. 'It won't be of any interest at all to you, I promise.'

'Who is it from?' he asks.

'It's from an old friend,' Asya says, 'a friend of both of us. It will probably mainly be a message for my husband.'

'But it's addressed to you: Asya al-Ulama.'

'Please, Gerald, give it to me.'

'No,' he says, looking at her. 'I'm sorry, but no.'

'Gerald,' Asya says, 'if you open that I'm going. I'll leave this house this minute.'

'OK,' he says, 'we'll keep it to the end.' He puts the yellow envelope down on his knee and holds up the remaining two. 'Which of these two do you want now?'

Asya looks at her name and address on the envelopes: one is in her father's elegantly spidery hand, the other is in Chrissie's rounded handwriting with the little circles above the i's that all the Manor House girls used.

'Whatever,' she says. Please God, please God, please God, she thinks, make them be in Arabic.

He opens Chrissie's envelope and takes out one sheet of paper torn from an exercise book and covered in green writing.

'It's all in Arabic,' he says, 'except for the word "Love" at the end.'

Asya shrugs.

'You'll translate it to me,' he says.

Asya stretches out her hand but he pats the bed next to him.

'Come and sit here, it'll be easier. It's all right,' he says when she doesn't move, 'I won't touch you. I might freeze.'

Asya sits on the edge of the bed and reads the letter.

'Who is it from?'

'It's from Chrissie.'

'Chrissie?'

'She's my best friend.'

'How come you've never mentioned her?'

'Haven't I?'

'Never.'

'I don't know.'

'OK. Read it.'

Asya reads: 'Dear Asya, I know you're having a problem of some sort because Tante Lateefa ran off to Athens to meet you. She hasn't told me what the problem is but since I am your friend and closer to you than your fingernails and also because I know your circumstances I think I can guess.'

'Will you please translate what you've read?' Gerald says.

'Dear Asya, I know you're having a problem of some sort because Tante Lateefa ran off to Athens to meet you. She hasn't told me what the problem is but since I am your friend I wanted to tell you that you are making us all quite worried.'

'I'll read the next bit, OK?'

Asya reads: 'Asya, if you've got yourself entangled with some man, please, I beg you, don't take it too seriously. Your circumstances are difficult and separation is bad. And you are not only separated from your husband but also from your family and your country and all those who love you. You can't judge anything while you are in this position.'

'Well?' Gerald says. 'Well?'

'She says: we are all worried about you. I have spoken to Kareem and Deena but no one knows why Tante Lateefa had to go to Athens to see you. I wish you had been able to come here but I know it would have been very difficult for you to get an exit visa since you have not finished your Ph.D yet.

'OK?' Asya looks at Gerald. He looks drawn and suspicious.

'Read the rest,' he says.

Asya reads: 'I want to say to you that if you have not yet told Saif don't tell him. I'm not telling you to do anything wrong: believe me, I am speaking from the other side and I know. I know also that you take things too seriously and that you might persuade yourself that you have a responsibility to this person – don't. Your responsibility is to your husband and your family. Please, please, finish your work and come back and everything will be much clearer to you when you're here. All your life you have taken your decisions yourself and that is right, but not when you are so far away. I think of you and I pray for you. Please write to me. Chrissie.'

'Have you finished?' Gerald asks.

'Yes,' says Asya.

'Read me the rest,' he says.

Asya wipes her face. Her voice shakes, but then it steadies. 'I do wish that you could be here so that we can talk things over as we always have. I miss you very much and there is such a lot I would like to tell you. Fuad still moves between Cairo and Suez. His work is going well. Ranya had a fantastic third birthday – she is very pretty and I can't wait for you to see her. I am in my fifth month now and I do so hope this one's a boy. My mother says it is, because I'm having an easier time with this pregnancy than I had with the last. But that could just be because it's the second. Please write to me soon, love, Chrissie.'

'Is that it?' Gerald asks.

'Yes,' says Asya.

'Every word?'

'Yes,' says Asya.

'All right. Who's this one from?'

'My father.'

'Your mother must have told him.'

'I don't know.'

Gerald slits open the letter. There are three paragraphs in Mukhtar al-Ulama's classic calligraphy. Gerald looks at the sheet of paper then throws it down on the bed.

'I'm not going to ask you to translate this,' he says bitterly. 'I know what it says.'

Asya picks up the letter. The Arabic says: 'I urge you not to do anything foolish – these things happen and the important thing is to know how to get out of them – Saif's roots go deep in your soul – I believe that they will be almost impossible to tear out –' There is one sentence in English. It says: 'You are making a mess of your life.' Why did Daddy write that in English, Asya wonders. Couldn't he have written it in Arabic? She thinks, but she can only come up with one Arabic approximation: 'You are destroying your life' – that would not be the same. 'You are making a mess of your life' can't be said in classical Arabic. Of course in colloquial Egyptian he could have said –

'Aren't you going to say anything?' Gerald says.

'What can I say?' asks Asya.

'You could say he's wrong. You could say he doesn't know what he's talking about –'

'Gerald, he's my father –'

'I know he's your father –'

'My mother tells him I'm – making problems with my husband, whom they've all known for ever, and I'm involved with a man in England – an *English* man – what do you want him to say?'

'He can say nothing. He can withhold judgment until he's met the man his daughter is leaving her husband for –'

'That's impossible.'

'*Impossible* – to give me a fair chance is *impossible?*'

'Given all the circumstances and the people involved it's impossible. The *situation* isn't fair –'

'So being with me simply means you're messing up? I like that. I *love* it –'

'You have to see it from his point of view –'

'Why are you always telling me about other people's points of view? I have to see it from *your* point of view, from your *husband's* point of view, for Christ's sake, and now from your whole *family's* point of view – what about *my* point of view? Why is nobody seeing anything from *my* point of view?'

'I told you,' says Asya, 'I told you this would never work.'

'What? What would never work? Speak up, man –'

'I *told* you you should go away and let things evolve. I *told* you you shouldn't get involved in this bit. I *told* you it would be terrible. This, this –' she waves the letter at him – 'is just the tiniest, tiniest bit of the beginning, and look how you're reacting. Leave it, Gerald, *leave* it.'

'No!' he shouts. 'I am not letting you go. I have found you and I am not letting you go. I am not letting them tell me what to do. I am not letting them judge me. I am going to prove to everyone that I'm not messing up your life: that you are only the real you when you are with *me*. I am going to make the world afford us the honour we deserve – the honour our *love* deserves –'

Asya hides her face in her hands. If only she were at home. If only home were just down the road and she could run there, now, in her dressing-gown and say, 'Daddy, I'm in trouble. Help me –'

'Let's get this over with,' he says suddenly, calming down.

Asya hears him tear open the last envelope and hears the rustle of the air-mail paper as he draws the sheet out. She snatches the letter from his hand and races to the bathroom and locks the door and leans against it, her breath coming fast.

'Dear Asya,' she reads. 'You may not remember me. We met a number of times in England – on one occasion you kindly invited me to a banquet in your home.' Gerald bangs on the door. 'I am writing to tell you that Mario died in a car accident on the tenth of January.' Asya reaches out and grips the basin. She holds the yellow paper up to her eyes and reads it again. 'I am writing to tell you that Mario died in a car accident on the tenth of January. He had been visiting his sister in Cape Town and was driving back to the farm. He was going over the speed limit and the Lancia overturned. He died immediately and no one else was involved.' The paper is shaking so much she can hardly read it. Gerald is still banging on the door. 'I feel sure that he would have wished that I write to you. Although he did not mention you often I know that you were in his thoughts. I am sure you will understand.' Everything inside her has gone: evaporated. She has become hollow. 'Please convey also my condolences to Saif. Mario spoke of him often. I know he will be very much saddened. As indeed we all are. His mother is still under sedation and his father blames himself. Here, we miss him very much. I know you will too. With my sad regards, Frederick Reimenschneider'.

Asya lets the hand holding the letter drop to her side. Her other hand is holding the edge of the wash-basin and she stands, slightly bent, leaning on it. The banging on the door goes on. She unlocks the door and Gerald pushes it open and stands in the doorway.

'What the hell –'

Asya holds out the piece of paper.

'Here, take it,' she whispers, and starts to cough. She sits on the edge of the bathtub with her arms wrapped around herself and coughs and coughs. Gerald stands in the doorway and reads the letter.

'Who is Mario?' he asks.

'A friend,' Asya says, her head bent, looking at the floor.

'Why did you run away with it like that? Why?'

'I don't know.'

'You were expecting something else. What were you expecting?'

'Nothing.'

'When did you last see this – Mario?'

'Sixteen months ago.'

'Here?'

'Yes.'

'And who is this German guy?'

'A friend of his. Will you stop, please?'

'I don't understand why you ran away with it.'

'Will you stop? Will you go away?'

'Oh, baby, you're shivering.'

Asya stands up and walks over to the toilet. She bends and retches but nothing comes out. She draws her hand over her forehead then bends and retches again. This time a small stream of bitter, greenish-yellow bile comes gushing out of her mouth. She straightens up and flushes the toilet. Then she goes to the basin and rinses out her mouth. There are tears, too, but they are just the tears that come from throwing up. She looks at Gerald.

'Do you mind?' she says. 'I need to use the loo.'

He goes out and she closes the door and locks it.

When she gets up from the toilet her legs are so unsteady with all the liquid that has burst its way out of her that she holds on to the window-sill as she lowers herself to sit on the edge of the bathtub. She washes and then sits there for a long, long time. She can think only two thoughts: 'Mario is dead' and 'Poor Saif.'

When Gerald knocks on the door and calls, 'Are you all right?' she gets up and dries herself and unlocks the door. He is in his black kimono.

'You look terrible,' he says. 'Come, I'll help you upstairs and I'll make you a cup of tea.'

Asya walks upstairs ahead of him and sits at the kitchen table. He pours boiling water over a teabag and stirs in some milk and puts it down in front of her. He sits down opposite her at the table.

'Was he a very good friend?' he asks.

Asya nods once, and then is too tired to lift up her head. She sits with it bowed and her arms stretched out on the table in front of her.

After a bit Gerald says, 'Why does it say his father blames himself?'

'What?' asks Asya.

'Why does it say his father blames himself?'

'The car –' She looks up. 'The car was a bribe – to make him go back to South Africa.'

'Didn't he want to go?'

'He wanted to – to try living in Italy.'

Asya starts to cough again.

'Have some tea, babe,' Gerald says.

Asya has a sip of tea and stops coughing. She can see him lying on the road. His white cotton shirt is immaculate, his arms are flung open. His brown curly hair is getting dusty in the road, his eyes are closed, his nostrils and moustache are caked with dark blood and from the corner of his half-open mouth a slow trickle of blood oozes out to add, drop by drop, to the dark pool which is gathering under him. She puts her hand to her throat. 'Do you mind,' she says. 'I think I –' She chokes and covers her face with her hands.

'It's all right, babe,' Gerald says. 'I understand.'

When she gets her breath back she says, 'I think I'd better go and lie down. I'll be all right later.'

'It's OK,' he says. 'It's OK. I'll come with you.'

'No,' Asya says. 'Please. I really – just – please. I just need to lie down.'

'You're going to shut me out?' he says. 'Even now you're going to shut me out?'

'Please, Gerald,' Asya says.

He is looking at her with curiosity now.

'You know,' he says, 'you're really strange, man. You get a letter saying your friend has died and there's just zero reaction. All you can do is sit there. You don't cry, you don't talk about him. You don't do anything. What are you made of that you can't even fucking grieve for a friend?'

Asya leans on the table and stands up. She walks slowly down the stairs. When she gets to the bedroom she closes the door and climbs into bed. She pulls the quilt up over her head and huddles on her side under it.

7.15 p.m.

Gerald comes heavily up the stairs.

'This is it, babe,' he says. 'I'm going. This is killing me. You're destroying us – smearing acid all over us – and I can't sit around any more and watch you do it.'

Asya continues to sit in the black leather armchair in her lilac dressing-gown.

'Did you hear me?' he asks.

Asya looks up at him. He stands at the entrance to the living-room. He is wearing his cowboy boots, his jeans and his sheepskin coat.

609

'I said I'm going,' he says. 'I can't take it any more. I've tried to help you, babe. I've given you everything I've got and more. I've given you what I didn't even know I had to give. But you're beyond help. You're out of reach, man.'

He walks a few steps into the room, looking at her.

'You're not going to stop me, are you? No. You're not even going to say anything.'

He stands in front of her on the cream rug.

'Look at you,' he says. 'Look at you: this is the woman I wanted to share my life with, this is the woman whose aura I could sense from across the room, the woman who wanted me to teach her about meditation, the woman whose power and fire shook me to the depth of my being, the woman who trembled and wept with passion under me –'

He waits.

'You really aren't going to say anything, are you? Nothing at all.'

Asya moves her hands.

'There's nothing to say,' she says.

'You're just going to sit there and let me walk away.'

He shakes his head slowly in wonderment. After a moment he takes a key from his pocket.

'Here's your key,' he says. 'I'm sure you're happy to have it back.'

He drops the key into her lap.

'Sit there then,' he says. 'Just fucking sit there all night. Here, I'll give you some entertainment in case you get bored – although I don't believe you're even capable of being bored.'

He walks over to the television and switches it on. He holds the remote control in his hand.

'D'you want to choose a channel? *The Satan Bug?* No, of course not: we'll get you the intellectual's channel, shall we?'

He turns the volume up loud.

'There,' he shouts. 'That might get through to you. It's a machine,' he shouts. 'You'll feel safer with it than with a living breathing person who might ask you questions, might even *want* something from you: like some emotion maybe. *Emotion? Fuck!*'

He hurls the remote control away from him. It strikes the wall and falls to the floor behind the sofa.

'You don't know the meaning of the word,' he shouts.

He looks at her for another minute, then turns and walks quickly out of the room. The television is so loud that she cannot hear his steps on the stairs. Then she hears the front door slam shut.

Asya sits in her chair. Her legs are curled under her and she can feel that they have gone numb. But she cannot move. When she thinks of moving the noise from the television beats her back into her seat. 'The *Washington Post* is to publish tomorrow – Sunday – a list of world leaders who it is alleged are – or have at one time been – on the payroll of the CIA –' She watches the newsreader. The sound is so loud. If only she had the remote control; she could switch it off – and then she could think and then she could move. But the remote control is behind the sofa – on the other side of the room. She looks at the sofa: it shines black and glossy in the lamplight. He is not sitting there. He is gone. He is gone and she feels nothing. She feels nothing except a longing that this noise should stop. '– is understood to include the the former German Chancellor Herr Willy Brandt, Archbishop Makarios of Cyprus, President Jomo Kenyatta of Kenya –' She stares at the television. It is more bearable if she sees where the sound is coming from. Slightly more bearable. It's going to make her sick. It's beating at her brains and it's going to make her sick. Asya holds on to the arms of her chair. She tries to move her legs. But a thousand pinpoints of pain rush into them and she gasps. She takes her right hand away from the chair and pushes at her feet. She grits her teeth and gives one hard push and her feet fall to the floor and the pain stabs through them upward from the rug. She presses her feet into the rug and the pain darts up her legs. 'This is following disclosures that King Hussein of Jordan has been receiving funds from the CIA since the ending of British influence in the Hashemite Kingdom in 1957 –' Bit by bit she pushes her weight on to her feet. If she tries to stand up now she'll fall. The noise is hitting at her stomach. She lowers her head and inch by inch she levers herself away from the chair. Her right leg gives way but she holds on to the broad arm and starts again. The pain is there but now her legs hold. '– his death in the Radcliffe Infirmary in Oxford early this morning deprives the Prime Minister and the Labour Party of one of the sturdiest and most indepen-dent intellects at call on a wide range of political –' She hobbles quickly on the sides of her feet to the television. 'Tributes have been –' She reaches for the power button and presses it. Silence. Oh, silence. She leans on the television and stands there till her heart slows down and her legs come back to her. Silence. Mario is dead and Saif doesn't know. And Gerald is gone.

When she lifts her head she is facing the blackness outside the window. Black as though a black curtain were drawn behind the glass. But there are no curtains on these windows. There never have been. What if he is outside? What if he's driven off just a little way and is parked on the bridge and is watching her now? She drops to her knees and crouches down on the rug. He can't see her like this. He can't see her if she stays close to the floor. And downstairs there are curtains. And they're drawn. The bedroom curtains have been drawn all day. She has to get downstairs. She has to get downstairs and lock the door. He's left his key but the door is unlocked. Oh, thank God he's left his key. Asya crawls quickly back to her chair, and just under it she finds the key that had fallen off her lap as she tried to stand up. She has to get downstairs and lock the door and then she'll be all right. She has to switch off the lamp that lights up this room like a stage-set and get downstairs. But the lamp is on the window-sill. She can't go near the window. She'll just go downstairs and lock the door. And if he comes back and bangs and hammers she won't answer. She just won't answer. He can't get in. Even if he breaks a window the lights are too small for him to get in through. And tomorrow morning she'll go away. She'll leave. She'll take her work and drive down to London and hole up in some hotel. She'll have to use Saif's money but he won't mind. He won't mind if she uses his money to escape. If she has to come back she'll come back to a room on campus. She'll never come back to this house again. Not ever. But now she has to get downstairs. She has to get downstairs without being seen. She crawls along the rug. If he climbs the hill she climbed with Mahrous he can practically look down into the living-room. But he won't do that. He's more likely to have driven off in his anger and then maybe decide to come back. She has to get downstairs quickly. She crawls over the bare wooden floor of the kitchen till she gets to the top of the stairs. At the top of the stairs she sees the socket with the long wire from the lamp plugged into it. She reaches out and switches it off. Now there is total darkness. He must have switched off the lights downstairs. She leans her head against the wall for a moment and takes two deep breaths. Then she swings her legs round and sits on the top step. She sits on the top step and looks down into the darkness and waits for her heart to stop hammering. It's OK now. It's just dark, that's all. She holds the key tight in her left hand and keeps her right on the wall as she starts to walk down the steps. Down there she can switch on the light because she can't be seen from the outside. The curtains in the bedroom are closed and all the other doors are shut. She feels for each step with her bare feet. When she feels carpet again under her right foot she leans, over, over, to where she knows the light switch is and presses it. She hears it click, and as the bright light floods the hall she hears Gerald say, 'You didn't even try to stop me –' and she hears her own scream, impossibly shrill and long but stopping suddenly as she feels the wetness on her legs and between her thighs and crosses her legs and sits down quickly on the steps.

'You didn't even try to stop me,' he says. 'You didn't even cry when I'd gone.'

Asya sits on the step with her legs crossed and stares at him. He is standing behind the door exactly where Mario had stood as he hesitated on that last night. The night he'd hugged her and gone and next day her foot had kicked against the wrappings round his white tulips –

'You didn't even cry. You just sat there till you thought I'd gone. You didn't follow me –'

Thank God the stairs are wood – otherwise she'd be staining Jenny's carpet. Now there must be a big wet patch on her dressing-gown. She's got to get to the bathroom. She's got to wash herself. She's got to change before he sees it –

'Baby,' he says. 'Baby. You must have known I couldn't do it. I can't walk away from you. How can I walk away from you when you are my life?'

He comes towards her. He kneels down at her feet.

'Baby,' he says. 'Baby. Help me. For God's sake help me, babe.'

He puts his head in her lap and his arms around her waist. He's going to smell the wee-wees, she thinks. As she thinks the word 'wee-wees' Asya starts to laugh. She presses her thighs tighter together – no, please, no, but the laughter burbles up and she presses her face to the wall, clutching the key in her left hand and sobbing and crying with laughter.

Gerald sits back on his heels and looks at her.

'You're not human,' he says slowly. 'You know what you are? You're a monster, man, you're *dangerous*, you really are –'

Monday, 14 March 1977: 3 p.m.

The North of England

The big brown suitcase lies open on the bed. The black kimono, the other pair of jeans, five shirts, the long belted cardigan, four pairs of white socks and a few underpants are already in there. The sneakers are in there too, inside a green Marks and Spencer's bag. Asya runs upstairs to the living-room. She picks up Gerald's five books from the floor by the sofa and runs downstairs again. She stacks them in a corner of the suitcase. She checks her watch: it's three-fifteen. OK, she tells herself. OK. She has at least one hour and forty-five minutes. Slow down. She has to do this really carefully, methodically – otherwise she'll make a mistake. She has to stop rushing about. She has to think. OK.

First: is the door locked? Check that. At least if it's locked she can't be taken by surprise. At least she can stop running and gasping as if she were being chased. She's on her own – and before she can be not on her own there will have to be a knock on the door and she will have to open it. She'll have a couple of minutes. So slow down. She walks over to the door and checks that it is locked, that the key is in the key-hole and that the bolt is drawn. OK. Now it's OK.

Next: get Gerald's things out of here. Before anything else. Before he comes back. Before he comes back and stands in this hall and declares that he's not going anywhere – that he's going to stay here and face Saif – oh God, God – she races up the stairs but when she comes to the living-room she stops. She's got to do this properly: she can't slip up. Now: *living-room* – she looks around her: books she's already removed. Plants?

613

No, none are his. Records? Yes. She leafs quickly through the records and isolates six. She tucks them under her arm. What else? Tapes? No. Magazines? No. She looks around: there's nothing in the room to give her away; nothing at all. Not that she's planning on concealing anything – if he wants to know she'll tell him; she'll tell him everything. But there's no need for objects to rise up and hit him in the eye; there's no need for her to be insultingly careless as well as cowardly and treacherous. She walks across the room.

Kitchen: anything? No. She opens the fridge. Yes: the Aludrox for his stomach cramps. She wraps the medicine in a small plastic bag and looks around the room one more time before she starts down the stairs.

In the bedroom she tucks the records between the legs of the jeans and wedges the medicine into the corner behind the books. She looks around her. She opens the cupboard and checks it once again. Nothing. She remembers something: she drops to her knees and fishes his Japanese slippers out from under the bed. Lying next to them, on its side, is his almost empty bottle of Essence of Eucalyptus Massage Oil. She pushes the bottle and the slippers into the Marks and Spencer's bag next to the sneakers.

She goes into the boiler-room. Three T-shirts are hanging on the line. She feels them. They are still damp. She collects them quickly and runs upstairs to the kitchen for another plastic bag. Then she remembers something else and collects two plastic bags. She runs downstairs again. She folds up the damp T-shirts and puts them in one of the plastic bags. She turns and empties out the laundry basket. Quickly she sorts out the used clothes: hers she stuffs into the washing-machine, his she puts into the second plastic bag. She goes into the bedroom and puts both plastic bags into the suitcase.

Now for the bathroom; this is the last thing: green toothbrush, Palmolive shaving-cream, disposable razors, spray deodorant, hairbrush and yellow comb, Braun baby-dryer. She runs back to the bedroom and puts the things in the suitcase. She pauses for a moment and thinks back over everything, counting the rooms off on her fingers. She runs out to the hall and opens each of the three drawers under the telephone. Nothing.

Back in the bedroom she closes the suitcase. She puts on her dark brown low-heeled shoes and her camel coat. She wraps a blue and beige scarf loosely around her head, picks up her handbag and her keys and lifts the case. It isn't heavy. She carries it through the hall and out of the front door. She opens the back door of the white Morris and puts the suitcase on the back seat. She goes back to the cottage and locks the door, then she climbs into the car and sets off for the university.

As she drives through the narrow lanes she notices that her hands are frozen and that she is sitting hunched up over the steering-wheel. A car

614

coming the other way hoots at her as she takes a corner in too wide an arc. Steady on, she thinks, steady on. She forces herself to slow down, to sit back, to lean against the back of the seat. She breathes deeply several times. If she's going to get herself killed she'd better not do it now with the suitcase in the car. She imagines Saif arriving at the morgue to identify her body. He nods and they draw the sheet back over her face before sliding her back into her refrigerated compartment. As he leaves someone says something about effects and points out the suitcase. He looks at it puzzled; he doesn't recognise it. When they open it for him he looks at the clothes and records. He opens a plastic bag and sees the Japanese slippers and the massage oil – oh God, oh God – she finds that she is hunched up again and gripping the steering-wheel. No, no, if it is to happen let it happen on the way back – after she's got rid of this suitcase; then he need never know, then everything can stay the way he always wanted it – for ever.

At the university she swings the car into a parking-space outside the Indoor Rec. She drags the suitcase through the big doors, past the old porter sitting in front of the big noticeboard with the squash-court bookings, and down the dark corridor. At the door of the gym she pauses and looks through the glass panes. Gerald Stone is standing with his back to her. There is no one else in the room. She watches as he shakes out his hands, jumps a couple of times on his toes, then bends and grips the weights. His buttocks strain against the red shorts – and then he's up, legs braced apart and trembling slightly, the weights held high up above his head, the golden hair quivering with effort. A count of ten and he swings forward. The weights clatter to the floor and he straightens up, hooks his hands behind his head and stretches twice.

Asya opens the door. He turns. His face registers surprise as he sees her – and then he frowns. Asya steps into the gym and closes the door behind her.

'Hi, babe!' he says. 'What's up?'

Asya folds her arms. She holds on tight to her upper arms with each of her hands.

'Saif,' she says, 'is coming back.'

'What?' he says. 'Here?'

Asya nods.

'When?' he says.

'Any minute now,' she says.

'This is it then,' he says – and smiles. 'OK, OK. It's good.'

Asya looks at him.

'Don't look so frightened, man,' he says. 'We'll face him together. We'll tell it like it is.'

Asya shakes her head.

'No,' she says.

'No?' He stares at her, his hands at his waist. 'What do you mean, "No?" '

'No.' She looks down at the floor and shakes her head again.

'Baby,' Gerald says. 'Baby, what are you saying?'

'This is between him and me,' Asya says. She looks up. 'I told you, I always *told* you,' she says desperately, 'this *has* to be between him and me.'

He looks at her, and then he nods. 'OK,' he says. He pushes his hands through his hair. 'What do you want me to do?'

Asya looks at the floor again. She draws a tiny circle on the polished wood with the toe of her right shoe. 'Nothing,' she says in a small voice.

'Nothing?'

Asya looks up. 'Gerald,' she says, 'why don't you go home? To Canterbury? This is going to be a bad time and –'

'Am I hearing this?' he says. 'Am I really hearing this?'

'And I really can't bear to think of you sitting around –'

'Sitting around? You think I'll be *sitting around*? Man, I'll be waiting for *you*, waiting for my destiny. You're going to need me, babe –'

'Where?' says Asya. 'Where will you wait?'

'I'll get a room on campus,' he says. 'They've got guest-rooms – as you know.'

'Gerald,' says Asya. 'Gerald, that'll cost you money, please, I don't want that on my conscience – I – I don't know how long this is going to take –'

She wants to look at her watch but she doesn't dare.

His face changes.

'How long have you known?' he asks.

'Known what?' Asya says.

'How long have you known that he's coming?'

'Just for an hour,' Asya says. 'The –'

'How did you know? Who told you?'

'They phoned a telex through to me an hour ago.'

'A telex from him?'

'Yes.'

'What did it say?'

'Just that he wants to talk to me and that he's coming over, that's all.'

'And he gives you an hour? He wanted to take you by surprise –'

'No, no, he didn't,' says Asya. 'The telex was sent last night. If he'd wanted to take me by surprise he would have just arrived. He's being fair – more than fair.'

'How come it was sent last night and you got it just an hour ago?'

'I don't know. They mislaid it. I don't know. Gerald, please, I have to go –'

'You have to go? Just like that? She has to go,' he announces to the

empty gym. 'The lady has to go; she has to go and meet her *husband* –'
He takes two steps and Asya flinches, but his fist slams into the wooden wall. It must have hurt, but he doesn't even shake it. 'And you want me to pack my bag and trot off to Canterbury like a good boy and wait there for the royal summons –'

'I don't want you to wait *anywhere*,' Asya says. 'I want you to get on with your life.'

'My *life*?' he says. 'My *life*?' He comes forward and grips her shoulders. '*You* are my *life*, man. Hasn't that got through to you yet? There *is* no life for me without you. All right, all right.' He drops his hands and raises them to show he meant no harm. 'You don't have to be scared of me, babe. You never have to be scared of *me*. I'm worried for *you*, babe. I don't want to leave you alone with him –'

'Why?' Asya asks, her eyes round with surprise.

'He's going to do something terrible to you –'

'Saif?' asks Asya.

'A man doesn't just get up and catch a flight –'

'No,' Asya shakes her head. 'You don't understand. He isn't like that. And anyway – he doesn't even know – for sure –'

'He isn't like that,' he says. 'He isn't like that. I'm sorry, I'd forgotten: he's a saint –'

'I'm going,' Asya says, and turns to the door.

'OK,' Gerald says, 'OK. I'm sorry, Babe.' He holds the door. 'You have to know how hard this is on me –'

'It's hard on everyone,' Asya says.

'Yes, yes. I know it is. OK. I'll have to come with you and get my things –'

'I've got them,' Asya says.

'What?' says Gerald.

'I've got them,' Asya says again.

She opens the door and steps out. In the corridor Gerald sees the brown suitcase.

'You packed my bag?' he says.

'I just thought –'

'You're throwing me out?' he says.

'Gerald, it isn't like that –'

'What's it like then? You pack my bag and bring it over –'

'I just thought it might be too painful –'

'That isn't what you thought.'

Asya is silent.

'You were just getting rid of me. You've been planning all along –'

'I have to go,' Asya says, and turns and starts to walk.

'Wait,' Gerald cries.

Asya stops but does not turn around.

617

'Look at me. *Please* look at me.'

Asya turns and looks at him. His face in the dim corridor is tinged with green. His nostrils quiver and two dark veins throb in his temples. He stands helplessly next to his suitcase in his red shorts and yellow singlet.

'I love you, babe,' he says in a hoarse voice. 'Always remember that. I love you and I'll be waiting for you.'

Asya turns and runs down the corridor. She runs through reception and out of the swing-doors and into her car.

Now, she thinks as she speeds down the country lanes: *now* it doesn't matter if she crashes. On her own, of course – like Mario – 'no one else was involved' – it doesn't matter. Except her mother's heart would be broken. And then there's Daddy. And Kareem and Deena. And Chrissie. And Khalu Hamid and Tante Soraya. Oh, Asya thinks, oh, and Saif? What would happen to Saif? But what is going to happen to Saif anyway? What is she about to do to Saif? What blow is she going to deal him in – she looks at her watch: four-thirty – in half an hour? In half an hour he could be there and what is she going to tell him? What is she going to say? Maybe she need not say anything. Maybe she can just run into his arms and hold him and hold him and he would know that whatever had happened she had always always loved him and they could just take it from there – But not to where they were before. No, but where? Where else is possible now? Where can they go? They can't go to bed because she knows she doesn't want to sleep with him. But maybe that was just in Athens? Maybe now it would be all right. But she doesn't want to. She *knows* she doesn't want to. She just can't imagine it any more. But Asya, Asya, she thinks, you love him. Yes, she does. She wants to stay with him. If he wants to – if he touches her she'll say yes. Yes, yes, *yes*. Because that would be the best thing that can happen. She needn't seize up and go all stiff any more: she knows now that it won't hurt. It won't hurt because of Gerald Stone. If she should run into his arms the moment he arrives. If, without a word, he should take her to bed, she'll go. She'll go with him into the bed she has shared with Gerald Stone – the bed – she'd better change the sheets – oh, she'd better get there quick and change the sheets – she imagines Saif throwing back the quilt: a faint yellowish stain spreads across the middle of the bed. 'What the hell's that?' he says – and like her friend so many years ago she'll dance and jubilate, 'Semen, semen, Gerald's SEMEN,' and Saif, in a flowered house-dress with broderie anglaise and red ribbons fluttering at the sleeves, will clap his hands over his ears and flee up the stairs –

Asya can feel her brains shaking and the asphalt quivers in front of her eyes. She pulls in to the side of the road, switches off the engine and puts on the handbrake. She sits. She sits until her breathing eases and the world stops shaking and, looking out, she sees the hedgerows stretching along the side of the road. They dip and rise in a long lazy line, bump bump bumpety-bump: hedgerows like elephants walking trunk to tail – and off they go: off into the distance. Out of the passenger window to her left she sees the branches squashed up against the glass: brown and spiky but each spike loaded with tiny green buds. It's March, she thinks. Next week it will be spring again. Spring: Wherein Each Thing Reneweth Itself Save the Lover. She leans her head against the back of the seat. Peace. The hedgerows, the sky, the road, all are bathed in a serene light – as though she were seeing them through a filter, or through water. Peace and silence everywhere. She closes her eyes for a moment and opens them again. It is all still there. A golden, celluloid world. Asya starts the car and drives carefully back to the cottage.

6.10 p.m

Asya hears the engine growl under the window and then cut out. She hears the car door slam and then she hears two knocks. She runs down the stairs and opens the door.

He stands outside in the fading light. He is shorter than she remembers him.

'Come in,' Asya says, and steps back to make room in the narrow hall.

Saif walks in and closes the door behind him.

'You got the telex?' he says.

Asya nods. 'Yes. But only at three o'clock today.'

'Still,' he says, 'you had enough time to get your friend out of the way?'

Asya looks at him without speaking. He wears dark beige cords and the big Burberry they had bought together in London last year. He looks terribly tired.

'Take off your coat, darling,' she says, 'and let's go upstairs.'

He takes off his coat and Asya takes it from him. She motions to the stairs and he starts walking up. She hangs the coat on the peg in the hallway. Then, before she follows him up the stairs, she bends down and quickly unplugs the phone. She tucks the end of the wire in behind the chest of drawers. Then she locks the front door.

In the living-room Asya says, 'Shall I fix you a drink?'

'Yes,' Saif says.

'Whisky?' asks Asya.

Saif nods. He sits in one of the leather armchairs and stretches out his legs. He watches the fire burning in the stove.

Asya puts ice into a glass, pours some whisky over it and brings it to him. She puts the glass in his hand and sits on the rug by his feet.

'You've been travelling all day,' she says, 'since what? Six in the morning?'

'I had to see you,' he says, looking into the glass.

'When did you decide to come?' Asya asks.

619

'Yesterday – more or less.'

'But how did you manage to get away?'

'I just left,' he says.

Asya frowns. 'How, just left?'

'They're not holding my passport. I left.'

He tilts the glass and drinks.

'But – didn't you tell anyone?'

'I told Sami, my second man.'

'But – for how long can he manage? How long can he cover for you? Can you trust him?'

'Yeah,' he says, 'I can trust him,' and takes another drink.

'But Saif,' Asya says, 'you said it was tricky. You said they were mean. You said they owe you a lot of money.'

He puts his head against the back of the chair and closes his eyes.

'My cigarettes are in my coat pocket,' he says.

'I'll get them,'

Asya jumps up and runs downstairs. The coat is hanging on the peg. For a moment, as she rummages in the pockets, she buries her face in the soft material and breathes in his scent; she can see him, standing at the open doors of his veranda, waiting for her; waiting for her to come and put her arms around him and rub her face against his back. He knows. He knows already and his answer is to come to her. Her fingers close on the car-keys. She runs out and opens the car. On the back seat his black case and his briefcase lie side by side. She takes them out, locks the car, carries them into the house, then locks the front door again. She slips the keys back into his pocket, gets the packet of Rothmans and the lighter and runs back up the stairs. She'd left the cases in the hall. Which room should she have put them in?

'I brought your things in from the car,' she says, handing him the cigarettes and the lighter. She brings an ashtray over from the kitchen and sits down again at his feet.

'You shouldn't have,' he says.

'It's OK,' says Asya. 'They're not heavy.'

Saif lights a cigarette.

'Saif,' Asya says again, 'you shouldn't have left like that really, should you? I mean, if you were working on Intelligence then that's – serious, isn't it?'

'Yes.' He blows out smoke. 'But this is serious too, Princess, isn't it?'

'Yes,' says Asya. 'But Saif, *I* could have come to *you* –'

He shakes his head.

'I told you that wouldn't have been a good idea.'

'Well then, I'd have sorted myself out –'

'Well, this way maybe we can sort you out together.'

'But I never ever meant for you to abandon your work –'

'It's all right, Princess. Maybe it'll hold.'

'And all the money you've worked for –'

'Look,' he says. 'Stop worrying. We've got lots in the bank. If we're all right, and we need money, I'll make money. If we're not – then who cares what happens next?'

Asya is silent.

'OK, Princess.' He leans forward to flick the ash off his cigarette and pick up his drink. 'Are you going to tell me about it?'

'In a nutshell?' Asya asks, looking up at him.

He leans back in his chair.

'You've made your point,' he says. 'Give it as long as it deserves.'

Asya is silent. When she glances up he is looking at her, waiting for what she has to say.

'Why did you decide to come now?' she asks. 'I mean, it's been seven weeks since Athens.'

'OK,' he says, 'so I'm slow.'

'That's not what I mean,' Asya says. 'I just meant, why now? Why not last week – or next week?'

'Was "now" particularly inconvenient, then?' he says. 'What should I have done? Filled a form in triplicate?'

'No,' says Asya. 'No. I'm sorry –'

'I just decided,' he says. 'I just suddenly saw what was happening and that I'd been a fool not to see it all along. I put a call through to your mother yesterday but she'd gone to Alexandria and I couldn't get through to Alexandria – so I decided to come to you and find out what the hell is really going on. Is that a full enough explanation for you?'

'Yes,' Asya says. 'I'm sorry.'

She pulls at the cream tufts of the rug. They look so soft and cuddly but when you touch them they're rough – sharp, almost –

'So,' Saif says. 'Are you going to tell me?'

What does he want her to tell him? Does he want 'the truth'? But the truth, the *whole* truth, would take so long to tell. Or does he want something in a couple of sentences? But he knows already. He said 'your friend' –

'Asya?' Saif says.

'Yes. Yes,' says Asya. 'I'm sorry.'

'Is it that bad?'

'No,' says Asya. 'I mean – yes, maybe – I – oh, Saif,' she says, and leans forward and puts her face in her hands.

'OK,' he says.

She feels the leg of his trousers brush against her as he stands up. He stubs out his cigarette and walks away a couple of paces.

'I'll make it easier on you,' he says. 'You've been having – some kind of a thing – with someone. Yes?'

Asya nods dumbly, staring at the rug, pulling at it.

'Yes,' Saif says. 'I thought so.'

Asya says nothing. It's happening, she thinks, it's happening. This is it. She has to be careful, careful what she says, she has to make absolutely sure he understands. But the words, 'It's happening, it's happening,' drum in her mind and drown out all other thoughts.

'How serious is it?' Saif asks.

Asya shakes her head. She cannot find words. It isn't – it wasn't – it was just – she makes a helpless movement with her hands.

'Who is he?' Saif asks.

'It's not,' whispers Asya, her face to the floor, 'it wasn't anyone – it wasn't anyone you know.'

'*Where* is he?' Saif asks.

'Gone,' Asya says.

'When?'

'Today.'

'He ran away? Left you to face the music on your own?'

'He would have stayed,' Asya says. 'He wanted to stay.'

'And why didn't he?'

'I wouldn't let him.'

'You were afraid for him? Protecting him?'

'No.' Asya looks up. 'No, that wasn't it.'

'What then?' He stares at her. 'What?'

'He's – irrelevant,' Asya says.

'You've been having some thing with a bloke up until the minute I get here and you tell me he's irrelevant?'

Asya nods, then shrugs.

'Did you tell *him* that too?' Saif asks. 'Did you tell him he was irrelevant?'

Asya moves her head. 'More or less,' she whispers.

Saif walks over to the window. He stands there for a moment looking out. Then he turns.

'OK,' he says gently. 'OK, Princess. I want it straight. How far did it go?'

Asya looks up at him, wide-eyed. 'What do you mean?'

'How far did it go? Christ, do I have to spell it out for you? How – far – did – it – go?'

Asya holds his gaze for a moment, then looks down. 'I don't see how you can ask –'

'How far did it go?'

Asya looks up at him.

'What do you think?' she asks.

From across the room he looks into her eyes.

'Did you sleep with him, Princess?' he asks softly.

And into his eyes Asya says, 'Yes,' and watches him crumple. He stands his ground but she can see him collapse. He looks like a man in a film the moment after he's been shot and before he falls to the ground –

'Jesus Christ!' he breathes. 'Jesus Christ!'

But he doesn't fall to the ground; he drags his eyes from hers and turns slowly away. He leans on the window-sill and Asya hears what must have been a groan. She springs to her feet and runs over to him. She throws herself on to his back.

'Oh, Saif, Saif darling, I didn't care – I swear I –'

'Get away from me,' he cries. '*Get away from me –*'

He shakes her off and straightens up and turns round to face her. His eyes are red and his face shines wet and his mouth has gone all wobbly like a child's.

'Five years,' he says. 'Five years. The *pain* is too much for you to take, you feel *sick* if I so much as put my hand on your tits, you *sneeze* if I come near you – then you go and open your legs to some fucking *stranger –*'

'This isn't fair,' cries Asya. 'For *years* I begged you – I *begged* you – to make it happen – and you *wouldn't*. And I *knew* it was going wrong – it was *all* going wrong –'

'So you go and *fuck* some bastard, you actually *fuck* some bastard –'

'What did you *expect*, for Christ's sake –' cries Asya.

'I *expected* my wife to be loyal. I *expected* my wife to have some sense of honour. I *expected –*'

'But you've been saying you thought *something* was happening – what did you think –'

'I *thought* – I *thought* it was some romantic hand-holding shit –'

'I'm *twenty-six*,' Asya screams. 'I'm not twelve. I'm twenty-six and I've been waiting for *nine years –*'

'You bitch,' Saif says slowly. 'I wouldn't have thought you could even *speak* like that.'

Asya throws herself into a chair and sits watching him. He looks at her for moment, then he walks across the room. He stops at the table and picks up his cigarettes and his lighter. Before he reaches the top of the stairs Asya has leapt across and is blocking his path.

'What are you doing?' she says. 'Where are you going?'

'I'm going away,' Saif says. 'Away from you.'

'No!' Asya cries, stretching both arms out across the top of the stairs. 'No!'

'I'm going away,' he says, 'before I kill you.'

'I don't *care*,' she cries. 'I even *want* you to.'

'Get out of my way,' Saif says.

'No!'

'Get out of my way. If I push you you'll break your neck.'

'No! I'm not letting you go. Not like this.'

Saif moves forward and grips her upper arms, trying to push her to one side, but she clings to him.

'Saif, please, please don't go, Saif, I beg you –'

'Get *away*,' he says, trying to free himself. 'Get away from me – I don't want to *see* you –'

'Please please *please*,' Asya cries. She clings to any bit of him that she can. She slides down two steps and wraps her arms around his legs. 'Please please please,' she sobs. 'If you have to leave me, leave me tomorrow. Oh please, oh please, don't leave me now. Oh, Saif, you've got to understand, Saif, I love you –'

'Don't say that,' he cries, kicking, trying to free himself.

'OK, OK.' She holds on tight and wipes her face on his trouser leg. 'I won't – I won't say *anything*. Only you can't go away like this. You've been driving, you've been travelling all day. Just stay tonight and if tomorrow you still want to go I promise, I promise I won't say one word to stop you. I'll never *ever* ask you for anything again, only don't go tonight –'

He stands still. 'I can't bear to be with you,' he says quietly. 'I can't bear to look at you.'

'You don't have to be with me,' she weeps. 'You don't have to *see* me. I'll go downstairs –'

'I can't stay here –'

'Saif, please Saif, you don't have to – the bed in the spare room is made up –'

'You'd already planned on tucking me away there?'

'No, no, no, I hadn't. You can sleep in my bed –'

'I don't want to come anywhere near you.'

'Then use the spare room – but stay.'

'Let go of my legs.'

'Will you stay?'

'*Let go of my legs.*'

Asya lets go and Saif walks back into the kitchen. He pours himself another drink. Then he turns and sees her sitting on the top step looking at him.

'Go away,' he says. 'Just get out of my sight.'

Asya stands up and walks slowly down the stairs wiping her face with her hands. In the hall, she feels in his coat pocket and gets out the car-keys, holding them very tight so that they don't make a noise. Then she takes the front-door key from the lock.

When she goes to bed she leaves the door of her bedroom slightly ajar and puts all the keys under her pillow.

Next day: 3 p.m.

Asya turns around in her chair and looks at him. He has been sitting at the head of the kitchen table since the morning. The bottle of whisky stands at his elbow. The full ashtray next to it. He hasn't spoken and she hasn't dared to speak – except to offer him coffee once and toast once. He had refused both.

Through the window beyond him, the sky is flat and pale. Inside, the room glows with the light from the two lamps and the fire burns in the stove. Asya wonders dully that the world should be so unchanged, so unaffected by what is happening here; to them. And then she wonders at her own dullness – that she should sit here, thinking these thoughts – with everything seeming to her so far away – so unreal – even Saif, her own beloved Saif, sitting there at the kitchen table – she might be looking at a statue of him for all she feels – for all she is doing about him, about his misery. What's the matter with her, she thinks, can't she *see* him, can't she *feel* his pain? She sits and watches him as though he were on film, but if this was a film she'd be crying; she'd be sitting in the cinema snivelling and liking the feel of the tears on her face because they meant she was so sensitive. And Gerald – she had watched *him* suffer too, he must be suffering now – she grips the arms of her chair and stares at Saif and prays, please, God, let me feel his pain, let me think his thoughts and feel his pain; whatever he is feeling let me feel it too – but when she loosens her grip she is still there: marooned within herself. She gets slowly to her feet.

'Saif,' she says. She stands by the kitchen table. 'Saif. We have no more teabags – or milk – or bread – or anything. I have to go and get some. Will you come with me?'

He does not answer.

She bends closer. 'Saif, will you come with me?'

He shakes his head without looking at her.

Asya turns and walks down the steps. But she can't leave him here on his own like this. What if after she'd gone he wanted her? What if he needed her? What if he thought maybe she was meeting –

She goes back up the steps.

'Saif, please,' she says. 'I don't think I can drive.'

He looks up. 'Why? What's the matter with you?'

'I – I feel very shaky. And I can't see terribly well. Please, will you come?'

He leans on the table and stands up. Without looking at her he leaves the kitchen and walks down the stairs.

Outside, Asya glances round quickly. He wouldn't be here, would he? Waiting? Watching the cottage? If he'd been looking through the uncurtained windows last night he'd have seen her throwing herself at Saif's feet, begging him not to go. But there is no one there. The path to the bridge stretches empty before them.

In the rented car Asya pats the seat and says, 'It had to be a Daimler?'

Saif shrugs. 'It was what they had,' he says. He eases the car into first gear. 'Where do you want to go?'

'Do you think we could just go for a little drive?' says Asya. 'We don't need much shopping. Any small shop will do.'

It is only when they cross the bridge and reach the end of the path and turn right on to the road that she is sure Gerald Stone is not there – for the moment.

Saif swings the car into the parking bay, pulls up the handbrake and turns off the engine. He gets out of the car and slams his door.

Asya winds a big shawl around her head and Mina's scarf around her neck and then fastens up her coat. She pulls on her woollen gloves. Outside, she can see the breath steaming from his mouth as he stands by the rails looking out to sea. He keeps his hands in his pockets. She gets out of the car, slams the door, pulls her head down between her shoulders and shivers in the cold. He starts to walk and she follows him.

Two years. It's been just over two years since last they were here together. The sea is still out: still a dreary expanse of mud and stones. And down on the beach this time there is no stone-throwing figure with a leaping dog; just one old couple, trussed up in grey windcheaters, bumping gently against each other as they progress slowly across the mud. Time was, thinks Asya, when she would have wondered about them – wondered what the home they would return to was like. If they had grandchildren who lived nearby. What they would do with the rest of their day. What it must feel like to be so old. Do they think about what it had been like when they were young? Now she does not wonder. Her eye rests on them neutrally – unreal figures in an unreal day.

Saif turns on to the pier and Asya follows him. If he finds it painful to see her she'll stay out of his sight. She doesn't want to cause him any more – suddenly she notices: his walk has lost its spring. That little bounce which she'd loved so much. It's gone. Now he walks like everybody else, his whole foot falling, rising – like everybody else. She hurries to catch up with him and tucks her gloved hand into his arm. But his arm is stiff and unyielding and when they reach the end of the pier he shakes it and steps away from her.

With the toe of his shoe Saif dislodges a pebble that had got stuck between two planks and kicks it down on to the beach below.

Asya shivers. He looks at her briefly.

'Are you cold?' he asks. 'Have you had enough?'

Asya shakes her head.

'Saif,' she says after a moment.

'What?'

'Don't you think you should call someone in Damascus?'

Saif stands with his hands in the pockets of his coat, looking out to sea.

'We agreed,' he says. 'We made an agreement. And you said it would be all right.'

He speaks sadly and slowly, as though she weren't there. Asya is silent.

'You couldn't wait,' he says. 'You couldn't wait. The first guy that came along you forgot everything –'

'That isn't fair,' says Asya.

'Isn't that what happened?' he says.

'No,' says Asya. 'No. I waited until it seemed I was going to wait all my life for something that was never going to happen –'

'We were going to be together –'

'When?' Asya says. '*When?*'

'When you'd finished your lousy Ph.D.'

'And what would that have been like?' Asya asks. 'Just like the times we were together in all those hotels, only longer. You didn't do what you promised,' she says. 'You promised that the bits we were together would be the real bits –'

'You're blaming me?' he says. 'Blaming me for doing my best for you? You think I was having fun out there in Damascus? You think I wanted to be out there –'

'No –' says Asya.

'Jesus Christ, I'm out there in the desert working twenty hours a day, putting my life on the line, mixing with ass-holes and shits I wouldn't mind strangling with my own hands, while my wife is going for woodland walks with some layabout with nothing better to do, and she blames me for not showing up on the dot once a month to hold her hand –'

'It isn't that –' says Asya.

'What the hell is it then?'

'It was never that. I would have waited twenty years if for five minutes when we were together we were really together.'

'So we didn't fuck,' he says.

Asya winces, and then she says, 'It isn't even –'

'Whose fault was that?' he says. 'Don't you even remember whose fault that is? You're going to lay *that* at my door?'

'We didn't *talk*,' cries Asya. 'When you phoned me from London you'd switch on the television before you called me –'

'You grudge me –'

'I grudge you nothing. You needn't have phoned – you could have phoned at some other point – when you didn't want to watch television –'

'Listen, you try saying this to any sane person: my husband used to phone me while he was watching television so I decided to go and fuck a stranger. Try telling that to one of your aunts –'

627

'You make it sound absurd –'

'It *is* absurd –'

'On its own, yes. But it's part of everything. We – we did *nothing* –'

'Nothing? We did nothing?'

'Any time I mentioned something we could do you said you'd done it already. You'd done *everything* already. You closed the world to me –'

'I *showed* you the world. I –'

'You took me with you like you'd take a magazine – no, not even like you'd take a magazine: you would *read* a magazine, you would flick through it and look at the *pictures* –'

'You showed *him* the pictures, did you?'

'Please. There's no need to talk like –'

'Like what? Like I'm talking to a whore?'

'Saif –'

'Cut it out. We've had the pure act. Five years of it. Five years of you turning on the taps every time you went to the fucking *loo*, for Christ's sake –'

'What on *earth* does that have to do with –'

'Five years of thinking she's young, she's fragile –'

'I *wanted* you –'

'And all the time she's just waiting for some stud to come along –'

'Saif,' Asya says. 'Please, *please* believe me. There wasn't a moment – not a moment – when I didn't love you –'

'Don't,' he says. 'Don't give me that shit.'

'It isn't shit,' says Asya. 'It's the truth.'

'Sure,' he says. 'You've got your legs wrapped round the bastard and you're loving me. *Shit.*'

Asya bends over the railings and sobs into her hands.

Saif watches her with his hands in his pockets, then he turns.

'It's starting to rain,' he says.

When she doesn't move, he says, 'Are you coming? Or do you want to walk back?'

Saif is sitting at the table with his head in his hands. Asya stands at the top of the stairs and looks at him. She's never seen him sit with nothing before: no drink, no book, no magazine, no blue squared paper – nothing. She says, 'Shall I make you something? A coffee?'

He lifts his head.

'What?'

'Shall I make you a coffee?'

'No,' he says. 'Thank you.'

He sits upright for a moment, then his head sinks once again into his hands. She runs over to the table and hugs his shoulders.

'Saif, Saif, darling –'

He straightens up. 'Don't,' he says. 'Don't do that.'

Asya removes her arms and takes two steps back. Above the round neck of his navy sweater the collar of his white shirt looks fresh and crisp. Behind him, the room is unchanged. The sofa and chairs sit empty, the rug lies quiet and fluffy, the stove is burning low. The rain comes down outside the windows. Asya walks across to the stove and puts a log gently down on the red embers.

'Will you tell me something?' Saif asks.

'Of course,' Asya says, turning. 'What?'

'When did you decide to do it?'

Asya stands in the middle of the living-room and says nothing.

'When did you decide to do it? *How* did you decide to do it?'

Asya says, 'I was lonely.'

'You were lonely?'

'I was –'

'So what's the big deal? *I'm* lonely. Everybody's lonely. My mother's mostly lonely; she doesn't go round picking up strangers –'

'I was *deep down* lonely. Lonely for *you*. I've been lonely for you since we got engaged –'

'Don't give me –'

'Everything was all wrong –'

'So you fixed it. And now it's all just fine only I haven't noticed.' Wearily, he rubs his forehead with his hand.

'Saif, please. Are you really asking or –'

'You think you're lonely here? You should try being in Damascus.'

'Saif, if this had happened to *you* I'd –'

'You'd have understood.'

'Yes, I would. I *would* have. Because of the way things have been –'

'So I might as well have screwed around. I might as well have screwed Ummu Salma –'

'It *could* have happened –'

'I could have done but I didn't. Because I chose not to. And I want to know how you chose, actually *chose*, to do it.'

'It just happened,' Asya says.

'It just happened? Just like that?'

Asya says nothing.

'It just happened that you stuck a knife in my back? It just happened that –'

'I didn't stick –'

'– you betrayed me. That you lay down and opened your legs to some bastard you hardly knew?' He stands up.

'I did not betray you,' Asya says.

'Who is he?'

'He doesn't matter –'

629

'Who is he? I want to know his name.'

'Why?' Asya cries. 'Why? I've already told you he doesn't –'

'*He* knows *my* name.' Saif slams his hand down on the table. '*I* want to know *his* name.'

'Gerald. Gerald Stone.'

'An Englishman. You fucked an Englishman.'

Asya turns and sits in an armchair.

'You fucked an Englishman,' Saif says again.

Asya looks at him: he stands by the kitchen table looking like a sleepwalker.

'Would it have been better,' she asks, 'if he'd been Egyptian? Or Iraqi? Or Palestinian?'

'You didn't know him,' Saif says. 'You can't have known him. You fucked an Englishman you didn't know –'

'Saif,' Asya says, 'why are you going *on* about this? Why does it *matter* whether I knew him? You'd rather it had been a friend? You'd rather it had been Mario?'

'Shut up,' he shouts. '*Shut up.* Don't even mention Mario –'

'You should have seen it coming – you *must* have seen it coming –'

'Don't *dare* mention Mario to me –'

'You even said, don't you remember –'

'Mario is my friend – Mario –'

'You said if I took a lover I should have the decency –'

'He knows about friendship – he knows about loyalty – he knows about honour – you don't deserve –'

'He's dead,' Asya says.

'What?' Saif says.

Asya watches him. 'Mario is dead,' she says. 'I got a letter – from Frederick – he died in a car crash.'

Saif turns away. He leans over a kitchen counter and puts his head against the cupboard above it. Asya watches his shoulders tremble. She stands up slowly and walks towards him.

'Saif?' she calls.

When she is next to him she puts her hand on his shoulder.

'Saif?' she says.

He shudders and moves away. He holds on to the edge of the kitchen sink and stands with his back to her.

'Saif?' she says.

'Go away,' he says. 'Just get away from me.'

Asya walks slowly to the top of the stairs. She walks down. When she gets to the dark hall she stops. She stands by the chest of drawers and waits. After a while she starts hearing sobs: terrible, rasping, suppressed sobs, separated by minutes of silence. She climbs slowly up the stairs. His glasses are lying face-down on the table and his face is covered by his

630

hands. When he lifts his head his face is wet and soft. Without his glasses he can only be seeing her very vaguely: a fuzzy sort of blob –

He says, 'Why didn't you die? Why didn't you die instead of killing the baby?'

Asya turns and walks back down the steps and into her bedroom.

Asya does not know how long she has been in bed. She does not know whether she has slept or just lain in the darkness with her eyes closed. She hears a soft sound at her door and opens her eyes. Saif stands in the doorway, swaying. Asya lies still. He takes a few steps into the room and stops. He stands, a dark shape in the darkness, then he moves again until his legs bump into the bed. Asya shrinks away.

'Will you let me in?' he asks, and his voice is uncertain. 'Sweetie, will you let me in.'

'No,' Asya says, lying still.

He turns and walks slowly, unsteadily, out of the room. When he turns the corner and she cannot see him any more the pain in her heart jolts Asya out of bed. She runs out into the hall and into his room as he falls on to the bed.

'Oh, Saif,' Asya breathes. 'Oh, Saif.' She sits on the edge of the narrow bed and puts her face against his back. 'Oh, Saif,' she whispers. 'Oh, my darling, oh, my love.' She unlaces his shoes and draws them off. She peels off his socks. She undoes the belt and the waistband of his trousers and draws the single quilt over him. She whispers endearments and strokes his back and his shoulders and kisses his head gently and holds his forehead in her hand until he falls asleep. When he turns on to his back and takes up the whole of the narrow bed she curls up on the floor at his side. When he moves and his arm dangles over the edge of the bed she takes hold of his hand. She lies on the carpet and holds on to his hand all night.

Next day: 5 p.m.

Saif puts a log on the fire. He squats in front of the stove for a while and then he turns. Asya is doing the washing-up.

'Where,' he says, 'did you do it?'

At the sink Asya pauses. She pushes her hands in their red rubber gloves under the soapy water. They had managed to get through today until now. They had done ordinary things and left each other alone –

'I'm curious,' Saif says. 'Tell me.'

Outside it is still raining. Who would think that spring is almost here? Yet the rain must be helping it along; soaking all those little buds on the hedgerows –

'Will you answer me, please, when I speak to you?'

'I don't think,' Asya says, looking into the soapy water, 'that this is a good idea.'

She hears the lighter strike. After a moment he says, 'But it was a good idea to fuck him.'

Asya takes the last plate out of the water. She stacks it on top of the two others on the side. She fishes out a fork and rubs it with the sponge.

'I want to know where you did it.'

'Why?' Asya asks.

'What?' he says.

'Why?' Asya says again.

'So I know what to imagine,' he says.

'Saif —' Asya says shaking her gloved hands and turning round. 'This —'

'I can't quite see Her Majesty going into some flea-pit in town —'

'Please don't do this,' Asya says, looking at him.

'Tell me,' he says. 'Humour me. Humour your old hubby. Please?'

Asya dries her gloves on a kitchen towel. She does not take them off. She might still get to finish the washing-up.

'Where did you do it?' he asks. 'Did you go to his room with all the chaps on the corridor knowing what you were going for? Did you?'

'No,' says Asya.

'So it was the flea-pit,' he says.

'No,' says Asya.

'Where?' he says.

Asya does not answer.

'Not *here*?' he says. 'Here?'

Asya takes off one glove and puts her hand to her neck. Her neck aches. Everything aches. It must be sleeping on the floor.

Saif laughs.

'You invited him in for coffee — and you let him fuck you.' He shakes his head. 'Here in this house. In *my* house.'

Asya watches him.

After a moment he says, 'What else did he do — apart from fuck my wife in my house? Drive my car? Try on my clothes?'

'No,' says Asya.

'Drink my whisky? Leaf through my books?'

'Saif, please,' says Asya. 'I know there's really nothing I can say that would make it less awful —'

'Read my letters?'

'I kept everything away from him. I put everything downstairs —'

'I've seen it. I'm sleeping there, remember, in the mausoleum you made for me —'

'Saif, please, you can't turn that into —'

'Everything packed away in there as though I were already dead. Was that what you wanted? For me to be dead and out of the way —'

632

'Saif, I sat there and loved you and wrote you letters. I lived there –'

'Except, of course, when you were being fucked by him. Don't make me laugh.'

'Why do you go *on* like this? Why do you go *on*? Don't you *want* to understand –'

'I understand. Of course I understand. I understand the whole fucking low, vile, disgusting –'

'You don't. You're seeing only one *bit* of it. You *insist* on seeing only one bit of it. You don't know what it felt like –'

'I sure don't,' he says. 'I sure don't. But we can fix that –'

'Saif –'

'You can invite him back and he can fuck me too. Then I'll *really* know what it felt like.'

'Oh,' cries Asya. 'Oh.' And runs out of the kitchen and down the stairs, her left hand still encased in the rubber glove.

When she feels Saif's presence she sits up on the bed and faces him. He looks around the room.

'So,' he nods, 'this is where it happened. What did you do?' he says. 'Did he carry you in or did you walk in on your own two feet?'

'I'm through,' Asya says. 'I'm not going to answer any more. Nothing is any use any more.'

He looks at the bedside table.

'You burned incense,' he says, holding up the small brass incense-burner.

Asya's heart stops. How could she? How could she have overlooked it?

'I might have known,' he says. 'It's the kind of thing that would appeal to you.'

His voice sounds amused. He looks at Asya, then he turns and hurls the incense-holder at the window and there is a great crash. For a second Asya's mind splits in two: one half remembers Uncle Sidki throwing the ashtray at Chrissie, the other imagines Gerald Stone crouched under the bedroom window – zapped by his own incense-burner – then she says, 'You've broken the window.'

'Is that all you have to say? "You've broken the window"?'

Asya is silent.

'I've broken the window,' he says. 'I'll pay for it.'

For a moment they look at each other, then he turns and leaves the room. There is silence in the hall. Asya hears him walk up the stairs, then she hears him walk down. She hears the front door open and slam shut, then she hears the engine rev up.

'No!' she cries. 'No!'

She starts up from the bed and out into the hall. She opens the front door and runs out. She hammers hard on the car with her fists. She tries

633

a door but it is locked. She calls out his name and bangs on his window with her open hand. He does not look around. The car shudders to a start. It sends droplets of mud flying off the road, and then it is gone.

Asya runs a couple of paces after it, then stops. She stands on the muddy track in her bare feet and cries. Then, hugging herself, she turns back to the house. At the door she stops and wonders how she will get in and into the bathroom without getting mud all over the hall carpet. She kneels down and, raising her feet off the ground, crawls on hands and knees into the hall. She balances on her knees and one hand and pushes the door shut. Then she crawls into the bathroom. She gets into the bath and turns on the tap to wash her feet. She sits on the edge of the bath and shivers with cold while the warm water runs over her feet. Then she pulls her dress and her slip up over her head. She stands up to take her pants off and sits down in the bath. She puts the plug into the plug-hole and lies back. Her hair is wet and frizzy with rain so she doesn't have to worry about it. When the bath is full she turns off the taps and lies back again. Her hair floats round her face. She stares at the ceiling. Her mind can think enough to think that it is blank.

When the water cools she sits up and rubs some shampoo into her hair. Then she closes her nose with two fingers and falls back under the water. If she could stay – if she could just stay there; drown like Ophelia – only Ophelia was chaste – she rises sputtering and climbs out of the tub. As she dries herself she remembers the telephone. What if he should call her? What if he's calling now? She runs out into the hall. The bedroom door is open and the hall is cold with the wind coming in through the broken window. Asya kneels, shivering, and hunts behind the chest of drawers for the plug. Her hair gets in the way, falling in front of her eyes and dripping on her shoulders and on to the carpet. She holds it back with one hand and plugs in the phone with the other. Silence. She gets up. Her knees have left two wet patches on the carpet. She goes back into the bathroom and wraps a big towel around her head. She starts drying herself again with the other towel. The phone rings. She holds the towel around her and runs into the hall. But what if it isn't him? What if – she picks up the receiver and holds it silently to her ear. She hears a click and a woman's voice calling, 'England? Alo, England?'

'Yes?' shouts Asya.

'I have a call for you from Damascus.'

Another voice comes on the line, a man's voice.

'Alo?'

'Yes?' says Asya. 'Alo?'

'Can I speak to the mister?'

'I'm sorry, he's not here,' calls Asya. 'Can I help?'

'He is come back?'

634

'Yes,' calls Asya. 'Later.'

'You are the madame?'

'Yes,' calls Asya. 'We can speak in Arabic.'

'No,' he calls. 'No. You can tell him. Tell him the situation is dangerous. Tell him he must to come back –'

'Who are you?' calls Asya.

'I am a friend,' the voice shouts from far away. 'His friend. He will know. Tell him they are unhappy and the work it cannot go.'

'Yes,' calls Asya.

'I have tried before many times but it is difficult –'

'I'm sorry.'

'Sorry? I cannot hear –'

'I am sorry,' Asya shouts.

'Tell him I cannot to go much longer. Tell him he must to come back.'

'Please,' Asya shouts. 'Please, can I come with him?'

'You? No, no, madame. It will be very bad. Very dangerous. Say I tell him he does not come back soon he does not come back never. And he better watch out. Tell him also –'

The line goes dead.

Asya says, 'Hello? Hello?' a few times and waits, then she hangs up. Her teeth are chattering now with the cold. She runs into the bedroom and gets her woollen dressing-gown, then she runs out and closes the door. In the bathroom she gets into the dressing-gown and hangs the towel on the towel-rail. With her head still wrapped up she goes upstairs to the living-room, throws a new log on the fire and sits down on the floor in front of it.

Later, when she hears the car roar up to the house and the door slam, she jumps into a crouching position. She hadn't locked it, oh, she hadn't locked it. Please God, *please* let it be him. Let it not be anyone else, *please* – she crouches, watching the corner that leads to the stairs. As Saif turns the corner she sinks back into a sitting position.

'You're washing your hair?' he asks. 'Why are you washing your hair?'

'I – it got rained on. I didn't know what to do with myself when you'd gone.'

'So you wash your hair.' He nods. He walks to the kitchen cupboard and pours himself a drink.

'Saif –' Asya says.

'Who else?' he says. 'Who else knows?'

'No one,' says Asya. 'Saif, there was a –'

'Does your mother know?'

'No.'

'Who else?'

'No one. Saif, there was –'

'I don't believe that.'

'We – I haven't been seeing anyone. There's no one –'

'You've been seeing your professor.'

'He wouldn't know, and besides he's gone away –'

'So you just holed up here and screwed all day.'

'Saif, please, I'm trying to tell you there was a call for you from Damascus.'

'Why did you plug the phone in?' he says. 'Were you trying to call lover-boy?'

'No,' Asya says. 'I thought *you* might call me. And the moment I plugged it in practically the call came through. It was a man and he didn't actually mention your name or tell me his, but he said he was a friend and you would know.'

'Sami,' Saif says.

'He said you had to go back.'

Saif takes a pack of Rothmans out of his pocket. He takes out a cigarette and throws the pack on the table. He fishes out his lighter and lights the cigarette.

'He said the work isn't going without you.'

Saif gives her his old, wide grin.

'Of course it wouldn't,' he says.

'He said "they" were very unhappy.'

'Sure,' he says. 'They would be.'

'Saif, who are "they"?'

'They're a bunch of ass-holes.'

'You said they were mean – and dangerous.'

'Yeah,' he says. 'They're still ass-holes.'

'He said if you didn't go back soon you wouldn't be able to go back at all. He said you'd have to watch out.'

'They can go fuck themselves,' Saif says.

'You can't do this –'

'Don't tell me what I can't do.'

Asya is silent. After a bit she says, 'He insisted on speaking in English.'

'Yeah,' he says. 'That's how sophisticated they are out there. They think if you speak English the censor won't know what you're saying. And they're probably right. They can go fuck themselves. Unplug the phone.'

'But Saif, he hadn't finished what he was trying to say –'

'He'd finished. Unplug the phone.'

Asya stands up and goes downstairs. She unplugs the phone and goes upstairs again. The towel around her hair is getting loose. She puts up her hands to tighten it.

'When,' Saif says, 'did you decide to do it?'

'Do what?' Asya asks.

636

'Let him fuck you.'

'Saif, please –' Asya begins.

'It's a straight question. Give me a straight answer. Come here and talk to me. Come and sit down.'

Asya sits in a chair at the kitchen table.

'When did you decide to let him fuck you?'

'It wasn't like that –'

'The hell it wasn't like that.' His voice is normal, conversational. 'We're not talking spiritualist shit now, are we? A guy has a prick, a dick, a dong, he wants to fuck you with it. When did you decide to let him?'

'Saif –'

'Here,' he says. He puts his glass down, reaches for his briefcase, opens it and pulls out a pad of blue squared paper. He throws it on the table in front of her. He takes out his Gold Cross biro, opens it and puts it down on top of the paper. 'Draw me a flowchart,' he says.

She looks up at him.

'Draw me a flowchart of your decision-making process. Go on.' He sits down in a chair next to her.

Asya looks at him. 'If you really want to know,' she says. 'If you really want to know about what was going on in my mind, then I'll show you.'

She gets up and walks downstairs. When she comes back she is carrying a bundle of envelopes. There are eleven in all – all sealed and numbered and fat. She puts them down in front of Saif and sits down, tightening the towel around her hair again.

'What are these?' he asks.

'These are the letters I wrote you. They are as honest and as truthful as I could make them. And I promise they won't hurt you any more than you're hurting already.'

'When did you write them?'

'All the time.'

'After you'd started –'

'Saif, I beg you –' She puts her hand on his arm. 'I beg you to give me a chance, to give *us* a chance –'

'You'd get up from your sweaty bed and then you'd write to me?'

'Saif, I've put everything there; everything that matters –'

'And you seriously expect me to sit here and read your post-coital ramblings?'

'You don't have to read them now. You can do what you like. Only *please* –'

Saif stands up. He picks up the letters and walks into the living-room. When he gets to the other end he bends down and puts them in the stove. Asya watches as the flames spring up, bright orange with yellow and blue tips, and the envelopes curl and blacken. Saif walks back to the kitchen table and sits down.

637

'Now,' he says. 'Let's be serious. Draw me a flowchart.'

Asya puts her face in her hands. The towel slips to her shoulders and her head feels cold.

'I have to know,' he says. 'Draw me a flowchart.'

Asya pushes the pen and paper a little way from her.

'I can't.'

'Yes you can. You know how. I taught you, remember?'

'Saif, it isn't like that –' Asya feels the tears rolling down her face.

'The hell it isn't. Draw me a flowchart.'

'Saif, these things –'

'Draw me a flowchart.'

She flings the note-pad away from her and he immediately reaches out and grabs a handful of her hair. He pulls it so that she is forced to lean across the table, her head twisted to one side.

'You're hurting me.'

'Pick up the pen.'

'Saif, please –'

'Pick up the pen.'

He pulls at her hair, hard. Asya picks up the biro. He lets go of her hair and she straightens up and tosses it back over her shoulder and looks at him. His face is blank.

'Draw me a flowchart.'

Asya throws the pen from her hand and jumps up, pushing her chair back. He catches her arm.

'When did you decide to fuck him?'

'In September.'

His eyes flicker and the rigid line of his mouth softens. He stands up. He walks to the kitchen window and stands looking out. Then he says, 'But I was with you. We were together in August.'

'What does that mean, we were together?' Asya's voice rises and she speaks fast. 'What does it *mean*? I hung about in London while you did your work. We had a dreadful fight at Howard Hotel and I followed you to Uxbridge and hung around some more –'

'But I was here, *here*,' he says, looking round at the room.

'You were here for five days and we tiptoed round each other, never ever talking about any –'

He has stepped forward and the blow catches her around her waist. She bends over and gasps and holds on to the edge of the table. So that's what it feels like to be hit: one flash of pain and then the edge of it pulls back – leaving everything very still and silent. The towel slips to the floor and her hair is wet and cold around her neck and shoulders. She turns her head to look at Saif.

He looks surprised, almost shocked. But he meets her eyes and says, 'So you decide to go and fuck some bastard you hardly know.'

Asya holds the edge of the table and draws shallow breaths to try and avoid the pain in her side.

'We've been,' she says, 'through that bit already.'

Saif draws both hands across his face. He throws the butt of his cigarette into the ashtray. He walks across the room and sits on the arm of the sofa while Asya eases herself carefully into a kitchen chair. She lays her arms on the table and puts her head on them. So this is what it feels like to be hit: it feels good. It feels peaceful. It feels clean. It feels as if, for once, they've been in something together – engaged in the same act, not clawing at each other through a glass pane. It must have hurt him though: hitting his princess like that.

'You'd better dry your hair,' Saif says after a while. Asya does not move.

'Come on, Princess,' he says, 'you're going to catch cold.'

She hears him move and feels his hand gentle on her cold, wet hair.

'I can't,' she whispers, 'I can't bear to.'

'Come on,' he says, 'I'll help you. Stand up now. You'll feel better when your hair's all – nice. You know you will.'

Asya raises her head from the table but when she tries to stand the pain makes her double over.

'I think,' she says, 'we've broken something.'

Saif puts his arm around her and holds her till she stands straight.

'Is it very bad?' he asks.

'Yes,' she says softly. 'Particularly when I breathe.'

'We'll get someone to look at it,' he says.

'What is it, Saif?' Asya asks. 'What's just in *there*, next to my lungs?'

'It's probably a rib. Come. Let's get you downstairs.'

Asya leans on him all the way down the stairs. At every step she feels a stab of pain – and feels his arm tighten around her.

'The bedroom's so cold,' she says.

'Why?' he asks.

'Because of the broken glass.'

'I'll fix it up with something,' he says. 'Tomorrow we'll get someone to change it.'

Seated in front of the mirror Asya raises her arms to her head and drops them again.

'I can't,' she says, 'I can't. Oh, I'm so tired.'

'I'll do it for you then,' Saif says, turning away from the window. 'Give me the comb.'

He stands behind her and Asya leans against the back of the chair and closes her eyes. Then she opens them again and watches in the mirror while he separates a too thick strand of hair, winds it untidily round a roller and then tries several times to pin it in place. When he leaves it, it stands loose and wobbly on her head. She moves her head and the roller comes tumbling down followed by a long tress of hair. In the mirror he looks perplexed and disappointed. Asya laughs and then bends over and gasps as the pain hits her again. Saif leans over her and holds her head against his chest.

'I'm sorry,' he whispers to her, 'I'm sorry, Princess.'

'Here, give me the comb,' Asya breathes after a moment. 'You're hopeless. I'll do it.'

'Can you manage?' he asks.

'Yes,' she says, 'better than you anyway.'

'OK,' he says. 'I'll get you some tea.'

'Yes please,' she says, and as he leaves the room she says, 'And a biscuit?'

Next day: 6 p.m.

Saif takes a mouthful of tea, picks up a slice of cake and looks at it, then puts it down again. He takes off his glasses. He leans his elbows on the table and presses his forehead with his fingers. Asya picks the glasses up from the table and breathes on them. She takes a paper napkin and starts to polish them.

'I'm really worried about your work, darling,' she says. 'Even if you don't like the people there, you've stuck it out so far. You really ought to finish the job.'

'They can stuff their money,' Saif says with his eyes still closed.

'I'm not thinking so much about the money,' Asya says. 'Both you and Sami have said that these people are dangerous –'

'I don't want to talk about this.'

'OK. But you're building a business; a business based on *your name*. That means you can't walk out and leave a job unfinished.'

Saif opens his eyes. 'Are you trying to get rid me?' he says.

'Of course I'm not,' says Asya. 'I'll come with you if you'll take me. And if you won't, I'll come with you as far as London. I'll find a tiny flat or a room and I'll just work there until you come back.'

Saif stands up.

'The thing is,' he says, 'I just can't understand how *you* could have done that to *me*. I thought, I really *believed* you were my friend.'

'I *am* your friend –'

'You let a man into my house. You let him live here. You let him fuck you. And you're my friend?'

'Saif –'

'I phone from the middle of the fucking Jordanian desert and my "friend" answers like she's never heard of me. And why? Because some stud is out there waiting to shove his prick into her fanny and she can't wait to get back to him –'

'It isn't true –'

'What isn't true? You didn't answer me like I was the man from the moon? Time and time again and I think, give her time – let her finish her work –'

'Saif, I beg you. It just isn't true –'

'What's true, then? Tell me, tell me what's true.'

'What's true is that I love you.'

'You love me but you fuck him.'

Asya is silent.

'Answer me!' Saif shouts.

'You didn't – you wouldn't talk to me –'

'And he talked to you, did he? The stud? He could talk as well as fuck? That's terrific. What was he doing up here?'

Asya says nothing.

'Come on, tell me; what was he doing?'

'I want to leave him out of this.'

'He can't *be* left out – what was he doing?'

'We could have been having this argument any time in the last four years – except you wouldn't – he doesn't matter –'

'What was he doing?'

'He was doing a Master's.'

'He was doing a Master's in what?'

'Business Studies.' Asya puts her head in her hands.

'Business Studies? Jesus! I thought you'd go for a mad scientist or a poet with lilies in his hair – Business Studies! What sort of Business Studies?'

'Marketing,' she says quietly.

'Marketing? An MA in Marketing? How could you? How *could* you?'

Asya lifts up her head and looks at Saif.

'What does it matter what he was doing? It was just –'

'Sure: it was just what he did for a living – except he didn't because he was living off me and that's how come he had time to do all this talking I keep hearing about –'

'He was not living off you –'

The bruised rib jabs at Asya's side as she stands up.

'No? What was he living on then? He slept here. He ate here. He paid you board and lodging did he? Did he even offer to do the shopping? No, I bet he didn't. So? You two lived on the thirty pounds a month you'd have left over from your grant if you paid the rent? One pound a day? You wouldn't begin to know how to live on –'

'You know you've always kept on about your money being *our* money –'

'Until you use it to fatten up some stud, sure –'

'Please will you *stop* talking like that?' Asya suddenly slams her hand down on the table. 'I've had *enough* of you talking like that –'

Saif reaches out and takes hold of her hair. He pulls it, and as she bends forward the back of the kitchen chair presses against the pain in her side.

'Saif –' she gasps.

'You've had *enough*?' he asks. 'I thought you couldn't *get* enough of talking? Or were we just talking about fucking all the time?'

'Saif,' Asya whispers, 'the chair is hurting me – it's exactly on the spot that –'

Saif lets go of her hair. He puts his hand on her waist and pushes her hard into the back of the chair. Asya chokes. She feels as if there should be blood gushing out of her mouth but there is nothing. When she tries to let go of the chair she crumples slowly to her knees.

7.25 p.m.

She hears his footsteps coming up the stairs. When she looks up he is standing at the entrance to the living-room. He is shaved and showered. He wears dark trousers, a white shirt, a plain wine-red tie and his beige linen jacket.

'The Spartans,' he says, 'combed their hair before they went to Marathon.'

Asya looks at him. He looks at her, but she knows he does not see her.

'Where are you going?' she asks.

He says nothing, but after a moment he turns and vanishes down the stairs.

Asya hears the front door slam. Then she hears the car door slam. She hears the engine starting up – and moving away. She still sits on the floor by the kitchen table.

Silence. The birds have gone to bed.

But what if he's out there? What if he's parked the car and is hoping she'll come looking for him? What if everything has suddenly become clear to him but he can't bring himself to come back? What if he's sitting in the car thinking, if she comes now everything will be all right? Asya gets slowly to her knees. She holds on to the leg of the table and levers herself to her feet. She leans on the chair and straightens her back as much as she can. She walks slowly across the kitchen and, leaning against the wall, she climbs down the stairs. In the hall she pushes her feet into some shoes and wraps a shawl around her shoulders and walks slowly out of the cottage. As far as she can see down the path there is no car. But he might have crossed the bridge. Asya walks down the path. She walks with a slight limp as she tries not to jolt her left side. She keeps her breathing shallow. He might have crossed the bridge and come to where the path forks out and, not particularly wanting to take either road, he might have stopped. And if while he's sitting in the car she goes to him he might look up and see her. *Really* see her – and he might lean over and open the passenger door, and as she got in he might

642

hold out his arms and she could just slide into them and he would gather her to him and stroke her hair and say, 'It's all right, Princess, it's all right. Don't cry any more. It's all right.' And in his arms she would say, 'I'm sorry, I'm sorry, I'm sorry – but I *love* you,' and he would say, 'I know.'

At the bridge there is no car. Asya can see all the way down the road and there is no car. But she walks across the bridge anyway, and down the path to where it meets the asphalt branching to left and right. She stands at the fork for a bit and then she turns back. What a fine night it is. On the hump of the bridge she pauses and presses her hand to her side. She has to take a deep breath even though she knows how much it will hurt. She breathes – and the pain doubles her over the railings of the little bridge. When she opens her eyes, she can see nothing beneath her except a mass of darkness and moving shadows. But she can hear her stream running busily along. It must be quite full now with all the rain that's been falling. Holding on to the rails, she straightens herself slowly: up above, the sky is clear and soft and very far away and there are so many, many stars. When you first look you can only see the bigger, brighter ones, but after a while, if you keep looking, you can see that there are lots and lots more: tiny stars all twinkling away until – when you're *really* seeing it – the sky is absolutely covered in glimmering dots. And those little ones, thinks Asya, are probably as big and as bright and as important as the others – only they are further away.

It is after ten o'clock when the phone rings.

'Yes?' says Asya. 'Darling?'

'Oh, baby, baby, thank *God* I've found you,' says Gerald Stone.

'Gerald?' Asya says.

'Oh baby, this has almost killed me. I've been ringing you night and day.'

'. . .'

'Babe?'

'Yes?'

'Are you all right?'

'Yes, yes, I'm all right.'

'You don't sound all right.'

'I *am* all right.'

'You sound terrible.'

'. . .'

'Is he there?'

'No.'

'Where is he?'

'He's gone out.'

'OK. It's OK. Don't cry, babe. It's all going to be all right. Listen – are you listening?'

'Yes.'

'I'm coming over. I have to see you. I have to talk to you –'

'No, Gerald –'

'This can't go on, babe. I can't live without you.'

'No, Gerald, please –'

'You need me, babe. I can hear it in your voice –'

'No, please *listen* to me –'

'Yes?'

'Well – he – he'll probably come back soon and –'

'Then I'll be there –'

'No –'

'I'm not hiding out here any more. My place is with you and that's where I'm going to be. I'll see you soon.'

'Gerald –'

'I'll see you soon.'

Asya stands and holds the receiver. She wipes her face with the back of her hand. She mustn't cry because crying makes her breathe and breathing makes the pain worse. Don't panic, she tells herself: don't panic. He's in Canterbury, and he's driving a Mini, he can't get here before five hours. She'll go. She'll get into the car and drive away. But would that be fair? To bring him all the way here to stand in front of a locked door? She can't see him, she can't, she *can't*. And if Saif comes back? But Saif might not come back. But if he comes back? Don't panic. She's got time to think. He'll probably pack some clothes. Five hours, five hours *at least* from Canterbury to here – *if* he's in Canterbury. Oh no, no – he can't be calling from just down the road? From a motorway services? Oh no – holding on to her side she goes into the bedroom and finds her handbag. In her handbag she finds her diary and she finds the number she had last called at Christmas. She dials. Please God, please let him be there.

The ringing stops and a woman's voice says, 'Hello?'

'Is that Mrs Stone?'

'Yes.'

'I'm sorry to be phoning so late. This is Asya? Gerald's – friend?'

'Yes, I know.'

'I – Gerald just called me.'

'I know he did.'

'Is he there? Is he with you?'

'Do you want to speak to him?'

'No. I mean – Mrs Stone, he says he's coming up here – now.'

'Yes, he's gone into his room to pack.'

'Mrs Stone, please, I'm really sorry about all this – but please, could

644

you not let him come? I tried to tell him it wouldn't be a good idea. My husband is going to come back any minute and it would be just terrible –'

'I thought you had asked him to come up?'

'Oh no, no. I don't want him to. I really –'

'I see. Well, I'll tell him. But he's very set on going –'

'Oh please, Mrs Stone. Tell him I'll call him first thing in the morning. I promise. Only don't let him come.'

'All right. But will you make sure you do ring him in the morning? It's very hard on Gerald, you see, not knowing anything –'

'I promise: whatever happens I'll ring in the morning. Only don't let him come.'

'I won't. Don't worry now.'

'Thank you, Mrs Stone. Thank you for being so kind.'

'It's all right, dear. Look after yourself now.'

Asya limps to the front door and checks that it is locked and bolted. She goes upstairs and switches off all the lights. Downstairs she checks that the windows are locked and the curtains drawn. She digs out her hot-water bottle from the bottom of her wardrobe, takes it to the bathroom and fills it. When she sits down on her bed and presses its warmth to her side she knows she will not be able to stand up again. She eases off her shoes and lies down. She draws the quilt over her and holds the hot-water bottle tight. Tomorrow, if Saif does not come back, she'll go to London.

Next morning

'Hello? Mrs Stone? It's Asya.'

'Good morning, dear.'

'Good morning. Is Gerald still there?'

'Yes, he's asleep. He's had a very bad night. But he said I must wake him when you call –'

'No. No, Mrs Stone.' Asya drops her voice to an urgent whisper. 'We're going away. I can't talk. My husband is out in the car waiting for me –'

'But Gerald will be –'

'I really have to go –'

'Asya dear, listen: will you just call some time and let him know how you are? It's –'

'I can't – oh, I shouldn't speak to him –'

'You can just call *me*, dear, and let me know what's going on. And then I can tell him.'

'Yes,' says Asya. 'I'll do that. I'll call you. And, Mrs Stone, I'm sorry. And thank you.'

Asya picks out some clothes on their hangers and takes them to the car.

She collects her things from the bathroom and puts them into her case. She puts in her hair-rollers, hair-grips, two nightdresses and a dressing-gown and lots of underwear and stockings. She packs her make-up and empties her jewellery drawer into a plastic bag and puts that in the case. She dismantles the hood and the tripod legs of her hair-dryer and puts them into a bag. She goes up and down the stairs three times carrying her work and her typewriter. She switches off the boiler. She carries everything out to the car. By now she is limping again with the pain in her side. She needs to lie down and let it ease up a little. But she'll have to do that later – when she's out of here. She waits a moment by the phone. What if Saif should ring her? He'll think she hasn't plugged it in – either because she doesn't want him to call her, or because she's forgotten that he might. Asya hesitates. But she can't stay. She can't stay here any more. When she's in London she'll try the hotels where he stays. She'll leave him messages. And then what? What will she do? She doesn't know. She'll hole up somewhere and try to work – and she'll wait. She unplugs the phone.

Scene 7

Monday, 4 April 1977

London

'Saif,' Asya says, 'can I just ask you, please, what are you planning to do about the Syrians?'

Saif continues to stand at the open window.

'Nothing,' he says.

'It can't be nothing –' says Asya.

'It can,' Saif says. He reaches into his pocket and brings out a pack of Rothmans and a lighter. 'That, at least, can be however I want it.' He shakes out a cigarette and lights it.

'Please, Saif, this is just so wrong –'

'Wrong?' He turns and looks at her. 'You're going to tell me what's right and what's wrong?'

'Please, can't you forget about the quips for the moment? Forget that it's me talking to you? Those people can't even get in touch with you any more; they don't know where you are. Go back. I'm sure it can still be done –'

'Leave it.'

'Just finish it. Finish it and come back. Nothing will change. We can take it all up again from here if that's what you want –'

'Take what up? There's nothing to take up. It's all finished.'

'Then go. If it's all finished –'

'And what will *you* do? Go back to your stud? Or find yourself a new one, or what?'

'I'll do anything you want. I'll sit in this chair, I'll not leave this room until you come back. Only I can't bear for you to blow up your whole career like this –'

'*You* blew up my career. You blew *me* up the moment you opened your legs –'

'I swear – I swear by anything – I swear by the head of my mother that I didn't think it would matter so much to you –'

'What did you think I was then? A natural cuckold? A pimp?'

'Please, I beg you, I *know* you know what I mean. Five years ago I would have thought it would matter. Five years ago I wouldn't have done it –'

'And if you really thought it didn't matter, what were you doing in Athens? What was the point of *that* little farce?'

Asya makes a helpless movement with her hands. 'I was trying –'

'Getting my permission to get screwed? *After* the event?'

'Saif –'

'What the hell did you bring me there for? You'd already *done* it. You'd already *had* your arms around his pimply white back –'

'Stop it. Will you *please* stop it –'

'What? Am I wrong? It wasn't pimply?'

'Actually,' says Asya, 'it wasn't.'

'You bitch,' he says dully. 'You bitch.'

He turns back to the window.

Asya sits in the chair and waits. Beyond him, the leaves of the trees in the garden square rustle in the open window. Some time, he will turn around. He will turn around and say something. It might be, 'I'm going.' Or it might be another question. What if he took a deep breath – what if he turned and said, 'OK. Here's what we're going to do. We'll go to Damascus by separate flights. I'll have someone meet you at the airport. I'll get you another flat in the same building and no one will know you're there. What's happening with your work? You need to analyse your data? I'll teach you. I taught you how to draw flowcharts, remember? I'll finish my job, you'll finish your thesis and we'll come back here to hand it in. We'll take it from there, OK?' The fantasy does not for a moment unclench the vice that grips her heart, but she'd go – oh she'd go; she'd do *anything* –

'That cable you got in Athens – it was from him?'

Saif turns from the window.

'Yes,' says Asya.

'And you just picked it up – just like that – and put it in your handbag?'

'What would you have me do?' cries Asya. 'What on earth would you have me do? The guy's handing me a cable – and you're standing there – of course I took it and put it in my handbag –'

'How were you able do that? To say, "It's nothing important"?'

'It *was* nothing important –'

'*He* thought it was important – our hero – important enough to cable you while you were with your husband. Or didn't he even know I was there?'

'Of course he knew you were there –'

'And he thought it was OK – you *let* him think it was OK to cable you while you were with me? "Don't worry about him. It's only my husband –"?'

'I didn't let him think anything –'

' "He doesn't matter" –'

'Saif, please. I thought it was wrong of him to send –'

'Good. I'm glad you managed to think *something* he did was wrong.'

'Saif, please, we've been –'

'What did it say?'

'What?'

'The cable. What did it say that was so important?'

'It didn't say anything.'

'What was in it? What were the words in it?'

'Do we really have to –'

'What were the words in it?'

' "I need you." '

' "I need you"?'

'Yes.'

'What a *jerk*. "I need you." But then you'd been out of range of his prick for two whole days.'

Saif turns suddenly and faces out of the room. Asya shifts in the one armchair. Outside, a car engine starts up. A girl's voice shrieks with sudden laughter.

Our relationship stabilised. I had found her in the flat she had taken in Beaufort Gardens. A tiny flat – with 'her' money. She said, 'I'm taking nothing more from you.' And where had 'her' money come from? On her government scholarship she was going to live next door to Harrods? I rang the bell, and when she heard my voice on the entryphone she let me in. At the door I asked, 'Is he

648

here?' and she shook her head. I walked in past her. One room; a bedsit with a couch in the corner, a writing bureau by the window pretending to a sort of shabby elegance. A table with her typewriter, an obviously untouched stack of papers, five blue card-index boxes, one armchair. A kitchen in a cupboard. A bathroom. At least it was all muted greens and greys – but all the same –

'So the Princess has developed a taste for slumming?'

She did not answer. She looked pale, and her face was thinner than I remembered it. In her bare feet she was small.

'So this is the happy love-nest? This is what you prefer to Duke's?'

'He doesn't come here.'

'Why not?'

'He doesn't know where it is.'

'Why not?'

'I haven't told him.'

'Why not?'

'I just need to be on my own for a while.'

'Ah! So that's what Her Highness wants now? It's not "communication" any more, but "solitude". Would you like me to leave?'

'No.'

That was not how I had meant it to be. But that was how it turned out. I kept my room at Duke's but I was always with her. Hadn't that been her complaint? That I was never with her? That I did not 'know' her? I sought to know her. I could not leave her alone.

That first evening we went to Mr Chow's. We ate in silence. I remember I was mainly thinking of Mario. Mario and two summers ago when we ate here so often and what it had all looked like then. Maybe she was too. Or maybe she was thinking about him. Thinking about him and how he couldn't afford to take her there. Maybe that was what she was thinking. And deciding to stay with me. Would she have thought like that? I don't know. That was what I was finding out: that I didn't know her.

We did the things we'd done before. We ate in restaurants. She still laughed at my jokes. We went to the movies. We even went to the zoo.

She was watching the tiger prowl half-heartedly malignant around his enclosure and I was watching her back and remembering how it had used to feel to bury my face in that long black hair and how cool its top layers felt but how when you burrowed into it close to her scalp it would always be warm and scented with her own particular smell. She turned round: she looked sad, and her mouth moved as she said something, and I saw it close around a pink uncircumcised penis. I saw the penis slide up so that the hanging testicles were pressed to her lips and her nose was buried in the curly yellow tufts, and I saw white hands holding her head, the fingers threaded through her hair urging her to move faster, faster – I turned away. She caught up with me and pushed her hand through my arm and we walked in silence until I was able to say, 'Did you?'

'Did I what?'

'Did you go down on him?'

She didn't take her arm away; just closed her eyes for a moment as we walked and put her forehead against the sleeve of my jacket.

I said, 'Did you?'

'Saif, please –' she murmured against my sleeve. I could have steered her into a lamp-post: her steps just followed mine.

I said, 'Did you suck him off?'

She lifted her head and opened her eyes. She took her arm away and stopped walking. She looked at me.

'Why do you go on like this? What do the details matter?'

I said, 'I need to know.'

She said, 'No. No, I didn't.'

I said 'You're lying.'

She pushed her hands into the pockets of her raincoat and walked on alone. Of course I didn't know whether to believe her.

This was how it was. We fought. Or rather, I fought and she occasionally answered. I told myself to let it go. I told myself that she'd been vulnerable, that maybe he'd drugged her or doped her and she was too ashamed to say. That maybe he'd even forced her and, alone with him in the cottage with no one around for miles, she had been afraid. And then, once it was done, she'd been paralysed by guilt and shame and hadn't been able to get out. I told myself that maybe Athens had been a cry for help and I should have taken her with me to Damascus – but of course I couldn't have. I told myself all this over and over again. I was trying to remember her. To remember her as she'd been before this happened. To remember her walking down the white library steps with her blue clipboard, or hurrying to meet me in Alexandria, not daring even to hold my hand lest someone should see us, or wide-eyed at the spectacle of two sailors smooching together on the dance-floor upstairs at Elite, or hesitant in front of the pretty china in Beirut . . . It worked while I was on my own, but seeing her in front of me I could only see her with him.

And as the days went by her answers got fewer and fewer. I felt her slipping away. Slowly. Every day taking her further from me. And yet she waited. That was all she seemed to be doing: waiting. If I didn't go to her she did not call me. If I went in the afternoon she would still be in her dressing-gown. She would let me in and go back to her chair and sit. If I asked, 'What have you been doing?' she would say, 'Nothing.' And it was true. Her work lay undisturbed. Sadat went to Washington. Hussein went to Washington. Rabin resigned. Podgorny fell and Brezhnev came to power. The miners grew restless and Rossellini died and she was moving between that ridiculous small bed, the drab bathroom and the sagging armchair – and waiting. She still washed her hair, depilated her legs, filed and painted her nails, but she'd have done that if she'd been living under nuclear fallout or dying of cancer – so it meant nothing.

At first she cried a lot, but then she stopped. The last time I saw her cry was in

Harvey Nichols. I'd insisted we go shopping. I'd used to like buying her clothes, watching her come out of the changing rooms slightly shy at presenting herself for inspection but proud at looking so good. She came but dragged her feet. 'I don't want to go shopping. I can't afford to go shopping.'

'We've got loads of money –'

'It's your money –'

'OK. I feel like spending some of my money –'

'And you're not making any more. You shouldn't –'

'Shut up telling me what I shouldn't do.'

'I don't want to go.'

'Look,' I said. 'This is for me. OK? I can't stand seeing those two dresses any more.'

'I couldn't bring everything down from –'

'OK. We'll just get some more.'

'It isn't right.'

'Look,' I said, 'they're for me. They're mine. When we split up I'll take them away.'

We didn't buy anything. There was a model on a pedestal wearing a classy suit and I said, 'That would look good on you,' and she started to cry.

'Why does it have to be beige?' she wept. 'Why does it always have to be beige?'

'You want psychedelic pink flares, do you? Is that what your taste runs to now?'

'It's always beige. Always, always beige. Your mother could wear that suit –'

'Go back then,' I said. 'Go back to the acrylic tartans and the mattress covers you used to wear when I met you. Paint spikes around your eyes, dye your hair purple. Let's see what you'll make of yourself on your own.'

I do not believe that she was seeing him. The telephone was mounted on the wall and could not be unplugged – that's the kind of dump she'd chosen to live in – and it never rang – at least not while I was there and I was there most of the time.

Mostly I took her back after dinner, saw her into the flat and left. But once I stayed. When she saw I wasn't going she hesitated, then sat down in the armchair. The room was dark apart from the street-light that came through the still-open curtains.

I'd finished a bottle of wine over dinner but I still needed a drink. I crossed to the depressing cupboard that served for a kitchen and poured myself a whisky. 'Do you want one?' I asked. She didn't. There was nothing odd about that; she normally didn't. I sat on the edge of the bed and looked at her; she looked tired.

I said, 'You look tired.'

'Yes,' she said.

'Come with me to Duke's,' I said. 'You'll have a separate room. Get out of this dump, for Christ's sake.'

'No,' she said, and shook her head. She sat very straight in the frayed chair.

651

Her red dress just touched her knees and her legs were crossed and slanted, the feet absolutely parallel.

'You know,' I said, 'you used to hesitate in doorways. Now you walk into a restaurant and stand there looking as if God himself should come and show you to your table.'

She said nothing. She wasn't looking at me; she was looking at the window where the tree was a great, restless shadow. After a moment I saw her face change.

'What is it?' I said.

She looked at me and her face went blank again as it had been before and she said, 'Nothing.'

'What did you think just then?'

'Nothing,' she said. 'Really.'

'You saw his face in the window? You heard him cry, "I need you"?'

'No,' she said. 'I just remembered a dream I had last night. I'd forgotten it.'

'So why wouldn't you answer?'

'Because you don't like being told about dreams.'

'Try me.'

'Saif, you know you get –'

'What did you dream?'

'OK,' she said, 'I dreamed I was back at Cairo University, teaching. I was standing behind the desk in Room Thirteen and the benches were full of students. Only it wasn't just Room Thirteen, it was also the hall in my grandfather's house. There was something about the walls and about the way the light fell through the windows that made it my grandfather's house. But I was behind the desk and all the students were there and I had to teach them, and I opened my mouth to speak but my mouth filled with ice: small cubes of ice like you put into a drink. I was embarrassed and pushed them out into my hand and dropped them behind the desk, but as I straightened up my mouth filled with more ice.'

'And?'

'That's all. It just kept happening till I woke up. It wasn't coming from anywhere; it was like my mouth was making ice, just very fast.'

'So you never got to give the lecture?'

'No.'

'That's a shame. I'm sure you'd have had some pretty interesting things to tell your students.'

I stood up and walked across the room towards the door. Then I stopped.

'I suppose you told him your dreams?'

She, of course, said nothing.

'What would you do? Wake up in the morning and cosily swap dreams? Mull over them over coffee since he had nothing to do and nowhere to go?'

She had stood up. She raised her arms and pushed her hair back over her shoulders and said, 'It's one o'clock. And I'm tired.'

'So?'

'I'd like – to sleep.'

'Who's stopping you?'

She walked across the room and opened the wardrobe. She picked out a nightdress and moved towards the bathroom. She had to pass me.

I said, 'Where are you going?'

'To the bathroom.'

'You can undress here.'

She did not answer but she did not attempt to pass.

'Go on,' I said, 'I'll watch.'

She did not move.

'What's the matter? Aren't you used to that by now? Togetherness. Being watched. Did he watch you undressing?'

The first time she had undressed for me in my bungalow at the Omar Khayyam she had just turned eighteen and she was so shy she was as stiff as a wooden doll. She had taken off her blouse and stepped out of her skirt and had stood there in a pretty white lace slip, obviously new – and then, not knowing what to do and since I just lay on the bed and watched her, she had wandered over to her handbag on the dressing-table and put on a few more dabs of Carven 'Ma Griffe'. And then I took pity on her and called her to me and she came and lay in my arms, round and brown with still a touch of puppy fat, taut and bursting with love and need.

'Did he watch you?'

'Please don't do this.'

'Do what? I'm just asking you a question. Did he watch you undressing before he fucked you? The first time. Let's start with the first time. Tell me about it.'

'Please. Please. We've been through this –'

'We've been through nothing. You've told me nothing. You've explained nothing –'

'It's impossible to explain anything to you. You don't want to understand –' She raised her voice. 'What you want is either flowcharts or empty sentimental –'

I hit her. I hit her with my open hand across her face. I caught her left cheek and felt my fingers graze her nose. She fell. From surprise, I think, as much as anything. I had hit her before: back in the cottage I had bruised one of her ribs. But I'd never hit her face. And I hadn't touched her at all since the battle-scene had shifted to London. She crouched down on the floor still holding on to her nightie and staring up at me. So I took a step forward, stooped a bit and hit her again. She covered her face with her hands. I knelt beside her. I pushed her and she lay back. I did not wait to undress her but just pulled her pants down and over her feet. Then I rubbed them in her face and forced the gusset into her mouth. I held her hands above her head and fucked her, truly fucked her, for the first time in our marriage. She fell asleep afterwards, right there on the floor, and I kept my arms around her all night, but in her sleep she turned away from me. I thought then that I would do anything to hang on to her.

Tuesday, 24 May

London

'No,' says Asya, 'No. I won't, I won't, *I won't.*'

'Baby, please. *Please.* I just want to feel you one more time. Even if it's the last time. *Please.* How can you say no?'

'No,' says Asya, standing by the chipped dressing-table.

'Just take off your coat, then,' pleads Gerald. 'Just your *coat.* What is it you're so afraid of, man?'

'No,' says Asya.

'Please, babe. I can't *talk* to you like this. You can't just stand in the middle of the room and pass sentence on me like this. I *need* to hold you. It's been the one thing I've thought about for three months. Please, let me just hold you one more time.'

He looks exhausted, worn out, ghost-like. He sits on the edge of the bed. When he stands he leaves a crease in the brown candlewick cover. Asya retreats till her back is touching the hand-basin in the corner of the room.

'Gerald,' she says, 'I only came here because you wouldn't let me speak to you any other way. Because your mother said I ought to tell you face to face –'

'How can you be so cold to me?' He puts his hands on her shoulders and looks down into her eyes. 'How can you be so cold to me after three whole months? Have you been making love to him, baby?'

'No,' says Asya. 'But I'm staying with him.'

'Oh, baby. My love.' He folds his arms around her and moves in close, 'If you knew the thoughts I've had – imagining you –' He lifts his head to look down at her. 'He hasn't touched you? Not once?'

'No,' says Asya. The wash-basin presses against the small of her back. 'Gerald, please, I'm not comfortable.'

'Come to bed.'

'No. I've *told* you. *No.*'

'You want to. I know you want to –'

His hand slips in underneath her hair and closes round the back of her neck. He bends his head but Asya turns away. His lips move along her cheek and down her neck –

'Will you please, please, let me *go* –'

'You're trembling –'

'The sink is hurting my back – let me *go* –'

'OK OK.' He steps back, 'You don't have to scream the place down.'

Asya pushes her hair back from her face. Her cheeks are hot. Her hands are cold and shaking. She pushes them into the pockets of her beige gaberdine.

'You look good,' Gerald says.

'I don't feel good,' says Asya. She looks around for somewhere to sit but there is only the bed.

'You know, the first time I saw you, you were stepping out of that red Lancia – you looked like an adman's dream –'

'I'm going to have to go soon; I said I wouldn't be long –'

'Where does he think you are?'

'He knows I'm seeing you. He knows *why* I'm seeing you.'

'To tell me to go fuck myself. He must be a happy man.'

'Gerald, please. I'm sure that under the circumstances –'

'Don't start talking like a fucking barrister –'

Asya turns and leans against the sink.

'What's the matter?' Gerald asks.

'I feel sick.'

'OK,' he says. He puts his arm around her shoulders. 'You've gone all pale,' he says. 'Lie down and I'll get you a glass of water –'

'No.'

'I won't come near you, I promise, I'll stand at the other end of the room. Don't be an idiot now, come.'

He steers her to the bed and Asya sinks down on to it. He arranges the pillows for her and takes the shoes off her feet –

'No,' says Asya.

'I won't touch you,' he says. 'Just relax, man.'

He walks over to the sink, takes his toothbrush out of the glass and fills the glass with water, and brings it back to the bed. He holds the glass to her lips and Asya sips. He puts the glass on the bedside table and sits down on the edge of the bed.

'There's someone I want you to meet,' he says.

Asya looks at him.

'Eesee,' he says. 'Remember?'

'The Vietnamese girl you went to South America with?'

'She's in London. She's been in London for a week. I've asked her to come here. I want you to talk to her.'

'Gerald, why?'

'She's clairvoyant, babe. She can see everything. She'll tell you what you should do.'

'I don't need to be told what I should do,' says Asya, 'I *know* what I should do.'

'Babe, I don't doubt that you're acting from the highest principles –'

'Gerald, please –'

'But even your husband would agree that you shouldn't stay with him just because he's ill –'

'You don't know –'

'You can't go against yourself –'

'There really is no more room for all this –'

'And I know you: you won't be content just nursing a sick man. Your true nature will assert itself sooner –'

'I've told you, I've told you, I've told you –'

'– or later. I'm not saying you should ignore him –'

'I am staying with him.'

'And if he really has cancer –'

'What do you mean, really?'

'– and if he is the man he must be, I'm sure he would *wish* you to live your life –'

'You don't understand –'

'You can still give him all the support he needs.'

'I am staying with him.'

'If he can be made to respect our love then I'm sure –'

'There is no way he is going –'

'We can *find* a way –'

'Gerald, it's over. I've been telling you –'

Asya starts to rise, but Gerald leans over and puts his two hands down on either side of her.

'You've always been prepared to sell us down the river,' he says. 'That was always your first thought; the first solution you'd come up with. I'm not going to let you do it.'

Asya lies back on the pillows.

'Gerald. Please listen to me. *I am sorry.* I *hate* myself for what I've done to you. *This* is the *only* decent thing I can do now. To tell you that it's finally, definitively over –'

'You've maimed me and now you'll do the decent thing and kill me off. Is that it?' Gerald smiles at Asya.

'You choose to put it that way, but there is nothing else I can do. I've done him more wrong than ever I did you, and he had no hand in it. None. He thought I was his friend and I betrayed him. I stabbed him in the back. He's taken it very badly – and now there's an extra reason why he needs me. I am staying with him. For you and me it's over. Will you let me get up now, please?'

'No,' he says softly. 'It will never be over between us. Never. Baby, you've got to know that.' With his right hand he strokes her neck. 'I'd rather strangle you right now,' he says.

'Go ahead,' whispers Asya, looking into his eyes.

He moves his hand down and starts to unbutton the red dress.

'I'm not going to struggle with you –' says Asya.

'It won't do you any good,' he says.

'But I'd really rather you didn't do this.'

' "I'd really rather you didn't do this." ' He slips his hand inside her bra. 'You don't talk to me in that schoolmarm voice –'

Asya tries to twist away but his mouth lands on hers and pins her head

656

to the pillow. She lies still, willing herself not to move. His tongue moves slowly in the corners of her mouth. His hand leaves her breast and wanders down to her knee. He strokes her stockinged thighs, up and up to where the stockings end, and then he strokes and scratches at her flesh. He slips his hand inside her panties and his fingers find all those secret paths they'd found before. He groans into her mouth. He lifts his face from hers and looks into her eyes as his fingers play with her, separate her, enter her –

'Tell me you don't want me to do this,' he says.

'I don't want you to do this,' she says.

'The shit you don't,' he says. 'You're hot for me –'

'It won't change anything,' Asya says.

'Can you bear it, babe? Never to feel this again? *Ever?*'

'I'm staying with him,' Asya says, and bites her lip as he pushes his fingers into her.

'Babe, you're going to force me to do something bad.'

Asya turns her face away.

'Listen,' he says. 'I wasn't going to tell you this, but I must. I read that paper.'

Asya turns her head back and looks at him. 'What paper?' she asks, but the cold hand is already on her heart.

'The paper you wrote in Athens. To remind you how you felt.'

'Let me go,' cries Asya. '*Let me go.*'

She tries to bring her knees together. She pushes at his arm. He puts one arm across her neck and keeps his other hand between her legs.

'Let me go,' she cries, pushing at his shoulders. 'You went through my drawers? You went through my clothes? How can you face me? How can you be here? How can you be doing this?'

'I told you I was fighting for my life –'

She scratches at his face but he holds his head further back.

'I'm telling you this so you know how much I love you –'

'Let me go, I can't stand you –'

'Even reading that didn't shake my belief in you – in us. I told you I know you better than you know yourself –'

'I want you to take your lousy fingers *out* of me. I –'

'I love you, babe. You're mine. You'll always *be* mine.'

'I *hate* you,' Asya says. 'You're *choking* me –'

'I thought you said, "Go ahead" –'

There is a knock at the door. Two quick knocks. Gerald takes his arm away from her neck.

'That's your friend,' Asya says.

'She's early,' Gerald says.

'You can't let her in,' Asya says.

'I'll take her downstairs,' he says. 'I'll give her a quick drink and bring her back. I want you to wait here till I come back. Will you do that?'

Asya does not answer. He stands up slowly and puts his fingers in his mouth.

'You're something else, babe. You know that?'

Asya says nothing and there is another knock at the door.

'You won't go anywhere?' he says. 'I'll be right back.'

Then he bends and picks up one red shoe from the floor. He holds it up.

'I don't trust you,' he says.

When he's gone Asya gets up. Quickly she adjusts her underwear, and buttons up her dress and smooths it down. She puts her handbag over her shoulder and looks at the one shoe on the floor. Well, of course she'll take it. She might get the other one back some day. She pushes it into the pocket of her gaberdine. It shows, but it doesn't matter. She listens at the door. She hears nothing. She opens the door and peeps out into the corridor. It is empty. She steps out and closes the door gently behind her. She runs for the stairs. They're sure to come up in the lift. Heart pounding, she races down the stairs. When she gets to the bottom she waits behind the door. They must be on their way up by now. She opens the door and looks out. The hotel lobby is full of people, but she can't see Gerald. She steps out into the lobby, and, as normally as she can, crosses it in her bare feet and walks out. In the street she runs along the pavement until she sees a taxi. She puts up her arm and it stops.

'Knightsbridge,' she says, and gets in and sinks back into the seat. Safe. She puts her head back and closes her eyes and tries to breathe deep and slowly. Under the gaberdine she presses the still throbbing heat between her legs, trying to make the ache go away. On Piccadilly she thinks she'd better sort herself out. She takes out her mirror and brushes her hair and checks her face. Then she remembers her feet. She leans forward and says, 'Excuse me?'

The driver inclines his head backward.

'Make it Bond Street, please.'

A pair of plain red shoes. And a new pair of stockings. Saif won't notice the difference. And he won't notice the odd shoe in the bottom of her cupboard. Gerald wouldn't package her shoe and send it to him, would he? Nonsense; where would he send it? He can keep it. He can get his Vietnamese clairvoyant to put a spell on it. Saif won't notice the new shoes. He's got enough to think about without noticing her shoes.

658

Wednesday, 22 June

Saif appears at the door of the waiting-room and Asya rises from her seat and follows him down the red-carpeted corridor. At the desk he pauses and writes out a cheque for the receptionist. In the street, Asya puts on her sunglasses and asks, 'What did he say?'

'He said we'd wait for the result of the biopsy.'

'That's it?'

'Yeah, more or less.'

They walk slowly up Harley Street.

'Didn't he say anything else?'

'No.'

'What about your chest?'

'I'll have to do some X-rays.'

'Is he setting that up?'

'Yes.'

'For when?'

'I don't know. His secretary will call me. Where do you want to go for lunch?'

'Why don't we call your father and see what he's doing?'

'No. He said he'd be in meetings all day. We're seeing him tonight.'

'Saif?' says Asya after a few steps. 'Are you going to tell him?'

'No. Not yet. There's no need. Do you want to go to Julie's?'

'I can't really face two restaurants in one day. Can we have sandwiches in the park?'

'Sure. We can do whatever you want.'

In the coffee-shop in Regent's Park Saif buys four cheese and pickle sandwiches and two Cokes.

'Are you going to eat three?' says Asya. 'Because I only want one.'

'Two for us and two for the ducks,' he says, 'otherwise you'll feed them yours and start tearing corners off mine. Let's go.'

They walk across the lawns and into the Inner Circle. They sit on a bench by the pond and unwrap the sandwiches and pop open the Cokes.

'Saif,' Asya says, throwing a piece of bread into the pond and crumbling another for the sparrows, 'before you do anything, will you check with Nadia?'

'Nadia?' he says. 'Why?'

'Because she's good. I know she's good.'

'You think she knows more than all these Harley Street guys?'

'No. But, however good they are, to them you're just another patient. But she'll really care. I'm sure that'll make a difference.'

'Don't look so worried, Princess. I'm really not too bothered.'

'I know,' says Asya, 'but I am. So will you? Promise?'

'What if they want to do something right away? This swelling is pretty painful.'

'We can courier her the reports. I can call her tonight –'

'What can she do over the phone?'

'I can describe it – a swelling under your left arm – and tell her when it started and what it looks like –'

'No, that's just silly. And it'll get back to my mother –'

'OK. But will you promise? Before you do anything? We just ask her opinion?'

'OK,' he says, 'whatever you want.'

At the flat Asya says, 'What time are we meeting Uncle Madi?'

'I said we'd pick him up at eight,' Saif says.

Asya looks at her watch. It is four o'clock.

'What are you going to do?' she says. 'Won't you have a siesta?'

'What about you?' he says. 'If I use your bed?'

She shrugs. 'Oh, I don't mind. I can just lie down on the floor.'

'Look,' Saif says, 'you're being ridiculous. Why are you staying in this dump? You like the flat I've taken –'

'I just want –'

'You want what? What is it you want? Tell me, because I'm damned if I know.'

'I'm just used –'

'You're just used to slumming –'

'It isn't –'

'What is it, then? Are you still seeing him? Is that why you won't move out? Are you still in touch with him?'

'No, I'm not. I've told you a hundred times –'

'Tell me again. Tell me he's not hiding behind some lamp-post out there waiting for me to leave so he can come up for a quickie –'

'Please don't start this again –'

'Why not? It isn't finished yet, is it?'

'It *is* finished. As far as I'm concerned it's finished. We've been talking about it for more than three months –'

'It isn't finished,' he says. 'You've no idea. There are a million things I still have to ask you.'

'I'm not answering any more questions. It's pointless –'

'You'll answer what I ask you –'

'It's pointless.'

'It isn't pointless to me. It isn't pointless to me to know, for example, how it was possible for you to tell me not to come to you last Christmas – after I'd arranged it all. I phone you and you say don't come. You feed me some shit about your work while what it is is that you can't bear –'

'Please, Saif –'

660

'– to do without him.'

'He wasn't even there.'

'What d'you mean he wasn't even –'

'He'd gone away. He'd gone to his parents.'

'You're lying.'

'I'm not lying. I don't lie.'

'The hell you don't. You lie all the time.'

'I am not lying. He wasn't there.'

'But you still couldn't bring yourself to see me. What was it? You were under a spell. You had to sit and *think* about him –'

'You see,' says Asya, 'I told you it was pointless.'

'Shit,' Saif says. He leaves the room and Asya hears the bathroom door slam.

Asya throws herself into the armchair. Underneath her are the mirror and the tweezers she had been using in the morning. She digs them out from under her and puts them on her lap. When he comes back into the room he stares at her.

'You're doing your *eyebrows?*'

'No –' says Asya.

'Is that all you can think about? Whether a hair has grown where it shouldn't?'

'They were lying on the –'

'You used to do that in private. You'd never let me see you. Has your skin grown that brazen?'

'I wasn't –'

'Did you let him watch you?'

'Saif –'

'Did you let him watch you?'

'No.'

'Maybe you did. In the cosy intimacy of the morning I've been hearing so much about. While you were swapping dreams. Maybe he even helped you. Held the mirror for you –'

'Saif –'

'Did he hold the mirror for you?'

'No.'

'Why not? He fucked you. You let him do that. So why quibble about holding a mirror or plucking a hair from the bridge of your nose?'

Asya is silent.

'Will you answer me? Since he was fucking you, why should he not assist you with the tweezers?'

Asya frowns. Then she says, 'Because that's – intimate.'

The back of his hand catches her right cheek and knocks her head into the armchair. She stays still. Her eyes closed. Her hands on top of the mirror and the tweezers in her lap. Saif looks down at her.

'I'm going,' he says quietly. 'I'm going before I kill you.'

After a while Asya opens her eyes. Oddly, she finds she is thinking about Chrissie. If Chrissie were here – she closes her eyes again. Oh Chrissie, Chrissie, what's happened? What's happened to the Arabiscos and the tea and the long chats and the feel of his hand on mine even after I'd left him, and the 'admirers' we used to notch up, and feeling so good diving into the pool or just walking down the street with our hair swinging behind us? Old Heraclitus and his river. Now when a man looks at me I feel someone should tell him he's making a mistake. Now I'm surprised when I catch a glimpse of myself in a mirror: if I'm walking in the street or sometimes when I'm going into the bathroom and I see someone in the mirror and I realise it's me, I'm surprised – not because I look good or bad or anything in particular, but just because I'm there. I can't believe I'm there any more. What is it that can't see itself in a mirror? Vampires. That's it. I am a vampire. I don't feel anything. I just watch it all. Saif and his helplessness – and his cancer. Do you think he's got cancer, Chrissie? Even that isn't touching me – not really really deep down touching me. And what if he's making it up? What if he is? It doesn't matter. I'm sure even if he is lying he'd rather he wasn't. He *wants* to have cancer. He'd will it on himself if he could. And maybe he isn't lying. He isn't, you know. We've been to all those clinics. And he even had a biopsy. And I've seen the swelling. Under his arm –

In front of the bathroom mirror Asya considers the spreading darkness around her right eye. It takes her a few moments to realise what it is – and then, 'A Black Eye,' she whispers to herself, happy to have labelled it. She sits on the edge of the bath to think – but no thoughts come: her mind is blank – and her headache is terrible. After a bit she stands up and looks in the mirror again. She gazes at the bruise and tentatively touches the edge of it, following the line of her cheekbone; it is just as it should be: sore. The other edge, just under her eyebrow, is sore too, but less so. The eye itself is red and seems to have grown smaller. Asya looks into the eye for a long time then wanders back into the room and lies down on the bed.

'You're not ready yet?' Saif asks as he closes the front door behind him.

Waking, Asya sits up quickly and looks at her watch: a quarter to seven.

'Jesus Christ!' Saif says.

'What?' says Asya as he stares at her.

'Oh Jesus!' he says again and switches the light on. 'Oh, Princess,' he says, 'Princess.' He folds her face carefully to his chest. He bends to place his face against the top of her head. He kisses her hair. After a few moments he says, 'Did you do anything? Did you put some ice on it?'

'No,' says Asya.

Saif goes into the kitchen. He breaks off a piece of ice and wraps it in his handkerchief. When he returns to the room Asya has lain down again. He sits next to her on the bed.

'Hold still,' he says, and lowers the cold damp parcel on to her eye. 'Oh, Princess,' he says, 'Princess. What have you made me do?'

Asya lies quiet under the ice.

'Look at you,' he says. 'You look terrible.' He holds the ice gently on her eye with one hand and with the other he smooths back her hair. 'OK, Princess,' he says, 'this is it. That was the last time. It's never going to happen again. I promise.'

'It's OK,' says Asya.

'But you mustn't provoke me,' Saif says.

'Don't ask me any more questions. Please?'

Asya pushes her cheek into his leg as he sits beside her on the bed. The roughness of his trousers feels comforting against her skin.

'OK,' he says, 'no more questions. No more questions, Princess.' He lifts the ice away from her face. 'I knew, really, in Athens,' he says quietly. 'I knew something was up. But I didn't imagine –'

Asya looks up at him. He frowns with concentration as he places the ice-cube on the inner corner of her eye.

'I knew when I opened the door of the room and saw the twin beds – and then saw you, at the dressing-table, choosing that moment to paint your nails.'

'Why – then?' whispers Asya. 'Why didn't you at least say something?'

Saif shrugs slightly. 'I just wanted everything to stay the same. I didn't want anything to change.'

Asya is silent. After a moment she says, 'You're going to be late for your father.'

'Get up and get dressed, then,' Saif says.

Asya says, 'I'd better not come and meet him with my face like this.'

'What will I say to him?'

'Say I'm not well.'

'He'll want to come and see you.'

'Can you call him and make it tomorrow?'

'This won't be gone by tomorrow,' Saif says.

'Well, what shall I do?'

'You can wear dark glasses. Come on, Princess, get dressed.'

As she carefully pats her skin dry, Asya looks at her face in the bathroom mirror. The oddest thing really, she thinks, is how untouched the left side of it looks. You'd think *something* would have happened to the left eye in sympathy with its partner: it could at least have closed up a fraction or gone pink or looked sad or something. She looks at the right eye, now swollen closed and bruised to a dark purple. She covers the left side with the towel: that's better, now she looks more – real, more like she feels she should look. She takes the towel away and once again the untouched eye looks neutrally out at her –

Saif knocks on the bathroom door.

'Are you all right?' he says.

'Yes,' says Asya. 'I'm fine. I'm just coming.'

Saif opens the car door for Asya and lets her in. He closes it behind her. He walks round the car, gets in and starts the engine. The radio splutters to life.

'– the future *is*
About to unfold –
Up*stairs* before the night's too old, *'cos* –'

'Crap!' says Saif.

'Switch it off?' says Asya.

'No,' Saif says, pulling out. 'We can't go round switching everything off.'

'– To*night's* the *night*
It's gonna be all right
Ain't *no*-body gonna stop us now-ow –'

Saif reaches out and switches off the radio. These days all the hits could have been designed with them in mind: Torn Between Two Lovers, Lucille, Winner Takes it All, I Don't Wanna Talk About It – not one that misses its mark. Songs here are so – so specific, she thinks; if they'd been in Cairo and switched the radio on they would never have got 'there's been another man –' and 'she'd made him look small'; they'd have got 'farewell, O world of happiness' or 'I shall not submit to what is written' –

'Do you want to eat at St Catherine's Dock?' Saif asks as he cuts from Knightsbridge to the Mall. 'Or shall we take him into town?'

Does he remember? Remember them circling this roundabout with Mario following in his car –

'I don't really mind,' says Asya. 'Whatever you prefer.'

'We could go to Chez Solange,' he says. 'You like that.'

'Yes,' says Asya. 'Or you can ask *him* what he'd rather.'

As they come out into Parliament Square Saif asks, 'How are you feeling?'

'I'm fine,' Asya says.

'Is your eye hurting?'

664

'No, not really,' Asya says. 'It's just throbbing a bit.'

On the Embankment he says, 'That bastard of yours had better keep out of my way. If I ever get my hands on him, I'll kill him. If I ever get a chance to do him a bad turn, I'll do it: I'll make sure he's ruined.'

Asya stares out of the windscreen.

'Is he in London?' Saif asks.

'I don't know,' says Asya.

After a moment he says, 'Do you have a photograph of him?'

'No,' says Asya.

'Truly?'

'Truly.'

'The leave-taking was too hurried for the exchange of mementos, huh? It's OK, Princess.' Saif leans over and pats her thigh. 'I'm not starting on you again. I just wanted to know what he looked like in case he ever crossed my path.'

Asya says nothing.

'I wish he would,' Saif says. 'I really wish he would. I'd make him regret the day he took advantage of my wife.'

As they pass Howard Hotel he says, 'It stinks, you know. It really stinks; taking advantage of a woman on her own: a defenceless woman. You know,' he says, lighting a cigarette, 'they billeted a girl on me for three days. A Palestinian girl.'

'Oh?' says Asya. 'Why?'

'Something they were up to,' he says. 'And, "You have an extra room, brother Saif, and the Boss will consider it a favour and the whole matter is three days –" '

'What did she look like?' asks Asya.

'Oh, OK.' He shrugs. 'She was no beauty queen but she was OK. Very gentle – her voice was very soft. She came to my room the second night. Knocked and came in: "The favour you have done me is big, Ustaz Saif, if there is any way I can repay you –" ' He is silent.

'What did you do?' asks Asya.

'I sent her back to her room. And the next night I stayed at a hotel.'

Asya says nothing.

'You just don't take advantage of a woman like that.'

'Why would it be taking advantage?' says Asya. 'I mean, since she offered?'

'What? Because she was in a weak position, hiding out in my flat –'

'But *you* hadn't made a move. She didn't feel she *had* to come and make her offer. Maybe she just liked you –'

'She wasn't a tramp – she wouldn't have –'

'Why would liking you make her a tramp?'

'Just to come to my room and –'

'Why does her offer have to be either an act of self-sacrifice or the act of a tramp? Why can't it be simply –'

665

'Look, let's not go into one of your theoretical arguments. What I'm saying is that it is wrong to take advantage of a defenceless woman. Do you disagree with that?'

'No. I agree. Just as it's wrong to take advantage of a defenceless man.'

'So?'

'Nothing, really.'

'What is it you're saying?'

'I just think it's – patronising to assume that where there's a – situation – between a man and a woman it's the woman who is automatically defenceless.'

'So, you're telling me you weren't defenceless?'

'I'm not talking about *me* –'

'You weren't taken advantage of?'

'I'm only saying –'

'You knew what you were doing –'

'Oh, *Saif* –'

Saif pulls the car in by the pavement and stops. He turns to Asya.

'What are you telling me?' he asks.

'I suppose,' says Asya slowly, 'I'm telling you that I'm not some idiot who'd let herself –'

'You're some idiot who what, then?'

'Why won't you ever –'

'Answer me. What would you admit to doing?'

'I'm not *admitting* –'

'What, then? What the hell *are* you doing?'

'I'm only saying –'

'Yes?'

'Well, that one shouldn't go around with preconceived –'

'Are you saying you actually –'

'– ideas and insist on fitting things into them.'

'– you actually suggested – *you* suggested –'

Asya is silent.

'*You asked him to fuck you?*'

'Saif, all I meant was –'

'*You* asked *him*?'

'Saif –'

'Just answer me straight: you invited him to fuck you?'

'It wasn't like that –'

'Just answer yes or no.'

'I asked if he wanted to stay the night.'

Saif opens the car door and gets out. He moves immediately to the rear of the car where Asya can't see him. She sits and waits. Her heart is cold and heavy. Every few beats it gives a lurch that leaves her breathless. She knows she should not go to him. In front of her is a maze of roads and bridges. They look very smooth and hard: white concrete and black asphalt. The street-lights shine yellow and regularly spaced. From time to time a car whooshes by, leaving a brief tremor in the air.

Saturday, 2 July

'Asya! Can you come in here a moment?'

Asya leaves Saif standing at the window looking out over Hyde Park in the gathering darkness and follows her mother into the kitchen of the flat Lateefa has borrowed for her two days in London.

Lateefa closes the kitchen door and crosses to where Asya stands by the cooker.

'Take off these glasses,' she says.

Asya takes off the glasses and her mother looks at her face. She draws in her breath.

'He did this to you?' she says. 'He did *this* to you?'

Asya knows that her face looks better now. The bruise has faded to a sort of olive green shading off into yellow along the borders; the eye itself is almost completely open again with only one red splodge radiating out from the inner corner.

'I'm going to speak to him,' Lateefa says, heading for the kitchen door. 'What does he think? Just because you were alone with him in this country he treats you like –'

Asya runs forward and catches her mother's arm.

'Mummy, Mummy –' she cries in an urgent whisper, 'don't be like that – how can you *be* like that –' She pulls her mother back to the other end of the kitchen. 'How can you be like that when you know what happened? When you know what I've done? You're the only one who –'

'I can't just keep silent –' Lateefa says.

'Yes you can,' whispers Asya, keeping hold of her mother's arm. 'I know it looks bad but what is it? A black eye? I've done worse to him than that: I've broken his *heart*, Mummy, I've ruined his *life*. Just because it doesn't show – just because he's walking round with no visible sign of damage – it's so unfair –' Asya lets go of her mother's arm. 'It's just so unfair,' she goes on. 'People look at him as if he's a brute, and one woman came up to me and said, "There's a shelter for battered wives in Chiswick now, you know. You shouldn't stand to be knocked about," and I said, "But I'm not a battered wife." She looked quite disgusted.'

'I don't understand you –' Lateefa says.

'He doesn't *mean* to harm me,' Asya says. 'It's just that – he just doesn't know what to do – about anything. He's walked out on his project in Syria – he says he doesn't care and won't talk about it but it *must* be on

667

his mind – and now he thinks he's got cancer and – when he turns to me he can't help but remember what I've done – not just remember but imagine – he's imagining it all the time – he just doesn't know what to do.'

'So he hits you? What are we? Brought up in the streets?'

'Oh Mummy, don't go all bourgeois –'

'So what are you going to do? You're planning to wait until he kills you?'

'He isn't going to kill me.'

'How do you know? How can you tell what he'll do next?'

'He's going to leave me.'

Lateefa looks at her daughter. Asya's eyes have filled with tears and she nods.

'I think he is. He hasn't said so, but that's what I've felt over the last week –'

The tears start falling slowly down her face. She wipes them away and shakes her head impatiently.

'I have to be in Oxford the day after tomorrow,' Lateefa says. 'Come with me.'

'No,' says Asya. 'As long as he's here – I'll stay.'

When they go into the living-room Saif turns from the window and says, 'I want to speak to Dr Lateefa – alone.'

Asya turns and goes back into the kitchen and shuts the door. She sits down on a wooden chair and waits.

Monday, 11 July
Oxford

When he leaves her she does not cry. She stands outside the barrier and watches him until he turns the corner of the screen at the door of the departure lounge. She stands and waits until she sees him once again: he crosses the narrow gap that is visible between the two large rubber plants at the top of the stairs inside the lounge – and disappears.

She turns round. The thought of buying a newspaper and sitting in the coffee-shop passes through her mind but she finds she is walking towards the car-park. He has left her. He hasn't said he's leaving her, but he's left her. He helped her empty the flat and get her things into the car. They drove to the airport together. He said he was going to Boston for two weeks – maybe longer. Once more the reflection walking towards her in the plate-glass doors administers a mild shock, a feeling of inappropriateness: there she is again; wearing a dress and shoes, her handbag slung over her shoulder like a normal person, still upright, still walking, still *there* –

She turns the key in the ignition. She has the keys to the car, the keys to the cottage and a copy of the keys to his flat. 'You can use it if you like,' he'd said.

She drives along the M4 looking for the exit to Newbury. She can get to Oxford from there. On the passenger seat beside her lies a big brown envelope. He had taken it from his briefcase as they got out of the car. 'You can mail this to your aunt if you like,' he'd said. 'It won't make any difference.'

'They haven't got a vacant room,' Lateefa says, coming back in, 'but this *is* quite big and I've asked them to put another bed in it –' She looks at Asya questioningly.

'That'll be fine, Mummy,' Asya says. 'Thank you.' She puts her four hangers in her mother's wardrobe and sits down on her mother's bed. 'That'll be fine.'

Lateefa looks at her daughter. 'Listen,' she says, 'it's the conference dinner in half an hour. Why don't you come and meet everybody?'

Asya shakes her head. 'I can't,' she says.

'Why not, darling? You look wonderful –'

'No,' says Asya. 'You go, Mummy. I'll wait for you. What did he say to you when you spoke alone?'

'Oh' – Lateefa's back is to Asya as she looks into the mirror and dabs at her face with the powder-puff – 'nothing much.'

'But what did he say, Mummy? What did he actually say?'

'What's in that envelope?' Lateefa asks, half turning, pointing her powder-puff at the big brown envelope lying on Asya's bed.

'That envelope addressed to Nadia?'

'It's his medical reports,' Asya says. 'I made him promise to show them to Nadia before he actually let anyone do anything to him.'

'What are you going to do? Mail it?'

'I'll courier it. Tomorrow. Mummy? What did he say to you?'

'He said some bad things about you, but –'

'What did he say?'

'Asya, dear, why?'

'I have to know, Mummy, please. Exactly.'

'All right then.' Lateefa puts down her powder-puff. 'He said, "Dr Lateefa, your daughter is a whore. She wasn't –" '

'He said that to *you*?'

'Yes.'

'I'm sorry, Mummy. I'm really sorry.'

Asya covers her face with her hands. Lateefa says nothing.

'Would you – please – go on?' says Asya through her hands.

'He said, "She wasn't a whore when I married her but she's changed. She'll pick up any man she likes the look of and I can't live with that." '

Asya raises her face. 'Is that all?' she asks.

'Did you want more?'

'What did *you* say? You weren't horrible to him, were you?'

Lateefa looks at her daughter. 'I said, "If that's what you think of her, why are you still with her?" '

'And what did he say?'

'He said, "I couldn't just leave her alone here. What would she do?" So I said, "Well, I'm here now, so she won't be alone." '

'Is that all?'

'He also promised not to tell anyone about this whole story –'

'Did *you* ask him for that?'

'No. He volunteered. He said, "I want you to know that I will never tell anyone what has happened. I don't want to ruin her life. She can say what she pleases." '

'Because I don't care,' says Asya. 'He must say whatever is least hurtful to him. And I shan't say anything.'

Lateefa turns back to the mirror then turns round again.

'Have you seen those reports?' she asks.

'No,' Asya says.

'Why don't you read them before you send them?' Lateefa says.

'Read them?'

'Don't you want to know what he's got?'

'But I *do* know.'

'You should read them.'

'But they're his.'

'He gave them to you.'

'Yes, but in a sealed envelope.'

'Did he say you shouldn't open it?'

'No.'

'If he didn't want you to read them he would have sent them himself.'

'He couldn't have. They were only ready just before he left and –'

'He could have mailed them from the airport.'

'But we wanted to courier them –'

'Still, if he didn't want you to read them he wouldn't have given them to you.'

'Do you think he wants me to read them?'

'What harm can it do?'

'But do you think he actually *wants* me to?'

'Yes. I think he probably does.'

Asya picks up the envelope lying beside her.

'I don't feel right opening it,' she says.

'Have done with empty talk, child,' her mother says. 'You'll know what's in it anyway as soon as Nadia opens it.'

Lateefa turns back to the mirror. Asya tears a corner of the brown envelope and slits it open with her finger. She slides the papers out into her hand and draws in her breath with a little gasp. Lateefa turns to her. Asya tries to slide the papers back into the envelope but her mother has seen the glossy picture on top. She comes forward and takes the envelope out of Asya's hand. She shakes it over the bed and all the brochures come fluttering out: BMW, Rover, Alfa-Romeo –

'Brochures for cars?' Lateefa says.

Asya sits and stares at the bed.

'So he was lying to you about being ill?' her mother says.

'No,' says Asya. 'He can't have been. He's been to doctors, I've gone with him –'

'Did you go with him inside?'

'No, but he *did* go in – he paid bills – he spent a day in hospital –'

'Maybe they've found that there was nothing wrong with him.'

Asya stares at the brochures.

'Did Nadia ask him for these?' she asks.

'I don't know,' Lateefa says. 'Did he actually say to you they're medical reports?'

Asya thinks. 'No,' she says, 'he just said, "You can send these to Nadia." '

'Well then, maybe you misunderstood him?'

'Yes,' says Asya, 'I must have.'

She can't have misunderstood him. He'd said, 'They won't make any difference.' He wouldn't say that about car brochures. He knew she would think they were his medical reports. He meant her to think that. It was the only thing they'd talked about sending to Nadia. He knew, of course he knew. But then, what if she'd opened the envelope? He must have known she wouldn't. And he was right. She wouldn't have if it hadn't been for her mother more or less making her. So he wanted her to think he was ill. But why? So she would stay? But she *had* stayed. *He* was the one who had left. But he hadn't *said* he was leaving, definitively leaving – leaving *her*. Yes he had: he'd told her mother – it must have been terrible for her, the worst thing, to sit there and be told your daughter was a whore and not be able to defend her – not be able to defend her because you knew it was sort of true. But he'd stopped saying anything to *her*: the questioning, the insults – everything had stopped and all there was was silence. Silence and coldness and – nothing. Just nothing at all. But what had he thought when he gave her the envelope? Even if she hadn't opened it she'd have phoned Nadia in a few days and asked what he should do. He must have known she'd do that. And then she would have found out. What then? What had he thought would happen then? Asya can't think of the answer to that. So she goes back to why he had done it: collected the brochures, put them into the envelope, sealed it and put it into his briefcase. He had tossed it on to the car seat

671

just before he locked the door: 'You can send these to Nadia; they won't
do any good.' Did he decide at the last moment to give them to her?
Might he have just taken them with him to America and thrown them
away there? 'You can send these to Nadia –' Why? So that for another
three days she would have gone on thinking he was ill? But she would
have thought that anyway. And why would he want her to think he was ill?
So that she would stay? She would have stayed. He was the one who had
left –

In the night Lateefa sits up in her bed. She throws off the covers and gets
up. She walks across the room and leans over Asya and puts her hand on
her shoulder.

'Asya?' she says.

'I can't – I can't –'

Asya's teeth are chattering so hard they make her whole body shake.

'Get up,' Lateefa says. 'Get up, darling.'

'I – can't –' Asya stammers.

Lateefa pulls the covers back, unclenches her daughter's hands and
feels them.

'You're frozen,' she says.

She unfolds Asya's rigid arms and pulls her up.

'Come,' she says. 'Come into my bed.'

She leads a stooped and shivering Asya across the room and sits her
down on the larger bed. She gets a glass of water from the bathroom and
puts it to her lips. Asya's teeth clatter against the glass. Her mother rubs
her hands and asks, 'Have you got a hot-water bottle?' Asya nods.
Lateefa switches on the light and looks through Asya's suitcase. She fills
the hot-water bottle and brings it back to her. She puts it in her arms and
smooths the hair away from her face.

'Look at you,' she says. 'Look at you. Would anyone do this to
themselves? Lie down now, lie down.'

She lifts Asya's feet into the bed and pulls the covers over her. She
switches off the light and goes back to the bed.

'Can you move over a little?' she asks, but Asya lies rigid, clasping the
hot-water bottle and shaking.

Lateefa climbs in over her. She sits up in bed behind her daughter and
rubs her back and her shoulders.

'Why, dear, why?' she murmurs. 'Why all this? Hush now hush –'

She rubs her shoulders and her back and talks softly to her until bit by
bit the continuous shaking stops and is replaced by irregular convulsive
starts and Asya turns on to her back and buries her face in her mother's
large, comfortable side –

'Oh, Mummy,' she gasps. 'Oh, Mummy –'

'There now, there. Never mind, darling, never mind.'

Lateefa smooths Asya's hair and strokes her face.

'Oh, Mummy —' Asya wails, holding on to the hot-water bottle as the tears start coming out with great choking sobs.

'It's all right, darling. Hush, it's all going to be all right,' Lateefa says.

Tuesday, 12 July

Asya walks to the post office. She buys another brown envelope, addresses it and mails it to Nadia. Then she walks back to the college and sits and waits for her mother.

Asya's days are taken care of now. In the morning she has breakfast with her mother, then sits and waits for her outside the conference room or the library. At half past eleven they have a cup of tea together, then Asya waits till lunchtime. After lunch Asya waits till half past four and then she waits again till seven. At night she lies in her narrow bed and listens to her mother's regular breathing and her odd gentle snore until she too falls asleep.

At last Lateefa says, 'All right, we'll go up north tomorrow.'

'Oh, but Mummy, why?' says Asya.

'Because this won't do. You're just wasting your time sitting around here —'

'No, but Mummy —'

'You're not doing any work. And now I don't think you *will* do any work until you're back in your own place. So we're going.'

'But Mummy, what about your fellowship? What about *your* work?'

'It's all right,' Lateefa says. 'I can do my work any time.'

'But you can't,' Asya protests. 'You really need to be here —'

'I've got all the material I need and now I want to see you start working again — seriously.'

'OK. I'll try and start —'

'No,' says Lateefa. 'We'll go back to your university and if I need anything I can come back here for a day or two.'

Scene 8

August 1977
The North of England

According to the methods described in Chapter 12, a corpus of 160 poems was compiled. This yielded a data set of 1750 minimal metaphoric units (MMUs).

These MMUs are divided into 10 sets of categories according to 10 factors. (The number of categories each factor permits will be called that factor's 'levels'.)

Lateefa puts a plate down near Asya's elbow. Asya glances at it.
'What's in the sandwich, Mummy?'
'Roast beef,' Lateefa says, and puts a mug of tea down next to it.
'Thank you,' Asya says, and takes a bite off the corner of her sandwich.

The levels of three of these factors were predetermined at the time of the compilation of the data set: AGE (which has 9 levels: see list 1); SCHOOL (which has 9 levels: see list 34); and STATUS (which has 2 levels: see lists 31 and 32).

The levels of two more factors were suggested from the beginning by the nature of this study and by the data. These are: PRIMARY SYNTACTIC UNIT DUPLICATION (which takes 2 levels: see Ch. 4) and SEMANTIC TRANSFER DUPLICATION (which takes 2 levels: see Ch. 7).

Asya stretches and looks up. At the other end of the room her mother sits in the corner of the sofa. Her feet are tucked under her. She munches at her sandwich and turns a page of her book. There was a time when Asya had longed for her mother to be slim and beautiful; to wear a pearl clasp in her chignon and drift abstractedly into her room in the evening to kiss her goodnight; to go out to a ball leaving the smell of her perfume lingering behind; to stand at a mahogany table, arranging tulips in a crystal vase with a shaft of sunlight falling across her slender hands. She had wanted to adore her instead of just loving her. And she had felt guilty – guilty for wishing to improve upon Mumsie, who frowned up from her book and pushed her spectacles back on to her nose when you walked into the room, who when she walked quickly thrust her head and shoulders forward as though she were charging at something, who always woke up in the night to help you be sick or comfort you out of a nightmare – and once when Asya was fourteen and they had had dinner in a small German village and were walking back to their hotel and her mother, slipping and breaking the heel of her shoe, had taken both shoes off and walked barefoot on the shining cobbles, Asya had been outraged. Outraged because her mother was not embarrassed or uneasy but enjoying herself; actually enjoying walking barefoot in the street. And her father had had to take her aside and whisper, 'Leave her alone. If she's enjoying herself why don't you let her? What harm is her walking barefoot doing you?' And she had felt ashamed of herself – but still angry. Now she wonders – in her heart she had always accused her mother of trying to shape her, of pushing her in certain directions, of imposing her view of things on her – but how much had *she* imposed *her* views on her mother? Her views on motherhood, on adulthood, on –

Lateefa looks up.

'What is it? Why aren't you working?'

'Mummy,' says Asya, 'what would you have done if you hadn't had us?'

'What do you mean?' Lateefa frowns, pushing her glasses higher on her nose.

'Well, do you sometimes – ever – wish you hadn't had children?'

'No,' Lateefa says.

'But having us must have terribly influenced what you did with your life. Especially me since I came first.'

'Yes, of course it did. That's what happens when you have children.'

'So don't you – just sometimes – wish we hadn't happened? So you could have done something else?'

Lateefa's eyebrows are now way above her glasses.

'No,' she says. 'One doesn't think like that. You can think like that about other things in your life, but not about your children. A child – once a child is there – well, there it is: you love it. You can't imagine your life without it. You don't *want* to imagine your life without it.'

'Is that really true?'

'Yes.'

'Completely completely true?'

'Yes, of course it is. You and Deena both couldn't have come at more inconvenient times – but the minute you were there – well, that was it, really. You were – part of me.'

'But one can wish one didn't have certain parts of oneself –'

'But not your children. You can wish they were a bit different: more tractable, less headstrong –'

'OK, OK. But that's not what I'm talking about –'

'I don't see why you should be talking about *any* of this right now –'

'But Mummy, are you the way you *want* to be?'

'Asya, darling, for heaven's sake –' Lateefa slaps her book impatiently against her knee.

'But I really want to know. If you could have it all back – if you could go back to – when was the first time you thought about what you wanted to be?'

'I can't remember. Now why don't you –'

'But you *must* remember. You must remember the first time you read something or saw something and thought, "*That's* what I want to do"?'

Lateefa looks down at her book for a moment, then she raises her face and looks at Asya.

'Yes,' she says. 'Your Mama Deela was in hospital. I was thirteen. The hospital was on Rameses Street and I was standing at the door waiting for your grandfather when a convoy of British Army lorries came slowly up the road heading towards Heliopolis. It was night-time and at first I could only see their lights, but when they came past me I looked up and I could see into the cabins and they were all driven by women. Young girls, sitting up there driving those huge lorries. And I thought, "That's what I want to do." I've always remembered that.'

'But you didn't,' Asya says. 'You didn't do it.'

'You can take it as a metaphor,' Lateefa says, waving towards Asya's typewriter, 'for what I wanted to do. And yes I have: I've done it.'

'But have you really?' says Asya. 'I mean –'

'Asya. I'm not chatting any more. It's only seven o'clock. You can easily do three more hours.'

Lateefa looks determinedly back into her book.

The remaining five factors are FORM, MEANING PATTERN, TENOR, VEHICLE, and TRANSFER. For these, the levels were in no way predetermined but were constructed simultaneously with and according to the process of analysing the data. They thus represent categories into which metaphors were found to fall rather than those into which they were made to fit.

She can see her mother. She can see her at thirteen: with intense eyes and untidy hair standing at the door of the hospital in the darkness watching the trucks go by. If that was the kind of yearning she had, a yearning to be driving a truck away into the darkness, then how much life at home must have irked her. It would have been impossible to turn round and say to Mama Deela, 'I want to be like those British girls driving Army trucks' –

'Mummy?' says Asya. 'Did you ever lie to your mother?'

'What *is* the matter with you?' Lateefa says looking up. 'What have me and my mother got to do with you right now?'

'Did you?' asks Asya. 'Did you always tell her the absolute truth?'

'No I didn't. How could I have? It wouldn't have been possible –'

'What did you lie to her about?'

'I didn't lie to her. I just didn't tell her some things. Asya –'

'Like what, Mummy? What didn't you tell her?'

'Well – I never told her I was reading novels. I just said they were school-books. And she couldn't read English so I got away with it.'

'What else? Something specific, Mummy.'

'Well –' Lateefa sighs. 'You know I told you about Miss Sage, my English teacher? She had a summer house up in Mansoura and she invited me to go and stay with her –'

'And you wanted to go.' Asya nods in anticipation of her mother's reply.

'Oh yes. Very badly,' Lateefa says. 'She came to the house to ask my mother formally, and she brought some pictures with her. Well, they sat in the drawing-room and I sat between them and Miss Sage would pass me the photo and I would pass it to my mother –'

'What were they photos of?'

'Of the house – and of the garden. Anyway, I looked at one picture in my hand just before I passed it over – and it was a photo of a whole group of young men playing volleyball: British airmen –'

'Gosh!' says Asya, wide-eyed.

'So I hid it. Quickly. I knew my mother would never let me go if she saw it.'

'Didn't she see you hide it?'

'No. I had a little bundle in my hand by then – photos my mother had already handed back to me – and I slipped it among them.'

'Did you go to Mansoura?'

'Yes, I went.'

'Was it fun?'

'Yes. Asya –'

'As much fun as you'd thought it would be?'

'Yes. But then it was enough for me just to be with Miss Sage.'

'And the airmen? Did you meet them?'

'They were around. I talked to some of them, that's all.'

'You didn't have romantic –'

'No I didn't. Asya dear, please –'

MEANING PATTERN is the distribution of 'literal', 'figurative' and 'neutral' meaning among the elements of the Primary Syntactic Unit (see 1.3). It is only applicable to syntax-dependent metaphor. Since no metaphoric PSU containing more than four elements was found (see 6.3), this factor consists of four sub-factors: 'subject' (S), 'verb' (V), 'object' (O), and 'prepositional phrase' (P). Each of these factors may take any one of three levels: (1) 'literal'; (2) 'figurative'; and (3) 'neutral'. Not all sub-factors, of course, are present in all PSUs: only the presence of the first two is essential. The 'neutral' level can only occur when the MEANING PATTERN is made up of more than two sub-factors; this is obviously because the simultaneous presence of a 'literal' and a 'figurative' element in the PSU is necessary for the occurrence of a syntax-independent metaphor.

'This is completely stupid,' Asya mutters.
'What is?' says her mother.
'This stuff. It's just useless.'
'I'll make you some supper,' Lateefa says, getting up and heading for the kitchen.
'I can't bear it –' says Asya, putting her head in her hands.
'Have a break,' says Lateefa. 'I've made you some lentil soup –'
The telephone rings and they look at each other.
'Why don't you just not answer?' Lateefa says.
'I can't do that,' says Asya.
'I'll answer it. I'll tell him you're asleep.'
'He won't believe you,' Asya says, walking slowly down the stairs.
'Hello?' says Asya.
'Hi, babe.'
'Hi!'
'How are you doing?'
'I'm – fine. And you?'
'I'm still alive.'
What should she say to that? 'Oh good'? What he wants her to say is, 'Only still alive?' So then he would say, 'What do you expect?' and it would all start over again. She could say, 'Well, that's *some*thing,' and then he'd be angry –
'What have you been doing?' she asks.
'Still looking around.'
'Has nothing – happened yet?'
'No.'
'Well, I'm sure it will.' She puts an encouraging note into her voice.
'I'm glad *somebody's* sure.'
Asya can't think what to say. 'At least you've got the dole'? She had been amazed when he talked so naturally about 'signing on'. She hadn't even known what he meant. 'Signing on what?' she'd asked. 'Unemployment. Money,' he'd said. He didn't seem at all ashamed. And it seemed to work. You signed on and you showed up every week and the government would give you enough money to live on till you found a job; a job that *suited* you even. All she'd known about getting money from the social services was the sight of desperate people who'd spent months getting various forms filled and getting them to the right desks, and finally ended up at the cashier's window on the eleventh floor of the Mugama' building where Tante Soraya worked, and crowded and yelled and elbowed and

pushed to collect their three pounds a month; three *Egyptian* pounds a month, as her mother would point out. And Tante Soraya said some cases were so bad that the staff who worked on that floor gave them money out of their own pockets – not that they were well paid themselves. And the Mugama' was built around a huge stairwell and Tante Soraya said they were trying to move the department to the ground floor because of the people who couldn't manage any more and threw themselves down the stairwell from the eleventh floor, and it was so crowded downstairs they always landed on someone –

'Babe?'

'Yes?'

'I said how about you?' he says. 'How are *you* doing?'

'Oh, OK.'

'Just OK?'

'Well, I'm – working.'

'Look, babe. I really have to talk to you properly. I'll come up to you and –'

'No, Gerald –'

'Look, this is ridiculous. You won't let me come and see you, you won't come down and see me – I *have* to talk to you, man – and not with three people standing staring at me – look, can you call me back? I'll pick up an extension somewhere else.'

'Yes, OK,' Asya says.

She sits on the bottom step for a minute. In the kitchen she can hear her mother moving about and she can hear the clatter of cutlery in the drawer. She dials the hotel number in London and waits while they find him.

'Hi!'

'Hi! You've found somewhere better?'

'Yes, at least they're not queueing up behind me. Listen, babe, I was saying we've got to talk properly.'

'Gerald, what is it that we really have to talk about right away like this?'

'About everything. About what you've done to us. About what we're going to do – do you realise that I have to live from day to day with the knowledge that you left me? That you were prepared to leave me, to *walk out on me*, because of another claim on you? You can't just come back and expect everything to be the same.'

'But I didn't come back. You rang here and found me –'

'I phoned every day – *every day* since you walked out on me – since you yet again –'

'Gerald, you can't –'

'*You* created a situation and *you're* responsible for it – you have *got* to make me understand how you did what you did. You have got to help me come to terms with it –'

679

'There is nothing I can do until I've finished my work here –'

'Do you expect time to stand still for you? Do you –'

'I expect nothing –'

'– expect people to keep their emotions in cold storage until it suits you to deal with them?'

He's going to use that dreadful metaphor, Asya thinks. Oh please please don't let him say it –

'If I were to tell you that your baby was in a burning house, would you say I've just got to finish what I'm doing? Or would you pick him up and run?'

Asya says nothing.

'Well? What would you do? Any mother – any *normal* mother – would pick up her baby and run.'

'I've told you: I can do nothing until I've finished this work.'

'You'd let your baby *burn* to *death*? Is *that* what you're telling me? This is criminal, man –'

'Look, just because you've chosen to use an image –'

'You'd let your baby burn to death?'

'You're not my baby and you're not burning.'

'I am telling you that what you have done to me needs to be attended to. That it is your human responsibility –'

'Please, Gerald, please. I've said I'm sorry. I don't even know how we got back into –'

'Because you refuse to see me. You refuse to do what any normal person – any normal warm-hearted person with a sense of what it means to be human and dealing with humans –'

'I've told you I can't –'

'– would do automatically without needing to be told –'

'I can't see you until –'

'You reduce me to begging you to take the knife from my heart, to staunch my wounds, and you say, "Just lie there and bleed a little longer until I finish my Ph.D" –'

Lateefa comes to the top of the stairs and peers down at Asya, who is sitting with the receiver to her ear and her head on her hand.

'Supper's ready,' Lateefa says.

Asya glances up and nods at her.

'– well it's not on, man. You can't do that to people.'

Asya says nothing.

'Are you listening to me? Are you hearing me? *Are you still there?*'

'Yes, I'm still here – but my mother's calling me –'

'Tell me, just tell me *why* you can't see me.'

'Because my mother's here. Because she's left her own work to stay with me and help me and she would be furious if I let everything go again –'

'You're afraid of your mother? You're twenty-seven and you're *afraid* of your *mother?*'

'I'm not afraid of her: I *care* for her. She's been through a lot with me already and this degree means a great deal to her. I'm going to get it.'

'And meanwhile, babe, I can rot in hell.'

Yes, yes, yes –

'No, Gerald, please, it's not *like* that. I don't see *why* it has to be like that. You're doing what you have to do and so am I –'

'I'd drop everything in a second if I could be with you.'

'We can see each other after. I promise. We can talk all you want –'

Lateefa comes to the top of the stairs again.

'Your lentil soup is growing cold,' she says. Asya glances up and nods.

'OK?' she says into the phone.

'No it's not OK.'

Asya closes her eyes. Oh shit, she thinks, *shit*.

'You're just dying to get off the phone, aren't you. It doesn't suit Brenda to talk to me just now. I'm being fucking inconvenient. What are you going to do about it?'

'There isn't anything I can do. It's no use going on and on at me like this –'

'Oh, baby, baby, if you knew how much I miss you, how much I *need* you. You *can't* know, or even *you* wouldn't have the heart to be like this –'

'Gerald, *please*, Gerald. Can't you just –'

'What? Hold on? Bleed for another six months or as long as it takes you to finish that damned Ph.D?'

'It won't be six months. I'm working very very hard. I'll be through by the end of the year –'

'Well, I might not be here by then. Don't say I haven't warned you.'

Asya hears the click on the line. She puts the receiver down, rubs her face with her hands and climbs the stairs.

'What on earth is all this?' Lateefa says. 'Every night – every night you sit on the phone by the hour, and it isn't even as if you come out of it looking happy; you look *dead*, your face turns yellow – what does he find, child, to say to you that takes all this time every night?'

Asya shrugs and sits down at the kitchen table.

'Nothing, really,' she says. 'He's just very unhappy and he thinks I should do something about it.'

'Like what?' Lateefa ladles soup out into a bowl and puts it down in front of Asya. 'Go to him and neglect your work for another year?'

'I don't think,' Asya says, stirring the thick lentil soup with her spoon, 'that even that would be enough.'

'What does he want then? What can he want from you?'

Lateefa puts a basket with three chunks of French bread in front of Asya and goes back to the saucepan to fill her own bowl.

'He wants me to explain to him how it was possible for me to leave him; to leave him completely, you know, and choose to be with Saif. He believes we were *meant* for each other –' Asya shrugs.

Lateefa puts her own bowl of soup down on the table and looks at her daughter.

'I can't, of course,' Asya says.

'But Saif is your *husband*,' Lateefa says.

'I know,' says Asya.

'And *you* don't even believe you were meant for each other, do you?' Lateefa reaches over for a piece of bread.

'No,' says Asya.

'Well, then, there's nothing to explain.'

'I know,' Asya says, stirring her soup. 'But I can't tell him that.'

'Why not? Why should you let yourself be bullied –'

'Because if I was going to say that I should have said it ages ago; I should have said it last summer –'

'And why *didn't* you?'

'Because – well, because, it would have seemed awfully – rude.'

'*Rude?*' Lateefa stares at Asya.

'Well, I mean, he was here in my house and everything – he was kind of – like my guest or something – I know, I know,' Asya says defensively. 'But if I was going to say something like that I'd have had to say it at the very beginning, and at the beginning I wanted him to stay – but I never said I *did* believe that we were meant for each other – I just didn't say anything – and he assumed – although he shouldn't have really, I mean he ought to have realised – oh –' Asya lets her spoon fall into her bowl.

'Eat your soup before it really grows cold,' her mother says. 'Go on, eat. I just don't know what to do with you, I really don't.'

'Well, he does have a point,' Asya says.

'And he's certainly making it,' Lateefa says, tilting her bowl and scooping the last drops of soup into her spoon. 'These phone calls must be costing him the earth.'

Asya says nothing.

'You can't hammer someone into believing something –'

'He's a marketing man.' Asya smiles. 'And anyway, he probably does believe that I believe that we were meant for each other – and that I can explain what happened –'

'But you can't. Will you please drink that soup –'

Asya puts a spoonful of soup into her mouth.

'This is delicious, Mummy,' she says.

'It's probably stone cold,' says her mother.

'No, no it's not,' Asya says, eating some more. 'I mean, I could think of things one *could* say –'

'Like what?'

'I don't know, things about human frailty or something – or about how there was some sort of task, you know, that I had to perform before I could reach the golden fleece –'

'This is just nonsense.'

Asya shrugs.

'You can't possibly say anything of the sort,' her mother says.

'No, I know,' Asya says. 'But I'm going to have to do *something* about him.'

'Change your phone number.'

'Mummy!'

'I'm serious. Do you *want* him to go on ringing you like this?'

'No.'

'Then change your phone number.'

'I couldn't possibly.'

'Why not?'

'Well, it wouldn't be fair. And besides, I'd know he was still out there thinking these thoughts – and he'd probably come and find me and then that would be another thing I'd have to explain –'

'Let him come here. I'll soon send him packing.'

'Oh, Mummy –'

'I would. He's ruined your marriage, he's wasted a year of your time, he'd stop you getting your degree if he could –'

'He didn't ruin my marriage, *I* ruined my marriage – and *he* would say I had wasted a year of *his* life and put him through hell into the bargain – I mean, if you look at it from *his* point of view, he's been used –'

'*Used* –'

'And his only crime is that he refuses to take it lying down – I mean, I know he's trying to shape things to what he wants, but we all do that, don't we –'

'Asya, you have *no* responsibility towards him. If you're actually – fond of him – which I don't think you are – you can join him after you've finished your –'

'But that's what you'd *always* say, don't you see? That's what you've always said even about Saif –'

Lateefa looks at Asya in silence.

'I'm not saying you're wrong or anything –' Asya says. 'Just that I can't imagine you ever saying, "Oh well, never mind about the work, darling, go and follow your heart," or some such –'

'Follow your heart!' Lateefa says scathingly. 'This is Mills and Boon talk – look where following your "heart" has got you now –'

'But maybe that's because I've never followed my heart,' Asya says. 'Not really. I mean, I don't even know about my "heart" any more. The last time I really knew what I wanted was when I wanted to live with Saif when I was eighteen – maybe if I'd done it then everything would have been different –'

'Look, Saif is still there if you want him: he's sitting in the Boltons spending his money hand over fist. Go back to him.'

'Oh, Mummy,' Asya says. 'You know that can't be done –'

'Why not?' Lateefa says. 'Why else is he still in touch? Why is he still in this country?'

'Yes, but it wouldn't work. I know I can drift into his flat and set up my typewriter and he'd let me – but then what? I mean, it wasn't really working even before any of this happened, and now –' Asya sits back in her chair. 'I don't know what I'm going to do,' she says.

'You're going to finish your Ph.D,' Lateefa says. She stands up and collects the soup bowls. 'You're going to finish your work and everything else will wait. Do you want some more soup? Or some cheese?'

'No, thank you,' Asya says.

Lateefa carries the bowls to the sink. 'Are you going to do any more tonight?'

'No,' says Asya.

'Right. I'm going to watch the news,' Lateefa says, moving towards the living-room.

Some days later

More recently, attempts to classify metaphor have taken the form of the construction of a 'tree' representing a semantic 'map' on which 'any' lexical item may be placed. Such 'maps' have been suggested by L. Ionesco, Lucy Wynn and Rosemary Gläser. Gläser's system is the most convincing, but as she points out:

The classificatory scheme touches a general problem: it is extremely difficult to classify the whole material and immaterial world on a logical basis and even more so on a linguistic principle. (1971, p.273)

The solution I have adopted lies in accepting a particular limitation for the typology but attempting, within its framework, to meet certain constraints which validate it.

Outside it is a brilliant, sunny day. If she were in London with Saif they would walk along the Old Brompton Road and buy two double cones of Dayville's caramel crunch ice-cream. When Mario was there –

Asya stands up and switches on the kettle.

'Would you like some tea?' she asks.

'Yes, please,' Lateefa says, not looking up from the letters she is reading in her corner of the sofa.

Asya stands at the kitchen window waiting for the kettle to boil. In the field behind the cottage a brown horse is grazing. He has a black tail and a black mane and glossy black patches near the points of his ears. He has a slimmed-down, elongated white Africa on his forehead. The riding-school must have bought the field, Asya thinks – or the meadow. Is it a field or a meadow? It must be a meadow if a horse is grazing in it. Would it be a metaphor to call a field a 'meadow' – or a meadow a 'field'? The dissimilarity, the semantic clash, would be in FUNCTION. 'She came upon a meadow planted with ears of corn' – but then it would *be* a field. Could you have something that was intrinsically, naturally, a meadow, but made to perform the function of a field – without its actually turning *into* a field? 'She, who had for so long been a meadow, now turned overnight into a field' – but the transfer here is between PERSON and LAND – where else could you have a FUNCTION clash: 'iron chains adorned her wrists and her neck' – no, because the TENOR and the VEHICLE here are still different things –

The kettle clicks and Asya makes the tea. She carries one cup over to her mother and comes back for the other. The horse lifts his head, swishes his tail, and sets off on a diagonal trot.

The limitation under which this typology operates is that it is mainly useful for the classification of semantic transfers *in poetry*: to fore-ground the transfer of meaning (or the incompatibility) between tenor and vehicle, and to capture important similarities and differences between the natures of the various transfers.

Certain distinctions appear to be central to poetic transfer. The most obvious, perhaps, is the concrete/non-concrete distinction; in a syntax-independent, unsignalled example:

The merchandise which thou hast brought from Rome *Are all too dear for me.*

Or, in a Verbal and Attributive syntax-dependent construction:

Today *deep thoughts* resolve with me to *drench*
    In mirth, that after no repenting draws; . . .
To measure life, learn thou betimes, and know
    Toward *solid good* what leads the nearest way;

'Toward solid good –' Asya pauses with her fingers on the typewriter: there's a big thought for you now; how can anyone know that? Know for sure? Aha! There it is: the nearest way to solid good; Asya sees a figure, triumphantly pointing – David's Napoleon, his cape swirling behind him, his arm outstretched, his horse rearing up – you'd have to know what was the 'solid good' first – and even then, 'the nearest way'? And anybody who thought they knew was more than likely wrong – like William, like Gerald, like –

Lateefa looks up.

'Are you all right?' she asks.

'Yes,' Asya says, and bends her eyes to her work again.

It has been remarked that metaphor is a 'concretising' trope. Our data bears this out: it yielded 946 non-concrete → concrete transfers as opposed to only 28 concrete → non-concrete transfers.

Another transfer is the one which involves the +PERSON feature. The most common occurrences of this transfer involve the movement towards +PERSON:

I turned my head and saw *the wind*,
   Nor far from where I stood,
Dragging the corn by her golden hair,
   Into a dark and lonely wood.

Much more rare are transfers moving towards -PERSON:

O in turns of tempest, and fan *me heaped* there;
   me frantic to avoid Thee and flee?
Why? That *my chaff might fly; my grain lie*,
   sheer and clear.

Now that's more like it: to lie still and wait for God – for *something* – to blow away your chaff and reveal the true, clear grain – and here, of course, the tenor would be – inexpressible; there's the thesis: 'a metaphor is that transfer in which the TENOR – or either the TENOR or the VEHICLE – cannot be adequately expressed by other means', and then it would be over in a day – in a minute – instead of four years . . .

The data yielded just 102 metaphors where PERSON is the TENOR, i.e. the object of inquiry, as opposed to 835 where PERSON is the VEHICLE – the defining element. Table (22) shows that metaphors where PERSON is the TENOR occur most frequently during the Renaissance and Jacobean periods, and to some extent during the twentieth century. The pre-Romantic, Romantic, post-Romantic and Pre-Raphaelite periods have virtually no metaphors of this kind. On the other hand, these latter are the periods in which 'personifying' metaphors (metaphors where PERSON is the VEHICLE) abound; the Romantics alone giving more than a quarter (26 per cent) of the total of personifying metaphors in the data.

Asya closes her eyes and stretches her arms above her head. She shrugs her shoulders hard several times and bends her neck and draws circles with her head until when she opens her eyes the keys of the typewriter are a blur.

'I'll have to drive in to the computer in a while,' she says. 'Will you come with me?'

'Yes.' Lateefa looks up. 'I can go into the library.'

'What's the news, Mummy?' Asya looks at the letters lying on her mother's lap.

'They're all fine,' Lateefa says. 'The baby's just lovely, Deena says. She says he's sleeping through the night already and he's only just completed three months.'

'He'll probably do his Ph.D when he's sixteen,' Asya says.

'His mother will have to do hers first,' Lateefa says, 'and it won't be easy with a baby to look after.'

'I'm sure she'll manage,' Asya says, resting her chin on her hand and gazing at her mother. 'Deena takes after you.'

'Well, she isn't without her faults,' Lateefa says, frowning at the letter. 'Her handwriting and spelling are still atrocious.'

'They don't need handwriting and spelling in her line of work.'

'You always need handwriting and spelling: there's a bit here I can't make out at all.'

'Let's see –' Asya stands up and goes over to the living-room. She takes the letter from her mother's hand and scrutinises Deena's scrabbly writing. 'It says – it looks like: something "is madder than ever" –'

' "Madder" is it? Let me see –'

Asya puts the letter back in her mother's hand.

' "Zeeko", that's it: "Zeeko is madder than ever but he's very good with the baby and babysits for us sometimes –" so she can't find anyone to babysit for her, it has to be Zeeko?'

'Who's Zeeko?' Asya asks.

'He's one of their crowd; the one who believes in "the inevitability of the armed struggle" –'

'Does he really?'

Lateefa waves her hand. 'There's always one of those –'

'You sound like Saif.'

'It's such a waste of time.'

'What is?'

'All that sitting around talking that they do.'

'Oh, Mummy.' Asya leans back in the sofa and stretches out her legs. 'You always want people to be getting *on* with things –'

'Well –'

'Get on and finish your work, get on and finish your food, get on, get on, get on and finish your *life* in the final –'

Her mother laughs. 'That's how you see it?'

Asya yawns. 'Well, that's what it amounts to. What's wrong with being a lotus-eater?'

'He's going to get them into trouble, that Zeeko.'

'You just said all they did was sit around talking; how can they be ineffectual and get into trouble at the same time?'

'Because they're in Egypt,' Lateefa says, 'and Deena would do better to –'

'– concentrate on finishing her MA,' Asya intones.

Lateefa shrugs. 'Well, it's true,' she says.

Asya stands up and walks over to the window: the path, the low wall, the nettles, and the hidden stream –

'How's my uncle?' she says.

'She doesn't mention him, so he must be all right. And Meedo has passed his primary school certificate, so your aunt Soraya must be all right too.'

'And Daddy? And Kareem?'

'She says they're both fine. Your father's been made head of the central committee that promotes everybody so he'll be busier than ever. You know Kareem is going out with a Christian girl?'

'No, I didn't know.' Asya turns back from the window. 'Is he?'

'Yes. Since the winter. She's very nice.'

'But you foresee problems.'

'Well, not from our side, of course. But I shouldn't think her parents are very happy about it.'

'Maybe they don't know.'

'Parents always know.'

'No they don't: Chrissie's parents didn't know about Fuad.'

Lateefa shakes her head. 'Now there's another story,' she says. 'You know when I went to visit Chrissie in May – when she had her little boy – her mother practically reproached *me* for Fuad's behaviour? "It's like this, Lateefa Hanim?" she said. "On our part we only took him because he was a friend of Saif's." What's she going to say when she hears you've left Saif?'

'*He* left *me*,' Asya says.

'Oh Asya,' her mother says, 'you know very well you're the one who's leaving him.'

'I would have stayed,' Asya says.

Her mother looks at her and says nothing.

'Mummy,' says Asya, 'have you ever fancied anyone other than Daddy?'

'No,' Lateefa says.

'Come on, Mummy, really,' says Asya.

'No. I haven't. Really,' Lateefa says.

'I suppose you *would* say that,' Asya says.

'No, not necessarily,' her mother says. 'I could tell you that I did but I didn't give in to it.'

'So you really never ever fancied anyone else?'

'My darling, I think the world was different in our day,' Lateefa says. 'Our circumstances certainly were different –'

'How?'

'Well, we had less – money, less freedom, we were never separated for as long as you were, and we took certain things as – given, I suppose.'

'Did *he* ever fancy anyone else?'

'I don't think so,' Lateefa says.

'You never thought maybe he did? You were never –'

'No, I never thought he did. But maybe he did, I don't know.'

'But if he had, what would he have done?'

'I don't know. When you go home you can ask him.'

'Mummy,' Asya says, going back to the sofa and sitting down. 'I don't want to go home.'

'You what?' Lateefa says, turning so that Deena's letter rustles from her lap down on to the sofa.

'I don't mean not *ever*. I mean I just don't want to go home straight away – as soon as I've finished.'

'Is that because of this Gerald?'

'No,' Asya says. 'No, really. It isn't. It's just that I want some time on my own –'

'You've had *years* on your own –'

'No, but I mean without this Ph.D hanging over me. You see, I've always had *something* hanging over me, Mummy: the BA stopping me getting married, then the marriage and the Ph.D stopping me from even thinking about what else I could do –'

'But that's what life is like, child –'

'But it doesn't *have* to be. I don't *want* my life to be like this. I feel as if I've never ever made a real choice –'

'All the choices you made were yours –'

'Yes, but were they *real* choices? I mean, I was born *into* a road which had "to the Ph.D" signalled on it; I hardly *knew* anyone who didn't work in the university – I mean, I don't even know that I want to be in the university for the rest of my life –'

'But what else can you do?' Lateefa stares at her daughter.

'I don't know. But maybe I can find out.'

'And your contract?'

'I'll honour it, of course I will. D'you think I'd let anyone say "Professor al-Ulama's – *and* Dr Lateefa's – daughter welshed on her contract"? I'll come back and I'll teach for the three years or whatever it is – but not straight away. I just want some *time* –'

'But what will you *do* with this time?'

'I don't know. Just *think*, just *be*, and see what happens.'

'You'll get yourself into some scrape –'

'I don't think so. I really don't. And anyway, what would be worse than the scrape I'm already in? Nothing I can do can have such – repercussions any more. And I don't want to go home till it's all died down.'

'But nobody will –'

'Yes they will. You've already said about Tante Muneera. And can you imagine Tante Soraya? And what do I say to Tante Adeela? And Kareem

689

will be very upset with me; he adores Saif. I know he loves me and he'll try to be fair, but I can't go round telling the whole story to everyone and I just know that I'll be under a whole lot of pressure. I just want to be *free* for a while –'

'But you can't just sit around doing *nothing*.'

'But why *not*, Mummy? Just for a while? I mean, I happen to have been born Egyptian – but if I'd been American or something, it wouldn't have been at all strange to take a year off between things and just bum around the world with a rucksack or something –'

'I can just see you with a rucksack.' Lateefa looks satirical. 'Where would you wash your hair and sit under the dryer for an hour and a quarter every five days?'

'Mummy, I'm not saying that's what I *want* to do and I *know* that one can't be free of one's own – character, but can't I just find out what it's like to be free of everything *else*; to find out what I would do if I could do what I wanted?'

'But you've *always* done what you wanted –'

'Oh, *Mummy*,' Asya cries jumping up. 'You're going round and round in circles.' She stands in the middle of the room. 'I've done what I've been *conditioned* to want. I've woken up every morning and done what I already *knew* I had to do. I want to know what I would do if I didn't *have* to do *anything*: what would I do when I got out of bed? Or would I just stay in bed all day? It's a beautiful, beautiful day outside' – Asya flings her arm at the window – 'and I *think* I'd like to go out and walk in the fields and look at the horses, and I'm not going because I have to work on my Ph.D – if I didn't have to work on my Ph.D, *would* I go out for a walk? Or would I sit here with a book and think I'd like to go out for a walk? I don't know. And I *want* to know.'

'Oh, Asya,' her mother says sadly. 'You always make such a problem out of everything.'

September 1977

That's it, thinks Asya, pausing with her hands in the soapy water and looking out at the empty field; that's it: 'Rather a ditch in Egypt/Be gentle grave unto me –' a transfer caused by a clash in FUNCTION –

'I've been thinking about what you said,' Lateefa says, 'and I'll tell you what to do. You're almost finished with this now, aren't you?' She moves her head towards Asya's typewriter.

'Well, there's still an awful lot to be done,' says Asya, turning away from the washing-up.

'Yes, but none of it is problematic, is it? It's just hard work.'

'Yes.'

'So how long do you think it will take you? Four months?'

'Maybe. But maybe six. I could run into problems with the computer.'

'I don't know why you did something that was so dependent on computers and statistics and all that.'

'I thought I'd have Saif to advise me.'

'Well, he would still help you, you know. If you asked him.'

'He's too busy with Lady Caroline Lamb.'

'That's not her name, is it?' Lateefa's voice takes on a sharp interest.

'No,' says Asya, peeling off her rubber gloves. 'But it's Lady Caroline something.'

'Are you upset about that?'

'No.'

'Why are you looking depressed then?'

'Because I'm not upset. What were you going to say, Mummy?'

Asya fills the kettle and switches it on.

'Well,' Lateefa says, sitting down at the kitchen table, 'we're in September now –'

'How long are you going to be able to stay, Mummy?'

'Teaching starts on October the first,' Lateefa says. 'I'll have to be back for that. But you'll be all right now, won't you?'

'Oh yes,' says Asya, 'yes, of course I will.'

'Well, listen. We're in September now. Say you finish by January. You're free then, aren't you?'

'There'd still be the viva.'

'Yes, but you'll have finished your work.'

'Yes. Would you like some tea?'

'Yes, but let's have it with mint this time.'

Asya opens the cupboard and brings down the jar of dried mint. She pours the boiling water into a small kettle which she puts on the cooker. She measures two teaspoonfuls of mint into it and lights the flame.

'Say your viva will be in March – at the earliest. There'll be only two months of the term left in Cairo. You'll write a letter to the university and ask for unpaid leave until October '79 to turn your thesis into a book. They'll stop your grant but we can talk about that later. You'll have a year and a half then to do what you want –'

'But I don't want to turn my thesis into a book –'

'You don't have to –'

'I want to put it away and never *ever* have to look at it or think about it again –'

'This is just silly –'

'You'd have me spend the rest of my life expanding on it – turning chapters into papers for academic journals –'

'Asya. We're not talking about the long term.'

'But you want me to write some letter –'

'You want some time to yourself –'

'I know I do –'

'But you are under contract. A contract that says that you will return as soon as the purpose for your study leave is accomplished.'

'Yes.' Asya spoons some tea-leaves into the kettle and lifts it off the fire. She switches the cooker off.

'So you have to have the university's permission not to return.'

'Yes, but I don't want to say –'

'They're an academic body. They have regulations –'

'Can't I just say –'

'What? That you need to find yourself? You have to give them something to which they can agree.'

'But I don't *want* to turn this thing into a book.' Asya stares at her papers.

'You're being so stupid,' Lateefa says. '*Don't do it*. Just *say* you're going to try to do it. Are they going to come and watch you?'

'No.'

'So?'

'But *you'll* think I might.'

Lateefa stares at her. 'No I won't.'

'Not at all? You won't be secretly harbouring the hope that I might – just *might* be doing it?'

'No.'

'You won't even *want* me to do it?'

'Well, maybe one day you will.'

'I won't. Not ever, ever, *ever*.'

'All right. You won't.'

'And that's all right by you?'

Lateefa sighs. 'Yes, that's all right by me.'

Asya pours the tea into two glasses and puts one glass and the sugar-bowl in front of her mother.

'OK, Mummy. Thanks.'

'Now, about money: have you thought of what you're going to do?'

'No, I –'

'Will you take some from Saif?'

'No, of course not.'

'Why? What's "of course" about it? He has plenty and he's not doing anything particular with it –'

'It's his money. He earned it –'

'He had nothing when you married him.'

'I've done nothing to help him earn it. I mean, if I'd cooked his dinners or ironed his shirts –'

'He'd give it to you gladly; he hasn't closed down your joint account –'

'Look, Mummy: if we wanted to be really strict about this, I should give him back everything he's ever spent on me –'

'You're mad.'

'– because I took it under false pretences. Because for him I was an investment that didn't work out – only I knew I wasn't working out and he didn't –'

'I tell you, you're mad.'

'But of course I can't do that. But I'm not taking any more.'

'Well, what are you going to do then?'

'I don't know. I'll find some kind of work, and I'll live very cheaply.'

'I can't see you living cheaply – you're not in the habit –'

'But I will. Honestly.'

'Look, I'll give you whatever I've got left before I go home. But it won't be very much –'

'Thank you, Mummy. That'll be very nice – and I'm sure I'll be all right.' Asya picks up their two glasses. At the sink she turns back to Lateefa. 'That letter: will you tell me what to write?'

'Yes,' Lateefa says. 'I'll take the letter back with me and when you've had your viva I'll hand it in. Let's just hope your father isn't Dean by then.'

'Might he be?'

'He probably will be the next Dean. But the elections will be in the summer. I'll push this through for you before then.'

'He'd never agree to it, would he?'

'For someone else he might – but he wouldn't want to look as though he were favouring his daughter.'

Some days later

Asya climbs up the stairs.

'I'm going to have to see him,' she says.

'No,' says Lateefa.

'But Mummy, he sounds desperate. He says he can't go on – can't do his work or anything –'

'They always say that.'

'Don't be so hard-hearted. He really is very unhappy.'

'And what can you do for him?'

'Maybe if I just talked to him –'

'You yourself said you couldn't say anything that would make him feel better.'

'I know, but –'

'You said that what he'd need would be a whole age of devotion –'

'Yes, but every day that passes with me sitting up here doing my work and ignoring him makes it worse –'

'You think that if you went down and saw him for a day, for two days,

693

that would be enough? You think he'd say, "Now you've explained it all to me, everything's fine? Now go back and finish your work"?'

'No, but –'

'But what?'

'I could at least *try*.'

'How can you try when you know it won't work?'

'At least it would look like I cared –'

'You care enough to sit on the telephone for hours every night listening to him.'

'I don't know why this lousy, wretched Ph.D should always take precedence over everything –'

'Because you're almost there and anyone who –'

'I wasn't almost there when I chose to come here instead of going with Saif to Beirut –'

'But that was never an option. Saif himself never considered it –'

'Yes, because he thought I had to have this university career or I'd die. But now that I don't want that –'

'You still have to finish *this*. And anyone who really cared for you would tell you that. Look at Saif himself, sitting down there in London. Is he trying to disrupt your life –'

'He doesn't *want* to disrupt my life. He's glad to be finally shot of me –'

'How do you know that? Why isn't he going home if it isn't to be near you? What else is there for him in this country?'

'There's Lady Caroline.'

'Oh Asya, be sane. You think he's staying here because of her?'

'No, I don't. But he's not staying because of me. He's staying because he's here and he has no particular reason to go anywhere else. But I can't *do* anything for him and maybe I *can* do something for Gerald.'

'Darling, what are you? Florence Nightingale? You're going to help Gerald because you can't help Saif?'

'Maybe I've always got it wrong: I've always let things stand in the way of what I really should do –'

'Look, Gerald Stone lived with you here for six months and you didn't do a stroke of work. He is not going to let you finish this Ph.D if he can help it –'

'Well, isn't it possible that he may be right? That there has to be a moment when I give *everything* –'

'Sacrifice all your work? For what? Someone who isn't even worth it?'

'But you would never think *anyone* was worth it. If God *himself* came down and stood here –'

'Look, I have had it with you.' Lateefa stands up suddenly and the kitchen chair she had been sitting on falls over with a loud bang. 'I have *had* it with you,' she shouts. 'You don't want your husband? *Fine*. You don't want your job? *Fine.* You don't want to come home? *Fine.* But *you are doing this Ph.D.* You have worked on it for four years. You've used up four years of your *life.* You've used *money*: two years of British Council money and two years of government hard currency that could have financed other people who are *rotting* in the department making do with ten-year-old periodicals while you sit here thinking the world was made for you and going on and on about not knowing whether you want to go for a stupid *walk.*' She slams her hand down on the kitchen table. 'You are going to do this Ph.D if I have to resign and stand over you to make you do it. I am not letting you ruin your life. You will finish it and then you can go to *hell.* You can do as you bloody well please – *I wash my hands of you –*'

'You said "bloody",' says Asya.

'What?'

'You said "bloody", Mummy.'

'I don't care if I said "bloody". You heard what I said and you're going to do it.'

Lateefa pushes her glasses back on to her nose. Her hand is trembling and her eyes are red with angry tears. Her breathing is loud as she walks across the room and sits down heavily on the sofa. Asya picks up the chair that had fallen over and stands it up on its legs. She waits for a moment and then crosses the room and sits down next to her mother.

'I'm sorry,' she says.

Her mother waves her away as she takes off her glasses and wipes them with a piece of tissue-paper.

'No, look, I'm really really sorry.' Asya plucks at the skirt of her mother's dress. 'I was horrible,' she says, 'and I really really don't want to upset you. Please?'

'Get away from me. Go do something useful,' Lateefa says. 'What do you think this is? A novel? A game?'

'Please, Mummy. I was wrong, I know I was. Only I feel so wicked I don't know what to do. But I shouldn't go on at you like that. I'm sorry. I really am. And of *course* I'll finish the Ph.D. If I was going to walk out on it I'd have walked out long ago. I've always been going to finish it.'

'So what's all this then? You're just amusing yourself with me? You're giving me a hard time for nothing?'

'No, no. I'm sorry. I don't know why I argue with you. I mean, if you weren't here I'd probably just shut up and do it.'

'So I'm just here to be harassed and tormented?'

'No, you're not. But there's just no one else for me to talk to. But I *am* sorry. Please will you stop being angry now?'

Lateefa puts her glasses down on her knee. She rubs her face with her hands and sighs.

'I don't know what's going to become of you,' she says. 'I really don't.

Your sister is supposed to be the madcap of the family and she never gave me half as much trouble.'

'I'll be all right,' Asya says. 'I know I will. You won't need to worry about me any more. I promise. OK?'

Lateefa says nothing and stares sadly into her lap.

'OK, Mummy? OK?'

'What have I done wrong?' Lateefa says.

'You haven't,' Asya says. 'You've done right. Given everything, you've done absolutely right. And *more* than right. And it's all going to work out just fine. Will you be all right now?'

'Yes,' says Lateefa quietly, 'yes. Go and make me a coffee.'

Tuesday, 4 October

Asya puts away the dustpan and brush, the polish and the yellow cloth, the bucket and the sponges. She takes off her rubber gloves and straightens her back: the bare floorboards she has just polished stretch from her feet to the wall at the other end of the room. She draws her arm across her forehead. What a lot of dust there had been. Even the few pieces that had been here had attracted so much dust – this is much cleaner, she thinks, much better: empty. The rented television still stands in the corner, the music centre sits on the floor. Balanced on a speaker, her one table-lamp throws a large pool of light on to the wooden floor and a smaller elongated one on the white wall. There is nothing else.

Behind her the electric kettle sits on the range of empty cupboards. There is no cooker, and no fridge. The kitchen table is still there – and one chair. Now she has no choice: if she wants to sit she has to sit in front of her typewriter. She leans against the sink and pulls off the rubber gloves and looks at her hands. Hands are always damp when they come out of rubber gloves; does the water seep in? Or is it because hands sweat with work and the rubber lets in no air? Under her arms and between her breasts she feels hot and sweaty. She goes towards the stairs. It's good that the shower is electric; the oil for the central heating is about to run out and it would cost a hundred and ten pounds to fill the tank. But the shower is electric. And the garage is still full of logs – well, not full, but there are enough to last the two months till the cottage is sold. Jenny had said the latest she could make the completion date was the first of December. So now she really *will* have to finish by then. Jenny had been very sweet and concerned but what could she do? She had to sell the cottage and she'd postponed it as long as she could – but she did need her furniture – and it was kind of her not to take it till Lateefa had gone *and* to offer to leave the chair and table. In the bedroom Asya pushes her jeans down then finds she has nowhere to sit to take them off. She leans against the wall and eases one leg, then the other, over her feet. She folds the jeans up and puts them down on the cement floor. She pulls her black pullover up over her head and folds it and puts it on top of the jeans. This room, the whole downstairs, is going to be freezing without the central heating. But she can sleep upstairs – sleep in front of the fire.

In the small bathroom mirror she pins her hair into a knot and covers it with her blue shower-cap. No more long hot baths. But she's always had showers for cleanness; baths are a luxury – and this is no time for luxuries. Under the shower she scrubs herself all over, then stands for a few moments enjoying the hot water on her skin. She mustn't let herself get sleepy; it's only eight o'clock and she hasn't done any work today, what with the removal men here and then cleaning up the house after them without a Hoover, but she's just *so* tired. She sits on the edge of the tub to rub in her body lotion. Gerald will be calling soon, and she'll say no. She has to go on saying no until she's finished.

In her nightdress and woollen dressing-gown, with woollen socks on her feet, she climbs the stairs. She switches on the television but kills the sound. Then she sits down at the table. The black art paper she'd bought on Thursday when her mother left is pinned into place on the window-panes. In the living-room she takes it down in the morning, but down-stairs now she might as well leave it up all the time. The stove is unlit but she'll save the logs till the oil runs out. She pulls the typewriter into position in front of her.

The second broad set of categories is that of the 'predications'. These are usually nominalised, and in most cases are tenors of transfers whose vehicles are arguments. They fall into five categories; the first is the 'emotive predication':

1. 'Emotive Predications'
Here I have grouped all predications which describe emotions such as 'love', 'pleasure', 'joy', 'passion', 'desire', 'despair', 'terror' etc.:

My Love is of a birth as rare
As 'tis for object strange and high:
It was begotten by Despair
Upon Impossibility.

No more – no more – Oh! never more on me
The freshness of the heart can fall like dew,
Which out of all the lovely things we see
Extracts emotions beautiful and new
Hived in our bosoms like the bag o' the bee:

Not, I'll not, *carrion comfort*, *Despair*, not feast on thee:

The 'emotive predication' is the category with the highest frequency of occurrence as a tenor (59 per cent) in all the transfers involving predications. It takes a wide variety of vehicles –

When the telephone rings Asya walks slowly downstairs.

'Hi, babe, were you sleeping?'

'No, why?'

'You took a long time to answer.'

'No, I was – upstairs.'

'Your voice sounds like you've just woken up.'

'No.' Asya clears her throat. 'I just haven't used it for a bit.'

'Were you working?'

'Yes.'

'Am I interrupting you?'

'No, not at all.'

' "No, not at all." '

'Sorry?'

'You.'

'What about me?'

'You just sound very formal: "No, not at all." '

'I don't mean to sound formal.' She is so tired.

'Poor babe, you can't help it: it's just the way you are.'

Asya leans her head against the wall.

'And now you'll go silent on me,' Gerald says.

Asya looks for something to say and finds nothing.

'Babe?'

'Yes?'

'It's OK. It was only a joke.'

'OK.'

'Don't be so serious, man.'

'I'm not – particularly.'

He sounds like he's in a good mood. She has to keep it that way.

'Have you been doing something nice?' she asks. Can he find fault with that?

'Not as nice as what I'd like to do.'

Oh. Well –

'Oh,' she says. 'Well –'

'Well?'

'Well, what *have* you been doing?'

'Did you hear what I said?'

'Yes.'

'Well?'

'I don't know what to say.'

'I want to make love to you, babe.'

Asya feels her heart skip a beat and her legs tremble. She braces her feet firmly on the hall floor and says nothing.

'You still don't know what to say?'

'Gerald –'

'Won't you say you want it too, babe?'

'Yes,' says Asya, 'but –'

'Meet me. Come to me –'

'No.'

'Why? Why not?'

'I've got to stay here till I've finished.'

'Then I'll come to you.'

'No, no you can't.'

'Baby –'

'My mother's here. You know my mother's here –' Asya remembers to drop her voice. 'It's not possible,' she whispers.

'Look, this is evil. This is criminal. How can you –'

'Gerald, Gerald, *please*, we can't go over this every night.'

'We'll go over it. And over it and *over* it until you see the crime you're committing –'

'Please, will you stop this, it's completely senseless –'

'No it isn't. It's the one thing which makes sense in this world. I want to be with you. Do you hear that? Do you *understand* that?'

'Yes, I do. And you will be.'

'When you've finished.'

'Yes.'

'What are you made of, man? Ice? Ice would have melted – but not you. You'll just go on, come what may –'

'I'm coming!' Asya calls up the stairs.

'Your supper's ready, is it?'

'Yes.'

'Brenda's supper is ready. It's all laid out for her on the table and all she has to do is go up there and eat it. You won't forget your napkin now, will you?'

'Gerald –'

'It's disgusting.'

'Gerald, I know you're having a hard time. But so am I. Why don't we *help* each other through this –'

'Tell me one thing.'

'Yes?'

'Are you seeing your husband?'

'No.'

'Is he there with you?'

'*No.*'

'Where is he?'

'I don't know where he is.'

'You're not in touch with him?'

'No.'

'Are you telling me the truth?'

'Yes.'

'Because if you're not –'

'*I'm coming, Mummy,*' Asya calls urgently.

'OK, babe. I have to go out tonight anyway.'

'OK.'

'You're going to be all right?'

'Yes.'

'OK. I'll call you tomorrow.'

Asya sits on the stairs and folds her arms tight. If he ever finds out – but he can't find out – even if he suddenly comes here she can say her mother's gone out, gone for a walk – in the middle of the night? Gone to Oxford then; she had to go to Oxford for one day and she's meeting her there tomorrow – because she's bringing a lot of books and papers back and she can't carry them on her own. He couldn't say he'd come with her to Oxford. And in the morning she'd see him out and lock the door and drive away. And make sure he wasn't following her. And she would have had him again for a night: one night, on the floor, in front of the fire – oh, but he'd talk, heavens, would he talk . . .

Asya switches on the kettle and pours the contents of a packet of tomato soup into her big blue mug. She cuts off a piece of brown bread and rewraps the rest of the loaf in the plastic bag. She can't stand at the kitchen sink and stare outside any more. But outside it is black, and this paper is black. So why is it different? Why can't she stand here and stare at the black paper? The kettle clicks off. Asya pours the water into the mug and stirs the soup. She takes it and the piece of bread to the table and sits again at the typewriter. On the television, a man in casual clothes walks in a green open space. His face is to the camera and his mouth is moving. He lifts his arm and points to something in the distance. The camera zooms out. When it stops the pointing man has become very small and the screen is filled with a postcard picture of a mountain.

> *Glory is most bright and gay*
> *In a flash and so away,*

Love is the fire, and sighs the smoke, *the ashes* shame and *scorns.*

The fifth category – exemplified above – is that of the 'Evaluative Predication' –

When the phone rings again Asya hesitates – but he can't have come back already, it's only – she checks her watch – half past eleven – he

700

might have come back – but what if it's Saif – or her mother ringing from Cairo. The phone stops. It had only rung three times. She runs down the stairs and dials Saif's number in London.

'Saif?'

'Hello, Princess.'

'Did you just ring me?'

'Yes. I decided you were asleep.'

'No, no I wasn't.'

'Are you working?'

'Yes.'

'I just wanted to know if you were all right.'

'Yes, yes I'm fine.'

'Good. OK, then –'

'Saif. I – thank you. For paying the rent. It's very kind.'

'How did you know?'

'Jenny MacRae called me –'

'She wasn't supposed to tell you –'

'But I'd have found out anyway –'

'She was supposed to just put it in your account –'

'And I wouldn't have noticed seven hundred pounds?'

'Well – how is it without your mother?'

'It's a bit spooky –'

'Have you put something up on those windows?'

'Yes I have. Saif, are you – managing?'

'Managing what?'

'Well – things –'

'What things?'

'Well – laundry and things.'

'Come on, Princess.' He laughs. 'Laundry? Since when have you worried about my laundry?'

'I've *always* worried about your laundry –' Asya remembers a game of tug-of-war with a green plastic bag in Howard Hotel. 'I did it when you were around. What could I do if you were in another country –'

'The laundry gets done. There's always someone who'll do the laundry.'

'How's Lady Caroline?'

'Fine. Gone.'

'Really?'

'Yeah, she couldn't stand the pace.'

'You mean she didn't want to sit around reading all day.'

'No, it was all riding and parties. You'd have loved it.'

'Well, maybe I'll join in with the next one.'

'This one's into politics. Another of your things.'

'You mean there's a new one already?'

'What can I do? I can't seem to keep them away.'
'Who is she?'
'She's Scots.'
'What's her name?'
'Clara. Her name's Clara.'
'Did you know her before?'
'No, I just met her.'
'But how? Where do you meet these people?'
'Come on, Princess. You get back to your work.'
'What about *your* work?'
'I haven't got any work. I'm unemployed.'
'But Saif, seriously –'
'Seriously. I'm unemployed. I'm a full-time playboy.'
'You're going to run out of money.'
'Not for a while.'
'But when you do?'
'I'll put a bullet through my head.'
'Saif –'
'Get back to work, Princess –'
'But Saif –'
'We don't have to talk about this right now, do we? It's almost midnight.'
'No. OK. I'm sorry.'
'Can I go to bed now?'
'Yes.'
'Right. Goodnight, then, Princess. Call me if you want anything.'
'Yes. Goodnight –'
Can I go to bed now? With Clara? Can I go to bed (with Clara) now? Well that's OK. That's fine. She doesn't mind. Asya walks up the stairs. A quarter to twelve. He can go right ahead. He puts the phone down and walks over to the window at the front of his living-room. Asya sits in front of her typewriter and watches him put a match to his cigarette as he looks out into the lamp-lit street. Behind his voice on the phone she'd heard Dylan's nasal demand:

'*Sa*-rah, *Sa*-rah,
Don't ever *leave* me
Don't ever go –'

Now he crosses the room and presses the button that lifts the stylus from the turntable. He turns off the power. In the silence he walks out of the living-room door. He walks slowly, as though he were preoccupied with something else, and Asya watches him disappear with his cigarette down the long dark corridor with the Victorian tiled floor that leads to his bedroom. Whether Clara is lying in bed waiting for him or not – Asya does not care to follow him there. Not that she minds. She doesn't mind. But what if he looks into her eyes and says, 'I love you, Princess'? He wouldn't do that. She knows he wouldn't do that. 'I love you, Clara.' *That* she can't even imagine. But if, this minute, he is lying on top of her – sliding his hand behind the small of her back, urging her body up to meet his – she doesn't mind. She doesn't mind.

In the course of her analysis of Shakespeare's 'Sonnet 73', Winifred Nowottny makes the crucial observation that 'retrospective redefinition can be of massive importance to the total effect of a poem.' (1965, p.80) 'Retrospective redefinition' is, I believe, an ongoing process by which we continually adjust our interpretation of previously perceived elements in the light of elements *just* perceived. It is particularly pertinent in the interpretation of Spenser's 'Sonnet viii' from the *Amoretti* (1595) –

At half past one, Asya cannot keep her head upright any longer. She pushes her chair back and stands up. Downstairs she brushes her teeth and collects the Sinai bedu rug that used to lie on the floor of the boiler-room and takes it upstairs. She goes down again for her quilt and her hot-water bottle. Back in the living-room she switches off the dancing dots of the television and spreads her rug out on the floor in front of the cold stove, then shakes her quilt out over it. She crosses to the kitchen and fills the water bottle from the kettle and switches off the light. She lies down on her rug and feels the wooden floor hard under her shoulder-blades and her head. But it can be done: this is how a peasant sleeps every night of his life – but maybe an earth floor is gentler than a wooden one? Well, the Japanese sleep on wooden floors; their – what are they? Tatamis – can't make much difference . . . Asya sits up and folds her dressing-gown into a pillow and lies down again. She puts out her hand and switches off the lamp. The lighthouse keeper in Tyre, the one with the little dress-shop with the sign 'Haute Couture de Paris' next to his lighthouse, he knows every single thing about the Roman city buried under his patch of sea; from the top of his lighthouse he can see its marble columns rising through the water, but he knows nothing about the ships that have been sunk in his harbour. 'It is difficult,' he says, 'to know the facts about recent events.' As she curls up on her side hugging the rubber bottle the wooden floor bruises her hip-bone. Dulce et decorum est, she thinks, pro – pro what? To suffer, to suffer anyway –

The mornings are dark and the days are brief. The rain falls and the cold wind blows. Figures move and mouth silently across the lit screen. The

703

oil runs out and the power-cuts begin. And all these things bring comfort. Dulce et decorum est. To wake up with an aching body. To remove a black screen and uncover a grey day and look out on an overgrown stream. To subsist on powdered soup and cold bread. To sit on a wooden chair till you can sit no longer and find relief in lying on a wooden floor. To complete a task that brings no joy. This is how it should be. This is fitting, and seemly, and right.

Sometimes a thought, an image, will catch her unawares as she crosses towards a window or steps downstairs into the cold darkness below: a dark shape swaying in her doorway – *'Will you let me in?'* – a loved familiar figure in an armchair – *'I did a bad thing today'* – or huddled on a rainy pier – *'How can you say that?'* – or softly, very softly, *'Did you sleep with him, Princess?'* – and she will find herself cowering against a wall, gasping, clutching herself against the pain that pierces through her just there: there in the soft centre of her body where the chest wall ends in an inverted V. At first the sudden violence would shake her, but then she came to know it; a familiar assailant whose intentions and whose limits she had fathomed and who causes her a pain so tangible that when it passes she can still feel its shadow like a bruise. And that too is as it should be.

And there are other images; scenes that shape themselves gently in front of her when the room is lit only by the stove and the three candles balanced on an empty shoe-box next to the typewriter: Dada Zeina rubs her feet after the torment of the *halawa* on her henna day: 'You were always the cleanest, prettiest child, and tomorrow you'll be the prettiest bride. May God, my darling, give you happiness, and not let time work its changes on you, may he be your man and above you in this world and the next, Amen O God of the two worlds,' or his arm round her shoulders in Bond Street as they pause to listen to a stooped and ragged man with a violin playing 'La vie en rose' under the arches outside Elizabeth Arden. Or Tante Adeela in her kitchen showing her how to rub the boiled pasta with raw egg beaten with salt and pepper before settling it into the baking-tray – these scenes cause another, more final kind of pain: an anguish already tinged with nostalgia that makes her bend her head down to the typewriter and weep. Once, as she lifted her head and opened her eyes, she found the keys of the typewriter all raised and jammed like cramped, protesting limbs.

And there is the dream. The dream comes often, but she never remembers. Each time, with a fresh heart, she sees him, in a Michelin-man type space suit, drifting slowly away. Through the visor she can see his face: surprised, frightened, bewildered. She calls out and reaches up, but, weightless, he drifts away: up he goes, slowly up, spiralling and turning – but, far though he may drift, she can still see his face. She can always see his face.

704

Scene 9

New York
Wednesday, 28 December 1977

Dear Mummy,
  I am writing to you from New York – although by the time you get this I'll be back in London. We're visiting (or 'visiting with' as they all say) some friends of Gerald's. He had his heart set on coming here for New Year and on me meeting them, so here I am. This is our third day here and I haven't seen anything of the city yet – but I will soon –

Asya sits at the chrome and glass dining-table with the letter-pad in front of her and the black biro in her hand. In the white laminate kitchen Marie slowly stirs something in a giant red Le Creuset pot. She is pregnant, in her fifth month, and her growing tummy is starting to bulge prettily through the light smocks she wears around the house.

I saw Saif in London just before I left and he seems OK. I found I envied him his pretty flat dreadfully. This trip has put off the accommodation problem for a bit – but I really think Gerald and I are beyond working out and I am going to try and find a place of my own as soon as I get back to London – although there *is* something quite bracing about having all my possessions in the car and being 'of no fixed address'.
  Gerald doesn't think so at all, of course. He's ravenous for the three-bedroomed house – preferably in the Boltons – and the garageful of Porsches. Maybe he'll get them some day; I wish him luck but I'm truly fed up with him being angry with me for 'having once had them' –

Gerald had been leafing through a magazine. He must have been looking at the car ads and thinking which one he'd buy when he got rich because he'd suddenly thrown down the magazine and said, 'What's the use? What the hell's the use?'
Asya looks up from her book.
'The use of what?'
'How can I buy you anything? How will I take pleasure in giving you anything when you've had it all?'
He sits cross-legged on the bed looking miserable.

705

'Well,' Asya considers, 'I haven't got anything now.'

'So what? You've had it all.'

'Yes, but I'd probably be more grateful to be given things than someone who's never had them. Because I'm not used to doing without – so giving me a nice car would be like giving me a necessity, not just a –'

'That stinks. That argument stinks.'

'OK.' Asya goes back to her book.

'How can you –' He jumps up, suddenly furious. 'How can you *be* like that? How can you have *done* the things you did –'

'Look,' she says coldly, 'if what you wanted was some half-starved waif who'd never tasted a steak in her life, why didn't you go to an orphanage? Why did you pick me in the first place?'

She was probably wrong, not wrong in the argument, but wrong in that she didn't love him. If she really loved him he probably wouldn't even think these thoughts – and yet there are times when she feels tenderly towards him: when his eyes light up with surprise at some tiny thing, or he falls in love with a smelly vegetarian basement restaurant on the Tottenham Court Road, or she hears him talk to his mother on the phone – and the fact is that some of the things he accuses her of are true. 'The trouble with you,' he'd said, 'is that all your ideas are second-hand; they're derived from art – not life.' That's true. And, 'OK. You're intelligent, you're bright, you're good at taking things to pieces, but you're no good at putting them together again. You're not clever enough for that.' That's true too – except maybe that's where love would have come in –

Anyway. Saif has got himself a lean-looking one too. Female, of course. And American. Yes. I'm afraid the days of Lady Caroline of the tiger-shooting, coolie-whipping father are over and the chances of her riding for the Gezira Club as plain Mrs Madi have quite disappeared. He brought this new one up north as well in my last fortnight. He was taking her on the Windermere round. To a little hotel run by two gay chaps where we once had dinner. He was taking her there for a couple of days and phoned me and said could he come up and borrow the Lancia. And I said I'd rather he took it because I was going to be finishing soon and how was I going to drive two cars away from that place? So they came up on the train and I met them. I paid two pence and went down to platform 3 as I had done so many times before, and the train came in and he stepped out as he had done so many times before – and, as usual, he was a bit shorter than I remembered, and, as usual, I wasn't quite sure what I was doing there, and then she stepped out after him and solved my problems. She was dressed up like a Lichfield ad. A Country Casual outfit that he'd wanted me to buy back in 1975: a just-below-the-knee camel skirt, a russet cashmere jumper and a *cape* – would you believe – with a Burberry check scarf, brown Charles Jourdan boots and an Etienne Aigner handbag to match. She even had fawn gloves. She looked terribly lost inside all that. It didn't suit her at all. Anyone could see he had only just bought it for her. Her name is Mandy. She's the small-boned wiry NY type. Arty-looking with frizzed-out brown hair, an amazingly clear, lit-up kind of skin and a very slight cast in her left eye which is actually quite appealing.

Anyway, seeing her in those clothes was weird. They're just the kind of thing he's always thought elegant women should wear and I'm sure she would never, ever have chosen them for herself. Do you remember that scene I told you about in Harvey Nichols where he stopped in front of a mannequin and said, 'That would look good on you,' and I started to cry and kept asking, 'Why does it always have to be beige?' Well, seeing this free-wheelin', verse-writin' (he says she is a poet and a photographer – both!), dope-smokin' (you mustn't be shocked, Mummy, everybody does it here; and you mustn't worry: I'm not doing it) New Yorker dressed like English County brought that side of it all back to me, and I was so relieved to be through and out. But, I must admit I felt a pang of jealousy: it was the idea of him 'looking after' her, I guess. Like seeing you or Kareem being really nice to someone other than me! I mean, I wasn't *jealous* jealous: I didn't want to swap places with her or anything – and I certainly didn't wish her any harm: I felt sorry for her: she looked so out of place, so uneasy and so determined. I suppose it must be rough being dragged off to meet 'the wife' – even an 'estranged' wife – as he once put it (neither of us has mentioned a divorce yet). Anyway, he was looking great: better than any time since we got engaged. He's stopped trying not to smoke and is back to forty cigarettes a day, except it's Freiburg and Tryer now, not Rothmans. He's terribly 'chic' and he's in a bearded phase. He looks like a gentleman sea-captain. We all shook hands and smiled and I asked about the journey and we said they'd picked a lovely day for it, then I took them to the best that the town had to offer in the way of cafés, which was a large room full of Senior Citizens and irate, too-young mums, and it all smelled of frying, and they, in their Bond Street outfits, looked like posh relatives come to give a poor student a treat.

So, we had tea and I felt terribly like some mother being shown her son's new girl, and like a mother I thought, she's not good enough for him, which she isn't. She isn't pretty enough and she doesn't have that unwavering serenity which he needs. She probably is in love with him, it's hard not to be. But also I think she's edgy and restless and won't be happy with him and won't make him happy. I also fear there must be some gold-digging element there because she's so obviously on the

707

make and he looks so prosperous. I don't think his money can possibly last very long, though. A year maximum and I don't know what he'll do then.

Well, they drove off to the Lakes, a battery of cameras on the back seat and all that. And he phoned to say the hotel was every bit as lovely as we had thought it was when we had dinner there with Mario two and a half years ago. Three days later he came back alone to say goodbye. He said she had some shopping to do in town – which can't have been true since they were on their way to London; she just didn't want to go through the wife routine again and I don't blame her –

Asya watches Marie pick up a herb jar and pour some of its contents into her hand. Marie tilts her head and considers the herbs, and her straight black hair swings slowly to the side. Her hair reaches way down to her bottom, where it is cut across in a stylish blunt line. She cups her hand and tips some of the herbs back into the jar. She shakes the herbs that remain in her hand over the pot and languidly rubs the palm of that hand with the forefinger of the other. Then she lifts her hand to her mouth and nibbles delicately at the nail of her little finger as she gazes at the pot. Everything about Marie is small and dainty, and yesterday and the day before Asya had found her incredibly pretty. She still thinks she is pretty, of course, but she has been waiting for two days now for Marie to do something other than vaguely look after the house. Not that she isn't right to look after her house, and of course she is free to be whichever way suits her, but you wouldn't have thought somebody could spend two whole days wandering round a small flat re-arranging knick-knacks and straightening the pictures on the walls and cooking a basic dinner. And that's what she must be doing *every day* – not just these two days –

Gerald's friend is called Leroy. He's black and terrifically handsome. His wife is called Marie and she's from one of the Pacific Islands – very exotic and dreamy and pregnant. They have the most amazing bedroom, with candles and fake tiger-skins and tropical plants (real ones) and speakers built into the headboard of a king-size bed – and I keep thinking, but what happens when they don't want to do 'it' any more – I mean, in a neutral bedroom you can tell yourself that's just the room you happen to sleep in, but you can't go into a room all done up like that and pretend it's normal to just go to sleep –

Anyway, it's supposed to be idyllic. It's OK, I guess, but it's all terribly terribly modern and – kind of hard-edged. And there's something wrong with it à la *The Stepford Wives*. Also, it seems almost oriental in the division between men and women: Marie stays home all day, Leroy (and Gerald) go out in the morning, come back at seven, sit down to dinner and talk about 'deals'. At least, that's what they did

708

yesterday, and I guess it's what they'll do tonight. There's really no other news from here –

Gerald said Marie used to work but Leroy had made her stop when she got pregnant and that it was better like this anyway because she had tried to leave him two years ago and so he wasn't completely happy about the freedom that having a job gave her, although now of course he trusts her completely again – maybe it's being pregnant that's doing this to her. Maybe she is genuinely slowed down and blissful. She certainly shows no sign of rebellion or even minor discontent. Marie turns to Asya. 'You want some tea?' she asks in a voice in which the shadow of some distant Far Eastern language can be felt in the fractional pauses between the words and the cooing, birdlike intonation.

'No, thanks, I'm all right,' Asya smiles at her.

'OK,' Marie says. 'I have to go prepare myself psychologically for my husband.'

Asya finds herself staring and drops her eyes. Prepare herself psychologically? This has just got to be phoney. This is unbelievable – to come up with a line like that – even if she *was* going to go prepare herself psychologically – how could she *say* it? Asya glances up – no, there is no irony, no joke, nothing: Marie is dead serious. She's going to spend the next two hours preparing herself for her husband's return – his normal, daily, regular return home from work.

'I was thinking,' Asya says, before Marie vanishes down the corridor, 'I was thinking I might go out for a while.'

'Out?' Marie turns. For the first time in two and a half days she demonstrates a reaction; she is alarmed.

'Yes,' Asya says, quickly stuffing her note-pad and biro into her handbag. 'Just for a while. Leroy and Gerald won't get back before seven, will they? and you'll be – resting.'

'But you can't go out?' Marie says on a rising intonation.

It isn't a question though, and Asya says, 'Why?'

'It is dangerous,' Marie says, frowning. 'You haven't been to New York before. This is a dangerous city.'

'It seems pretty quiet to me.'

'This bit is not bad. But –' Marie shakes her head. 'You have not told Gerald?'

'I don't need to tell Gerald,' Asya says.

'Asya –'

She remembers my name, Asya thinks, as Marie steps forward and takes her hand.

'You and Gerald are going to be very happy together. You were meant for each other. I feel it. Gerald loves you so much. He is a very good man. He is like a brother to us.'

709

Everybody's going around talking about brothers, Asya thinks; at the airport Gerald had stood with his arm around Leroy's shoulders. 'This man is my brother,' he'd said. And Asya had thought how good they looked together, the black man and the white. Now she looks down at Marie's hands holding hers: Asya had always thought her own hands were slim and delicate, but Marie's are positively childlike next to them.

'I know,' she says. 'I'm not planning on running away: just on going for a walk.'

Marie drops her hands and looks at her helplessly.

Downstairs there are some trimmed patches of grass, a few trees, apartment blocks – Asya pulls her coat tightly around her. It is sunny but a cold wind is blowing. This is nowhere. She'd checked it out on the map: it's way, way north; past Harlem, past the Bronx; it's practically not New York City at all. Tomorrow, she promises herself, tomorrow.

Eventually she finds a small supermarket and goes in and buys a newspaper and then shops at random: cheeses, yoghurts, olives, fruit. Not too much, so it wouldn't look as though she were criticising their fridge: just enough to look friendly. She'd hoped to find a café where she could sit and finish the letter to her mother and maybe write to Chrissie, but there isn't one. She walks back to their block. Before she buzzes the entryphone she remembers what Marie is doing. She shouldn't disturb her. She puts her bag of groceries down on the ground. She sits on the low marble-clad wall and wraps her coat around her. It isn't going to work out with Gerald. She'd known all along it probably wouldn't – but she'd thought she'd try all the same. In good faith. She hadn't gone to him with evil thoughts. And she hadn't blamed him for Saif: she knows that wasn't his doing. She'd joined him in his dreadful King's Cross hotel and she'd paid half the bill and she'd listened to him and listened to him and *listened* to him – and it just isn't going to work out.

Gerald opens the door of the bathroom and comes out.

'Are you trying to stifle me?' he says.

'It's the steam,' Asya says.

'The what?'

'The steam. The steam comes pouring out of the bathroom and it ruins my hair.'

'Well too bad, man. There's no ventilation in there. I can't have a shower without ventilation.'

'OK. You'll just have to live with me with curly hair then.'

'What are you talking about, curly –'

'Damp makes my hair curl. The only way it can look good again is if I wash it and put it in rollers and dry it. That takes three hours, and I'm not going to do it every time you have a shower. So, from now on my hair is going to be curly. OK?'

Of course he thought she was making trouble. And of course he thought she could do something about it. And she could: she could run and pin up her hair and wrap it in a scarf and hide it under a thick towel every time he had a shower, but she wouldn't. She could be grateful that they live in days and lands of showers; that she doesn't have to heat water for him and carry it steaming and heavy from the kitchen and pour it into a tub – and she had lain on the bed and thought, this is like a scene from some gritty northern novel, a novel of cramped spaces and procreating resentments that swell up and press on you until you can no longer even breathe.

And there were the harangues – about everything: the plain shoes she favoured – 'Look at them: a whole row of them, looking exactly the same –'

'They're different colours –'

'It's like you're at school –'

'We didn't wear high heels at school –'

'You are so conservative, man.'

'I don't like shoes with – things on them.'

'I don't want to *see* these shoes any more.'

'OK. You go buy me a pair that you like: with a bow on the front and a zigzag round the back and blobs of brass here and there –'

And now, of course, because he isn't in her house any more, because her tongue isn't tied by hospitality and guilt, she answers him. Oh, she still doesn't say everything she could – everything she *might* say. She doesn't say, 'You looked mean as hell standing in Cecil Gee trying on suits and snarling because you could only afford a forty-pound suit that looked like it was made out of cardboard and had ripples across the shoulders – what do you think? You think the world *owes* you a Bond Street suit? You think you have a *right* to luxury? Why? What have you given the world that it should owe you anything –'

When a woman with a baby unlocks the front door Asya fumbles in her handbag as though looking for a key and – not finding it – slips in through the slowly closing door. She takes the lift up to the ninth floor, then walks down the corridor to the 'Service Door Keep Shut'. She opens it and goes in and sits on the stairs. She should be OK here for another hour. She takes out her note-pad.

Anyway, Mummy – just before I left London I contacted Professor Murray and he told me my viva's been set for 15 February. It's a Wednesday. And Mummy, I can't tell you how weird it is not having to do the Ph.D any more: it's like – floating – and also there's nothing

711

after it: it's like suddenly I'm in possession of eternity. I mean, when I finished my MA I thought straight away: it's the Ph.D next. Now I don't have to think anything particular is next. It's going to be wonderful I know – right now it just seems strange, the days seem – flatter somehow, but that's because I'm not doing anything with all the time I have –

No, it isn't going to work. There's so much about each other that they actually don't like. Asya shakes open her newspaper: Sadat and Begin are on the front again with Sadat trying to put as good a face as he can on his Ismailia fiasco, poor man.

'You must be very proud of your president,' Leroy had said at dinner on Monday.

'Why?' Asya had said, although he was only trying to make conversation and she should have just smiled or something. 'Why?' she'd asked. Deena would have been proud of her.

'Well' – he'd looked taken aback – 'he's a man of peace. He's the first Arab leader to meet with the Israelis.'

'He's the first Arab leader to meet *publicly* with the Israelis,' she'd said. 'And being a man of peace isn't always the best thing to be.'

'You mean you want to go to war? You know you can't beat the Israelis.'

'I don't want to go to war, no –'

'Don't get me wrong: I'm on your side in this –'

'And I do think he has made a "visionary leap", as they keep calling it –'

'It was very courageous of him to go to Israel,' Marie had said.

'Yes it was, but –'

'It was the act of a brave man.'

'Or a blind one.'

'Come on, man –'

'You said I must be "proud" of him –'

'Yeah, sure –'

'Well I think that before he made that "bold, visionary" move he should have found out if the Israelis were going to meet it with a bold, visionary move of their own, but they haven't: they've given him nothing.'

'They've offered to give you Sinai back.'

'And that way they divide the Arab front. The issue has to be Palestine –'

'Maybe that's down the line –'

'It isn't –'

'How do you know?'

She doesn't – not really – it's just that watching that Knesset speech on television she'd felt – well, there he was upfronting away, centre-stage

712

as he'd wanted to be all his life, and there were Mr Begin and Mr Shamir et al., poker-faced, knowing that the game was one of nerve and concealment and giving nothing away – unless America made them, and America wouldn't. But as far as Leroy and Marie – and Gerald – were concerned, she had plenty to be proud of: the Sadat initiative and the queues outside the Tut Ankh Amun exhibition –

Later that night
Gerald comes to the dinner-table holding a book.
'Who's reading this?' he says. 'It was on the coffee-table.'
'Oh, this is a wonderful book,' Marie says. 'It is truly inspired.'
Asya glances up: *Notes to Myself: My Struggle to Become a Person.* She'd picked it up earlier and thought, oh, if only Saif were here –
' "I don't want to listen to just what you say. I want to feel what you mean",' Gerald reads. 'This is good,' he says.
'It is full of wonderful things,' Marie says as she ladles a meat and vegetable stew on to his plate. 'You want some rice? Wild rice, I know you like it.'
'Mmmm, please.' Gerald smiles up at her. ' "This book was written in moments of pain",' he reads, ' "and I think it shows." '
'He ain't in no pain, now, brother. The man's a millionaire,' Leroy says.
'Yes?' Gerald says, and passes the book to Asya. 'You seen this, babe?'
'Thanks,' Asya says and opens it: twenty-fourth printing.
'*You* can do that, Gerald,' Marie says, sitting down in front of her own plate. 'You have a gift with words. You can write a book about your experiences.'
Gerald gives a little smile and looks at Asya. Asya smiles back and looks down quickly at the book. Other titles by the same author: *I Touch the Earth – The Earth Touches Me.* Oh, if only she were with Saif –
'What do you think, Asya? Don't you think Gerald could write a book like that? Inspirational?'
'Yes,' Asya says, not looking up. 'Yes, I'm sure he could.'
Gerald reaches over and clasps her hand.
'The lady believes in me,' he says.
'Shall we see a bit of the Carter interview?' Leroy asks. 'I'm sure Asya will be interested.'
'Yes please,' Asya says, gently disengaging her hand.

He's had it now, Asya thinks, as Marie switches to Channel Seven and *Charlie's Angels*, he's had it. He must be raging mad now, furious with disappointment to have his negotiating position so completely undermined by his friend Jimmy. Carter couldn't have said it more clearly: the

United States does not want to see a 'fairly radical new independent nation in the heart of the Middle East'. Well, if the United States doesn't want it, then it's not going to happen – so what are they even pretending to negotiate about? Is this it, Asya wonders, has he made his historic blunder; taken the step from which all things will now evolve? She thinks again of the photograph of the Knesset address: a Rembrandt-like scene with the heads of Sadat and Begin emerging out of the darkness; the light catches the two men's foreheads and their shirt-collars; the whorls of Sadat's left ear are an exercise in chiaroscuro. His mouth is open, his brow furrowed, he is unmistakably sincere – but what manner of sincerity is it? Wasn't it just the sincerity of an actor who's landed what he thinks is the plum role? But why 'just'? He believes himself; that's what matters. But should he? Next to him Mr Begin leans back; the bald lower rim of his left eye is visible behind his spectacles. His face betrays nothing.

When Asya concentrates again the ice-cream is on the table and the men are no longer talking about cheap oil from Libya – they're talking about pigeons.

'It's amazing,' Gerald is saying with a lit-up face. 'Even if you take a bird that's always raced from Berwick – you take it in a closed box and let it loose in San Sebastian, it'll still know where it is. It'll change direction and fly north.' He smiles at Asya.

'That's amazing.' She smiles back.

'That's why they were useful in war-time.' Leroy pushes back his chair and stretches out his legs. 'Wasn't there an Army Pigeon Service attached to Mongomery?'

'Yes,' says Gerald. 'They used it to target caravans in the desert and the pigeons were virtually impossible to intercept. But the best racer,' he says, digging a raisin out of his ice-cream and putting it in his mouth, 'the very best, is a bird that's sitting on eggs.'

'Why?' Asya asks.

'Well, what you do,' says Gerald, 'is you take the eggs and you make two small holes in each of them with a pin and you blow them –'

'You "blow" them?' asks Asya.

'You blow into them: you empty them. Then you push a worm into each egg and tape the holes and you give the eggs back to the bird. When the bird sits on the eggs it'll feel the worms moving and think it's nearly time for the eggs to hatch. Then you take the bird and race it. It's in such a hurry to get back that it'll break records. It's got one instinct: that the chicks won't survive if their mother's not there when they hatch –'

Asya pushes her ice-cream bowl away.

'I think that's dreadful,' she says.

Both men look at her. Marie stands and picks up the heavy casserole from the table. As she turns to go into the kitchen, Leroy gives her a light smack on her bottom. 'You look after my son now,' he says. Marie turns to smile at him.

'Why is it dreadful?' Leroy says, turning back to Asya.

'Because you're taking a creature's powerful, natural instincts – which you would call "good" instincts, like mothering – and making them work against her. That's awful.'

'Come on, babe,' Gerald says. 'These are racing pigeons.'

'They don't *know* they're racing pigeons,' Asya says. 'They think they're just pigeons –'

'What're you talking about?' Gerald smiles at Leroy. 'They don't think anything –'

'Yes they do. That bird thinks she's got eggs that are about to hatch. That's why she hurries back to them. If she didn't think that she wouldn't hurry, would she? Then she wouldn't break any records.'

'Yeah, the lady's got a point.' Leroy smiles at her easily.

'And why don't you at least leave the eggs alone?' says Asya. 'Why do you have to empty them and put a worm in them? A *worm*! Why don't you do it when they *are* about to hatch? That way when she gets back at least she'll find her chicks there waiting for her –'

'Take it easy, babe.' Gerald puts his hand on hers. 'You can't time the races to suit the birds. I'll tell my dad not to race any more pigeons if you want.'

After a decent couple of minutes, Asya takes her hand away.

Gerald takes his hand off her breast and sits up in bed.

'What is it, babe?' he says. 'Why have you gone all frigid on me?'

'I haven't,' Asya says, pulling the shoulder of her nightdress back up.

'Don't give me that, man. It isn't the first time.'

'Gerald,' Asya says, 'why don't you ever use my name?'

'I asked you a question,' Gerald says.

'I just don't feel – that way, tonight.'

'But why? What is it?'

'I don't know. Maybe that pigeon story just depressed me.'

'That's just shit.'

'It isn't. I keep thinking of those eggs with the worms inside – and the bird thinking she can feel her chick moving.'

'Look, babe, it was just a story.'

'No it wasn't.' Asya sits up. 'It was a description of something which happens. Which is probably happening right now. And *you* didn't think there was anything wrong with it.'

'If that bird was in the wild the cats would get its eggs.'

'Yes, but that's *natural*. That's a risk the pigeon *knows* about. She takes precautions, she takes steps to prevent it happening. She doesn't know about some omnipotent human with a pocketful of worms piercing holes in her eggs –'

715

'Look, babe. You're really trying my patience. You know that?'

'Yes.'

'Yes what?'

'Yes, I do know that.'

'Are you being bloody-minded on purpose?'

'No.'

'Well, what the *hell* is going on then? And it's not just tonight. You're freezing up on me –'

'I don't know.'

'It's like trying to start some clapped-out old motor, getting you going.'

Asya sighs. 'Maybe it's all got too real,' she says.

'What does that mean?'

'I don't know.'

'*Will you stop saying I don't know.*'

That used to bug Saif too – long ago. Asya says nothing.

'What do you mean "too real"?'

'Well, before, it was like a fantasy; an escape. Now – well, we're around each other all the time –'

'That's how it's *supposed* to be. People who love each other *want* to be around each other all the time.'

'I know.'

'So?'

Asya shrugs. 'Maybe it's just that – well, we're not in perfect sympathy with each other. I mean, you keep going on about – I mean there's so much you don't like about the way I *am* –'

'How can you say that, babe?'

'Well, you know what I mean. I'm not –'

'You're perfect. You're lovely, man. You're beautiful and clever and kind –'

'Thank you.'

'Come on, babe. This is me: Gerald. Remember? Come on, lady' – he holds her face in his hands and puts his lips gently to hers; he's been saying 'lady' since they came to New York – 'Beautiful, beautiful lady. Let go, let go, baby. Come on. Let me warm you up.' His mouth closes gently on her upper lip. When he releases it, he whispers, 'Take your nightie off. Go on. You do it. Take your nightie off, I want to look at you.'

Asya slips her nightdress down over her shoulders.

'Oh, you are beautiful,' Gerald breathes, 'beautiful.' He puts his hand under her right breast and, bending his head, starts to flick at it gently with his tongue.

In the morning, as Gerald stoops to brush his hair in the mirror inside the door of the built-in wardrobe, Asya says, 'I'm going out, later.'

'Going out?' he says. 'Where?' He turns around and straightens up.

'To Manhattan.'

'Where in Manhattan?'

'I don't know. I'll look around.'

'You can't just go wandering in the streets.'

'Why not?'

'It's dangerous. This is a dangerous city.'

'Oh Gerald. This is day-time, and I won't be –'

'Look, babe, I know you've been sitting in the house for two days, but I'm just trying to get something going with Leroy and I thought you and Marie would be getting to know each other.'

'Yes. Well, I'm just going out for a bit today –'

'But where is it you want to go?'

'I don't know. I might go to a museum –'

'OK. Look: I'll get Marie to phone around some of her friends. She used to be big on Art. She must know someone who'd go with you –'

'But I don't want anyone to go with me –' Asya sits up in bed.

'It would be much better. You don't know your way around –'

'I've got a guide –'

'It's much better to go with someone –'

'Gerald. I'm not going with anyone. I don't *want* to go with anyone. *I want to go on my own.* OK? I'll phone you from town.'

'You mean you'll stay out till dinner-time?'

'Yes. I'll phone you, and then, if you want, you can join me.'

'Look, babe, I don't like this –'

'We can agree now if you like.'

'Agree what?'

'When and where to meet.'

'But I don't know what I'll be doing – when I'll be free –'

'OK, then, I'll try you here at seven.'

New York, Thursday, 29 December 1977

Dear Chrissie,

This is absolutely the most brilliant city and I've fallen in love with it. I only wish you were here: we could have such fun together. It's desperately crowded right now because of the New Year and all that – and it is just *wonderful*. The people are great: everybody sounds like they're straight off the Muppet Show and you don't know whether they're serious or sending themselves up. I stopped for coffee and croissant at a café and this man (a customer) walked up to the serving counter with his plate and said, 'This is shit, man. You feeding me shit?'

Waiter: 'Whaddya mean this is shit?'

Man: 'Shit. Horse-shit. You feeding me horseshit?'

Waiter: 'Hey, Luigi, take the plate offa this jerk –'

I thought they'd beat each other up but they didn't and it all died down with the customer leaving, having had his say. It's really *exactly* like it is in the movies. And it's going on all the time: with taxi-drivers and everyone. It's terribly like Cairo that way, with people yelling at each other and making jokes and blowing their horns, but I haven't seen an actual fight yet. It's like Cairo in other ways too (I know it sounds silly, but it's true) – like the taxis are all beat up – most of the cars have dents in them one way or another – and there's a general untidiness about the place: bits of paper blowing around, little piles of rubble here and there, puddles and pot-holes and some people in a great big rush and others standing in doorways picking their noses. And people *look* at you: men look at you in the street, which they never do in England, and I had a whole chat with a woman in Bloomingdale's about which earrings she should buy. I've been to Bloomingdale's and Bergdorf Goodman. And tomorrow I'm going to Saks and Tiffany's – not to buy anything, of course, but just to look. I tried to go to the Museum of Modern Art (they call it MOMA, isn't that brilliant?) but the queue to get in was curling down the street as far as I could see because there's a Cézanne show, so I gave up and went to the Frick instead – there was a queue there too but I got in – and it was *fantastic* – you'd have really liked it, I promise you, you wouldn't have been the tiniest bit bored, but I won't go on about it now.

Oh, and Chrissie, I saw a sign on Park Avenue which said 'DONT EVEN *THINK* OF PARKING HERE' – isn't that terrific? I mean, it wasn't just 'No Parking' or 'Verboten Parking' or something, but DONT EVEN THINK – and the green traffic light says WALK and the red says DONT WALK. It's all kind of informal and abrupt and humorous. And there are fifty million movies, I can't even decide which one to go to – and I had lunch in a huge restaurant with thirties décor that reminded me of places I used to go with Grandfather with waiters yelling out orders and racing through the room with dishes balanced all the way up their arms, and there's absolutely nothing weird about being a woman on your own here because there are plenty of them – of us!

Anyway, I'm writing this in the bar of the Hilton with a wonderful hot advocaat with nutmeg in front of me, and the waiters keep coming round with nibbles, and there's a piano playing and everything feels wonderful. I've fixed to meet G. here at half past eight but I think he'll be sulking because I went out on my own today. Can you imagine, he thinks I should come to New York, then sit in his friends' house all day until it suits him to take me out? And the house isn't even down-town so you can't wander off for half an hour and come back: it's way, way away, like Helwan from Cairo for example – Chrissie, darling, I

718

haven't heard from you for ages and I don't know how the kids are or Tante Muneera or how you're doing with Fuad or anything. Do please send me something. You can always (well, not always, but for the moment) write to me c/o Saif. He doesn't mind and that's what I've agreed with Mummy that she should do until I get somewhere of my own. My viva's been set for 15 February, but I'm going to look around for work as soon as I get back to London because although I still have some money it isn't much. I don't think Gerald and I are going to stay together, we object to too many things about each other – I know one is supposed to adapt, but if I couldn't adapt to Saif – and that was *Saif* – why should I even *try* to adapt to G.?

I saw him up north last month (Saif) – I've written Mummy a long letter and you can read it if you like – but basically he seems OK – and he has a girl-friend – although I'm very uncomfortable about the fact that he isn't working – you know Saif and what he's like about work, and also I can't believe that the Syrian matter is closed – that he can walk away from it just like that –

Asya takes a sip of her advocaat and nibbles at a burnt almond. Maybe she should take up smoking? The timing had been terrible – if only it could all have waited until he'd finished the Syrian job – if only she hadn't brought them all rushing over to Athens in January; she'd been wrong to think it wouldn't matter that much to him: yes, he took her for granted, of course he did, but he took her for granted – not like an old coat in the corner of a dark cupboard, as she'd put it to herself, but like the very air that he breathed – oh – oh, if only she'd waited till – till when? In March he hadn't yet finished and she has no idea when he *would* have finished – and maybe by the time he'd finished this job he'd have started on something else. No, things happen when they happen, and that's just how it is. But how nice it would have been to be sitting with him here now – 'What is that stuff you're drinking? Baby-puke? It looks putrid. Why can't you just have a straight whisky? Why does it always have to be something odd?' That would be fine, she'd welcome that; it would be indulgent and joking, not mean; it would make her laugh. They would buy all the magazines and leaf through them, they'd sit and comment on the people passing through, and then – and then? And then he'd want to have dinner in the hotel restaurant and later go to bed with a magazine. And she would be wanting, *yearning*, to wander the mean streets in the night: to go to the Village or Times Square or 42nd Street –

In the bar Asya draws lines on the cold glass of her Bloody Mary and looks up at the dancer. She's so pretty and so aloof, so – above it all. Asya notices her pun and smiles. The blonde girl struts the bar in her shiny

719

black heels. She does the odd bump, the odd grind, walks to the end of the bar, does a little jump as she turns and walks back. She isn't exactly killing herself, she knows she has to keep it up for a while. Around the horse-shoe the men sit back with their drinks, some keeping a vague eye on her while they talk, others gazing up, bleary or vague or stony faced or encouraging – what is Gerald thinking? Asya glances at him: he is looking up with a pleasant, friendly open face. Asya thinks he is thinking how coolly he is behaving and what a great guy he is and how the poor dancer isn't going to get lucky and find out just *how* great because he's tied up – for tonight. He might even be thinking how 'horny' she looks. Asya imagines Gerald saying to the dancer, 'You are the horniest woman alive!' The dancer looks at him coldly. 'How do you know?' she asks. Asya smiles. Right now he's making sure that if the dancer looks down and sees him she'll think wow! This guy sure is different – but she isn't looking down; she looks straight ahead and goes through her movements: down the bar and wriggle and jump and around and up the bar and bump and grind and around and down the bar and – how smooth her legs are: all soft and tanned with not a spot or a blemish, the knees completely of a piece with the rest. How do you get legs like that? Chrissie and Asya had debated that once while a woman with perfect legs crossed them as she sat with her head safely stuck into one of Hassan's giant hairdryers: you'd have to have never fallen down in the school playground, never bumped into a desk or a chair, never needed to pluck a single hair out of them – smooth and tan right up to the G-string, with not a hint or shadow of a hair showing through, and still the gentle bronze goes on: up over the smooth belly and the dimple of a belly button to the breasts, so touching from this angle, the globe of their underside quivering gently with every movement, bouncing with the jump at the end of the bar, their tips pink and erect and indifferent – Botticelli *Venus* rising from the bar-top, hair in a coil over her left shoulder, G-string spangled, breasts vulnerable and proud – oh, if she were a man she would want to take her home and look after her – wrap her in a soft fine cloak, bring her a cup of tea in bed and put gentle kisses on that soft flesh – ah, but that is thinking like a man – how do you know she needs wrapping up? What if she's doing what she wants to do? Using her – assets; making money and being free – not locked up at home out in the sticks spending two hours a day preparing herself psychologically for her husband's return, or marooned in a classroom teaching something she doesn't much care to teach to kids she doesn't much care to teach it to – they must have rules here; she must be able to get down from the bar-top safely, put her clothes on and walk through the snow to a small, warm flat with a patchwork quilt and maybe a pussycat – but what if there's someone waiting for her outside – some pimp-figure ready to take her money, shoot her up with heroin and push her into bed with some fat slobbering drunk with dirty fingernails –

'Hey, man?'

Asya turns to Gerald, smiling. 'Yes?'

'Why don't you let your hair down, man?'

'Sorry?'

'Why don't you let your hair down? You look like you're sitting in front of your typewriter.'

'What should I do?' Asya says.

' "What should I do?" Oh boy.' He looks really fed-up. 'You really are great to be out with, you know. Can't you just let go? Be yourself?'

'I *am* being myself,' Asya says. 'And I'm *enjoying* myself. I don't know what you want.'

'I want you to let your hair down.'

'You've already said that but it doesn't mean anything. Tell me how.'

'I don't believe this lady –'

'Well, I can't imagine what I can do that would be letting my hair down. You want me to strip and get up there on the bar?'

'I'm leaving, babe. This is no good. You're even putting *her* off.'

Asya slides off her bar-stool and follows Gerald's back down the long dark room. The door of the bathroom had been – as usual – open and he had been standing at the basin with his back to her. Lying in bed, she had watched his pants vibrate with the vigour of his brushing of his teeth – and she had hated him: hated his bloodless heels on the brown slippers; hated his long legs and the vibration of his white cotton pants and the dark shadow that divided his buttocks and the white vest slightly crinkled at the waist and the muscular shoulders and the arm upraised with the toothbrush and the energy and dedicated precision with which he brushed his teeth. And then she had felt ashamed and she had felt compassion for him as he stood there concentrating and unaware of the blackness of her heart – unaware of the treachery brewing behind his back – yet why *should* he be unaware? He of all people should know of what treachery she was capable – had she not betrayed her husband with him? Why should he think he could turn his back on her without fear? Look to her, Inglese, if thou hast eyes to see –

They walk side by side through the light snow. The coloured lights of 42nd Street wink and bleep and blaze. Asya can't stop looking round: at the women in amazing costumes and make-up standing on the sidewalks, at the guys lounging comfortably in doorways, at the pictures and the signs: '*Hot "PUSSY!"* 'LIVE NUDE ACT!'

'It's just a waste of time taking you to a place like that,' Gerald says.

'Look,' Asya says, 'if you suddenly got uncomfortable for some reason don't blame it on me –'

'Yeah, I got uncomfortable, sure I got uncomfortable with Miss Goody Two-Shoes sitting next to me –'

721

'OK. So I don't know how to behave in a topless bar. I've never been to a topless bar before. Why don't you *show* me instead of just being –'

'Show you? What can I show you? You've seen it all, man. There's no one alive can show you anything –'

'THREE IN A BED!' 'BOND-MAIDS –'

'I don't know what you're talking –'

'You come into a city for the first time and you're off – it's like you know it already – it's like you fucking *own* it, man – you don't wait for anybody –'

Three men push past them on the pavement. One turns to look back. Asya returns his look.

'That isn't fair. I sat around for two days –'

'I bring you to New York –'

'You don't bring me anywhere,' Asya stops walking and faces Gerald. 'I paid my own fare, remember? I've made sure I've gone at least halves with you on everything –'

Behind him there's the street with traffic moving slowly through the slush. At the other side a big sign winks on and off: 'GIRLS! GIRLS! GIRLS!'

'Wheel on the accountancy kit –'

'Just don't say "I bring you to New York" like you'd flown me here in your private jet with the limo purring on the tarmac, OK?' Asya stands her ground.

A loudspeaker behind her belts out, 'You're a *native* New-*York*er –'

'No, well, even your husband didn't quite run to *that* –'

'PUSSY! PUSSY! PUSSY!'

'Let's leave my husband out of this –'

'We're leaving nothing out of this. They've made you what you are, man –'

'OK, OK –' Asya stamps her foot in the soft snow. 'So I am what I am and I'm probably not changing, or not that much anyway –'

'Look at you: stamping your foot like Little Lord Fauntleroy. You are so – *petulant*. You were brought up thinking you were better than anybody else – you hit a city and you make a bee-line for the Hilton –'

'It's just an obvious place to –'

'Sure it's obvious – to you –' His face above his sheepskin jacket is pinched and cold.

'Look, if you're talking about money, you don't even have to *spend* money to meet in the Hilton. You can use their loos, buy a newspaper and sit in the lobby'

'That isn't what you did –'

'No. I had a drink. What on earth's the matter with that?'

'Nothing. Nothing at all. It's your right.'

Asya stares at him. 'It *is* my right, yes.'

'*You're a native New-Yorker –*'

'Sure, like the whole way you were brought up is your right: dancing away the nights at Embassy balls while the peasants starved outside –'

'You – oh, you –'

'Wasn't that the scene, babe? Isn't that how you grew up? What's it called, that club your lot used to go to?'

'You know what you are?' Asya says. 'You are mean – and ignorant – and boring with it –' She's said it, she's said it – she's said it and nothing's happened. '*You* are going to stand here and tell me about Egypt? Tell me what was wrong with how I grew up?'

'But of course you'd think there's nothing wrong with it' – Gerald's voice is reasonable, persuasive – 'because you were one of the privileged class. But privilege stinks, babe, you've got to know that – and it stinks specially in countries where there are people who can't get enough to eat –'

'Gerald,' Asya says quietly, 'why have all your girl-friends been from "developing" countries?'

'What?'

'You've never had a white girl-friend, why?'

'I don't think that way, man.'

'Yes, you do – and the reason you've gone for Trinidad – Vietnam – Egypt – is so you can feel superior. You can be the big white boss – you are a sexual imperialist –'

'You don't even believe what you're saying' – Gerald laughs.

'Yes I do. You pretend – to yourself as well – that it's because you don't *notice* race – or it's because these cultures retain some spiritual quality lost to the West – you pride yourself that you dance "like a black man" – but that's all just phoney –'

'Hold on a minute –'

'No, I won't hold on. You've pushed me and pushed me and *pushed* me and I've had it. I hate it. I hate people who go around trying to change people. The hypocrisy of it. "I know you better than you know yourself" – *shit* – what you mean is that the way you think I *should* be is better for *you* than the way I *am*. Well, I've had it –'

'I told you you were pleased with yourself –'

'That's not true. *You're* the one who's pleased with himself. You think the only thing that's wrong is that you don't have any money and that's not your fault: it's the fault of the world – but *I'll* tell you what's wrong with you –' Asya jabs at the air with her index finger.

'Hey, babe, you're great when you're angry –'

'Don't *touch* me – what's wrong with you – *one* of the things that are wrong with you – is that you are *mean* as hell. You haven't an ounce of generosity in you – and it's going to be dreadful for the woman you're with when you do have money because every time you throw a trinket her way she'll have to roll around on the floor and yelp with delight – there's nothing, *nothing* that you'll give for free – oh, *man*: "Though I speak with the tongues of men and of angels, and have not charity, I am become as sounding brass, or a tinkling cymbal" You ought to know that –'

'Welcome back, Aries. See? I wasn't wrong after all. All that fire –'

'No. Keep away.' Asya jumps back and bumps into a huddled figure shuffling along by the wall. She holds her hands up. 'No. No marketing techniques on me. No alternate hard sell and soft sell and "it's when they say no that the adrenalin starts to flow". Isn't that what you and Leroy were saying? Well, you can go back and talk that language with your friends because I am out.'

'Come on, babe –'

'No. I'm out. I'm through. I'm *taking a powder*, as you'd say. I'm finished. It's over.'

'What are you talking about out? How? What –'

'Now. Tonight. I'll get my bag and go. I'm sure they'll be glad to see the back of me – at least Marie will –'

'Look, babe. Don't do this. At least wait till we get to London. Then it can be private.'

'I'm not staying at your friends' any more.'

'Why not?'

'I can't bear it. I don't want to. Why should I stay if I don't want to?' The Botticelli *Venus* wouldn't, that's for sure – when she didn't like a place, she *walked* – these *boots* were made for *walk*ing –

'Look at you: look at the spoilt brat talking.'

'I'm not spoilt. These people are not my relatives, or my friends – they have absolutely no claim on me –'

'You move out like this you're insulting their hospitality –'

'Fuck their hospitality,' Asya cries, throwing out her arms – and almost laughs out loud for joy – she's done it, oh, she's done it – she could clap her hands and dance in the street. '*Fuck – their – hospitality.*' Oh boy oh boy oh boy, she digs her clenched fists deep in her pockets and stamps her feet to stop from jumping about and punching the air like a goal-scoring footballer – if she can say that she can say anything, anything at all – *nothing* can stop her now –

724

Scene 10

Saturday, 18 February 1978
London
Asya knocks at the big wooden door in the Little Boltons. She still has the key but she leaves it in her bag. He'd asked her to pick him up – she isn't sure why –

'But wouldn't it be better if we just met outside?' she'd said.

'No. Why?'

'Well – I don't want to upset Mandy –'

'Why should it upset her?'

'Well – you going out –'

'That's all right. She'll probably go out later anyway. And if she doesn't she's got Clara to keep her company.'

'Clara?'

'Yes. She came back.'

'But – why?'

'*I* don't know. How would *I* know?'

'So, what – they're both living with you?'

'Clara's sleeping in the spare room.'

Clara opens the door – at least, it must be Clara because it isn't Mandy and it isn't Saif –

'Hi!' Asya says, holding on to the strap of her handbag to keep from holding out her hand, a habit she's still trying to break herself of. 'My name is Asya –'

'I know. Come in.'

In the living-room Saif is putting away some papers; he gives her a quick smile.

'Hello, Princess. Do you want a drink? I won't be long.'

'I'm OK,' says Asya, leaning against the door.

Mandy waves at her from behind the back of the bedragoned sofa. Mandy is playing 'kept woman' with some flair: she has obviously just got out of bed and had a long bath, and now reclines in a scarlet silk kimono surrounded by yellow and white carnations – in February! Her kimono is open to show a lot of leg and she is painting her toenails shocking pink and rocking gently to 'Bye Bye Miss American Pie' on the new music centre. Clara sits down in a nearby armchair, shakes her long red hair out over one shoulder and opens a copy of *Private Eye*. A scene from a modern harem, Asya thinks, except that here the women ignore each other; there's none of that mutual grooming and gazing you find in the classical stuff. If this had been a Delacroix, now, you would have had Clara leaning over to paint Mandy's toenails, while Mandy lay back, eyes dreamy, lips half parted, one hand lazily extended to toy with the red tresses that flowed over Clara's smooth, creamy shoulders – she shouldn't stare, Asya thinks, and turns her eyes to the books lying on the coffee-table: *Tinker, Tailor, Soldier, Spy*, she knows that one; and then *White Nights, Decent Interval* –

'Shall we go?'

Saif stuffs his wallet into his pocket, picks up his coat from the back of a chair, splits a 'See you' between the two women and opens the door for Asya. In the hall he stops.

'Hold on,' he says and goes back into the flat. He comes back with two letters.

'These came for you,' he says.

Asya looks at the envelopes. One is from her mother and one is typed. Both have the same London postmark. She puts them into her handbag.

'What are you going to do about them?' Asya asks as they walk down the street.

'About what?'

'Clara and Mandy, of course.'

Saif looks surprised. 'Why should I do anything? They can stay as long as they like – and leave whenever they like – what's there for me to do?'

'Oh, Saif –'

'What?'

'Well – they're waiting for you to do something.'

'Like what?'

'Like express a preference.'

'But I haven't got one: they're both fine.'

Asya glances at him. He's serious. He really doesn't have a preference. And if they both went tomorrow, he wouldn't mind. Why had he wanted her to see all that? *Had* he wanted her to see all that? Or had he just wanted the convenience of meeting her at the flat and wasn't bothered about the women? Is it or is it not odd, Chrissie, that after nine years with him I can't ever decide what is deliberate and what isn't? Is he a terrifically good actor or is he a total innocent? His mother always claimed that he simply didn't notice things that he wasn't actually focusing on. But then Tante Adeela thinks all men are guileless, stray beings, and it's up to their women to keep them in good social order. I think he's too clever for it to be that simple. Do you have any idea how much she knows, Chrissie? I mean, I know she knows that there are problems, but does she know what *sort* of problems and why and what's been happening? Does she know about Gerald? I feel so dreadful when I think of her: much more as though I'd been treacherous to *her* rather than to him – in *her* terms I can't justify anything I've done and she must feel as if she had mistaken me all those years. Does she know –

'So, you've done it, Pussycat?' Saif is smiling down at her fondly. 'It's Dr Pussycat now!'

Asya shrugs and makes a little face. She feels herself on dangerous ground and does not want to be congratulated. They turn into the Pontevecchio and sit opposite each other. After they've ordered and handed back the menus Saif puts a black leather box on the starched white tablecloth.

'What is it?' asks Asya.

'Open it,' he says.

'Oh Saif, I –'

'Open it.'

Asya opens it. Nestling in a bed of dark blue velvet, utterly confident, relaxed and serene, is a thirties Baume & Mercier watch. Asya looks up at Saif.

'Congratulations, Princess,' he says.

'Thank you,' Asya says.

'Well, don't sound so miserable.'

Asya shakes her head silently.

'OK. Here's your soup,' Saif says when the waiter arrives. When after a few minutes Asya still sits silent without moving he says, 'Are you going to eat it?'

Asya nods, two big tears rolling down her cheeks.

'You can eat it and cry in it at the same time. They won't charge us extra,' Saif says.

He watches her as she dips her spoon tentatively into the minestrone.

'Stop crying,' he says. 'I've had enough of women blubbing all over the place. If the watch makes you so unhappy, give it back.'

Asya shakes her head, but leaves her spoon in the soup-bowl and puts her white napkin to her eyes.

'If you don't eat your soup,' Saif says after a few minutes, 'I shall do to you what my father did to me. I've always wanted to do it to someone. Did I tell you what my father did to me?'

Asya nods without taking the napkin away.

'Well, I'll tell you again. He said, "Are you going to drink your *mulukhiyya*?" And when I shook my head he said, "Very well," and he leaned over and took the bowl and emptied it over my head. Then he left the table. It wasn't hot – the *mulukhiyya*, I mean – but my mother sat stuck to her chair and cried for Wageeda, "Help! Help, Wageeda! Look at the boy! Look what your master's done to him –" and Dada Wageeda came rushing in from the kitchen and – I must have looked a sight with all that green slimy stuff over my face – and she shrieked and got hold of her smock at the neck and tore it down the middle to the hem –'

Asya is laughing now and Saif points his spoon at her bowl,

'So eat,' he says, 'before I'm tempted, and then you'll have to go and spend three hours washing and drying your hair all over again.'

As they wait for their steaks Asya says, 'Did you see the news of the Helwan crash?'

Saif nods as he lights his cigarette. 'The whole place is collapsing,' he says. 'Buses falling into rivers, mysterious fires, trains crashing –'

'And the President is busy making new friends,' Asya says.

Saif shrugs. 'He needs arms. He has an air force that can't fly, planes that sit in hangars because they can't get spare parts –'

'He's been getting arms from the Russians; why does he have to go and break off with them?'

'He doesn't like their style; he likes the good life: to swan around saying my friend Henry and my friend Reza Shah –'

'So it all boils down to – *vanity*?'

'Most things boil down to vanity.'

'"Abd el-Nasser didn't.'

'Sure he did. It was just a different type.'

'It was still better than this.'

'It landed him in '67 – landed us all in '67 –'

'That wasn't vanity – that was – he trusted people whom he shouldn't have trusted.'

'Well, you can say the same about Sadat.'

'Do you think they'll give him anything?'

'They'll sell him the F5Es –'

'I meant the Israelis.'

'They'll give him Sinai.'

'I know that, but I meant for the Palestinians.'

'Well, they've made their offer –'

'Their offer amounted to annexation of the occupied territories – he can't accept that.'

'The Palestinians have turned it down anyway. And the Israelis won't make a better one.'

'Not ever?'

'I don't think so. I don't see why they should.'

'Saif! Because it would be *just*.'

'But what's in it for them? Think about it. If you take the question of justice away. Why should they give back the West Bank? It gives them more space; it gives them a captive source of cheap labour; it gives them a carrot to dangle in every negotiation –'

'Because it isn't right to hold on to –'

'I said forget the morality –'

'Because they would have peace.'

'Would they? A Palestinian state would be another enemy state on their borders – would be *the* enemy state on their borders. And why would they want peace anyway? Their government consists of men who have spent their lives in war and resistance and conspiracy – and the nation thrives on being embattled: it gives them a cohesiveness they wouldn't have by nature; it gets them a great deal of sympathy and cash from the world; it keeps all sorts of possibilities open for them. And when things boil over into actual war, they win it. I don't see why they should give up anything.'

Asya stares at him.

'Then you think it's all quite hopeless?' she says.

'I think time will take care of it. In two hundred years or so another situation will have evolved –'

'But Saif, people will have lived out their lives in wretched refugee camps, thinking that this is just a phase, their whole lives – thinking that one day they'll go home – "Oh, I don't think I'll bother to mend that tear in my tent; we'll probably be going home soon –" '

'Oh, Princess, you still think there's a bit that's just preparation for life, and a bit that's life itself. You think you come to a day when you think, Ah! The prep's done, from now on it's The Real Thing –'

'You thought so too,' Asya says, stung. 'Real life was going to be in the house by the pyramids with the fountain in the courtyard –'

'Well,' Saif says, as the waiter arrives at their table. 'You put me straight.'

Over the steaks Saif says, 'Have you told your mother about the Ph.D?'

'No, not yet,' Asya says. 'I'll write to her tomorrow.'

'Why don't you phone her?'

'Well, I –'

'Some stuff about money, yes? Phone her from my flat after dinner.'

'No, I –'

'Don't be silly. What will it cost? Five pounds? And it's sure to be on her mind.'

'OK,' says Asya. 'Thanks.'

'You'd better read her letter first, though.'

'Oh, I can't sit here and read –'

'Of course you can. Go on.'

He leans back in his chair and lights a cigarette.

Cairo, February 1978

Dear Asya,

I am sending you this with Vivien Roberts who has been in Cairo for our conference on 'Aspects of Orientalism: the Twentieth Century'. Vivien will be writing to you too.

I am enclosing a cheque for three thousand pounds made out to your name. If you still feel the way you felt when I last heard from you and if you do pass your viva (which I'm sure you shall) and get the job that Vivien has been telling me about and feel that you can manage, then you must use this money for a down payment on a small flat. If you don't get the job or if you've changed your mind about wanting to stay, then tear up the cheque and leave the money where it is. I've collected it from various sources here and there and I want you to have it so that you do not pay exorbitant London rents and start off handicapped from the beginning. But it isn't to be wasted or frittered away!

I have signed a contract to go to the University of Kuwait next year. The way the economy is going here now, somebody in this family had better make some money. I had thought *you* at least were well taken care of in this respect, but now you've gone and thrown it all away. Deena, of course, has always been hopeless about money, and Muhsin is very nice but is even more hopeless than she is. I thought Kareem as an electronics engineer would be all right but he is talking the most hare-brained schemes you can imagine about setting up an old van as a workshop and driving round the countryside fixing up peasants' radios and getting to know 'Egypt and its people'. And as for your father, you might as well put your hands in the earth and bury them as far as he is concerned: all his life he has turned down anything that so much as smelt of money in the interests of 'independence and purity'. He does not, of course, approve of my going to Kuwait. He believes I am 'selling out', betraying the principles we had when we married back in 1948, ratting on the university, contributing to a deplorable trend which we ought to be fighting and proposing to prostitute my brains and my training to a few ignorant nouveau-riche Arabs. I've told him that that was all very well in socialist times in the fifties and the sixties when the salary of a university lecturer was enough for a family to live on reasonably well. But that is no longer so – prices are soaring beyond any decent person's reach, and the way I see it you children will all need subsidies for a long time to come. Also, there was always your grandfather when we were really stuck for a hundred pounds or so: he didn't *like* giving it but he always gave it in the end. Now your uncle is running the business and I don't feel it's doing that well. He's taking a risk and expanding into aluminium and I think that needs energy and health, and he has many ideas but I don't know if he's strong enough to carry them through. I've thought lately that he isn't looking very well. Also he is far too lenient and open-handed with his workers and they take advantage of him. He did suggest – before he started the aluminium project – that we sell the business and divide the proceeds between us, but Soraya and Nadia and I all agreed not to. For some reason we'd all rather keep the old shop on Morgan Street and have Hamid taking Father's place and being there under the sign that says 'Ismail Mursi and Son'. Maybe it's sentimental – but it's what we all want. And of course your uncle is generous with help and offers of help at every turn, but he too has sons and has to provide for them. Anyway, I've decided. I think it is the right time. I could not have done it before, but now you're not here and Deena is married and Kareem will do his finals this year, and anyway he has a life of his own – I think it is right that I should go. I had vaguely thought for a while when I saw how things were going that I would probably take early retirement at fifty-five and go then for Deena's sake – but now, after what you've done and after that heart scare we had back in 1974, I think I'd better seize the day and go now. After all, I've been teaching in Cairo University for twenty-seven years and no one can say I have not done my duty by it.

The thing that makes me sad is that by the time you come back to Cairo to fulfil your contract to the university and teach, I will have gone. And if you do get this job and a flat and have one foot here and one foot there, then when I come back to Cairo in the holidays you will be in England. That makes me sad. There have been so many things I have postponed or neglected to do, thinking that we would do them together when you came back – just simple things: I would have liked us to drive together to Luxor and spend a few weeks there. I have only ever been there supervising a university trip and never been able to do the things I would have liked to do. Still, I am sure we shall manage somehow – and of course if you have a flat in London then it will be quite easy for me to come and see you. But even for that I will need the Kuwaitis' money. So you see?

I do not really feel that bad about it – after all, you could see it as continuing a tradition: it was always us Egyptians who educated all those Arabs and civilised them; us and the Levantines. And not only educated but supported them too. Why, we used to give King 'Abd ul-Aziz an allowance before he found oil, and if the Kiswa hadn't come from Egypt every year the Ka'ba would have remained without any clothes. So now they have money and we don't – and they can pay us and we need paying – it's no reason to stop helping them.

Anyway, that's one way of seeing it.

I can't write more because I have to meet Vivien and give her this letter. We are all well and everybody asks after you and sends you their love and congratulations for having finished your Ph.D and in advance for the title. They are all missing you very much and waiting for you to come back.

Oh, by the way, I have spoken to the Dean about applying for one year's unpaid leave for you starting from October this year. He was surprised but of course he won't turn it down. I said you were going to use the time to prepare your thesis for publication in the Longman series – but he wanted a firm assurance that you would be here and teaching on 1 October 1979. I gave it. As soon as you have your viva result I will put the application in formally.

Look after yourself, darling, and write very soon and tell me what you are doing. I am sure you will be all right now but I still need to know.

Your mother
Lateefa Mursi

Asya looks up at Saif.

'Well?' he says.

'Oh, it's all fine,' Asya says. 'Do you want to read it?' She holds it out to him.

'It's too long,' he says. 'Is she OK?'

'Yes,' says Asya. 'Do you mind if I just glance at the other letter? It's from a friend of my mother's.'

'Sure, go ahead,' Saif says, and spears a baby carrot with his fork.

Asya glances first into her mother's envelope. Sure enough, the cheque is there. She opens the other letter.

London, 14 February 1978

Dear Asya al-Ulama,

I have just spent a most enjoyable week in Cairo where I saw a great deal of your mother and other members of the department of English.

I understood from Professor Mursi that you are here in London and will be looking for work over the next few months. I told her that I'd heard that Citadel Publishing were planning to start a Middle East Division and that there might be an opening there for you. You could just phone and ask to speak to the Managing Director's secretary, or if you'd like to chat about it with me first, please feel welcome. My number is –

'It's a job,' Asya says.

'What's a job?'

'This letter: it's about a job.'

'What? Offering you one?'

'No, just telling me about it. Suggesting I apply.'

'What is it?'

'Something in publishing.'

'Should be OK,' Saif says. 'Do you want some wine?'

'Saif,' Asya says after a while, 'what about *your* work?'

'What about it?'

'Well, what are you going to do?'

'Nothing.'

'Well, what about the Ph.D you were doing?'

'What about it?'

'I don't want to sound like my mother, but –'

'Then don't.'

'OK. But you *did* start it – why not finish it?'

'I thought you said you didn't want to sound like your mother?'

'Yes, but –'

'Leave it. OK?'

'OK.'

As they walk back to his flat Asya links her arm to his and shelters against him from the cold. Oh, that she could shelter against him always –

'Saif?' she asks.

'Yes?'

'What are we going to do?'

'About what?'

'Us.'

He says nothing.

'Are we getting a – divorce, or what?' Asya makes herself say.

'If you want,' Saif says.

'I suppose we should,' Asya says.

'If you want,' Saif says again.

'It's not what I *want*,' Asya says passionately. 'I never *wanted* it to be like that.'

'What *do* you want then?'

'I don't know – I want – yes, I do know: I want everything to be all right between us – basically – in whatever way –'

She sees Saif shake his head with a sad little smile on his face.

'Can't there *be* a way?' Asya pleads. 'Can't we make a pact or something? To meet at a certain point?'

'Come on, sweetie, this is life, not a Gothic romance –'

'No, but *why* not? Some point in the future – however far –'

'What am I, Asya?' Saif asks gently. 'An elephant's graveyard? That's unworthy of you, isn't it?'

'That isn't what I meant,' says Asya, but she is shamed. 'What I meant was that I want to carry on being – being –'

'Yes?'

'Oh, Saif! Can't we agree to be *friends*, to be best *best* friends?'

'No, sweetie, we *are* friends – but we can't agree to be *just* friends.'

'But why? Why?'

He shrugs. 'Things don't work like that.'

'But I don't feel we can – be – anything else right now.'

'Maybe you're right.'

'Well, what's the answer?'

'The answer is to let go.'

'But I can't, because if I do you'll make it be completely and for ever.' Asya is crying now. 'You won't agree to *anything*: any little barrier or milestone or anything – just *something* – something like those buoys out in the sea –'

'Hey,' he says, stopping and holding her shoulders. 'Now, honestly, even if this were a novel, what kind of a novel would it be? It would be pretty crappy, wouldn't it, if it had us standing here now agreeing to meet in twenty years' time? You could have a sequel then: *The Flame of Friendship: Part Two*.' He grins.

'It's just that – oh – I love you – so much,' Asya sobs.

'I love you too, Princess,' he says, and lifts her hand briefly to his lips. 'Are you going to stop crying before you come in and call your mother?'

When she leaves him, Asya crosses the road, then stops. She can't bear to go away. Why *should* she go away? Why *should* she leave him? Why shouldn't she just run back – or, better still, *walk* back quietly – and just stand in front of him and say, 'I come in a taxi, I did'? And then? Would he lean back in his chair, tip his hat over his face, and say, 'Asya, where the *hell* are my slippers?' Oh – she stands under the now bare tree on the pavement opposite his house and looks into his living-room. He is already in his favourite armchair by the reading-lamp, with *White Nights* open on his knee and a pile of magazines and books lying in readiness at his feet. Concealed from her view in the corner the television gives out a flickering light – and at his side there is his walnut coffee-table with his whisky, his ice, his Freiburg and Tryers in a silver box, his ashtray, his antique lighter and a couple of gold fountain pens filled with black ink – and some sheets of pale blue squared paper. Later, when she thinks back, she will not be able to remember how much she actually saw through that lit window and how much she simply knew was there. She will always remember standing and watching him: loving the set of his head on his shoulders and the movement of his hands with the cigarettes, the drink, and the magazine. Well, why not go to him, then? Why not go? She imagines going inside and sees herself vanish. It is like vanishing into one of those black holes they are talking about these days – a black hole brimming with a kind of still, secret energy that sucks you in effortlessly – like quicksand; that can't *help* sucking you in – until there's nothing of you left, nothing at all.

Walking along the Old Brompton Road a little later, Asya sees Mandy walking in the opposite direction on the other pavement. Mandy wears a black, lurex skirt, short and tight, with very high heels and a big, fluffy, sequined pullover. And she wears huge dangly earrings that show clearly from across the road. Asya thinks Mandy looks more like herself (even though she remembers that she doesn't know what her 'self' is like) . . . And, Chrissie, I suddenly thought: she's had enough; she's had enough of the mellow lights and the Japanese atonal music and the Burberrys and the Poetry of the Thirties and the whisky. She's had herself a fix and a good screw. And I saw what she would see when she got back to the flat: Saif in his armchair, with his music and his cigarettes and his smokescreens – and I missed him so terribly that it was an actual *ache* – but I could not bear to be sitting in the other armchair turning the pages of a magazine –

Epilogue
April 1980

We shall go back by the boltless doors,
    To the life unaltered our childhood
knew—
To the naked feet on the cool, dark floors,
    And high-ceiled rooms that the Trade
blows through—

The wayside magic, the threshold spells,
    Shall soon undo what the North has
done—
Because of the sights and the sounds and
the smells
That ran with our youth in the eye of the
sun.

—RUDYARD KIPLING
'Song of the Wise Children'

Thursday, 10 April 1980
Cairo

Sheikh Zayid's arm, the hand holding a rolled-up copy of *al-Ahram*, comes out of the passenger window of the car ahead and waves them down. Asya steps on her brakes, honks and smiles at two women who stand talking on what should have been the edge of the pavement. The women smile back, then move slowly out of the way, and Asya pulls in behind the battered old Mercedes. Sheikh Zayid gets out and walks to the cart loaded with reeds and flowers and parked where the shadow of a wall will fall on it when the sun rises higher in the sky. Asya gets out of her Fiat and waves a reassuring hand at Deena, who is calling out after her, 'Don't go and spend ten pounds now, this is Egypt, remember.' She walks over to the Mercedes and bends at the driver's window.

'How're you doing, Khalu?'

Hamid Mursi smiles up at her. 'Fine. How about you?'

'I'm fine. But if I lose you I'll be sunk. I don't know my way around this bit at all.'

'Stay on my tail, then.' He grins.

'Take care!' Tante Soraya cries out from the back seat as a heavy truck lurches by. Asya moves closer to the car.

'They drive like donkeys,' Tante Soraya says. 'Can't they see the world is crowded?'

'I don't know how these children don't get run over by the dozen,' Asya says, looking at the small crowd milling round the swings set up at the side of the road. Two brightly painted boxes hang from the bars and in each a little boy is furiously swinging, urging his creaking craft faster and faster, higher and higher, until one of them manages to complete the loop and force his box up and over the bar while the children on the ground push and shove and hold out their hands with the piastres clenched in them and clamour for their turn.

'You wouldn't think it was a day for visiting the dead,' Tante Soraya says.

'They're children, Soraya,' Khalu Hamid says. 'What do they know?'

Asya bends to her uncle again. 'It's amazing how you manage,' she says. 'How do you steady her while you change gears?'

'That's where this thing comes in useful,' Hamid says, lifting his false left arm slightly. 'I wedge it into the steering-wheel –'

'He shouldn't be driving at all,' Tanta Soraya says. 'If the police catch up with him –'

'They haven't caught up with me in six years,' he says. 'Why should I start worrying now?'

Asya walks over to where Sheikh Zayid is picking out bundles of green reeds and orange flowers.

'Let me get some, 'Am el-Sheikh.'

'No, no, it's done,' he says, digging some money out of his pocket. 'Are you able to drive here, Asya? You're not used to all this any more, child.'

'Yes I am,' Asya says. 'I've driven in the countryside and everything.'

'God give you health,' he says turning back to the car. 'Let's go before the winds rise again.'

Asya goes back to her car.

'There: I've spent nothing at all,' she says. "Am el-Sheikh wouldn't let me.'

'He always gets the flowers,' Nadia says.

Asya follows her uncle as he bumps on the cobbles, overtakes donkey-pulled carts loaded with women, runs on the tram lines for a while, then swerves to avoid a child –

Many, many years ago, as she rode in the front seat on Sheikh Zayid's knee, he had told her about the tradition of the green reeds. 'The Prophet (the blessings and prayers of God be upon him) was out walking when he chanced upon a fresh grave. He stopped and asked who was buried there and they said, "It is the grave of so and so, O Prophet of God." Now this so and so was known for uncleanliness and not washing himself after doing what is necessary and the Prophet stood and thought for a moment and he knew that the man was even then being tortured. So he bent and plucked a green reed that was growing near his feet and he laid it on the grave and he said, "O God, I ask that You lift this man's suffering for as long as this reed stays green." And that is why,' he'd said to Asya, 'we place green reeds on the tombs of the dead.'

'But why did he only pray for the suffering to be lifted as long as the reed remained green?' Asya had asked. 'Why didn't he pray for it to be lifted completely?'

'Is it not enough that he is asking a favour of God?' Sheikh Zayid had said. 'And after all, the man had been unclean. How could he have prayed if he didn't wash? It must mean that he didn't pray.'

'The reeds stay green for a long time,' Lateefa's voice had said soothingly from the back seat.

But Lateefa is not here and Asya wonders again what that reprieve was worth. Was there any chance that if the torture was unremitting you would get used to it? No; they say in Hell your skin is periodically renewed so that the flames and boiling oils strike you always afresh – 'they shall not die, neither shall its tortures be lightened for them –' Asya tries to imagine the man: the man at the instant when the torture stopped. Yes, he would be grateful, he would be grateful for one second without it – and he would hope that it wouldn't come back – that somehow he would slip through the system; that they'd forget him – Asya sighs.

'What's wrong?' Nadia asks.

'I was just thinking – thinking of Mummy, all alone in Kuwait.'

It wouldn't do to come up with 'I was thinking about torture' with Deena sitting there in the back seat.

'She won't be sorry to miss this,' Deena says, reaching in the big basket of mercy at her side and taking out a piece of *shoreik* to nibble at, 'She never liked this trip.'

'Would you be able to find our place on your own?' Asya asks Nadia.

'No, not really. I've always come with your uncle,' Nadia says.

'I think *I* could find it,' Deena says.

'I'm sure you could,' Asya smiles at her sister in the mirror. 'You can find anything.'

Deena had, it seemed to Asya, taken on the Egyptian government single-handed; she had secured her husband and his friends' release from their illegal imprisonment in the Citadel Jail, and by the time the official warrant for Muhsin's arrest had come round she had smuggled him away to some place on the Mediterranean coast west of Alexandria. There she had joined him with their son, and they had hidden out for the two months it took her to get pregnant. In early November they had come back to Cairo and, in the company of his wife and two lawyers, Muhsin Nur-el-Din had given himself up. The trial had lasted three months. In February, he and el-Prof and Zeeko had been convicted of possession of a potential weapon and sentenced to five years each. Zeeko, because he was paralysed, would serve his sentence in hospital. The earliest any of them could hope to come out is August 1985. By then Deena's son would be eight and the baby she is carrying would be five. And she takes it all in her stride: the Faculty Union, the Palestine Committee, the new opposition, the committee to fight Sadat's proposed 'Law of Shame', the teaching, the child, the Ph.D, the pregnancy, the husband in jail thirty hot and dusty kilometres outside Cairo – none of it phases her in the slightest, and there isn't a minute in the day when she isn't doing something that she knows she ought to be doing – and what's more, that she *wants* to do –

'Are you OK back there?' Asya glances at her sister in the rear-view mirror. 'All this jolting can't be good for you.'

'I told her not to come,' Nadia says.

'I'm used to it,' Deena says.

'And she's going out to Tora tomorrow,' Nadia says.

'Are you really?' Asya asks.

'Of course I am. It's visiting day.'

'How are you getting there?'

'By bus. And walking.'

'No you're not. I'm taking you.'

'Will you really? Muhsin would be very pleased to see you.'

'No, this time I'll wait outside. You have your visit in private.'

'It's hardly private with fifty other people in the room.'

'Still, it's not the same as having your sister sitting right next to you. I'll wait.'

Khalu Hamid's car takes a sharp left and Asya follows. Now they have left the main road and have entered the cemeteries. The groups of children still play by the roadside, but they are thinning out. No winding alleyways now, only long straight paths bordered by low mausoleums, on and on –

The last time Asya had taken Deena to Tora they had had to wait outside the prison gates for two and a half hours. She had sat on the stump of what had been a tree, her feet surrounded by Deena's plastic bags, and stared at what she now recognises as a particularly Egyptian landscape: stretches of hard, cracked land suddenly sprouting patches of grass or the odd, twisted tree; the earth shading off into sand at one end of the clearing and dissolving into muddy puddles at the other – you could see both the mud and the sand in one line of vision. To the right of the great prison doors stood a full-size Greek or Roman youth, his right foot firm, carrying all his weight, the left behind him – about to lose contact with the ground. His face and his genitals have been obliterated as though by the fine strokes of a chisel. The rest of his body – although grey and streaked with dirt – is intact. How does he come to be standing here, Asya had wondered. Was he there on purpose? An attempt at decoration? Or had he been found nearby and was waiting to be moved to a museum? Maybe she could ask Deena. But Deena had come up and said, 'If they don't open by one o'clock it means they won't open today.'

'And then what?' Asya had asked.

Deena had shrugged, 'We'll have to come back tomorrow.'

Asya had looked at their nine plastic bags.

'Oh, I can probably get them to take these in,' Deena had said.

People had stood around in little groups waiting for the gates to open. The odd soldier wandered by, carrying his rifle by the barrel, walking with that stoop so typical of the peasant male. Peasant *women* don't stoop – although they too are burdened. But their burden is different: the men bend to plough and plant, the women walk erect with pots of water on their heads and children on their shoulders. Most of the women waiting outside the prison had been from the countryside; they wore black smocks and carried covered baskets filled with food for the men inside.

'What is all this?' Asya had asked as Deena had come struggling down the stairs of her home with four heavy carrier bags. She had jumped out of the car to help her.

'There's more upstairs,' Deena had said, and they'd gone back up the stairs to her flat and come down with five more bags.

'It's not just for Muhsin.' Deena had laughed as she saw the look on Asya's face. 'It's for all of them. There are seven in the cell.'

'I thought it was just Muhsin and el-Prof?'

'There are other prisoners.'

'All from the same organisation?'

'Oh no. There's one other leftist: an independent. And four from the Islamic currents.'

'But I thought they were supposed to be enemies?'

'Outside, yes,' Deena had said, 'but inside they're all "Politicals". They don't read the same books, but they eat the same food.'

It had taken an hour to get from Pyramid Boulevard to Tora. They had had to park outside the prison grounds and walk the last dusty five hundred metres to the prison gates, loaded with the bags of food and books and clothes. Asya had looked at her pregnant sister and said, 'If I hadn't been here, how would you have carried all this?'

'One of them would have helped me,' Deena had said, nodding towards the group of soldiers sitting on the sandy verge with their rifles between their knees.

Asya had sat on the stump of the tree and watched Deena talk to a bewildered-looking grey-haired lady in a pale green suit. She must be the mother of the other leftist: the independent, Asya had thought. Occasionally one of the black-smocked women would walk up to the great wooden doors and bang on them and a small inset door would open and a guard would shout, 'Not yet, not yet. Patience is good.'

A small boy with a bucket had shown up and everyone had crowded round to buy Seven-Ups.

'You ought to sit down,' Asya had said to Deena, and Deena had sat next to her on the stump of the tree.

Deena had looked at her watch several times. At half past twelve, the inset doors had opened and an elderly guard had come out carrying a small wooden child's school-desk. He'd set it up just outside the door and gone back for a chair. When he sat down everybody crowded round him.

'In turn,' he'd shouted. 'In turn.'

'We've been waiting for three hours,' the women shouted back.

'Patience,' he said, 'patience. We have to get through the procedures.'

One by one they had shown their identity cards, been checked against a list, made their mark in a book, uncovered their baskets and gone inside.

'You don't speak,' Deena had said to Asya; then she had gone up to the guard and shown him her card. When the guard had waved at her to go in she had taken hold of Asya's arm. 'And she's with me,' she'd said.

'And who is she?' the guard had said, looking up. He had a heavy body and a grey moustache and looked kindly, like an old bus inspector, or the keeper of some benign animal at the zoo – the giraffes maybe.

'She's my sister-in-law,' Deena had said.

'The identity card.'

'She hasn't got one, 'Am Sergeant. Her husband has their family card and he wouldn't let her have it.'

'She can't go in without proof of identity.'

"Am Sergeant, she's come all the way from Alexandria to see her brother. *Haraam*. Let her in on my cognisance. I'll leave my ID with you –'

'Go in,' he'd said, 'go in. But it's the last time. Next!'

As they stooped through the small door and into the cobbled passage Asya had thought how medieval it all looked – how picturesque. And the guards all look like kindly, elderly, family men. Would they be able – if they were given the order – to strip a man? To hold him down? To stamp with heavy shoes on his face, on his stomach –

'The next left and we're there,' Deena says from the back seat.

By the time Asya has pulled up at a slight distance from her family's mausoleum both Tante Soraya and Sheikh Zayid are out of the Mercedes and the inevitable crowd of ill-kempt children with expectant faces is already gathering. A man in a *galabiyya* has come running round the corner and opened the iron gate and Tante Soraya is scolding him.

'Is it like this then? Is every time going to be worse than the one before? Why isn't the place swept and washed? You know we are coming today – every time we come here we must sit on the dust?'

'I swear, Sett Soraya, I swear on the head of my father I washed it only yesterday – but it's the season, Sett Soraya – it's the Khamaseen –'

'This is empty talk – and you're using it as a store-room? What are all these bricks doing here?' she exclaims as she walks into the building. 'Last year it was bags of cement – this year it's bricks? Have the dead no sanctity?'

A woman with a dirty cloth comes running in and starts to wipe the seven chairs ranged against the walls. On the raised platform at the far end of the room Sheikh Zayid is untying the bundles of reeds and flowers and arranging them on the marble tomb and in the vases around it. Asya watches him: he arranges the plants with matter-of-fact care, his lips moving as he works. How many, many times he must have arranged flowers around this tomb – Tante Soraya walks over to the big pots with the dusty cactus.

'Have you no compassion in your heart?' she cries out to the man who is now coming in with one of the big baskets. 'How long has it been since these plants drank any water?'

The man puts the basket down on the floor.

'I swear I watered them the day before yesterday –'

'Don't swear, man, how can you swear? Do you think I'm blind? Look at them – they haven't seen water in weeks –'

His wife comes in with the other basket.

'He watered them just yesterday, Sett Soraya –'

'But I'll water them again for your sake,' he says.

'Not for *my* sake,' Tante Soraya says, 'for the sake of God who is up there and sees you –'

The man goes out and comes back with a big tin can full of water which he empties into the four pots. The parched earth drinks up the water immediately. He spills a lot of it on the tiled floor beside them. Deena and Nadia have come in and settled each on a chair. Asya thinks how nice it would be to take off her shoes and go and stand barefoot on the tiles in those pools of water. The children cluster round the doorway. Khalu Hamid appears behind them and puts his hand on the head of one of the boys.

'Make way, kids,' he says.

Sheikh Zayid has finished arranging the reeds.

'I'll go and send for the reciter,' he says as he walks out of the room.

Hamid nods and walks over to Soraya.

'I think you should hand out the *rahma* now, Soraya,' he says, 'so that we can sit in peace.'

'They don't deserve anything,' Tante Soraya grumbles.

'This is *rahma*, not payment,' Hamid says. 'Come on, kids' – he turns back to the door – 'in a line now so Hajja Soraya doesn't get cross with you.'

The children line up and Asya watches Tante Soraya's face soften as one by one they come to stand in front of her. She calls them by their names, asks how they are doing at school, puts a brand-new fifty-piastre note into each little fist and then drops a handful of dried dates, an orange, and a three-finger bar of *shoreik* into the laps of their *galabiyyas*, which they hold out like little sacks then gather to them and run out to their mothers waiting by the door. When a very small child with large black eyes in a dirty face toddles up Tante Soraya takes his hands in hers and looks at the group of women gathered round the doorway.

'Whose son is this?' she asks.

A pretty, smiling young woman carrying an even smaller child steps in.

'He's my son, Hajja,' she says.

'And already you've brothered him?' Tante Soraya says. 'He isn't even two.'

'It's God's will, Hajja,' the woman says.

'And she's carrying again!' one of the women at the door calls out, and they all laugh and hide their faces.

Tante Soraya is doing her bit for the family-planning campaign.

'Have mercy on yourself, sister.' She smiles. 'What are you? A factory?'

And like all the women in all the villages Asya has been to, the woman giggles and says, 'What can we do? It's God's will.'

745

'What's your name, little one?' Tante Soraya says to the boy.

'Ahmad,' he whispers.

'His name is Ahmad,' the women shout from the door.

'Here, Ummu Ahmad.' Tante Soraya digs out a precious plastic bag and fills it with food. 'Take this for the children. And this is for your baby.' She hands her a pound note. 'Ahmad,' she says to the little boy, 'this is for you.' She puts a fifty-piastre note into the small hand and folds his fingers over it. 'Don't let them take it away from you. And eat this up' putting a bar of *shoreik* into his other hand – 'so you can grow and be a man. And Ummu Ahmad,' she says before she lets go of the boy, 'clean him up. The boy – may my eye be cool on him – is beautiful and his face is like the moon. Clean him up. God will count it a good deed and reward you.'

And what would Gerald Stone have made of this little scene? What would he have said? That it was seigneurial? Patronising? Perpetuating the evil system of privilege? And so they should have come empty-handed to visit Geddu and Mama Deela? And the children would have crowded round, and they would have said, 'Sorry, we think that the "mercy" we bring here every season delays the process of your liberation; we've decided to speed it up, to help you by increasing the pressure on you just that little bit more –' And what would the children have done? Asya can see their faces turn sullen and uncomprehending as they retreat and watch them from across the road. Of *course* it would be best if there were no children living among the tombs, if they all lived in clean little houses with a bit of garden like in some Bavarian village – and who would look after the graves? A uniformed security guard employed by a company – an 'open-door' company to run the City of the Dead – well, they've given Transport to the French, Sewage to the British, Telecommunications to the Germans and Defence to the Americans; they could give the Cemeteries to the Swedes or the Japanese –

Asya smiles, and a little girl with matted blonde hair who has been staring at her smiles shyly back. She is so pretty. Asya could adopt her: she could take her home and spray her hair with insecticide and then put her into a warm bath with bubbles and scrub and shampoo her clean. She would buy her clothes and send her to school and that would be that: it would take care of the whole question of 'the child'. But she wouldn't be her own; Asya would not be able to look into her face and trace its features back to herself or to other, loved people. But it would be doing good; it would be giving this little girl more of a chance than she is going to get – no, there is no use in thinking like that: she wants one of her own. She wants to look into a small face and see her own eyes look back at her, to catch a fleeting expression and think, ah! that's Grandfather's twist of the lip; to hold the soft feet and think, there's Daddy's second toe: slightly longer than the big one . . . Tante Soraya could have adopted a child, or given up on children. But she had put her life at risk to produce Meedo out of her own body – 'And look where that's got me!' Asya suddenly hears her say in one of her crosser moments. 'Two years of changing nappies, thousands of bottles of warm milk, a support system that would have propped up an army, and what have I got at the end of it? A rhinoceros who won't even buy yoghurt on his way home from school –' But Tante Soraya's view of things is jaundiced – which isn't surprising: she has worked all her life with the deprived, from 'Abd el-Nasser's 'People's Clubs' to the 'Productive Families' to God knows how many other schemes – how many miles she must have walked down muddy lanes, how many glasses of stewed tea she must have been served by how many legless and legged women, how many scraps of embroidery and crochet she must have checked and corrected – and after thirty years of it to find that the misery and the squalor had simply increased: that the poor were poorer and more numerous and had less hope – to find that after thirty years in the service of the government you could actually afford less than you could when you started – to be called Director-General and have to think about whether you could afford the new shoes your son was demanding –

Tante Soraya had suddenly looked up from ironing Meedo's school shirt. 'Why did you leave your husband, child?'

Asya had been sitting in her usual corner of the sofa, turning over the pages of one of Nadia's 1959 *Woman's Weeklies*:

'You shivered when I touched you,' he said and his voice betrayed his hurt.

'A woman may shiver when a man touches her, Neil,' Julie said softly. 'It doesn't always have to mean she doesn't like him.'

Her husband lifted his eyes to hers and in them she saw the beginnings of understanding.

'You mean –' he said.

'Yes,' she said in a whisper, her eyes shining bright with love.

'Oh, my darling,' Neil said. In two strides he was close to her and she could feel the strength of his lean body as he gathered her up in his arms. 'Oh, my darling,' he groaned. 'All these months I have lived in torment –'

She had looked up. Tante Soraya was resting the iron on a corner of the dining-room table and looking at her. Why had that scene appealed to her so? She remembers it almost word for word –

'We were not happy together, Tante,' she had said.

Tante Soraya had raised her eyebrows. 'Not happy?' she had repeated.

'No,' Asya had said.

'Is this sane talk?' Tante Soraya had asked. 'Who's happy, child?'

A cough at the doorway. The women and the children have all

disappeared and a plump young man names the Name of God and crosses the threshold. As he enters with the light behind him Asya can see the white boxer-shorts and the vest he wears underneath the thin white *galabiyya*.

'You are the Fekki?' Tante Soraya says disbelievingly.

'God willing,' he replies, stepping off his Korean platform clogs and sitting down on a chair facing the women. Asya looks across at Nadia, who raises her eyebrows briefly and then glances at Tante Soraya.

'The truth is, son, I've never seen a Fekki without a *djibba* and a *kaftan*.' Tante Soraya smiles slightly to soften her words.

'In any case, the measure is in the reading,' Sheikh Zayid says.

He motions to Asya. She stands up, and he lifts her chair and carries it to the other side of the room so that she is not directly facing the Fekki. 'We want good, intoned reading,' he warns. Then he sits down and takes out his prayer-beads.

' "Yasseen" God willing,' he says.

'Where is Hamid?' Tante Soraya asks.

'Outside,' Sheikh Zayid replies simply.

The young man has hoisted his legs up on to the chair and now begins straight away.

'I take refuge in God from Satan who is to be stoned. In the name of God the Compassionate, the Merciful –'

The pool of water by the cactus-plants has already dried up. Where, Asya wonders, have all the old men gone, the real sheikhs who had to be led along by small boys as they muttered and rolled their sightless eyes, who sat and swayed and coughed on the straw mat before raising their hands to their ears and their strong, melodious voices to heaven? There isn't one of them left in the cemetery? This fat young man perched cross-legged on top of the chair with his undies showing and his high-heeled clogs waiting for him under it is a joke: he has no *'imma*. How can he be a sheikh without an *'imma*? He wears a straight *galabiyya* with cufflinks and a gold wristwatch, and his hair is slicked back like a car mechanic's on holiday. His eyes are everywhere. He pretends to close them as he recites, but from under his lids he is examining the legs of the women. Things change, she thinks, but hold on to their names. Like Midan El-Opera which is now a gigantic car-park. Forget tradition, forget the fanfare and the laying down of the foundation-stone: a huge, concrete multi-storey car-park, smelling of car exhaust and urine, stands on the site of Khedive Ismail's opera house. And they still call the midan 'Midan El-Opera'. If at least they used its real name: Midan Ibrahim Pasha – that would make more sense since his statue is still standing there – dusty and ill kept, but standing. But no, buses go to 'Opera'; 'Where did you park?' 'In Opera' – and there isn't an opera anywhere in sight. Deena says she is sorry, of course, that the old opera house is gone, but the carpark is of more immediate use to more people – so it's the old pinball versus poetry argument all over again. 'But it's so hideous,' Asya had said. 'Just look at it!' and Deena had shrugged. 'If they'd built a new opera house it would have been hideous too,' she'd said. And that was probably true – and yet – can it be right that everything should go like this? *Everything?* Even on the drive home from the airport six months ago – even as she had greeted with joy the familiar badly drawn posters, the lamp-posts, not one of them aligned with another but leaning crazily every which way like melting candles on a crumbling birthday cake – she had realised that she would not have found her way home alone: new roads, new buildings, new roundabouts, the great statue of Rameses II, once an imposing landmark outside Cairo Central Station, now slips by insignificantly below them as they speed along '6th October Bridge'! – it used to be that if you didn't want to call a street 26th July Street you could carry right on calling it Fuad Street – and everybody did – but this bridge has no other name: it was *built* as 6th October Bridge – and of course it's better for traffic, much better. Oh, she knows, she knows. She knows you can't step into the same river twice, but this is ridiculous. All her memories – the Omar Khayyam has been taken over by the Marriot and turned into a huge building site; the maze where Saif had held her against the rock and kissed her and whispered, 'Marry me,' has been bulldozed to the ground – why have a maze where a pair of lovers can whisper and kiss and lose themselves, when instead you can throw up a hundred rooms yielding a hundred pounds a night each? The Semiramis where they had had their wedding has gone too, and a monolithic Intercontinental Semiramis is rising in its place. Gone is the roof-garden with the dinner-jacketed band where she had gone with her parents one magical evening when she was eleven and seen a foreign woman in blue chiffon tango round the floor. She had decided then that being grown-up would mean being romanced on that roof, would mean being able to sit all night at a table overlooking the Nile in the 'Night and Day' – with a pot of coffee, a packet of cigarettes and a note-pad, looking up briefly to greet the odd acquaintance who walked in, and then down again at what she would be writing. Now it was all gone, she would never ever be able to do these things – she would never be grown-up now – not like that. And when she had gone to the university she had prepared herself. She had said to herself: Remember: 'Am 'Ali is dead, he won't be looking up and smiling reluctantly from under his grey shawl to greet you; he's dead. Remember: your professor is retired and no longer to be found under the faded portrait of Shakespeare. Remember: the students will be all new to you – and young, and many of them will be wearing the *hijab* and the *thob*, and they won't know who you are; they won't automatically smile and make way. Remember: there will be changes – but when she had got

749

there and had seen the old clock-tower and heard it chime and then had glimpsed the figure stalking through the central campus garden and recognised Napoleon by his stately gait and the books under his arm and the angle of his haircut, she had thought, Ah! it hasn't changed, and rounding the corner of the main Faculty of Arts building she had kept her eyes trained on the library steps as though she would once again see a man in cords and Hush Puppies standing in the sunshine on the bottom step watching a girl with a bandaged knee who hesitates at the top. The stairs were crowded with students walking up and down and she had turned to look at the parasoled cafeteria at the bottom of the garden and her heart had stumbled. The cafeteria was gone, and in its place there was yet another semi-finished building. And she had felt so desolate –

'Yasseen. By the Qur'an full of wisdom. You are one of those who have been sent. On a straight path. With a Revelation of the Precious, the Compassionate. To warn a people whose fathers were not warned and who are unaware. The word is true of most of them for they do not believe. We have put chains round their necks even to their chins. And we have put a barrier in front of them and a barrier behind them and blinded them so they do not see. It is all the same whether you warn them or you do not warn them, they do not believe. You warn only him who follows the Word and fears the Compassionate in secret. To him bear tidings of forgiveness and a generous wage. We it is Who bring the dead to life and write down what they have put forward and what they have left behind and all things we have recorded in an accurate book –'

His recitation is efficient; not tremendously heartfelt, he does not repeat a line for the pleasure of it, but he is efficient. Is that enough, though, to win mercy for those they have come to visit? Somewhere underneath the raised platform to Asya's right, Geddu and Mama Deela lie. Or what is left of them lies: two long bundles of white cloth. If you lifted them now they would be very light; light and crumbly. Asya feels the bundle flop as she slides her arms under it and tries to raise it gently as you would a sleeping child; she feels it flop and disintegrate. And once upon a time they were solid. They were solid and walked and talked and thought secret thoughts, and were happy and angry and loving and miserable – until one day it had all stopped. But they had known it would stop. When Grandfather was twenty-five and had set up his own business, he took a wife, he rented the big flat in 'Ataba, and he bought this plot of land and built a mausoleum and commissioned a marble tomb. These things done, he was ready for his life. It seems pretty clear-cut from here, but had it seemed so to him? Was there a day when he had stood at the door of his thriving shop on Morgan Street and looked out at the busy marketplace and – knowing his bride was in his house getting

750

ready for his return; knowing his grave had been built to his specifications – had stood and thought, This is it. My preparations are complete. From now on every moment counts as My Life? Asya looks at the tomb she has known all her life, the tomb that has always terrified her: a big cuboid of white marble, towering above her when she was a child, but now shoulder-high if she stands close up to it. The inscription on one side reads 'Enter in peace and safety' and on the other 'He rewardeth thee for thy patience with honey and milk'. Above it the ceiling ends and the room is open to the sky. When she was very small Asya had imagined that the marble was hollow – a sarcophagus inside which the dead were placed – and she had worried because she could see that it wasn't long enough for a grown-up to lie comfortably. 'No dear, no, it's solid,' her mother had said. 'They are under it.' And then she had imagined that the block of marble was hinged to the floor; that when it was pushed open like the lid of a box only very very heavy there would be a hole underneath, that *that* was where they had put Mama Deela. But later, just before her grandfather died, she had learnt that there is a trap-door somewhere. Somewhere, concealed under one of these big stone tiles on the floor, there is a trap-door. And there is a flight of stairs. And down below there are two chambers: one for women and one for men. She does not know what they look like. She imagines them dim and cavernous like the tombs of the Capulets in the film, with Sheikh Zayid instead of Friar Lawrence standing holding a light above his head. Khalu Hamid has been down there twice: once to bury his mother, and once his father. And both times Sheikh Zayid was with him.

'And there came from the furthest ends of the city a man. He said: O people follow those that have been sent to you. Follow those who ask you no payment and who are on the right path. Why should I not worship Him who created me and to Whom you shall all return? Should I take gods other than Him? Should the Compassionate intend harm to me their intercession will do me no good nor can they save me. I would indeed be lost. I have believed in your Lord so hear me. It was said: Enter Paradise. He said: O that my people should know; know that my Lord hath forgiven me and I am one of those honoured.'

The prayer-mark in the middle of Sheikh Zayid's forehead is clearer than Asya remembers it. She had thought of it as a vague shadow, but it isn't; it is a real, vivid presence. He sits back in his chair with his eyes closed, fingering his beads. He hasn't changed much, Asya thinks, and neither has her father. It is the women who change most. The men just dry out slightly, withdraw, get a faintly pickled look, the women expand and overflow. She looks over at her two aunts and her sister. Tante Soraya sits upright and ample in her black dress, her thickened ankles crossed, her handbag squarely on her knees; she has metamorphosed from a slim girl in a cloche skirt, her hair blown by the wind, into a substantial matriarch – but the girl in the cloche skirt was – what? Twenty-six years ago? Asya works it out and is amazed; is that how she has thought of Tante Soraya all this time? As she was in a photograph taken twenty-six years ago? No wonder then that the grown-ups still treat *her* like a child – if time stands still and you live by the images of the far-away past – and Deena, Asya has been thinking of her as her kid sister, outspoken, impulsive, a bit loony, thin and restless in jeans and a sweatshirt – and there she sits, swollen with her second child and given substance by the life she has managed to accumulate: the husband in prison, the child, the flat on Pyramid Road, the students, the research, the politics – twenty-four years old and already partaking of Tante Soraya's solidity. Asya looks at them sitting side by side: they look so – anchored; as though they have never known a moment's indecision – a moment's doubt. But Nadia – Nadia's face occasionally looks uncertain, her eyes look vague, but then she is trying to decide to leave her husband. She isn't vague with her children – or with her work. Asya has been with her on her rounds, young interns flapping at her heels in their white coats with their stethoscopes dangling from their necks. She has seen her sitting in her office with the patients brought before her: a young woman with a heart-shaped face, with a perfect nose and wide, clear eyes, carried in by her father, her atrophied legs dangling uselessly over his arm. Her face had been so serene, so patient, it had made Asya think of the paintings of saints.

'Is she in pain?' she had asked.

'Yes,' Nadia had said as she washed her hands after the woman and her family had gone.

'A lot?'

'Probably.'

'Will she get better?'

'I don't think so. But you never know.'

'Will she die?'

Nadia had tilted her head to one side. 'Yes, it's possible.'

'What will you do for her?'

'Try another treatment – and give her pain-killers.'

A child with a huge, swollen, misshaped head, and then a skeletal man in a peasant *galabiyya* who has to get down on his hands and knees on the examining table while Nadia inserts a gloved finger into his rectum. The frame of a screen stands unused in the corner. The nurses and the cleaning-women come and go with trays of instruments and buckets of disinfectant.

'Why don't you use the screen?' Asya had asked later, in the car.

'It was filthy. I made them take it down to wash it.'

'Is there only one set of covers for it?'

752

'Yes, apparently.'

'That can't be right. Why don't you get another? I'll get you some –'

'Asya,' Nadia had said, manoeuvring through the cars parked on either side of Museum Street, 'the hospital has no money. We've begged and borrowed enough to get a cobalt – we don't possess a CAT-scan, sometimes I prescribe medicines for patients knowing the dispensary has run out and they can't possibly afford to get them privately. No one worries about screens. That man was terminal. We're beyond screens.'

But Asya in the second before she looked away had seen a thick, long penis spring to life as the gloved finger entered the anus. He wasn't beyond screens. No one is ever beyond screens –

'We have not sent against his people after him a host from the sky and We shall not send. It is but one cry and they are extinguished. Woe to My people, no prophet is sent to them but they mock him. Do they not see how many We have destroyed before them over the centuries and they shall not return?'

– and they shall not return. In a way they are right: the girls who wear those horrible long pastel-coloured gowns, the gloves and the angled veil; they've screened themselves off entirely, held on to their privacy. They're preferable anyway to the halfway ones, the ones who wear the long gown but leave their made-up faces bare and deck out their *tarhas* with bits of ribbon and coloured braids – and yet how dismal it would be to think that it is for them and only for them that there will be forgiveness and great rewards. But that is what they think. They are certain of it. And there are so many of them in the university now. Of them and of the young bearded men in short white *thobs*. And on the other hand there are girls in short skirts and tight trousers and amounts of make-up that no one would have dreamed of wearing ten years ago when Asya was a student. She has three of the veiled girls in her classes – and they always sit in the front row. The first time she'd gone into her Seventeenth Century Poetry class she'd asked the sixty-three students to write a paragraph explaining why they had chosen to enter the Department of English. 'And, ladies and gentlemen, I would be grateful if you could give me an honest answer. Please do not write "because I love Wordsworth" – particularly if you have never read him. I don't *mind* whether you like literature or not. I just want to adjust my teaching as much as possible to your needs – so it would help us all if you could give me a true, and brief, answer.' And the answers came back, depressingly predictable – every single one of them to do with learning English in order to get a job in a bank or one of the new agencies or import companies – every single one jaggedly constructed or scarcely legible or managing to cram four grammatical errors into one sentence – and one had stood out by its simplicity.

'I want to learn the language of my enemy.' Asya had read the student's name out, and sure enough the girl who sat shrouded in the front row, dead centre, had put up a gloved hand.

'This is yours?' Asya had held up the paper.

The hooded figure nodded. It was spooky talking to one of them directly – seeing nothing except the movement of a pair of eyes through the narrow slit of a white *tarha*.

'Why is English the language of your enemy?' Asya had asked. She knew the answer, but she wanted to hear her speak, to engage her in dialogue, to ask whether she did not think there was a commonality of human experience beyond politics, beyond forms.

The veiled head shook once silently and was still.

'I'm sorry?' said Asya, and nothing happened.

'Are you all right?' she had asked, and another – an unveiled – girl had spoken up.

'She cannot speak,' she had said, 'because the voice of a woman is a *'awra.'*

'How is she going to participate in seminars then?' Asya had asked. The class was silent. 'Why did she not go to al-Azhar? Or the Girls' College? Then at least she would have been able to answer her teachers.' Still silence. And the eyes watch her from the slits in the veil. 'Very well, then.' Asya had turned away. 'We might as well begin. I think, rather than start with a long introduction about the age, we'll start with the poetry itself. Then, later, we'll try to find out *from* the poems about the age. Would you open your books, please, at page sixty-nine: "When I consider how my light is spent –" '

That should be safe enough to start with, she had thought. The voice of woman is a *'awra*. Of course, she'd always known that theoretically, but she'd never come across anyone for whom it was a living truth before. So as far as this girl – and the others who thought like her – were concerned she was doing a sort of porno-spread up here on the podium for the world to see. So now it was not only a class that wasn't bothered about literature, that didn't know English, that didn't know about sentences, that was too numerous to be taught properly anyway, but also a class holding people who were sitting and scrutinising her and thinking she was doing something shameful by merely being there – something worse than shameful; something for which the fires of hell were being stoked in readiness. What if they knew – what if they had looked through the window of the cottage and seen a blond, blue-eyed man kneeling, his head between her thighs –

'They sent me a little delegation,' she'd told Deena. 'A delegation to say they could see I was a good sort really only it was a shame I was destined for hell.'

'That's all right,' Deena had said comfortably. 'They do that with the ones they like. They did it with me.'

'What did you say?'

'I said maybe God would show me the true path in His own good time. What did *you* say?'

'I said that I believe each one of us has to find his own way to Paradise. The thing is, they spook me, and I know if ever they had their way we'd all be finished – at least, I would – but I do have a kind of sneaking admiration for them. I mean, they've sorted out some kind of answer to what's happening all around us – all the manifestations of the West that they see here are no good for them, for the way of life they want to hold on to, the values they feel comfortable with, even to their standard of living. And their answer is genuine, it's not imported or borrowed from anywhere –'

'How genuine is it, though?' Deena had asked. 'I mean, it's essentially an urban phenomenon –'

'But don't most of the young men come from the countryside?'

'Yes, but they only get like this when they move to the cities – no, I don't see it catching on here like in Iran.'

'Because we're not a warrior people like the Persians? We're essentially a submissive peasant race?'

'Well.' Deena had smiled. 'That's been true so far.'

'And a sign for them is the dead earth We revived it and produced from it grain whereof they eat. And we placed on it a paradise of date-palms and vines and watered them with gushing springs. That they may eat of its fruit although it is not the work of their hands and will they not give thanks?'

The women in the villages Asya has been to visit cover themselves up too. But there they do it naturally, without fuss. They do it because that's what their mothers and grandmothers have always done – because that's the way it is in Baraket Sidi Ahmad or in el-Managel or wherever they are living their lives. In a village near Sohag, she had stood behind the lattice in the harem quarters of the headman's house and watched the women flocking to the trial session. As she watched them covered in their black *shoggas*, moving fast and with an air of stealth, staying close to the walls except when they had to avoid a group of men sitting smoking in the sunset with their legs outstretched, she had been conscious of her mid-calf skirt and her bare head. But the women had come into the house and thrown off their *shoggas* and revealed themselves resplendent in satin smocks of purple and green and shocking pink, radiant with bright plastic jewellery and the glittering discs on their headkerchiefs, and they had crowded round to kiss her and make her welcome.

'Oh Father, how beautiful the women of the city are,' they had laughed as they patted her and examined her rings, her hair, the material of her clothes. 'How happy her husband must be with her!'

'Do you have children?' they asked.

'No.' She'd shaken her head. 'Not yet.'

'Never mind,' they said. 'The days are coming in their numbers. God will give you what you want.'

They had sat on cushions around the room and Asya had thought of giant anemones –

'All praise to Him who hath created everything in pairs, all that the earth produces and they themselves and other things of which they know not. A sign for them is night, we strip it of the day and Lo they are in darkness. And the sun runs to its resting-place by the estimation of the Precious, the All-Knowing. And the moon, We prescribed its mansions until it returned like an old withered palm-leaf. Neither the sun can catch up with the moon nor the night can outstrip the day – each swims in its separate sphere.'

She had hesitated as she looked at the images fanned out in her hand. Then she had looked up at the women. 'Ladies, you know I have come here in connection with the government campaign for family planning to ask for your opinion and your advice. They say there is no embarrass-ment in knowledge, but these teaching aids are going to be in the hands of the village leaders and shown around the whole countryside, and if there is anything in them that is considered wrong or unseemly it will make problems –'

'Show us, doctor, show us,' they had urged. 'God willing there will be nothing wrong –'

And they had laughed and commented and nudged each other through the demonstration, and when she came to the barrier methods she had hesitated for a moment and then held up the drawing of the erect penis with a blue condom being fitted over its head, and they'd all fallen over laughing and pointing and covering up their faces.

'Don't worry –' The woman sitting nearest her had leaned over and patted her shoulder. She was a plump, merry-looking woman who had arrived bundled up on the back of her husband's motorbike. The other women had explained this unorthodox arrival – 'Her husband is the village photographer, not a *fallah*' – and she was the unofficial make-up artist and hairdresser to the women, painting and coiffing them on the very rare occasions when they had to have their photographs taken, arranging them and then chaperoning her husband when he came in to perform the final click. They were the 'arty' set. She had an elaborate braid showing through her purple kerchief and her eyes were shadowed in green powder. 'Don't worry, darling,' she'd said, 'your lesson is fine and there's no offence between women, let's just laugh and untie our

756

bonds for a while. What shall we take with us from this life?'

And in Zenein, as the men had sat in the mosque listening to the tame sheikh and the doctor from the Family Planning Council, Asya had sat upstairs on the floor with the women in the harem gallery. And when the young women had tried to hold aside the curtain so that they could see the board and the pictures the doctor was talking about the old women had scolded them and even smacked their hands to make them drop the curtain. And the children had opened the packets of 'valuable gifts' their mothers had been handed at the door, taking out the condoms and blowing them up like balloons and turning them loose to zoom their way round the gallery with loud farting noises, and one delicate-looking young woman had crawled up and squeezed in next to her where they sat on the floor and said, 'Doctor my period hasn't gone away for seven weeks now. What should I do?'

'Go to the clinic,' Asya had whispered back.

'My mother-in-law doesn't like me going there; because they examine me –'

'But you have to go –'

'Can't you just tell me what to do?'

'I'm not a doctor.'

'Then why do they call you a doctor?'

'Because I have a degree, but it's not in medicine.'

'What's it in then?'

'In literature.'

'Literature?'

'You know: poetry – and stories –'

'And what use is a degree in that?'

'It's not much use.'

'Stop it, girl, don't be rude to the doctor,' another woman had said.

'She isn't being rude,' Asya had assured her. 'It's all right. Medicine *is* more useful.'

'My sister, a degree is a degree. And better than nothing. Don't you have a medicine for my legs? They ache so much.'

And up near Mansoura they had come to the alphabetisation class carrying their children on their shoulders, their papers and pencils tucked into old plastic bags. 'Stay with us,' they had urged, 'stay with us until we get the certificate. This is a beautiful project.' Tante Soraya says they're only doing it for the thirty pounds they've been promised if they pass the test, but why shouldn't they, Asya thinks, get thirty pounds as a reward for working so hard? They work all day at their houses, their children, their washing, their poultry, their cooking – and twice a week at sunset, they pack their papers into the old plastic bags they'd bought their rice in from the co-op, put their smallest children on to their shoulders and trek out to the school. They sit on the floor and Asya sits with them and watches: a seven-year-old boy kneels close to his mother watching her work; again and again he prises the pencil from her tight grip and places it back in her hand, folding her fingers round it properly. Another woman holds a baby on her left knee: with closed eyes he sucks at her breast. On her right knee she balances her writing-paper and labours over the first three letters of the alphabet. She smiles at Asya when their eyes meet, and holds her paper out proudly for inspection. Asya is in love with these women – oh, she knows her view of them is romantic – but they are worthy of romance: they walk erect balancing heavy pitchers of water on their heads, barefoot they drive huge buffalos along the streets of the village, they are surrounded by children whom they produce and care for with seeming lack of effort, they are beautiful and adorned; there is not one without an ornament of some kind: a heavy silver anklet, a pattern of henna on the foot or hand, a fancy braid, a coquettish gold earring, a discreet tattoo on the chin, a line of antimone in the eyes – each one of them is – as Dada Sayyida had put it – a tree: bearing fruit and offering shelter to all who come near. Walking through the streets of the village, she sees the women through their open doorways preparing food – and always they call out to her – 'Come, come and eat, come and honour us.' They live their lives with open hearts. 'Just stay in our village for a while so you plump out and come back to yourself. Our village is bountiful.' And they live with a complete certainty about the things that matter. 'Sister, may God make you happy and grant you a bit of a child to fill the world around you –'

'They will get their thirty pounds at the end, won't they?' she had asked the project chief at Mansoura.

'Of course they will,' he'd said.

'You have control over that? They're not going to wait to get it through US AID?'

'No, no, of course not. We've got it in our budget.'

And what could she do except hope that that was true? Hope that at the end of the day the government would not once again fail these people. The low, white buildings of the health units look derelict and unused. The plaster busts of 'Abd el-Nasser in their courtyards survive because no one in Cairo has remembered to order them removed. Nothing has been done here since 1967 – but people go on simply living their lives.

Asya had watched the women as they stole along the streets like small black gliding tents – and that is all that the outside world of men will ever see of them. No wonder then that when their patience occasionally comes to a temporary end and they gather, for example, around the police station, throw off their outer garments and untie their kerchiefs and – with their hair spread out and their house-smocks revealed to every passer-by – they raise their voices and wail through the night demanding the release of their menfolk who have been rounded up in the coffee-houses a few hours earlier – no wonder that the bravest station commander will not come out to face them, that the machine-gun carrying soldiers will only shout at them from behind the walls, and that, by dawn, the men are free.

'But why did they pick them up, Dada Sayyida?'

'Does anyone know, Sett Asya? It's the government. They went round the coffee-shops with the black box and anyone who didn't have his identity card got put inside and driven away.'

'But didn't anyone ask why?'

'It's the *government*, Sett Asya. Will anyone stand in the face of the government?'

'But you stood in its face. You and the other women. Didn't you go along to the police station and make them set the men free?'

'We're only poor women. Can we do anything?'

'But you did: *you made them let the men go*.'

'That was by God's command.'

'A sign for them is that we carried their race in the crowded Ark. And We have created for them similar on which they ride. And if We choose We could drown them and none would hear their screams nor would they be saved. Except by Our Mercy and for temporary comfort –'

Each thing is by God's command and no thing may come to pass except He command it. They live and they die by God's command. The cotton comes good or the buffalo falls into the well by God's command. The government picks up their men and sends them to dig the Canal or die in the Yemen or the Sinai or sit all day holding bayonets in armoured cars outside the university, and it is all by God's command. They have twelve children by God's command. Some of the children die and others grow up and work the fields or get an education or turn into robbers or God opens it in their faces and they get work in Libya or Iraq or the Gulf – it is *all* by God's command. And why should it not be so? This is what they know; this is what they feel most comfortable with. The lot of that particular peasant woman is not going to be bettered through having two children instead of nine. She might feel less worn out by the time she is thirty but she's stacking the odds against herself – it's no good telling her about exponential growth, about the economy of the country, about the per capita income – since when has a piastre of the per capita income come her way? And what are the alternatives: to turn them into regiments of blue-suited Maoists or into the degraded lowest rank of a capitalist society forever hankering after refrigerators and washing-machines? No. Money and children are the ornaments of this world; so, since they can't have money, let them at least have children. Children to fill their lives, to look after each other and sleep in a warm, breathing heap next to the oven, to look after them when they are old, and weep over them and visit their graves when their day – which has already been written down and determined – finally comes –

759

'And they say when is this promised day if you be truthful? They shall not wait but for one cry that shall take them even as they dispute. And then they can leave no instruction nor can they return to their people –'

The arched doorway is set into a stone wall, dusty yellow like all the walls along this path, like the stones of the pyramids, like the sands that surround them. And through the doorway the glare of white, sand-filled sunshine. A narrow, stony track and then the earth falls away. Beyond, there are the domes and small minarets that belong to other people. They stretch as far as one can see, until another sandy ridge provides the eye with a horizon. In English books and magazine articles they call it 'The City of the Dead'. Here it is more differentiated; people refer to it by the names of its districts. 'We're going up to al-Imam tomorrow,' or al-Khalifa, or al-Basateen – or simply, 'We're going to visit.' When the object is unspecified, it is understood to be 'the dead'. Only the living need to be specified. When they had gone to visit Muhsin three weeks ago Asya had been surprised by how well he looked: tall and relaxed and confident. The politicals are respected by the other prisoners: they are top rank, along with the killers – the brave killers, the ones who have killed in an open fight, or killed for reasons of honour. The leftist politicals – Muhsin, el-Prof and the independent – were continuing a fifty-year-old tradition: they had organised the prisoners to plant the yard with vegetables and flowers. They were running literacy classes. They had fixed up the latrines and established a rota to clean them. They had even stepped in between the prisoners and the boss-man, Abu-Dra', who had killed seven people and was in for life and controlled access to the water-heating facilities – and persuaded him to allow one free gallon of hot water per week to each prisoner and to fix the price of each subsequent gallon at five piastres. Asya had studiously not watched Muhsin and Deena as they sat on the wooden bench with five centimetres of empty space carefully preserved between them, but she had been struck by how adapted, how comfortable he'd seemed. It was all settled. He was no longer waiting for the knock on the door. He was no longer held naked on his own in a dark room knowing that at some point they'd come for him again, sick with fear at what they would do to him the next time. They had done it – and it was over. Here it was like normal life only a bit narrower. Instead of being confined to Egypt, he is confined to Tora. He has to work at certain times, but he would have to work outside anyway – and he likes the work he does here. In their cell they take it in turn to cook for dinner using the food sent by their families and the produce of their own plot of land. It's a life. It's different, but it's a life. What he is really deprived of is the comfort of his wife and the company of his son. But even that – Asya looks at Deena: she is listening to the reciter with a small smile on her face. Deena is with him. Deena is *always* with him. And seeing them in the prison, chatting easily like old friends and comrades, Asya had been sure that he knew it. That he knew it completely.

As the gates had closed behind them and they had started back down the path to where their car was parked, Asya had put her arm around Deena's shoulders. Deena had pushed her spectacles back on to the bridge of her nose and said, 'I'm just sorry I couldn't bring Ahmad with me today. I'll bring him next time.'

'Yes,' Asya had said.

'And I'll bring the new baby as soon as she's born.'

'Yes,' Asya had said.

'I'll try and make it as normal as I can for the children. It's not impossible. After all, their father could have been working on a project in the desert somewhere and they'd still have only seen him once a month.'

'And the trumpet was blown and Lo they hasten to their Lord from their tombs. They say O Woe is us, who is it who resurrects us from our resting-place? Verily it was the promise of The Compassionate and His messengers were truthful. It is but one cry and they are all brought before Us. Today no spirit shall suffer an injustice and your rewards will be but for that which you were used to do –'

A child. She will have to have a child. A little girl whom she can love and cuddle and dress, and whom she can teach all the things that she now knows. A little girl who would grow up beautiful and confident and strong with the world open before her. A girl who would brush her mother's hair for her and say, 'Why don't you wear it this way, Mummy? There, that suits you better.' Who would rifle through her clothes and her make-up and her jewellery as she had rifled through Tante Soraya's. Who would come here to visit her when at last she was with Mama Deela in the women's chamber – to visit her and remember. A girl who would grow into a woman who thought, this is what my mother would have done, but *this* is what I shall do. On the balcony in the flat in Kensington, when Khalu Hamid was definitely getting better, Asya had said to her mother, 'How can I ever repay you?' And Lateefa had said, 'You don't repay *me*. You pay it back to your own children. That's how it works.' That's how it works. That's how it *has* to work. And if he had lived, her little boy, he would be eight. Eight and three months. A tall child, with his father's dark eyes and his father's light step and warm colour. And there isn't even a place where she can visit him. Flushed down the loo. The hospital loo. Ten years, twelve years of her life, gone, with nothing to show for them. Not even a child's grave –

'Those who will inherit Paradise are today happily employed. They and their spouses recline on soft cushions in the shade. They shall have fruit and they shall have all that they call for. And they shall have a

greeting of peace from a Beneficent Lord. And those who are guilty –
let them today stand apart –'

Saif is no longer her friend or any part of her life – even though she still
dreams of him. He had come to see her in her flat in London and brought
her an antique telescope for a house-warming present. He had smiled
over her flat and said, 'Very nice. Just the thing to invite someone up for
coffee and impress him.' And then he had gone. Chrissie had said he had
come home and for three months he had locked himself up in his room
and would speak to nobody – 'They even had to put his meals on a tray
outside his door,' she said. 'Tante Adeela was going mad –' Asya imagines
Tante Adeela sitting in the kitchen: she looks up as Dada Wageeda comes
back without the tray. Dada Wageeda shakes her head and Tante Adeela
looks down silently at the bits of fila pastry she is carefully folding around
spoonfuls of spinach and ricotta cheese. 'Like this, Asya? Like this? You
sell my son so cheaply? All the days you came here, all the times we sat
together in this kitchen – I gave you his photographs when he was a little
boy – my daughter, he put you in his eyes and he would have been loyal to
you for the whole of your life – for him the world was one thing, and Asya
was another, and you do this to him –'

'But he seems to be all right now,' Chrissie had said. 'Fuad says he's put
together a company and he's started to work – he's basing himself in Cairo
now –'

A Cairo without the Omar Khayyam, without the Semiramis or the
little Pizzeria in Tawfiqiya where they had gone so often and eaten pizzas
runny with cheese for ninety piastres and joked with Alphonse the old
waiter who was always half drunk – a Cairo without their flat which was
sitting deserted – a Cairo without *her* –

'But don't you *want* to go back to your flat?' Chrissie had asked as she
helped her unpack.

'No,' Asya had said. 'I feel much more at home here in Zamalek –'

'But nobody lets go of a flat in Cairo these days –'

'Never mind, Chrissie. I really don't want it.'

'And your furniture?'

'There are some things I want. I'll take them eventually – but not just
yet.'

Not just yet. She can't go back there while she is still visited by that
dream – where every night when she goes to sleep there is the possibility
that she might see him, in his odd space-suit, floating silently away from
her –

'Did I not charge you O children of Adam that you not worship Satan
for he is your clear enemy? And that you worship Me for this is the true
path? He has led a multitude of you astray and will you not come to your
senses? This is Hell which you have been promised. Taste today its

762

tortures in which you disbelieved. Today we set a seal on their mouths and their hands shall talk to us and their legs shall bear witness to that which they have gained –'

'Muhammad is the Messenger of God.' Asya had unclipped the piece of paper from her passport and handed it to Chrissie. Chrissie had rooted about in her large handbag, brought out her purse and opened it, and from a zipped compartment she had drawn out the other half: 'There is no god but God.' She had held it up to Asya. She had sellotaped the pieces together, folded them carefully and slipped them back into her purse. Asya had reached over and held on to her friend's hand –

Home. On the wall above the mahogany and ormolu cabinet Uncle Sidki clasps the hand of a smiling Gamal 'Abd el-Nasser. Nowadays you only come upon photographs of 'Abd el-Nasser in private homes – in private homes or on the walls of coffee-shops, or in the countryside. In Midan el-Tahrir the granite pedestal stands empty; the plans, sketches, proposals for his statue probably gathering dust in some office of the presidency. But here in Chrissie's house the gladiators still salute the crowd above the red plush sofa to the left of the piano. Tante Muneera looks up at the camera from beneath the little hat of black tulle and, on the opposite wall, Uncle Sidki still clasps the hand of the President. But it is not only in photographs that time is arrested; it is also arrested in the mind – even though it continues to flow: Tante Muneera is eighteen and shyly brave; Tante Muneera laughs as she puts food in front of her family; Tante Muneera collapses against the dining-room door with her hand to her chest; Tante Muneera weeps in the hospital corridor ('We're losing him, Asya, we're losing him'); Tante Muneera rocks Chrissie's little boy to sleep – and every time a new image is added the eye wanders back to the first one and the whole configuration shifts slightly. How can one keep up with it all? It is like – like – Asya closes her eyes as she tries to concentrate, to capture the thought. It is as though the brain were a split screen, one half examining a frozen frame, a moment where time has stopped, the other vaguely registering the continuation of the action; storing up the passing frames for closer inspection later. The lighthouse keeper at Tyre had the right idea; how *can* you tell about recent events – much less about events as they happen? The only way to proceed is by a series of catchings up. You may have an intimation that this is a moment that will merit freezing later – a moment that you will come back to and come back to and come back to – not to think, if only I had turned left instead of right, but to wonder at the fixedness, the immovability of that right turn; how every time you play it back there you are: unseeingly turning right. Blind, blind, blind. But these intimations seem pretty haphazard; if you start paying attention to them you get superstitious, you avoid walking on cracks, you race to get to the phone before the third ring, you kill yourself getting

763

through those traffic lights before they turn amber –

'Chrissie? How old would you say you were? If you had to say it suddenly without thinking?'

'Thirty-one,' Chrissie had said, coming in with the tea-tray.

'You'd know that right away? You *feel* thirty-one?'

'Yes,' Chrissie had said.

'I don't feel thirty,' Asya had said. 'I have to keep working it out. I keep thinking there's a mistake somewhere and I'm really twenty-four.'

'It's because you've been away,' Chrissie had said. 'You'll catch up soon enough in this place.'

Chrissie turns laughing from the blackboard; Chrissie screams at Fuad in a grey Portakabin; Chrissie shivers and cries in Tante Adeela's kitchen the day she met Fuad and then turns round in the front seat of the car with her hair all messed up on Asya's wedding night; Chrissie snips at the stitches of Asya's wedding dress and, big with Ranya, hugs her clumsily at the airport –

'They don't make Arabisco any more,' Chrissie had said, putting the tea-tray down on the Queen Anne sofa between them.

'No,' Asya had said. 'I tried, and the chap at the grocer's just smiled at me: "Welcome back, lady." He pointed at shelves of biscuits, French, German, Austrian, you name it.'

'Except no one can afford them,' Chrissie had said, handing Asya her glass. And when later Asya had asked why the doors to the balcony were closed and shuttered, Chrissie had thrown them open, and there, just level with them, the cars were roaring past on 6th October Bridge.

'We can't use the balcony any more,' Chrissie had said as they retreated into the room and pushed the doors closed against the dust and the noise.

'But Chrissie, that's terrible –'

And Chrissie had shrugged. 'Yes. But the traffic would have been impossible without the bridge.'

Impossible too to imagine Issam el-Uthmanli covering his cousin's hand with his own on the railing of that balcony, whispering his declaration with the cars belching black fumes at him as they lurch past. For that scene the 6th of October Bridge would always have to be cancelled out and the street transformed again into a quiet, wide, rather sandy road, lined with eucalyptus trees. And from the balcony you could look one way and see the river, and look the other and see the dim form of the great pyramid in the far distance. And in the whispering silence, you could listen out for your brother's footsteps coming up behind you –

'Did you ever get any news of Issam?' Asya had asked Chrissie, and Chrissie had shaken her head.

'No,' she'd said –

'And had We pleased We would have blinded their eyes and they would

764

have groped for the path – for how could they see? And had We pleased We would have transfixed them where they stood and they would have been able neither to go forward nor back. And he to whom We grant long life We weaken him among people so will they not see reason? We have not taught him poetry nor is it fitting for him. This is but Remembrance and a clear Recitation –'

To see the end in the beginning. But in life you can only see the end when you come to it. And do you then have time to look back at the beginning? To look back at all the frozen moments and see the completed pattern? To think, ah! So this is what it all amounted to? How terrible if it comes upon you suddenly – as it had come upon Mario, speeding along the motorway with music on his radio, or as it had come upon King Faisal, his arms open to receive his nephew. How kind and gentle it would be to go slowly – to have a week, say, to think about things, to add it all up – a week of quietness and a clear mind and not much pain, and then – the arched doorway set into the stone wall, the tile lifted, the trap-door and the stairs. They say two angels come to question you right away; it all begins right then and there, not on that far day when the thousands of millions rise up and flock towards the Throne – save us, everyone prays, save us from the torments of the grave. Through the doorway the white glare has turned red with swirling sand. On the narrow track Khalu Hamid paces slowly, his scarf wound around his nose and mouth, his beige shooting-cap on his head. His eyes are covered in dark glasses. His right hand is in his pocket, the left hangs stiffly down at the end of his sleeve. Beyond him the earth falls away and there is nothing except red and swirling sand. The six months Mr Haygold had given him are up and his latest scan has come out clean. The small shadow on his right lung has not changed and what remains of his left lung is perfect. He has been permitted time; time to look back and time to look forward. And he has used it: he has done his adding up. Sitting in the flat in London, walking through the mellow Kensington streets, drinking double espressos at Italian coffee-bars, recovering in the Cromwell Hospital, he had worked it all out. Now, even if the next scan should show something bad – and pray God please please that it doesn't – it cannot take him by surprise, for he is prepared –

'To warn those who are alive and to prove the charge against those who doubt. Do they not see that among the work of Our Hands We created for them cattle which they own? And We made them docile so that some they ride and some they eat. And from them they draw benefits and drink and will they not be thankful? Yet they take other gods in place of God and hope that they will give them victory. They cannot give them victory even though they be equipped soldiers. Let not their speech sadden you. We know what they conceal and what they

765

proclaim. Does man not see that We created him from a drop of seed that now he stands before us a clear adversary?'

Both Nadia and Tante Soraya cast anxious glances at their brother as he walks past the door. Nadia starts to fidget with her handbag, but Sheikh Zayid holds his hand up slightly with the prayer-beads hanging from his fingers and she sits still. They worry about Khalu Hamid – particularly Tante Soraya. At lunch on Fridays Asya sees her watching him. But he says he feels wonderful. His hair has started to grow again, and to see him throw back his head and laugh or jump up to cheer an Ahli goal you would not believe there had ever been anything wrong with him. 'Say I take refuge in the Lord of the dawn,' Asya whispers just in case she evil-eyes him thinking these thoughts, 'from the evil of that which He hath created –' After lunch he had settled in Geddu's old chair – now Khalu's chair – and smiled at Asya when Nadia's little girl had overturned the coffee-table and sat in it and chugged like a train.

'They built a table like a table in those days,' he'd said. 'How many kids have sat in this one and dragged it round? And there it is, still solid.'

'I don't remember me,' Asya had said. 'But I remember Kareem and Deena.'

'Every child in this family has turned it into a train,' he'd said. And then he'd fallen asleep with his tea at his elbow. And Asya had watched him as he slept, his head resting where his father's head had used to rest, his mother's display case standing behind him with the gilt coffee-cups that were only taken out for weddings or funerals, the small blue opaline vase and the impossibly delicate soup tureen that you could see the light shine through, still there, still polished even though Mama Deela had now been dead for twenty-four years. He slept, and a new lot of children played noisily around him, and when he woke they had stolen the arm that he had left lying on the sideboard and he chased them down the long corridor and caught them in the sunny front room where Mama Deela had nursed him back to life forty-nine years ago, and tickled them and retrieved his arm.

'And he put an example to Us and forgot the very fact of his creation. He said: Who can breathe life into dead bones? Say He can revive them Who built them in the first place for He is well-versed in creation. He Who made fire for you out of green trees that you may have kindling. Is not He Who created the skies and the earth able to create their like again? Yea, He is the Creator the All-Knowing. His command if He intendeth a thing is but to say to it Be! and Lo it is. Therefore all Glory to Him in whose hands is the dominion over all things and to Whom ye shall return –'

'Verily God hath spoken,' they all murmur.

Sheikh Zayid sits on his chair for a few seconds more: his eyes are closed, his fingers on the prayer-beads are still, only his lips move silently. Then he lifts his hands and draws them over his face. He opens his eyes.

'You have done well, Sayyidna,' he says to the Fekki.

The Fekki raises his hand to his head in gratitude and fumbles with his feet under the chair for his clogs. Khalu Hamid appears at the doorway, puts his hand on the young man's arm and leads him out of the door. The women all shift and rummage in their handbags and cough and frown up at the sky which is red with dust. Nadia takes a blue silk square out of her bag, unfolds it into a large scarf and puts it over her head.

'The children must have driven Sayyida mad by now,' she says.

'But Meedo is with them,' Deena says.

'Meedo? Meedo is worse than the lot of them put together,' says his mother.

'Shall we go?' says Asya, and steps out of the door.

All the children have vanished and the air of the City of the Dead is opaque with dust and sand. Asya follows Khalu Hamid's tail-lights through the narrow lanes and out to the Salah Salim periphery road. On Shari' al-Azhar, the wind catches at torn sheets of paper, at broken straws and old plastic bags, and swirls them around in an intermittent dance. A small, empty can that used to hold tomato sauce bowls merrily along, clanging on the empty pavement. People everywhere have rushed home and fastened their doors and windows and sealed every gap that connects them to the outside world with an assortment of rags. But still their floors and furniture are turning gritty with sand and when they open their drawers a fine film of dust will be lying on their clothes.

Chrissie had shaken her head as she straightened out Asya's beige cashmere. 'This has a mark on the back, here.'

Asya looked at the stain she'd made when she sat on the ground next to Mahrous. 'I know,' she said, 'the grass was wet.'

'You sit on the grass in a cashmere coat?'

'I'm sure Madame Zouzou will manage to get it out.'

'This is very pretty,' Chrissie said, holding up the turquoise silk Mario had held in his arms in Paris. 'You should wear these deep colours more often, dear; not all those beiges and blacks you've got –'

'Yes,' Asya had said, 'I'm trying.'

'And this is still not made?'

Chrissie held up the fuchsia silk Tante Adeela had bought in Hong Kong. Asya had looked at it as Chrissie unfolded it and for a moment her breath had gone as she waited for the plastic penis to fall out. Then she'd remembered: it is in London; in a drawer in her flat in Kensington where no one will look, and even if they did it wouldn't matter. The fuchsia silk had travelled with her, from the flat she had shared with Saif, to her room in college, to the flat above the college, to the cottage in the north, to four months in a suitcase in the car, to her flat in Kensington, and now it had come home.

Chrissie held it on her knee. 'This is what married me to Fuad,' she said sadly. 'If I hadn't come with you to the dressmaker that day I might not have met him. Or I might have met him when it was too late.'

'Do you wish you had never met him?' Asya had asked. 'I mean, *really* wish that?'

'Sometimes I do. And then I think about the children and – no, I don't wish I had never met him. I did at first; when I found out.'

'That must have been terrible, Chrissie.'

'Yes.'

'But it is all right between you now?'

'Well,' Chrissie had shrugged. 'It goes. Nothing stays the same.'

'But nothing stays the same for anyone. Look at me. Look at Noora.'

'I know. Mimi's the cleverest of us. She gives herself an easy mind. She concentrates on her children and her husband comes, goes, it's none of her business.'

'I thought she was OK.'

'She *is* OK. But only because she doesn't put things together – she doesn't sit and add things up. Her husband climbed on the shoulders of her uncles and now he has an air-conditioned office and a Mercedes and a secretariat, and one day he says he's in Washington, the other he says he's in Rome, and she says go in safety. As long as he supports the household and takes her on holiday once a year she asks him nothing.'

'Mimi was never given to – examining things.'

'It's better for her. Because her husband is up to all sorts of things. I know it.'

Sometimes when Chrissie talks now Asya thinks of Tante Soraya: a clever, good-looking, disappointed woman –

'How clever of you to find a parking-space,' Nadia says.

'Asya won't park in Opera on principle.' Deena laughs. 'Not until they call it Midan el-Parking.'

Tante Soraya waits for them on the pavement.

'Isn't Khalu coming up?' Asya asks.

'Yes, but he's gone to park at the shop,' Tante Soraya says.

The women walk along the uneven pavement. Asya and Nadia each carry a basket now empty of mercy.

'There's no doorman, no car-park man, no one to help with carrying,' Tante Soraya says.

'You know this lift of yours,' Asya says as they turn into the wide lobby sprinkled all over now with sawdust to save on the cleaning, 'they've got a model of it in the Science Museum in London. It's a genuine antique.'

'We're all genuine antiques,' Tante Soraya says.

The first time she had come here to Tante Soraya's after her return she

768

had been stopped by a voice just as she was about to close the gates of the old lift. 'Wait a minute, please!' She had turned, and there, coming up the lobby towards her, was a young blonde girl: her friend who had first brought heartache to Mariana all those summers ago. Asya had stepped aside to let the child in and then, staring at her as the lift creaked its uncertain way upwards, she had realised it must be her friend's daughter; a product of one of the drops of 'semen, semen, my husband's SEMEN' that had *not* stained the sheets. Her daughter, already – 'Thank you, Tante,' the child had said politely as she stepped out at the third floor – and why not 'Tante'? She is her mother's age and the girl could see it. Time passes, oh, time passes – she had better take note, she had better do something about it. Up on the fourth floor, Zio Philippe, grey-haired now, still gets into his pyjamas and dressing-gown when he comes home from the office. He settles in to his wood-carving in the room where he was born, where his mother's bridal wreath lurks mummified in the display cabinet – and Nina herself still cooks and keeps house for him, even though her eyes have become so bad that she has to knock on Tante Soraya's door every time she needs a needle threaded and she has given up on plucking the three hairs that now grow long and wavy out of her chin. Across the landing, the flat which had been so darkened by the grief of Madame Biba when her four sons had died in one night is now filled with sunshine and the noise of the dead young men's nieces and nephews who spill out on to the landing to chase the cats or greet their father or simply sit on the landing rolling plastic cars to one another. The world above the old Averino store will never be mended; the most one can hope for is that it is not completely blown away. And downstairs, the barrier wall that had gone up after the war in 1967 has been taken down and a new component has been added to the buses, cars, bicycles, carts and trams on El-Geish Street: the private minibus taxis with the drivers raising their voices above the din of the road to call 'Waili – Waili – Waili –'

The children stampede out of Grandfather's old room towards their mothers. Dada Sayyida follows them.

'We worried about you,' she says.

'Where is Meedo?' Tante Soraya says.

'He's in his room, Sett Soraya. You've visited, praise God?'

'Praise God,' Tante Soraya replies. 'Have you fed the children?'

'They've been fed and they're full.'

'Right. Let's feed the grown-ups now,' says Tante Soraya and goes into the kitchen.

'Undress first, Tante,' Asya says. 'We're not going to die.' But Tante Soraya is already in the kitchen and tying an apron around her waist.

Asya takes off her shoes and sits on the floor in Grandfather's room,

769

and immediately Lola, Nadia's two-year-old daughter, climbs on to her knee.

'Pussycat!' she says. 'Pussycat!'

' "Oh you little pussycat, With the rounded eyes –" ' Asya sings.

'No,' Lola's five-year-old brother Kamal interrupts, 'tell us a story.'

'What story do you want?' Asya asks.

'We want a story from olden times,' says Ahmad, Deena's son.

'Invent us a story,' Kamal says.

'Pussycat!' says Lola.

' "You have a long tai-ai-ail, And such pretty fur –" '

'Your professor's got a piece in today's paper,' Deena says, rustling the pages of *al-Ahram* as she lies on Grandfather's bed. 'He's getting very spiritual.'

'Invent us a true story,' Ahmad says.

'Pussycat!' says Lola.

'You've had "Pussycat",' says Asya.

' "I flower like a plant",' reads Deena, ' "and I live – I live and flower by the command of the god Ra', for He knows me and I am of Him." '

'It was, oh how it was, honourable gentlefolk, and talk is not sweet, except by mention of the Prophet, praise and blessings be upon him –' Asya begins.

'Praise and blessings be upon him,' the children respond.

'It was, oh how it was, in a time and era long past, there was a pretty girl and her name was Sett el-Hosn –'

'It's an old story,' Kamal says.

'What do you mean it's an old story? You haven't heard it yet.'

'I've heard the story of Sett el-Hosn. Dada Sayyida told me.'

'There are many stories about Sett el-Hosn. You haven't heard this one. It'll break, Lola,' Asya says, disengaging Lola's hand from her necklace.

'Tell the story,' says Ahmad.

'There was a pretty girl and her name was Sett el-Hosn. And she lived with her step-sister whose name was Mankousha because she never brushed her hair –'

'Was her mother dead?' Ahmad asks.

'Yes, her mother was dead.'

'How old was she when she died?' Kamal asks.

'Very old,' says Asya, 'a hundred and ten.'

' "Time and change are the basic elements of man's life," ' reads Deena.

'And every day one of the two sisters had to go to the river to fetch water,' Asya says.

'Why?' says Ahmad.

'Because they didn't have taps,' Kamal says. 'Right?'

'Right,' says Asya.

'Put some perfume on me,' Lola says.

'I haven't got perfume,' Asya says.

'Yes you have. In your bag,' Lola says.

'OK. Go get my bag.'

Lola jumps up and runs out of the room.

'What happened next?' Kamal asks.

'Well, one day, it was Mankousha's turn to get the water. So she picked up the pitcher, and put her *tarha* on her head, and grumbling as usual – she was always grumbling – she set out on the road –'

'Why was she always grumbling?' Ahmad asks.

'Because she was grumpy.'

'This kid was messing with your handbag,' Nadia says, coming into the room with Lola in one hand and the handbag in the other.

'She wants some perfume,' Asya says.

'She's so vain,' Nadia says.

Asya takes out her atomiser and sprays Lola's neck and wrists with Capricci. Lola screams with laughter and settles back on Asya's lap sniffing at her hands.

' "The moment of Eternity is the end and the means at one and the same time," ' Deena reads.

'What is that?' asks Nadia.

'Asya's professor turning mystical,' says Deena.

'Move over,' says Nadia, and lies down next to Deena on the bed.

'Oh, my back,' she groans.

'You shouldn't wear those very high heels,' Deena says.

'Someone open for Khalu,' Tante Soraya shouts from the kitchen as she hears the lift doors clang shut. Kamal runs out, opens the door and runs back.

'What happened next?' he asks.

'Well, Mankousha walked and walked,' says Asya, 'and when she got to the river she saw Mother Ghoula sitting on the bank. So she stopped and said "Salamu 'aleikum, Mother Ghoula," and Mother Ghoula replied –'

' "If this meeting had not begun with your greeting –" ' Kamal and Ahmad say, ' "I would have munched your flesh and crunched your bones." '

'Right. "Come here, daughter," said Mother Ghoula. "My head is itching and driving me mad. Come and delouse me." So Mankousha came slowly forward. She had to do what Mother Ghoula asked but she didn't like it. So she came, stepping forward with one foot and dragging the other, and she squatted down behind Mother Ghoula and started to pick the lice from her hair. "Phew," she cried each time she picked out a louse –'

'They've colonised you already?' Khalu Hamid puts his head round the door.

'What can I do?' says Asya, and tickles Lola, who squirms and giggles on her knee.

'What happened next?' Kamal asks.

Khalu Hamid calls out, 'Come on in, 'Am el-Sheikh,' and throws open the doors of the drawing-room.

' "Phew," cried Mankousha. "Your lice are disgusting, Mother Ghoula. Ugh!" she cried, as she killed the louse with her nail. "Your lice are horrible, Mother Ghoula." And do you think Mother Ghoula liked this talk?'

'No,' say the children shaking their heads.

'Well, in the end, Mother Ghoula got so fed up and so cross that she reached over for Mankousha's pitcher and hit it with a stone and broke it into a thousand bits. "There, you uncivil girl," she said, "you won't be getting water from the river today."

'Mankousha saw that Mother Ghoula was cross so she put the hem of her *galabiyya* between her teeth and flew home. Sett el-Hosn saw her come running and stepped out to meet her.

' "What's the matter, sister?" she said sweetly, and Mankousha, still panting from her long run, told her what had happened.

' "Don't worry, sister," said Sett el-Hosn, "I'll go and get the water." So Sett el-Hosn picked up her pitcher and she stuffed some sesame seeds into her pocket and walked down the road to where Mother Ghoula still sat muttering angrily to herself.

' "Salamu 'aleikum, Mother Ghoula," Sett el-Hosn said. And Mother Ghoula replied –'

' "If this meeting had not begun with your greeting –" ' the children say, ' "I would have munched your flesh and crunched your bones." '

'Right. "Come here, daughter," said Mother Ghoula. "My head is itching and driving me mad. Come and delouse me." So Sett el-Hosn stepped eagerly forward and squatted down and started parting Mother Ghoula's hair. But Sett el-Hosn had come prepared –'

'The food is ready,' Tante Soraya calls down the corridor.

'Finish the story,' Ahmad says.

'But Sett el-Hosn had come prepared, and she didn't even look for Mother Ghoula's lice, she just parted her hair and stroked it, and every once in a while she would take out a sesame seed from her pocket and put it in her mouth and crunch it and say, "Ah! Your lice are so good, Mother Ghoula!" And after a moment: crunch! "Your lice are so delicious, Mother Ghoula!" –'

'What a creep!' Deena says.

'I said lunch is ready!' Tante Soraya calls.

'We'd better go,' Nadia says, struggling up.

'Finish the story,' Kamal says.

'I'll finish it after lunch,' Asya says.

'No, now,' Ahmad says.

'No,' says Asya, 'you think about it while I eat and we'll do the ending after. Get off, off' – she tickles Lola – 'my leg's gone to sleep.'

'How are you going to end it?' Deena says in the corridor.

'It's up to you and Nadia,' Asya says. 'They're your kids. Mother Ghoula can break Sett el-Hosn's pitcher and tell her she's a creep and a hypocrite, or she can fill it with gold in reward for her tact and diplomacy.'

'I know what Deena wants to happen,' Nadia says.

'The food's getting cold,' Tante Soraya says.

'Have you heard this?' Khalu Hamid sits at the head of the table and fiddles with the aerial of his transistor radio.

'What?' says Nadia.

'He's offered to go and talk to the Knesset again.'

'That'll do a lot of good.'

'They won't even let him. Anyway, he's played that card once.'

'Where did they say that? On the news?'

'The BBC.'

'Let's catch the five o'clock news, see if *they* say anything.'

"Am el-Sheikh, please eat. Asya, pass the chicken to 'Am el-Sheikh.'

'In the name of God –'

They eat silently as they listen to the headlines. Behind Khalu Hamid the great glass-panelled doors that lead into the drawing-room shine with a thousand tiny pinpricks of light. Grandfather is dead but his backdrop remains. Sixty panels – and not one of them broken in fifty years. The road has been opened between Egypt, the Gaza Strip, the West Bank and Israel. Homah erupts against the rule of Hafiz al-Asad. Fighting breaks out on the Iran–Iraq border. The Iranian students threaten to kill the American hostages. The dust storm ends today. Elephants are in danger of extinction.

'They're not the only ones,' Tante Soraya says.

'And that's it,' Khalu Hamid says as he switches off the radio.

'No mention.'

'Of course not. He's in a lousy position.'

'Why doesn't he do something about the problems here first before he goes rushing off to Israel?' Soraya asks. 'Look at us: bread queues, cooking-gas queues, pension queues, the housing crisis, the transport crisis, the sewers bursting in the streets –'

'He can't do anything about the problems here –'

'He's hoping the Americans will help him –'

'This whole AID thing is a terrific swindle –'

'I don't really see the way forward – I mean, you can't suddenly change tack again, with the economy of a whole country, and swing back to protection –'

'It was wrong to open up so thoughtlessly in the first place –'

'Of course it was –'

'Something is bound to happen –'

'We're always saying something is bound to happen –'

'Well, something *is* bound to happen.'

'Like what?'

'The army –'

'The army is nothing now –'

'Or the Brethren – no offence, 'Am al-Sheikh.'

'It's all right, daughter, I don't support those short-*thob*ed fanatics –'

'We need another 'Abd el-Nasser –'

'And what did we get from 'Abd el-Nasser, God have mercy on him?'

'We got plenty – the country got plenty –'

'Not even 'Abd el-Nasser could do anything now.'

'Eat. Deena, eat for the baby you're carrying. Asya, forget the salad, have some stuffed courgettes –'

Khalu Hamid rests his head against the back of the chair and sleeps, his glass of tea steaming at his side. Nadia and Deena are lying down in Grandfather's room while their children play around them. Sheikh Zayid and Uncle Muhammad al-Fadl drink tea and talk in the drawing-room. Tante Soraya and Dada Sayyida are still busy in the kitchen. Asya opens the dining-room window slightly and looks out: the dust storm is indeed dying down. And possibly elephants will become extinct. How sad that would be; to have to tell your child when he came across a picture in a story-book that there were no more elephants because people had killed them all. All? All. Not one left, not one teensy weensy elephant to plod along and raise his trunk and – and what? What good would one elephant be anyway? For a start he'd be dreadfully lonely: the only elephant in the world –

Asya moves the tea from next to Khalu Hamid's right hand and puts it on the sideboard. She sits down in her corner of the sofa and opens the newspaper: two hundred and thirty-one thousand students to sit the Thanawiyya 'Ama this year. She turns the page. Why shouldn't the Professor turn mystical in his old age? It is fitting that he should. It's an answer anyway. 'The choice for man is between "having" and "being" –' Is it? If it is, then the choice has to be obvious, for what is the use of having without being? Asya closes the paper. It is here in this house that she feels most at home – or, rather, that the part of her that feels at home feels most at home. In the flat in Zamalek she constantly looks around for the grown-ups. In her parents' bedroom she often feels like a child doing something she shouldn't. The first time she had opened her mother's wardrobe and caught the scent of her powder lingering in the polished, empty shelves, she had thought, this is it: I've graduated. I'm grown-up now, really grown-up – but the scent still lingers in the wardrobe; it continues to be her mother's wardrobe even though it is now filled with Asya's clothes. Every time she turns the key in the secret jewellery drawer she feels she should have asked permission. She looks up to speak to her mother – but her mother is not there. She spends long stretches of time contemplating objects her parents have left behind: the slim black stork with an upraised head standing on his tiny wooden platform; her father had brought it back from a conference in Nigeria when she was ten. It had stood on the mantelpiece in his study – where it still stands now, its long delicate neck stretched upwards, its head elegantly poised with the beak pointing to the sky. Asya had loved to take it down and hold it in her hand, feeling the weightlessness of it, the smoothness of the ebony, the impossible fragility of the slender legs. Now she carries it to a chair and sits down with it in her lap, running a finger over it. It is so very small. They probably sold them by the dozen on the streets of Lagos, it was probably worth less than a pound, yet what feelings are evoked by those angled legs, by the ever-so-slightly parted beak, with what care she puts it back on the mantelpiece and turns it just so: so that it is half facing the room where Daddy no longer works and where she is now free to sit or stand or dance or sleep or use the telephone all night if she so wished. For he is out in the new flat that they took because it was bigger – except he is now alone. Deena in her own flat, Mummy in Kuwait, Kareem in the middle of the sea, and Asya here in Zamalek. And it was here, here in this very chair, that Uncle Sidki had sat, big and full of life, the night he had almost caught Bassam studying with them. Uncle Sidki is dead and Bassam is gone. Picked up the night of Camp David and given twenty minutes to pack a bag and then driven off into the night leaving a distraught Noora helplessly to cry her heart out while their little boy slept on. 'It was in the evening of the next day that he was able to call me and tell me he was in Beirut,' Noora had said. 'They had just driven him to the airport and put him on a plane.' And that was it. Noora and her son had gone to Malta to meet him last summer. As far as anyone could tell he would not be able to come back for a long time – perhaps not ever. Not to return ever – even to the things that do not change – like the kitchen where Dada Zeina had made escalopes and chips after school and Asya, still in her green and grey uniform, had told her true and invented stories about everything that had happened from eight-thirty-five to three-thirty that day – in the kitchen where Hasna, now practically blind, had wept when Asya had told her she'd bought a washing-machine.

'So it's finished, Sett Asya? My washing isn't good enough for you any more?'

'Dada Hasna, your washing is like flowers – but are you in love with sitting in front of the tub?'

'It's finished – it's finished – my day is over –'

'It isn't, it isn't. Listen. You'll come on washing-day like always. I'll just put the washing in the machine and you take it out and hang it out to dry –'

'And these machines ruin everything anyway. It's a sin to put precious things in them –'

'All right. I'll just use it for sheets and towels. You do my own things by hand. Agreed?'

Asya walks out on to the balcony. From up here the street appears almost the same: the two florists still spread their buckets full of flowers out on the pavement. Gadallah has expanded and actually built a glass display-case around the tree in front of his shoe-shop. The greengrocer's wife, big and scarred, but no longer terrifying, sits on a low stool by the courgettes, still growling occasionally, but unable to raise the thin bamboo stick she holds in her hand. Her husband lies in the back of the shop – surrendered now to the bliss of a round-the-clock hashish stupor. 'Am el-Sunni stands behind his counter, his *galabiyya* and *'imma* as gleaming white as ever, his shop still an austere counter wedged into the wall. Across Hasan Sabri Street, the lights in the bakery still glow all night and Maison Zamalek displays an assortment of pots and dusters and clothes-pegs, but the Pharmacie Nouvelle Victoria has given up half its space to a new boutique selling imported clothes. The petrol station is still on the corner and beyond, the curtain of the open-air theatre in the officers' club is always closed.

Khalu Hamid stretches and yawns. He rubs the back of his neck with his hand and says, 'I slept.'

'You did,' says Asya. 'I'll make you some fresh tea.'

'It's not necessary –' he says, but she takes his glass and goes into the kitchen.

'Your uncle has woken?' Tante Soraya asks.

'Yes, I'm making him some tea. Shall I make you some, Tante?'

'Yes please, dear; I haven't had any yet.'

'I keep telling her to go and rest. I can manage on my own,' Sayyida says.

'It's done, it's done,' Soraya says, rinsing her hands under the tap and shaking them dry. 'Is it still dusty outside?'

'No, it's died down,' Asya says.

'Praise God,' Sayyida says. 'It makes the roads very difficult.'

'I'll give you a lift when you're going, Dada Sayyida, you're on my way.'

'May you always be safe, Sett Asya, pray God.'

In the dining-room Khalu Hamid and Tante Soraya sip their tea.

'How come Sayyida's on your way home?' Tante Soraya says.

'Well, she's only a little bit out of my way,' says Asya.

'She's in Giza and you're in Zamalek.'

776

'It'll only add ten minutes on to the drive,' Asya says.

'You're a good girl,' Khalu Hamid says. 'Is Sheikh Zayid still here?'

'He's in the drawing-room with Uncle Muhammad,' Asya says.

'It's sad that your mother and Kareem aren't with us,' Tante Soraya says.

'Yes,' says Asya.

'It would be nice to be all together again.'

'Yes,' says Asya. 'And we could sit up and watch Fuad el-Muhandess like we used to. They've got *Eve at Twelve o'Clock* on tonight.'

'Why don't you stay the night, dear?'

'I can't, Tante. I've got papers to correct for Saturday.'

'Do them tomorrow.'

'I can't, I'm taking Deena to Tora – and then I've promised to go to Daddy's in the evening.'

'Your crazy sister,' says Tante Soraya. 'She's planning on going out to Tora tomorrow?'

'It's visiting day.'

'And she can't skip a visiting day in her condition?'

'But Tante, her condition is, God willing, going to last another three months –'

'She's in a sensitive stage. It's no good for her, all this jumping around. The road is bad, and when she gets there she's kept waiting for hours – it's very bad for her.'

'You don't approve of anyone.' Asya smiles. 'Not the ones who leave their husbands nor the ones who stick to them.'

'Reason,' Tante Soraya says. 'Everything should be done with reason.'

'You know your aunt,' Khalu Hamid says, levering himself up against the arm of his chair. He stands up and shakes his legs to wake them up. 'When is Nadia going back to Alexandria?' he asks.

'Tomorrow evening,' Tante Soraya says.

'Right. Well, I'm going to wash my face and put my harness on,' Khalu Hamid says, picking up his arm from on top of the sideboard.

'You're going back to the shop?' Tante Soraya says.

'Yes,' he says. 'Do you need anything?'

'Only your safety.'

'He'll stay in the shop till nine, then he'll go and play chess till after midnight,' Tante Soraya says after she hears the bathroom door close.

'What *is* your problem with his chess, Tante? He enjoys it. Let him be.'

Tante Soraya says nothing but looks grim. After a moment she stands up and leaves the room. When she comes back she is carrying something wrapped in a white handkerchief. She hands it to her niece.

'Open it,' she says.

Asya opens the bundle and there, coiled in the white cloth, is the belt of silver fish-scale sequins that had once belonged to Mama Deela's grandmother and that Tante Soraya had worn on her wedding night. Asya looks at her aunt.

'You have it,' Tante Soraya says. 'What am I going to do with it?' She pats her comfortable tummy and smiles. 'It will look good on you.'

Asya leans over and hugs her aunt and kisses her. Tante Soraya pats her head.

'Are you not my daughter?' she says, and smiles at her. Then she stands up. 'I'm going to see what Meedo's up to. His exams are in a couple of weeks and he's spending his whole time sleeping.'

Asya opens the window and stands by it holding the bright silver belt. She slips it on and it fits her waist perfectly. She unclips it, coils it, and wraps it up in the handkerchief. Who will she pass it on to? She looks out of the window. The air is perfectly clear now. She should be going soon. She has sixty-three essays to mark between now and Saturday. She'd better sit over them tonight. The sun is setting and they say the dust storm is over. Tora will be dreadful if there's another storm tomorrow: waiting around in that clearing with no shelter anywhere. It would be nice to go to Alexandria soon. If there's a storm there it means the wind blowing and the sea rising high –

The waves had been beating against the rocks of Bir Mas'oud, and from time to time she had felt the droplets of spray cold against her stockinged legs. The sun had gone down in a spectacular blaze and all the oranges and purples it had left in the sky had died away, and still she had sat and watched the twilight turn the sea into a darkening silver. It still strikes her as odd – her freedom. Driving along the corniche she had thought how nice it would be to stop and climb these rocks she had not seen for so long. And then she had realised that she could – that she had no reason not to. And it had been simple. She had parked the car, got out, and climbed. And she had thrown a scarf over her head and pulled her coat around her and walked along the rocks, empty in the November evening, then sat down to watch the sun set. On summer evenings she had used to come here, first with Mama Deela, and Khalu Hamid, and then with Dada Zeina and Kareem and Deena, and later, much later, with Saif. And she had always watched in fascination the little boys who with a shout would jump into the churning waters of the Bir itself and vanish for what seemed such a long time and then come out in the open sea beyond the rocks, purple-faced but laughing and shouting and waving in triumph. In November there were no little boys playing around on the rocks. She had stood up and, pushing her cold hands into her pockets, had walked over to the well. There it was: a deep narrow hole in the rock, and way down the black water seething and hissing and churning itself into white foam. She had shuddered: the courage it would take to break free of the solid ground, to surrender yourself to the air and leap into this chaos; to dive

beneath the wall of rock and hold your breath and swim through the dark
till once again you could see the light above you and rise up into the air.
And little boys of eight and nine did it every day. She had used to hold on
to Kareem for fear he would take it into his head to jump. 'I'm not going
to,' he'd say. 'Of course you're not,' she'd answer, and keep her hand on
his arm just the same. In February he had come back for home leave from
his oil-rig and they had had dinners and long walks and talked about
everything – everything except Saif. And she had held on to his arm as
they walked the length of Shari' Al-Mu'iz, all the way from the gold
market to the Gates of Victory with the voice of Ummu Kulthoum
following them from doorway to doorway.

'How could they remind me?
Had I ever forgotten you?'

And she had thought how odd it was that this tall young man who had
Daddy's hands and Khalu Hamid's eyes was also her baby brother who
had climbed on to a chair to sing 'There is no "I"/Only "us" my friend' –
that this was the solemn ten-year-old who had sat with Saif for endless
hours poring over books on cars, on aeroplanes, on computers – how did
he feel about her now? It was not a question she could ask, but when she
had driven him to the airport at the end of his leave and stood on tiptoe to
hug him at the departure gate she had been so happy – so happy and so
relieved to see – just before he gave her shoulder a quick pat and turned
away – that the hazel eyes were wet.

'I'm ready, Sett Asya, whenever you want.'
Asya turns from the window. Dada Sayyida is already in her black
outdoor dress, with her *tarha* round her head and her green plastic
shopping basket in her hand.
'OK, Dada. Let's go,' says Asya. 'Let me just say goodbye to everyone.'
In the car she looks through her tapes.
'Shall I put a tape of the Lady on, Dada?'
'And is anyone like the Lady?' Dada Sayyida says, and settles back
happily.
In the cool, dust-free evening, the streets have come to life once again.

'They took me back – your eyes
To my days that are gone
They taught me to regret
The past and its wounds –'

Ummu Kulthoum sings. In Shari' Abd el-'Aziz the shops are bright
with lights, and in Midan el-Falaki the trams clang their way through the
traffic. Asya circles Laz Ughli, crosses Qasr el-'Eini Street, cuts through a
narrow lane in Garden City and comes face to face with a taxi. They flick

779

their lights and start inching past each other. As her window draws parallel with the driver's, Asya says, 'Is this a one-way street? I'm sorry, I didn't know.'

'Never mind,' he says. 'There's room for all of us, God willing,' and gives her car an encouraging pat.

'Everything that passed
Before my eyes beheld you
Was all lost time
How can they count it against me?'

After one more street they come out on the river. Asya loves driving through Cairo at night. She would willingly have driven Dada Sayyida to Heliopolis or Ma'adi had she lived in either. But she drops her by the railway crossing behind the university and turns back towards the Nile.

'How much of my life before you
Has passed, passed and gone, my beloved.
And the heart before you did not know one joy
Or tasted in this world other than pain.
How much of my life has passed –'

Asya crosses Gala' Bridge and turns left. She turns right by the wall of the Exhibition grounds and left again by the Flower Gardens. What is it that the song makes her nostalgic for? How can she be yearning for Cairo and the feel of the Cairo night and the voice of Ummu Kulthoum while she is actually here in the middle of it all? If it were a pool she would dive into it, but as it is, what can she do more than just be, just be here? She turns into the club and parks. Time was when she would have given anything for this – for less than this: for just half an hour more, half an hour beyond sunset to stay with him. She gets out of the car and walks through the Lido. The young girls of the water-ballet team are practising in the Lido pool. She wanders out to the Pergola and round to the racing track again. The scent of jasmine is gentle on the night air. If you try to smell it, it disappears. But if you stand quietly and think of something else it steals up on you and fills you with its fragrance. She leans on the barrier and stands as she had stood that first time after she had come back. 'I love you,' she had heard herself whisper as she leaned against the white wood and gazed out at the racing track and the golf course. Twilight, and all edges had been blurred. The grass and the hedges were no longer green, only a deeper shade of dark than the sky. Even the 6th October Bridge which now cuts across the once free skyline was gently smudged, and the cars speeding across it were silently moving headlights. Behind her, sheltered by a group of trees, was the pet cemetery: fifteen small weathered headstones. You would have to know all about Cairo – all about Egypt – to understand the quaintness of this place. 'Lucy: a friend for fifteen years'. She had walked through it and found that none had been added in the ten years since she had last looked; since they had become engaged and stopped wandering through the grounds of the club and the Omar Khayyam. At seven o'clock she would have been lingering for a few last moments with him before panicking about her curfew and setting off for home. The chirp of a cricket rose from the ground, breaking briefly into the stillness. The day had ended and the whole of the night protected the world from tomorrow. The crows which lived in the club were doing a final slow circle before they settled into the trees. Two grey-haired ladies in trainers walked briskly in step around the track. 'I love you,' she had whispered, and smiled and shaken her head when she heard herself. It was early October and there was no scent of jasmine on the air – but she had known it was there somewhere, hiding in the bushes, waiting for April. 'I love you.' Who was she talking to? Saif still? Saif who had stood here and adjusted his lens and then handed her the camera, and through it she had watched the dragonfly dip its head to a drop of water on a leaf? Or Hilal, with whom she had first walked here, the easy camaraderie of the classroom suddenly gone and its place taken by a shy silence? Or Chrissie, who had sat here with her and tried to comfort her when she had wept in anger because she was pregnant? Or Deena, who had lain under that bush over there and waited to die after she had swallowed the mercury? Or Kareem, whom she had watched as he trained in shorts and a singlet in 1974 and suddenly realised that he was sixteen and tall and handsome and no longer her baby brother? Or just this place where so many things had happened? Over there was the spot where the helicopter bearing 'Abd el-Nasser's body had touched down and his coffin had been transferred to the ambulance standing by to take him to the start of his funeral route and the waiting crowds – 'I love you'. Or was she rehearsing for the day when she would put her hands on a man's shoulders and look into his eyes and say carefully, her words well considered, 'I love –' But would she? Would she ever again? Who could it possibly be who would take her on now? Knowingly take her on, for it would have to be knowingly. Who *could* know?

'Know what?' says Chrissie.

'Everything,' Asya says.

'That you had an affair?'

'That too, but not just that.'

'What then?'

'Me, Chrissie. *Me.* Everything about me: from the moment I hid in my mother's skirts when Daddy said you're three now, you mustn't suck your thumb any more, all the way through to Saif – and to now. And add it all up.'

'No one can know you like that.'

'*You* know me – almost.'

'No *man* can know you like that. Men aren't like that.'

'Then I won't be with anybody.'

Is that true then? Is that how it will be? That she will be with nobody? And if not nobody, who? Asya amuses herself by describing him. He would have to be at least forty – or maybe thirty-eight – but not younger. He would have to be doing something serious – something she could respect and understand and something only he could do. He would have to have money or really really not care about money; he would have to be generous; he would have to be serious and yet have time for what people would call trivialities; he would have to be big and strong and good-looking – but in a worn kind of way, not sharp and brand-new – he can't wear anything with a pattern – except ties – and even then they would have to be discreet and he must prefer not to wear them – he must wear shoes with laces – he would be cynical but kind – he would be ironic and funny but serious, yes, serious but interruptable – and fun: his pleasures should be dolphin-like and show his back above the – he can listen to Mozart and Ummu Kulthoum and Bob Dylan and Genesis – he likes to dance but not to show off – he would love to talk to her – but he would want to listen, he would want to know her, really *know* her, and he'd take her as she came and explore her and not want her to be any particular way. He would be kind. He would be wonderful to watch, to talk to, to listen to and to make love with. And he would want a child – children. And he must be unmarried. And why should he be unmarried if he is such a paragon and forty already? No. It isn't going to happen. And the list that she had drawn up that Christmas five years ago is still as incomplete as ever. 'Family' and 'Friends' are still 'as above'. 'Work': there is still a question mark in front of 'something that matters', and 'Love' may for all she knows be behind her. The roof-garden on top of the Semiramis is gone and the Botticelli *Venus* dances the night away on a bar-top in 42nd Street.

Asya walks back to her car, turns on the ignition and starts driving slowly out of the club.

'Only now I've started to love my life
Only now I've started to fear that it may pass too quickly.
Every joy my imagination ever yearned for
Was found – in the light of your eyes –
by my heart and my mind –'

She turns by the Belgian Embassy, which used to be a beautiful yellow stone villa and is now a modern white fortress, and decides to do a small detour to see the huge baobab tree that blocks the road near the Italian Cultural Centre. That will always be there. Please God let that always be there. It is there. She parks and looks at the tree for a few moments and then drives home.

'Oh life of my heart,
More precious than my life –
Why? Why? Why did your love not meet me,
Oh my darling, sooner?'

'Am 'Abd el-Hadi, the old doorman, is dead, and 'Am Salih, the new doorman, salaams her from his bench. Asya returns the salaam and gets into the lift. As she gets out in the vestibule of the flat and hunts for her key, and looks – as she always does – at the niche in the wall where a statue should have been and where Kareem used to perform his ritual of jumping out on one foot to say goodbye, she suddenly thinks of the idol.

Driving back from Sohag she had seen a sign saying 'Akhmeem' and pulled in. The silks she buys in the charity bazaars in Cairo come from Akhmeem. She had turned towards the village, passed through some scattered houses, come to a large bare clearing and stopped. Even as she stepped out of the car she was chiding that tiny corner of herself that she suspected was looking for a busy market square, for the lengths of freshly dyed silk stretched out in the sun to dry – and a small cathedral, no doubt, is she looking for? And a welcoming sign saying 'The Pig and Whistle'?

Two little boys in the standard striped *galabiyyas* tug at her skirt.

'Baksheesh, baksheesh,' they cry.

'Stop it, kids,' she says. 'Do I look like a tourist?'

'She's Egyptian,' one boy says to the other.

'But you've got a camera. There,' the other boy says, pointing at the car.

'Take a photo of us, then.'

They laugh and strike clowning poses against the dusty background. And, laughing too, Asya had taken her camera and shot three photos of them.

'Have you come to see the idol?' they ask.

'What idol?'

'The new idol; the one that's still buried. Come, we'll show you.'

They run, and she follows. They turn down a wet alley between two houses. How can it be wet? Asya wonders. The land looks as though it hasn't seen rain for months. They come out on another clearing with a big crater-like hole in the middle.

'Here, here,' they cry.

Asya approaches the edge, and there, just a few feet from her, a stone woman lies face-down in the sand. A lady, Asya corrects herself – for there is no doubt that this is a lady. She has been lifted slightly: her chest is propped on several planks of wood, her forehead rests on three large stones. Her arms are either hanging straight at her sides or they are broken off, for from the elbow down she is still entombed in sand.

A shout from the far side of the ditch sends the two boys scampering away and an old man appears waving a stick.

'Forbidden,' he cries. 'It's forbidden. No photos.'

Asya lets her camera dangle at her side and raises two hands to show she means no harm.

'Get away from here, you boys,' the man shouts as he advances, and the boys vanish from the edge of the clearing.

'Salamu 'aleikum, 'Am el-Hajj,' Asya says.

"Aleikum es-salam, Sett,' he answers suspiciously.

'They've just found her recently?'

'Photographs are forbidden,' he says.

'I won't take a photograph,' she says.

'You're from the press?'

'No, I was visiting relatives near Sohag and I was driving back to Cairo. I saw the sign that said Akhmeem and stopped. I know your silks.'

'Ah!'

'I stopped here by chance. The kids said come see the idol.'

'Damn kids.'

"Am el-Hajj I won't harm her, or tell anyone about her. But she is so beautiful.'

'The place is full of the likes of her. Everyone knows that.'

'But who is she?'

'They think she's from the time of Rameses the Second.'

'But who? A princess?'

'They've found things that say a queen, and things that say Rameses' sister, and things that say a dancing girl at court. Who knows? They used to marry their sisters in those heathen days.'

'She is so beautiful.'

'All right. You can look as much as you like, but no photographs.'

He sits down in a wavering patch of shade and takes out an old tin full of tobacco. Asya puts her camera down next to him and walks back to the princess. She can only see one side of her, from the head to just above the elbow. Her eyes are open but cast down. Above her eye the long slim eyebrow is perfectly drawn. Her nose is straight and ends on an upward tilt and a delicate nostril. Her lips curve into a slight smile, still rosy with the paint they used for lipstick. On the lobe of her ear is a great disc decorated with a scarab, and on her head a crown carved with the ankh. Her hair is arranged in a fringe over her forehead and curves back behind her ear in a folded wing and then down over her shoulder in an intricate braid. Where the braid ends a small, pointed nipple finishes off a perfect breast. Of course these statues are stylised: everybody looks straight and slim and stately – and yet this woman is beautiful. Like this, not standing at the door of a temple or at the knee of the great pharaoh, she is beautiful.

Asya had sat down on a rock to look at her. Lying face-down in the sand, uncovered now after what? Three thousand years? Her forehead resting on three bricks – the very indignity of her posture makes the pride and grace of her expression – of her bearing – all the more remarkable. Who was she? A dancing girl whom the great Rameses took a fancy to and elevated into a Sister-Wife? But she has none of the arriviste about her. The composure, the serenity, of her smile tells of someone who had always known who she was. The mummy of Rameses the Second, which they had finished delousing in Paris around the time Khalu Hamid was in London, was but a paltry, shabby thing, small and shrivelled, hardly recognisable as human. Since she had seen it Asya had looked at the pharaoh's statues with new eyes. But this woman who had in some way belonged to him, and who now lies here in the sand – she has indeed found a gentle grave; for here she is, delivered back into the sunlight still in complete possession of herself – of her pride, and of her small, subtle smile.

glossary

Abu-l-rish: a popular district in South Cairo.

'Afreet: someone's ghost or – more commonly – a sort of independent mischievous spirit.

Ain Shams: second university in Cairo, on the road to Heliopolis.

Akhmeem: town in upper Egypt which retains its pharaonic name and is noted for its heavy silks and cottons.

Allahu Akbar: God is greatest. The opening phrase of the call to prayers and of the prayers themselves. The battle-cry of the first Muslim armies.

'Am: literally 'father's brother', used colloquially as title of respect for older man.

Amshir: the name for February in the old Coptic calendar, by which the weather in Egypt is mostly designated.

'Antar: Arab name, most famous bearer of which is the pre-Islamic poet 'Antar ibn Shaddad, famed for his courage in warfare (which earned him his freedom although he was born a slave) and for his happily concluded romance with his cousin 'Abla. Both are celebrated in 'Antar's famous *mu'allaqa* poem and in folk *siras* (folk romances).

'Asr: afternoon. **'Asr prayers**: third of the prescribed five daily prayers. To be performed somewhere between two o'clock and sunset.

'Attareen: the old 'Quarter of the Herbalists' in Alexandria, known for its antique and junk shops.

'Awra: parts of the body which should never be shown in public.

Baqsheesh: pronounced 'baksheesh' for the foreigners; the Egyptian pronunciation is 'ba'sheesh': a tip.

Bamia: okra, or Ladies' Fingers, a vegetable.

Basbousa: also known as **baseesa**, a dessert made by mixing a special toasted breadcrumb with sugar syrup and then baking. The effect is supposed to be exceedingly soft and melty and sweet.

Bey: Turkish honorary title, above 'Effendi' and below 'Pasha'.

Bir: well.

Borek: triangular cases of fila pastry filled with a savoury.

Dada: polite middle-class title for nanny, nurse or other serving-woman.

Djibba and **Kaftan**: traditional clothes worn by a sheikh or man of learning. The *kaftan* is the long inner robe, made of a satiny cotton with thin dark stripes on a white background and fastened with a broad cloth belt. The *djibba* is the outer robe, in dark brown or grey, worn loose and open to reveal the *kaftan* underneath.

Dorra: a co-wife; the verb *darra* means to cause harm.

'Eid: the festival. There are two 'Eids in the Muslim year: the 'little 'Eid' or "Eid al-Fitr' comes at the end of the month of Ramadan and lasts three days; the 'big 'Eid' or "Eid al-Adha' comes at the end of the season of the pilgrimage and lasts four days.

Fallaha: feminine of *fallah*: a peasant, literally a tiller (of the soil).

al-Fatiha: the opening *sura* (chapter) of the Qur'an; reciting it is an indication of sealing a promise.

Fekki: degraded form of 'Faqeeh' (man of learning in Quranic sciences), used for a man whose job is to chant the Qur'an at functions.

Fool: a small bean which is used to make a very common Egyptian meal.

Fuad el-Muhandess: a comic actor who contracted an immensely successful partnership with the actress Shueikar Toob Saqqal in the late fifties and early sixties. The partnership (they were also married for a while) resulted in a number of comedies which were extremely popular in the Arab world at the time. Phrases from these plays have entered into everyday Arab vocabulary.

Galabiyya: long, loose gown worn by traditional men to relax or sleep in.

Geddu: endearment for *geddi*: grandfather.

el-Geish: the army.

Halawa: a sticky, sweet-smelling paste of caramelised sugar used for depilating unwanted hair. It is customary before using it to twirl a bit around a stick and give it to any child in the house as a lollipop. When it is used as a sweet it is known as 'Ali Loz'.

Hanim: lady. Formal title of respect for a woman. Turkish.

Haraam: adjective denoting something which is sinful or taboo. It is also used as an adjuration, e.g. to stop someone harming someone, and as an expression of pity.

Hassan Fathi: celebrated Egyptian architect who adopted traditional Islamic architecture in the houses he built.

Henna Day: a day of beautifying for the bride before the wedding, so called because traditionally, on that day, a bride used to have her palms and feet decorated with patterns in red henna.

Hijab: the Islamic veil.

'Imma: turban.

Imru' al-Qais: Mu'allaqa poet from the pre-Islamic period in Arabia.

In sha' Allah: if God wills.

Jameela Bouhreid: heroine of the Algerian resistance, imprisoned and tortured by the French in the late fifties; a long popular poem was composed in her honour by the Egyptian caricaturist and colloquial poet Salah Jaheen.

Jinn: supernatural beings who live their own lives parallel to the lives of human beings.

Ka'ba: the holy house in Makkah, built by Abraham and purified of idols and reconsecrated to God by Muhammad. It is towards the Ka'ba that

Muslims face five times a day at prayer, and around it that they perform the annual ritual of the pilgrimage.

Khalu: endearment form of *khali*: my mother's brother.

Khamaseen: The hot winds that blow across Egypt for fifty days in March/April. They carry sand from the desert and can sometimes amount to sandstorms in the heart of the city.

Khiyana: treachery, betrayal.

Khosheshban: in a folk-tale, a princess has to assume a disguise. She wears a suit made of wood and calls herself 'Khosheshban'. 'Khashab' is Arabic for wood.

Kiswa: a new suit of clothing. Here used for the Ka'ba: a cloth of black velvet embroidered with gold that covers the entire building and is changed once a year. Traditionally the Kiswa used to leave Cairo in a huge caravan procession through the city and then through the desert to Makkah. The Kiswa is nowadays provided by the Saudi government.

Kofta: balls of minced meat; can be grilled, fried or cooked in a red sauce.

Kohl: antimone. Black powder used for lining the inner rims of the eyelids.

Koshari: popular dish made with rice, lentils and fried onions.

Kushuk Hanim: nineteenth-century Egyptian dancer and courtesan who set up house in Minya in the Sa'id during a drive against prostitution in Cairo and was visited there by many of the powerful and famous, including Flaubert.

Mabahith: the Egyptian secret service, used for domestic purposes.

Mankousha: dishevelled.

Mashta: a woman who attends to the grooming of women's bodies.

Ma'thoun: official who performs marriages and divorces.

Mousky: the long, always crowded market street that connects 'Ataba to the Bazaar area in Cairo.

Mu'allaqa: the name given to a poem which won the poetry prize at the Ukaz Fair in Hijaz in pre-Islamic times. The name derives from the root *'allaqa*: to hang (something up), because the practice was to hang the winning poem up in public.

Mudiriyat al-Tahrir: a big project to reclaim and plant land in the Western desert.

Mukhabarat: the Egyptian intelligence service, supposed to be used for foreign matters.

Mulukhiyya: a green soup made of chopped *mulukhiyya* leaves, the perfection of which distinguishes an Egyptian housewife.

Muhasanah: from *hasanah*, to fortify. A woman who is fortified (through having her desires satisfied in marrage) from the sin of adultery.

'Orabi: Ahmad Pasha 'Orabi, nationalist army leader who led the resistance against the British Occupation in 1882. He fought the occupying army with a small force in the battle of Tal el-Kebeer and upon his defeat was sent into exile by the British command.

Osta: master craftsman, used as respectful title for working-class man.

Qaf: the name of the letter which is denoted in English by the 'q'.

Qasr: literally 'castle' or 'palace'. Used in Cairo with just the definite article it always refers to the Qasr el-'Eini, the huge public hospital which houses the medical school of Cairo University.

Qatr el-Nada: Egyptian princess whose wedding became a legend for its splendour and extravagance.

Qibla: that towards which one faces, i.e. the direction of Makkah. From *qibal*: in front of or facing.

Rahma: mercy. Also food and money given to the poor in supplication for God to grant mercy to a dead person.

Sa'd Zaghloul: famous Egyptian nationalist politician, head of the most influential political party, the 'Wafd' or Delegation. He travelled to Paris after the end of the First World War to discuss Egypt's independence and returned believing it would not be willingly given. He led the 'revolution' of 1919 in which women demonstrated in the streets for the first time; this marked the beginning of an overall cohesiveness in the struggle against the occupation. He died in 1927, but for many years afterwards if you asked a *fallah* in rural Egypt whom he would vote for in the coming elections you could get the answer, 'Sa'd Pasha.'

Sa'idi: from the 'Sa'id' of Egypt, i.e. Upper Egypt.

Salamu 'aleikum: 'peace be upon you', traditional greeting upon meeting or taking leave of someone.

al-Sayyid al-Badawi: al-Sayyid Ahmad al-Badawi, a saint of great importance in Egypt, is buried in Tanta in the Nile Delta; the season of his nativity is massively celebrated by pilgrims from all over the country. Although 'al-Sayyid' simply means 'Mr' or 'the gentleman', the invocation 'Ya Sayyid' would always be addressed to al-Sayyid al-Badawi.

Sett: literally 'lady', used similarly to the Elizabethan 'mistress'.

Sett el-Hosn: a heroine of Egyptian folk-tales, literally 'Lady of beauty'.

Shahada: literally 'statement of a witness'. Here used in its most dominant use as the statement of the Muslim Creed: 'I bear witness that there is no god but Allah and that Muhammad is his prophet.' This is the statement with which Islam is embraced and the statement every Muslim needs to make on his deathbed.

Shahid: witness, also tombstone.

Shari': street.

Shari'a: Islamic Law.

Sheikha Sabah: a bride-saint buried in Tanta whose tomb is decked out with lace and tinsel.

Shisha: waterpipe, hubble-bubble, Turkish *nargile*.

Shogga: Upper Egyptian dialect for long black tent-like garment worn by women out of doors.

Shoreik: a particular bread for distribution as alms.

Sidi: my master.

Sidna or **Sayyidna**: our master; title of respect for a religious man.

Sunni: someone who follows the example of the Prophet in daily life. Hence, a good man.

Sofragi: a man servant, part waiter, part footman.

Tabbouleh: a Lebanese salad made by chopping parsley up very finely, mixing it with crushed wheat and then seasoning it.

Tabliyya: low round wooden table traditionally used for eating by the poorer classes.

Ta'miyya: small fried cakes made of ground beans.

Tani: second, or again.

Tarboosh: fez. Men's headwear made of red felt with black tassel. Turkish in origin.

Tarha: length of chiffon – usually in either black or white – worn as a loose headcovering by women.

Thob: a white robe reaching to just above the ankles.

Ustaz: Mr.

Waili: the name of a district in Cairo – also, in classical Arabic, 'woe is me'.

Zaffa: a traditional wedding procession with music and dancers.

Zaghrouda: ululation – a long joy-cry uttered by women on happy occasions; plural: *zaghareed*.

Zebibah: a raisin; a brown mark that appears on the skin of the forehead as a result of much praying.

A NOTE ON THE AUTHOR

Ahdaf Soueif was born in Cairo and educated in Egypt and England.